THE JAGUAR PATH

By Anna Stephens

Godblind
Darksoul
Bloodchild

The Stone Knife

THE JAGUAR PATH

ANNA STEPHENS

HARPER
Voyager

Harper*Voyager*
An imprint of
HarperCollins*Publishers* Ltd
1 London Bridge Street
London SE1 9GF

www.harpercollins.co.uk

HarperCollins*Publishers*
Macken House
39/40 Mayor Street Upper
Dublin 1
D01 C9W8
Ireland

First published by HarperCollins*Publishers* 2023
1

A catalogue record for this book is available from the British Library

ISBN: 978-0-00-840405-5 (HB)
ISBN: 978-0-00-840406-2 (TPB)

Typeset in Sabon LT Std by Palimpsest Book Production Ltd, Falkirk, Stirlingshire

Printed and bound in the UK using
100% Renewable Electricity by CPI Group (UK) Ltd

*For the Bunker, without whom this book
would quite literally never have been finished.*

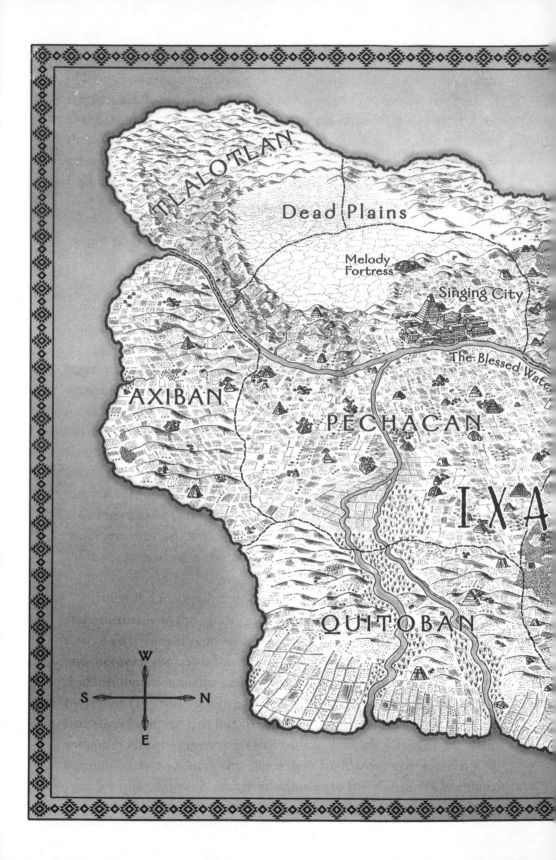

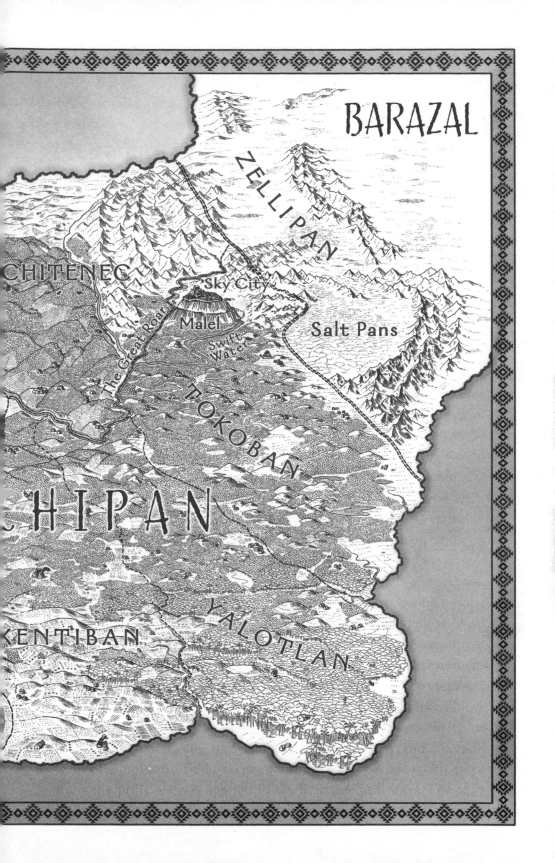

LILLA

*Melody fortress, the dead plains, Tlalotlan, Empire of Songs
182nd day of the Great Star at evening*

'Pod one, advance!'

Lilla and his hundred warriors sprinted forward, howling, and threw themselves at the dog warriors of the Fifth Talon. They were a mix of Chitenecah, Tlaloxqueh and Xentib, and the Yaloh of Lilla's pod were brutal in their determination to best the latter, their ancient rivalry alive even here and now, more than two sun years under the song. Two sun-years as slaves of the Melody.

Lilla's pod, Lilla's whole Talon – the Eighth – were Tokob and Yaloh, unlike the mix found in other Talons. He'd thought it idiotic at first, putting together all the people most recently enslaved and training them to fight in the Melody style, but as weeks and then months passed, he understood it. They fought harder because they were surrounded by kin, they defended the fallen with more ferocity because they were tribe, children of Malel and siblings to the Jaguar and the Snake. They were still kin, still bound to each other, even

1

though they'd been stolen from their homes and jungles. But now they were bound too, to the Melody, and the false promise and sweet submission that the song encouraged and the eagles demanded.

Day by day, the Pechaqueh were moulding them into an unbreakable force, united by shared pain and history, and rewarded or punished equally. Lilla hated it, even after all this time, but not because he wanted to be apart from his people. The thought of that, of being trapped in this place but apart from other Tokob, made the skin on his back crawl. No, what he loathed was how effective it all was. The training and the bonds forged through shared suffering were one thing, familiar to him from his warrior training back home. The beautiful, insidious poison of the song was something else entirely.

Tokob and Yaloh were connected by family, blood, and ancestors and Lilla knew that this, their greatest strength, was being turned against them. The song steadily unpicked the bonds that made them the children of Malel, even while it appeared to strengthen them. He'd known it to be true since their first days in captivity under the song, and he'd spoken against it for just as long. And for just as long, he'd been ignored.

The song itself seemed designed to shape them into a tool for the Melody's use – it was harsh and hungry today, spawning violence in his heart, lending strength to his arm as he parried his opponent's blunted axe with his own and smashed the small wooden shield in his other hand into her chest, sending her over backwards. He barely resisted the urge to cave in her head. Lilla didn't know if he wanted to kill her because she'd helped bring his people under the song, or if he wanted to do it to impress Feather Ekon, the tall, proud eagle who commanded his Talon.

His heart and blood thrummed with the need to paint the dirt crimson, but he forced himself to step back and let her up. Others were not so cautious and screams and blood were bright in the morning air.

The dog warrior saw how close she'd come to death at the hands of a slave and scrambled backwards, abandoning the front line to put distance between them with a sneer that didn't mask her chagrin. Lilla let out pent-up frustration and self-doubt in a bellow and surged against the next dog in line. Their axes clashed above their heads until he twisted his wrist to free his own and disengaged, stamping hard on the man's foot and taking a shield to the face for his trouble.

Lilla's attack faltered as tears sprang to his eyes and his nose gushed blood. His lips drew back from his teeth and he roared again, spraying red mist. What he wouldn't give for a spear, but this moon they were fighting only with axes; the Melody liked their warriors to be skilled with all weapons and able to fight in all situations.

He ducked another axe blow, took a third on his shield and felt it crack, but his upswing thumped into the warrior's armpit and he squealed and fell back, hand up for mercy. Again, Lilla had to hold back the urge to use his blunted axe as a bludgeon and end the man's life.

These were the dog warriors who'd torn through Yalotlan like locusts? Who'd taken his own land? They were nothing special. He beckoned a third, grinning despite the blood dripping into his open mouth. '*Come on,*' he screamed.

'Pod one, withdraw!' Feather Ekon's command overruled his invitation and Lilla snarled in frustration but stepped back, trying like the rest of his warriors to disengage without leaving himself open. By the time he was back on his side of the vast drill yard, his shield was a splintered mess hanging from his left arm, the flesh beneath bruised to the bone, and his right shoulder was a hot throbbing agony from the blow he'd taken, just steps from the line scratched in the dirt behind which they were deemed safe.

He disentangled from the remains of the shield and threw it to the floor, dropped his axe and bent over, hands on knees and gasping for breath, staring at that same line. He saw the feet approaching an instant before something slammed into the back of his head so hard he dropped to the dirt, his much-abused nose taking the brunt of the impact and his wrists jarring as he failed to break his fall.

Groggy and furious, he rolled onto his back and made to get up. Feather Ekon pressed an obsidian-headed spear into the soft vulnerability between his clavicles. 'Safety is not always safe,' he growled, 'whether it's a line of warriors or a line in the dirt. And as pod-leader, you should know that. You should check your people are out of danger before dropping weapons. Instead, you took your attention from the enemy. You fail this day's training.'

There were soft murmurs of protest and dark looks cast Lilla's way as Ekon pulled back the spear and let him up, his eyes on him the whole time.

'Three laps,' the Feather said and the groans were louder this time. The drill yard was a stick in length on each side, a vast square larger than all of the biggest plazas combined back in the Sky City, big enough to train a full Talon – three thousand warriors. It would be highsun by the time they'd run three laps of it, and they knew without asking they'd get only half their ration at duskmeal as added punishment. But that was the way of the Melody. Rewarded together; punished together.

Lilla looked at his pod and grimaced. 'I'm sorry,' he began, but Kux, the warrior of Yalotlan he'd fought beside during the war, pushed past and led them off in a ragged stream of angry runners. Lilla waited for them all to start – it would be his job to support any stragglers and make sure everyone finished, even if he had to run back and forth a dozen times to help his people complete the punishment.

Ekon pushed Lilla in the back, not hard, and he set out after the rest, the Pechaqueh disappointment making his cheeks flame. Despite all his time here, despite his bloody nose and the irritation of his pod, despite everything, knowing he had failed Ekon cut at him.

It hadn't always been that way. For months, for the first year even, Lilla had held true to himself and his people, working at increasing the number of warriors who would side with him when the time came to rise up. Ekon and the other Pechaqueh – and all the free who strutted around the fortress, clean and independent and wealthy, had provoked nothing but contempt. Chitenecah, Xentib, Tlaloxqueh, Axib and Quitob, all came to the fortress to trade in beer and obsidian, skins and slaves, their brands scarred through to proclaim their freedom and disdain dripping from their scowls. As if they'd never been where the Tokob were now.

Lilla had seen the envy in the faces of his Talon, the desperate, gnawing need to *be like them*, blind to what it had cost, and he'd resisted that need. At least half the free who came to sell weapons and salt-cotton wore their hair and jewellery in the Pechaqueh style, their own traditions and ancestors and even gods forgotten. He'd never do that. Never.

But somehow, somewhere, perhaps through the song that was an endless whisper in his bones, he'd come to want, then need, then *crave*, Feather Ekon's approval. Lilla had nothing left but his prowess as a warrior and the desire for someone, anyone – *Ekon* – to notice it and appreciate it was a constant fire in his belly. To be appreciated as more than a slave. A thing.

He told himself it was arrogance to want such things, that it was another manipulation by the endless, hungry song, which no matter its stutters and stumbles and roaring surges, promised glory in return for obedience. It ate at him like a maggot in dead flesh: patient, mindless, ceaseless. *Give in,* it whispered. *Give in to glory and power and unity. Breathe me. Live within me and know peace.*

It was hard to remember life before the song, before this thing – this will that wasn't his – that lived beneath his skin. Now, with nothing but an hour of running ahead of him, he made himself chant praise to Malel in his head, even if the words came in time with the song.

They all lived to its beat, automatic as breathing. Its claws were already fixed in Tokob and Yaloh alike. Now it was down to how many could resist its pull and remember who they were, what they were, and what they could be again once this long nightmare, this horror sent by the lords of the Underworld, came to an end. Because it would. It had to, or what was the point in living?

Glory. He pushed away the thought; the lie.

Even those warriors who, like him, had pledged to destroy the Empire from within, and who plotted with him to light a fire of rebellion that would spark in every slave, strove to please the eagles and prove themselves. Lilla was no different. He told himself it was necessary; in his more lucid moments, when the song was perhaps a little weaker, he knew it for a lie.

Tinit of Yalotlan was near the back of the straggle of warriors and he caught up to her easily. She slanted a look at him, her mouth thinning at his apologetic smile.

'Sorry,' he said, 'I never meant for you to—'

'Get punished as well? It's how they make us stronger.'

Lilla was silent for a few paces, shortening his stride to match hers. 'They make us accountable for one another so it's easier to control us,' he began, his voice beginning to labour as they ran along the base of one of the towering walls.

'Don't start,' Tinit warned. 'Not again.'

'Please, Tinit,' Lilla tried now they were out of earshot of Ekon and his dogs. 'Just listen. I'm not asking you to do anything. I'm not asking you to change your behaviour, even. Continue being the exceptional warrior you are, continue to gain their trust, get promoted into the dog warriors and—'

'And then, when you've got enough suicidal fucking idiots determined to die for nothing, you'll rise up and get your-selves slaughtered,' the Yalotl panted. 'I know. I know your stupid fucking plan, Fang Lilla. *Pod-leader* Lilla. But it won't just be you and your rebels who die; it'll be us, too. Won't it? We're running this drill yard because of you. What do you think they'll do when you start killing eagles? Punished together, remember?'

'Once we're trusted, we can get close to the High Feather,' Lilla tried desperately. 'We can—' But Tinit put down her head and accelerated away from him. The Toko ground his teeth in frustration. Couldn't they understand that all they needed to do was kill the High Feather and his subordinates and the slaves and dog warriors would come to their side? They'd break out of the fortress and cut a bloody swathe through the farmland towards the Singing City, calling on farm, house and body slaves to join them.

And they will, in their hundreds, their thousands. When they see freedom dangled before them, when they see us uncowed and unbroken, they'll join us and we'll be unstop-pable. We just need enough warriors on our side. I have to make them understand, to see that it will be worth the risk. That freedom is worth any risk.

He'd spoken the words so often to himself that they were rote, almost trite, but that didn't make them any less true.

With Tokob and Yaloh warriors at the forefront of a new war, the enslaved peoples of Ixachipan would heed their call and overthrow their owners.

It was a distant dream, a goal so far away it was but the glint of a single star in an expanse of unending night – and it would take three more years of lies and deceptions. Two if they were lucky. Once they were dog warriors, they could act. Just three years. More than enough time to bring the others to the cause.

None of that made Lilla feel any better when he caught himself laughing at one of Ekon's jokes or flushing under his praise, given rarely but honestly. Lilla concentrated on running, emptying his mind as best he could and giving himself up to the repetitive movement, almost soothing in its difference to the stresses of combat.

Of the three thousand warriors in his Talon, eight out of every ten spoke openly and excitedly of war and the chance to prove themselves, to hasten the long process of earning their freedom by spilling the blood of others. Those rebels who hadn't forgotten who or what they were countered the bloodlust with memories of home and family and Malel, of their cities and traditions, the dances of their ancestors, the paint of their kin. They were, increasingly, ignored. Derided. Forgotten.

Kux lagged back, letting Tinit and others pass her until she was at Lilla's side. 'Leave my people alone.'

Resentment flared in Lilla's chest. 'Your people?' he panted, flicking his gaze deliberately at her hair. In the last half-year, Kux had begun braiding it in the Pechaqueh fashion.

Kux's cheeks were already flushed from the exertion, but they darkened some more. 'Fuck you. I focus on the positives, as do the rest of us who don't listen to your moon-madness.'

'What positives, Kux? What positives are there to this?'

Lilla's gesture was violent enough that she had to dodge sideways; when she came back, she was snarling.

'My family. I, at least, still have one. I won't tell you again: leave us alone.'

Like Tinit, she accelerated away before he could reply and left him chewing over words unsaid and pleas unmade. It was resentment, he was sure of it. Kux had been a Fang in Yalotlan, the same as him, but here he was pod-leader and she was under his command. She hated it and it was poisoning . . .

No. That was Pechaqueh thinking. Song thinking. Lilla was Tokob; he was better than this. And he wouldn't convince anyone of anything if he went around making bitter accusations. They had hundreds on their side already and three years to recruit the rest. He needed to be patient. Dedicated. True to the cause. He'd come too far to falter now.

Although he didn't believe Kux and the others like her would betray the rebels when the time came, neither could they count on their aid, and when it did come to a fight, he was terrified of the choice they might be forced to make. They'd embraced the Empire's promises – the Empire's lies – wholeheartedly, convinced they'd see their families again if they only did as they were told. But what if what they were told was to kill the rebels among their number? If they were ordered to do so to prove their loyalty and save the lives of their families? And what if the rebels then had to defend themselves to the death? Could either side actually go through with it?

His blood sang in his veins, and it sang warning.

The sun was lowering to the west when the Eighth Talon was dismissed to their barracks, handing in their practice weapons to the labour slaves who kept the enormous fortress running.

9

Every one of the hundred warriors in Lilla's pod ignored him as they made their weary way out of the drill yard and through the high-walled passage to the living compound with its barracks, kitchen, latrines and washing area.

The walls here were even higher than those of the training square and Lilla felt as if they closed in on him alone, compressing him, crushing his spirit. In here, there was nothing but dark stone and baked dirt and three thousand mostly hostile Tokob and Yaloh, with guards on the walls above them armed with bows and blowpipes. Stone and dirt and the pale, undyed maguey of slave clothes. It was as if all other colours had been leached from the world. As if freedom was blue and green and red and yellow, and slavery and submission were these drab, dull tones only ever brightened by the spilling of blood.

The only freedom was the slice of sky he couldn't reach. Lilla found he could stare at that square of blue for hours if he was left alone to do so, watching as it paled into dusk and then blackness across which the stars that had been scattered by a playful Malel began to burn. The evening sky – the only sky he had time to watch – wasn't the same shade of blue as the paint of Tayan's shamanic finery, but it was all Lilla had and he held it close; wrapped that strip of sky around his heart and his memories of his husband and imagined he could feel the gentle press of fingers in his hair, across the cut of his jaw.

Breath shuddering in his chest, Lilla stripped and walked onto the washing area – wooden planks stretched over a wide, shallow, limestone trench that carried the spent water into a narrow drainage channel leading under the compound wall. It never failed to elicit a bitter amusement in his heart that a people who thought the Drowned were gods would go to such lengths to keep them out of the places where they lived. Tokob invited and encouraged Malel, Jaguar-brother and Snake-sister to visit; they communed with spirits and ancestors and kept the long line of history unbroken and close. They respected and feared their gods, as was natural and healthy, but they did not hide from them the way Pechaqueh did.

Lilla scrubbed the sweat and dust from his skin, the dried blood from his face. His nose was swollen and sore but unbroken. He poured saltwater over his head and watched it swirl down his legs. The faded yellow cord of his marriage to Tayan was still wrapped around his left ankle instead of adorning his throat. Widower. Pain and shame burnt anew in his chest and he scrubbed them away along with his sweat, then combed his fingers through his hair – his Tokob hair, long and braided at the temples, tied with threads picked from his blanket. The perfect slave warrior, yes, not a perfect fake Pechaqueh. He'd seen enough fiercely loyal dog warriors who retained their people's traditions to know it was possible to be trusted and wear Tokob fashions at the same time. He could at least pretend to loyalty without making his appearance into the shadow of those who owned him.

Lilla rewrapped his kilt and made his way to the queue already forming at the great fire-pits, tucking his tunic into the back of his waistband so the breeze could dry the water beaded on his skin. Kitchen slaves sweated and ladled and raced back and forth to feed thousands of other slaves and, as he did each day, Lilla forced himself to remember they too were people, with families and pasts and the hope, however faint, of a better future. It was all too easy to be impatient with them, or snarl when they didn't serve a large enough portion to sate his combat-tired body. It was all too easy to treat them as less than he, though they shared the brands on their shoulders. They were all property.

He could see, even among the rebels who'd pledged him violence for freedom, the unconscious way the warriors separated themselves from the rest, thought themselves different, better. *We are warriors; you serve our food.* When he was handed the small wooden bowl of broth and triangle of cornbread, his stomach already protesting how little there was, he thanked the server, quietly and genuinely. As always, the slave smiled back with real warmth and stood a little straighter. A small and simple gift – *I see you. You are not nothing.*

Lilla sat alone, knowing his pod wouldn't welcome his presence after the punishment run that morning. He concentrated on his food – the broth was heavy with corn and bamboo tips and squash. It was bland, without spice, but it was food. And food meant strength. And strength meant the opportunity to get close to Feather Ekon. As pod-leader, Lilla had the most opportunity to interact with the man and gain his trust. He imagined sliding a glass blade into Ekon's throat, the edges almost too sharp to feel, just a sudden inability to inhale and then the hot, hot rush of liquid down his chest. Ekon's eyes on him as he died, betrayed. Uncomprehending.

Lilla breathed through the discomfort of the image. This plan, and the lives they had to lead to make it work, were worse than the worst moments of the war. That was a fight, and Lilla knew who and what he was during a fight. This was patience more suited to the snake path of the ejab than the jaguar path of warriors. This was a stealth that would last years, not hours, a deception breath-taking in its scale and audacity. They had to be lucky every day; their enemies only needed to be lucky once, and it would all come tumbling down like the ash on an incense cone caught in the wind.

Lilla's appetite left him but he forced himself to eat, as he forced himself to do so much these days. Despair threatened at the edges of his resolve and he fought against it, silently repeating the prayer that had become his driving force since they had decided on their plan.

Ancestors, hear my vow. Malel, witness it. I will break this empire from the inside. I will make them love me – and then I will kill them for it.

'I thank the Feather for the lesson,' Lilla panted. It wasn't a lie. He did thank Ekon, because despite being badly beaten, he knew a little more of the Melody's fighting style than he had the day before. And, perhaps, the Pecha trusted him a little now, to gift him this extra time and practice.

Lilla rested on one knee, chest heaving for breath and running with sweat so his tunic clung to him, hands aching from the jolting of his axe in his grip as Ekon had battered it down and away time and again, a relentless, flowing attack Lilla could do little but withstand. He hadn't managed more than a dozen counterattacks, and only one had landed, and even then without force. The Feather well deserved his title: he was power and grace and ruthlessness. All-seeing and cruel but only as necessary. A wild hunter and one it was both easy and prudent to respect.

The rest of the Eighth had finished training when the afternoon began to lilac into dusk, but Ekon had called him back for extra sparring. Now he grinned. 'Better than last time,' he said. 'Not quite a rancid monkey turd today.'

Lilla managed a wry smile in return. 'The Feather's praise is mighty indeed.' He snapped his mouth shut as soon as he spoke, unsure how Ekon would respond, but the man only laughed, genuine and from the belly, pulling a crooked grin from the Toko that he was unable to quell.

'The Feather is a little less disgusted with your ability than yesterday,' he agreed and then startled him by offering a hand. Lilla took it and Ekon hauled him to his feet without apparent effort. His palm was hot and calloused yet dry, unlike the sweat slicking the Tokob own. 'You learn quickly. That is good.'

'You honour me,' Lilla said. 'But it is your teaching that makes me better. I . . . forgive me. This slave speaks out of turn.'

'Please, continue.' Ekon was warm with curiosity, a small smile hinting at the dimple in his cheek.

Lilla looked away. 'As a Tokob warrior, I believed myself capable, and then I fought the eagles of the Melody. When I was first brought here, I tried to learn well. And yet still, after all this time, there is more I do not know. It is humbling.'

Ekon was silent and then he sighed, light as the breath of a lover. 'There are few things that will take a warrior's honour faster than knowing they are not all they thought they were. It is why we ensure new slaves are in a weakened state when they swear the oath. We keep you captive to allow you to absorb the song uninterrupted but also so that the first time you fight us again, or see us fight, you can't win. It made you angry, didn't it? That you couldn't beat us in those early days here?'

Lilla ran his tongue across his parched lips, swallowing the first retort that sprang to them. 'It did, high one.'

'And yet in the last two years we have moulded your fighting style to one that fits with ours. We have brought you from below your previous standard to better than you were, not just as warriors, but in what you know. In what you are, and what you can accomplish. Warfare for us is as much an art form as pottery or weaving or painting. You fight – fought – very well, you and the Yaloh, but now you fight in the Pechaqueh style, and so you fight better. Our gift to you, alongside the song. Among so much more.'

'And yet dishonourable.' Ekon's face went hard and Lilla's eyes widened in alarm. 'F-forgive me,' he stuttered, throwing himself back on to his knees and pressing his face to the dirt.

There was a long, pregnant silence above him and his shoulder blades twitched, awaiting the blade that would ram past them into his lungs. 'Why dishonourable? And stand up to answer me.'

Lilla's heart was pounding so hard his vision was pulsing with it, but he stood. 'I . . . you said you ensure we are weak and broken before you fight us the first time. That is not the way of my people. Not the way of the jaguar path. You put us at a disadvantage so you might trick us into thinking you are better than we are.'

Ekon snorted. 'Trick? We *are* better than you; it is why your people have been brought under the glory of the song. It is why you fell.'

How easily he spoke of Pechaqueh superiority, as if Lilla should feel nothing but gratitude for being in the presence of one so far above him. And how easily he dismissed the Tokob jaguar path as having no worth. Lilla breathed and bowed. 'Your patience for this slave's hasty words is generous indeed, high one, as is your skill and the wisdom of the lesson. With your permission and his kind thanks, this one will take his leave. Under the song.' It was the best he could do, all he could offer if he did not want to rage and scream and take the eagle by the throat and force him to listen.

'Wait, Lilla.'

Lilla's eyebrows rose. He didn't think Ekon had ever used his name before. The Pecha handed off the axes to a waiting slave, who took them and trotted off ahead, and began to walk slowly to the yard's gate. Lilla fell in just behind, as was customary, and Ekon gestured that he should walk by his side. Another surprise. 'That was perhaps unthoughtful of me,' he said, but didn't look in the Tokob direction.

Lilla startled, but to acknowledge the apology would shame the man.

'I would ask you about the Tokob ejab. No, no, there is nothing to fear,' he added when Lilla pulled back on instinct and began again to kneel. 'Please, stand. As you know, it is a . . . horror to us, what your people have done to our gods. Your heresy, your ignorance – though of course you could not be expected to know any better.'

The man seemed oblivious to this further offence and so Lilla kept breathing and let the insults wash over him. *He can't help it. He truly believes these things about us.* But he was surprised at how much it still stung.

'I would try and understand it,' the eagle continued. 'And try and make you see why it is wrong. If you are to live under the song, if you are to earn your freedom and live among us, we must know we can trust you as we trust the Chitenecah or the Tlaloxqueh, for example. That means trusting that your ejab will not begin their wickedness again as soon as they are free.' He paused a moment and glanced sidelong at Lilla, as if weighing his words. 'Many of your people are proud of their god-killers and wear that pride like eagle feathers. But not you, I think.'

Be Pechaqueh in your heart, Lilla. Believe what they believe, the better to end them all. Betray everything to save everything.

'I was proud,' he said softly, Xessa's face mocking him, calling him a traitor, from the depths of his memory. Malel, but he missed the bite of her ire. 'This slave wished to walk their path himself, though it was not to be. You must understand, ejab are respected and honoured among my people for everything they do, not just the risk of the hunt itself, but all they suffer under the spirit-magic that deafens them to the Drowned's song. Forgive me, the holy Setatmeh song.'

Ekon's expression was a mix of disgust and curiosity as they passed through the gate and down the long, open passageway.

'They are our . . . the holy Setatmeh are our greatest predator, high one. To us, the concept of human sacrifice is inextricably bound up with our god, Malel the mother of all, on whose skin we live. A sacrifice to her is rare and only offered during the greatest need. And, of course, our numbers are not enough to sacrifice to the Dr— the holy Setatmeh regularly, as you do here. So what other choice did we have? Water is life, but they are death. High one.'

'But they are gods,' Ekon said, and though his voice was soft it echoed back from the walls hemming them in.

'They are *your* gods,' Lilla corrected, his scalp tightening at daring to speak so. 'Tokob histories tell of these creatures appearing in our waters hundreds of years ago. The shamans of that time could find no link between them and Malel. They were simply a new, terrifying predator, deadlier than the jaguar. What else were we supposed to do?' Ekon didn't answer and Lilla dared again, his heart beating hummingbird wings against his ribs.

'If an unknown creature, something you had never seen or heard of before, suddenly began slaughtering your people, would you name it god, high one? Or would you fight against it?'

Ekon glanced at him, anger and possibly something else tightening the muscles around his mouth. 'You said "I was proud",' he said in a neutral tone, evidently unwilling to address anything else Lilla had said.

The Toko ducked his head. He had pushed, possibly too far. But had he made the Feather think, at least? *What does it matter if I did? These people can't be educated, will never see reason.* Why, then, did he feel compelled to try with Ekon?

'Yes, high one, this slave was proud, all his life he was proud of the ejab, honoured them, revered those who died performing their duty. This slave danced and drummed for them, prayed for their spirits to find rebirth. And then . . .' Lilla lost the formality of his speech as he spoke, the words coming from deep within. 'I came beneath the song. I know I have not heard it for long, and I know from the talk of the dog warriors that the song is not how it used to be, but . . . but it is a wonder, is it not? It,' he paused again, not because he worried he would sound foolish, but to find the truth of the words he wanted to speak. 'It tells me things. Tells me who I am and what I can be. What I should be. Is it so for everyone?'

Ekon's disgust faded and his face became still, almost wondering. He gripped Lilla's forearm and drew him to a halt. 'Yes. Or I believe so. The song finds our deepest truth and shows it to us. What does it show you?'

'That I am not worthy,' Lilla said honestly. Pain flickered at the admission and he looked down at the Pechaqueh hand on his arm, then further down, to his own dusty feet and legs. 'That I, this slave, will never be worthy.' His voice was husky and rage and loneliness battered against his ribcage, straining to break free in a roar of sound that would never end.

'That will change,' Ekon promised in a low voice, squeezing his wrist. 'As your status changes, the song's truth – your truth – will change with it. It is already in your heart, Lilla. Now you must let it into your spirit, into every part of you, your breath and blood and balls. Drink it like honeypot and feel its warmth steal through you. Alter you. The more you bathe in it, the cleaner you will become. The higher you might rise.'

Ekon's fervour was a physical warmth on Lilla's skin.

'I have always sought to give myself to something greater,' he whispered. 'For Tokob, it is Malel and the spiral path to rebirth. The drum-dances to the ancestors used to pull my spirit free of my body and send it soaring. I never thought I would feel anything like that again when I was stolen from my home and brought here. I never thought there was anything else, anything I could cling to.'

'The song is but the beginning,' Ekon said and though his hand gentled on Lilla's arm, it didn't release him. 'The song leads us to the world spirit. The song is our call to it and when it wakens from its long sleep, everything will change. *Everything*. Soon, perhaps.' He moved closer still until Lilla could taste his breath. The Feather wasn't particularly handsome, but in this moment, in this yearning for Lilla to understand, he was almost beautiful. The Toko shivered and longing poured through him, entwined with the song. Longing to possess and be possessed by one so far above him. So much greater than him.

And then Ekon stepped back and began walking again. 'Rest. And remember the lesson of the punishment run. I don't expect to see you make a mistake like that again.'

'As the high one commands,' Lilla said, but the Feather was already gone.

ENET

Chosen's quarters, the source,
Singing City, Pechacan, Empire of Songs
185th day of the Great Star at evening

Thirteen sun-years. One and a half cycles of the Great Star's appearances in the morning and in the evening. Singer Xac was one of the strongest and most accomplished holy lords in the last hundred years.

Enet's mind was well-trained and it was easy to wake with the dawn and with the Singer's glory and majesty foremost in her thoughts. She stretched in the cool of her suite in the source and let images of the Singer dance behind her eyes. The Singer of a few years ago, at the height of his power and the height of his desires. The height of his beauty.

All gone now.

She cut off the thought before it was even half-formed and rolled over in the pillows to fumble among the contents of a low shelf until she found the cup and the small jar next to it. She sat up and tipped some of the fine silvery powder from the jar into the water and drank it down, licking greedily

20

at the last drops in the cup and the thin rime of gritty powder coating its inside and her own gums. The tonic soothed her almost immediately, settling her heart and allowing her to bring her thoughts more firmly under control as the familiar burn made its way down her throat and through her chest to her stomach.

Almost, Enet could feel the magic in it begin its work as it mixed with the countless other tonics she had drunk in the last two years, brightening her eyes and sharpening her mind. Limitless possibilities presented themselves before her; all the things she could do and accomplish with the tonic's magic working in her.

She clapped twice and her body slave appeared from the adjoining room to lead her through the lavishly painted corridors to the bathing area. The song was a low rumble, only occasionally jarring into dissonance or jagging up into clanging disharmony. It was always most peaceful when he slept, and so the Great Octave encouraged the Singer to rest often, overseeing the council herself, intercepting reports from songstone mines and the Melody and anything else that might disturb the holy lord. Doing all she could to soothe the Singer, as was her duty as Great Octave. Anything for the Empire.

Sleep also curbed his . . . other urges.

His only urge. Blood.

The Great Octave and Chosen of the Singer carefully put that thought, too, from her mind, for even if the holy lord could not read it while he slept, a Listener might. Some, at least, had become practised at navigating the turbulent waters of the song in its mighty new configuration. Communication was no longer impossible from one end of the Empire to the other, though it remained extraordinarily difficult. Enet's loyalty was absolute, but her enemies were many. It would not do for idle thoughts to suggest otherwise.

21

Instead, she reminded herself that under Singer Xac's firm hand, the conquest of Ixachipan and all its tribes and lands was finally complete. He had done that. His might and majesty, his glory and the power of his song, had stiffened the spines of the warriors of the Melody and driven them to victory. The Singer's power and accomplishments were all, and if the song was different these days, waking and sleeping, then that was his right. Who were the citizens of the Empire of Songs to question his will? Who was Enet?

For two years, there had been peace.

Two years in which the gossip had faded and the continuing supply of slaves to the pyramid had become routine, commonplace. Hadn't they won, despite – or because of – the song's new rhythm and harsh, discordant melody? Hadn't it brought them victory and brought peace to Ixachipan? How then could it be anything other than a marvel?

If the streets ran with blood a little more often and the newest slaves were fractious or outright rebellious, well, that was the will of the Singer. Blood was the way, now. Strength was the way. If punishments were harsher and deaths more frequent, that too was the Singer's will and the Empire's glory. At least until the world spirit's awakening, when all sickness and disease and unhappiness would be wiped away.

Enet would bathe and then go out into one of the pyramid's gardens to watch the sun rise over the Singing City, the heart-city, and imagine what that waking might feel like. She would let the city's slow stretch into consciousness brush over her skin, its people press against her like a babe wanting to suck.

Enet blinked away sudden pain and the image that went with that thought. *Pikte; my boy. My precious diamond child.*

The courtesans' quarters were silent but for the low, urgent sounds of two or more taking their pleasure together. As with Enet, so with them; the Singer's long seclusion as he forged the song into a new melody had left them bereft of his divine touch and they must make do with only each other.

The Great Octave turned down the corridor to the bathing room, passing a pretty, scarred Chorus warrior stationed there. The warrior fell in behind her body slave and then, as they reached the door, slid ahead to check it for danger. Enet waited, serene in the promise of a future of change and strength and glory, until the warrior nodded and gestured for her to enter.

The old slave stripped Enet's tunic and helped her into the cold water. She gasped, shivering, but ducked beneath the surface, her eyes closed against the sting of the salt that made the pool undesirable to the holy Setatmeh. When she surfaced, her long black hair thoroughly wetted, the slave was already in the water with her, her soft, wrinkled body even more puckered at the chill. She used a cloth to wipe saltwater out of Enet's eyes and nose, and then stroked it in long, firm lines across her chest and back and down her arms. She hummed a low lullaby that Enet remembered from her childhood, soft and soothing. The Great Octave rested her head on the side and let herself float, enjoying the firm pressure of washcloth against skin and how the woman's lullaby wove through and around the notes of the song, gentling it. A small smile played on her lips, here in the privacy of the baths with none but her oldest and most loyal to see.

When she was clean, Enet lay on a low couch while the slave massaged oil into her hair and skin. She let the old woman's expert touch probe tight muscles and soothe unwanted worries alike. Enet's fingers brushed at her throat and the single feather tattooed there, a nervous gesture she mostly managed to resist, at least in public. Chosen to ascend with the Singer when his time came. Not chosen to replace him.

23

The slave's humming shifted into a different tune, the hymn of triumph and success that told of Tenaca, Pechacan's first Singer, and all she had accomplished. Again Enet smiled, this time in appreciation and acknowledgement of the wordless reminder. Of the woman's perception and loyalty. She still had time; not much, but perhaps enough, if she was diligent.

For the last two sun-years she had waited, the very public, very beautiful face of generosity and competence, drawing the citizens of the Singing City to her like hummingbirds to nectar, the reputation of her philanthropy and capability spreading through the Empire and slowly superseding the rumours which had gone before, buried now beneath her wealth and the freedom with which she distributed it.

Wealth she spent without regret on ensuring her three songstone mines in Tokoban were productive. The huge veins of songstone discovered after that land was brought under the song were a source of immense status and she'd acquired the mines outright as soon as they were discovered. Despite the prestige they brought her, it wasn't quite complete: there were four mines in Tokoban, and she knew well who had managed to buy control of the last one.

Fucking Pilos.

The Great Octave grunted and sat up, and the slave reached quickly for Enet's huipil and helped her back into it, then shrugged into her own and scurried after her. Enet stalked back through the corridors, past the warriors and the first early-rising courtesans heading for the baths now that she was done. All of them gave her the respect and obeisance she was due; it didn't restore her mood. Her fingers drifted again to trail over the tattoo decorating one side of her throat before she changed the gesture into a brushing back of wet hair. She was in public now; any sign of weakness would be like blood to a jaguar.

Yet Enet knew her history: nine times since the discovery of the song-magic and the founding of the Empire had a Pecha with no feathers been gifted the magic in preference to any of those Chosen. Once, even, an unchosen Pecha had become Singer over the two-feathered heir themself. It could happen again.

Then it will happen.

I do none of this for myself. I do it for the Empire. For all people and all time. Nothing will change that.

The sun was half a golden disc on the horizon when Enet stepped into gardens lush with dew and heavy with scent. Up here, it smelt of earth and growth and wealth rather than the press of humanity in the city all around, and it was easy to believe all was right with the world. Easy to watch the line of the rising sun claim the landscape a stick at a time so that a thousand shades of green burst into life beneath its caress. Easy to know that what she was doing was right. That the gods approved.

A million people, content in the Empire and under the song. 'All for you,' she whispered as the dawn shattered and its colours faded into the blue of morning. The words were a prayer and a promise spoken upon the breeze this time, not just within the privacy of her heart. 'I do it all for you.'

The song hitched and rumbled, the familiar cadence that was the Singer beginning to stir, and Enet hurried back indoors. Outside his sleeping chamber, her slaves were setting out a cushion, a low table and a stack of bark-paper and inks and brush. She bypassed them to her own rooms and let other slaves dress her. The one who had been in the pillows with her during the night clutched the first reports that had been delivered for her attention, his gaze demurely fixed on the floor.

Enet exhaled a tiny snort. Demure? She knew those wide black eyes would flash with loathing if they dared meet her own. How he hated and wanted her – and hated himself for the wanting. It was among the reasons she most often chose him; the bite of his hate was as hot as chillies in her belly, a sensation that brought her almost as much pleasure as his lean body and clever hands. She smiled as her body slave fixed the huge, elaborate headdress into her hair with pins.

When she was dressed as befitted her station, Enet settled herself at the low table outside the Singer's chamber and took the first report the slave handed her. He'd collated them in order of importance, and she drank honeyed water and picked at fruit as she read of the latest songstone yield from Tokoban. The report covered her own mines and Pilos's too – she paid well for the information, and it pleased her to see that his mine was less productive than any one of hers.

'How big is the quarry where the cave used to be now?' Enet asked with sweet malice.

The slave licked his lips, but his voice when he answered was devoid of emotion. 'Almost a stick wide, high one, and in three places has reached two hundred paces deep. The upper part of the Sky City has been demolished to accommodate it.'

'What was it the Tokob used to call that place?' she asked, feigning forgetfulness.

'The womb of Malel, high one.'

Enet laughed. 'The womb of Malel,' she echoed. 'How quaint. And that was the place where you yourself were taken by the famed warriors of the Melody, was it not? For torturing one of the holy Setatmeh like the savages your people are? Shaman? Is that not right?' She reached back and slid her palm beneath his kilt and along his inner thigh. 'Back when your name was . . . oh, let me think.' She pinched suddenly, hard, and he flinched. 'Remind me what your name used to be, slave, back when you were permitted one?'

He dared meet her eyes for a heartbeat, no more, and her smile broadened at the naked loathing she saw there.

'Tayan,' he said. 'My name is Tayan.'

'Tayan,' Enet said, rolling the name around her mouth and making it a caress. His lips thinned. 'Shaman of this Malel, and now witness to her destruction. And what does she do in retaliation, shaman of Malel? Nothing.'

She caressed his thigh again and despite her words, despite his loathing, heat bloomed in his cheeks and he swallowed again. Enet laughed and withdrew her hand. She gestured towards him. 'Take this thing away,' she snapped, her voice suddenly cold. 'His stink disgusts me.'

The slave handed the reports to another and then pressed his forehead to the mats, before rising and backing away. Enet paid him no more mind, for there was a low, comforting murmur of voices from the room opposite. The Singer was awake.

'Spear of the Singer Haapo, you have something to say?'

The traditional daily council meetings no longer took place. Singer Xac was weaving his own traditions. Together, he and his Great Octave reviewed reports and made judgments and issued them to the councillors via a seemingly limitless number of slaves. Today, though, the council had been summoned peremptorily and at short notice when Enet had ascertained the Singer had rested well and would oversee his council's efforts and review their accomplishments in person.

As expected, the increasingly contentious question of the fate of the Melody was being raised once more. It was a question Enet herself had yet to decide upon, but she could not deny that those councillors who had tentatively voiced their concerns at intervals over the last half-year made a compelling argument: now that all Ixachipan was under the song, what need for the Melody at its current capacity, its current size?

Other words, spoken softly and not to Enet – though she had heard them nonetheless, of course – ventured that a smaller Melody would mean smaller tithes to the great pyramid, resulting in greater wealth for the rest of the Empire. Or greater wealth for the councillors and most of the noble families, at least. The Great Octave knew that not a single bead of those savings would be passed down to the merchants or farmers, crafters or artisans who performed the bulk of the Empire's necessary transactions.

She was surprised, though, that the dissenters had managed to seduce Haapo into speaking out, especially now that he was Spear of the Singer, the holy lord's military adviser. If anyone was loyal to the Melody, it should be him.

Haapo, formerly only a councillor until Enet herself had elevated him – with the Singer's agreement, naturally – shuffled on his mat and cleared his throat several times. Pretty and pliable and oh-so suggestible, he had made a perfect, and completely different, replacement for Pilos after the latter's disgrace.

'Holy lord, Great Octave, I have been tasked by members of the nobility across the Empire to broach a delicate matter. The matter is the future of the Melody in these times of glory and peace.'

Enet noted that High Feather Atu, newly arrived from the Melody fortress to the south, twitched in place. Blood rushed into his cheeks. He too was young and pretty, but very much the product of Pilos's teachings rather than her own. That one would not bend to her gentle persuasion, no matter what form it took. She ignored him and gestured for Haapo to continue. Behind the rose-cotton hanging, the great Singer was gazing mindlessly out into the garden. The Toko slave shaman, Enet's earnest, reluctant bed-mate, was at his side, his fingertips drumming almost silently against his knee in the peculiar rhythm of his shamanic practice. She felt a flash of discomfort when she realised it was a similar nervous tic to her own stroking of the tattoo along her throat.

Blinking, she focused back on Haapo.

'For more than two sun-years, holy lord, Ixachipan has been at peace under the song. There is no more war to be had, there are no more peoples to bring into the glory of our Empire. The question, then, among many nobles, is why the Melody needs to continue. Surely now is the time for plenty, for peace and for prosperity. We do not need blood and war and horror. We ask the great Singer's wisdom on this matter.'

A thorny question prettily phrased. Nothing about it spoke to greed. The Melody was the only other true power in the Empire and the Great Octave did not have control over it. She had her own people within their ranks, of course, loyal to her above all, but it was not enough. She had ruined Pilos and she could probably ruin Atu, but so far she didn't have an ally in a strong enough position to take over as High Feather in his stead. And until she did, better to leave that scorpion sleeping than invite it to strike.

Atu spoke. 'May I address the honoured Spear's remarks before the holy lord renders his wisdom?'

Enet blinked in surprise and then turned the full power of her attention on the young warrior. 'High Feather, it is always a pleasure to listen to you speak,' she murmured.

Atu's eyelid twitched, but he merely inclined his head in acknowledgement. 'Thank you, Great Octave. Holy lord, with respect, the Empire of Songs is far from as peaceful as the council and the nobility seem to believe. There is unrest across much of our lands, with most of it – as expected – arising from Tokob and Yaloh. Not even those captured in the very earliest days of the conflict have lived three years under the song; for the vast majority, it is only two. That is nowhere near enough for them to embrace their new home, religion and way of life. Those who have survived their first years as slave warriors would rise up against us if they were sent instead to be farm or house slaves. Also, the Xentib dog warriors are not yet a full Star cycle under the song. They fought hard to bring Tokoban under the song and are trusted in principle, but they may still falter if Tokob encourage it in them. Yes, we have peace, but it is as delicate as a butterfly's wing. Even to breathe too roughly over it could tear it.'

Enet's eyebrows rose; she had not expected the High Feather to have the spirit of a poet. Her curiosity grew. She would have to contact her informants to gain knowledge of the man, this time of a more intimate nature.

'High Feather, it sounds as if you don't trust in your own methods,' Councillor Haapo said with a small smile as he cooled himself with a fan woven from bamboo leaves.

Atu scowled and his eyelid flickered again. 'Spear, the Melody contains fifteen thousand highly trained slave and dog warriors. Would you have me free them all here and now? What do you think they'd do with that freedom?'

Who was this boy to speak so eloquently?

Another councillor laughed and waved her hand in dismissal. 'If you don't trust them, tie them up and use them as target practice,' she said dismissively. 'Or offer them to the holy Setatmeh.'

'Target practice, Councillor?' Atu asked and his voice wavered just a little as he fought back the scorn that flashed in his eyes. Enet's interest grew apace with her amusement, both – for now – outstripping her indignation. 'Why would anyone need to perfect their archery if we have peace? If there is no more war? In fact,' he added, 'I believe a part of your wealth comes from the sale of weapons, does it not?'

Enet sat up a little straighter: the High Feather was very well-informed indeed. She saw the moment the councillor understood his implication, saw the sudden confusion and then wariness slip across her features. She was loyal to the Great Octave – they were all loyal to the Great Octave – but only as long as it didn't cost them anything. Atu was pointing out it would cost a great deal in lost sales and Enet couldn't even refute it.

'They, we, we still need hunters,' the councillor spluttered, and although it was true, it was also weak. Atu offered a polite smile and dismissed her from the discussion as if she were a slave.

'Without the Melody, Councillors, wild and ungovernable slaves in their thousands will be released upon the Empire like a virulent disease. And without a Melody, there will be no one to end their uprising when it surely begins. That is not a risk I and my warriors are prepared to take without the direct word of the Singer.' Atu pressed his forehead to the mats for a moment and then sat back again on his heels. His face was calm, giving no hint of any turmoil that might be within.

'Is it the holy lord's will that the Melody be disbanded and the fifteen thousand slave and dog warriors be released into the Empire? It will be as the great Singer commands.'

As one, the councillors turned to face the rose-cotton and the faint outline of the Singer behind it. Enet, too, turned to face the holy lord, though from her vantage parallel to the hanging, she could actually see him. She waited a few seconds to see whether he would answer and, when there was no response, she turned back into the room.

'At this time, it is not the great Singer's will that the Melody be disbanded. The slaves must all complete their time in its Talons until they come to fully embrace the song and their place within our civilisation. We will not risk unrest because we have hurried the education of those who need it most. There will always be some who refuse the song's glory and Pechaqueh wisdom. They can be disposed of in the usual manner. The rest will serve the Empire of Songs and be content with their place within it.'

Atu bowed to the mat again and, an instant later, Councillor Haapo and the woman who had spoken did the same. The question would be raised again, in a half-year or a sun-year or perhaps less, but for now the High Feather and his warriors were secure and power in the Empire remained balanced between them and Enet in the source.

She breathed. *All as the gods decree.*

The Great Octave's estate was cool and secluded, the perimeter wall blocking many of the sounds and scents of the city so that the song rang supreme across the lush gardens surrounding her palace. The wall itself was screened by a small orchard of fruit and pom trees, bamboo and watervine. Despite her haste, she paused to wander through the trees and shrubs, to breathe in the shade and dappled light, to centre her spirit within her body and the world.

It was rare that she got to come home; usually only a few times a week, whenever she ran out of her tonic and the Singer was suitably distracted. His order for her to never leave his side, made in the aftermath of his great blooding of the song so long before, was not strictly enforced; besides, the only people to have heard him make it were her own guards and they would never betray her.

The gardens of her home were sculpted but natural, and the murals decorating the walls of most of the rooms and corridors of her palace were beautifully drawn, of animals and legends and the holy Setatmeh. Of herself in the Great Octave's headdress. Visible signs of her wealth and status.

If there was anywhere within the Empire that Enet was safe it was here, and she relished that feeling of security as she padded up the path alongside the thin, deep stream she had had diverted at huge cost from the Blessed Water to her private offering pool.

'Open the sanctum,' Enet said as soon as she was inside and her old body slave bobbed acknowledgement, her knees clicking. The Great Octave followed her through the entertaining rooms to the centre of the house, where they paused beside a beautiful painted wooden screen. The slave folded it away to reveal a thick mahogany door. Enet stepped inside as soon as it began to swing open and the old woman took up a candle and followed her in. The room had no windows and the light was small, but she lit wood shavings in a brazier and piled on sticks infused with citrus that crackled and popped until the glow brightened enough to see properly.

Shelves lined each wall, crammed with books and scrolls, artefacts from across the Empire and even beyond its bounds. Books of legend and of prophecy, books of old magic and forbidden magic. And, in the centre, the songstone cap. *Her* songstone cap. Her future and that of the Empire of Songs.

Its paleness was unremarkable until the flames caught the flecks in its surface and lit it up like a tiny, inverted sky littered with stars. She had not expected it to be so difficult to carve, but now, finally, it wore its sacred shape – a pyramid. The wooden angle she'd demanded from a master craftsman sat on the nearest low shelf, along with her chisel and hammer. It was so close to completion; to perfection. Looking at it now, she believed for the first time that it would be ready when the day came – soon now – that she finally needed it. When it would secure her in her power and together they would remake this world.

It was so close to finished, with just one final bump of stone that needed smoothing, a bump that had proved resistant to her efforts thus far. But not for much longer.

Enet's gaze flicked up to the books beyond the capstone, books that had introduced her to this laborious but powerful magic many years before. And years it had taken for her to acquire the right size piece of unworked songstone under the cover of absolute secrecy and have it brought here. To learn to carve and shape not just the stone but the magic within it.

The books were of immense power in and of themselves, but this . . . this was a magic lost to the storms of history and not performed in generations until she found it. Lost in the same way the use of the stone knife had been lost. She wondered, fleetingly, how many other forms of magic and ritual Pechaqueh had forgotten, what other paths to power she might have taken if only she'd learnt them first. Still, this was her path and she was almost ready to walk it.

To work the songstone oneself, with dedication and with prayers on lips that were unknown even by the Pechaqueh master masons who usually shaped it for use in the pyramids, that was where the magic lay. In the chanting and the asking and the slow, patient working of the stone. There and the tonic, of course, at least in Enet's case.

The Great Octave's blood pulsed at her wrists and the base of her throat as she knelt on a blue mat and took up the hammer and chisel. Delicately, like a lover about to touch for the first time the object of her desire, she began to shape the songstone a little more.

Behind her, the old woman hummed one of the ancient,

forgotten prayers, and Enet chanted the words with her. Slowly, the magic gathered, in the stone and then the tools, in the air and in her skin. Slowly she shaped it and drew it to her will and then offered herself to it. A cycle like the Great Star's, like the sun's and the moon's. Reciprocal. Binding. Powerful.

Tiny puffs of songstone drifted from the pyramid's surface and Enet breathed deeply, feeling them catch in her lungs with a sweet fire, begging them to adhere to her insides and deposit their infinitesimal load of magic within her. More fell in a soft cloud into the wide-mouthed basin at the song-stone's base, collecting there for her use in the tonic that strengthened her bond with the song-magic and the world spirit whose voice it was that spoke through the Singer.

Enet ran through the cycle of chants and prayers as she worked, lost in contemplation of the future she was creating with her own hands and will. All she did was for peace. She would not – could not – allow her plans to go awry. Whatever actions she needed to take to accomplish them, she would. She wouldn't be stopped; she wouldn't *allow it*. She was Enet, devoted, implacable, pure of intent. She would take this power and—

A sharp crack echoed through the room and she blinked back to reality as the old woman's hum broke off into a cry and Enet's own prayer stuttered and fell silent. She didn't understand what she was seeing, not for long moments. The songstone had cracked a quarter of the way down its tapered length, a jagged seam like lightning jagging through the entire capstone, beginning at the tip of her chisel. There was a faint grinding as the pieces slipped and then settled, a fissure opening between them. A canyon. A chasm into which they would all fall, screaming.

The songstone was broken.

No. *She had broken* her songstone.

Broken her magic.

The tools fell from Enet's numb hands, the chisel's sharp edge scraping the skin of her knee as it fell to the mats. 'No,' she breathed. And again, louder. 'No no no *no no!!*'

Enet's slave grabbed her around the shoulders, pulling her in against her side as if to comfort her. The Great Octave allowed it for a single moment as she lost herself in the awful reality of exactly what had just happened to all her plans, to *everything*, and then pushed herself roughly upright.

She stared at the broken capstone, willing it to restore itself, for it *not to have happened,* and then she put both hands over her mouth to muffle the raw scream as it clawed its way out of her chest. Her fingers tasted of stone dust and she inhaled the fine powder and immediately coughed it back out, great hacking coughs that mingled with sobs in a tight throat. The magic was gone from the stone, that ancient and forgotten magic she had needed so badly, and so the dust choked her when it never had before. It didn't gift her its magic now; it punished her with it. Punished her arrogance and thwarted her ambition. The songstone didn't care that all this was for peace; it didn't care for her or what she was going to do to heal the Empire of Songs.

'It's over.'

The words came out harsh and ragged, coughed from the depths of her chest like blood, and Enet shoved away from the stone and onto her feet. Ignoring her slave's inarticulate cry, she bolted out of the room, frightening other slaves and ignoring them all, running to her bedchamber and scrabbling on a shelf for her divination bones and mat.

It might not be so bad. It might not be the end despite her own raw words.

With trembling fingers, Enet laid out the painted depiction

of the world, rolled the bones between her palms and breathed on them, and then cast. They bounced and skittered across the mat and came to a halt. The Great Octave gripped the edge of the table and stared down at them, eyes flickering from one to the other and comparing their relative positions. Reading her future, the Singer's future, and the fate of Ixachipan in their pattern. She uttered another hoarse scream and swept them all onto the floor, the mat spinning away across the room, and then upended the table when the violence failed to soothe her.

Calamity was coming. And she was its author.

THE SINGER

The source, Singing City, Pechacan, Empire of Songs

I am the blood.

I am the blood and the songstone and war without end. War to feed the songstone. War for blood. More and more blood for the songstone's thirst.

I am the blood. I am. I am the blood.

. . .

. . .

I am the song. The broken song I must fix as the shaman says. He tells me.

Tells me who I am, what I am. What I was, once. What I should be, still.

Shaman tells me no more blood. It hurts. Without blood, everything hurts. Songstone is angry. The song is angry. It wants.

I broke the song.

Shaman . . .

Shaman says Enet broke the song. Broke me, broke the song. Shaman says fix the song. But not with blood.

The Jaguar Path

Enet says . . .
Shaman says . . .
But the song . . . the song says blood.

TAYAN

The source, Singing City, Pechacan, Empire of Songs, 185th day of the Great Star at evening

After Enet had dismissed him a little past dawn, Tayan had hurried to the slave bath, where he'd scrubbed his skin, rolled the saltwater around his mouth and dragged his fingers through his hair. Still, he could smell her on him. He could always smell her on him. It wasn't unpleasant; that was the problem.

Eyes stinging from the saltwater, Tayan dried himself and dressed, rubbing a cloth through hair that hung halfway down his back. It had taken Enet summoning him to her bed more than half a year ago for him to finally begin to use the baths instead of a bucket and cloth, as all right-minded people did.

Once every three days, there would be a small jar of oil he could massage into his hair and skin afterwards, leaving it soft, lightly scented and glossy instead of dull with salt residue.

Not this morning, though. His skin was tight and dry, a little too small. Much as he had to be, here in the heart of the Empire. Meek and shrunken, his talents hidden.

One of Tayan's brands caught his eye as he pulled the tunic over his head, a tall, narrow-based triangle on his upper right arm, its twin on his left. Slave brand. Property.

This one had cut through the spiral inked into his shoulder, as if severing him from his path as a shaman. He'd had the thought many times before and shook his head as he finished dressing, before dragging his fingers through his hair again to clear the worst of the tangles. He was more than a skin-deep shaman; it was in his bones and muscles, his spirit wedded to the spiral path and the spirit world that lived beneath this one of flesh. It was no different to the warriors who took wounds that carved through their jaguar tattoos. He refused to let the symbolism mean anything. Slave he might be for now, but shaman he was forever, in this life and all those that had come before and would come after. Wedded to Malel.

Wedded to Lilla, he reminded himself, though the previous night and this dawn gave the lie to his assertion. They'd both known and been friends with people back in Tokoban who brought others into their marriage or married more than one partner; neither he nor Lilla had wanted that sort of relationship. *Not that this could ever be that.*

Tayan shivered; his ability to resist Enet's charms was sporadic, and last night – and this dawn – he had given in with an ease that clawed at him, desperate for the forget-fulness that came with taking and with surrender. He scraped at the guilt shrivelling his heart as he began plaiting the heavy weight of damp hair.

In the last months, Enet's and Tayan's mutual spite and disgust had become a part of their play, so that while he hated the Great Octave with every strand of his spirit, he wanted her just as much. She knew that; she liked that.

As ever, he put Lilla's face in his mind and focused on it,

and then Xessa's and Toxte's and his parents'. Tiamoko, Lutek and all the others, one after another. All his people. Every Toko who had ever been or ever would be. Tayan was going to tear this empire to pieces, and until that day came, he would do whatever was needful.

Including betraying Lilla?

Yes. No. Yes.

He didn't acknowledge what Enet had told him when he'd first been given to her by Pilos, that Lilla had not claimed him as kin or husband, hadn't tied their fates and lives together in slavery. He had never acknowledged it because it wasn't true. It couldn't be true. Tayan had been claimed, and Lilla's family and Xessa too, probably. Lilla would have claimed him so that they might rise from slave to servant and then to free together. He would have; of course he would have.

And so you repay him by fucking your owner every time she clicks her fingers? The voice in his head spoke in the Great Octave's amused, mocking tones. It was better than the times he asked himself the question in Lilla's voice.

I am a slave. I do what I must to stay alive so we can be together again. What other choice do I have? She can kill me any time she decides I've displeased her; rebuffing her charms would certainly do that.

He'd repeated these words so often as well, but unlike his belief in his identity as shaman, these had almost ceased to have meaning and were now as thin as morning mist over the gaping chasm of his betrayal. Because *he wanted her.* Gods and ancestors, but he wanted her. Craved her touch and the bite of her scorn in equal measure, her slick wet heat and lithe strength and sharp, piercing fingernails.

Tayan paused to swill another mouthful of bitter saltwater around his teeth and tongue. This time, a small gesture of penance, he grimaced and swallowed it. As soon as they were reunited, he'd tell Lilla what he'd done to survive. Tayan wondered what would disgust his husband more: the fire that Enet could kindle in his belly with little more than a lingering glance; or that he bent all his skill and knowledge to saving the life of the Singer, at whose will they had all been torn from their homes in the first place.

Not quite covering myself in glory.

A promise that had been made in fear and desperation and which he was now trapped within. A promise to save the life of a man dedicated to destroying theirs; a man who had already done so and who deserved nothing but the horrific death he still seemed destined for despite Tayan's every ministration.

And yet. *And yet.* Tayan was a shaman dedicated to the healing arts, to medicine as well as ritual and the gods and journeying. And he'd never seen anyone so in need of healing as Singer Xac. Physical healing, yes, but also spiritual. The man was lost so deeply inside his uncontrolled desires that it was almost impossible to reach him in the flesh world. And so, these days, they didn't.

Tayan finished braiding his hair and twisted the thick plaited rope around and up, pinning the tail high on the back of his head as all the Singer's slaves were required to do, and then slipped from the slave baths and made his way towards the source. Snakes slithered anxiously in his gut.

Before his audacious, desperate declaration that he could save the Singer – a promise he had made only to try and save his own life – Tayan had known that there were four worlds: the flesh world of life; the Realm of the Ancestors; the spiral path trodden by spirits; and the Underworld. Now, he had learnt of the fifth: the song world.

A world he had never even suspected existed, one not mentioned in any of the Tokob histories. A space inside the song of Pechacan and the Empire. A connectivity, an immensity, previously hidden to him. The shaman was forbidden from using his journey-magic in the source, for the Pechaqueh feared it and his powers when the magic was in him, but despite not having that familiarity or the comfort of his spirit guides, Tayan had still learnt the secrets of the song-magic. Just not on purpose.

He had been in the small, bare-plaster room he shared with the rest of Enet's slaves, sinking into trance despite the lack of his journey-magic. He had been seeking something, anything, that would remind him of home and give him a reason to live, perhaps even a way to reach his ancestors and the spirits so that he might not be quite so alone. He knew of the Listeners and had thought that perhaps, now there were pyramids stretching across Tokoban, he might use the song to cross the endless sticks north to the soil of his people. The skin of Malel. *Home.*

What he had found instead was the song-world, a concept unknown to him, one he could not understand and didn't quite know how he had reached. A place without colour or shape or form, and yet in which he had all three – there was the golden thread connecting his shamanic-blue spirit to his flesh. There were and other blazing lights, too. Living people, perhaps? He didn't know. Through and over everything, the song, its individual notes and melodies structures through which he must move. He didn't experience it the way his flesh did, as something inescapable that curled within him. It was so much more than that. It was in him as he was in it, this world made of music and magic, as if all the worlds were one world; all the spirits one spirit.

Tayan had known, instinctively, that he'd always be able

to come here, vast, and alien and terrifying as it was. He'd found the path to the song, and he could learn to walk it just as he'd learnt the path that was a spiral.

But then Shaman Kapal had discovered him within the song's currents, her spirit a great blue snake trailing wings of black shadow: fear. She had rammed her mind into his, seeking to force him from this strange new world and back into his body – or perhaps to snap the thread connecting them entirely.

Tayan had fought ancestors desperate to steal that same golden thread and invade his body; he'd been tricked by his guide Young Jaguar and pushed onto the path to the Underworld; he'd been confused and torn at by wild, ancient spirits. When Kapal threatened him, he'd seen the way to overwhelm her and reduce her spirit to tattered threads that would blow away on the current in an instant. Yet he did nothing, instead allowing her to push him out of the song, feigning confusion and fright of his own.

Distressed, Kapal had taken his deception at face value when she burst into the crowded little room moments later to confront him, Chorus warriors on her heels. He'd been close to death in the source before, more times than he cared to remember and for infractions of far less import, but never this close. Tayan had babbled thanks and pressed his face to the mats in shivering adoration, tears streaming down his face. It wasn't entirely fake; the journey had been brutal and exhausting without the journey-magic, the risks enormous, not to mention that the revelation of the song-world itself had shaken the very foundation of who Tayan was and everything he believed in.

But it had been something unexpected and utterly new, something his insatiable curiosity needed. Tayan was a sun-loving plant growing in perpetual shade without anything to engage his mind and so, as the weeks passed, he fed Kapal's curiosity, performing his small devotions and rituals within sight or hearing of her when Enet was absent. He no longer had the figures of his spirit guides, but that didn't stop him honouring them, or his ancestors and the spirits. Malel herself and her god-born, Snake-sister and Jaguar-brother.

Eventually, Kapal's curiosity won out and they exchanged knowledge of medicine and ritual. Tayan had had weeks to formulate a plan and he spoke openly of the Tokob shamanic tradition of journeying with a sick spirit to uncover the cause of their illness and see if it could be treated. With all the charm and subtlety of a peace-weaver that he possessed, he planted seeds and watered them until Kapal came to the idea as if it were her own. The idea of steadying the Singer from within the very song, spirit to spirit, providing strength and even a structure for him to draw upon.

She couldn't develop this medicine without Tayan and they both knew it. Still, she impressed upon him how unlikely it was that he would succeed in journeying again: according to her, only Pechaqueh shamans and Listeners could enter the song-world. What he had done was some monstrous accident and nothing more.

Tayan snorted at the memory and the warm satisfaction that had come from her stunned surprise when he'd slipped into the song again, easier this time. Yet he was under no illusions about his abilities. If the Pechaqueh didn't believe a single shaman of any of the stolen peoples of the Empire knew how to move through the song, that just meant no one had yet been discovered doing it. Unlike him. Pechaqueh arrogance often blinded them to the abilities and sophistication of those they owned, and Tayan relished every little example of it that he saw. Each was a taste of honeypot, the caress of a loved one, the soft blackness of a moonless night.

That blindness would be how those they underestimated rose against Pechaqueh rule and tore their Empire apart.

Kapal presented the medicine to the source's principal Listener, Chotek, and with his approval to Enet. Tayan had been there for that conversation and the Great Octave had stared at him unblinking, snakelike. As if she knew he had a hand in this somewhere. Tayan kept his head down and his face blank, the attentive, unthinking slave. He – or Kapal, officially – had backed her into a corner and she knew it, but there was no plausible reason to refuse. The medicine could help restore the Singer and the song both to glory, after all. How could she not want that?

To his surprise, Kapal had chosen him as one of the shamans to administer the medicine. He still couldn't tell whether it was a punishment or a reward: the exhaustion that came from hours within the song without the aid of journey-magic was deep and relentless. It was ostensibly for that reason that he had been chosen over any of the source's other shamans, whose strength was given to the holy lord's physical form. Privately, Tayan thought it more likely that if this final medicine didn't work – and they'd exhausted every other treatment he knew of – then the failure of it would be laid at his feet and his life would be forfeit while Kapal's and Chotek's were saved.

And yet, despite everything, it was working.

Not all the time, and not as well as he had hoped, but over the weeks and then the months, and then the turning of the seasons and the Wet, the Singer stabilised and his song with him. Tayan, Kapal and Chotek between them were accomplishing the impossible, dragging a blooded song and a blooded Singer back from madness – and the Empire with them.

A song that had been wild and painful to the ear and the spirit was smoother, at least in the way a porcupine with its quills laid flat was smooth. A Singer that demanded blood every few days and was absent the rest of the time was now a Singer who took offerings once a week and managed the occasional coherent sentence on other topics.

It was working.

And how Enet loathed them for it. Tayan supposed her position as Chosen of the Singer meant she would succeed upon his death, and so every day they healed him was a day she resented. The knowledge he was frustrating her plans brought him a hot rush of pleasure, but as always it was followed with sick apprehension. His life was in danger every second of every day.

As it would be if I did nothing to aid the holy lord. Enet can have me killed or offered to the holy Setatmeh – or the Singer himself – at a moment's notice and no one will question her. I am her property.

The words did very little to comfort him.

Tayan came to the entrance of the grandest chamber within the source, the long oval with the colonnaded wall out into the gardens where the Singer spent most of every day. He cleared his mind of the tumult of his thoughts, for he was soon to enter the song. He glanced reflexively and with a shudder towards the offering pool at one end and his stomach dropped into his feet at the alien, big-eyed face watching him, chin pillowed on forearms as it leant on the pool's edge with the rest of its body hidden in the water.

They were being honoured with the presence of a god. One of the gods his people were dedicated to destroying. Tayan's throat tightened and the breath squeaked out of him. He fell to his knees. Would it be today that he was killed by one of Singer Xac's living ancestors?

The holy Setat lifted up slightly, enough to tilt its head to one side like a bird or a dog, curious, and he saw from its size and the toughened hide like armour covering its torso that it was one of the Greater Drowned. A former Singer, then, not a councillor. It blinked and then opened its mouth, revealing row upon row of tiny, wickedly curved teeth. Whatever it had been before meant nothing: the song of a Lesser Drowned – *holy Setat, not Drowned!* – was just as lethal.

The god drummed its claws on the edge of the pool, four loud *ticks* against the stone as it watched him. Tayan stared at it in terrified awe, sweat beading on his salt-dry skin and his pulse fluttering like a bird in a net in the hollow of his throat.

'Holy Setat, ask and I shall answer.' He breathed the words that were spoken at each new moon offering when Pechaqueh would send slaves to their deaths but pay lip service to offering up their own lives if the holy Setatmeh asked. This wasn't lip service and both he and the water god knew it. Not that Tayan *wanted* to die, but as they locked gazes, he felt a strange pull. A knowing; almost a . . . kinship?

The holy Setat studied him, as if contemplating his offer and analysing the truth with which he made it. He'd seen this particular god before, so perhaps that explained the familiarity. The mottling of its grey-brown skin had a distinctive pattern on the right side of its face, three dots across its cheekbone in the approximate shape of Malel's Bow, the constellation that rose bright in the eastern sky each evening.

No, it was more than familiarity. He knew it. And it knew him. Slowly, Tayan placed his hands flat on the mat in front of him and lowered his head. He didn't drop his gaze, though. Not even the threat of death would make him break eye contact with the monster, the Drowned, the *god*, before him.

'Slave!' Enet called from the far side of the room, where she sat with the Singer. Where Tayan was supposed to be.

Tayan didn't move, watching the holy Setat watching him. It cocked its head the other way and then pushed up on the edge, lifting itself out of the water. The pool gurgled and sloshed as water was pumped into it from the pyramid's belly, only to tumble away down the channel carved in the building's side. The holy Setatmeh personal entrance and exit to visit the Singer.

Beyond the roar of blood in his ears, Tayan could hear Enet's angry voice and the low murmur of someone answering her. Footsteps. And then a kick to the ribs that knocked him off his hands and knees and onto his side. The flare of pain and sudden movement broke the gaze he'd locked with the holy Setat and by the time he'd breathed, and blinked, and scrambled back onto his knees, the Chorus warrior who'd kicked him had followed the direction of his gaze to the pool. She gasped and prostrated herself next to him, murmuring the same prayer, and Enet's protest cut off into a reverent hush. She, too, understood his behaviour now. *Eat her*, Tayan prayed at it. *Eat her and put us all out of our misery. Holy Setat, please. Eat Enet's face off.*

A hysterical laugh bubbled on his tongue and he swallowed it back. He didn't make eye contact this time; instead, he angled his chin up just enough to see its shadow. He waited until it slipped back into the water and then out through the stream and away, down into the tributary from the Blessed Water that cut through the centre of the Singing City.

A murmur of reverence and thanks rose from the group waiting at the other end of the source, and Tayan made his way to them on his hands and knees, as all slaves were required to. He didn't mind the humiliation this time, unsure if his legs would carry him if he tried to stand upright.

The Singer, Shaman Kapal and Enet sat together near the colonnade, patterned in alternating bands of sun and shadow, while a handful of Chorus warriors were dotted around the large space. Enet's body slave, the mute old woman whose name he didn't know even after all this time, sat in her usual place by the wall, alert to the smallest hint of need from the Great Octave.

The Singer slumped among a swathe of pillows, staring through the colonnade into the morning. The sun lit a fire within the flowers of the garden and the feathers of the birds and the faint iridescent gleam of gold in the holy lord's own flesh. Why was the magic moving in his skin? What did the Singer want?

Tayan crawled to a point halfway between Singer and Great Octave and waited, forehead touching the mats between his palms. He closed his eyes and listened to the echo of his breath and his own heartbeat, still a little too fast for a shaman preparing to journey. He made a conscious effort to slow it, to settle into his body in preparation to move his spirit out of it as it joined the song and found the holy lord within its vastness.

'Slave.'

Tayan twitched and looked up; Shaman Kapal beckoned and then gestured for him to rise. He stood and walked to her side, knelt again. Up close, the grey in her hair was visible and the lines around her mouth and eyes were carved deep with weariness. He didn't turn his face in Enet's direction: despite what had passed between them in the night, he was nothing to her. Of as much interest as a plate or comb. Tayan told himself he was relieved not to have to suffer the weight of her regard.

'The great Singer slept well, but there is more . . . agitation in him now,' Kapal said with effort. The Toko had yet to master the art of communicating in the flesh world while his spirit resided with the Singer.

Tayan nodded his understanding of Kapal's euphemism; the song was hungry. The *Singer* was hungry. That explained the glow of magic on his skin, then. 'Thank you, high one. Under the song.'

He admired the Pechaqueh resilience, though of them all, Listener Chotek was by far the most accomplished. The tall, emaciated man with the shaved head lived so much of his life within the song that he could speak and move and hold entire conversations while his spirit rode its currents and depths. It was both fascinating and frightening.

Tayan shifted until he was sitting cross-legged and began to tap his fingers on his knee, the rhythm that should be beaten on a drum and accompanied by journey-magic of herbs and frog poison and mushrooms. He should have the totems of his spirit guides and blue paint on his forehead and lip. That he had none of these things endangered his spirit and the flesh he left behind, but the Pechaqueh were unbending in this.

Kapal waited, holding her place within the song until he joined her, sliding between the individual notes and feeling their edges ragged and sharp scrape against his spirit. It wasn't so dissimilar to the ancestors when he tarried too long in their realm and they became hungry for his life-force, to seize the golden thread that connected spirit to flesh and race back to his empty body before him in an attempt to claim it and so live – almost – again.

Even after the initial tentative weeks of practice, and then the eventual approval from Chotek, it took him time to welcome the song-world and move his spirit into and through it.

It was like and unlike the spiral path he had walked countless times before. The biggest, most incomprehensible difference was that, as far as he could understand it, the spirits of dead Pechaqueh never moved on. They remained within the song, without anyone – without Malel – to lead them to rebirth.

Instead, it was as if they each became a note within the song – it was the only way he could think of it. The spirits didn't leave echoes of themselves behind in the form of ancestors and then travel on to rebirth. Instead, they lived only until their deaths and then became . . . this. Aimless, adrift within the song itself, unremembered, unloved. Unalive.

The knowledge, and those trapped and empty spirits within the song, were so abhorrent that he'd thrown up the first time he realised what he was witnessing. What he *moved among*. But it was the danger inherent in this practice that frightened him the most. The Pechaqueh seemed ignorant of the fact that there weren't an infinite number of spirits in existence. Every one trapped like an insect in amber within the song was one fewer to bring forth new life in the world. Eventually, the song's greed would consume every spirit in the world and no new creatures or plants would come into being. The green earth would wither and the dead trees would be empty of birds and animals. The skies, even the waters, would languish unbrightened by life, because every spirit Malel had created would be trapped in the song.

Far from the glory they thought it to be, the song was killing the world.

And they know. Surely they know. This must be why they're so desperate to wake this world spirit of theirs – perhaps it can free the other spirits.

Or perhaps the dead plains of Tlalotlan and the salt pans beyond Tokoban's border were the first visible signs of a disease living deep in Malel's own body, one not even she could cure. Perhaps they would grow, eating away flesh and life and laughter until Ixachipan became a barren wasteland bordered by dead seas.

Tayan shuddered and turned his thoughts from the monstrousness of the idea. Without a tranquil spirit, he would become lost within the song. Some Tokob shamans were practised at learning the shapes that spirits had worn before, and the flesh they occupied in each new life was often attuned to those same abilities. Tayan's own spirit had been shaman before, but also the spirit of a waterfall and the spirit of a great, ancient mahogany that had stood watch over Tokoban for two dozen Star cycles. His shamanic ability was more than just hard work and luck; it was the accumulated wisdom and magic of his spirit, ancient, young and eternal, combined with the stoic strength of the mahogany and the patient carving of the waterfall that dug its own channel through Malel's skin.

But the spirits of Pechaqueh within the song . . . he shuddered again, his own brushing against them as he made his way to Kapal and the Singer. He could feel their apathy whenever they made contact, the slow suck of the song that trapped them and kept them quiescent, unable to see or yearn for more, for new life, new flesh. In contrast, his spirit and others' who still lived and moved through the song were blinding, incandescent suns. Aside from the Singer himself, there was no god within the song that he could discover, and the Singer did nothing to soothe the spirits or usher them to rebirth. They simply . . . waited, stagnant.

Shaman Kapal's spirit pulsed and called to him and he pushed closer. Every day from mid-morning to early evening he came into the song to soothe the jagged edges of the Singer's magic. In turn, the holy lord was able to modulate it into something that didn't scrape Tayan's – and every no-blood's – insides raw, day and night. Shaman Kapal and Listener Chotek helped him through the remaining daylight hours so that it was only during the night that he was unattended. Then, sleep did their work for them.

This was the medicine that Tayan, a Tokob shaman, had made to save Singer Xac, back before he'd known of the captivity of the spirits that, he suspected, somehow helped power the song that held them all in thrall. Medicine meant to drain the poison building up in the song with each bloody offering. His time inside the song had shown Tayan that it was more than just the songstone that let the magic out into the Empire. The spirits themselves – did the Singer feed off them? Were they like this, apathetic and powerless, because he daily drained them dry to fuel his magic? Or had the broken song made them like this?

Tayan, called the stargazer, shaman and peace-weaver, was a slave. And no one would answer a slave's questions, not even Kapal. Not even to save the spirits. The mystery of it ate at him, a puzzle he couldn't solve but one that kept his mind nimble and which gave him something other than his precarious status in the source to ponder.

Within the song, he finally reached the shaman and allowed her spirit to seize his, not fighting against the alien tug of another consciousness. She was tinged sickly-white with fatigue and dragged Tayan roughly through the symphony of song and spirit to the Singer. He pretended obliviousness to the myriad golden veins, pulsing with life and magic, that led to the holy lord. Before him stretched a vast golden pool of power, like a great lake reflecting the sunlight, or the very disc of the sun itself. Blinding. Radiant.

And broken.

Because they did not know that he could see within the song – and because he didn't know whether he should be able to at all – Tayan couldn't ask them about the shattering of the disc, the pool, the Singer's very essence. He was covered in a fine tracery of veins, like those in a leaf held up to sunlight, but black and poisonous. Like cracks leading to the Underworld itself, perhaps. Tayan had probed at their edges and slipped inside one and nearly been consumed by the madness roiling within. Even if Kapal hadn't had his spirit in her maw, he wouldn't have ventured near to them again. Those chasms were like some illnesses: beyond his skill to heal.

But what he could do – what he and Kapal and Chotek were doing – was to close them, bury them under new, healthy skin. Perhaps they would rupture again, abscesses of putrid filth spewing into the song, or perhaps they would heal from the inside out, the way burns did. He didn't know; none of them knew. All they could do was attempt something that had never been done before – and pray.

They neared the edge of the disc that was a lake that was the Singer, its edges flowing and rippling and, here and there, cracking as if they had hardened and then split. Kapal began to loosen her grip on him and Tayan made a show of pretending to gather himself and his bearings, sending out cautious blue feelers of spirit to probe at his surroundings until he found and identified the Singer. The Pechaqueh shaman would stay close for a while until he was settled in his task and the holy lord had accepted his presence – if he was aware of him at all.

Here in the song, unlike in the Realm of the Ancestors or upon the spiral path, Tayan's spirit did not share the shape of his flesh. As the Singer was a disc as vast and shining as the sun, Tayan was, in imitation of Kapal, a thin ribbon-like snake, the deep blue of the shamanic paint he was no longer allowed to wear.

The Pecha was the same and Tayan was careful to keep himself smaller and less vibrant than her or Listener Chotek, who was likewise a snake, but a deep arterial red. He let Kapal guide him to the very edge of the Singer's presence, in between the thousands of strands of gold spilling from his centre that were, he suspected, the connections between the Singer and each of his pyramids. From there to one of the cracks marring the Singer's edge. Kapal poured questioning at him and he responded that yes, he was ready, so she retreated far enough to observe, but close enough to intervene should he need her.

Tayan began to draw on the song itself, all the awe and adoration of the million people living within its music. He channelled it through his spirit into the Singer, balm and sweetness and tenderness, pasting it like mortar into the holy lord's cracks and filling them in, his blue overtaking the black in the veins, shamanic magic turning love into medicine.

He held the connection to his body and carved open his spirit until it was a tunnel and he took worship in and poured strength out, and all the while the notes of the song scored his spirit and snagged on him, cutting.

Kapal's presence vanished from the song and he was alone with the Singer's life force. He rested then, gathering himself for what was to come and the danger of it. Still, this was how he helped the Singer, whether they were aware of it or not. And this was how he helped the slaves of the Empire of Songs, too. The Toko was supposed to remain in the snake form, gently filling the cracks at the edges of the disc until the black of poison, the black of brokenness, faded under his blue, which in turn was absorbed into gold. He did not.

Tayan extended his spirit until it was a thin translucent blue blanket that drifted onto the golden disc of the Singer and settled upon him like smoke lying on still water. Gently, slowly and without acknowledging what he was doing, Tayan pressed onto, and through, *and into,* the holy lord. Merging, two into one.

What he did had its origins in the Tokob shamanic ritual of communing with Malel herself, a secret known only to the members of the shamanic conclave and certainly not to Kapal and Chotek. It was fraught and exhausting, but the reward of it outweighed any risk. Back in Tokoban, Tayan had successfully communed with Malel on four impossibly heady occasions, being absorbed by her and held safe in her immensity, separate and joined, everything and nothing, the world and a single grain of soil, all at once. He had *been Malel.*

Now, here, he became the Singer.

When he had first begun to enter the song, he had done as instructed, remaining in snake form and smoothing the cracks on the Singer's expanse. He'd learnt immediately that Xac was not a god in the way Tayan thought of gods – of Malel and Snake-sister and Jaguar-brother. His power, though incomprehensible, was tangible.

When he'd seen what the Singer was here, when he'd brushed against his surface and learnt that the magic was alien and possibly stolen from the trapped spirits, and that the song-world was unknown but the principle of communion *the same*, he knew he could attempt something similar. And so he entered Singer Xac's vastness as he had done Malel.

Within the song, within the holy lord himself, the imperative of his desires was stronger even than those in the source and the flesh, and at first, like an animal in a snare, the shaman thrashed against them. He was drowning, consumed by hunger and confusion and a terrible, red-edged need that was bigger, brighter, toothier than yesterday. It was a lust he had never experienced, a thing he had never craved the way some warriors did – the urge to conquer, to be victorious in death. Within the Singer it was vaster even than that. The holy lord did not want to pit himself against a foe and win; he just wanted to taste blood and death upon his tongue, his limbs bathed in crimson.

It sickened Tayan, but he pitied the man too; the Singer didn't even know any more why he craved these things, only that they dominated him and he could no more resist them than he could fly.

Like the roots of the water vine, the shaman drank deep of lust and need and craving, sucking it out of the Singer and replacing it with love and adoration – his own, and that of the million spirits who lived under his song. He could feel it in himself, sickening and oily and threatening to twist him into a creature of blood and darkness. But he could also feel the Singer's immense power, the deep cenote of the magic he drew upon and filtered through himself into song. With the same intensity that he rejected the bloodlust, Tayan was drawn to the magic. The urge to dip his spirit into it, to soak in it, soak it up, was almost overwhelming.

Instead, he soothed the spine-sharp edges and ridges of the Singer's spirit, strengthening him, merging with him until they were one creature of gold and blue, existing within the Singer and within the song and barely within himself any more, until his mind and his senses doubled and he was Tayan and Xac both, four arms and legs, two heads, one immeasurable power within two spirits.

A kernel of the holy lord not drowning in blood recognised what he was trying to do and he didn't fight Tayan, other than the instinctive animal kicking against restraint, which the shaman could and did ignore. Instead, he concentrated on filling the Singer's spirit with serenity. Through the thread of his life, he was aware of the song steadying, smoothing as the golden disc smoothed, Tayan filling its cracks and crevices, pouring worship and love and all of himself into the ruin, brushing against the magic but holding himself – just – separate from it, though it strained every thread of his will to do so. To be merged with the Singer but not with the magic was an exquisite torture, and one that he knew he might one day fail.

It was different when he merged with Malel, for her magic was already in everything – every person and plant, animal and tree. The harvest was magic, and the Wet that drove it. Spirits and ancestors were magic, and eternal, dancing the spiral from the world's birth to its end. Magic was every-where, in them all, a fact irrefutable and ordinary. The Empire's magic was very, very different, hoarded with greedy fingers and packed down small into this one thing – song.

Small, and yet fiercely, hotly powerful.

Tayan could feel it drifting across him. What would happen if he seized the magic here in the song? Could he? Would the Singer fall dead and the magic become Tayan's? Would he be the first non-Pechaqueh to become Singer of the Empire? And if so, what would he do with that power?

The holy lord's spirit thrashed and convulsed and the song, which had been steadying, brayed out of control once more. Fatigue and ambition had overcome Tayan and he knew Listener Chotek would be hurrying his spirit into the song to find him. The whole day had passed in this timeless place, and the Singer had sensed his distraction, his desire for the song-magic, and was fighting him.

The shaman pulled himself out of the Singer with an aching sense of separation and loss, the heartache and spirit-ache of abandonment, and coiled himself back into the small, slender blue snake Kapal and Chotek expected of him. The thread connecting him to his flesh was weak, almost transparent, flickering and tenuous. He had been here too long, but he could not leave. And not just because Chotek was not here yet.

No matter how much Xac the man was a physical wreck, no matter the daily indignities of being a slave and the nightly betrayals of Lilla in Enet's hateful, expert arms, Tayan loved the Singer. Despite all his efforts and the bright burning seed of vengeance in his heart, he loved him. And the song. And the Empire itself. Beyond reason and into madness and, increasingly, away from Malel, Tayan loved him.

Despite it all, he had become Pechaqueh in his heart.

PILOS

'High Feather Atu. You grace this house with your presence. Under the song.'

Atu winced as he sat before the low table. 'Under the song. And please, my friend, just call me Atu,' he said with clear embarrassment. Still. More than two sun-years had passed since Pilos had commanded the Melody to victory against the Tokob and Yaloh. Eight hundred and one days, to be precise, not that anyone but him was counting, and still Atu treated him with deference, as if their positions were reversed.

Pilos inclined his head. 'As the High Feather commands.' Atu blushed again and Pilos was bitterly amused to see the man had carefully braided the command fan of a Feather into his hair, twin to Pilos's own, instead of the elaborate fan of the High Feather he both deserved and was entitled to.

Atu had been here in the Singing City for a fortnight,

62

reconnecting with home, family and allies. It was unlikely he'd be able to get back here again for the festival marking the Great Star's little absence from the sky in a few months' time. In fact, it would probably be half a year or more before they met again, now that Pilos was trapped here.

Not trapped. Atu did what he could for me in the aftermath of my disgrace. He restored a portion of my status and reputation to me, at risk to his own.

'Forgive my presumption, High Feather, but you should wear the full command fan,' Pilos said with an effort. 'I know why you are not, again, and I appreciate the gesture more than you could know, but you shouldn't give the vultures here any excuse to treat you with less than the respect you have earned. The last thing the Melody or you need is to be scorned or defied. If I may be so bold, you need every advantage you can get when you meet with the council, including appropriate attire.'

Atu's hand half-rose to his hair and then fell back. He shook his head. 'I will, I do. But not today. Not . . . here,' he said quietly, gesturing at Pilos's home.

Pilos met his eyes and held them, sun-years and Star cycles of meaning drifting unspoken, never spoken, between them, sweet as pollen, sharp as thorns. His heart hurt at what might once have been and never had, but then he forced a laugh and slapped the younger man on the arm and the moment passed, to wither with all the others, a lifetime of others. The gesture was one he'd always allowed when Atu was his second in command, and he was pleased the High Feather echoed him in this. Not that he was Atu's second in command; he'd never rise that high again.

'And please never use the phrase, "if I may be so bold" again,' Atu added and gave a theatrical shudder. 'You and I are far beyond all that, my friend.'

Pilos snorted. 'As you wish, and I thank you for sparing my feelings, High Feather, but there is really no need. The stars have turned since the Singer understood that the Melody needed a fresh approach, one that I could not provide, but that the holy lord saw in his wisdom that you could. I gave my life and all that I could in service, and I know that you do the same.' He quirked a smile. 'How could I not, when I receive so many requests for advice from you?'

Atu had still been in Yalotlan the day Pilos lost everything – position, Melody, honour – to Enet's machinations. He'd been fighting to bring the last of that intractable land and its people under the song when a Listener had informed him of Pilos's disgrace and his own elevation in status. Whatever his private feelings about that – and the circumstances surrounding it – his response had been swift and decisive, securing the former High Feather's status and income by putting him in charge of the thousand eagle warriors stationed within the Singing City, a private army dedicated to the holy lord's protection and the city's prosperity.

That he was also a knife poised at Great Octave Enet's throat went unmentioned; she had done her best to disgrace him and Atu had countered her the only way he could, without hesitation or, seemingly, regret. And Pilos's position, so close to the heart of power and magic, made it impossible for him to be ignored or ridiculed as Enet had no doubt planned. He was the Feather of the Singing City, and that honour forced people to respect him and his status as one of High Feather Atu's most trusted subordinates.

It also meant that his fighting pit remained popular, at least with those patrons who were not firmly wedded to Enet, supplementing the reduced income that came with his demotion.

'You do me too much honour, Feather Pilos. And yet I thank you for your faith. Though it isn't the Melody or the command I struggle with,' Atu admitted with an eloquent sigh. 'It'll be the politics that kills me.'

Pilos leant forward, a half-smile playing across his lips. 'It's politics that kills us all in the end,' he laughed. 'Kills or ruins.' He gestured at his estate. 'If not for your generosity, this would be all I have left in the world now; this and my fighting pit. Oh, I've got a few farms in Axiban and a song-stone mine in Tokoban that I am pleased to work to the Singer's glory.' He said the last with conviction in his voice and his heart, though in truth the mine drained his resources rather than supplementing them. Still, the increase in his status was worth the high cost in slaves and masons to work the stone and gift it to the Empire.

Atu blushed again, for Pechaqueh were rarely so open in their admissions of poverty, not that Pilos was actually poor, though there had been an . . . adjustment period when it came to managing the flow of jade and cotton and slaves in and out of the estate.

Pilos cursed inwardly at Atu's discomfiture. 'Let me be a lesson to you, High Feather, if you will accept advice from a disgraced old warrior.' Atu nodded and drank to hide his embarrassment. 'Learn those politics that make you want to scratch your own skin off. They are nothing but a great game, a dance if you will, in which everyone seeks to dance closest to the Singer, basking in his favour. The council are nearly all – presume all – Great Octave Enet's creatures. You have no friends among them. There will be those within the Melody, too, who will sell your secrets to increase their status. Choose who to trust with extreme caution.'

Pilos raised his cup. 'But you know all this, and you know those fluctuations and flows of influence better than I, by now. Forgive your Feather's ramblings.' The words came easy, at least. Convincing. Pilos himself had ignored all that advice, given to him over the years by his predecessor as he was groomed for command. Instead of listening, he had trusted his warriors and the councillors both, and it had led him almost to ruin. It was a lesson hard learnt – but learnt nonetheless. He did not want Atu to suffer the same fate.

Still, it was not his place to offer such advice any more. Detta was Atu's second, a firm and steadfast Feather and skilled warrior; together, the two of them would protect Pilos's Melody. *Atu's Melody*, he reminded himself.

Atu saved the moment with a laugh that sounded genuine. 'What are all these claims to being old?' he asked. 'There are not even two Star cycles between your birth and mine. Has all this easy living made you soft?'

'Perhaps,' Pilos admitted with a small smile, 'though I train with the warriors at the compound, and when my duties keep me here Elaq still gives a good showing of himself. I can still beat him. Most of the time.'

Elaq turned from where he was sitting at the window watching the gardens. 'Ever the richest of praise, Feather,' he said, so mildly it took Atu a moment to sense the friendly mockery beneath it. Pilos snorted at the shock on his face. 'And it's a little less than most of the time these days. The High Feather is right; the lack of real opponents and long forced marches has blunted your edge.'

That bit, deeper than Pilos had expected, and he chewed his lip to keep from responding. He was a Feather of the Melody, a warrior committed to the Empire of Songs and a commander of a thousand exquisitely trained warriors. Elaq was right, he should be better than this: stronger; faster. Yet even after all this time, the lessening of deference between them still sometimes caught him unawares. *And yet I'm the one who insisted on it. Demanded he do it, the better to help me adjust.*

Pilos took in a slow breath, recognising the need within him for the High Feather to still consider him useful, formidable, and not just because of the wealth and status of a position in the Melody. Because it was the hard seed around which Pilos had grown. If he didn't have this, he had nothing. So he would have this, for as long as he could.

He raised his cup and saluted Elaq. 'You're right. On the days I'm at the compound, I'll train there and we'll spar in the evenings. When I'm not there, we'll train twice a day or with the fighters at the pit. And we'll use live weapons from now on; that should add some fire to my softening belly.'

Elaq raised an eyebrow. 'As the Feather commands,' he said, but there was a glint of approval in his eye that made Pilos uncomfortable. The fury and disbelief that had consumed him in the immediate aftermath of his disgrace had numbed into apathy in the subsequent days, and then into a lingering depression. He battled it as surely as he battled the flesh merchants selling new fighting stock to the pits. Used the need for delicate negotiations with the Empire's Choosers over which of them got the choicest specimens from among the destitute Pechaqueh living on the streets to remind himself, week on week, who and what he was. Pilos wanted them for the hawks of the Melody, the caste he'd created in between war seasons in Yalotlan. The Choosers, of course, wanted them for the holy Setatmeh.

That same depression swirled in him now, a slick, low voice that whispered of failure and helplessness, at odds with his genuine pleasure at seeing Atu again. He forced it away, as he always did, swallowing more bitterness along with a sip of his drink. He resisted the urge to put his palm against his gut to check the firmness of muscle he'd never before had to worry about. He had been a child of the song for forty-four years; it was natural he wasn't as sharp as Atu anymore.

Should be sharper than Elaq, though.

He swallowed that thought, too, keeping only the burn of it high in his chest as a reminder. A challenge to himself to be better.

'I'd be happy to cross spears with you, Feather,' Atu said. Pilos choked on his drink and the High Feather blushed. Elaq snorted, very quietly. 'In the compound, tomorrow morning before I leave?' he managed.

'As the High Feather commands,' Pilos said, blinking away a very different set of images than those of combat. There was no point sighing over lost chances.

He waited for Atu to ask, obliquely as ever, about what Pilos had learnt over the last weeks that he might not have trusted to a written report. The High Feather sipped his honey-water and glanced at him from beneath his lashes. The source of such information still made him deeply uncomfortable, but as Pilos had pointed out on the single occasion they'd discussed it, it had been an act of desperation to keep the Singer safe and Ilandeh was now so embedded in the pyramid's hierarchy it would be difficult to remove her without arousing suspicion.

He would have preferred for Atu to never know the looseness of the order he'd given the Whisper in those desperate moments after learning of the breaking of the song, that she find a way to keep the Singer safe no matter what. He'd have preferred it if Atu didn't have to know that a half-blood, wearing one of Pilos's own eagle feathers – an act of madness that made him wince every time he remembered gifting it to her – was now ensconced in the great pyramid. And not just in the pyramid as a servant or administrator, either, but disguised as a full-blood and a member of the Chorus dedicated to the Singer's personal protection. Closer to him than his own courtesans.

And yet the risk had been too great that Atu would see

Ilandeh unexpectedly and react in a way that aroused suspicion. If anyone were to discover that not only was she a spy but a half-blood and a Whisper, and so more often used in political assassination and the quiet undermining of governments, she wouldn't even be granted the honour of a death at the holy Setatmeh hands. Her death would take hours and involve humiliations he couldn't begin to imagine. Pilos himself and everyone employed and living on his estate would be stripped of all wealth and status and either cast onto the streets or thrown to the water gods like no-blood criminals.

Pilos had risked losing everything a second time when he told the High Feather of Ilandeh's presence in the source, and he'd come close to it, too. Atu's disgust at the Whisper's deception of everyone, but especially the holy lord, was only diluted because he knew that if not for her, they wouldn't get anything from the source but that which Enet wanted them to know – which was very little and most likely untrue. Now, to avoid implicating himself in the deception, Atu always avoided asking for Ilandeh's intelligence directly. In deference to that choice and because Enet could have a Listener spying on him through the song at any moment, Pilos himself never mentioned her name.

'High Feather, you're not here to listen to Elaq and me bicker. How may I serve the Melody?' he asked, allowing him an opening to ask without asking.

'It came up again in council today,' Atu said instead. 'The suggestion to disband the Melody. I made the points we'd agreed on and some definitely struck their marks, not least the lack of jade from the sale of weapons and the release of the slave warriors on an unsuspecting populace. And yet,' he sighed and rubbed at his cheek; Pilos heard the rasp of his callouses against his smooth skin. 'I do not think the question will stop being raised. And it was Spear Haapo himself who spoke for what he said was a number of concerned citizens across the Empire.'

Pilos's answer was an eloquent and eye-watering gesture. Despite himself, Atu snorted.

'Do they not have enough, Pilos? Most of these snakes already have more than they could ever spend or eat or wear and still they want more?' Atu drained his cup and put it down with a little more force than necessary. 'How do I counter such sheer stupidity? Especially if it is raised when I am not present?'

Pilos blinked and a warm rush of pride flashed through his chest. Atu still needed him, still trusted him to offer sage counsel. He pushed it down. 'You call it stupidity, so you believe the Melody is still needed?' he asked, although he knew the answer and Atu knew he knew. Still, the High Feather nodded. 'Indulge me,' Pilos said.

'Uprisings, rebellions, external threats. Disease or catastrophe sent by the gods. An attempt to wrest control of the Singer or the song-magic itself. Landslides during the Wet; droughts the rest of the time. Anything that could lead to death or loss, to desperation among the lower classes. Even the changes that will come with the waking of the world spirit, when that sacred day arrives.' Atu hadn't paused, hadn't even had to stop to think, the words tumbling over themselves in their haste to be spoken.

Pilos's throat tightened. *I taught you well, High Feather.* 'Then those are your answers, every time this cursed question is raised. And if you speak to the council with the same passion that you do to me, they must listen.'

Hope warred with caution on Atu's face, making him appear younger than he was. There was a hint of vulnerability around his mouth. 'Do you really believe so?'

'How many warriors retire from the Melody each sun-year?' Pilos asked, refilling Atu's cup and then his own. He raised the jug to Elaq, who wandered over from the window and, at his nod, sat at the table.

'Taking age, ill-health and injury all into consideration, some hundreds. Sometimes thousands.'

'And how many warriors does the Melody currently boast, from slaves up to eagles?'

'Nine full Talons; twenty-seven thousand warriors,' Atu said promptly, though again all three men already knew the answer. 'Fifteen thousand slaves and dogs, three thousand Whispers, three thousand hawks, seven thousand eagles.'

'I for one wouldn't trust a Tokob house slave around my children,' Elaq said, 'and they're nearly full-grown. It's not worth the risk. Tokob and Yaloh can't be trusted until they've been under the song a Star cycle or more.'

Pilos and Atu nodded their agreement.

'Even discounting the no-bloods, that's ten thousand eagles and hawks suddenly in need of farms or trades and homes, slaves and servants. And why should the hawks be rewarded? The whole point to their service in the Melody was to wipe out their debts and regain their status. We can't give them land when their obligations remain unmet.'

'Exactly,' Atu interjected. 'We'd be putting them straight back on the streets when the whole point was to clean up the cities and towns.'

'If the council still cannot, or will not, see the sense in your words, you could offer them something more solid,' Pilos said and glanced at Elaq; the older eagle pressed his lips together and folded thick arms over a broad chest. He knew where this trail led. They'd passed enough evenings in the last weeks musing over it, after all. Still, something twisted in Pilos's chest as he spoke. It felt like betrayal.

'No more recruitment. As the years pass, the Melody will shrink as warriors leave its ranks and are not replaced. This will decrease the size of the tithes while ensuring that the Melody in some form survives at least until after the waking of the world spirit. After that, all will be harmony.'

'Halting recruitment will destroy the dreams of thousands of young Pechaqueh and the children of free. It shatters our very way of life. All so the rich can be richer.' Elaq's words were bitter. 'My children's dreams included.'

'Yes,' Pilos said sadly. 'There is that.'

'Of course, that could lead to thousands of idle, hot-blooded young Pechaqueh with nothing else to occupy them besides causing trouble in the cities,' Atu mused. His face and voice were guileless, his body relaxed and carefree, and Pilos felt a smile tug at the corner of his mouth.

'It would be a shame if that were to happen.' Pilos glanced at Elaq. 'I have no doubt that many of them will have been raised with weapons in hand to prepare them for entry into the Melody. Skirmishes and bloodshed in the streets of the Singing City would be a terrible thing. And without even a single Talon to stand against them, things could turn very ugly very quickly.'

It was almost treason, but in the last two years Pilos had learnt that he could forgive himself much if he acted with the Empire's and the Singer's best interests at heart. It was dangerous, too, though, this newfound, almost reckless disregard for the law and the possibility, however thin, that someone was Listening to him through the wavering, uncertain song. His reputation was ruined, even if his status as Feather forced people in the city to respect him. But that very ruination made it simple for him to heed his own counsel and ignore that of others, excepting the High Feather's requirements and orders. And so he did. And where had it led him but to here, a conversation with the foremost warrior of the Melody that skirted the edges of encouraging riots in the Singing City.

But how else to secure the Empire from our enemies and guarantee enough people to provide aid where needed? If there is no other way . . .

'It could even lead to the ban being lifted after only a year, perhaps,' Atu finished, inspecting his fingernails. He exhaled and raised his cup to Pilos. 'Thank you for your wisdom, High Feather. No, in this let me do you that honour,' he added as Pilos began to protest and Elaq grinned. 'As ever, you see through the mud to the seed waiting to be discovered. In time, perhaps, the Melody will reduce in size, with only eagles and hawks allowed to serve in its ranks. But that is a problem for a future commander; I hope to serve out my time in relative peace now that Ixachipan is secure.'

Elaq saluted Pilos too and he felt a blush of pleasure, a hint of his old fire, warm him. Setatmeh, he had lived for this. This camaraderie, this trust and confidence and strategy. This family.

'The honour is mine, and always will be, High Feather,' Pilos said formally, and they drank.

'I find I enjoy the idea of our warriors being used to help in times of flood or famine instead of worrying how many will die at the hands of the unenlightened. It would be a legacy I would be proud of.'

'As would I,' Pilos said softly, without meaning to, and then stammered an apology that Atu waved away.

The afternoon passed in memory, stories and laughter, easing a knot in Pilos's chest that had been there so long he had forgotten about it. When the High Feather left, with brags about their dawn fight at the compound tomorrow, it began slowly to tighten again, twist by twist, loss and shame and humiliation and uselessness all wrapped around each other and his heart.

Pilos sat in the house that had only recently begun to feel like a home. Before, for sun-years and Star cycles, he hadn't been in it more than a couple of months a year. Now it was the only place he had left and he was comfortable here. Though it wasn't the Melody. It would never be the Melody. Because of Enet.

Pilos stood with the small crowd on the processional way. During their match, Atu had beaten him with ease and rekindled Pilos's pride in the process. Already, he felt more alive than he had for too long, a sense of renewed purpose in him.

There was a rising murmur from the crowd and he leant forward, squinting. There. The Melody. His Melody.

Not any more.

A song rose up from beneath the jangling, harsh dissonance of *the* song, a song from the three thousand throats of the First Talon, who'd travelled with Atu to visit family and friends in the heart-city. It was the new one, the hymn of victory and praise hailing the bringing of Tokoban and Yalotlan into the Empire. The one that named High Feather Pilos as the architect of that victory. A distant memory of the man he once was. The Melody sang it, and he knew without arrogance that they sang it for him.

He let the grief come, let it climb his throat into his eyes and overflow. High Feather Atu and Feather Detta marched past, and each looked at him directly as they sang, and they touched bellies and throats in salute of him. Pilos returned the gesture, Elaq and his other eagles, all those who lived on his estate with him – no slaves for Pilos, one of his eccentricities – doing the same. Arrayed behind him were the one thousand eagles of the Singing City and they too saluted the Melody as it marched past. Pilos couldn't tear his gaze from the command fan of eagle feathers standing proud around Atu's head. Had they ever looked so regal – so right – upon him? *Setatmeh, I hope so.*

Pilos stayed as the long lines of singing warriors marched down the pale limestone road into the south. His beloved eagles. His home. It wasn't until the last of them were gone that he relaxed and let his shoulders droop. It took an effort to force the emotions back into his stomach and contain them.

In front, the silence of the road. Behind, the bustle and muted roar of the Singing City. All around, within and encompassing, the song of the Empire, an erratic growl of need and power that twined uneasily together. A cool breeze eddied through the city and its thick necklace of farmland and wide, slow rivers. Pilos sighed and turned away from the open freedom of the road. He smiled and thanked the detachment, and the eagles returned to the compound or their rest day activities or their patrols with nods of respect.

He and Elaq walked back through the gate and along the wide road, past the first of the flesh markets and artisans, weavers and potters. He found a grin for Elaq's offspring and flipped them a short string of jade; they vanished like jaguars into shadow within the press of the crowd.

'You spoil them,' Elaq murmured.

'I apologise,' Pilos said, as he always did and, as ever, Elaq waved it away, secretly pleased at the interest the former High Feather took in his children.

He was hosting Yerit's pit for a day of fights and there was much to do before the first bout, so he set off fast across the Singing City towards the entertainment district, Elaq his armed and ever-watchful shadow. Pilos probably wasn't worth the effort of assassinating these days, but habits well-learnt were hard-forgotten and they moved as one, always alert, hands near their knives.

'The Mute fights today?' Elaq asked as the crowds thinned.

'She does. Masked. It was all I could get her; you know what Yerit's like whenever she's listed for a death match.'

Elaq grunted his understanding. Masked fights were unpredictable at the best of times, the warriors' peripheral vision limited, but even more so for the Mute – the deaf Toko Enet had "gifted" Pilos in an attempt to humiliate him. Yerit had figured it out the first time he'd watched her fight, and now he always pushed for masked bouts with her to even the odds for his own fighters, who were generally of a poorer quality than Pilos's. *Because the man has no idea how to train fighters. No idea how to coax the best out of them, preferring to threaten instead. To beat and starve instead of reward.*

The Mute was loathed among the pit's audience because of her status as a killer of the holy Setatmeh, and that hatred made Pilos rich when the betting ran against her and she won. But still, this was her third masked fight out of nine bouts and her opponent – he knew from observing during free practice – was talented. And it was to the death this time, not first cut.

The morning was still early when they arrived and took the long looping road down and beneath the amphitheatre to inspect the cells and see those fighters who had been injured during the bouts the month before.

They followed Kalix, a former pit-fighter herself and now the overseer of Pilos's pit, into the underground training hall, where the newly recovered fighters were moving slowly through drills. Those still injured sat lining the walls, watching, criticising, their voices soft and good-humoured. There was little dislike and a lot of genuine respect among his fighters, another reason his pit was popular – Pilos didn't allow brawling or bad blood, though he knew the Mute was disliked by the majority of his fighters and even the trainers. Dislike was fine as long as it didn't turn into anything more serious.

He ran the pit like a Talon and treated the fighters with the respect he would warriors of the Melody and they responded in kind. When arguments arose that couldn't be solved, Pilos sold both fighters so as not to take sides. The knowledge that they could be traded to another pit, more profitable but inevitably less comfortable and prestigious, was another reason his fighters kept the peace.

Now, when his presence was noted, the injured scrambled onto their knees and bowed, hissing to those sparring. The room dropped into stillness as all faced him and offered him respect.

'Continue,' he said, voice echoing through the gloom. Sunlight slanted through the wooden planking above and cast beams of gold through which his fighters darted like birds. Above was a second, smaller and open-air practice arena where the free fighters, those who'd hired themselves to the pit on set contracts, trained during the day and relaxed and joked in the long, warm evenings.

The harsh clack of spear shafts and wooden knives and clubs began again, and the injured fighters settled back, one eye on Pilos, one on the fighters, hoping for a word or a nod. Pilos made sure to speak to all of them. None of them would fight today, but he checked their progress and how much their wounds slowed or hampered them.

'They look good, considering,' Elaq said as they left the hall and made their way along a dark corridor past the comfortable barracks of the free to the cells of the slave fighters.

'As ever, the shaman knows her trade in healing,' Pilos said and Kalix grunted agreement. They stopped outside each slave fighter's cell for Pilos to examine them and exchange a few words. Some responded sullenly, some with pride and many with fear, but all responded. Until they reached the second-last cell in the row.

'The Mute,' Kalix said, unable to hide the scorn in her voice. Even after so long, the trainer disliked the extra effort she had to make when working with her. Xessa of the Sky City in Tokoban. *The Mute*. They all called her that now, in here and out in the city. Even Elaq. Even, on occasion, Pilos. As ever, she sat with her back to the bars as if unaware of their presence, staring at the stone wall at the rear of her cell. As ever, Kalix tutted. As ever, Pilos stamped hard, three times, and then she turned, rolled onto her knees and pressed her forehead to the dirt. A show of obedience so correct it was an insult.

Pilos felt the irritation jump from Kalix to Elaq; he looked at neither. He didn't share their frustration because the Mute was a treasure. He tapped his foot again, in her eyeline, and she sat back on her heels, watching him. Her face was blank. Her eyes were empty. Dead. He crouched down, holding one of the bars for balance, and leant close. Elaq shifted behind him, uncomfortable that Pilos would stray so near.

'You fight today,' Pilos said, pointing at her and then up over his shoulder in the direction of the arena. 'To the death.'

The Mute shuddered once, a hard ripple of movement, and then nodded. Pilos held out his hand and Kalix put the mask in it – carved of light wood, painted red and yellow, decorated with small, bright feathers around the top. 'You will wear this.'

Xessa's face was as carved and still as the mask, and the eyes he'd thought were already dead went cold and distant, as far from him and the world as the Great Star himself. He'd learnt it was better to tell his fighters when they'd be masked early on, so they had time before their matches to get used to the idea. Too many balked when confronted with it at the last second, knowing they'd need to adjust for the lack of peripheral vision.

Her tongue darted out to cross her lower lip and he caught a flash of her teeth, almost a snarl, and then she held out her hand. Pilos slid the mask through the bars and she stood and came forward, kneeling again before him.

'Feather,' Elaq warned.

Pilos met the Mute's eyes and her fingers brushed against his as she took the mask, gentle as a dog taking food from its owner's hand. She put it over her face and tied the cords behind her head, one mask on top of another, her eyes vanishing into shadow. The mask's mouth was carved in a wide savage grin and painted with pointed teeth, and her own mouth was a thin slash within its confines.

'Fight well, Xessa,' Pilos whispered. The mask bowed to the floor again and stayed there, and he knew she wouldn't look up until they were gone. He stood, rubbing the knuckles she'd touched so lightly, unsettled in the way she always made him. He couldn't say why even after so long.

It was with something like relief that they moved on to check the final cell in the row. 'Zimio,' he said and the Chitenecatl approached the bars.

'High one,' she replied and knelt, bowing. He waved her up. 'I'm ready. I won't let you down. Under the song.'

'I know it, Zimio. Under the song.' Her eagerness was the complete opposite to the Mute's, and familiar to him from his time in the Melody; she vibrated with the same energy as those dog warriors who were close to earning out their worth and being freed.

Zimio had only three bouts left on the contract she'd agreed when she'd sold herself to the pit to clear her family's debts.

She was free and a child of free, but her family had been unable to sustain that freedom and selling their daughter to a pit or the Melody was their only option. It was a common enough tale among no-bloods who hadn't served in households or who made poor trade or planting decisions, and it ensured a steady flow of returning slaves or servants to manage Pechaqueh estates and houses.

They returned along the row, not looking in on the fighters now, and then climbed out of the shadows into the seating around the arena, leaving Kalix to make the final preparations. The packed earth oval was swept clean and smooth and the tiers of wooden benches that encircled it were already beginning to fill, excited chatter rising all around.

'Here he comes,' Elaq murmured and Pilos stood in time to welcome pit-master Yerit and his body slave.

'Master Yerit, under the song,' he said, rolling the 'r' in his name as Quitob did, a measure of respect Pilos didn't have to accord him, but chose to. 'Have your fighters settled in below? Do they require anything?'

Yerit was out of breath from the climb to the seats of honour and waved away the question before settling himself on the cushion his slave placed on the bench. 'They are well,' he said when he was comfortable and Pilos had taken a place at his side. He noted the pit-master didn't respond to his welcome, a distant insult. 'I am glad for the breeze,' he added as his slave produced a cup and stoppered jar of beer from a basket.

Pilos raised an eyebrow at Elaq, who quietly summoned a pit-servant and ordered refreshments. Yerit was starting early, even for him.

'I was surprised at your request for a masked bout,' Pilos said conversationally, sipping water. 'And especially with the

Mute. My other fighters, yes, but not her. I didn't think you had the correct stock.'

'The crowd enjoys them, so I spent time and wealth in the flesh markets looking for someone to match her,' Yerit said. He looked sidelong at Pilos. 'I expect to make it all back today.'

Pilos raised his palms. 'As the holy Setatmeh decree,' he said quietly, aware of the irony of invoking the gods that Xessa had dedicated herself to slaughtering. That she'd survived nine bouts since making her debut a year and a half ago without their protection, three of them masked, was extraordinary. Unsettling. Much as she was herself. She had taken every lesson they'd taught her and combined it with her own natural and unpredictable talent to become one of his most sought-after attractions – though only because the other pit-masters were desperate for the glory of seeing her fall to one of their fighters.

Xessa was both a gift and a burden to Pilos, who regularly faced calls for her to be executed due to her past, and yet at the same time she drew immense wealth into his pit. Her continued existence was both a lessening of his status and a burnishing of his reputation as a warrior and trainer. Whichever fighter finally took her down would know fame, wealth and status for the rest of their life. Their name would be spoken for a generation among Pechaqueh and free alike. Pilos did not think that fighter would belong to Yerit today, though he'd been wrong before. Still, that dead look in Xessa's eye made even the former High Feather respectful of her ability. And he was one of the ones who'd had a hand in honing it.

Yerit grunted. 'They'll fight last,' he said. 'Give the crowd something to look forward to.'

Pilos's smile showed none of his displeasure. He nodded

to Elaq. 'Ensure Kalix knows the Mute fights last,' he said. 'I don't want any mistakes today.'

'As the Feather commands,' Elaq said. Yerit twitched at the title, just a little. Perhaps he was rethinking the tone he'd taken so far.

They made idle conversation as the benches filled and the sun strengthened and Yerit picked at the platter of food and drained the pitcher of beer. The first bouts were fought to blood only to warm up the crowd, and then the first to the death as highsun came and went and jade flowed like beer flowed like water, and Yerit sweated and slurred and shouted for, and at, his fighters.

Pilos laughed and joked with the nobles seated around them, ensuring a steady supply of food and drink, dropping hints about fighters that encouraged them to bet more heavily, discussing those from other pits, asking opinions of people who'd never raised a knife in anger, let alone a spear or a club. This was what his fall from grace had made him.

Pit guards began moving easily, casually, around the wall separating the arena from the first tier of benches, armed with long spears and nets. It was time.

'You think this fight will go so poorly we'll need to urge them on?' Yerit asked with sneering belligerence.

'I think a masked fight is always dangerous and I would prefer to have protection for my honoured guests.'

'Are you saying you can't control your fighter?' Yerit demanded. 'Or that I can't control mine?'

A small pool of silence opened up around the pair and Elaq raised a hand to Kalix, hovering in the arena entrance, pausing her. Pilos faced the other pit-master. 'I mean no insult to your honour, Master Yerit. I presume you intend none such towards mine?'

Yerit squinted at him, bleary with drink, and licked his wet lips. 'What? Of course not,' he stammered. He flailed a burly arm towards the guards and his slave nimbly scooped up the fresh pitcher of beer and moved it away. 'They're marring the view of the crowd. You overreact.'

'I care for my patrons' safety,' Pilos said as the silence spread.

Yerit scoffed but made no further comment. He leant forward and waved at Kalix. 'Get on with it, then,' he bellowed. 'I bet fifty jade.'

There were murmurs as Yerit pulled five cords of ten beads from around his neck and shook them together – not at Pilos, but near enough. The Feather let nothing but cool amusement show on his face, though sweat prickled across his shoulder blades. Fifty was a ridiculous amount. *Unless he knows more about his fighter than I managed to observe. Or he's too drunk for caution.*

Pilos didn't need to check his own strings to know he couldn't match the other pit-master. He had the wealth, just not with him, but even that admission would cost him. 'Master Yerit,' he began, shame thickening his throat and sure, suddenly, that this had been Yerit's plan all along. Attract the attention of the wealthy patrons sitting around them and then force Pilos to admit he couldn't match the bet. Anger coiled in his chest.

'Feather? Your spare strings.' Elaq passed him two cords strung with jade, jet and obsidian beads and discs. They were Elaq's own; it was probably a large part of the disposable wealth he and his family had. He forced them into Pilos's hand before he could object and then turned calmly to the arena, where Xessa had emerged from the gloom beneath the seating.

The mask made her unknowable, monstrous, and violence drifted from her like smoke as she prowled in a slow circle around the arena. He knew she'd be checking the dirt for broken weapons or patches where it had been softened to mud with spilt blood. She'd check, too, for anything on the pit walls, splinters or bits of weapon lodged in the wood that might give her an advantage or see her slaughtered. Cheers broke out along some of the benches, boos from others, as she stalked. Most people hadn't forgotten what the Mute really was, but there were some – even some Pechaqueh – who saw her simply as a champion and feted her accordingly.

Pilos knew he was a hypocrite every time his heart lurched when she fought, and he reminded himself that she was nothing but a spectacle, and one that would eventually fall. Until then, she was wealth.

Yerit was watching her with narrowed eyes as Pilos counted out beads and discs and held the strings in a sweaty fist. If she didn't win now, not only would he lose one of his best earners, he'd lose status among the pit-masters. Yerit was ranked lowest in their number, and to lose the main bout to one of his . . .

The rival fighter emerged through the arena's other gate. Xessa's opponent was tall and broad-shouldered, and from what Pilos had seen at open practice, he'd been a trained warrior before being brought under the song. Had the Mute finally found her match?

Elaq gestured; Xessa turned to face her opponent. His mask was black with stark white painted around the eye holes and the leering mouth. Like the Mute, strips of material covered his arms and legs, hiding any identifying marks or tattoos.

Xessa circled until she faced Pilos and Elaq on the bench, with Kalix on her left. The bout was to the death, so she only needed to know when to start, but bitter experience had taught them she needed visual confirmation that the fight had begun. Others had taken advantage of her incomprehension before now.

'Fight,' Yerit shouted and Elaq and Kalix both flung up their arms. In the arena, the two figures erupted into motion.

XESSA

Pilos's fighting pit, Singing City,
Pechacan, Empire of Songs
186th day of the Great Star at evening

It was hot inside the mask, the light wood blowing Xessa's breath back against her cheeks despite the opening over her mouth. The edges of the eye-holes narrowed her vision so that she couldn't turn too far or she'd lose sight of her opponent and get herself stabbed.

Beneath the mask, she'd drawn the symbols for strength and protection on her brow with spit and dirt, as she wasn't allowed paint. Nothing that might summon her people's magic and ancestors. Nothing that might slow her integration under the song, or so she presumed. There were other warriors, some even members of this pit, who went out to fight in the paint of their people, and it had taken Xessa months to realise that to them, it held neither blessing nor magic. Instead, they wore their people's sacred symbols as an attraction, a flash of colour to draw the audience's eye, to make them bet on them. It made Xessa sick – and it

86

made her jealous. If she could pretend not to care, would they allow her paint? Not that she would ever pretend not to care.

She'd signed the stories of her people and drummed her own death rites before leaving her cage. She was eja. She was Toko. Malel would guide her and when it was time, Malel would welcome her onto the spiral path to rebirth. Until then, Xessa would fight – and she would live.

And I will kill. Not a Drowned, not an enemy in war. A person. A slave like me. Who has no choice like me.

Xessa cleared her mind and circled to her right. Thoughts like that didn't help her. She'd been a warrior before and she was a warrior now. She still killed only out of necessity – only this time the deaths bought her a few more months of life in a cage. Her life and Tiamoko's.

The presence of Tiamoko in this pit was a blessing unlooked for and treasured all the more for it. A flash of home, a flash of pain from the memories that followed every glimpse of him, but she would trade neither for all the jade in the Empire. What use had she for wealth anyway? She knew a little of the system here, the idea of buying freedom through time served, in her case as a killer. She also knew, without anyone having to tell her, that such was not the fate of an eja. Xessa would never see freedom.

She'd managed a few moments with the big Toko before the bout. Tiamoko had signed luck and Malel's blessings to her, told her not to hesitate, not to show weakness or mercy. He wasn't fighting this month, still recovering from the wound of his last bout, so they hadn't had long together, but it strengthened her as always. His belief in her. His love for her.

They'd long since claimed each other as family, licking their thumbs and pressing them to each other's temples, gifting each other spirit and courage. She could feel it inside her now as she continued to circle. Tiamoko's spirit stirred in her chest, coiled and strong, ready to spring. It nestled alongside the spirits of those who loved her – Toxte, her husband, lost during the fall of the Sky City; Tayan, her childhood friend and his husband, Lilla; her fathers, Kime and Otek.

Ossa, her dog, whose lavish pink tongue had gifted her with love every single day before war and madness had torn them apart.

Xessa gathered all those splinters together and held them close, a second layer of armour beneath her salt-cotton and the bindings on her limbs that hid her tattoos – another of the strange affectations of these masked fights. The crowd betted blind, she guessed, unable to identify either fighter before the bout began and relying solely on the promises of the trainers. Perhaps it made the fights more exciting for these soft civilians who had never in their lives raised a weapon in defence of home or family or tribe or land or gods.

No weakness. No mercy.

Snake-sister, Jaguar-brother, guide my hands and feet. Malel, guide my spirit. Ancestors, I honour your teachings and your lives. Watch over me.

Xessa rolled her shoulders, spear in her left hand, right one empty. What she wouldn't give for a net, to fight the way she'd been trained against the Drowned, lessons and drills that Kalix and Pilos and Elaq had refined and then altered as they made her the fighter they wanted, not the warrior she was.

What she wouldn't give to have Ossa by her side, his lithe black form racing in and out, alert to her every click and whistle and his strong protective instincts keeping her safe the way he had done throughout their years together at the

Swift Water and in the war against the Pechaqueh outside the Sky City.

Her opponent was big and muscular, angling the obsidian point of his spear to try and reflect the sun into her eyes as Elaq and Kalix both flung up their arms to tell her the bout had begun. Xessa glided sideways and he moved with her, twisting easily on the balls of his feet, holding the centre of the arena. Making her do the work. So be it. She closed the distance at a run, brought the spear around in an arc at the last moment instead of the jab he expected, the butt driving for his midsection as her right hand closed on the shaft and pulled, increasing momentum.

He was unused to parrying someone left-handed and although he got his own spear in the way, it was weak and she still made contact, only a little of the blow's force deflected. The spear butt slammed into his flank above his hip. The salt-cotton absorbed much of the blow, but he took a step to the side, off-balance.

Xessa didn't waste time reversing the spear. She pulled it back and jabbed for his throat; he blocked; she swept it low and cracked it into an ankle as he stepped over it – stepped back. His own spear stabbed and she batted it away, spun hers and lunged again, with the point this time. He took another step, fighting for a rhythm she wouldn't allow him to find. She moved with an unpredictability that Pilos and Kalix had tried to train out of her and which she'd resisted. If they made her predictable, they made her easier to kill. That tactic was Melody thinking, where cohesion was their greatest strength. Xessa didn't have anyone to fight alongside, and so an erratic rhythm and sudden changes of direction made her better, stronger. More likely to survive.

More likely to step into a feint instead of away from it, the twinge from a healing puncture wound in her upper arm reminded her as she thrust low. She flipped her spear away from the answering parry and drove it back in, shoving upwards with all the power of her thighs.

The spear tip bit into salt-cotton over the belly and Xessa ripped it free as the fighter staggered backwards. She was aware of the noise from the crowd as a vibration in the dirt beneath her as hundreds of feet stamped and mouths howled. He sidestepped to her left, trying to crowd her, and Xessa lunged at him. He danced back again.

No blood. She'd punctured his armour but not the flesh beneath, and he was warier now, pacing around the arena out of range. Sweat glistened gold on the backs of his hands and in the hollow of his throat. Xessa sucked hot air through the too-small slit in the mask. Couldn't let him get out of her eyeline, turning with him, muscles thrumming, bare toes digging into the earth, anchoring her to Malel's skin, the goddess's body. *Bless me. Forgive me.*

He leapt in without warning, a smooth, almost invisible transition from retreat to attack that she didn't see until it was too late. He could be unpredictable too. She smashed his spear upwards with the haft of her own, impact vibrating through the wood, and then she was flying backward with the imprint of his sandal in her armour. Like the Drowned, like the Drowned by the Swift Water back home, knocking her flat. Xessa tucked her chin as she landed, right hand slapping the ground to break her fall, losing most of her breath but rolling over her shoulder and coming up onto her feet, blind. The tumble had knocked her mask askew. She didn't hesitate, leaping backwards and to the side as she scrabbled at it, dragging it back into place. Vision returned, bright sunlight, screaming faces glazed with bloodlust, and her opponent, black mask, black eyes outlined in white, close. Too close. *Right there.*

Xessa twisted as he thrust and the glass blade ripped through several layers of salt-cotton, across her upper chest and shoulder. Flesh parted, blood flowed, heat and agony spiking. The ejab hand loosened on her spear and she leapt away again, barely managing to hold on to the weapon, scrambling backwards too fast to set her feet and fight back, trying to assess how badly she was hurt, whether her lung had popped.

But she breathed and she moved, and though she was dizzy, she lived. Not fatal, then, unless she was too busy staying alive for her body to realise it was dead. He came on again, spear a blur of movement and Xessa blocked on instinct, but his spear shaft mashed her knuckles and her grip loosened even more. She struck back, driving the spear up between his legs and twisting at the last instant as he instinctively hunched against a strike to the balls, scooping behind his right knee and buckling it. He went down, lashing out with his spear and she scrambled sideways, dragging her own from between his legs and managing a shallow slice to his inner thigh as she did, little more than a scratch. By the time she'd settled her loosened mask again he was back on his feet and she'd gained nothing but a few drops of his blood compared with the steady leak down her breast and ribs, saturating her salt-cotton from the inside. Soon it would soften, become nothing more than padding.

He was better than her. He was bigger than her. Stronger than her. Unhurt. And he moved in a way that she found familiar; likely they had fought to first cut before, unmasked.

Xessa couldn't get enough air in the confines of the mask and she didn't know where in the arena she was, whether she was backing into a wall, couldn't take her eyes from him long enough to check. The faces of the crowd blurred into one raging animal, screaming for her blood. Toko blood.

Eja blood. She was glad not to know what it was they were screaming – just the pressure of their hate against her skin was enough.

The fighter came at her again, not slow in the surety of his victory, but fast and hard, unstoppable, the charge of a jaguar out of the shadows. He leapt at the last second to come in over her parry, to fall on her from the sky.

It was what killed him.

The world went still and slow, sunlight smearing through the sweat in her eyes. Drowned, leaping to come down on her, taloned hands and feet extended. Drowned, flat dead eyes in the mask of its face, needle-teeth exposed in writhed-back lips, coming down out of its leap to tear into her belly and chest and throat.

The man didn't jump as high as a Drowned, but he landed almost the same, hands stretching for her, only they had a spear in them instead of claws, a spear that would take out her throat well before his body crashed into hers. Xessa fell to both knees and slammed the butt of her spear into the dirt, right hand slapping down as a backstop, shaft pressed tight to her right hip. His spear caught the side of her mask and ripped it from her head as she ducked to her left, digging a trench above her ear, and then his full weight came down and he impaled himself through the chest on her spear. It scraped backwards under his weight, the butt ripping through the flesh of her palm and making her scream.

His feet touched the ground but Xessa didn't give him time to recover; she planted a foot and heaved, pushing him back and crashing her head into his chest so she was too close to stab. His legs wobbled and blood cascaded over her left hand and still she pushed, twisting the spear, shoving him back and back until he hit the wall and she was screaming with ugly triumph as well as pain now, so hard her throat was tearing.

She ripped her spear free, stepped back and sliced the point through his throat in a shower of gore. It caught beneath his mask and ripped it free to spin high through the clear blue sky as he fell onto his side at the arena's edge, hair curtaining his face.

Xessa set her spear and took five wobbling paces back, waiting for him to rise and come at her again. His blood soaked the dirt. So did hers. His stuttering breaths stirred the hair over his mouth and his eye watched her, bright as a bird's but dulling, smoke over the sun.

The spear fell from the ejab hand as she looked into that eye, as she traced the jawline and cheekbone she knew so well. He scraped his hair back from his face with a bloody, trembling hand and Xessa's heart was engulfed in flame. She knelt again, not in blood and death this time but in horror and in shame.

'Xessa,' he signed. 'Sorry. Hoped you'd never know.' He managed a ghastly approximation of a smile and she saw his teeth were coated in blood. 'Drum for me? Please?'

Xessa nodded, numb, the pain – all her pains – dull and distant. 'I will,' she tried to sign, but her hands were shaking too badly to form the words. He understood anyway, another smile, this one relieved, lightening bloody, well-loved features.

His hand fell to the dirt, curled softly like a child's, and Oncan eja of the Sky City, child of the Tokob and of Malel, was dead.

Xessa didn't feel the steady leak of blood down her chest or the sharp heat in her torn palm or scalp. Didn't feel the cautious footsteps approaching to kick away her spear. She didn't think she'd feel anything ever again that wasn't this cold burning, this hollow rot, these hooked teeth tearing from the inside until she was a shell, her spirit fled with Oncan's but never welcomed by him.

Shadow fell on her and she blinked, looked away from his dead face, his dead eye that she had gifted him. Kalix and Ilam, whips in hand. Behind them, the benches full of faces, some gleeful, others furious. Many laughing. Others were already filing out now the entertainment was done. Xessa saw Pilos and Elaq rise to escort the rival pit-master, drunk and stumbling, down the steps and out. Pilos spared her a glance, his face smooth but his eyes wary. Perhaps concerned. It slid off her skin, meaningless.

She had a sudden, horrifying foreboding that someone was going to fetch Tiamoko to translate for her and he'd know what she'd done. Would know she'd killed one of their own, an eja condemned like they were condemned, that she'd slaughtered him for the entertainment of Pechaqueh just so that she might live a little longer.

Xessa's fingers twitched and under-trainer Ilam grabbed her arm; she wrenched it free and leant forward, began beating a soft tattoo on the dirt. The monster inside her had eaten her tears already, and she couldn't cry for Oncan. She could drum his death rites, though, as he'd requested. Even though she had no right to do so.

Ilam grabbed her again, ruining the rhythm, and she spun on her knees and slammed the heel of her bloody hand into his crotch. The under-trainer dropped the whip to clutch his balls and sank to one knee behind her, curled around his pain. She ignored him and the deep wrenching hurt in her hand, turning back to Oncan and resuming the beat. Three slaves entered the arena and shuffled over to his corpse and hoisted it up between them. Oncan's head lolled on a boneless neck, obscene and gaping, the pale white-pink of the severed windpipe splashed red and showing through the tear left by her spear point. His hair hung sweat-lank, clumped and clotted with dirt and blood.

Xessa lunged onto her feet, wobbled as dizziness rushed through her, and ran at them, bellowing. Kalix's whip snaked out and lashed the back of her leg with fire; she didn't stop. Another lash, and another, and then she was on the slaves and wrestling the Tokob body from their arms, mindless, savage, desperate. Her chest was tight and pain washed through her as she took his weight. Kalix whipped her again and again, laying open the skin on the backs of her arms and legs, and then a wiry arm came around her neck and wrenched her backwards.

Xessa grunted, dragging Oncan with her, choked screams vibrating in her throat. Another arm around her waist and then someone else, too, wrestling her back and she fought harder as Oncan was torn out of her grip. A foot swept hers and she slammed into the dirt and then knees and hands drove into her thigh and ribs and the side of her head. Crushing. Immobilising.

A snarling face appeared in the corner of her eye – Ilam, and he was angry. It was his knee pressing her head into the bloody dirt, using far more force than necessary. Xessa prayed to Malel that he would crack her skull like an egg and she could flee to the Realm of the Ancestors after Oncan, and beg his forgiveness, pledging her spirit to subservience in all its incarnations to come. Agony rushed through her head and jaw, spiking up into her back teeth and she writhed on instinct.

The pressure eased, Ilam's head jerking up before, reluctantly, he shifted some of his weight off her. Xessa didn't move, letting all her various hurts build – chest and hand and head and ribs and heart, heart, *heart*. She begged Malel that they were enough to kill her, that her blood might mingle with Oncan's in this dirt so far from home, a blessing she didn't deserve and still craved.

The hook-toothed monster inside her gibbered and jeered and fought against the pain and her weakness, instead reliving the impact of Oncan's body on the spear and his blood running over her hand, the resistance of muscle and then the soft slide of meat and organs as the obsidian went in. Bile stung the back of her nose.

Ilam and Kalix hauled her onto her feet, arms twisted up behind her regardless of her wounds. The slaves collected Oncan's body again and staggered off, leaving his spear behind – spoils of victory for the pit to use. A tally against Xessa's name. They left his mask, too, and she watched it as though it might speak. And then he was gone. The trainers marched her out of the arena and down the corridor to the healing hall. Free fighters watched, cold that she had shamed them or laughing at her response to killing. Casiv, one of the free Tlaloxqueh twins, held up three fingers and then drew them across his throat as she passed. She stared in dull, uncaring incomprehension. Maybe he was going to kill her? She hoped so.

A hand higher. Why wasn't his spear a hand higher? He'd have torn out my throat if it had been higher. It should have been me.

It should be me.

They roped her uninjured arm to a stone ring in the wall and Ilam held a knife ready as the shaman, Tleote, and an assistant stripped off Xessa's salt-cotton and the tunic beneath. The pain was distant again, roaring and futile behind a high, numb wall. Everything was distant – the rope too tight around her wrist, the point of the stone blade hovering in her eyeline, the man holding it, the woman examining her wound.

Nothing mattered. Nothing. More people came into the hall, fighters and guards; she paid no attention. Tleote scrubbed at the long slash across Xessa's chest; the pain screamed but she stared into the distance, through the bodies of the small crowd and all the way home. She could never go back now, she realised. She had no right to the comfort of her ancestors or the warm embrace of Malel and the Sky City.

She had nothing. She had become the weapon Pilos had trained her to be and then he had turned her against others and she had slaughtered them. And now one of her own. One of the first children, Malel's chosen. Xessa had killed an eja, dedicated to Snake-sister and the snake path as she was herself. Oncan had trained and fought and killed the Drowned and then been dragged here in ropes and pitted against one of his kin and she'd killed him. *She'd killed him.*

A name threatened in her mind and Xessa pushed it away. A name she couldn't think without breaking. A name she had no right to now that she was a murderer. The crowd parted and she blinked, slowly, as a figure stepped through it and stopped in front of the tall stool where Xessa sat, Tleote bending over her, Ilam threatening like a storm cloud.

Pilos.

She was off the stool before the under-trainer could react, before she even knew she was moving, but the Feather was ready for her, parrying her punch an instant before the rope jerked her arm and pulled her back. She was screaming, spit flying from her mouth, as Ilam and Elaq wrestled her back and forced her to sit. Ilam's knife dug in under her ribs and Xessa grabbed his hand and shoved herself onto the blade.

Elaq's arms were like mahogany as they dragged her back, pinned in his embrace, the blade leaving nothing more than a scratch and a bead of blood on her skin. Pilos was shouting at the under-trainer, words she didn't care to read. Ilam blanched and sheathed his knife. Elaq bound her arms and legs and pinned her until the shaman had treated her wounds, and then he hoisted her over his shoulder and carried her to her cage. Ilam and Pilos followed, with Casiv and his twin Vorx at the back.

The Pecha put her down and Ilam threatened her some more as he untied the ropes. They backed out and tied the door shut and she knew from weeks of trying when she'd first come here that she couldn't reach it. Couldn't quite bend her arm enough to unpick the knot of the rope threaded through the hollow bamboo. Not that it mattered now. There was nowhere she wanted to go but into death and Oncan's righteous vengeance.

Pilos crouched down and looked in at her. 'Rest and heal,' he said, offering neither explanation nor apology. 'Leave your wounds alone or you'll be restrained.' Xessa spat at him, but her mouth was dry with medicine and grief and emptiness. The hook-toothed monster laughed at her pitifulness. The pit-master stood and walked away, Elaq and Ilam following. The twins crouched in their place and put their heads on one side, so alike it was unnerving. They held up three fingers and then pointed behind her.

Xessa looked over her shoulder. Three masks lay against the back wall of her cage, on top of her mattress and blanket. One was Oncan's and grief surged fresh in her throat. The other two . . . she turned back to the twins and they nodded. Laughing, they left her to her ruin.

In the last year, she'd fought and killed three masked warriors, fought for Pechaqueh entertainment and Pilos's wealth. Masks to disguise identities. So they wouldn't know each other, recognise friends and kin and tribe.

Three masks.

Three Tokob.

TAYAN

Chosen's quarters, the source,
Singing City, Pechacan, Empire of Songs
187th day of the Great Star at evening

When Tayan dragged himself out of the song, dusk was tinting the sky and Ilandeh, eagle and Chorus warrior, was watching him, her eyes glittering in her shadowed face. She often did, and not just when he was around the Singer. As if she thought he was any sort of a threat. He wished he was a fucking threat; he wished he was dangerous. He wished he hadn't fallen in love with the song and its Singer, even though both were broken. They were beautiful in that brokenness. Irresistible.

He thumped his head down against the mats, more a collapse than an obeisance, and then rose unsteadily on numb legs. There was a familiar surge of bitter disbelief at the blank calculation in Ilandeh's eyes. He well-remembered the heat of his fury when he'd found her here, of all places, and realised just how deep her betrayal had run. Hours after he'd pledged to cure the Singer and thought he might be safe, she'd appeared and shattered his fragile world again.

100

'You? How can you be—' he'd managed before she'd stepped forward and broken his nose, her face first disbelieving, shocked, and then tight with anger. For good measure, she'd spat on him as he lay bleeding at her feet. Enet had been there, his new owner, but Ilandeh hadn't been able to restrain herself. The cold contempt with which she'd told the Great Octave, her other slaves, and the gathered Pechaqueh how she'd discovered him torturing one of the holy Setatmeh had marked him irrevocably as the most savage and untrustworthy occupant of the great pyramid. If he hadn't already promised to cure the Singer – and had the Singer believe him – Ilandeh's revelation would have seen him torn apart then and there.

He'd tried to explain that it wasn't like that, back before he'd learnt that Enet's slaves were not allowed a voice – one of them didn't even have a tongue. He'd been paying for Ilandeh's pronouncement, and his own actions, he supposed, ever since; he had the scars and the wariness of a wild animal to prove it.

Tayan was loathed by all and Ilandeh most of all, her presence a constant reminder of his so-called crimes. His solitude was almost physical despite the cramped room he shared at night with Enet's other slaves. He had to maintain an eternal vigilance against assault or incrimination from them, for some thought that by removing him they might take his place. They were fucking welcome to it as long as they didn't step into it over his corpse.

He woke exhausted, bathed exhausted, spent most of every day in the song exhausted, and then ate and fell into his blanket with a weariness so deep that nothing could wake him other than physical contact. Those nights he was summoned to Enet's bed took on a nightmarish, almost hallucinatory quality, as fatigue mingled with arousal. He had slept

101

through her summons more than once, other slaves having to wake him and send him stumbling and gritty-eyed into her suite.

Tayan's bed was furthest from the door, and from what he could gather that made it the place of least honour. He didn't care that he was the lowliest piece of her property except inasmuch as he'd never make it to the exit alive if the rest decided to gang up on him. Still, he collapsed into his bed now, his eyes falling shut even as he tugged the blanket up around his ear, a half-formed prayer that Enet wouldn't send for him stuttering into incoherence as sleep rushed over him.

Tayan woke in the pale light of pre-dawn and found a figure sitting on his chest, knees splayed up around their shoulders. He was half-asleep still and dry-mouthed, his mind working slowly.

'What?' he tried and a cold hand wrapped around his throat. It didn't squeeze hard, just enough that he knew he should be silent. The figure was tall and hard to make out among the shadows. They smelt of water and wet skin and Tayan realised that the hand and his blanket and chest were damp. The rest of the room was empty, tangled blankets testament to the haste with which the other slaves had left. No one wanted to be witness to his untimely death.

And then Tayan's tired brain made sense of who – what – was sitting on him. His heart stuttered in his chest and the shaman drew in a great shuddering breath, whether to scream or to beg he didn't know. The holy Setat leant closer, bringing its face down until it was only a hand's width from Tayan's own, fingers squeezing and then releasing his neck to trail down his naked chest, claws rasping against his skin. Large black eyes examined him with alien intelligence and Tayan became aware of the quiet ticking of its claws as it drummed the fingers of its other hand on the stone next to his head. Idle. Curious.

Or hungry.

'Holy Setat . . . holy Setat, I see you. Ask . . .' Tayan's voice cracked. Every muscle in his body was rigid, adrenaline bringing a startling focus to his mind, the sharpest it had been in months. He knew that if he so much as twitched in the wrong direction, the god would tear him open.

'Ask and we shall answer,' he breathed. The Pechaqueh prayer of submission left his mouth while others, these wild and half-formed, tumbled through his head and heart: prayers to Malel and his ancestors incoherently babbled among prayers to the Singer, the song and the holy Setatmeh them-selves. Prayers to anything, anyone, who might spare his life and keep the god's lips sealed and its song trapped within it. *Do not ask. I pray you, god, do not ask.*

The ticking of claws on stone stopped and Tayan's heart stopped with them. The holy Setatmeh face came even closer, its mouth opening. So close the shaman felt its ribs expand against his own as it inhaled.

'Please,' he begged in a broken whisper. This close, he could make out its features more clearly and he realised it was the same creature who had watched him from the offering pool. The one he thought he knew, and not just because of its frequent visits to the source.

And then he realised.

'Sweet fucking Malel, it's you. But, but how can you be here? How did you get all the way here?'

The holy Setat sat up a little and cocked its head to one side. It didn't seem capable of smiling, but amusement rolled from it in waves. Tayan was looking into the face of his own death and it was laughing at him. Because this was the Drowned that Xessa had captured and crippled and which he had studied in the womb above Sky City. The one Ilandeh said he had tortured when in fact he had sought only to understand. Xessa had trapped it; Xessa had cut it. Tayan had merely sought to communicate with and understand it.

'Forgive me that I didn't recognise you before. But . . . it is incredible that you have travelled so far. You are back in the heart of the song.' The shaman's voice turned thoughtful as his ever-present curiosity began to stir. 'I wonder how your life is different now you are under the song once more. Is your magic greater, or your hunger less? Are you more powerful or more connected?'

Are you harder to kill? was the question he did not ask. A voice in his head berated him for heresy; another hummed its approval.

His abrupt fascination had blunted the edge of Tayan's fear, but it came back with the strength of a mid-Wet storm when the holy Setat shifted backwards to sit comfortably on his stomach and then put one clawed hand upon his face. The shaman stilled beneath its touch, his breath trapped and his heart a wild bird beating against the cage of his ribs. He was too frightened to repeat his earlier prayer. He could do nothing but lie in his blanket and stare up into the face of holy nightmare.

He knew the bite of Drowned venom and he had the scars to prove it. He also knew that the Pechaqueh had no antidote to their gods' venom the way Tokob did. To them the touch of the holy Setatmeh was a privilege as well as an agony. If he was poisoned here and now, survival would depend purely on his own strength – of body and of will. The holy Setat dragged its claws down his cheek, scratching but not breaking the skin, the same as it had done on his chest. And then it lifted its hand away and held it up before Tayan's eyes as if presenting it for examination. It shifted off him and to the side, giving him space to move, to sit up. With extreme caution, the shaman did exactly that. The god's eyes narrowed as he moved and its lips pulled back from its needle-like teeth, but it neither sang nor struck.

Tayan sat cross-legged opposite it. 'I tried to communicate,' he murmured. 'I tried to find a way for us to be able to speak to each other. You know, I pray, that I never meant you any harm. Is that why you are here now, to continue that dialogue, that discovery between us? A way that we might talk to each other properly?'

The holy Setat uttered a soft, birdlike trill that made fear and then excitement flash through Tayan like a fire through wood shavings. There was no order or imperative in its noise, no demand for the shaman to offer his life to it. It was inquisitive. Intelligent. It proffered its hand again, palm up, for the shaman to inspect. It was mottled green-grey, its claws long and fingers webbed, but other than that it was exactly like his own. *Of course it is, for this was once a Singer, ancestor of the current holy lord, Xac. Of course its hand looks like mine. It was a person once. A Pecha.*

At the base of each claw was a small bulge – a venom sac, he guessed. The god could scratch, or it could poison, depending on pressure and angle. The claws themselves weren't venomous. That was a defence against predators. *Against ejab.* Tayan pushed away that thought.

Cautiously, he presented his own hand for similar inspection and again he got the feeling the god was amused by him. Nevertheless, it bent its head over his hand and stared at it. A grey tongue flicked between those piranha-like teeth and across Tayan's palm, tasting him. The shaman squeaked and flinched, but the lick wasn't followed by a bite, or his arm being torn off, or a song, so he proffered it again, turning it over this time. The holy Setat copied him, exposing long, curved talons as black and shiny as a beetle's back. A thrill coursed through Tayan's stomach.

'I believe you understand my speech,' Tayan said quietly. 'I believed it back in Tokoban and I still believe it. The question is what else you understand of me and what I can learn to understand of you. Do you still have the ability to write, for example? Could you write your name?'

The shaman had to pause and take a breath at that concept. A written dialogue between himself and the holy Setatmeh.

'I have so many questions . . .'

Ideas tumbled through his head with increasing vigour and it wasn't until the holy Setat flicked its fingers that he realised he was speaking to himself. Tayan's voice juddered to a halt and he looked up into its eyes again. It was showing teeth and he bowed his head instantly. 'Forgive me, sacred spirit, for any offence I have given you. I seek merely to know you and your kind that we might find a way to live together in harmony.'

'We already live in harmony with the holy Setatmeh, slave.'

Tayan and the god both turned to look at the doorway where Enet was kneeling in a hastily donned huipil, one shoulder showing through the square neckline. Her hands were on the stone before her and her head was bowed, hidden by the fall of loose, unbrushed hair, but her voice cracked with authority. The holy Setatmeh gills flapped in agitation at her tone.

'She speaks to me, god, not to you. The fault is mine and I beg your forgiveness. Yours too, Great Octave.'

'How dare you speak in my presence or the presence of one of our gods,' Enet hissed from the doorway. Did she think the holy Setat was here for her? Tayan was fairly sure it wasn't. It had come to him, after all. If it wanted the Great Octave, it could have found her easily enough. He did nothing to disabuse her of her arrogance.

'Sacred spirit, ask and we shall answer,' she said now in a tremulous voice. The holy Setat cocked its head towards her and uttered another birdlike chirp and this time there was an imperative: go away.

Enet sucked in a harsh breath and bowed her head to the stone. 'As the god commands. Slave, with me now.'

Tayan scrambled onto his knees and began to press his head to his blanket when the holy Setatmeh hand closed on his shoulder and held him still. The implication was clear; it was not Tayan who needed to leave.

Enet rose smoothly to her feet and stared at them, her face unreadable in the growing light. 'I will send a Chorus warrior to protect you, god,' she said formally and with another, longer glare at Tayan, she turned on her heel and left.

Tayan waited. He knew she wouldn't have gone far and was probably hiding around the corner listening in like a curious child. He had no idea what the god wanted and even less idea of how to provide it.

The holy Setatmeh hand moved from the shaman's shoulder up underneath his chin. It raised his head and he found himself looking into liquid black eyes once more. The fingers beneath his chin shifted and came up to cup his cheek in a gesture strangely, bewilderingly, intimate. It chirped again and Tayan's breath caught in his throat. If only they could speak to one another. A dialogue, written or spoken or signed, could change the future of all Ixachipan. Could change the relationship between people and gods. Could, potentially, end the sacrifices and killings.

The holy Setatmeh claws, framing his eye socket, dug in with sudden violence, five punctures – three above and two into the delicate skin beneath his eye. Tayan gasped and began to pull away and its other hand came up and cupped the back of his skull, holding him still. He waited for its fingers to flex and inject the venom into his face. It didn't happen.

The holy Setat pulled its claws free and let go, stroking its forefinger down the length of Tayan's nose the way he might to a child or a dog. *Good boy*. It rose to its full height and loomed over him and Tayan couldn't help but squeak and fall backwards, incoherent pleas falling from his lips. It trilled one last time, definite amusement, and then slipped from the doorless room and away. It had marked him, but not killed him. He had no idea what that meant.

Marked. Chosen?

But chosen for what?

The Singer's hunger was ravenous, demanding. It was in the set of his shoulders and the liveliness of his eyes as he stared at Enet, Tayan kneeling behind her and watching him through lowered lashes. It was in his broad, sure gestures, normally so wandering and inept. Hunger made him a predator; it made him live again.

Shaman Kapal was sweating as she tried to suppress the urges and heal the rifts in the holy lord. It would be Tayan's turn soon and he was filled with dread. The final few days before the Singer fed the blood-craving were the worst, a ceaseless barrage of petulant, dangerous want. It had been building for a week already and he could tell from Kapal's face that the hours she'd spent with him since before dawn had been hard. Now, faced with an empty-handed Enet – the supplier of his unholy medicine – it would be even worse.

His mind returned to the holy Setat and the implications of its marking of him. The mystery. The skin around his eye was puffy and swollen from the punctures, and when he'd finally been allowed to leave Enet's questioning for the baths, the saltwater had stung in the wounds – and burnt like coals in the lashes the Great Octave had laid into his back with her own hand. Punishment in the source was normally carried out by an administrator or slave-overseer, but not this time. She hadn't asked him for an explanation of the holy Setatmeh actions; she'd simply beaten him.

I could have admitted I know that god. I could have told her it was the one from the womb.

And then she'd have killed me for apparently torturing it. Even though it could've killed me and didn't. Because it knows I did no such thing.

So he'd remained pathetically silent and Enet had made him prostrate himself at her feet as she wielded the short whip with an ease and confidence that told Tayan much, before all knowledge was lost in the agony eating through his back. Twenty stripes, and her hand stilled only by the fact he would have to enter the song in a few short hours to support the holy lord.

And now here he was, preparing for that very ordeal while the wounds in his face and back throbbed in time with the pounding of his heart and the Singer spoke and moved with a coyote's slip-shadow grace.

'Don't come back without something for me,' Xac said, dangerous and petulant. Tayan glanced from under his lashes at the four slaves kneeling in held-breath silence on the far side of the room. Envy twisted in Tayan: what he wouldn't give to be so beneath Pechaqueh notice that it didn't even occur to the Singer that they could feed his hunger.

Enet reached out and put her hand on the Singer's knee. 'Three more days, holy lord,' she murmured. 'Only three.'

Xac growled and struck her hand away. 'You deny me? Deny your Singer? Deny the blood, the song?'

Tayan began to tap his fingers on his knee in the journey rhythm, breathing in time, slow and deep. Kapal was failing and would need his help if the transition was to be gentle on the Singer's emotions.

'You are overwrought, holy lord,' Enet said. 'Perhaps a walk in the gardens to soothe your spirit?'

'Perhaps your head on a fucking stick,' the Singer snarled and Tayan had to swallow a shocked giggle. Enet bowed under the lash of his rebuke and he copied her even as he kept tapping, kept breathing, his spirit loosening within him and the song-world, the fifth world, beginning to rise and coat everything with magic.

As ever, without the journey-magic, it was a monumental effort of will and training and if not for his spirit's past incarnations and his own extensive years of practice and journeying he would never leave his flesh at all. At first, Tayan had believed it would get easier with time, but it almost seemed as if the reverse was true. Perhaps that was his fatigue, but every day was a fight to free his spirit and move it into this unfamiliar, unknown and awful world.

Sweat broke out across his body, burning as it trickled through the broken skin on his back. He gave in to the urge to pant for a few seconds before forcing his breath back into rhythm with the tapping on his knee. He was barely aware of Enet leaving or of the Singer's snarled comments at her retreating form.

The memory of the holy Setat sitting on his chest with its hand around his throat flitted across his mind and Tayan flinched. His spirit shivered where it rested in the air just above his flesh and it took all his will not to pull it back inside where it was safe and hidden. The holy lord was watching him, his gaze sharp and glittering with a strange intensity – an intensity the Singer very rarely displayed – and the Toko wondered if the time for blooding had come after all, and whether the Singer had already chosen his offering.

There were Chorus dotted around the great oval chamber, but none of them would lift a spear or even a finger if the holy lord decided to take Tayan's life. First the holy Setat and now the Singer. Adrenaline left him shaky and nauseous, but with no options available to him but to proceed, the shaman closed his eyes again and focused on the song-world.

Slowly, like a snake emerging from its shed skin, his spirit poured further out of him. It glowed bright gold, vibrant and strong, as it rose from his flesh into the magic. The song was jagged, picking at him, seeking to sever him from his body, but Tayan held tight and flowed through the gaps towards the Singer. Towards Kapal.

He controlled his fear, packing it inside his flesh so it wouldn't taint his spirit; he would carry nothing with him but love and strength and healing. He made himself small and blue as he drifted through the stagnant, apathetic spirits and the swirling currents of the song, avoiding the patches where it jangled out of harmony, knife-sharp, knife-wicked, until he reached the centre and the vast golden disc of the Singer. Kapal's little blue snake was sickly-pale with exhaustion and Tayan was vibrant beside her.

She startled and flashed the deep red of alarm, purpling into anger. *How did you get here?*

The Toko realised his mistake: always Kapal had fetched him when she sensed his spirit enter the song. He thought fast, not allowing himself to bloom an anxious yellow. His blue was the deep afternoon sky shade of shamanic paint rather than the paler blue of caution that would make her more suspicious. Here in the song was the only time Tayan was allowed to adorn himself in the colour of his calling. He wouldn't let Kapal's questioning take it from him, no matter the riot of emotions swirling through him.

111

After so long, I have begun to recognise you in here. And to recognise the Singer's vast, divine spirit. He is becoming restless and you have been with him for many hours; I feared for you. Somehow, I think my desperation allowed me to find you.

She was suspicious anyway, but also too fatigued to argue. *Soothe him well, slave. And remember your place.*

She waited as he fastened onto one of the cracks in the golden disc and began to pour the love and worship of the Empire's citizens into it, his own spirit the channel through which it moved. The Singer . . . resisted. Or perhaps his unnatural urges did. Either way, the crack was slow to close, fighting the adoration, fighting the subtle imperative to resist the lust, which struck back at him with the speed of a snake, catching him in its maw. Its terrible, seductive darkness. The need for blood rose in Tayan too, swamping his spirit and pinning it in place.

Like a leech, he sucked that want out of the Singer and into himself and away, expelling it from his spirit as fast as he could. Replacing it with serenity for them both. Or trying to. Kapal slid away, leaving him locked in combat with the Singer's blood-maddened desires.

He had joined to the holy lord more than a hundred times in the last half-year, through his hungers and his periods of satiation, but he hadn't felt anything like this before. As if the Singer was so hungry he would devour Tayan himself. *Perhaps he will eat my spirit here in the song. Can he do that?*

The Singer's attention fixed on him, the weight of his regard a crushing vastness so big its edges vanished over the horizon. Tayan's spirit was spreading into Xac's as it always did, the better to pour healing balm into him, but that consciousness, that sudden looming *attention*, was enough to still him with only their edges mingling. They regarded each other in the depths of the song, floating together in the broken magic, and then the Singer's need rolled over him like an ocean wave.

A thousand golden arms, each tipped with desire, lashed out and gripped Tayan, dragged him closer, pulled him onto and then into the Singer's spirit. Tayan thrashed in the lust's grip, trying to free himself. Fuck the song. Fuck the holy lord if he refused to be helped. Tayan wasn't going to stay here and let himself be killed, either spirit-slaughtered by the Singer or torn apart in the flesh world. He wouldn't – couldn't – do any more. He was just a slave; it wasn't his place to fix something so badly broken, no matter his promises, no matter that this had been his plan, his medicine. Just a slave.

A fragment of his mind rebelled at that – Tayan wasn't defined by his status. He was a shaman, a husband, a friend, a son. He wasn't a slave, but a person enslaved. Words were important; words had power; and none more so than the words a person spoke to themselves.

His disgust at the mental slip was enough, just, to steady him. Tayan forced himself to focus, his mind a cracked eggshell held delicately in hand, but no matter how he bent his will, how he thrashed and wriggled and fought, there was no escape. The blood-craving had teeth and they were fastened in his spirit, joining him like a birth string to the Singer. The shaman thrust love, desperate adoration, worship that was all his own, at him, begging him to take it, to see it and be soothed by it and to release him.

Let me go. Holy lord, great Singer, let me go!

The song grew sharper and pressed in close, each note a blade of stone or obsidian, a holy Setatmeh envenomed claws, tearing, infecting, and weakening him. The song was a lust as deep as the night. Tayan's spirit was wrapped in that craving and the Singer's own spirit, tighter than a constrictor's coils. Crushing.

He tried to retreat to his body, but there was no escape. He tried to break out of the song; couldn't. He tried to balm the Singer; failed. The thread connecting him to his body was fraying as the Singer pulled him closer, deeper within himself. Tayan abandoned all attempts to distract him with the worship that was his due and concentrated only on escape, but it was useless. The need grew and grew, the song rushing towards that particular imperative no one in the source could resist. And it was going to happen while he was inside the song and the Singer both. Mingled; joined; vulnerable.

The great golden disc surrounding him flashed an intense, blinding purple and rage coursed through the song and Tayan. He writhed, clutching desperately at the wavering thread leading back to his flesh as the purple melted into a burning pink of pleasure and that, too, savaged the shaman's spirit in wave upon wave.

He was a bird blown in the storm, a leaf torn from a tree, a lost spirit wandering the twisting, endless pathways to the Underworld.

Lost in pleasure. In an ecstasy of violence. In the Singer and the song. No longer Tayan, or Toko, or shaman. No longer husband or friend. Nothing but sensation. The joy of death. Of killing. Blood burst behind his teeth and meat tore beneath his hands and Tayan sobbed his delight.

Every action of the Singer's in the flesh world, every movement of his body and every fulfilled desire, roared its fury through Tayan's spirit, staining, corrupting, *blooding* it.

He wavered on the very precipice of that surrender, wanting only to snap the spirit-thread to his body and cast himself headlong into the holy lord, there to rest within his depravity for eternity, when the connection solidified.

Someone – not him – was drumming. His spirit shivering, Tayan clutched at the thread and fled back along it, heedless of all but the overwhelming sensations that still reverberated through him, their echoes shaking the very fabric of his spirit. He wanted to go back there. He needed to get away.

Tayan reached his body and fell into it, scrambling to pull all of himself inside like a mouse into its nest, not even a whisker left visible. Afraid that if he didn't, he'd run back to the holy lord's spirit and beg for more – more destruction, more lust, more pleasure in death. He wanted it. He *wanted it.*

The shaman lay on the mats in the source, the scent of blood hanging heavy in the air, the mats themselves warm and sticky beneath him. The first sensations upon his return to his flesh, dazed and uncomprehending. The Singer was slumped opposite, bloody to the elbows, his mouth and chin and chest crimson, his eyes glazed not with indifference, but with satisfaction. Glutted on sensation.

The Toko lay in blood and stared at the ceiling as someone continued to drum on the other side of the source, the beat like enough to the one Tayan always tapped on his knee that it – and the drummer – had saved his life.

Ragged sobs of relief and loss clawed from his throat and his mouth was coppery and thick. Tayan raised his shaking hands: blood and hair beneath his fingernails. Blood on his aching hands and splashed up his arms and across his chest. Warm and pooled in the hollow of his throat. Matting his hair to his cheek and his back to the mats.

Tayan licked his lips, tasting life and death, as dread sank into his bones, weighing him down. Dread and delight. He rolled onto his side and saw the corpses. Three of them, stabbed and bitten and clawed and torn. Empty eye sockets stared back at him from a lipless, noseless, earless head, half its scalp torn free. Strands of its hair still wrapped around Tayan's fingers, connecting him to the corpse he'd made with his own hands and teeth.

The shaman raised his red fists to his red cheeks and shrieked.

LILLA

Melody fortress, the dead plains,
Tlalotlan, Empire of Songs
189th day of the Great Star at evening

The slaves of the Eighth Talon had learnt that nothing good came from the regular changes in the song a long time before, but they never failed to add anxiety to an already perilous way of life. The Pechaqueh eagles and overseers had no tolerance for mistakes or accidents in the run-up to the strange fluctuations that none of them would explain, and even less in the few days afterwards. Whenever the crescendo itself occurred, all training was immediately halted, with the slave Talons locked into whichever compound they were occupying at the time. The Pechaqueh retreated to endure the riot of impressions and emotions as best they could.

Every time it happened, all who heard it were affected by it. Brawls and even deaths among the slaves and dogs were common when the song began to veer and they were left to themselves.

Lilla and his secret rebels had discussed in furtive voices the idea of staging the rebellion during one such frenzy, for it was at those times that the song's grip on them was weakest, all its energy bent towards savagery. Savagery that they could use to strike at the eagles holding them captive and bolster their own courage. Surely, the Pechaqueh would be distracted; vulnerable? Discussed, but never more than that.

Despite the efforts that Lilla and the rest put into convincing the pods of the Eighth, they still didn't have the numbers necessary to gain a big enough advantage to risk rebellion. Each new moon, the Feathers and eagles offered people to the Drowned in the river outside, but still those who had pledged loyalty to the Melody did not falter. It seemed nothing could sway their conviction that servitude meant safety, for themselves and their loved ones. And each new moon, perhaps in an effort to hide from the Choosers who selected the victims to be sacrificed, more Tokob and Yaloh began abandoning the fashions and prayers of their people in favour of Pechaqueh hairstyles and vocal allegiance to the song.

But the maddened song of two days previous had been wild even by the standards of the last two years. There had been a depth of savagery and an edge of fear sharper than any Lilla had felt before. Fear in the song; fear from the Singer? And something else. A sort of . . . doubling, as if the song was being driven by more than one person. Two voices, one barely audible and out of rhythm, but there nonetheless. Struggling to keep up, to be heard. The frenzy had crested and driven them all to their knees, thousands of them crumpling as one.

Lilla had crouched on the stone with his hands pressed to his ears as a mass brawl broke out at the other end of the training compound, the screams and clash of blunted weapons drawing more and more into the fray. Not Lilla. Not Lilla, because of the disorienting, awful *familiarity* in the song teasing and tearing at him. As if it knew him personally and called to him alone. It would be the same for all of them, he knew, some new torment developed by the Singer to add to their misery and reinforce their lack of status so that they might never forget and might never rebel.

By the time the song gentled and slipped into languid satiation, Lilla had been shuddering and weeping and a full two dozen warriors of the Eighth Talon were dead or dying. It was the worst outbreak of violence since the earliest days of their imprisonment.

Hours passed before the eagles returned and ordered them into the small barracks compound and left them there. There was no duskmeal that night and little sound rose from the living quarters of other Talons, none of the usual clamour that was thousands of warriors existing in close proximity.

The conversations among the Eighth since were full of wild speculation. Those who were with Lilla in the plan to rebel lamented it as a missed opportunity; the rest – the majority – put their heads down and refused to meet anyone's eye. Lilla knew it was spiteful, but he hoped they were contemplating what their lives might be like under a song that so ruthlessly twisted their emotions. Perhaps it would be enough to finally bring them to their senses and to Lilla's side.

The day after it happened, the eagles had switched to unarmed combat drills, for even blunted weapons were dangerous and another seven warriors had been killed or crippled in the first training session. Others were still being hurt, only now with fists and feet and elbows, chokes and locks, but the eagles were brutal with their clubs and whips and maintained a fragile order. Too brutal in some cases, the same need to hurt living in them as much as the warriors they trained.

The song still hadn't settled and was a constant itch beneath Lilla's skin and an ever-present anger burning in his belly. It didn't speak of his inferiority so loudly, but rather gifted him a constant gnawing need to lash out in violence. A violence that could tip more than just his rebels into open revolt if Malel so blessed them. Perhaps now was the time after all.

And then came the summons to Ekon's quarters after training.

Lilla's pod watched with open suspicion or open worry as he followed the messenger out of the barracks. He hesitated when the woman leading him turned left at the end of the passage, towards the eagles' compound, glancing at the guards. They were dog warriors and they checked him for weapons with rough but thorough efficiency before letting him past. The passageway was long and narrow, leading between high walls and there were eyes on him the whole journey, from ahead, behind and above.

The check was repeated at the other end, even more thoroughly, but this time the warriors searching him were eagles and their professionalism couldn't quite hide their contempt for him. Lilla didn't know what he'd done to deserve it, other than existing, so he ignored it. Eventually, the thick, high gate swung open and he passed into an area of the greatest luxury he'd seen since his capture, so open and vibrant that he gasped aloud, earning scornful looks from the warriors within.

The eagles lived in two-storey stone blocks with exterior stairs and flat roofs for relaxing on. In between the blocks were stands of shrubs and small trees, almost painfully green, and Lilla let his fingers brush against the leaves as he passed – life from Malel, not stone and dirt and dust and sweat.

The first fresh, living green he'd seen since he'd passed under the fortress's great gate so very long ago. His heart stuttered and his throat tightened at the brush of those leaves across his palm, thick and waxy and alive. He could have wept; he nearly did.

Eagles passed him, all of them looking at Lilla with expressions ranging from indifference to disgust. Other slaves scurried back and forth while warriors lounged in the shade, eating food and drinking beer.

The compound was dotted with allotments and markets and dozens of kitchens from which a dizzying array of aromas rose. It was a village within the fortress. A rich village.

Feather Ekon lived on the ground floor of a two-storey block, his doorway sheltered from the worst of the sun by a tall stand of water vine and mixed bamboo. The messenger called in through the curtain, alerting him to Lilla's presence, and the Toko took a deep breath and sank into the focus he used in combat.

Ekon pulled back the curtain and nodded coolly to the woman, then beckoned Lilla in. He had been summoned while still waiting in line to wash the sweat and filth of training from his skin, and as he stepped out of his sandals and up onto the mats of Ekon's home, shame at his appearance and his filthy feet consumed him. He knelt and put his forehead to the floor. His heart thudded through his ribs, so hard the eagle was sure to hear it.

He knows. Kux has told him of our plans. She's betrayed us all.

No. If he knew, I'd be having my skin peeled off in the training compound in front of the whole Talon. This is something else.

The house wasn't large, but the mats were clean and pleasingly woven in red zigzags. Weapons hung from the walls, gourds and baskets dangling from shelves holding trinkets including broken arrowheads, bannerstones from the spears of three different tribes – spoils of war, he guessed – and small carved ornaments. Another held pots of dry paint, for war and for worship. Lilla's fingers itched to sweep them onto his own skin, to welcome Jaguar-brother and ask Malel for speed and strength and the way back home.

He breathed through the spike of hurt at the realisation he'd probably never wear his paint again and glanced around some more while Ekon used a square of maguey to scrub the sweat and dust from his face and arms.

The door-curtain was brightly striped and the spare clothes hanging from the roof beams were of fine cotton lavishly dyed. The blanket on the low bed— Lilla looked away from the bed, his gut twisting. Was that why Ekon had summoned him? If it wasn't Kux or word of the rebellion, was it . . . this?

He focused on the patterns and shapes and blinked away sweat. So much colour. So much opulence. And the sweet, much-missed rustle of leaves and branches outside.

'Sit. Relax,' Ekon said and Lilla took a deep breath and shifted off his knees to sit cross-legged, shoving his kilt down between his legs. His mouth was dry and his palms were damp. The eagle took a clay pitcher from a storage chamber under the floor and poured. The heady scent of beer filled the room and Lilla's mouth flooded with saliva. He hadn't drunk beer since the Sky City.

'You did not claim kin when you took the Melody oath,' Ekon said abruptly. 'You have no one at all? No children or parents?'

The man might as well have slid a blade beneath his ribs. Lilla swallowed hard as a slender frame and a high-boned face painted with shamanic runes danced behind his eyes, flicking back its long hair with familiar impatience. 'No, high one,' he said with an effort. 'This slave has no one any more. This— I am alone.'

The admission nearly tore his heart from his chest, the truth of it, the great gaping emptiness of it that was so much more than the lie he'd intended it to be. He didn't even know if Tayan was alive; he might have died fighting the invaders. If he did live, he too was a slave, somewhere in this vast and greedy Empire of Songs. A slave or a sacrifice to the Drowned. His husband was gone in every way that mattered, and his friends and family, those who hadn't been condemned to the Eighth alongside him, were gone too.

It's easier this way. I can't fail them if they don't even know what I'm attempting. Easier.

Not a single part of him believed the lie.

Ekon passed him the cup of beer, oblivious to the wound he'd just torn open in Lilla, but then, instead of moving away his hand dropped to touch the Tokob ankle. Gentle. He flinched anyway. 'What does this mean?'

Lilla looked at the cord. 'It is, was, my marriage oath. Each of the knots was a promise we made about our lives. Children, things we wanted to do, places we wanted to see. Those promises we had fulfilled have the charms on.' He faltered and then hunched down, spinning the wrapped cord around his leg. A bitter, broken laugh ripped from his chest and took away any curiosity or trepidation about why he was here.

'I've lost most of them now. All those kept promises, and I have no way to replace them. I don't even know when they snapped off. Gone, like everything else. Like everything that means anything.'

That last was too much and they both knew it. Lilla flushed and sipped from his cup to hide his face, but the beer was rotten all of a sudden and he put it down. Picked it back up again.

'What about the song?' Ekon asked softly. 'You told me not so long ago that it was a wonder and that it shows you things. And that you were becoming a better warrior. These mean nothing to you?'

Danger prickled the hairs at the back of Lilla's neck. He put the cup down yet again and bowed, fingertips to the mat. 'Forgive me, high one. Of course those things mean a great deal to me. It is just' – he patted his ankle gently – 'this was all I had left of us.'

'Ah. You said "was". So not any more? They're dead?'

'I wear it on my left ankle rather than around my neck,' he said with an effort, uncaring if Ekon didn't quite understand. He was so tired, and not just from the day's training.

'Tell me of them, your lost love. Perhaps it will ease the hurting.'

Lilla looked up. There was an intensity in Ekon, in the cant of his head and the relaxed but alert posture of his shoulders. He too was cross-legged, close enough to touch. The cord that bound them had loosened a little with the mention of dead lovers, and now Ekon looked . . . like a friend offering comfort.

Lilla swallowed and tried to answer without his heart falling out of his mouth. 'His name is – was – Tayan. He was a shaman. We'd been married for a Star cycle, were ready to adopt. And then,' he gestured, an all-encompassing sweep to indicate the world. 'This.'

'How did he die?' Ekon asked softly.

Lilla grimaced, but the Feather was silent, sympathy in the creases around his eyes. He sipped but didn't look away. Patient. As if he cared. As if he and his weren't the cause of all this, all Lilla's pain, his lies, his betrayals. The people he should have claimed as family and hadn't – not just Tayan but his mother and sisters, and Xessa. Tiamoko and Lutek. All of them abandoned. They'd think he was dead, for otherwise he would have claimed them. Would they have drummed for him? Danced his spirit to rebirth? Would Tayan have sought him on the spiral path and grieved anew at not finding him, presuming him lost in this unsanctified land, or cast to the Underworld? Would he have wrapped his own marriage cord around his ankle in a broken-hearted farewell that he didn't know was a lie?

'We were captured in Yalotlan. Ambushed. I didn't get to say goodbye.' He didn't have to fake the lump in his throat that strangled his voice. He stared at his clenched fist and willed it to open, but nothing happened. Let Ekon infer what he would; it was the truth, after all.

'I'm sorry,' Ekon said, and he sounded as if he meant it. 'It is hard to love a warrior, but I imagine harder still to love one who cannot fight but yet is lost to violence. That sense of helplessness is well-known among all our peoples.'

They were quiet and Lilla drank again, and this time the beer was good. It hit his thirsty stomach and warmed it, and he knew dehydration and his lack of tolerance after all this time would make him drunk after just a single cup. Suddenly he wanted that, and all the sweet oblivion that would come with it. Despite himself and his words and thoughts of Tayan – or because of them – his eyes flicked to Ekon's mouth as he licked moisture from his bottom lip.

'Sometimes it is good to talk of loss and know another understands,' Ekon said, staring blindly out through the door. His smile spoke of remembered pain. 'It lightens the spirit.'

The Toko rubbed the heel of his hand into the centre of his chest. 'It does, high one,' he agreed, and found it was true. Tayan was gone from his life, whether or not he still lived.

I didn't find his body. Dakto's words, at his final parting from the half-Xenti Whisper. The treacherous, betraying fuck who, along with Ilandeh, had wormed his way into Tokob lives and hearts and helped destroy them. And yet . . . *I didn't find his body.*

But what could Lilla do with that knowledge, other than use it to cut at himself? Tayan was gone. Even if he still lived, he was almost certainly being too curious, too loud, not subservient enough, and those sorts of slaves didn't live long.

And so the marriage cord on his ankle rather than around his throat felt right and true – he was widowed. He was alone. Back during the war, he and Tayan had never spoken of the things they might end up doing to survive, and how those things would impact the promises they'd made to each other, to the ancestors, to Malel herself. Lilla knew now that had been a mistake. Knew it from the tension in the air, his awareness of Ekon and how he took up space in this world that belonged to him.

He gulped beer and cast around for another topic. 'May I ask a question about the song, high one?' he blurted and then flushed and snapped his mouth shut. 'Forgive this slave's presumption,' he added. How easily that word tripped from his tongue now, he realised as he shoved over onto his knees and bowed again. The Tokob emotions veered off again, too many and too fast on top of the tiredness, the hunger, the alcohol. The constant, draining trepidation. The lies and the song that told him, over and over, to stop. Give in. Who was he to resist, to believe he was better or other or capable of anything that wasn't abject surrender? Who was Lilla, but a slave?

Ekon slapped his back. 'Speak.'

The Toko blew out a long breath and sat up. So tired. 'The song,' he began, thinking of what had happened a few days before. 'May I have the honour of knowing what it was like before . . . before the holy lord began his great magic?' It was what he'd heard said more than once, in a variety of tones and with many different implications. He was fairly sure it was a lie, but one everybody in the fortress seemed to have accepted. The Singer was performing a great magic and every so often the song would veer wildly; this was to be expected. It was the holy lord's strength growing.

The eagle blinked, astonishment painting his lean, angular features. 'That is not an easy question to answer,' he said, but he didn't seem angry. Or even particularly irritated. 'I'm not sure how I can explain it,' he added after a long silence in which he washed beer around his gums. 'It was . . . understand that the song is, was, and always will be, glorious. Different now, yes, but not less. Never less.'

Lilla nodded rapidly at his intensity. Even this small, nothing level of honesty was more than he expected. More than he deserved. *No. That's the song talking. The song, not me.*

'Of course, high one. Forgive this slave.'

Ekon waved away the comment. 'There is nothing to forgive. It is different now; to say otherwise would be a lie and eagles have no need of lies. The holy lord begins the work of waking the world spirit.'

'Thank you, high one. And what exactly will happen then? If you would honour me with an answer.'

Ekon drank to hide a small smile. 'Of course. To fully embrace the song you need to understand what it will accomplish, what we in the Empire of Songs are going to bring to Ixachipan. The world spirit sang the earth into being and then began its long sleep to recover its strength. It promised to awaken once all people were united and peaceful and change the whole world into a garden where there will be no suffering, no disease or famine. No war. The Pechaqueh ancestors discovered the songstone and the song-magic and knew this was the way to bring about that peace. The rest of Ixachipan refused Pechaqueh wisdom, trapped in their own incorrect beliefs. We have finally accomplished what it demanded of us and so the time for the world spirit to awaken is at hand. Soon the world will transform and the great Singer will walk at the world spirit's side for eternity. Its undying consort.'

Lilla was silent. If he opened his mouth, he wasn't sure he'd be able to control what he said. War, conquest, stolen land and people, brands in skin like a potter carving their name on the base of a bowl . . . this was not how you made a peace, even if your gods did promise a paradise in reward.

There was no peace when one person owned another. There was no end to disease when slavery itself was the sickness. No end to famine when people were starved of their gods and rituals, their soil.

'You don't believe me.'

The words were mild, but Lilla tensed. 'Forgive me, high one. It is just that there is much to think about. I had not realised you were so, ah, cut off from your gods. Malel is with us all the time, beneath our feet and in our lungs and blood. She is—' He stopped. 'This slave spoke incorrectly. He begs the Feather's indulgence.'

Ekon grunted. 'It is not— we are not cut off from our gods. The holy Setatmeh are everywhere, bringing us the Wet and the crops, watching over us and keeping the world balanced: day and night, sickness and health. The world spirit is different. Older. Our creator and the creator of the gods. The Singer is the path from the world spirit to us, and the song is the world spirit's gift to us. When it wakens, everything will be glory.'

'I am happy for you,' the Toko managed. 'That you will welcome your creator soon,' he clarified. Ekon's gaze was neutral and Lilla drained the last of his beer, wincing. 'Will the song return to normal with the world spirit's awakening?'

'The song is exactly as it needs to be,' the Pecha said, his voice sharp.

Lilla winced again. 'As the high one says,' he agreed. 'This slave's words were ill-thought. We have become accustomed to the changes that occur in the song every few weeks when the magic is, ah, woven. They are uncomfortable, but of course we do not understand as you do. I meant no disrespect.' Ekon glared and then subsided and Lilla breathed a little easier.

He raised the cup and found it empty, regretted how quickly he'd drunk it when the words slid from behind his teeth without his permission. 'This last one, though . . . it was so hard to bear. So fierce and ugly despite that edge of, of *home* within it. It has never been cruel before, not like that, anyway.'

That whisper of home frightened him more than anything, how comforting it had been. How beloved. For the first time, it felt like something he could let rule him. Something he *wanted* to rule him. Lilla had been both bereft and relieved when it had faded.

He had wanted to surrender to the song many times, in extremities of despair or pain or fatigue. This was the first time he'd wanted to surrender because of love. What did that mean? Why could he want such a thing?

'Home?' Ekon asked, sounding puzzled. 'Different yes, that I will concede, but I wonder at it feeling like home to you.' There was a touch of suspicion in his tone, and perhaps even a hint of envy, but that made no sense. The song was of Pechaqueh origin; its every manifestation would be home to him.

'Perhaps I misread my response to it,' Lilla said hastily. 'Or perhaps it is in truth becoming my truth. Becoming the core of me.' The thought was almost enough to shatter him. Break everything he was, and everything he believed. Convince him that there was nothing but the song and the Singer and the holy Setatmeh. The world spirit.

Lilla refused that truth, pushing it forcibly away. He would rather die. Malel's existence was real; this world spirit was not. And the Drowned were nothing but mindless predators who needed to be slaughtered. Familiar or not – home or not – Lilla would break this song and its hold on the peoples of the Empire.

His fingers clenched on his cup almost hard enough to crack the fine pottery.

'The song is beyond all our understanding, but if you feel that touch of home within it, then I offer you my congratulations, Lilla. You are a step closer to becoming Pechaqueh in your heart,' Ekon said and gave him a warm smile. 'Soon you will be whole, and all will be as it should be.'

'As it should be,' Lilla echoed hollowly. Why was the song beyond mortal understanding? If Lilla had ever had questions about Malel or her god-born – the Snake and the Jaguar – he could ask the shamans and historians, the keepers of the old truths. The only mysteries in Tokob society were around some shamanic practices, and then only to keep people safe. Walking the spiral path was perilous and it would be reckless for the ways onto that path to be openly known or attempted by foolish, pride-driven youngsters or grief-stricken mourners.

But the entire foundation of the Empire of Songs was built on secrets. The truth of the song. The way to waken the world spirit. The true nature of the Drowned. And the Pechaqueh had forced all the peoples of Ixachipan under their song while telling them nothing but that they must love it and serve. They were as ignorant of the song's truth as Tokob were.

It should be ridiculous. And yet.

The song shivered through Lilla's bones and heart, promising him glory through violence and acceptance through surrender. It was not beautiful, but it was so powerful it couldn't be ignored, a whisper in his blood. A promise breathed on the back of his neck. A kiss from an enemy.

'What are you thinking?'

The words were quiet, but they still made him jump, and Lilla looked up on reflex. Ekon wore a gentle smile, an expression almost of fondness, and something small twisted in his belly. Something soft and needy. When had someone last been gentle with him?

'Forgive me, Feather. There was much to ponder in your words.'

'Forgive me,' he echoed, tilting his head to one side with something very much like mischief. 'How many times this evening you have said those words. Another eagle would suggest that perhaps you just shouldn't do anything that required forgiveness.' Ekon held up his hand as Lilla began to stammer an answer. 'Another eagle. Not this eagle. Not here, anyway. I like to encourage curiosity in my warriors; it makes them resourceful, better leaders. More interesting to be around.'

He didn't know whether there was an implication in that, or, worse, an invitation. Either way, Lilla pretended not to understand it. Pretended, too, not to understand the small, needy thing in his belly that cried out for contact, connection. Touch. 'I should leave you to sleep, high one,' he said, putting his cup on a low shelf. His palms were sweating. 'I thank you for the conversation. It was . . . enlightening. Under the song,' he added when the man didn't respond.

Ekon pressed his lips together and exhaled, soft. 'I have to walk you back; there won't be anyone waiting to escort you out there.' He hesitated, and perhaps other words sat on the tip of his tongue, but then he stood and Lilla scrambled to bow his head to the mat before rising.

The Feather took a step towards him, fingers stretching towards his face, and Lilla rocked back on his heels but held his place. Held his breath, but then Ekon reached past him, pulled back the door-curtain and stepped out. The Toko shuddered, violently, and followed him into the low heat of evening. They put on their sandals and walked quickly and silently back to the compound's gate and the waiting guards.

'I want to see those elbow strikes improve,' Ekon said when they reached the gate. His expression was unreadable.

Lilla bowed his head and touched belly and throat. 'As the Feather commands. Under the song.'

ILANDEH

The sun had set and the wind was unusually strong for this time of year. Those Chorus warriors on duty at the great pyramid's entrances and gardens had muttered and exchanged meaningful glances, as if it was a portent of ill omen. Rumours of holy Setatmeh displeasure were rife across the city and even within the source. Ilandeh, as ever, listened and watched and threw in a quiet comment or observation only rarely.

They all knew her as the eagle who kept herself to herself, the warrior who had been promoted after Yalotlan fell. Most assumed her to be affected by the horrors she'd witnessed during the war, by her meeting with the Tokob ejab who slaughtered gods. Anyone would be withdrawn after being exposed to such atrocities. And that much at least was true, although the length and intensity of her association with them – her life with them – was unknown here in the Empire's heart. But their suppositions worked in her favour, adding another layer to the subterfuge she'd created and which she

133

refused to acknowledge even to herself, because if she stopped to think about the danger of her situation, she'd curl up in a corner and never move again.

Tayan's appearance in the source was a complication no one had foreseen when Elaq had installed her here in response to Pilos's command that she keep the Singer safe at any cost. Thankfully, she'd been firmly ensconced before his arrival and the Toko had had no reason to question her status as full-blood Pecha. Even if he did, he was a slave and she was Chorus. No one would believe him, especially not after she'd so publicly denounced him as the holy Setatmeh torturer.

She pushed the memory into the dark with all the others, names and faces and places she'd brought under the song or exposed to the Melody's swift mercy. For their own benefit, one way or the other. For their own good and the Empire's glory. It wasn't betrayal, no matter what they said; it was for their own good.

Tayan's time here may be over, anyway. A grimace twisted her lip and this time the flicker of unwanted emotion was sympathy. No one deserved what had happened to him five days before and from which he had yet to recover. He'd been a good friend back in the Sky City. Guilt tried to set its claws in her, and with the ease of long practice, she pushed that away, too. Ilandeh was a Whisper and her loyalty to the Melody outweighed loyalty to any one individual.

Ilandeh changed out of the bright yellow kilt that marked her as a Chorus warrior into a plain one with a decorated hem, then tied a square chequered shawl around her shoulders against the chill. She left her spear propped by her bed and tucked a knife in her belt and then walked through the lower corridors of the pyramid towards the warriors' exit. She nodded to the man guarding it. 'Strange night,' he commented, jerking his head out at the weather.

She shrugged. 'Drinking night,' she replied with a small smile. 'I'd put up with far worse than this for a few jars of honeypot.' Chorus couldn't be seen drinking in public, but the removal of her kilt and armour meant no one would mark her as such. Besides, time out of the great pyramid and away from the song's overwhelming power was a precious commodity.

The warrior waved her through. 'Have one for me.'

Ilandeh slipped past him and came out into the road between the great pyramid and the temple next to it. The wind lifted her hair and tugged at the eagle feather tied at her crown; absently, she checked the binding was still tight.

The air was cool and, with thoughts of Tayan swirling through her head, it was easy to be reminded of the Wet in Tokoban. Fighting in the Sky City and then fighting in the thick jungles of Yalotlan and then back to Tokoban again. Never really dry, always looking over her shoulder for danger within and without the Melody. Always watching Pilos's face and Pilos's back. In the last two years she'd lived and guarded and trained in luxury, sparring against exquisitely skilled eagles in a wide practice area deep inside the pyramid. When it rained, she could choose to stay inside and take her leisure time in the kitchens or her own quarters. She'd worried it would make her soft, make her careless. Instead, constant paranoia honed her sharper than she'd ever been.

Sharp, but perhaps brittle, like too-thin obsidian.

Ilandeh raised her face to the wind, relishing its bite. The grand plaza in front of the pyramid was almost deserted and no one marked her as she hurried past, shawl clutched tight for appearances. Torches burnt in the entrances to the temples and she moved through their flickering pools of radiance until she was deep in the noble market district, where only the finest Pechaqueh artisans and craftspeople were allowed to display their wares.

It was mostly deserted and Ilandeh slipped into the alley between two closed buildings. She stopped in a pool of black shadow and undid her shawl. Working by feel and guided by the tiny wooden beads sewn into the hem, she found the slit in the material and slowly worked the garment inside out. The red-and-white checked pattern vanished, and the inside of the shawl was backed with undyed brown maguey. Ilandeh retied it and then took the eagle feather out of her hair and slid it into the inside of her tunic's side seam. She gathered up the damp, tangled mass of hair and knotted half of it messily at the nape of her neck, the rest falling forward around her face.

Plain shawl, a mostly plain kilt, and no feather. Ilandeh emerged from the other end of the alley as a half-blood merchant, not a warrior. She hurried on through the wind, cold against her legs and face.

The walk to the entertainment district and the fighting pit took an hour, far longer than if she'd taken the most direct route. Despite the weather, the district was brightly lit with torches and bonfires, drinking huts, brothels, and gambling dens bright with flickering flamelight. The most exclusive had awnings of palm-leaf or even rubber-coated maguey to keep the rain off the customers sitting outside.

Ilandeh skirted the loudly shouting crowd surrounding a dogfighting pit. She had unpleasantly conflicting feelings about such entertainment these days. She'd spent hours in the company of ejab and their dogs, the animals fiercely protective but exuberant with people they knew. They'd known Ilandeh. After the fall of Tokoban, the dogs were a huge draw at any pit that could procure one, their killing instinct far more honed than even the dogs bred to fight for entertainment. Ilandeh lived in fear that she'd pass a dog pit and see an animal she'd once played with or laid prone

136

beneath, giggling helplessly as they bore her down with their full weight to lick her face and neck.

'I heard some greedy, stinking Chitenecah merchant tried to double the price of his stock when he realised he was selling to the source for the Singer's, ah, pleasure.'

The speaker probably thought they were being quiet enough not to be heard over the shouts and snarls from the dog pit. Ilandeh heard them anyway; her feet slowed.

'Great Octave had him tossed back in among his own produce and' – the stranger laughed – 'apparently they tore him apart with their bare hands. Still, that's the uncivilised for you. And he deserved it. Great Octave won't allow faithlessness like that. How she puts up with Xac's—'

'Enough,' the speaker's companion hissed, gripping their arm. 'All praise to the Singer, may he live forever,' she added quickly and without much conviction.

'He's crazier than one of the Tokob frog-lickers,' the first speaker insisted and Ilandeh realised they were drunk, not that it mattered. 'Things will be different once Enet's Singer, is all I'm saying,' they added, but this time the woman smacked them hard across the shoulder.

'Fucking stop,' she threatened. 'The Singer is—'

Ilandeh was clenching her teeth hard enough to send an ache through her temples. She took three rapid paces forward. 'The Singer is what?' she asked in cold, lethal tones. The Pechaqueh spun to face her, alarmed, and then suddenly furious when they took in her attire.

'Who do you think you're addressing?' the woman demanded and her companion squinted through a haze of alcohol and smeared charcoal that had once lined their eyes.

Ilandeh became abruptly aware that she wasn't dressed as a Chorus warrior. 'I—' she tried, just as the woman slapped her hard across the cheek.

137

'Filthy fucking half-blood,' she snarled, shaking the sting out of her hand as Ilandeh swallowed her instinctive response and hastily rearranged her face into something humbler. 'Get out of my sight before I report you to a Chooser. Disgusting creature,' she added, turning back to her friend as if they hadn't been caught defaming the Singer only heartbeats before.

The slap had cut the inside of Ilandeh's cheek against a tooth and she swallowed the hot metal taste and forced her way through the crowd, ruthlessly dragging her mind back to her body and appearance. She let her shoulders hunch and lowered her chin, shortening her stride until she was hurrying unobtrusively through the crowds, stepping wide around Pechaqueh so she didn't brush against their skin or clothes.

She'd forgotten that out here her disguise was actually her true self: Ilandeh *was* a half-blood. She had no right to question the words of Pechaqueh, no matter how seditious. She barely had the right to look at them, regardless that her own father had been a Pecha.

By the time she reached the fighting pit, she was the demure and respectful Whisper once again. Outwardly. The arrogance she cultivated as a Chorus warrior she held tight beneath her skin. Still, when Elaq opened the gate to her, he nodded in that mildly disapproving way that never failed to tighten her gut. Ilandeh gave him a bland smile and followed him through the passages to Pilos's office. It was warm, with candlelight reflecting off the plastered walls and waxed window-curtain. The former High Feather sat on a stool behind a low table, but he stood at her arrival and caught her hand before she could sink to her knees to bow.

He gestured for her to sit and Elaq handed her a cup of beer. 'Thank you.'

'Empire and song and Singer,' Pilos said and they echoed him and drank. 'Five days ago, Ilandeh. The song was blooded, but . . .'

Ilandeh grimaced and stared into her cup for a moment, collating her thoughts to give her report in the right order. 'There was an incident with the Tokob shaman. He was within the song at the time, performing the healing magic Shaman Kapal invented. They were connected through the song and the offering affected him badly. He's mostly delirious.' She took a deep breath and met Pilos's eyes. 'When the Singer began, the shaman . . . joined in. Full participation. Three slaves. Frenzied.'

It had been more than that, but Pilos didn't need those details. Ilandeh knew she'd never forget them. She'd been in the garden when it began; she'd caught glimpses and they'd been more than enough. Tayan's face, his curious, usually gentle nature subsumed beneath a feral lust, a raging need that perfectly matched the Singer's own.

Elaq stared between them, his brow creased. 'So? He's a slave. From the perspective of the song's, ah, hunger, it's interesting, I suppose, but what does it matter if some frog-licker is delirious? What's worse is that he thought to act alongside the holy lord. He probably increased the Singer's madness just with his presence. Kill him and have done with it.'

'How has the Singer been since? The song remains more troubled than usual,' Pilos asked, his voice tightly controlled, though he'd nodded along with Elaq's words.

'Tayan – the Toko I mean – is, as I said, incapacitated. Without a third to guide him in the song, the Singer is restless,' Ilandeh acknowledged. 'Shaman Kapal and Listener Chotek have had to split the duty between them, but they are struggling and these last days his sleep has been disturbed, too. And he . . .' The Whisper put down her cup and made herself focus on Pilos. 'He asks for Tayan. Screams for him. Not even the Great Octave can soothe him.'

The silence stretched long between them. 'What does that mean?' Elaq whispered in the end, his earlier ire vanished into the shadows leaping against the wall. 'Why would the holy lord want him? He's just a slave.'

'I do not fully understand what it is they have been doing in the song with the holy lord, other than that it is medicine, but whatever connection the Singer and the Toko shared before appears to have strengthened during the blooding.' Ilandeh scrubbed her hand wearily through her damp hair. 'The Singer is bereft. As if Tayan were his favoured courtesan taken ill. He has sat by his bedside, even, and held his hand.'

Both men inhaled sharply and then Elaq refilled their cups without asking Pilos's permission. Ilandeh wished it was honeypot, not beer.

'What does the slave do when the holy lord is near?' Pilos asked.

Ilandeh bobbed her head. 'If he is unconscious, then he remains calm and the song steadies. The Singer himself is more peaceful. But when he is awake, he raves and thrashes, tries to escape. He screams at sight of the holy lord, who is then distressed in turn.' The Whisper closed her eyes and let her chin drop onto her chest. 'It's such a fucking mess,' she muttered, and then blushed. 'My apologies.'

Pilos waved it away. 'It is a fucking mess,' he agreed. They sat in brooding quiet while the rain beat on the roof. Elaq stood and crossed to a shelf and took down a second, smaller gourd and three tiny cups. Honeypot. At last. Its sharp smell wafted into the room as the old eagle poured for Pilos and then passed the gourd to Ilandeh.

Pilos tossed back the honeypot in one. She copied him and the sweet liquor burnt down her throat, through her chest and into her belly. Her cheeks ached with it and she exhaled fumes in a long, slow breath.

'I will have to inform High Feather Atu, but I can't trust this to a Listener and I know my letters south are being read.'

'I'll go in person,' Elaq said immediately. 'Verbal only report. And I can check up on our friend Nara on the way.'

Ilandeh's scalp prickled. Nara. The former Chorus leader – the only survivor of the Singer's massacre two years before, the act that had broken him and the song and led to her being installed in the source as Pilos's spy and the Singer's protector. She remembered Nara's open hostility and absently ran her finger along the thin line of scar that ran through her cheek and over the bridge of her nose. He'd been smuggled out of the Singing City in the aftermath of Pilos's disgrace and owned a farm supplying food to the Melody fortress. He passed on any news he heard through the merchants who moved in a steady cycle between the Singing City and the fortress.

Passed on news. If I was doing it, it would be called spying. But Nara is a full-blood, and so has too much status and honour to stoop so low.

Ilandeh swallowed bitterness that not even the honeypot could sweeten and let none of her thoughts flicker across her face.

Silence fell on the room and she watched the candle flame on the table behind Pilos. Its wavering light alternately cast a glow around his head and highlighted the growing silver in the long, elaborate braid he wore.

'Though it pains me to say it . . .' she broke off, wishing for more honeypot. Wishing she hadn't opened her mouth at all.

'Well?' Pilos demanded. He held out his cup for a refill and then gestured to her. Elaq hesitated the barest instant and then poured for her – full-blood serving half-blood. She knew he felt it, too.

'Forgive me, High Feather. If we can reconcile Tayan to the Singer's presence, perhaps the holy lord's recovery will begin again. There had been progress before this that no one expected.' She grimaced at their matching expressions of ire. 'Forgive me: while that was ill-said, it is true. The Great Octave's patience is wearing thin and despite the Singer's affection for Tayan, he remains Enet's property. She may try and find a way to kill him. Do you want me to prevent that if I can?'

Ilandeh had no idea how she could accomplish such a thing. She had no reason to even acknowledge Tayan's existence, let alone speak with him or spend time in his presence when she had so thoroughly made her disgust of him clear in order to allay any suspicion. Yet if Pilos asked it of her, she would do what she could.

'Since when has the Great Octave required an excuse to kill a slave?' Pilos asked, and the Whisper was surprised at the bitterness in his tone.

'The shaman's place at the Singer's side, and his role in keeping the holy lord healthy' – she almost choked on the irony of the words; what passed for healthy in the Singer these days would be named a lingering death by anyone else – 'afford him a strange sort of protection. For all that he belongs to her, the Great Octave would need to wait until the Singer was occupied to kill the Toko. Kapal and Chotek would be aggrieved, but no one else would even blink.'

'Except the Singer?' Pilos asked. Ilandeh inclined her head.

'Why does he even bother?' Elaq demanded, frustration clear in his tone. 'The Toko, I mean.'

She spread her hands. 'His shamanic oath, perhaps.' She wanted to elaborate on how dedicated he'd been, how there had been no injury or sickness too small for him to treat back in the Sky City, but her training – and her paranoia – kept the words behind her teeth. Those were secrets known to Whisper Ilandeh, not Chorus Ilandeh.

'Perhaps he sees it as a professional challenge,' Elaq mused. 'Sees our holy lord's life and mind and fate as an interesting new breed of beetle that must be studied and poked and watched and interfered with until it is understood.'

'Perhaps he does,' Pilos acknowledged. 'But that doesn't change the fact he is one of the few people standing between the holy lord and an ignominious death – or he was, before this. So if possible, yes, he should be protected. I have a fondness for anyone who the Great Octave wishes ill, after all.'

Ilandeh inclined her head in acknowledgement. She hesitated and then reached into her tunic and drew the cords over her head and laid them down. Six strings of jade beads, jet beads, polished mahogany, tiny discs of metal strung through the holes in their middles. Elaq's breath hissed between his teeth. 'This is too much wealth for me,' she said and saw the moment they understood. She was paid so well because she was believed to be an eagle. 'Please, use it to increase your status, High Feather.'

'You earned this,' Pilos said, unable to hide his surprise or the tiny crimp to his mouth that told her he needed it and hated that he did.

It was wrong, what Enet had done to him, and again Ilandeh was seized with the urge to slide a knife between the woman's ribs. She focused back on her High Feather and shook her head.

'I know my worth and my place. I have kept that which is my due, but I need no more.'

'It will smooth our path, especially if you give in to the Mute's demands,' Elaq said in a low voice. Ilandeh arched an eyebrow and the warrior threw up his hands in open disgust.

'Our Tokob fighter discovered who was behind the mask of the last opponent she killed. Knew him well, apparently. She's refused to fight masked again and promised to take her own life if we force her to. Masked bouts are more lucrative, and hers most of all – the other pit-masters pay us much to secure a fight with her. And now her attack of fucking conscience will ruin us all.'

'Is there anything else?' Pilos asked, not even trying to hide that he was changing the subject. It was clear he didn't feel the need to ask Ilandeh for her opinion on this or any other matter related to his civilian life. She felt a pang of regret at the distance growing between them, wider and deeper each month, but she knew her duty and her place – as she had said.

'Nothing further, High Feather.'

Finally, the corner of Pilos's mouth twitched upwards. 'When will you stop calling me that?'

Ilandeh shrugged. 'When you stop being so in my eyes. It was you who gave me this assignment, and all that goes with it. It is you who is here, you who I report to, not High Feather Atu, Setatmeh protect him. You are my High Feather until the end,' she added with a fierceness that surprised her and warmed her equally.

Pilos shook his head, but the smile stayed tucked into the side of his mouth. He picked up one of the strings and untied a jade bead. 'Go and get drunk, Ilandeh. That's an order.'

Ilandeh smiled and accepted the bead. 'With absolute pleasure, High Feather.' She pressed her head briefly to the mat and then stood. The men rose with her and inclined their heads, then touched bellies and throats. She returned the salute and then bowed again at the waist. 'Until next moon, High Feather. Eagle.'

'Warrior,' they said instead of calling her what she was – Whisper. Half-blood. Spy. She stepped out of the room and into the warren of dark passages below the pit. Back into the night. Back into the sullen, brooding city.

She'd a mind to readorn herself in her eagle finery and then find those gossip-merchants from before. They wouldn't recognise her; no one looked a half- or no-blood in the face unless they had to.

Yes, she decided. She'd change her shawl and put Pilos's feather back in her hair so that her appearance matched what her heart already knew, and then she'd seek them out and remind them what it meant to be Pechaqueh.

ENET

The source Singing City, Empire of Songs
194th day of the Great Star at evening

The song had changed with the holy lord's awakening, its smoothness spiking, like flint suddenly knapped. With the ruthless efficiency of a Feather of the Melody, Enet forced her wayward thoughts into order. Since becoming Chosen, she'd learnt how to Listen through the song, and the inverse was also true: she was finally beginning to sense when she might be being Listened to.

Ever since the songstone's rupturing, the Great Octave's mind had been as undisciplined and open to investigation as it had been when she'd been a child. The breaking of the capstone had broken her grip on her own mind, which had run in circles like a stunned turkey as she tried to find a way forward. So far, she'd been unsuccessful.

And then that fucking Toko slave . . .

Enet didn't know where to start with that fucking Toko slave. With his medicine for the holy lord, which had seemed to be working? With his incomprehensible entry into not

146

only the song, but the offering? With his pathetic babbling in the days since?

With the holy Setat marking him?

But the song was spiking. The Great Octave turned back to her work where she knelt outside the Singer's bedchamber, reading through the latest reports and making those decisions too far beneath the holy lord for him to even know of. More and more of those each moon, it seemed. But of course, Enet would do all that was required of her.

The sun was fully risen before the slow, shuffling scuff of bare feet on rug and mat announced the holy lord's approach. The Great Octave gestured for the table to be set aside and then placed her fingertips on the floor. As the Singer's shadow crept across the mural painted on the wall, she bowed at the waist. Her body slave knelt half-facing her so she could hold the headdress in place as Enet leant forward, though it pulled painfully at the pins in the back of her hair. The Great Octave stared at the backs of her hands, at the stump of her little finger where it ended at the middle knuckle. Permanent reminder of all she had done – of who she had lost – to bring her to this point. *So close until the songst—*

'Holy lord, your glory is as the sun, and I must turn my face away from it,' Enet said as the Singer shuffled past her, leaning heavily on Shaman Kapal's arm.

The Singer said nothing to her ritual greeting and Enet doubted he'd even heard her. There was another week until the next blooding, but she saw when she dared a glance back at him that the shakes had already begun. Would the Toko slave be shaking too, she wondered.

Enet had decided not to offer him to the holy Setatmeh at new moon. Not until they had more information anyway, and preferably from his own mouth. Information that would condemn him and free the Singer from his enchantments. But that would only come once – if – he regained the power of coherent speech. Whatever the Tokob ultimate fate, it was entirely likely that the experience would provide vital intelligence in their quest to heal the holy lord, which was her greatest and fondest wish.

There had been some genuine progress in the Singer before this latest setback. The period between offerings was a little longer each time, and the Singer himself a little quieter, a little more docile. And now, perhaps, it was all undone. Again. Not at her hand, this time, but the hand of her slave. She knew not a single Pecha would make any distinction between the two.

The holy lord disappeared around a corner, his steps slow and unsure like an old man's, as Enet filled her mind with the desire that he might be made well again, holding the image of him as he'd been in the front of her mind: beautiful, his warm brown skin flushed gold from within as the magic cascaded through him, tethered to his will. His song magnificent, his mind sharp as an eagle's claws, and his heavy body powerful and unblemished by scar or infirmity.

She held that image and refused to compare it with what Xac was now: thin and broken, his skin almost grey except for when he was allowed to indulge himself, and his hair thinning and lank. Not all the perfumed oils and cunning cosmetics and paint could make the holy lord into his former glory. A glory that had honoured her body with his, and one that had conjured a child within her. A child gone now in service of a greater, wider purpose. Another of Enet's sacrifices to the promise of the future.

'The Singer is a glory to us all,' Enet said as she sat back on her heels and the headdress settled once more. When it was steady, she rocked up onto her feet and followed the

Singer through into the source proper. Her slave gathered up her papers and followed her into the great oval chamber.

The source was perfect, without a single hint of the blood and stink she remembered from that fatal day when the song was broken, and yet Enet's bare feet seemed almost to reject the soft mats. Her stomach tensed in unconscious horror at the memory of the sticky blood seeping up between her toes with every step, but she knew that nothing showed in her face but joy and awe at being in the holy lord's presence. She worked relentlessly to ensure it was so.

A rippling curtain of rose-coloured, translucent cotton hung near the colonnade, floating gauzy as spiderweb in the soft breeze from the gardens. Behind it was the square of blue mats covered in the finest, plumpest pillows in every shade of a hummingbird's wing. The Singer's place, where he sat to shield his glory from his council so that they might not look upon him and lose the thread of their thoughts.

Singer Xac did not sit there now. Shaman Kapal had helped him out into the garden, where the holy lord spent much of his mornings these days, his empty eyes staring at the trees and the tame birds who lived in their branches. He held a woven basket, a child's toy, full of ground corn-meal from the kitchens, and as she walked softly up behind him, he reached in and scattered a handful onto the dirt paths wending prettily through the shrubs and flowers and small trees.

Enet halted a pace behind him so that the birds wouldn't startle and heard the Singer's small chuckle as the first of the brightly coloured creatures dropped down to feed. Finches and flatbills, mostly, though a couple of flycatchers sat watching from the low branch of a stunted papaya. The Singer reached into the basket again and scattered more crumbs, and more birds flocked around his feet. Kapal murmured something to him and he reached in a third time and then held the meal in his palm and opened his hand. The shaman put her own hand under his to steady its tremble and take its weight, and soon enough a waxwing, its head and breast the peach of early sunset, landed on his thumb and bent to eat.

The Singer laughed again, delighted, and the sound was claws in Enet's heart, ripping. Their boy had laughed like that, their Pikte. *My son.*

The Great Octave forced away the pain and the images and the sudden upswell of black, bitter hate, so viscous and malevolent she wasn't sure who it was aimed at, Xac, or herself. She took a breath and smoothed her kilt, her face, her thoughts, plastering a smile onto a mouth that wanted to scream.

Empire and Singer and song. Glory eternal. The world remade. It will all be worth it. It will.

It must.

Shaman Kapal had turned at her movement and now studied her, and despite herself Enet chafed beneath the weight of that gaze, at once outraged and anxious, but then Kapal looked back at Xac's mewl of upset; the waxwing was gone. She soothed him and together they scattered the last of the cornmeal, enough to make bread for a starving beggar, and then the shaman led him slowly around the garden and back towards Enet and the entrance into the source. He'd be back out soon enough, but first Kapal would ensure he ate and drank, for the Singer craved only one thing and would forget to nourish his body if not reminded.

As they approached, Enet knelt again, fingertips on the ground and bent at the hips, head up but eyes closed so as not to look upon the Singer's glory without invitation.

They shuffled past her and Enet felt one of the feathers of her headdress catch on something, a hand or arm or shambling leg. There was a tug and a sharp pain in her scalp, and she knew he'd taken the feather as his own. Without volition, her eyes opened and met his, for just the briefest instant: they gleamed with childish malice.

Enet breathed in the morning until they were gone, the heaviness of building clouds in her lungs, and then stood, brushing soil and cornmeal from her knees and shins. She followed the holy lord back into the source to begin a new day at his side, governing the Empire of Songs while the Singer concerned himself with loftier matters.

Bloodier matters.

Great Octave Enet took a long, cleansing draught of early evening air as she stood in the entrance to the great pyramid, her slave fitting her sandals to her feet. She was exhausted, her multitude of worries overshadowing everything else she had to deal with. Personal matters should never exceed Empire matters, but they circled her like coyotes around a wounded deer.

Every beat of her heart reminded her that she'd cracked her capstone. Every blink spoke of her own slave's reckless endangerment of the Singer during an offering. Two calamities. A third would spell disaster and the end of all her plans. Not just disaster for her, but for Ixachipan.

She descended the pyramid's grand staircase on twitchy legs and climbed into her litter. 'Home,' she told her slave guards and then leant back on the pillows to think and plan. She would have preferred to walk off her nervous energy, but the city was taut with anger and unease.

And not just the Singing City. Unrest stirred everywhere, all the way out to the very fringes of the Empire of Songs. While Pechaqueh could and did affirm that the whole of

Ixachipan now belonged to them and to the song, the unpainted truth was less palatable. There had been almost a dozen slave uprisings and not just among the Tokob and Yaloh, which was always to be expected in a people's first year or two under the song. Xentib had revolted too, and they were much farther along in their civilisation. There had been tiny, brutal civil wars between rival cities in Quitoban. Burning fields marred the skyline and upstanding Pechaqueh had been found slaughtered by half-bloods and worse.

Enet had introduced a campaign of silence and brutal crackdowns on rumourmongers. Merchants and traders from the affected cities were threatened with ruin if they spoke of what they knew to citizens of the heart-city. The Choosers suppressed gossip at the best of times; they had taken this additional challenge in their stride.

Despite all her efforts, some word of the unrest had leaked but, so far, the council had managed to contain it, dismissing it as disputes over farmland and the price of slaves that had got out of hand. High Feather Atu had sent portions of the Melody to each of the restless cities to quell any disturbance, and Enet's network of informants was supplying her with names of citizens to bring to justice. There would need to be another purge, not just here in the Singing City, but Empire-wide, to drive out the persistent rot.

Enet shifted irritably. It wasn't only no-blood free bickering among themselves. It was Pechaqueh themselves, not scheming or trading or ruining each other as normal, but openly acting against the precepts of the song and the protocols of society. Pechaqueh questioning why they should tithe to the Singing City, just as the councillors and even Spear of the Singer Haapo had questioned their support of the Melody, never mind how prettily phrased. Others were hoarding wealth to set themselves up as nobility on the fringes of Empire, as if any noble worth their jade would live so far from the seat of power. Still more were prioritising their own cities' status over that of the Singing City, as if they believed themselves rivals to the very home of the song-magic.

In all, the Empire was more restless than it had been in two generations. Here at the very moment when every citizen should be pouring their love and devotion into the song to feed the Singer, ready to wake the world spirit, they were instead questioning every instruction and edict issued by the great pyramid. They had all Ixachipan – they should have peace.

The noise and bright chaos was all around her now, distracting her from the tumult of her thoughts and almost shocking after the cool tranquillity of the source. Out here, the song was less potent and it was easier to breathe, even if it smelt less inviting. Still, it was soothing in its very difference and Enet acknowledged, fleetingly, that she was safer out here surrounded by potential assassins or ungrateful slaves than at the very heart of power in the great pyramid.

She thought again of her slave's reaction to the offering to the Singer. It fascinated and disgusted her equally. Chotek and Kapal, who had been present and summoned to bear witness respectively, had both expressed their own morbid curiosity. It had become an unspoken rule among the Listeners and gifted shamans across the Empire that as soon they felt the swelling of the song that indicated an offering, they would remove themselves from the currents of magic for their own safety. Either the slave had not known that or he had not had time to exit. Perhaps he didn't know how to: Chotek fetched him whenever his time in the song was done.

Enet had watched fear and then ecstasy flood across his strangely still, absent face – more emotion than he ever showed when he was in the song – and then within moments he had thrown himself at the second offering she'd procured with a high-pitched wail of need that had made the hairs on her neck stand up. Enet had thought to pull him away, had even gestured towards one of the Chorus to drag him out of the source, but in the end fascination stayed her hand.

She didn't normally watch, though she was always present, but that day she'd made herself observe the slave's movements and where they differed, or not, from the Singer's. It was eerie, how synchronised they became. After the initial frenzy, they had moved and acted as one. Unsettling in their matched depravity, almost as if they shared a mind. And yet that sharing hadn't lasted: as soon as the offering was complete, and despite his clear enjoyment at the time, the slave had become immediately hysterical.

That hysteria – the nightmares, the screaming, the revulsion around eating, touching and being touched – had yet to subside. Kapal was using her observations of his condition to formulate a new treatment for the holy lord. She had some ideas about changes to the medicine that might make him more alert and less driven by his desires. It was a blessing, really, what had happened to the slave. Theories and medicines they wouldn't dare test on the holy lord could be tried on him. It wasn't perfect, for he wasn't Pechaqueh and therefore his connection with the song could never be pure, but it was a start.

Already Kapal had ventured a theory that if their strange link could be re-established, the Singer could be encouraged to channel his darker desires into the slave, thus purifying himself and the song so that he might return to them. The slave himself could then simply be caged somewhere out of sight and sound, so that he might not act upon those desires the Singer had gifted to him.

Before this, it had been clear to Enet, and she thought clear to Chotek and Kapal too, that the Singer was never going to be well again. And now, because of one ambitious, too-clever slave, Kapal was full of ideas and theories and plans. Plans to bring the holy lord out of his madness and into the world again. Plans that required the Toko.

The holy lord might be made himself once more. What will that mean for the Empire of Songs?

And can one person be allowed to prevent the culmination of everything I do, which is for the glory and prosperity of all?

Enet blotted out the thought as she blotted out the city around her, drawing the curtains against the sudden foulness of intruding humanity. She needed the solace of her estate and the hidden room; she needed her tonic and the stone.

And she had neither. The Great Octave had wasted two weeks in paralysed indecision, the monumental scale of her error, of the songstone's breaking, a knife in her spine. She had scoured every book in her personal library and the source's own collection, but not even melting down gold and attempting to fuse the two broken pieces back together was said to work.

Enet needed that capstone and she didn't have it. *Then I will find another. All is not lost, as long as I am decisive.*

I can still do this. I can. I will.

She slapped the bamboo pole supporting the canopy. 'Faster,' she snarled to the litter-bearers. 'I have work to do.'

Great Octave Enet had no eyes for her gardens or the birds and gave the offering pool and stream no more than a cursory glance to ensure it was empty – and came to an abrupt halt. It was not empty. She bit back a grimace of frustration and let adoration wash over her as she dropped to her knees, prostrating. 'Holy Setat, god of rivers and lakes, you who make the rain fall and the crops grow, I honour you. Ask and we shall answer.'

It watched her, its chin just skimming the pool's surface and its long limbs spidered up around itself: the pool wasn't quite deep enough for this particular holy Setat, one of the larger ones. A former Singer. Was it the god who visited – tormented – her Toko slave? Had it realised she was the one it should speak with?

The holy Setat pushed back from the pool's edge, sloshing water, and flapped its webbed hands at her in amused dismissal. Enet made herself rise slowly, walk slowly into her palace. It had acknowledged her; that was gift enough. She refused to run, even though the urgency beat anew beneath her skin. Not run from her god, of course. Never from that.

Her estate slave greeted her at the door and she brushed past. 'I want reports from all my songstone mines immediately. How many have capstones almost ready? Roughly shaped is no good; they must be almost complete. Almost ready to be installed. *Now!*' she added, cuffing him around the shoulders. The Chitenecatl fled into the records room and Enet stalked on towards her secret room. Her body slave slipped ahead to wrestle the heavy painted screen aside, puffing and grunting.

The Great Octave stood waiting, foot tapping impatiently. 'Move it,' she snapped, and then in her haste shoved at it herself, until between them they'd exposed the door just enough for her to slip through.

All the wondrous calm of this room that she'd experienced over the years carving the songstone was gone. It was the tomb of a dead dream, magic-less and tonic-less and a death sentence to anyone who saw it who wasn't Enet or her estate or body slave, the only people who knew of what she did in here. Not even her guards were permitted inside.

Enet stood in contemplation of the broken songstone until her estate slave returned. There was still a layer of disbelief painting her thoughts every time she remembered what had happened and seeing it anew did nothing to take that away. It was impossible. *And yet here it is.*

'What took so long?' she griped as the man bowed low.

'High one, I have collated the reports in order of priority. The secondary mine in Tokoban has capstones closest to being ready for transportation, but nothing has yet been chipped free of the rest of the stone. The latest information estimates three moons at least before anything would be ready to be transported to a finisher for final shaping. And the shaping itself would take another—'

'Three moons before it can even be finished? Absolutely not. Unacceptable. I need a complete capstone or one that can be transported here and finished within two moons. You hear me? *Two moons.*' The slave flinched but held steady. Enet paced around her ruined capstone. 'What about Pilos's mine?'

The slave bowed again and shuffled a different report to the top of the pile he held out for her inspection. 'Yes, the last information from there said there was a capstone ready to be chipped free. That will have happened by now. It will still need final shaping, like the others, and intercepting it will be complex and dangerous. We would need—'

'Steal it, buy it, slaughter everyone guarding it. I don't care. Just get me that capstone and get it here. You have three weeks.'

'I will contact our Listener here in the Singing City with your orders, high one. Under the song.'

THE SINGER

The source, Singing City, Pechacan, Empire of Songs

It hurts.

It burns in my skin, in me.

The blood is gone. The blood is mine. The blood is song and the song is mine and the song is gone.

It hurts. The song hurts. The songstone hurts. It yearns for blood, angry without it. Singer is angry. I am the Singer. I am the song and the blood. 'No more', they tell me. Yes, more.

Yes. More.

Shaman is gone. Shaman was with me, inside me and it was . . . good. And now gone. Why is he gone? Where? Shaman wanted the blood with me. Made the song with me. Shaman is good.

Shaman is gone.

Shaman told me I am broken. Broken by Enet, but he could fix me. Shaman said he could but then he left. He left me.

Enet is my Chosen. Where is my Chosen? Chosen says to wake the world spirit and all hurt will go. Tells me soon, soon I will wake it and walk at its side forever.

Shaman doesn't tell me that. Shaman tells me I will be well. Puts himself inside me. But I am not well and he is gone, too. All gone. Everyone gone and the blood with it.

Cannot be well until the song is fixed. Blood will fix the song.

'No,' shaman says.

Yes.

Give me blood. Or I will take it from all the world.

XESSA

Pilos's fighting pit, Singing City,
Pechacan, Empire of Songs
197th day of the Great Star at evening

Xessa lay on her cot, her face turned to the wall. Propped next to her were the masks, empty eye sockets accusing, empty mouths screaming. She could smell the blood on them, or on her. Still.

Always.

Eighteen days, and they wouldn't let her die. Not the spirits – those would welcome her with fangs and claws and plagued her nights and haunted her days for daring to live – but Shaman Tleote and Trainer Kalix and Pit-master Pilos. They wouldn't let her die.

She'd tried so hard, tipping out her water even when her body screamed for it and refusing food and medicine even when they put a blade at her neck. She prayed the knife would cut deep and swift; instead they took it away and left her there, another gourd of life-giving water in easy reach, the smell of it maddening. She'd kicked it over and then sobbed, dry and painful in her throat and chest.

160

And still Xessa lived.

As a child, she'd twice taken part in the beautiful, solemn ritual that encouraged death in the already-dying, a peaceful end to an agonising, incurable disease or injury. She didn't have any of the herbs or medicines, but she remembered the pounding of drums thudding through her ribs, the stamp and spin of feet in dance, and an ululating song that pressed on her skin like heat. The ritual of sought death, for the good of the individual, or sometimes for the good of the tribe, an honoured, honourable sacrifice to request Malel's intervention and aid.

Xessa wanted the same. It didn't need to be honourable or memorable or anything else. It just needed to be now. She had done everything she could: danced and drummed herself unconscious, woken up and danced again only to have trainers come and lash at the bars of her cage with their whips and yell at her to stop, or so she assumed. She didn't bother reading their words. On the third day they'd tied her ankle to the bars to restrain her; within minutes she'd unpicked it and fashioned it into a noose. After that, they moved her to the Grave.

Xessa had seen other pit-fighters talk of it, but she'd never been able to imagine it. It was just a stone-lined pit one pace long and two paces deep – not long enough to lie down, nor tall enough to stand up. Gagged and with her hands tied behind her, she'd been in there for four days, the gag removed three times a day so the guards could force food and water into her. They were brutally efficient, taking no pleasure in tormenting her, concerned only that she live to fight and die for them later.

Xessa had stopped screaming through the rough rope in her mouth on the first day and stopped fighting the guards on the third. She couldn't die in her cage; she couldn't die in the Grave. She who walked the snake path, whose every duty had spat in death's face, was unable to die.

Since her return to her cage, the days and nights rolled around in an endless, numb cycle of force-feeding, wound treating and ritual death-seeking. Images of the circle of death-dancers made up of swirling, sweating, painted bodies assailed her, the sweet smoke of incense wreathing them and the drums and voices vibrating through her ribs and fingertips as the old woman had gone, loved and loving and with little regret, to the spirit world.

How she had thanked them for easing the last of her life, for loving her enough to let her go. Xessa remembered how it had felt, the ancestors drawing close and the spirits too, the stamp of shamans, the wild joy and terror. The place of self-sacrifice and ending; the place of new beginning. How she yearned for it, for an end to this world in which she'd become more a monster than even the Drowned.

Xessa lay still but for the beat of her palm on her chest as she tried to find the bonds that joined spirit to flesh within her and prise them apart. Seeking not rebirth but an end. One without a new beginning. Annihilation.

Another dusk. Another change in the air that signalled guards bringing her food and water to force down her throat. Xessa didn't have the will to fight them. Wouldn't it simply be easier to eat?

No, that's my traitor body speaking. The harder I fight, the more likely someone is to lose their temper and choke me, or snap my neck, or crack my skull.

Determined to fight them again – always – the eja moved to the back of her cage. They'd have to catch her before they could force her to eat. Only it wasn't guards; it was Tiamoko. Xessa blinked, wondering if hunger was affecting her eyes. Perhaps she was having visions like some shamans back home had been able to conjure. He was balancing a platter on one hand and carrying two pitchers in the other. A guard was with him, but he merely reached past to untie Xessa's door, peered in at her without much interest, and then tied the gate shut again once Tiamoko was inside.

Xessa watched his slow, amiable approach. 'I brought us duskmeal,' he said when her gaze landed on his face. 'Thought you might be hungry.'

She flinched, almost snarling, the way Ossa had done when threatened with something big and imposing he didn't understand. Tiamoko had never been like that before, an unknown threat and something to beware. He'd been a friend, a piece of home. 'Not hungry,' she signed, her gestures abrupt and inelegant. 'Leave.'

Tiamoko shook his head and put the platter and jugs down on the ground, then sat cross-legged. He invited her to join him. 'I can't leave when I'm worried about you,' he signed. 'And I'm really, really worried about you, Xessa. You're all I've got left of home and under-trainer Ilam says you're committing a long, slow suicide.' His face softened, the hardness dropping from his features until she remembered exactly how young he was. More boy than man for all his size and prowess. A boy who'd laughed – once.

Still, she couldn't let any weakness past the cage she was building around her heart. The last years had taught her how effective cages were at containing dangers. She was in one, after all. Best for the raw wound that was her spirit to be confined to another until she could find a way to die.

Despite herself, though, anger wormed its way past the bars to bring a sneer to her mouth. She pointed to the food that her nose and stomach were insisting she fall on like an eagle. When they force-fed her, it was mostly corn gruel or mashed avocado, something liquid enough that she couldn't try and choke herself. Tiamoko's platter held meat and cornbread and peppers and underlying those tantalising scents was something sweet she couldn't place.

'And was this Ilam's idea?' she asked, swallowing a mouthful of saliva and fixing her glare on the boy's surprised face. 'You work for him now, for Pechaqueh slavers? Why do you want me to live just so I can kill for them?'

'That's not—' he began, but she slashed her hand through the air.

'Why didn't you tell me about the masked fights?' Her breath caught on the thorns clogging her throat until it stumbled.

Tiamoko stared at her for so long that Xessa experienced a sudden, wrenching panic. What if he didn't know? Tiamoko had fought masked as well, but what if he'd never learnt who was behind them? What if she had to tell him, here and now, that he'd slaughtered his own? The fear of it was stronger even than the shame that burrowed its fangs in her. She couldn't do that to him; she couldn't break him the way Casiv had broken her. Not this brave, beautiful and distant boy who'd already been twisted by the last few sun-years.

'I hoped you'd never find out,' he signed, the words so similar to Oncan's own that it took Xessa a few breaths to make sense of them. When she did, the battered, bleeding muscle of her heart rattled the bars of its cage and roared its fury and devastation. *Not Tiamoko. Not this boy.*

'I know why you're doing this, Xessa. Believe me, I thought about it myself when I found out, but isn't that just another victory for them? They already control so much and I thought at least this – my death – I could control. That I would go to Malel and my ancestors on *my* terms. And then Pit-master Pilos spoke to me.'

'Lied to you,' Xessa signed before she could stop herself. 'He'll say and do anything to feed his spectators with our blood.'

'Yes. But what about those we've claimed? Our families? Every bout we win, a portion of that wealth goes to their freedom. And if we did die, what would they be told? That we'd suicided and left them to suffer. Malel put us here for a reason, Xessa. She allowed us to lose the war so that we would be here, in the heart of their Empire.'

'To do what? We are slaves. We are *nothing*.' She finally sat as if someone had kicked her legs from under her, nearly upsetting the platter as she did. Her stomach continued to insist on eating, but she didn't have the energy. Finally signing her thoughts had stolen the strength from her muscles, as if each word was a poison.

Tiamoko dragged the platter and pitchers to one side and shuffled forward until they were sitting cross-legged knee to knee. He grabbed her by the shoulders and shook her, his fingers digging in hard enough to bruise. When he stopped, he spoke very clearly. 'We are not nothing. We are not defined by this state they have condemned us to. *We are people, Xessa*. Living, breathing, thinking, feeling people. We can embrace what they have done to us and use it to make us stronger, or we can fall and die under its weight. I am a warrior, a child of Malel, a son and friend and one day a parent, and I will let no one take that from me. *I will go home*. That is what I am; that is who I am. Nothing and no one will stand in the way of that.'

Xessa focused on his words with desperate force, but the thought of seeing Toxte again, or Tayan, and telling them she'd murdered Tokob for Pechaqueh pleasure just to win the right to reunite with them made bile scour her throat.

And besides, Xessa would never be free, no matter how much wealth she earned to pay off the debt that came with owning her. Xessa was eja, and no eja would ever be released to live in the Empire of Songs. She'd be murdered in the streets within an hour of leaving this pit. Everyone who came to watch her fight did so in the hopes she would die – the betting was always heavily against her and she knew that was the only reason Pilos tolerated her continued existence. She made him rich.

'We have to do what we are told,' Tiamoko continued with that youthful earnestness she normally loved. His wide-eyed, infectious wonder at the world had been a source of delight ever since he'd joined Lilla's Paw; now his naïveté set her teeth on edge. 'But we don't have to think of ourselves the way they think of us. They call us slaves, but we are people. Tokob. Every time we fight, no matter who our opponent is, we both step into that pit knowing it could be the day Malel calls us home. Is the death of a Toko at my hands any better or worse than the death of the same Toko at the hands of another? It's still death. At least this way we can learn their names and drum for them. Honour them.'

Xessa didn't know how to answer him. Everything he said was wrong – yet everything he said made sense. Wrongness coming from a right heart. Evil from an innocent spirit. How could she explain the difference between taking Tokob life and taking anyone else's? Tiamoko was a warrior, and while he hadn't been involved in any skirmishes with Yaloh before the war, he'd been taught that taking life in defence of the tribe was honourable. Xessa was eja and her enemies had been monsters and so her conscience had never had to wrestle with concepts like this.

Perhaps Tiamoko had the right of it. She couldn't say. All she did know was those words didn't belong to her friend;

they were Pechaqueh lies and the fact he used them to justify his actions indicated how far he'd fallen into their way of thinking. Which of them was right? Both? Or neither?

Xessa stared at him as he scooped up a piece of meat and popped it in his mouth. Tiamoko the easily teased, easily led boy was no more, and while she mourned for the loss of that boy, the man he'd become needed her support. *The support of a kin-killer? A maker of ancestors before their time?*

We are both that now. His hands are as red as mine and if he needs to lie to himself in order to live, that is his choice. But I don't have to live. I don't have to believe any of this.

'Thank you for coming here,' she signed, 'and for saying what you did. But I can't live with what I've done and I ask you not to try and convince me otherwise.'

Tiamoko's broad, muscled shoulders slumped and he sucked his bottom lip into his mouth. 'At least eat with me,' he pleaded, his eyes big and wounded. 'I had to bribe three different guards to get the food and beer and an evening with you. You must know they won't let you starve to death, and there are easier ways to die in a fighting pit anyway. Please eat with me. Tell me stories of home, Xessa, so we can pretend we're back there, just for tonight. Please.'

Ah, so that was what the sweet scent was – honeyed beer. More saliva flooded her mouth and she swallowed convulsively when he ate another piece of the smoky meat. In this, at least, he was right. Refusing food would never work, but if she let them think Tiamoko had convinced her to live, they'd put her in the pit again soon enough. As he'd said, there were easier ways to die when death itself was your trade.

Oncan's bloody, slack face flickered like a bat's wings across her mind. *Enjoy the food. We'll be waiting.*

Good, she thought, and picked up a triangle of cornbread. Tiamoko grinned and slid a pitcher towards her. *I'll see you soon, ancestors.*

Another day in the Underworld.

Ilam appeared with her dawnmeal, so unexpected that she took it when he shoved it through the bars at her. 'You have chosen to rejoin the living, I see. The other frog-licker's cock convinced you?'

Xessa blinked, slow and catlike, to cover her embarrassment. Even if she could have replied in a way he'd understand, she wouldn't. Ilam was a worm.

'Hope you enjoyed it; he'll be dead soon enough.' She couldn't help but react at that. Tiamoko was an exquisite fighter who surely brought a good amount of jade into the pit. Xessa shook her head and the under-trainer laughed at her.

'You know nothing of entertainment. He's too efficient, too remote. There's no passion in his fights.' Ilam squatted opposite her and ran his tongue across his lips as he stared at her. 'What the crowd spends its wealth on is betting against *you*, frog-licker, with your desperate, painful honour. We all know how much it hurts you to kill, how you loathe taking the lives of people, you who delight in the deaths of gods themselves. It's you they bet against, not the pretty boy who fights as if he's chopping wood. He'll fight and die in this pit and be forgotten the same day but you, god-killer . . . Oh, the fighter who ends your curse upon this world will be lauded for a lifetime.'

Xessa's stomach rebelled at Ilam's words and the horrible sense they made. She'd thought her disgust could get no stronger; she'd been wrong. Tiamoko was rarely injured in his bouts, and never badly. He won all his fights with that same cold economy she'd witnessed as they fought for Sky City and freedom. Emotionless. Swift and merciless, without a move or a step or even a breath wasted. A dance of destruction, beautiful enough to steal a heart and shiver a belly, and yet quickly over.

But the crowd came to be entertained, and Xessa's emotional, desperate bouts probably were more to their perverted taste. No distant, contemptuous grace and the certainty of an ending from her, as it was with Tiamoko. Rather fear and self-loathing and the possibility of defeat that hung like a cloud over her every movement. The spectacle of an eja meeting their end. Of an upstart Toko finally finding the justice she deserved.

Tiamoko gave them victory, but the crowd's enjoyment of him was centred around the jade they could earn, not delight in his movement, and because of that, Ilam said he was less important to the pit than her.

And Tiamoko knew it. Xessa finally understood the reason for the small line that had taken up residence between his brows some time in the last year, which she'd thought was merely homesickness or disgust at what they were made to do. But really, it was knowing that the very thing he'd been honoured for at home, the very thing that had turned the fortunes of more than one battle in the Tokob favour, was his biggest failing here. It was the thing that would see him killed or forgotten. Or killed *and* forgotten, more like.

Xessa could see the path of Tiamoko's life unwinding in front of him – fighting ever bigger, ever faster opponents. Multiple opponents. Using inferior weapons, maybe no weapons. Somehow never quite profitable enough to buy his freedom. And one day, years from now, he would die in this pit and be forgotten, as Ilam promised. There were no other outcomes for Tiamoko, for the boy with the dimpled smile and the tireless feet.

And there was nothing Xessa could do to help him. Surely he must know where the trail he was walking led. He'd spoken to her just last night of living and seeing his family again. Had he only said that to encourage her to embrace living herself?

Forgive me, ancestors. Forgive me, Oncan. Although I deserve death, I will not see Tiamoko die as well. If he is the only Toko I can save, then save him I must. I will.

She didn't know how, but she vowed to find a way. Xessa could feel the ancestors' aggression as a cold breath on the back of her neck, their rage at her refusal to join them so that they might chase her down the spiral path into the depths of the Underworld, never to return.

Xessa had thought her death was the only choice she had left to make, the very last thing she had any control over, and the Pechaqueh had taken even that from her by ruining Tiamoko.

So be it.

I'm sorry, ancestors. Malel and you spirits, Snake-sister and Jaguar-brother, please understand. I don't ask for your forgiveness, for I don't deserve it. But I will save Tiamoko, even if I don't know how. He is my people now. He is Tokoban itself. He cannot die because of Pechaqueh greed.

He must not.

I refuse it.

TAYAN

It was dark and close and cramped, and there was a figure looming over him in the blackness. A torn-open, keening figure with no tongue, no eyes, that nevertheless demanded to know *why*.

Tayan woke, a scream clawing into his throat. He slapped both hands over his mouth – both bloody, wet hands – and forced it back down. His pulse thudded through his chest and temples and he was slick with cold, sticky blood, his tunic clinging to his back.

Sleeping quarters. I'm in the slave sleeping quarters deep in the pyramid and it's sweat, not blood. Not blood. I'm safe.

He wasn't safe. The figure of the slave he'd slaughtered with his hands and fingernails and teeth resolved into the figure of the holy Setat who had, once again, come to find him. The one that had marked him; claimed him. Despite the shaman's best efforts, a muffled wail made its way past the hands clamped to his face. The god shifted backwards

171

slightly so that the light from the distant candle caught in its big, liquid eyes and highlighted the gentle swell of its cheekbone. It would have been beautiful when it was human.

It's beautiful now.

Tayan shifted one hand from his mouth to touch the tender points around his eye, almost healed into little red scars. Was it here to finish what it had started? Had it changed its mind about letting him live?

The holy Setat chirped as he fingered the scars, as if acknowledging the marks and pleased with them. The sound was like a rope around the shaman's middle, drawing him up out of his blanket and closer. Black, round eyes narrowed and it almost flinched and Tayan realised he'd been about to touch it. He sucked in a ragged gasp and jerked away.

'Forgive me, holy one,' he stuttered, shoving backwards out of his blankets instead, putting some precious distance between them. It chirped again, and the imperative this time was to stillness. Tayan's muscles locked. He wanted to look at the creature crouched beside him but didn't dare to make eye contact again. He settled for staring at its mottled chest in the dim light and *wanting*. But wanting what?

'How may I serve you, sacred spirit?' he managed to whisper. It watched him as if waiting for the prayer that he should have spoken first, and Tayan added it hastily. 'Ask and we shall answer.'

The song was disjointed and stabbed at Tayan's skin like ant bites. Distress and confusion, the emotions projected by the Singer even in the depths of his sleep. Violently, Tayan shied away from thoughts of the holy lord. The Singer had done this to him, had made him this crazed animal, made him gaunt and exhausted by too little sleep, too little nourishment, and too much panic. There was only one food the shaman wanted, and even as the thought crept at the edge of his mind, his stomach heaved and he wrapped his arms around his middle, consumed with need and pain and nausea.

The Singer hadn't done this, though. He hadn't woven this strange bond between Tayan and this particular water god. This was very much of his own making, though for it to have followed him through rivers and streams and cenotes all the way from Tokoban was a feat he still couldn't quite believe. Whatever link was between them – different as it was to his link to the Singer that he couldn't yet bring himself to examine – it was powerful enough to extend across the sticks of Empire, to have drawn the holy Setat from the waters of Tokoban to the Singing City.

It was with something like relief that he could focus on the god in front of him. The fear gave him focus and stopped him from concentrating on the images that rose, wave upon wave, in his mind's eye. Tayan hadn't been aware of his actions at the time, but his body remembered them. It had ached – the muscles in his hands and jaw in particular – when he came back to himself. The knowledge of *why* they ached a constant sliver of flint in his chest, working deeper with every day that passed. His spirit had been absent when it happened, but it had not stopped the holy lord's bloodlust infecting him. In fact, it had probably made it easier for Xac to sink deeper into Tayan because his spirit had been outside his flesh at the time. Vulnerable.

My spirit entered his in the song, so his spirit entered my body in the flesh world. Neither of us asked permission. But I did it to heal.

Didn't I?

His thoughts were bouncing from one hideous memory to another, and the holy Setat before him saw his distraction and was unimpressed. It sang a short refrain of clicking, atonal notes unlike anything he'd heard any of them make before, the rhythm irregular and the progression skipping and sliding. Tayan jerked as it tore a grunt from his chest; it *hurt*.

It took control of his body and forced it into a prostration, his lower back and hips twanging with pain as he pressed his forehead to the ground over his crossed legs. 'Forgive this one, sacred spirit,' he stammered. 'What is your will?'

Before it could answer, the song clattered and clamoured out of the shaky rhythm brought to it by the Singer's sleep. Had he woken? The holy Setat rose on its haunches and stared along the corridor, as if it could see all the way to the Singer's bedchamber four floors above. Tayan eased himself slowly backwards as it looked away, gaining a little more distance between them until it reached out and grabbed him by the arm, its attention still far away.

Obsidian-sharp claws pressed delicately against the veins of his inner wrist and the shaman fell still once again. He was barely breathing. This wasn't the first time it had touched him, but familiarity did nothing to lessen the gut-wrenching fear of its cold, strong grip. Its very lack of violence was more frightening than an attack would be. At least an attack would be over quickly, his throat torn out by impossibly sharp teeth. This slow perusal and increasing tension between them was more than he could bear, especially with the burden of the song and everything he had done while at its mercy.

A muffled sob made its way out of his chest and drew the holy Setatmeh attention back to him. 'I don't know what you want,' Tayan whispered despairingly. 'Either tell me or kill me. I can't stand it any longer.'

The god had dropped back to all fours when he began to speak and again it radiated amusement without making a sound, reminding him of the most unpredictable of his spirit guides, Young Jaguar. Perhaps the holy Setat was enjoying

Tayan's torment in the same way. After so many days at his and Xessa's mercy in Tokoban, he could understand that. He couldn't even blame it for wanting a little vengeance. While it might be a monster made of teeth and claws and magic, it had once been a person. Another clicking run of notes; another wrench of agony in his chest. Had it read his thoughts through the song?

There was a noise from the corridor and the shaman recognised it as the changing of the Chorus shifts, which meant that dawn would soon be upon them. Would the god go back to the offering pool once the sun had risen? How much longer until its lungs failed and it needed to retreat?

The holy Setat shifted on its haunches as if agreeing with him, but then its throat sac inflated. Tayan sucked in one disbelieving breath and scrambled out of his blankets, but before he could flee the god began to hum, a low liquid trill of notes that bypassed the Tokob conscious mind and spoke directly to the core of him. *Relax. Rest.* So at odds with its warning and the threat of its claws.

Yet the commands were inviolable. The holy Setat knew what Tayan had been through and was seeking to soothe him despite the ill-discipline of his thoughts. Gratefully, tearfully, he slid back down onto his cot and pulled the blanket up over his chest, a faint smile on his lips. He watched the god hum until he could no longer keep his eyes open, while knowledge and insights drifted into his mind through its voice. Sleep sweet and dreamless beckoned with grey-green hands. The last thing he was aware of was long, webbed fingers caressing his cheek and the faintest rasp of claws across his stubble. Tayan slept.

The next time the shaman awoke, the great pyramid was busy with life and movement, soft voices and footsteps echoing from beyond the end of the short corridor leading to his quarters. And those quarters were blessedly empty of everyone and everything but himself.

No god watched him from the end of his bed like a haunting spirit; no smirking Great Octave stood over him; and no crazed Singer mumbled and shuffled in his peripheral vision. Tayan sat up. The thin, cotton-stuffed mattress on which he lay was damp, as was the blanket and his tunic. Despite this evidence of nightmares he felt rested, as if his sleep had been undisturbed. His hair lay heavy and suffocating down his back and shoulders, wisps stuck to his sweaty cheeks. He scraped it away, desperate to get some air to his skin. The holy Setatmeh presence in his room would not have gone unnoticed and he could guarantee a visit from the Great Octave or Shaman Kapal. He needed to be washed and dressed before that.

The song was a stuttering jumble this morning and Tayan wondered who was inside it with the holy lord, trying to bring some stability to the magic and the madness. But for now, he was far from Enet's cold gaze and perfect face; far from the disdain that ate at him and the desire that filled him with confusion. And he was even further from the Singer. Tayan shuddered and fresh sweat broke across his brow.

Xac.

The unholy lord.

Tayan sat on the edge of his cot and stared blankly at the door-curtain. Something was different. The holy Setatmeh voice hadn't just lulled him into sleep; for the first time since . . . *it* . . . had happened, his thoughts were clear. The god had stolen the madness from his mind and replaced it with sweet sleep. The wave of grateful adoration that swept over him was shocking in its intensity. Shocking but not unwelcome. The holy Setat had saved him and the Singer loved him. These were irrefutable truths.

And I love them.

He had fought against ancestors on the spiral path who had been determined to tear his spirit out of his flesh and inhabit it, striving for life again. He had even faced wild spirits not tied to person or place or living creature, more powerful by far than an ancestor. Those, too, he had defeated.

But with the clarity the god had granted him, he knew there was no separating himself from the holy lord. It had been Tayan himself who joined their spirits within the song in his attempt to heal the Singer. He had chosen to merge their beings together and the Singer had responded, growing an unbreakable bond within the fifth world and the song and the blood.

He should, perhaps, have anticipated it, or at least been more careful. The song-world was still largely a mystery to him and yet he had taken a risk there, unblessed by spirit guides and unprotected by journey-magic.

Tayan's stomach cramped; he hadn't eaten in days. He slid off the mattress and fumbled for his kilt, tying it with clumsy fingers and slipping into his tunic before lurching out through the curtain and down the corridor. Cool air slapped him in the face and a Chorus warrior spun to face him: Ilandeh.

'You're alive, then?' she sneered. 'I had thought the water god might have finally ended your miserable fucking life as you deserve.'

She stared at him, something indefinable swirling in her wide, dark eyes and then gone behind a wall of blankness. Her lips parted as if she would speak again, but she held her tongue. The scar running through her cheek and across the bridge of her nose had faded since he'd been here, but it had puckered the delicate skin around her eye, pulling it just a little wider than the other one. As if half her face was startled. Or as if a part of her was innocent.

Tayan snorted beneath his breath as he bowed low, hands and forehead touching the stone. There was nothing innocent about that lying, manipulative bitch of a murderer.

'This slave begs the honour of using the baths, high one,' he said instead of any of the bitter thoughts swirling behind his teeth that had returned to him now that the holy Setat had removed his confusion.

'Wash and shit and then proceed immediately to Shaman Kapal's room. Now that you are *recovered*' – the word dripped with disdain – 'she will want to see you. Hurry, slave,' Ilandeh added as he hesitated.

Tayan bit the tip of his tongue and bowed again before pushing up onto his feet. 'As the high one commands.'

She followed him through the long, empty corridor towards the slave baths, the skin of his back prickling under her attention, attention that didn't waver even when he entered and stripped out of his grimy tunic and kilt, then squatted by a bucket and scrubbed his skin. He hung his head over a second bucket and wetted the length of his hair, then poured cold saltwater over himself and scraped his fingertips over his scalp.

He wished he had time for a proper bath, but Kapal would be angry enough at how long he'd been confined. Tayan wanted to reassure her that all was well now, that he was secure in the Singer's and the holy Setatmeh affections.

Despite his newfound knowledge, the shaman was still uneasy. The things he and the Singer had perpetrated together made him recoil, even if the sanctity of it made more sense to him now. Still, the calm peacefulness of the holy Setatmeh sleep was fading with every breath and the thought of putting something in his mouth other than water unsettled him.

Clenching his teeth, Tayan poured unscented oil into his palm and smoothed it across his body and face, then dragged some more through his hair to rub away the salt. Oil and water formed droplets against his skin and he rubbed them in, long firm strokes down his legs and arms and belly.

Lilla had used to do this for him whenever he came back from a spirit-journey, massaging the last of the journey-magic out of his system, easing him back into his flesh and making sure the connection was strong. Worshipping him.

Tayan blinked savagely. He didn't need his fragile equilibrium disturbed any more, and memories of his husband could do that even on a good day. He steadfastly ignored Ilandeh's huffed sighs of complaint. She could speak up if she had something to say; if the warrior thought she was anything like as frightening as the things he'd been through in the last weeks, she was sadly mistaken.

Tayan wrung out his hair, dragged a wooden comb through it and added a little more oil, and then plaited it at the base of his neck before wrapping the long braid around itself and tucking the end under. He barely registered the air against the back of his neck any more, though he'd always taken such pride in his loose hair braided only at the temples, rattling softly with charms and beads. *Lilla's hands stroking through it, brushing it back to put his lips on my neck . . .*

Tayan quelled the memory. Lilla hadn't named him, hadn't claimed him. His fingers ran along the faded yellow marriage cord at his throat as he dressed and then moved to the exit.

Before he could leave, Ilandeh seized him by the neck and slammed him hard against the plaster. She leant very close. 'What is it the holy Setat wants with you, little slave?' she snarled. 'Why would it grace you with its presence when your entire fucking tribe are dedicated to god-killing? Speak, you fucking heathen Toko. *Speak.*'

The shaman scrabbled against her grip, but her strength was implacable. He wheezed in her face and kicked ineffectually at her shins. Eventually, Ilandeh released his throat enough that he could choke in air.

'We knew each other in Tokoban,' Tayan spluttered, 'but I do not yet understand what it wants.'

Ilandeh shook him hard by the neck, her lips peeled back, as she took his meaning. 'You did not know it; you *tortured it*,' she hissed. 'Your curiosity is well-known even here. Your . . . improper interest in everything. That curiosity is liable to get you killed.'

The words sounded like a threat but there was something in Ilandeh's face, pressed so close to his own, that made him think it was more of a warning. *But that's impossible. She hates me as much as the rest of them.*

Tayan dared to meet her eyes for just an instant: the loathing he expected to see was there, but there was a shadow behind it that he couldn't identify. Ilandeh let go of his throat and he managed to slide sideways from between her body and the wall. 'I should not keep Shaman Kapal waiting,' he said in a raspy voice and walked away before she could respond. Even that was a risk, and he waited for her to call him back and punish him. Instead, she followed.

He hurried up two levels into the public and Pechaqueh areas of the great pyramid, massaging his throat as he walked. The walls were brightly painted with murals and geometric patterns here, and the stone underfoot was softened with finely woven mats of the highest quality. Ilandeh's sandals whispered behind him; the Chorus were the only people allowed footwear within the pyramid as well as the gardens. The better to fight in, Tayan supposed.

They reached Kapal's room and Tayan knelt to one side and knocked. He put his forehead on the backs of his hands on the floor and waited. Kapal opened the door herself.

'Ah, finally. Thank you, Chorus. Under the song.'

'Under the song, shaman. Call if he becomes a problem.'

'I will, thank you. If you could stay close for this? You: in.'

Kapal stepped back and Tayan stood and walked past her to the centre of the room and knelt again, prostrating himself. The shaman shut the door and crossed to sit on the thick, patterned mat opposite him.

'Up.'

He sat back on his heels, palms on his thighs, and stared at the floor between them. The last of the peace gifted him by the holy Setatmeh song hours before trickled away like water through limestone. The silence grew and stretched and thickened and a manic laugh began to build in his belly. Whatever relationship they'd built in the months of their combined treatment of the Singer was no more. Tayan's own actions within the song, with the Singer, seemed to have ensured that.

It wasn't me, he wanted to scream. *I didn't do it. He made me and I hate him for it.*

I love him for it. For the secrets and the power, and the secret of the power. I love him.

The song juddered and Tayan flinched, began to twist towards the door and then stopped himself. Kapal's words to Ilandeh came back to him: Stay close for this. *Why? What are we doing that she needs the protection of a warrior?*

'So,' Kapal said and he jumped again; she snorted. 'You have made some little progress in your recovery, it seems. Or you were never ill to begin with.'

Tayan eyed her in open disbelief and she twisted her lips in reluctant acknowledgement. 'Opinion is divided about you, slave. It may be you are even cleverer than I have long suspected. I haven't decided yet. Come out,' she added in a louder voice and Tayan frowned as another slave hurried from the inner room of her suite and knelt at the Pechaqueh side.

181

Kapal grabbed the man's arm. 'Watch and let us discover which it is,' she said and took a knife out of her belt, the blade black stone with a slight sheen in the candlelight. With a single, sudden move, she sliced open the back of the slave's forearm.

Blood sprang into the cut, welling fast – fast enough to alarm. Tayan shouted and lunged forward on instinct: he could already tell the man needed stitches. 'Your medicine box,' he gasped as the cut slave screeched and then clamped his free hand over his mouth to stifle his cries.

'No!' Kapal ordered. 'Sit and watch. Not as a shaman but as yourself. Watch and listen to the song. Feel it. Let us see how deep this supposed connection really goes.'

Tayan felt dread begin to slide through his limbs, but he sat back as ordered. Further disobedience would simply bring Ilandeh in to restrain him. Frowning, the Toko focused on the man kneeling opposite. Blood gathered on his arm and then ran down and began pattering onto the mat below. The slave panted against the pain, his nostrils flaring above the hand jammed into his mouth. His muscles corded as he fought the urge to drag his arm from Kapal's grip.

'High one?' he mumbled around the knuckles he was biting. Kapal ignored him.

Tayan watched, nauseated and fascinated. There was a lot of blood. A lot. It was bright and heady, the smell thick in the room. His mouth began to water. A thin whine eased from his throat, like a dog begging for food. His pulse thundered in his ears and his hands were fists on his thighs, clenched so tight the knuckles cracked.

'What do you see?' Kapal whispered.

The song jerked again, stumbling and somehow, suddenly, *interested*. Need rose in Tayan like water full of black claws and knowing eyes. His heartbeat was wild, uncontrollable, and he shifted on his knees as the song strengthened. His belly tightened, hot and wanting.

'Stop it,' he gasped, and then whined again. 'Stop it now.'

Kapal shuffled forward, dragging the bleeding slave with her. 'You want this?' she demanded, proffering the arm towards him. The man was cowering and uncomprehending, the muscles standing proud in his jaw and throat as he swallowed pain and fear.

'H-high one?' he asked again, his voice an octave higher.

Tayan whimpered and reached for him with a shaking hand as if the honorific was meant for him. With every last strand of his will, he tore his gaze from the blood and met the shaman's eyes. 'The song,' he slurred as his fingers curled into claws. 'Listen.'

Kapal cocked her head, her attention shifting outwards in sudden panic. 'You've woken it,' he managed as the tips of his fingers brushed the slave's arm. He groaned again and made a desperate, unwilling grab. Inside him, the need roared, golden and irresistible and terrible. The beat of a thousand drums. Outside him, the song pealed and skidded and demanded.

Kapal hauled the man away from him, her mouth and eyes round with shock, and Tayan lunged after them. The song was thundering now, a driving, relentless imperative and the Singer was, the Singer was . . .

'He's here,' Tayan gasped as the Singer's spirit entered his flesh, looking through his eyes, moving his limbs. As if he'd fallen prey to an ancestor while walking the spiral path. The massive, golden magic of his presence, his divinity, his *love*, flooded through every limb and Kapal let out a little shriek. Tayan's arms pulsed with a faint inner glow, a golden haze inside his skin. The Singer. He lunged for the bleeding slave again and locked one hand around his wrist, jerking him forward.

'Out, now,' Kapal shouted at the terrified slave, who began to struggle in earnest. 'Chorus!'

Ilandeh burst into the room and cracked the butt of her spear down on Tayan's wrist without hesitation, breaking his grip. The cut slave scrambled away and fled into the inner room, shrieking. Tayan made to follow, but then his hand fell into the spatters of blood soaking into the mat and he paused, fighting the urge to chase the slave by focusing desperately, to the exclusion of all else, on those bright, tantalising splashes. He brought his face close to the crimson smear and inhaled. A shudder of almost-ecstasy ran through him and the song battered higher, relentless. He growled. His tongue came out and he lapped, catlike, at the rapidly cooling blood.

'Holy Setatmeh,' Kapal breathed and then Ilandeh had him around the throat, hands and arms locked into an unbreakable chokehold.

Tayan opened his eyes on the brightness of the source. The oval inner sanctum was overflowing with sunlight, loud with hymns of praise and lively birdsong. Citrus and incense. The trickle of water. And the song, rambling and roaring and discordant and *hungry*. Angry. Denied.

Ilandeh's sleeper hold must have only lasted long enough to drag Tayan out of the shaman's chamber and into the Singer's presence. Off to one side, Listener Chotek was hissing angrily at a pale, apologetic Kapal, his gestures violent.

The holy lord paced the room with a vigour Tayan had rarely seen. A lightness that trembled in his own limbs despite the soreness in his throat and the aching of his head. The Singer's presence woke memories and sensations in his body, made him shake with a sickly mingling of need and revulsion. Mostly, though, he was hungry. Ravenous. His stomach clenched uselessly and the holy lord grimaced and rubbed absently at his belly.

The Singer's limbs were thin and spindling, although his gut and face were puffy. His skin was greasy and ghastly pale. In another person, Tayan would have said they had an internal disease that nothing could cure, or that a malignant spirit or ancestor had latched onto their flesh. He would have given them weeks to live and yet the holy lord strode back and forth as if the prime years of his life still belonged to him.

Despite his angry remonstrance with Kapal, Listener Chotek was at the same time within the song, sweating as he tried to bring harmony to the Singer's spirit. Tayan could feel that, too, the softest tug on his mind that urged him to calm. He wanted to find Kapal's slave and eat him. He wanted to tear apart every living thing in the source. He wanted to claw his own eyes out. Instead, he lay still, Ilandeh's short stabbing spear hovering point-first at his throat.

'*I hunger*,' the Singer roared. Great Octave Enet hurried to him with a platter of fruit and honeycomb and purple cornbread. He smashed it out of her hands. 'You tempt, you tantalise, and then you take away. I should have every one of you killed. I should do it myself.' His amber gaze fell on Kapal. 'You.'

Tayan, too, was hungry, and wanted what the Singer wanted. They were so closely aligned, in fact, that he could almost predict what the holy lord would say next. His muscles twitched as if he was the one striding around the room. As if they were one. One spirit in two bodies.

Still. 'Not Kapal, my love,' Tayan murmured. Kapal twitched; Ilandeh's spear jabbed downwards, grazing his skin.

'How dare you,' Enet began, but the Singer held up a hand, stilling her, his gaze fixed on Tayan. Tayan who wasn't nauseous any more; he was *starving*. He wasn't disgusted by what he'd done; he *relished it*. Xac had brought him into power and glory and might and right and he would have more of it, more and more until the room, the pyramid, *the world* was red with it.

'Yes,' Xac whispered.

'Yes,' Tayan whispered back. He felt the Singer's smile before it appeared on his face and returned it at the same instant.

'Holy lord,' Enet tried, her voice low and coaxing. Now there was disgust, rising in their two bodies as the woman wheedled and coaxed and petted and pretended a love and worship she had never felt, not even at the beginning and certainly not now.

The Singer's hand rose and Tayan's rose with it, a mirrored image. Together, as one, they pushed Enet away. The Great Octave stepped sideways under the pressure of the Singer's hand and Tayan felt her arm under his own palm. The coil and release of muscle in Xac's shoulder was echoed in his own and he rose fluidly to his feet, Ilandeh's spear pressing in and then withdrawing before it broke the skin. Perhaps she didn't dare; perhaps she understood the greatness he was stepping into. Becoming.

'What is this?' Enet whispered. They looked at her looking at them, jerking her gaze between them. 'How are you doing this, slave?' the Great Octave demanded, strident.

Tayan and Xac came together like a bird to its nest, like a lover to their beloved, and despite his emaciation the Singer broke the heavy leather collar around the Tokob neck, ripping it apart with song-strength that the shaman could feel running through them both. The slide of muscle, the application of force, and a tender brush of fingers over the flesh of his neck that made him shiver. The joining of spirits within the song

186

and to the song. Together. One. He fell into it. He fell into Xac who fell into him.

'No,' they said, their voices harmonising and the song swelling between them. 'Not slave. Shadow.'

LILLA

Melody fortress, the dead plains, Tlalotlan,
Empire of Songs
202nd day of the Great Star at evening

'Feather Ekon requires your presence.'

Lilla had barely finished his meal when the kitchen slave appeared at his elbow. His stomach clenched and threatened to reject the food and he had to swallow hard and carefully. Only the night before, he'd dreamt he'd been summoned to Ekon's quarters. Summoned and more. Desired. Wanted. *Begged.* It didn't mean anything, he knew. He'd been without Tayan for more than two years and desire was as natural for him as dreams were impossible to control. Still, when he stood it was too fast, too eagerly, and the blood rushed into his head and made him dizzy.

'As the Feather commands,' he said. 'Let me return this to—'

The man held out his hand and Lilla passed over the bowl; he preferred to return items to the kitchens himself, instead of leaving bowls and spoons scattered across the ground as many of the Talon had begun to do, knowing

188

others would collect them for washing. *As if the Eighth have forgotten they, too, are slaves.* Every day it grated, like sand in the eye. A constant irritation, a prickle of warning that Tokob and Yaloh were turning ever further from the ways of their people.

'Thank you,' he said and the slave darted a look at him and then away. Lilla made his way to the exit, walking slowly with his hands by his sides. 'This one is Pod-leader Lilla. Feather Ekon has sent for me.'

The guards nodded and opened the gate, one of them trailing him through the open passageway and past the drill yard towards the eagles' compound. Another guard took custody of him there and marched him through another gate.

Nerves and embarrassment – it really had been an explicit dream – were burning in Lilla's belly by the time they reached the complex where Ekon lived and the guard escorted him to the door and then called inside. Ekon pulled aside the curtain and then nodded. 'Thank you. I'll walk him back myself later.'

'As the Feather commands.'

Ekon gestured him inside and Lilla kicked off his sandals, stepped up onto the mats, knelt and pressed his forehead to the floor. 'Under the song, high one.'

'Sit up.' Ekon's voice was that of a Feather and one knot undid itself in Lilla's stomach while another tightened in his chest. He sat back on his heels, ready to prostrate himself, or stand, or curl up against the promise of pain. 'Your pod has failed two days' training in a row.' Lilla put his hands on the mat. 'Sit up. Explain yourself.'

Shame flushed hot across the back of the Tokob neck. He sat straight, watching Ekon's hands where they curled loosely in his lap. 'Forgive this slave's incompetence, high one,' he began. The eagle snorted. 'A member of my pod was informed by the administrator of our Talon that her family have been executed. She has been distraught and it has affected the morale of the rest of the pod.'

'I know,' Ekon said, to Lilla's surprise. 'My question, however, was why you have failed your training twice.'

Lilla frowned and then hastily cleared his face. 'High one, the pod's morale,' he began.

'Your pod is one hundred warriors. Did they all know this woman's family?'

'No, high one, but—'

'And as pod-leader, it is your responsibility to deal with discipline. Cohesion. You have failed to do this and so they have failed their training. Twice.'

Lilla touched the mat again, and when Ekon didn't speak, he put his head down as well. 'Forgive this slave's incompetence,' he said again and slowly sat back up. 'This is the first loss my pod has suffered. As warriors, we all believe – believed – that if lives were to be lost, they would be ours, not those of our partners and children. Slave warrior Tinit wasn't given much explanation as to why her husband and daughters were executed. She does not know their crimes. She is grieving and my pod – and I would say the whole Talon, high one – is . . . anxious. This is not what we were promised.'

Ekon's fingers twitched. 'And what was it you were promised, Pod-leader? What was it we told you when you pledged yourselves to the Melody?' His voice was sharp, tinged with mockery. 'Did we say your families would live in peace and luxury while their debts were worked out by you? Or did we say you were each responsible for the others' wellbeing? Your Tinit is lucky she was not condemned alongside her family. It was discussed,' he added pointedly.

Lilla's scalp tightened and his heart warned him not to speak. He ignored it. 'Right now, Tinit wishes for nothing more than to step on to the spiral path and find the spirits of her murdered kin,' he said, his voice low but throbbing with passion. Danger raised the hairs on his arms; he ignored that, too.

'Tinit is a remarkable warrior and gave herself to the Melody mind, body and spirit in order to keep her loved ones safe. Now they are dead and she wonders what is the fucking point in fighting any more. She wonders how easy it would be to lose her life in training and my pod is engaged in ensuring that doesn't happen, in shielding her from her own impulse towards self-destruction. I don't know what to tell her to convince her to live, or whether it is even my place or my right to do so. Why shouldn't she find them in the Realm of the Ancestors and ascend to rebirth by their sides?

'So forgive me, high one, if my pod is not full of the happy little slaves you've come to know and ignore.' He was gasping for breath by the time he'd finished, staring blackly into Ekon's eyes in full and furious knowledge of exactly how much trouble he was in. And fucking revelling in it. Something, anything, that would allow him to *feel* anything other than relentless pressure and tension and paranoia.

When the punch came Lilla moved without thinking, slapping it to the side so Ekon's arm was across his body and launching himself off his knees, wrapping around the man's chest so they crashed down together, the Feather on his back, one arm trapped between them. The other wasn't, and as Ekon's legs came up to seize Lilla's waist and squeeze hard enough to make him rear back in pain, that fist clipped his jaw and snapped his head to the side. Ekon twisted his hips in the same direction, rolling them so the Toko was the one pinned.

Lilla grunted and got his left hand under the man's chin and started to heave him backwards, the right scrabbling blindly to protect himself.

'Stop,' Ekon grunted between gritted teeth as Lilla slowly forced his head up. 'Lilla, stop.' He didn't, couldn't, and a second later he grunted as the eagle punched him in the face again and his other hand gripped his wrist, thumb digging into the pressure point. Pain flashed through his arm, pain followed by weakness, and Ekon wrenched the hand from under his chin and twisted it until he cried out. 'Lilla, stop!'

Ekon pressed him hard into the mats, his thumb still on that flaring spot of pain, ready to dig in again if he didn't relent. Lilla's right hand was free, but the fight had gone out of him. He swallowed blood and looked up at Ekon's face, hovering so close above his own. Looked into his eyes and saw something churning there, the expected fury, but also regret and something else.

Just feel something, I just want to feel something.

He lunged upwards, acting on some wild, impossible impulse, and crushed their mouths together. The Feather made a startled sound and then another, lower and from deep in his chest, and he kissed him back with almost that same ferocity he'd displayed during their brawl. Their teeth clicked together and Lilla gasped, his skin catching fire with need at the wet press of tongue into his bloody mouth, Ekon's hands pinning his wrists, the full weight of his body sinking onto him. He moaned and arched up, the Feather grinding down at the same time – and then Ekon tore his mouth away and scrambled gracelessly to his feet.

He stepped out of range and Lilla lay on his back, panting with adrenaline, with fight and fuck and the knowledge that he'd attacked his Feather. He'd be punished for this. His entire pod could be whipped for it. Perhaps even killed, and their families too. Still, his skin tingled and the impression of Ekon's grip on his wrists stoked the heat in his belly. He rolled over onto his knees and then pressed his face to the mats, seeking his scattered equilibrium. Blood trickled from his nose and he cupped his hand to catch the droplets. He wanted to continue the fight. He wanted to continue the kiss. He fought back both impulses with savage force.

'This slave accepts your punishment for his behaviour with grace under the song,' he said, voice unsteady. 'This slave accepts your judgment for the pod's disgrace with grace under the song and asks that any punishment due to them be lain into his own skin instead. The failure is his; so too he asks for the penance.'

The request was rare enough to be unusual and there was a very long silence.

'Face down,' Ekon said eventually, his voice gone hard and implacable. The voice of a stranger; of a Pecha. Of a high one.

Lilla did as he was told and stretched out on the mat, one hand still cupped beneath his nose and the other beside his head, all his senses reaching for the man standing behind him. The eagle could flay the skin from his back with a knife, beat him unconscious, whip him until his spine showed through tattered flesh.

Or he might kneel between my thighs and fuck me.
Shut up, Lilla.

The anticipation stretched and grew and tightened to breaking point until he was sweating, his face screwed up and his heart echoing from the mats and reverberating back up through his ribs.

Lilla's free hand had clenched into a fist and still there was nothing. The urge grew to look, seek some sign of Ekon's intentions, but he didn't. Despite the promise of pain, he licked his lips and tasted the Feather on them.

The lash cracked across his shoulders without warning and Lilla flinched, his breath hitching and a sound nearly escaping before he choked it back, surprise more than pain, though that would come. Nine more blows landed, each precise and almost in the same place – Ekon's mastery of the whip was as assured as every other weapon he wielded. And then he stopped. Ten blows that stung deep in the flesh, deep enough to bruise and yet, Lilla knew from two sun-years' experience, hadn't broken skin.

He waited, heart in his throat and the anticipation building again. What would Ekon do to him next for the unforgivable heresy of answering back, of attacking a Pecha? A small, angry part of him reminded him it wasn't heresy, but lying face down and humiliated on the Feather's floor, awaiting whatever punishment he saw fit to mete out, it was easy to ignore that voice. Easy and sensible. That part of Lilla would get him killed – *had* almost got him killed by encouraging his behaviour in the first place.

'If your pod is not back to peak performance tomorrow, every last one of them will be punished, and everything meted out to them will be doubled upon you to make up for today's mercy.' The words were as unexpected as that first lash and the Toko flinched as if they carried weight and bite.

He lay still and uncomprehending. 'As . . . as the Feather commands.' The words were slow and tinged with disbelief. The punishment was far too light for the crime, as if dealt for the sake of appearances rather than a genuine desire to correct.

'To your knees.'

He pushed back with one hand and rose to sit on his heels. He could see Ekon's feet and calves and the tip of the lash dangling next to one strong brown leg. Lilla wanted, so badly, to look into his face and find some explanation, some understanding, for what was happening here. Was it because of the kiss? Had he bought himself this leniency?

The blood had mostly stopped leaking from his nose, but he had nowhere to discard the small red pool glistening in his cupped palm. Lilla raised his tunic and smeared crimson across his belly, just as Ekon said, 'here'. He squatted and held out a small cloth.

'Ah. The Feather is more than generous.' Lilla looked up as he took it and found Ekon watching him. The Pechaqueh gaze had weight and texture, fingers that stroked across his skin so that he shivered. The hairs on his arms and legs rose as if he stood within a lightning storm, and he had to concentrate to clean the worst of the blood from his hand and face.

Was this as far as his deception might have to take him in order to rise against the people who held them in servitude? Was this how he became Pechaqueh in his heart? Even worse: would it be as difficult as he'd once believed? Ekon touched a scratch beneath his lip, put there by Lilla's fingernails when they'd been struggling, and the Toko found himself following the gesture. That mouth curved in a half-smile, the hint of a dimple creasing the eagle's cheek.

He looked away, blushing, and wiped the smeared blood from his stomach to give himself something to do, and then folded the cloth carefully. 'With your generous permission, this slave will wash the cloth and return it before tomorrow's training.'

Ekon hummed. 'Keep it.'

Lilla paused. Slaves were not allowed personal possessions, not even something as small and seemingly simple – but in reality luxurious – as a washcloth. And he'd been gifted it when he should have been beaten half into the spirit world. He didn't know what to say or what was going on, so he tucked it into the waistband of his kilt and then prostrated himself. He held the position without a second thought, gratitude coiling sickly with anxiety and both overlaid with the memory of Ekon's body on his. His eyes stung and he blinked savagely.

'I'll walk you back.'

'The Feather is kind.' Ekon rose fluidly and Lilla came out of his bow and stood, a strange weight in his chest he couldn't identify, one that compelled him to look into the Pechaqueh face. He found Ekon was staring back, eyes flickering up from his mouth and his own plush lower lip caught between his teeth as if to bite off words that shouldn't be said. Heat flashed between them despite the punishment – or maybe born of it. The Feather's hand rose and this time Lilla swayed into it; his fingers glanced across the Tokob cheekbone lighter than a feather, a kiss of skin that meant more in light of the brawl and the beating than it had any right to. Ekon blinked and stepped out of his home and into his sandals.

Lilla exhaled, shaky and bewildered, and followed him through the curtain in silence. The light was fading and it wasn't too hot, but he ducked his head against the glare and the stares and walked a pace behind, watching Ekon's slim heels flashing pale against the brown of his calves.

When they reached the turning leading to the Eighth's barracks yard, the Feather faced him. 'Remember what I said: get your pod working by dawn. You don't get another chance. None of you.'

Lilla touched his tight belly and then his constricted throat. 'As the Feather commands. Under the song.'

Ekon paused and then heaved a sigh. 'You do like to complicate matters, don't you, Lilla?' he murmured almost too low to hear, and then turned and walked away. 'Under the song,' he added.

The words were soft, easily lost under the susurration of sound from beyond the walls. But Lilla heard them. His feet slowed, but then he carried on, not looking back. Not wanting to read any expression on the Pechaqueh face because he didn't know what he wanted to see. He was a slave; the blessing of the song was not bestowed upon such as him. That Ekon had said it, after everything, made him feel like a muscle stretched to tearing – even the slightest twitch would have him howling.

It was a relief, somehow, to pass through the gate and hear it shut behind him; Lilla was safe here, among his own kind. His own caste. Still, as he walked towards his barracks to find Tinit and the rest of his pod, his fingers brushed unthinkingly against his mouth.

Lilla's pod was lounging in a loose group, its edges mingling with other pods as friends and lovers sat close to each other. Kux watched his approach with her usual blank disapproval and a tiny, shameful part of him hoped that there were still some traces of blood on his face. As if that might elicit some sympathy and make this next part a little easier. Or might somehow cover up that he'd kissed Ekon and been kissed in return, crushed into the ground and kissed as if he was the only man in existence for one beautiful, delirious moment, as if the evidence of it was branded on his skin as clearly as his slave marks. He pushed away the thought and threaded through the group towards Tinit, wondering what in Malel's name he could say to her.

The Yalotl was sitting in a circle of friends who'd known her from back home, a circle tight enough to be exclusionary, though he understood why. The last thing he wanted was to intrude on her grief and force her to shoulder the responsibility for the potential punishment that might be coming their way. She already carried enough burdens. Lilla couldn't add to them.

He returned to Kux, squatting opposite her. 'Fang,' he said, giving her the title that meant nothing to Pechaqueh but to which they both clung with a fierce pride. A memory of freedom. 'I need your help.'

Kux curled her lip. 'Not this again,' she began.

'No,' he cut her off in a low voice. 'Not this. Feather Ekon has decreed that if we fail tomorrow's training, all will be punished for it. I won't ask Tinit to stop grieving – it would just be another indignity heaped upon her head – but I need the rest of the pod working at full capacity tomorrow. I'm hoping that all of us combined might mask any issues with her performance. I know we're all tired, and we're all scared for our families—'

'We?' Kux demanded, her voice throbbing as she straightened out of her slouch. 'You count yourself among us now, then, do you? Oh no, of course not. How could you when you abandoned your family and husband at the first opportunity?'

It was an old accusation and one he'd long since stopped defending against – because there was no defence. It didn't matter how many times he told Kux and the rest why he and some of the others had made the choice they had. All of them understood it, on the surface. They just didn't *understand* it.

'The Feather has not told me what form our punishment will take,' he continued as if she hadn't spoken. 'It could only be physical. It might be more than that. It might be weeks or months or seasons added to our service. It might be our progress wiped from the records so that we must prove ourselves again. I need you to help me get the pod working so that we might all – whether we have claimed kin or not – remain on the path to freedom.'

Kux stared at him with undisguised loathing and he wondered whether it was incomprehension or jealousy as the bonds of her obligations tightened, day by day, until they must strangle her.

'Will you help me?' The question was quiet and delivered with a humility he didn't really feel, but if he had to play to Kux's ego, he would. He shifted as his shirt stuck to the welts on his shoulders. 'Please.'

'And if I don't?'

'Then I will do my best to convince our warriors to regain their focus. And if I fail, I will be punished alongside you.' He didn't bother mentioning how his punishment would be doubled; she wouldn't care. He missed their friendship from the war. He missed her.

'We won't get much out of Tinit,' the Yalotl said eventually. 'She can barely string a sentence together. She'll be no more use tomorrow than she was today.'

'Then the rest of us need to compensate for her. Please, Fang. For them, not me.'

Kux put her head on one side and then hawked and spat between his feet. 'But also for you, to save that pretty skin of yours from the lash, no?' She waved away his attempt at an answer. 'Fine. For them.'

Lilla gave her a smile. 'Thank you, Kux. However we can encourage them now is to their benefit, not the Pechaqueh. The speculation over kin will eat at everyone if we're not careful.'

Kux snarled. 'You speak as if you know what that feels like, that worry for those you love.'

Heat flooded through Lilla, a burning rage that had seethed in his belly with every altercation and might now explode to engulf everyone in reach in its fiery agony. 'You think I don't know worry?' he hissed, his tone so distorted with the promise of violence that Kux rose to her feet and those around them shied away.

Lilla stood too. 'You think I don't feel regret?' he demanded, spitting words like fire. 'Or despair? Tinit received word her family were dead and it broke her. It would break any of us and I bleed to see her grief and pray to Malel it happens to no one else. *But at least she knows.* My family might already be dead, and I will never find out. Never, unless and until I am free and can search this entire fucking shithole empire to find them again. So don't fucking talk to me about worry, and don't ever think I don't love Tayan and my mother and sisters. You can throw my choice in my face all you like, but you don't get to say I don't care. Not to me and not to any who chose with me.'

Lilla gestured, a broad, all-encompassing sweep of the warriors around them, whether or not they were aware of the commotion. 'I care about those I left behind, and I care about this pod. I care about every Toko and Yalotl in the Eighth and Ninth Talons and every one of us spread throughout this empire who are just trying to survive. I don't have the luxury of *not* caring. Now I have to make this pod work again and I have to do it tonight and all I want, Kux, all I *fucking want from you*, is your help. Not a lecture, not a glare or a condemnation. Your help. Do I have it?'

Kux was flushed and shaking, her rage almost equal to his, but she took a few deep breaths and then unclenched her fists. 'You have my help. Just . . . get out of my sight. I'll take my people; you talk to yours.'

He wrestled his voice back under control. 'Thank you, Fang. May your ancestors guide you.'

She twitched at that. 'And you yours,' she responded, as decency required, though her tone indicated she'd rather they broke free of their realm and devoured him. Lilla almost wished they would, an end to the smothering, ever-tightening tension within his skin. Instead, he nodded once and moved to the nearest group of Tokob and began to speak.

It was highsun when drums and bone flutes blared a cacophony that bounced and echoed across the enormous drill yards. All movement among the Eighth Talon ceased as the warriors lowered their weapons and tried to identify the source of the sound.

Lilla's shoulders had stiffened overnight, and the welts had been noticed when he undressed in the barracks, but none of his pod commented. They'd spent the morning sweating under a strengthening sun, the warriors around Tinit protecting her from the worst of the attacks another pod was making with their blunt-headed spears. The Yalotl had stumbled from one engagement to the next, but the pod had pulled together and performed well, and Lilla had hope that they might escape further punishment.

And then the flutes and drums. Feather Ekon shoved his way through the clumped warriors as if they were corn in a field, seeming oblivious to the fact that even with blunted weapons they could kill him. Lilla had thought it arrogance at first; now he knew it was confidence that wasn't entirely misplaced. Still, the constant show of strength to keep the slaves in line had to be exhausting.

'What is it?' Ekon yelled as he broke free of the crowd. Dog warriors prowled between the paired-up pods, idly cracking long whips. It accounted for at least some of Ekon's confidence, but the dogs never waded through the slaves like eagles did unless they were breaking up a brawl.

'Fourth Talon under Feather Detta returns,' came the reply, high and drifting on the wind.

A rustle of noise ran through the Eighth. The Fourth was

the Talon sent by High Feather Atu to subdue an uprising of slaves in Tlalotlan, less than a hundred sticks from the fortress. Lilla's neck prickled; Kux was staring at him, ugly triumph twisting her features, as though news of a failed rebellion should be celebrated, because of course it had failed. They wouldn't have announced Detta's return within hearing of the Eighth otherwise. *You really are becoming Pechaqueh, aren't you, if you relish this?* he thought churlishly at Kux.

'How went it?' Ekon called.

'As expected. Minimal casualties. Macaws gave a decent showing of themselves.' The dogs and eagles patrolling the drill yard began walking with a little more purpose, moving together to better defend themselves, as if they expected trouble.

'They're all dead, then,' Kux snarled, pushing her way through the pod towards Lilla. Loud enough for the warriors surrounding them to hear, but not Ekon or the dogs; or at least, Lilla hoped not. 'It was Tokob and Yaloh who rebelled, you know. Your people and mine. All dead, and every one of their loved ones claimed by them as well. That's probably what happened to Tinit's family. Slaughtered by the Melody, by Feather Detta and the Fourth. And still you tell us to rise with you. Still you think you can achieve victory.'

Lilla folded his arms and stared at Kux for a moment too long before he sought out and found Tinit, wan and distant, over her shoulder. The woman let out a wail and sank to the dirt, wrapping her arms around her waist and rocking on her knees. Other Yaloh moved towards her and a few of them cast poisonous glances at their Fang.

Lilla was tempted to do the same but instead he did his best to keep his expression neutral. 'For now we are slaves, Kux. But does that status wipe out who we are as people? Does it take away our minds and our wills, or just force us to hide both? Right now, we have no control. Whatever we thought we could do for our kin, as slaves we are helpless. Hopeless. But that very hopelessness gives us strength, doesn't it? If nothing matters, if our kin can be slaughtered anyway, then we're free to do anything.

'All those who rose out there, they're not warriors,' he added, jerking a finger towards the distant walls imprisoning them. Feather Ekon was nearby and Lilla had only moments to get his point across, not just to Kux, but to as many within hearing as possible. He had to seize this opportunity, maybe finally make them understand.

'They rose up without concern for kin or tribe because they knew that if they could just push through, could just find a victory, *one victory*, that others would rally to the cause. Civilians, not warriors, fighting for their freedom. And here you stand without the spirit to do the same. Don't ever tell me again you're not fighting out of worry, not when our farmers and potters and weavers *and children* can fight.'

The Yaloh face had reddened with each word, anger bubbling beneath her skin until it boiled over. Screaming her war cry, she shoved warriors out of her path and threw herself at Lilla.

Shit.

This was not how it was supposed to go. Tokob and Yaloh scattered, giving them room, as Kux used the momentum of her run to power the flurry of strikes she unleashed with her blunted spear. Strikes hard enough to cave in Lilla's head or shatter his knee or arm. She didn't need a stone or obsidian tip, or even a carved wooden one, to end his life here in the training yard.

'Peace, Kux!' Lilla shouted as their staffs cracked together hard enough to rattle his teeth. He parried desperately, backing away, deflecting the attacks to steal their power or push them wide.

203

'You're a traitor,' Kux snarled in his face, saliva flying, as Ekon and four dog warriors began to bellow and converge on them. 'You'll kill us all.'

Ekon was nearly at them. 'Peace,' Lilla shouted again, and then he saw the deception for what it was as the Yalotl dropped low and cracked her staff into his ankle bone hard enough to send him onto one knee, white agony blazing up his leg. Shrieking, he tried to force himself to his feet as she pulled a shard of obsidian from her waistband. The broken edge of a spear, probably from when they'd had target practice two months before. So long she'd kept it. For this moment. For him.

It was neither long nor wide, but it would kill him just the same if she used it right – and she was more than good enough to do that. She swung with the staff and then punched with her off hand, the obsidian protruding between two of her knuckles. Lilla had no choice but to defend against the first – it wasn't a feint and would crush his jaw if it landed – but he couldn't get the staff back across in time to deflect the second. He threw himself sideways and the wicked glass sliced across the side of his neck, catching in his tunic and tearing fabric and flesh.

Lilla rolled twice and rose, gasping at the flare of pain in his ankle – pretty sure a bone was cracked – and drove his spear in a humming lateral line towards Kux's ribs. And then Ekon was there, slapping up the staff with his club and moving in between them, roaring at them to stop.

Over his shoulder, Lilla saw the shift in Kux's eyes. Knew exactly what she would do next, and how she and those who'd sided with her would try and lay the blame at the Tokob feet. There was no remorse in her eyes; not a sliver of regret.

She lunged.

'*Blade!*' Lilla dropped his spear and grabbed Ekon by his salt-cotton, whipping them through a half-circle and using the momentum to fling the Feather bodily away. His fingers had only just let go when the obsidian punched in through his back, scraping over his shoulder blade and then sinking deep into the flesh behind it.

Lilla spun on until he was facing Kux again, ripping the little shard from her hand with the violence of the movement so that it stood proud in his flesh. There was a rush of heat down his back and a surge of sick pain. Empty-handed, he leapt backwards and yelled as his damaged ankle protested.

Kux's staff drove towards his temple in a blow that would kill him before he even felt it land. His ankle was agony and his back was pulsing a different type of hurt while the stress and adrenaline sent a spike of pain lancing through his head from where he'd had his skull cracked the day he'd been captured.

Blood ran down the back of his left arm, tickling. Each sensation was distinct, each sound and image unrelated to the others. Kux's face was tight with hate and effort as the spear continued its inexorable trajectory towards his head, and though Lilla managed to shove his weight back into his heels, there was no time to take a step away. 'Malel,' he croaked.

Again, a club batted up a practice spear, spoiling its strike, but this time it swept back around and down in a curve as elegant as an eagle turning on a wingtip to crunch into the back of Kux's skull, throwing her forward a step. She tried to take a second, but her legs had stopped working and she didn't even put out her hands to break her fall. Her face smashed into the hard-packed earth. Ekon's club swung down a second time, cracking her head like an egg.

Shocked silence fell across the compound, disturbed only by Lilla's harsh panting. The Tokob weight swayed back into his toes, sending a fresh flare of pain through his ankle all the way up into the joint of his knee. He grunted and stumbled forward, belatedly slapping a hand to the cut in his neck, though if the glass had hit anything important he'd be kneeling at the centre of a crimson pool by now. Still, his breath was laboured, and not just from adrenaline.

'Lilla? Pod-leader?' The voice was distant, coming through the storm roaring in his ears. Lilla couldn't look away from Kux's crumpled form. The breeze stirred what hair wasn't stuck down with blood, giving her a ghastly semblance of life.

A shadow fell over Kux and finally he let his gaze drift upwards. Ekon was in front of him and Lilla snapped back to where – and who – he was. He fell to his knees at Ekon's feet, yowling at the pain in his ankle, his back, his neck as he prostrated himself. 'Forgive this slave, high one. I should have seen . . . should have known she'd try something like this . . .' It was such a small sliver of obsidian. Why were the words tangling in his throat, choking him?

'Don't punish the pod, high one,' he croaked urgently and sat up so Ekon might hear him. His head swam. 'I take their punishment into my skin. I take their, I take—' A cough racked him and he put his hand to his chest to press on the pain. 'I take it into my skin,' he gasped and swayed and Ekon was, astonishingly, impossibly, kneeling opposite and supporting him.

'Get me a fucking shaman right now.' His voice buzzed in Lilla's ears. 'And get this Talon back in its barracks before I have one in ten offered to the holy Setatmeh.'

Lilla's hand groped at the air and then found Ekon's saltcotton; he seemed very far away. 'I take it into my skin,' he mumbled again, and fainted.

PILOS

Melody compound, Singing City,
Pechacan, Empire of Songs
202nd day of the Great Star at evening

Feather Pilos,

On the 198th day of the Great Star at evening, we were attacked as we escorted the bearers and the newest capstone from your Tokob mine to its place of honour in Yalotlan. Most of the bearers died, as well as nearly half the guards, but we drove off our attackers, who numbered at least forty. I believe they intended to seize the capstone for their own, but those in danger of being captured chose death instead. We do not know who sent them or why they might commit such sacrilege. If they attack again, we will strive to take captives for interrogation.

I have sent one of the bearers to the nearest pyramid with this report and a second requesting aid from Feather Calan; the rest of us are remaining with the capstone until a pod from the Sixth Talon arrives.

We will not lose the songstone, Feather, I swear. Under the song.
Yours in honour,
Oteom, free warrior of Axiban

Pilos read the Axib report three times; it got more unbelievable with every repetition. Oteom had been a dog warrior of the Melody and they'd saved each other's lives while bringing the Tokob under the song. In the aftermath of Pilos's disgrace, the man had resigned and pledged himself exclusively to the former High Feather.

Pilos had made him the warrior in charge of all the songstone deliveries from his mine in Tokoban in reward, and Oteom had never let him down. But it wasn't questions of the Axib loyalty or ability that disturbed him: capstones were never stolen. *Never.*

Who would even risk such a thing? And why? As Oteom had written, it was sacrilege. Not just forbidden but . . . impossible to contemplate. Or so he'd thought.

The Feather stood from the low table and paced the room. Around him, the everyday sounds of the Singing City's Melody compound proceeded without pause: the clash and thud of training warriors, the shush of brush on bark-paper from the adjoining room, a loud-voiced argument with a merchant over the price of peppers. Normal. Routine. Nothing to indicate that someone had tried to steal an almost-complete capstone for purposes unknown.

Pilos missed Elaq with a sudden fierceness, but his oldest friend was still in the south with Atu, awaiting his thoughts on the news about the Singer and the Toko slave. He paused in his restless pacing – Tokob mine; Tokob slave. No. Ridiculous. They couldn't possibly be linked.

But . . . his thoughts jumped from the slave to the one who owned him. Enet's compulsive need to ruin Pilos hadn't lessened despite the passage of time and her other concerns. Might she have attempted to destroy faith in his mine and his ability to deliver songstone to where it was needed? He snorted. Of course she would. She'd taken his position as High Feather from him; she'd slashed his wealth to tatters and his status with it. Now she was trying to finish the job.

As the only rival to Enet's songstone monopoly, it made sense for her to try and destroy his ability to deliver as promised, but . . . but it was *songstone*. The bones of the world spirit itself. What would she have done if she'd managed to steal it? Destroyed it? Pilos shuddered. No matter what Enet was, she wouldn't commit such an act.

Perhaps her wealth was finally at its end. The flesh merchants knew that Enet had to have the best stock to offer the Singer and tripled their prices accordingly. But even if that was so, songstone was never sold or traded. There was no point to such an act.

What was she thinking? With the Singer languishing and unrest growing instead of shrinking across the Empire, we need the surety and sanctity of the song more than ever.

The song. Enet's song?

'That's it,' he breathed, staring unseeing at the far wall. 'If I'm seen to mismanage the mine, it will be confiscated. She'll give it to some underling in return for their help in her bid for power. And she'd only ruin me now if she's making that bid soon. She's going to take the magic, by force if necessary. The snake is finally on the move.'

The idea was outlandish, but no more so than the attempted theft. Pilos's gut told him he was right. Enet would make her bid for power soon and she wanted him, at the least, out of the way beforehand.

Pilos couldn't use the Melody Listener who lived in the barracks to send a reply to Oteom, because this wasn't Melody business. He'd have to send a runner to a city Listener instead. He scrabbled for paper and brush and began a hasty letter.

'Feather?' Eagle Xochi called and then immediately opened the door to Pilos's office.

'What now?' he snapped, for his warriors knew better than to enter without permission.

'We have received a message, Feather,' Xochi said hurriedly. Pilos put down the brush before he snapped it in half and gestured for her to continue. 'It doesn't make any sense.'

She held out a piece of bark-paper and the Feather took it from her. "The hidden chulul must flex its claws." Pilos's heart climbed into his throat. *Not now, for fuck's sake.* He bit the inside of his cheek and then folded the paper in half. 'Anything else? Anything verbal?' he demanded.

'The messenger said: "in the shade",' Xochi said, her tone bewildered. 'Feather, what does this—'

Pilos cut her off. 'Thank you, Eagle, that will be all. I must attend to this, but I should be back before dusk. Oversee things in my absence and make sure we get a good price from that pepper-merchant; they've been arguing too long. Damn peddlers have no respect,' he added in an undertone as he ushered Xochi ahead of him out of the office. She turned right towards the training yard, frowning over her shoulder with obvious curiosity, and he waited until she'd turned another corner before ducking back into the office to snatch up his half-written letter – and his war club. He hurried out of the compound.

As Pilos had guessed, Ilandeh was waiting in his office at the fighting pit. She leapt to her feet as he burst in and touched belly and throat in the most perfunctory obeisance he'd ever received.

'What the fuck?' he demanded as soon as she straightened. 'We're not due to meet for—'

'Six days ago, the Singer and the Toko slave became . . . joined together. In the song. In spirit. I'm not sure, I don't understand it fully.' She paused, reluctant wonder skating across her scarred features, and then shook herself.

'It wasn't an offering this time, not truly. Shaman Kapal was experimenting on Tayan, showing him blood, and then she called for me and . . . but now, Tayan and the Singer move as one, as if guided by a single will. They speak the same words at the same time. The Tokob skin glows gold when the holy lord's does. I had to come, High Feather. Enet isn't allowing the news out of the pyramid and someone needs to inform Atu— Forgive me, inform High Feather Atu.'

Pilos didn't even notice her slip. 'What moon-madness are you speaking?' he said, hoarse and flat with disbelief. Laughter threatened.

'No moon-madness, not unless everyone in the source is infected,' Ilandeh said. She grimaced and squared her shoulders. 'That's not all. Not even the worst of it.' Now Pilos did laugh, a sharp, shocked bark. 'This morning, in Enet's absence at her estate, the holy lord put two feathers on Tayan's throat.'

Pilos stumbled back into the wall, the club dropping from nerveless fingers. Now he knew how it felt to have his legs cut from under him. His mouth opened and shut and then opened again. 'What?' he repeated helplessly.

'I was trying to find a way to send word anyway, because of the spirit-link – that's what Kapal and Listener Chotek are calling it. The Listener has confirmed they're, I don't know, tied together within the song? Joined, he said, and the bond is only growing stronger. But when the Singer put the tattoos on the Toko with his own hands, I came straight away. The

211

source is in uproar, not just the Chorus but the administrators, the courtesans, even the slaves. No one will notice my absence if I'm only gone a short time.'

Ilandeh stepped forward, right into his space, and grabbed Pilos by the forearms. 'We'll be out of options when the Great Octave returns and sees the dark feathers. And if I'm not back before her, she may become suspicious of me. I need to know what you want me to do.'

Two feathers. Two feathers tattooed across a Tokob slave's throat. Not Chosen to ascend like Enet, but the Singer's own future heir. The next Singer. A no-blood, destined to wield the magic of the Empire of Songs and the world spirit.

'It won't take,' he croaked. 'The magic won't take in a slave, let alone in a Tokob god-killer. It won't.'

Ilandeh shrugged. 'Probably not,' she agreed. 'But what about the Great Octave? She only wears the mark of a Chosen; this will be an insult too far. She has gathered almost all the strings of power into her hands, but the Melody and the succession she cannot control, though she has tried. She cannot act openly to undermine the holy lord's strength any further than she already does with the offerings. She must be seen to support the shamans and Listeners in their attempts to cure him.'

Pilos's skin was two sizes too small, pressing against his face and scalp and constricting his limbs until his fingers tingled and his pulse raced in his wrists and against his ribs. For one hysterical moment he thought he might faint, but then he hauled in air and locked his knees. 'How does this spirit-joining you speak of work? Does it strengthen the Singer or is it just another symptom of the illness the Great Octave has conjured in him? Speak quickly,' he added as Ilandeh hesitated.

'I don't know what any of this means, and I don't know what position the slave now holds or if he even is a slave any more – the holy lord himself tore the collar from his neck and said he was to be referred to as, as Shadow' – Pilos gasped – 'and I have seen the magic moving in him. I have seen him glow gold, High Feather. And the Singer is more present in his skin, more alive and aware and that already undermines Enet's control of the source. When she sees the tattoos . . . High Feather, please, what do you want me to do?'

Pilos knew that at some distant future point when everything wasn't so fucking catastrophic, he would find the idea of Enet being outranked by a slave almost unbearably funny, but for now amusement was the very last thing he was feeling. Ilandeh was still holding his arms and he was grateful for it; her touch reminded him where and what and who he was. There was absolutely not enough time to get a message to Atu: this decision would fall to him and the consequences of it would be his as well. Consequences that could determine the fate of the Empire of Songs – and its Singer. The song itself was strident, its rhythms unfamiliar. Its rhythms . . . Tokob? Would that savage land's traditions infect their holiest magic? What about their tradition of slaughtering the holy Setatmeh? Pilos's stomach churned.

'Is Enet a direct threat to the Singer's life at this moment?' he asked, breathing slowly.

The Whisper hesitated and this time he let her think. She shook her head. 'I don't believe so, High Feather, although I have no idea what she'll do when she sees the tattoos. She is absolutely a threat to Tayan, but I don't know whether that is the same thing when taking into account their, ah, linked spirits. She has been extremely hostile in the last six days and has openly questioned all the theories put forward by Shaman Kapal and Listener Chotek. She has even expressed doubt to the great Singer himself. I believe the tattoos will force her hand. And she has friends among the Chorus who will carry out murder even within the great pyramid.'

Pilos flinched at that: the majority of the Chorus was made up of warriors hand-picked by himself and High Feather Atu in an attempt to curb Enet's influence. If those warriors had also been seduced to her side . . . once again, he was confronted with the knowledge that the only person currently within the Singing City who he trusted implicitly was this half-blood Whisper living a lie in the heart of the source.

'Then our choices are to remove the slave without killing him and risk the Singer going into a frenzy at his loss, or remove the Great Octave,' he murmured almost below his breath. 'Or at least be prepared for either eventuality. There's a chance she might not do anything immediately.' Ilandeh puffed out her cheeks in silent scepticism. Pilos almost smiled; she knew Enet better than he did these days.

'If you're thinking what I think you are, High Feather, it needs to be outside the source. Not her estate; she has too many loyal guards. And within the source, well, as I said, if they'll kill for her then they'll absolutely kill to protect her. I can't tell you who among the Chorus to be wary of because I don't trust any of them. But if you would permit me, there might be a third option?'

Pilos raised his chin in permission for her to speak. 'Come back to the source with me. Be there when she sees the marks of succession on Tayan's neck. She can't act in front of you—'

'And if she has the Toko executed, she knows I'd tell everyone in the council and among the nobles that the Singer chose his heir and they mysteriously died. It wouldn't even matter if I couldn't prove it was her. Everyone knows she plies the Singer with death and covets his position; if the Shadow was murdered, they'd be forced to accuse her. She'd lose everything.'

Pilos straightened up from where he'd leant against the wall, suddenly energised. 'Yes. Yes, that could work. And if we get back to the source now, I'd know of it before her – there's no way she could guarantee I hadn't told anyone and given them instructions to make the information public if I suddenly went missing, too. She'll need to waste precious days carefully questioning the council and nobles to discover who knows what, and during that time we can come up with a better plan. I might even have time to reach High Feather Atu.'

Ilandeh looked a touch despondent that she wouldn't be killing the Great Octave today, even though it had been her suggestion to bring Pilos back to the source to avoid bloodshed. The emotional side of him shared her senti-ment. Killing Enet would absolutely end one of his own greatest threats, but despite his personal feelings and everything she'd done to ruin him – *the fucking songstone!* – Pilos couldn't deny that she would make a strong Singer if it ever came to it. There was growing unrest not just among the Tokob and Yaloh slaves but across the Empire, despite the truth of all Ixachipan being under the song. Despite the rumours that were flying from the great pyramid that the waking of the world spirit was near, the peninsula-wide peace that was supposed to herald it seemed, instead, to be fracturing.

On top of the civil and slave unrest, Calan had sent word of probing attacks from the people of Zellipan who sat just beyond Ixachipan's border in Barazal. Attacks on his song-stone mine; attacks over the border. At this rate, Tokoban would go up in flames of either rebellion or invasion before the next Wet – only three months away. And if it spilt over into Yalotlan, they could well be back at war instead of waking the world spirit and transforming Ixachipan.

And in spite of everything else she'd done, in spite of her clear and obvious ambition, Great Octave Enet was devoted to the cause of waking the world spirit. She was one of the Singing City's foremost experts on the ritual and magic that would be needed, to the extent that shamans and soothsayers alike consulted her. Before she'd destroyed him, Pilos remembered afternoons in the source listening to her tell the histories and the prophecies to an enraptured audience and an enraptured Singer. Whether the holy lord had the strength for the ritual now, Pilos didn't know, though he could guess, but of course Singer Xac waking the world spirit had never been Enet's intention. Pilos had no proof that she'd blooded the song and broken the Singer to hasten her own ascension, though he could make a guess about that too, but whatever the motive, the result was her own ever-strengthening position.

Unless the slave achieves the impossible and the magic chooses him.

Ilandeh was waiting for him to decide, her mouth crimped with an impatience she normally never showed. She needed to get back to the source before Enet arrived, and she needed to know what she was going to do when she got there. Pilos bent to retrieve his dropped club. The familiar heft and smoothness of the handle grounded him. A weapon. Pilos knew who and what he was when he had an enemy to fight and even as his stomach lurched with combined excitement and trepidation, he couldn't deny how much he'd missed this. Despite the very real worries of their situation, it was as if he'd woken from a long sleep, his limbs tingling with energy, ready to move.

A no-blood, god-killing, frog-licking slave. Or an ambitious, intelligent, murderous noblewoman. On the surface, the choice looked easy, but nothing concerning Enet ever was.

'Take me to the source, Chorus warrior,' he said formally. 'I want to see Enet's face when she learns she's outranked by her own property. And I want to make it very clear that harm to the slave will have lethal consequences. If it can buy us enough time to summon High Feather Atu, we might have a chance at some sort of peaceful resolution.'

'With pleasure, High Feather. Though I'll need a compelling reason to let you in,' Ilandeh said.

Pilos grinned and felt a little tension drain out of his muscles. 'Oh, I'm sure the holy lord will be interested in a possible disruption to the provision of songstone. And it's not even a lie,' he added when her eyes widened in shock. 'My latest delivery caravan was attacked by bandits and I'm keen to see if Enet blinks when I bring it up.' He lifted one shoulder in an innocent shrug. 'How could I not refer such a matter to the great Singer's attention?'

Pilos's lungs expanded as he drew in his first breath of the sacred air of the source in almost half a year. As Feather of the Singing City, he was – rarely – permitted entrance to the great pyramid to discuss matters of ritual that might lead to unrest with the city overseers, but this would be the first time he'd been in the Singer's presence since the day Enet had stripped him of his title, status and reputation.

Citrus and pom and cool water drifted to his senses, flowers from the gardens and a hint of breeze from deep below that held tantalising aromas of roasting meat and hot cacao.

He'd bought a new kilt and tunic as they hurried from the fighting pit to the pyramid, and then hired a litter so he could struggle into the new clothes in relative privacy. Ilandeh had slipped on ahead, running easily through the crowds towards where she'd hidden her own distinctive Chorus warrior attire, and it was she who greeted him at the warriors' entrance less than an hour later.

'Yes, administrator, most urgent news about the provision of songstone in Tokoban. If I could beg an audience with the Great Octave . . .'

'She isn't here,' the administrator said, fretting.

Ilandeh stepped forward. 'Perhaps Chorus Leader Acamah might hear the Feather's information and judge whether the holy lord should be disturbed. I can't imagine he'd come here on a whim; he is High Feather Atu's most trusted subordinate,' she murmured. The administrator looked at her with pursed lips and then waved him in, his relief at not having to make the decision himself palpable.

'Under the song, administrator,' Pilos said as he slipped past, following Ilandeh through dim, cool corridors painted with martial scenes and images of the holy Setatmeh.

'He may well send immediate word to the Great Octave,' Ilandeh murmured, her voice so quiet it barely reached him. 'But Acamah is in permanent attendance upon the holy lord and the, ah, slave, so by bringing you to him, you'll automatically be in the Singer's presence. Best you see for yourself.'

'You risk much, Chorus,' Pilos whispered.

Her shoulders tensed and then relaxed as she turned down another corridor. Not far now. 'We are warriors, Feather. Our lives are lived alongside risk. And this – your news, the Singer – is more important than my life.'

Pilos glanced ahead and then behind, checking they were alone. 'Ah, Ilandeh,' he breathed, 'what an eagle you would have been if your father had married right. Such a waste.'

She was silent for a few steps, then: 'I would hope not entirely a waste, Feather. People may not be able to change the circumstances of their birth, but surely loyalty and ability count for—' She cut herself off as two other Chorus warriors stepped into the corridor from a side room.

Neither of them said any more until they reached the source itself, pausing at the entrance to prostrate themselves until Acamah spotted them and approached warily. He paled when Pilos stood, which was interesting. Acamah had been hand-picked by High Feather Atu to dilute the number of Enet's creatures within the Chorus. Neither of them had ever had cause to question his loyalty to the Melody, but perhaps he'd spent too long in the Great Octave's company.

'Feather Pilos. What are you doing here?' he stammered.

The Feather stated his business again, pitched just loud enough to carry through into the oval chamber, and Acamah paled further. 'That would be, the Great Octave is the one who should—' he tried.

'No doubt the great Singer has already been informed by Listeners in Tokoban of what is happening there with regards to the Zellih,' Pilos interrupted smoothly, 'but perhaps not the songstone. And as it was the capstone from my own mine that was nearly stolen, I must of course come to offer my life to the holy lord for my failure.'

Acamah and Ilandeh both flinched at his choice of words, but he spoke the truth: Singer and songstone shared a sacred bond, and anyone who endangered it was supposed to present themselves to the holy lord in person if possible or communicate their remorse through a Listener if not.

'Shall I ask the holy lord if he will see the Feather, Chorus Leader?' Ilandeh asked while Acamah hesitated again. The man was an exceptional warrior, and Atu had chosen him for that as well as his loyalty, but he was a follower rather than a leader, and it was clear the position of Chorus Leader didn't suit him. Now he turned a grateful glance on Ilandeh, and she strode away before he could change his mind.

He waited in awkward silence, the conflict as to whether he outranked the former High Feather clear on his face as he shifted his feet. Pilos took pity on him – and perhaps earned a little goodwill – by taking a pace backwards so that Acamah had primacy when or if the holy lord graced them with his gaze.

'Tokoban?' The voice was doubled and layered with harmonies – and it spoke with the northern roll of consonants common to people of that land. Pilos twitched. He had not thought this new malaise would extend to the Tokob actually *having a voice in the source itself.*

'May we, my love?' the slave asked and Pilos twitched again, at the endearment this time. What the fuck was going on? Before he could think any further, there was a low, indulgent chuckle that sent a wave of affection through him, as if he was curled in a lover's arms.

'Bring him in,' the Toko continued. 'It's been too long since we saw him, hasn't it, holy lord?'

If the Singer answered, it was lost beneath Acamah's gruff 'Come.' Pilos stepped into the source proper, his mind buzzing with questions and crawling with unease, bowing at the waist. Despite the posture he stole a glance, forbidden though it was, and nearly lost his footing. The slave sat at the holy lord's side attired in glorious colour and painted in his shamanic finery. The Singer himself had a proprietary hand upon the Tokob knee, who was watching Pilos's approach with avid curiosity. Golden flickers curled in his cheeks and danced on the tips of the feathers tattooed into his neck.

The balance of power had shifted, and the ground with it, and the Feather would have to scramble if he wanted to keep his feet – and his life – in this new world.

ENET

Great Octave's estate, Singing City,
Pechacan, Empire of Songs
202nd day of the Great Star at evening

Enet stalked from the streamlet in her garden to the estate wall and back again, over and over, insensible to the chirping insects or the scents of flowers and blossoming shrubs rising around her. The lush green life and darting reds and yellows of birds and frogs and tiny lizards, these physical manifestations of the world spirit's power and generosity, couldn't touch her.

Slave-shaman. Slave-Shadow. *Slave.*

And yet Shadow.

It was impossible. It – he – was going to destroy everything she had worked for. All Enet's plans, which she'd had to refine over and over to face each new change and twist of prophecy, were once again as tattered and transparent as an old maguey kilt. Did she have the strength to overcome *yet another* obstacle to her destiny?

Yes. I have to. For all Ixachipan.

221

She would separate the holy lord from the slave somehow, once she understood how they'd been joined in the first place. There was nothing in the histories of Pechacan or the stories of the song-magic itself that had ever so much as hinted at it, Enet knew. She had studied every single book and scroll and stone tablet and temple painting that had ever been created, either in person or through copies made by talented artists. And nothing. Shaman Kapal theorised that their spirits had somehow merged within the song itself, wedded by the blood of the shared offering. Listener Chotek confirmed that the link was quite clear within the currents of the song-magic. A blue spirit – the Tokob – had inextricably entwined itself with the golden might and vastness of the holy lord's. A leech, attached to the Singer's glory and sucking it dry. Parasite.

He could not be allowed to continue his infection of the song or his manipulation of the Singer. It was in the holy lord's best interests and although it would be painful, in the way pulling a rotting tooth was painful, in the long term it was for the best.

If the Singer's foretelling agreed with Enet's – and she knew it would – then the ritual to wake the world spirit was only a few months away. That ritual would test all of them to their limits and the holy lord could not be distracted, let alone by something as unimportant as a slave. Not with chants and dances to memorise and magic to weave and gather and offerings to be made. There were too many things that could go wrong anyway; the slave could not add to that likelihood. He *would not*.

Enet stalked another path from the stream to the high stone wall behind the trees and back again. She knew what needed to be done, but she had no idea how to accomplish it. The Singer and the slave had not been apart from each other for the six days and nights since their joining. They ate and slept and bathed together and always the Toko murmured in his ear, of love and duty and strength.

But his grip on the holy lord wasn't perfect: she'd witnessed the Singer's sudden rages at something the slave had thought or said. Not all aspects of their beings were in harmony, and because the magic belonged to the Singer, his ability to Listen through the song was unparalleled. The Toko had no mental defences in place to keep him out, and his every stray or disloyal thought was read by the holy lord.

'Surely the Singer will kill him for heresy or faithlessness,' she murmured as she walked, oblivious to the brush of leaves against her bare calves or the sun like a warm hand cupped upon her skull. 'Accept him as an offering for his deceitful thoughts and words.'

There was a sharp knock on the estate gate and Enet looked up irritably. 'No visitors,' she barked as her estate slave appeared from behind a tree. He'd been with her since they were both children and he knew her moods as well as she did. *That's probably why he's hiding behind a fucking tree.*

He pulled open the gate a little way and murmured something quiet to whoever stood outside. Enet stalked back and forth again and when she turned and glanced over, he was still speaking. 'I said no visitors,' she shouted, loud enough this time that whoever was at her gate could hear. There was a scuffle and then the estate slave was stumbling backwards, his arms outstretched and his body a barrier. Not touching, which meant the intruder was Pechaqueh, but trying to slow their advance. Armed slaves ran from various corners of the garden to confront the trespasser and Enet took several steps towards the safety of the house before recognising the person forcing their way onto her property as Chorus warrior Lisek.

'Great Octave,' the man panted, sweat dripping freely down his face and darkening his salt-cotton. 'You need to come. Now.'

'What is it?' she snapped, dread coiling within her. To her astonishment, Lisek was already shouting for her litter-bearers.

'You need to see for yourself. Chorus Leader Acamah sent me to fetch you, but I have to go back. One of the other Chorus is missing and we don't know what she's doing. Just get there, Great Octave. Please.'

And he ran back to the gate, hauled it open himself, and fled.

Enet stood in the cultivated beauty of her garden and gazed after him. A waxwing whistled, shattering the fragile silence. Her estate slave watched her warily, but he also signalled for the litter to be brought out, as well as additional bearers so they might make the journey faster. 'High one?'

She jumped and focused on him. 'Yes,' she said and her voice was ragged. She stumbled over her own feet as she clambered into the waiting litter. 'You will come as well.'

'As the high one commands,' the man said and fell in behind the litter-bearers, his downcast eyes sharp with worry. Enet's guards opened the gate and pushed out onto the busy street, clearing a path. The litter left the ground smoothly and they began to run.

Enet flung back the litter's curtain and stepped down in front of the great pyramid, ignoring the panting, exhausted bearers. She'd brooded all the way there, panicked scenarios running through her mind of what might have happened that would cause Acamah to send for her. The most obvious reason was that the Singer was going to the waters, but the song was powerful, with only occasional hiccups and stumbles when it lost its newfound clarity. Every time that happened, it lasted only a dozen heartbeats before settling again into something that was very simple and yet still far more coherent than it had been since the renewed war in Tokoban. It contained none of the tell tale upset of an impending ascension.

Other options – war or uprising, disease or famine – would not have brought a Chorus warrior of all people running across the city to her estate. It had to be something to do with the Singer himself; she just *didn't know what,* and that not knowing had eaten at her all the way here, so much so that she'd been unable to calm herself sufficiently to contact the holy lord or Chotek through the song.

As Chotek should have contacted me – and didn't.

Enet hurried up the steep and narrow staircase towards the entrance. She was panting for breath and her thighs were burning by the time she reached it. The Great Octave kicked off her own sandals and stepped into the richly painted, cool interior of the pyramid, Chorus warriors stepping aside to let her through without looking at her. That was normal, but this time it felt ominous. She hastened along the corridors, eyes down as protocol demanded but her heart tripping faster even than her feet.

Courtesans and administrators bowed and hurried out of her way, hissed conversations cut short, while slaves flattened themselves against the walls to let her pass; she ignored them all. The song and its emotions were stronger here, of course, and Enet let it surge through her, seeking an answer within its regular repeating melody.

That *fucking slave* had done something to the holy lord, something far worse and more irreversible than her own offering of blood to the song to ensure strength and victory in the war. Which it had done. Enet had given the Empire a song of strength and rage and it had brought them all Ixachipan.

This song was sweet with Tokob magic, sweet like the sleep medicine from which the sick never woke. And like those who drank such medicine, this song would be the death of them all. And it was the Tokob doing, she was sure of it.

Enet couldn't stop the whirl of her thoughts, which were as unguarded as they perhaps had ever been. She barely waited for the Chorus on duty to announce her before sweeping around the corner and into the holy lord's presence. The Toko was there, of course, kneeling beside him rather than behind him, his head up and his eyes clear, if a little wild. They watched her approach with identical expressions. Watched her approach, watched her halt mid-step, watched her frown.

They weren't behind the rose-cotton, so there was a beautifully painted paper screen standing between them and the seated Feather Pilos. Enet blinked, trying to reconcile Lisek's garbled fear with the warrior's presence. He was the Feather of the Singing City; as much as she hated it, she had no authority to refuse him entrance in to the source. *Though I like not that he is here without me. What have they been discussing?*

The corner of Singer Xac's mouth turned up; the corner of the slave's did too. Identical little smirks. It had been a long time since the holy lord had smirked. Enet had almost forgotten what it looked like and the power it had to discomfit her.

The Great Octave slid smoothly to her knees and prostrated herself. She wasn't wearing her formal headdress, so she was able to put her face to the mats and take a moment in the darkness behind her eyelids to pause, and breathe, and think.

And make sense of what she'd only glimpsed in the instant her eyes had sought out the slave at the Singer's side, unable to quench the rage that tightened her throat each time she saw him there. Despite all her years of training and her familiarity with protocol, Enet's head snapped up before she'd been given permission. She corrected herself almost before she'd moved, but all those present would have seen her twitch. Would interpret that twitch. Pilos certainly would.

'Great Octave. We did not expect you back so soon,' the Singer said, the Tokob voice mingling with it – the same words, spoken with the same inflection at the same time. A doubling of sound the way vision doubled if one drank too much honeypot, and just as disorienting. Enet had had six days to become accustomed to the slave's absurd, heretical elevation, but his voice layering with the Singer's still grated at her ears and made her stomach writhe with snakes.

She sat up slowly, her hands in her lap and eyes demurely down. Under the pretext of pushing back a strand of hair, she darted glances at the Toko from beneath her lashes. She hadn't been mistaken. Waves of horror, or disbelief, or perhaps madness coated her in a cold, sickly sweat.

'Holy lord, great Singer Xac, you are a glory I do not deserve to look upon,' she said smoothly, her mouth moving without any conscious input from her mind.

Two feathers. The twin dark feathers. On the Tokob throat. The Tokob *throat, not mine!*

His clothes, too, were different, as if that could possibly matter compared with the great weight and significance of the tattoos, still raw but beautifully drawn, which claimed him and named him and placed him above her. No longer undyed maguey as his status demanded. Now, his kilt was a vibrant blue, even and rich and clearly coloured with the finest dye available in the Singing City. It was of a quality Shaman Kapal herself would wear. He wore no tunic, and his chest and arms were painted with the symbols of his people, a crime in itself here in the source. Beneath the paint, tattoos that she'd traced with her fingers in the dark decorated his shoulders and the centre of his chest, and his hair was unbound and rippling almost to his waist.

The only thing that gave Enet the tiniest hint of hope amid this madness was that his slave brands remained intact. Xac hadn't freed him – yet.

'That is not an answer,' the Singer and his parasite said, drawing her back from her open, horrified contemplation of the slave's decorated skin. A contemplation that no one had permitted her, but nor had they stopped it.

'Why are you back so quickly?' There was amusement in their voices, as if the holy lord knew exactly what had caused her breathless return.

'Holy lord, your wisdom is as boundless as all Ixachipan's bounty. The slave, though, has—'

'Not slave. Shadow,' they said in concert, echoing the words first spoken six days before.

'Slave . . . Shadow,' she grated, her voice unfamiliar in her ears. 'Slave-Shadow, I was dealing with some matters at my estate and realised that I had not formally given you your papers of freedom since the holy lord elevated you, and I wanted to hurry back to present them.' She held out her hand, knowing full well her estate slave had brought no such thing because it didn't exist.

She waited in silence, a small smile curving her lips, as he slid forward and bent to her ear, though he whispered nothing. Enet twisted to look at him and then slapped him across the face before bowing once more.

'Great Singer, Slave-Shadow, accept this humble one's apologies. The papers have been lost somewhere on our journey. The slave responsible will be punished, and in the meantime, I will have a new document readied within the hour.'

Enet flicked her fingers at her slave, who pressed the red handprint on his cheek to the mats and then fled to write up a document that gave the Toko ownership of himself – though Enet would ensure it was delivered to the Singer, not to him.

'Does he know how to create such a document?' Pilos murmured with a touch of humour in his voice. 'Your slaves are all held for life, are they not?'

'The Slave-Shadow is clearly no longer my property,' the Great Octave said, bowing slightly in the Tokob general direction. 'Are you sad that I am giving away your gift to me, Feather? You think I would presume to keep such a one the holy lord himself has . . . enjoyed.'

Singer Xac grunted, a small, discontented sound. Enet ducked her head just a little, coy and teasing in a way he had not responded to in months. The performance was more for Pilos than him: let the Feather see the strength of the relationship she maintained with the holy lord. 'Forgive me, is that not how your Chosen should refer to him? He is, after all, a slave, at least until he has the papers in hand. He cannot compare with your glory, holy lord. He does not have the potential to be your equal, let alone your successor, you must see that. You are divine, while he is merely an aid. Medicine, if you will, to keep you strong and focused. It would be wrong for us to call him something he is not.'

'He is my Shadow and you will name him such. Make no mention of his status; it is irrelevant.' Two voices, one will, stronger even than it had been the day before, as Xac again named the Toko his successor against all protocol, all tradition. Against everything Enet had worked for all her life. The mockery in their voices, mockery in the *Tokob* voice, stung like wasps. She bowed once more, turning her face down and taking a moment to breathe. He was serious, then. Xac truly was naming a Toko slave as his heir, not just with the title but the tattoos as well. It wasn't all some hideous, elaborate prank.

Xac could name the Toko his Shadow, but everyone must know he was no such thing. He was a disease, a strangling vine wrapped around the holy lord's glory. And he had used this never-before-seen link to claw his way to a power that should never be his. That couldn't be his.

The slave – Enet refused to use or even think his name, let alone his new title – looked at ease at the Singer's side, but there was a tightness around his eyes that spoke of exhaustion, or perhaps pain. He struggled to maintain his grip on the holy lord's spirit, no doubt, and the effort taxed his strength.

The Singer turned abruptly and glared at him, and he cowered. 'Not equal,' he grated, and this time it was only his voice that echoed through the source. 'Shadow, not Singer. Not self. Not yet.' He softened then and cupped the slave's cheek, straightening him out of his submission. 'Not yet, my love,' he crooned. 'My sweet love.' He pushed him away hard so the man fell onto his side on the mats. 'Not ever, if the world spirit deigns to wake at my calling. But you will love me and serve me faithfully still, will you not?'

'Always, my sweet lord,' the slave said, pushing himself upright again as if the shove had been but a playful nudge between lovers. 'In all things. Forever.'

"Not yet." Enet bit her lip. And, more telling perhaps, "not equal". So, she was right about the Tokob ambition. He truly believed that he would be allowed to take the magic, that the Singer would fulfil the promise of the twin feathers. More importantly, he remained unable to control his thoughts. Enet could use that.

In contrast to the Tokob lack of control, the Great Octave barely let the shape of the echo of the idea flit across her mind, like a bat black against the blackness of a night-time tree canopy. A hint of wings, perhaps the merest puff of displaced air, and then gone. 'Your Shadow expresses his desire for your magic, holy lord?' she said as fear for the Singer filled her mind. 'Perhaps—'

'I exist in the Singer's love only to serve, Great Octave, in whatever capacity he deems fit,' the Toko interrupted. 'My life and wants and death are all his. He need only ask. The holy Setatmeh need only ask.'

They all waited in silence to see whether the holy lord would indeed demand the slave's annihilation. When it didn't come, Pilos shifted.

'Singer, Shadow,' he said easily, as if the title of successor was already familiar to him, though Enet had done all she could to keep the information from reaching the world outside the pyramid. She almost twitched again; she'd forgotten he was here. The reason for his presence became clear then. She would need to ask Acamah which of his Chorus had fled, for they were surely suckling on Pilos's wealth in return for secrets of the source. Both Pilos and his spy would die for it.

'If we may return to the issue of the theft of songstone in Tokoban,' Pilos continued and Enet went very still. He met her eyes, calculating. 'Forgive me, the *attempted* theft,' he clarified and cocked his head to analyse her reaction.

The Great Octave tensed her feet where she sat on them, curling her toes hard enough that a cramp seared through the sole of her left foot. She focused on the agony for one long, breathless moment and then shifted slightly forwards to take the pressure off. Were her hands shaking? She didn't lift them from her lap to find out. She allowed shock to cross her face, her mouth falling open.

'Someone attempted to steal songstone?' she asked and Pilos

231

ran his tongue over his teeth, cold anger fading into reluctant approval in the squint lines around his eyes. 'Feather, have you been careless with the Empire of Songs's most precious resource? Such a thing is a crime punishable by death.'

'The holy lord in his merciful wisdom has already spared my life,' Pilos said and pressed himself to the mats even though the Singer couldn't see him. 'Feather Calan has sent three hundred warriors to search the jungle where the attack took place: the thieves will soon have nowhere to hide and, when they do, they will be questioned until they give us the name of their employer. We must know which no-blood, no-honour traitor would try to steal a capstone so that they might face the justice and the full punishment of every true citizen of our great Empire.'

The slightest emphasis on "true" and Enet felt that arrow sink home, yet her face told only of her relief. 'I am pleased to hear that Feather Calan may be relied upon, though I wonder that she can spare the warriors when there is unrest on Tokoban's border.'

She'd hoped to discomfit him with the realisation that she knew of the Zellih skirmishes, but it seemed that two years away from his position as High Feather hadn't dulled all his talent for politics.

'Feather Calan has more than enough warriors to deal with internal and external enemies,' he said. 'And of course, there are hundreds of freed dog warriors now farming Tokoban. They can be relied upon should there be need.'

'Of course,' Enet echoed him. She faced the Singer again and inclined her head, fingertips touching the mats. 'I will cast the bones to see if I might divine the identity of the thieves or their intentions for this despicable crime.'

The Singer nodded, his amber eyes sharp on her face. Intelligent and cutting, looking into her. Enet let him see her adoration and humility and her great hope that there would be peace throughout the Empire.

'Great Singer, Shadow, if it please you, I will hurry along my slave with those papers of emancipation. With your gracious permission, I will return soon. Feather Pilos, may I walk you out?'

Pilos's smile showed too many teeth. 'If the great Singer and his Shadow have no further need of me, then of course,' he said. 'It has been too long since we talked, Great Octave. Would you care to join me for duskmeal?'

It was that, in the end, that shocked her. She didn't know what her face did, but the Toko smothered something that sounded very much like a snort of amusement. Enet wanted her estate and her tonic and the sealed room where she could put down all her burdens and the weight of responsibility and expectation and the crippling paranoia. She could have none of them.

She gave him her brightest smile. 'How lovely,' she said. 'I fear, however, that I have many duties still to attend to here. Perhaps next time.'

'Perhaps,' he said. 'In that case, Chorus Leader Acamah, allow me to brief you on my detachment. They've been called out twice in the last month to assist Choosers breaking up brawls. It would be wise to coordinate a response now should anything occur closer to the great pyramid.' He shook his head as Acamah rounded the screen, frowning. 'Each approaching absence of the Great Star seems to make the unfilial ever more reckless, does it not? Holy lord, Shadow, you are a glory to this empire. Under the song.'

Enet and Pilos prostrated themselves and then stood, backing out of the source step by step with Acamah escorting them. The Singer didn't even glance in their direction, appearing too absorbed with gazing adoringly into the Tokob eyes.

'I am pleased the Empire of Songs has the stability of a Shadow,' Pilos said as they paced together down the wide corridor. 'It is a comfort in these restless times.'

'Indeed,' Enet agreed blandly as Acamah made a noncommittal noise in the back of his throat. If the Feather was hoping to provoke her into unwise words, then he had forgotten their history in its entirety. 'I am shocked to hear that your songstone was almost stolen. Was it much damaged?'

Pilos didn't glance her way. 'Not in the least. The thieves were poor warriors and most were slaughtered. Those few who escaped will not remain free for long. The capstone is under heavy guard and will reach its destination without further incident, I'm sure. My warriors will show no mercy in the event of a repeat attempt.' They turned a corner in silence. 'I am curious, though, as to what someone thought they might achieve with a stolen capstone. What do you think?'

Enet smiled gently. 'I couldn't possibly say,' she murmured, and then they reached her suite. 'Under the song. Chorus Leader, if I may beg a moment of your attention when you have finished strategising with the Feather?'

'Of course, Great Octave,' he said with a hint of relief that Pilos surely noted.

She closed the door on his suspicious glare, cutting off his words of blessing with her smile still fixed in place. Her estate slave knelt and held out a sheet of bark-paper. The Tokob freedom papers, presumably. Enet ignored it. She crossed to the bed and sat, bracing her elbows on her knees. She put her head in her hands and swallowed against nausea. Against the screams clamouring within her throat.

Against the future, once more unwritten and dangerous with possibility.

Against tears.

Enet reached automatically for the small clay vessel that contained her tonic before remembering, again, that there was no more tonic. No more magic to bind into her skin. And the acquisition of a replacement capstone had also failed. *And I had to fucking learn of it from Pilos himself – in the middle of the fucking source.*

So be it. It was attempted and it has failed. It was not my only chance.

But this is.

Enet had one final roll of the bones to make, more audacious by far than the previous scheme. Her headache spiked and she massaged her temples. Her estate slave sat quietly opposite her, awaiting orders. She stood and paced the room, the muscles in her legs twitching with anxiety and the need to move.

'High one,' he ventured quietly and Enet's shoulders slumped. 'We won't have Pilos's capstone.'

He sucked in a breath. 'The alternative, high one?' he asked. 'It's risky, but . . .'

'But,' she agreed. Still, she didn't say the words, tongue-tied and suddenly weary down to her bones. Enet had been working towards a point, a date, an outcome, for so long and now it was nearly upon her. She'd brought the world to a place of change and wonder and at the very moment of her triumph, she'd lost control. All she could do now was scrabble on her hands and knees to try and salvage something from the wreckage.

For the first time since she was a child, Enet could not see the shape of her own future. Her world and her plans were crumbling to dust between her fingers and she didn't know how to stop it. She felt an almost uncontrollable urge to laugh and bit it back with vicious discipline.

I can still do this. I can still save everything.

I will be worthy. I will.

She faced the slave. 'Do it. And then get me a mason. Don't even bother bribing them; just get them to my estate and keep them there. We'll need them when it arrives.'

The man took a deep breath and then bowed, fingertips touching the mats. 'The mason has already been selected and is being watched. I will give the order. As the Great Octave commands.'

'As the Great Octave commands,' Enet repeated in a whisper. She was so weary.

THE SINGER

The source, Singing City, Pechacan, Empire of Songs

We are the Singer and the song and the blood.

Not the blood, my love.

We are the Singer and the song. We are divinity and glory and we have all the world at our feet, worshipping us, for we are the sum and pinnacle of all life.

No, my love. We are servants of the song.

Servants? You mean slaves. We will not be slave to anything. We answer to no one. We rule, and all will bow before us and beg for our favour. Beg for the favour of their lives. Or beg that they might give their blood in our honour.

Not the blood, my love. We serve Ixachipan. It is our duty. Our privilege.

. . . You overstep. I am the Singer. Me. Only me. I am the Singer and the song and the blood. I am war and vengeance and you, you are none of those things, my sweet. My little Shadow. What I have given, I can take away.

Let me take the place of the blood, great Singer. I can give

237

you the same strength. More strength, if you will let me. Will you allow me that glory, that honour?

The song hungers. It always hungers. You have not the strength to sate it.

Let me try. Please, holy lord, my love. Just let me try.

It will please me to see you fail. And then your blood will water my song. My love.

PILOS

Pilos would bet every fighter and every bead of jade and jet he had that Enet was behind the attempted theft. The merest flicker in her eyes when he'd deliberately misspoken, that little jump of triumph swiftly quenched, wasn't enough to accuse her publicly, but they were far past flexing their claws out where anyone could see.

What happened next would be a dark blade out of the shadows. The only question was whose hand would wield it.

He'd spoken true about his eagles being called upon to assist the Choosers who both kept the peace in the heart-city and selected new moon offerings for the holy Setatmeh, but it had been an excuse to assess Acamah's continued fitness for command and his loyalty to the Singer. Pilos had come away from the meeting with a clearer view of why he was so forgettable and convinced of his lack of ability for leadership. Acamah was a skilled warrior and nothing else, and the set of orders he'd been given by Atu to follow as Chorus

239

Leader seemed to have been supplanted by Enet's own suggestions and instructions.

Acamah's attention was with the Great Octave whenever they were in the same space, but he didn't watch her the way Ilandeh did, the way a Chorus dedicated to the Singer's safety should – as if she could be a threat. He watched her as if awaiting his next order. Or his next fond glance. It made Pilos's skin itch with apprehension.

As had Acamah's clumsy question: 'What made you come here, Feather, today of all days?' The man might as well have asked which of his Chorus had alerted him to the Tokob elevation. As it was, he'd given the man a polite but quizzical head tilt: he'd stated his business on his arrival, to Acamah himself. The Chorus Leader had blushed and fallen silent and Pilos prayed he was the most competent of Enet's lackeys within the source, even as he feared the extent of her reach.

Brooding, the Feather made his way down the steep staircase to the plaza. 'High one?' a muscular slave asked and Pilos halted on the last step, suddenly aware of how alone he was. 'We have been assigned as your litter-bearers, high one.'

Pilos paused and then very deliberately took the last step onto the plaza. 'I don't need a litter. Offer my thanks to whoever hired you for me, but I don't accept favours. Or bribes.'

'Please, high one,' the slave repeated with deference. 'It would be our honour to carry you to the Melody compound.'

Not home. Whoever had ordered the litter – he snorted; Enet, naturally – had assumed he would scurry back to his warriors for their protection. Then again, he had told Xochi he'd be back before dusk. He hesitated a little longer, hating that his next worry was whether he could trust his eagle or whether she'd had someone follow him to the pit. Would they have seen him and Ilandeh? The Whisper's position was precarious enough as it was.

As is mine, it would seem.

He rubbed his stomach; so much paranoia was bad for his digestion.

'And may I know the name of my benefactor?' he asked, trying to waste a little more time and curious to see what the slave would do next.

'Great Octave Enet,' the man said easily, and Pilos could do nothing but blink. He hadn't expected her to be so open about this latest attempt on his life. Then again, he was without a single guard and she was obviously desperate enough to try. Not a dark blade in the night, then. She must have checked whether he'd sent a message out of the source during his visit that might indicate news of the Tokob new status was already abroad in the city. He should have realised she'd be astute enough to play the game to its conclusion. He should have actually sent word somewhere, anywhere, both to deflect attention from Ilandeh and to protect himself.

Instead, he was vulnerable.

The attack on his songstone was a genuine enough reason for Pilos to beg an audience with Enet or the Singer, though, and might be enough to protect Ilandeh from scrutiny a little longer. He'd made it plain that had been his only reason for visiting and whatever he'd discovered upon his arrival was merely coincidence. Still, no doubt Enet would speak to Acamah to get every detail of what had happened before she'd hurried into the source, panicked and sweaty and pretending to neither.

If I do die here, Ilandeh will get the word to Atu and, if she's got any sense, she'll flee the source to keep my name out of any investigation into the purity of her blood.

But that's if I die here.

He was abruptly grateful for all the extra training he'd undertaken in the previous weeks. He was faster and stronger than before, and he'd brought his war club and a knife to the source, leaving them at the entrance as protocol demanded. He spun the club in his hand now, loosening his wrist. Four slave warriors with nothing to lose and quite likely freedom to gain were bad odds. If this was a bout in a pit, he knew where he'd lay his jade.

'1 will send the Great Octave a note of thanks when I return home, but I prefer to walk.' He said nothing else, just walked at the man. The slave's life would be forfeit if he sought to halt Pilos or put his hands on him and they both knew it; the man pivoted and let him past.

They didn't pick up the litter. They let him get a few paces ahead as he strode towards the biggest knot of pedestrians he could find and then they followed him.

Pilos felt a prickle that was part awareness and part excitement crawl up his back. No one had actively tried to kill him in more than two years and he almost shivered at the brightness of the adrenaline coursing through his system.

Above and around and through everything beat the song, skipping and stuttering and then holding true again. It was stronger, a little more assured, as it had been ever since the holy lord had linked his spirit with the Tokob. And Pilos had seen the proof of that strengthening with his own eyes. There were no words to encompass the difference visible in the Singer, not just his voice but the energy and intelligence that suddenly animated him. The life.

Around him, Pechaqueh walked taller, prouder, and if violence sat just beneath the skin of the city, then at least it meant there were more armed eagles on the streets as well as Choosers. The Feather just needed to find some before his killers made their move. He strode towards a wide avenue leading into the artisans' residential quarter and found half a dozen people loitering nearby, sharp gazes belying their casual postures.

Pilos glanced at the next road and saw some more, and then at the narrow alley between the two, which was conveniently and unsurprisingly clear. With the four behind him, he was laughably outnumbered. The Feather turned abruptly left and wove through a tangle of mats laid out with goods for sale, stepping nimbly over traders and piles of their wares, dodging playing children and ducking behind a slave, who shrank from making contact with him.

He was almost at the temple in the plaza's corner and its resident shaman who could, if necessary, facilitate his entry into the song to call for aid, when two men and a woman closed off his route. Pilos swung back, ducking around the slave again and hurrying along the row of merchants until he found a knife-seller. And her four burly, armed guards.

'Spears up,' Pilos said low-voiced as he stopped before the mat. 'Feather Pilos of the Singing City. Three on my right, four somewhere in the crowd, and maybe another half-dozen coming from that direction.' He jerked his chin.

The guards gaped, staring between him and their employer, but the merchant rose fluidly to her feet and touched her belly and throat. 'Under the song, Feather. I served under you a decade ago. Eagle Matla of the Fifth Talon. You need an escort home?'

'These four?' Pilos asked, not letting relief cloud his voice.

'Retired dogs. They've worked for me for a Star cycle, give or take.'

'Good enough. Can someone watch your goods?'

Matla spoke to the merchant on the next blanket and then gestured for Pilos to lead the way. It was still a risk, but he distantly remembered Matla's face – she really was an eagle. 'Melody compound. Eyes open,' he said softly and led them away from the market, threading between shoppers and traders, hurrying slaves and playing children. All the chaos of an ordinary day in the Singing City. None of them were aware of the careful, calculating dance being played out in their midst.

They passed temples in their bright paint, incense drifting from every doorway, and smaller buildings where Listeners waited for the very wealthy to buy their services to send messages to homes, farms or businesses in other cities. Or they had, before the breaking of the song. Pilos wondered, as he always did when crossing through this area, how many of them were now those very same beggars that Choosers had once chased away from their doors. There were so few Listeners now, scattered across the Empire. The others had died or gone mad during the first breaking of the song.

'Is she getting bold, or is she getting desperate?' Pilos murmured to himself as Matla slid in front of him to keep an eye on the road.

'Feather?' she asked, glancing back before checking their surroundings again.

'Ah, thinking aloud, eagle, nothing more,' he said hurriedly and then paused in place, the others stilling with him.

The road was narrowed by racks of freshly moulded pottery lining the walls. Two had been pulled over, scattering distorted pots and folded bowls across the road amid the splintered racking. Slaves and furious free mingled among the wreckage, shouting conflicting orders. A man slapped at the head and shoulders of a cowering slave, his voice strident as he berated her.

Pilos didn't like it, but a quick look behind showed him the four litter-bearers trailing them into the road. 'Get us through as quick as you can,' he muttered. 'We've got company behind us.'

Matla nodded once, her gait smoothing into a predatory glide. Pilos and the dogs mimicked her, hands still and heads moving, checking all around. They edged to the right, away from the chaos and milling people, the laughing spectators attracted by the noise who alternated shouted advice with cheerful bets on the punishment the slaves would suffer for the calamity.

Matla went first, Pilos following with the four dog warriors in a half-moon behind him. The Feather let his eyes move of their own accord, looking not for a burst of movement but for stillness where there should be none. There. And there. And again. He gestured the right-hand dog up front to flank Matla, and the other three moved into a triangle, one either side and one behind.

Ahead, the three still points among the little crowd resolved into three warriors, salt-cotton snug against ribs and bellies. They unslung blowpipes from across their backs and Pilos and his escort broke formation, two ducking left and three right. Instinctive and fast. The Feather found himself at the entrance to the potter's shop and spun inside just as a dart clattered off the mud-brick wall. He tripped over a cowering merchant and then a sandalled foot took him in the kidney.

Pilos twisted as he fell and crashed down onto his back, tightening his hold on his war club so it wouldn't jar out of his hand. His assailant was already stabbing down towards him, falling onto his knees to drive the blade into his chest. Pilos kicked out and caught him in his off-hand shoulder, spoiling his aim – the knife went in under his chin instead, ripping open the line of his jaw.

Pilos uttered a hoarse scream and tried to ignore the surge of fear – had his throat been opened? Was this his death, here in a potter's shop in the Singing City at the hands, however distant, of the Great Octave? He got his left hand around the man's wrist, fingers digging into the muscle and wrenching it sideways. The knife came out of his neck-face-cheek and he couldn't help but squeal again, but then his club battered into a skull and the man dropped his knife as he canted over sideways, blood sheeting down his face. Pilos clubbed him again as he sprawled over the sobbing merchant and then scrabbled for the blade and punched it in and out of the assassin's belly in a frenzy.

Holding onto the knife, Pilos pressed the bottom of his fist to the right side of his neck and rolled onto his feet, brandishing his club, and ducked back out into the street.

Matla was pressed against the opposite wall, two attackers harrying her, coming at her from either side. The dog warrior he'd gestured to her side was dead, slumped against the wall with his legs splayed before him, crimson hands cradling his intestines.

Pilos bellowed a war cry and the killer on the left flinched, hesitated, and Matla stabbed him low in the belly and then shoved past, putting him between her and the other assassin. The other two free dogs were still fighting, and the slaves, merchants and jeering crowd who'd filled the street had vanished. The litter-bearers were gone, too, their taste for murder quenched by the spills of blood soaking into the clay dust choking the street.

'Take them alive,' Pilos croaked at Matla as one of his attackers pawed weakly at the spurting jet of blood from his thigh. He'd be gone in seconds. The eagle knew her business and she and her surviving dogs cut the remaining two onto their knees and disarmed them. Matla wrenched one's head back by his hair and put her blade to his neck while the dogs stood guard over the other.

Pilos looked down at the prisoner. He had an ear missing, blood pissing down his face and neck, and a cut across his chest. 'Enet's orders?' he slurred. He wasn't in a much better state himself. The man wouldn't meet his eyes. 'I can kill you fast or kill you slow. I'd enjoy slow. Enet's orders?'

The assassin screwed shut his eyes and jerked his head in a nod. 'Holy Seta—' he began, and Matla slit the man's throat.

'No salvation for you,' she said and spat on him as he jerked and fell to the side. Her dogs killed the other. 'Feather? You said the Great Octave?'

'You have my thanks,' he said instead of replying. 'You're all retired; none of you needed to spill blood, yours or theirs, for me. And I grieve the loss of your comrade. I will see your status and reputations polished accordingly. Your honour is your own, and it shines bright. I trust it also shines with discretion.'

Matla gave the others a meaningful look. 'It does, Feather. The utmost discretion. But your wound.'

'I'll live,' he said grimly. 'The rest of you?' The warriors shrugged and nodded. 'Then if you're still willing, get me back to the compound, Melody warriors. I need honeypot and stitches, in that order.'

'As the Feather commands. We'll not let you down,' Matla said. 'Diamond formation,' she added. 'I've got the front.'

Pilos retrieved his club and they set out, the eagle and her dogs surrounding him, and he studied her back as they moved. Wondering if he could trust her despite the blood they'd shed for him. Wondering if he could trust anyone, here in the heart-city at the centre of Enet's web.

He took some deep breaths and accepted a torn piece of material from Matla to wad against the bleeding slash in his face. The pain was bright and threatening to overwhelm him;

it took every shred of discipline he had to push it to the corners of his mind and try and think.

Was it the failed theft in Tokoban or his knowledge of the Shadow's creation that had led Enet to try and kill him this time? But even if it was to do with the theft, he still didn't understand why she needed a capstone. Pilos knew from Ilandeh that the date to enact the waking of the world spirit was being debated and that it was likely to be very soon, despite the Singer's illness. That, of course, was Enet's desire, to entrap the Singer and force him to commit to a difficult, draining ritual when his strength was waning. It was a clear, if subtle, bid for power and one that everyone in the source and the council would be aware of, possibly excepting the holy lord himself.

Enet wanted to be Singer and so she must seize the magic before the waking of the world spirit, for once the ritual was complete, the Singer who performed it would become its immortal consort, eternally bound to their human form and not transformed into a holy Setat. Likewise, no more water gods would be created, for there would be no more ascensions. Whoever on the council wanted that chance at immortality and godhood would side with Enet in her bid for power so that they might ascend with Xac when he was forced to the waters.

His thoughts circled around yet again to the capstone, a cat returning to its kill. Pilos, like all noble Pechaqueh, knew the basics of the ritual to wake the world spirit and none of them required the use of a capstone. And if they did, the Singer would simply demand one. He would need no subterfuge: anyone who owned a mine or had the wealth to procure a capstone would beg him for the honour of providing it.

Enet wanted it for something else. *Which is why I can't let her have it, no matter what. It's clear now she must never be Singer, not if her route to it is by murdering the holy lord.*

He pictured her, beautiful and arrogant and manipulative, ruling Ixachipan as the vessel between world spirit and people. Its voice. How much of Enet's own autonomy would remain? How much of her own will, her own contempt for all the world, it sometimes seemed, would become a weight beneath which the Empire of Songs must labour forever?

How much more must Pilos do to secure peace? He jammed the cloth harder against his wound. 'Hurry, eagle.'

TAYAN

The source, Singing City, Pechacan, Empire of Songs
206th day of the Great Star at evening

Nineteen days since the offering that had joined him to the holy lord in spirit, in mind, in love. Nineteen days and the hunger was growing in them both.

Tayan told himself it wasn't his, but that didn't stop his guts from cramping or his temper from shortening. He was the Singer's Shadow now. He was free, and chosen, and powerful. He would inherit a magic greater and stronger than any he had known; he would live in the song-world and bend all to his will; he would—

The Singer's arm snaked around his neck and tightened fast, dragging Tayan's head against his chest and squeezing until he couldn't breathe. 'I am Singer,' he murmured in a voice that fluttered with harmonies and was laced with threat. A voice that didn't, this time, tremble in the Tokob own throat. 'I will wake the world spirit and walk at its side all my life. You will do none of these things, and none of those petty little desires you think so very loudly, either.'

He squeezed until Tayan was dizzy and swamped with love and obedience for the holy lord, promises of loyalty and support, adoration and help sparking in his mind. No more. Nothing more. His only desires were those the Singer granted him. He wanted what his sweet love wanted; would do what he was told; would be whatever Xac needed him to be.

'I tire of your thoughts, little shaman. I tire of your ambition. Go away from me.' The Singer shoved Tayan aside.

'I am sorry, my love,' he murmured, bowing low. 'I am sorry for my thoughts. All I want is for your glory to last forever.'

The Singer turned his cool, amber gaze on him. 'It will.'

Those two words sent a thrill of fear through Tayan's gut and he bowed again, face to the mats, and then rose and hurried away. Ilandeh detached herself from the wall of the source and followed. She'd taken it upon herself to be his escort on those rare occasions he and the Singer were not together; she appeared to be the only person in the great pyramid who could stand him, though he knew it to be a lie. Ilandeh hated him more than most.

But even Shaman Kapal looked at him with unveiled suspicion now. He'd thought there might have been the beginnings of, not a friendship, but possibly a professional acquaintance, growing between them. Before. Her original diagnosis of their spirit-linking had been cautiously positive. Tayan had an obvious steadying influence of the holy lord, which she appreciated, yet as the days passed and the Singer insisted on him being called the Shadow and treated accordingly, any goodwill he'd bought with his medicine and his obedience was lost. Pechaqueh spat his new title as if it was poison, their disgust evident whenever the holy lord wasn't there to see it.

251

The document of freedom Tayan had once longed for now rested in the Singer's possession, though it bore the Tokob name. Likewise, the brands on his upper arms remained unblemished. Tayan had discovered that the loss of his collar and the addition of his paint counted for very little. Rather than free him, Enet had simply transferred ownership of him from herself to the Singer and while he no longer had to perform her every whim, he was subject instead to Xac's.

Serving him is my greatest honour and deepest fulfilment. The reason for his expulsion from the source into the gardens was not lost on him, and Tayan filled himself with love and worship. It was easy to do.

As the Great Octave's slave, Enet could have had him killed at any point, despite the promise he'd made to the holy lord to cure him. As the Shadow – as the Singer's toy – she would have to move against him subtly, as if he were a worthy and powerful opponent, but that didn't mean she wouldn't. He'd seen Enet destroy people over the last two years, both behind their backs and to their faces. None had withstood her cunning. And every lapse in Tayan's thoughts, every stray idea that pushed him away from Xac's side, only served to give her another opportunity.

I have no friends here, he reminded himself. *I am devoted only to the Singer. If my death will protect him, I offer it willingly.* A sour smile twisted his mouth. *Ask and we shall answer.*

But not you, Enet. You don't get to ask. My death to save Xac my love, yes. Not my death to further your ambition.

Tayan turned his face up to the faint breeze. The heat was stifling, a heavy blanket laid over his skin. The air moved desultorily, stirring the fall of his hair and the loose, blue-striped kilt he wore. Sweat had ruined some of the designs he'd painted onto his skin, but the affectation was one he was only grudgingly afforded. Now would not be the time to refresh them.

Tayan wandered along the paths among the plants and ferns, the lush leaves of rubber and the stands of bamboo. He rubbed at one of his slave brands and then the dark feather tattoos, the irony of bearing them both bitter at the back of his tongue. What would Lilla think of all this?

Lilla didn't claim you, slave.

That's a lie.

He'd ask him one day, when he was free, when they both were. The golden thread of his spirit jerked at a sudden pull and he clutched at his chest, gasping. He put ideas of freedom and of Lilla from his mind and replaced them with love for his sweet lord. Again.

Always.

The Singer's attention was unrelenting. Tayan had no privacy even in his own mind. His body was owned, his spirit tied, and his emotions subject to another's will. He was but an extension of the Singer now, joined, an egg with a double yolk. *A part of something greater. A part of greatness itself. Singer Xac will wake the world spirit and I will do all I can to help him. And all the world will be a garden.*

Yet the words were hollow. What would happen to Malel, Snake-sister, Jaguar-brother? What would happen to the Tokob ancestors, to the spirits, even the lords of the Underworld? What would happen to him?

Another tug in his chest, a sharp reminder. Tears started in Tayan's eyes, of frustration rather than pain. He blinked rapidly. He was a gifted shaman, a gifted journeyer through realms and worlds and along the spiral path. He would explore the Singer's strength and discover where and how he might supplement it. He would do what Malel had brought him here to do, what the holy Setatmeh marks on his flesh had chosen him for. What the sacred bonding of his spirit promised. He would not let down any of his gods.

Tayan walked to a low carved-wood seat looking over the tiered garden and down into the city. He couldn't clearly see the base of the pyramid, let alone into the plaza, but the seat gave him a sense of space and freedom that he relished. He'd rarely been allowed into the gardens before his elevation, and never alone – he glanced at Ilandeh – and the novelty had yet to wear thin.

He sat cross-legged, smoothing his kilt over his knees and letting himself fill with sun and heat and the whisper of the breeze, the call of birds and rustle of leaves. He closed his eyes against the glare and sought within, grasping the red vine that grew from the Singer's spirit into his own with delicate fingers. If he was to aid the holy lord, he needed to understand the magic that lived in and around him. To know how it worked. To follow its currents and use them to travel.

Lilla.

Tayan's breath caught. Finding Lilla by traveling the song-stone had been his original intention, back before he'd realised it could be medicine for the Singer. Distance in the song meant nothing, not in the way that the length of the spiral path did. Tayan could cross all Ixachipan if only he had a place to aim for – a spirit to seek. He could do it. Find him. *And find out why he didn't claim me. Or whether that was one of Enet's lies.*

Another thought stopped him. Why not visit Enet's mind? Find the truth from her? *No. Lilla first. My love first.*

I thought I was your love, the Singer said in his mind and Tayan gasped and jerked, but there was no tugging hurt this time. Amusement at his rush of fear – someone else's amusement – bubbled within his ribs instead.

Forgive me, holy lord. I thought . . . I am, was, being selfish. Tell me how I might serve you.

Instead of an answer, Tayan was flooded with images, most flickering past too fast to really understand, but he had impressions of hunger, anger, lust, vengeance. Of death and dying, of Enet in its midst. Images that all centred on the great pyramid and others, fainter as if with time or distance, that must have been from Xac's youth. Before he became Singer.

Do you understand?

Tayan didn't, but he understood the imperative to return to the holy lord's side well enough. He stood again, banishing thoughts of journeying to Lilla with a vague promise of "next time", and walked quickly back through the gardens and into the source, Ilandeh his silent shadow.

'My love?' he murmured as he knelt at the Singer's side.

'Go into the city,' the Singer said. 'Go and live for me, my Shadow. You, Chorus, will protect him with your life. I want him to see everything and feel everything. The fighting pits. The entertainment district. The flesh markets. I want to see, hear, taste and feel everything you do, Shadow. Hold nothing back. I will know if you do and I will exact my price for it.'

Tayan could feel Ilandeh's hesitation and sat up eagerly before she could voice her concerns. A rush of excitement flooded him, not all of it his own. 'Great Singer, I will be your eyes, ears and tongue in the Singing City. I will show you the world, my love. We will live in it together.'

'Great Singer, may I recommend your Shadow changes his attire? The kilt and paint say one status, but the brands say another. And . . . that his Shadow-mark is covered up?' Ilandeh's voice was perfectly calm, as if they weren't discussing Tayan's first foray into the city as Shadow. Almost free. *And the first one without Enet. The first one where I might walk where I please and see what I wish. What the holy lord wishes.*

One corner of Xac's mouth twitched at that last, hasty amendment, and Tayan ducked his head, then dared to glance up at the Singer through his eyelashes. The holy lord was looking especially beautiful, his skin regaining a healthy glow with each day of their linking, fat and muscle and magic carving him anew. He was so easy to love when he wasn't being terrifying. Though when he was . . . well, that had its own special allure, too.

The Singer laughed aloud at that. 'What say you, my sweet? Do you wish to hide who you are or shall we show the world my Shadow has been chosen?'

'Let us show them,' Tayan said over Ilandeh's bitten-off protest. 'Chorus Ilandeh will keep me safe.' He glanced back at her, giddy with possibility.

'I recommend the Shadow wears a tunic and also a shawl to cover the marks on his arms,' she said. 'Both the brands and his Tokob tattoos. Unless, great Singer,' she added, suddenly blanching with realisation, 'your intention is for your people to know the Shadow is not of Pechacan? Forgive this one's presumption if—'

The Singer waved her silent, as excited as Tayan. 'No, cover him up as you see fit. My little Shadow will just have to endure the heat.' There was a touch of malice to that last, and the Toko bore it with as much grace as he could muster. A shawl would make him look suspicious, but he supposed once the news spread, everyone would be looking at his throat, not his clothing. He'd be the centre of any attraction, the person to whom all eyes would be drawn. Not dismissed and overlooked as he'd spent the last two years, nor commanding respect as a shaman of the spiral path or even a peace-weaver. Tayan was Shadow of the Singer, and everyone who saw him this day would know it.

He stroked his forefinger along both sides of his throat, where the tattoos sat, still a little raised, a little scabbed, but beautiful. He smiled wider than he had since before the war. He smiled for Xac alone. 'We will have so much sensation, my love. So much fun and enjoyment. Tell me where I should go and what I should see. Tell me what will make you happy.'

'All of it,' the Singer breathed, and Tayan laughed and leant forward to press an impulsive kiss to the corner of his sensuous mouth. 'I want to see it all.'

'Then that is what I will show you, my love.'

Tayan was dizzy with delight and all the sights and sounds of the city. At Ilandeh's insistence, he was seated in a litter with the translucent curtains closed. The litter-bearers were of the highest quality and regularly hired to transport coun- cillors to and from the source. They were servants, not slaves, and their employer or a member of their family accompanied every journey as a guarantee of loyalty.

Ilandeh knelt opposite Tayan in the litter, festooned in so many weapons it would have been laughable if not for the intent glitter of her eyes and the way her lips had pressed tight into a thin, anxious slash. He'd almost teased her about being worried for his safety, but held back. Teasing implied friendship, and as he'd reminded himself not an hour before, Tayan had no friends.

Biting his lip, he drew back a curtain just enough to peek out and immediately forgot the Chorus's presence. So many colours, so much movement and life. The smells drifting from food stalls, the raucous normality of voices raised in sales and barter, argument and laughter. He drank it in like honeypot and could feel Xac's delight sitting alongside his own. 'It's so loud, my love,' he murmured with a private, inward smile. 'So loud and so . . . normal.'

'Where would the honoured Shadow like to go first?' Ilandeh asked, her fingers twitching as she visibly fought the urge to pull his hand away from the curtain. Tayan grinned at her, full of joy and curiosity, and her mouth softened just a touch. Was she, too, remembering their past friendship? Tayan saw her suddenly in a new light, not as the betrayer of his city and people but as a person out of place, thrust into a new world she wasn't used to and to which she'd been forced to adapt or die. As he was now.

'We're not so unalike, are we, Ilandeh?' he asked softly in turn. He felt Xac's interest stir at that, but before he could elaborate, the warrior gave him a polite, puzzled frown.

'I could never compare with the Shadow of the Singer, high one. Perhaps the entertainment district first? A fighting pit? It is only to first blood today – no death matches,' she added as he instinctively recoiled. 'I have jade should you wish to bet on the tests of skill and it would, ah, the pits have many guards dedicated to keeping the peace among the patrons. Should your status cause too much excitement.'

The Singer was amenable, so Tayan agreed and Ilandeh leant through the curtains to tell the litter-owner their destination. The entertainment district was a few sticks away, giving Tayan plenty of opportunity to stare out through the curtains and ask every question he could think of. How long had it been since he'd been able to speak freely, to question anyone at all, let alone a Chorus warrior with the highest Pechaqueh pedigree? Question her as if they were equals, at least.

When the initial rush of excitement faded, he drew the curtain open a little further and then, in deference to the warrior's discomfort, leant back against the padded rest so his face – and throat – fell into shadow. He quirked a smile at her sigh of relief and felt something unknot in his chest that had been tied for so long he'd forgotten about it. City life. The noise and smells, the swirls of colour that were all his eyes could make out in the distance. The sheer vibrant *life* of a city. He'd missed it.

'Will we cross the Blessed Water?' he asked when the scent of moisture drifted to his nose.

'Not today, Shadow. Not unless you wish to visit?' There was a hint of challenge in Ilandeh's voice and the Singer stirred within him again, stronger this time. Tayan narrowed his eyes at her and felt magic seep through his skin. Golden sparkles fluttered through his hands and up his wrists.

Ilandeh put her face to the cushion. 'This one begs your forgiveness, Shadow,' she said.

'It is a valid question, Chorus,' Tayan said despite the Singer's displeasure puckering the skin between his shoulder blades. 'I am only newly elevated to the holy lord's regard, after all. But I would like to gift today's experiences to him in all their glory. Sensation and pleasure and enjoyment, rather than the ritual he knows so well.'

The warrior nodded as if this pretty little evasion made perfect sense and the rest of the journey passed in pleasant quiet. The entertainment district was loud even a few hours before duskmeal, raucous crowds gathering around dog-fighting pits and dicing tables. Brothels and drinking huts lined the streets and jugglers, tumblers and fortune-tellers wandered through the small plazas.

The litter-owner passed him a long skewer of roasted palm hearts and lizard and Xac enjoyed the novelty of food that didn't come served with beauty and ritual. Tayan licked grease from his lips and fingers and felt the Singer's delight squirming within him. Happiness drenched him.

A troupe of Tlaloxqueh vision-dancers occupied another, larger plaza, vibrant in their paint, wailing as they spun and leapt to the beat of skin-drums and the shriek of reed flutes. Tayan's heart lurched, the smile falling from his face. These weren't shamanic dances as he understood them, but they were close enough to wake a painful longing. He hadn't danced for Malel in too long, in a lifetime it felt like. He watched avidly, craning his neck until they vanished.

'You let them worship their gods for your entertainment?' he asked, faintly nauseated but deeply envious at the same time.

Ilandeh snorted. 'They are not Tlaloxqueh,' she said as if it should have been obvious. 'Likely they were Quitob – those people are gifted dancers and actors – who learnt enough of the steps and the painted symbols to appear to be vision-dancers. It's just a performance, Shadow.'

Tayan stared at her in shocked silence, while inside the Singer rumbled amusement again – at him this time. 'But. But their dances are sacred, their paint is sacred. How could someone impersonate something so personal, so intrinsic to an entire people?' He was aware that his tone was strident with disbelief and burgeoning anger. 'Who gave them the right to steal something so precious?'

'Precious, Shadow? The Tlaloxqueh are happy, productive members of the Empire who have embraced the song and Pechaqueh ways. Their dances mean nothing to them – why shouldn't they sell them for entertainment?'

'Sell them?' Tayan squawked.

'Of course. Some may be stolen, I suppose, but those are easier to tell – the performances are never as good as those who bought their instruction from people who had the dances passed down from their ancestors. Still, a poor show is only to be expected in those who reject Pechaqueh values. If you stoop to thievery, you can never guarantee the quality of what you'll get.'

Tayan scoffed. 'You speak of Pechaqueh values and pretend to be disgusted at others for stealing culture and ritual, yet you steal entire peoples and the lands they come from and call it liberation? Your hypocrisy—'

Anger suffused Ilandeh's face, but before she could respond – if she would dare – Tayan's chest exploded into agony. He grunted, didn't have the breath for more, and curled around the pain, fingers clawing at his tunic.

Did I steal you, little shaman? I think you came to me willingly. I think you want this, and everything that goes with it that I have gifted you. Could your Malel have done this, made you this? When the people's adoration washes over you, then will you understand what I have made you?

'I would never sell Tokob knowledge and secrets,' he protested in a croak, the hard seed of that truth sticking in his chest, weighty and full of conviction.

Haven't you already done that, my sweet love? the Singer crooned within him. *All those shamanic medicines you tried, your strange little journey-rituals that let you enter my song? Do you think I don't know them all? You've already given me everything worth taking.*

Except this.

There was another pull within his chest, the Singer's spirit feasting on his own. Tayan shuddered. It hadn't been like that. He was a shaman dedicated to life and to healing; of course he'd used his skills to help the Singer. It was his duty, his calling.

Was it? Or was it your own ambition?

Tayan didn't know who that voice belonged to. He bit the inside of his cheek, swallowing the urge to scream, at the pain or at the words, he didn't know. Ilandeh was still watching him and he forced himself to sit upright, spine straight and trembling. 'Silence until we reach the fighting pit,' he snapped.

The warrior bowed her head. 'As the Shadow commands,' she said mildly. He searched her face for contempt or amusement and found neither. It didn't reassure him: he of all people knew Ilandeh could conceal her true thoughts behind a smiling mask. Still, she didn't speak to him again until they reached their destination, instead conversing very quietly with the litter-owner who walked beside them. Leaving Tayan alone, as he'd ordered. Or as alone as he could be, sharing his skin with the living god of the Empire of Songs.

The crowd at the fighting pit was riotous with excitement and alcohol and the thrill of winning and losing wealth. Pit fights were different from the contests between warriors that Tayan was used to back home. Here, the fights were between rival pits and exclusively for entertainment. In Tokoban, they'd been to honour the gods, or between student and teacher, or occasionally rival Paws, but always with blunted weapons and always with honour. Even if bets were laid, the warriors were honoured equally for their skill and dedication to the jaguar path – here, Tayan could already hear jeers from the crowd as someone lost their bout.

He dragged his shawl back on over his shoulders despite the heat, keen to leap out of the litter and drink in the noise and bustle and *freedom* of the fighting pit.

'Shadow, a moment please,' Ilandeh said and leant to the litter-owner once more. 'Please tell the pit-master that Chorus Ilandeh has brought a special guest and requires the utmost security and a private space with a view of the arena.'

'Never mind that,' Tayan said as impatience, belonging to both him and the holy lord, brought a light sweat to his skin. 'Let's just get out there.'

262

'Shadow, I cannot. I am but a single warrior. The risk is too great. It should only be moments before guards arrive to escort us.'

The Toko remembered Ilandeh's polite requests for fifty Chorus to accompany them, and both his own and the Singer's insistence otherwise. With the litter curtains drawn and on the move, he supposed the risk had been worth it, but here and now she wasn't taking any chances with his safety. Tayan felt a tiny thrill at her care for him. How long had it been since anyone had considered his welfare? He nodded once.

'And it is only to first blood today?' he confirmed as they waited.

'Yes, Shadow. Exhibitions of skill alone, to stir the appetites for when the fighters appear next month. Others who are returning from injury will test their health and the power of their shamans' medicine. Those are often less exciting but also a necessary part of the life of a pit. A favourite fighter who has been wounded will be keen to show their supporters that they are recovering. The crowd can be fickle and quickly lose interest,' she added at his frown. 'Indentured fighters need to keep their attention to earn their way out of the pit.'

'High one, Chorus Ilandeh,' a familiar voice said from without the curtains and Tayan snorted.

'Feather Pilos,' he said, examining Ilandeh.

'Pit-master Pilos,' she said smoothly. 'His pit has the highest reputation among all those within the Singing City. If you would allow me to check our surroundings before you exit?' she added and he waved her on. She vanished through the curtain. 'Pit-master, your pit is graced with the Shadow of the Singer. We require adequate protection and a private viewing area.'

Tayan grinned at the stunned silence from behind the curtain, his pride drinking it in. He imagined Pilos's handsome face contorting with shock and panic.

'The Shadow of the Singer honours this pit beyond all reckoning,' he said and there was a faint tremble in his voice. 'They are only exhibition matches today.'

'No death-fights,' Ilandeh said smoothly. 'The Shadow wishes only to be entertained by the skill of strangers.'

There was a hint of emphasis on the last word that had him frowning, but then Pilos was urging her back into the litter and they were moving again, up a winding path with the sounds of the crowd growing ever louder.

The next time the curtain was drawn back, he saw the whole pit spread out beneath him. The litter was surrounded by seats clearly recently vacated, grass fans and a few pieces of fruit scattered along the benches. A ring of guards held back the rest of the murmuring, staring crowd. Ilandeh and Pilos stood side by side, both armed but in his defence. Tayan stepped out and down, sucking in a great lungful of heady, dusty air. He turned in a slow circle, taking in everything he could see and lamenting, yet again, the blurriness that soured his vision for things far away.

When he faced Pilos again, his breath hissed between his teeth and he rocked forward on his toes. 'That's a nasty wound, Feather,' he said, gesturing at Pilos's face as if the man might not be aware of the ugly, swollen slash beneath his jaw. It looked clean enough, but angry. 'I have a medicine good for treating knife wounds – I presume a knife? Stone blade or obsidian?'

Pilos blinked rapidly. 'S-stone, Shadow.'

Tayan nodded. 'I will have it sent over with instructions for its use.'

'You honour me, Shadow.'

He waved away the comment. 'I was shaman before the holy lord saw fit to grace me with his favour,' he said. 'It is no trouble. Now, do your fighters win today?'

Pilos shifted with the topic as smoothly as if they'd rehearsed it – a warrior's instinctive repositioning. 'More win than lose, by the grace of the holy Setatmeh. Would you care for a demonstration of skill, Shadow?'

'Very much. Who should I bet on?'

Pilos began discussing the relative merits of his warriors, but Tayan turned inwards, towards the red vine and the golden love. *Holy lord?*

Turn around, little Shadow. Let them see you.

The litter had vanished and the bearers added their presence to those protecting him from the crowd, so he turned in a slow circle again, not looking outwards over the city this time but in, towards the spectators and the fighters. Head raised high and proud, he let them all see the dark feathers tattooed upon his throat.

There was a long silence, Pilos's voice fading into it, and then cheering erupted from every corner of the seating and washed over him. Tayan drank it like honeypot. It was his due.

LILLA

Eighth Talon's training compound, Melody fortress,
the dead plains, Tlalotlan, Empire of Songs
208th day of the Great Star at evening

Feather Ekon didn't do him the dishonour of asking if he
was ready. The shaman had insisted that the wound left by
the sliver of obsidian Kux had wielded be bound so that it
wouldn't be torn open again. It was small but deep, and the
hurt of it lived somewhere beside Lilla's shoulder blade.

It would be insignificant by the time the day was over. He
stared out at the Eighth Talon drawn up in formation, with
his own pod a dozen paces to the front so they had an unob-
structed view.

Tinit and a few others nodded at him and he nodded back,
carefully avoided Ekon's gaze, and stepped up onto the
platform holding the two crossed beams. Dog warriors
secured his wrists and ankles to each point until he was
spread wide and exposed. Vulnerable.

'Six days ago, a member of this slave's pod attempted to
kill their pod-leader and myself, Feather Ekon of the Melody.

266

Pod-leader Lilla saved my life and begged for the pod's punishment to be taken into his own skin. I agreed.' Ekon's voice carried across the silent expanse of the drill yard. There was no emotion in his tone and Lilla was glad he couldn't see his face. He didn't know what expression he wanted Ekon to be wearing. Despite Kux's death and the promise of this day, this punishment, it was Lilla's moon-mad decision to fight – and then kiss – the Feather that haunted him. How much of that would bleed into this?

'One hundred lashes.'

Lilla's every muscle tightened at the pronouncement. *One hundred?* One hundred would likely kill him. It was too much. It was a death sentence. It also made a sick sort of sense: one hundred members of the pod, one hundred lashes with the whip. Rewarded together; punished together. The inviolable law of the Melody.

Ekon appeared in his line of sight and Lilla made an effort to compose his expression. The Feather's face and eyes were remote as he offered him a thick fold of material to bite down on. Lilla accepted gratefully. He had no urge to hear his own screams echo across the drill yard. He worked his jaw until the material was comfortable and then nodded; Ekon let go and stepped back. Something flashed across his face, too fast for the Toko to recognise, but he said nothing. Perhaps he, too, was lamenting that their first kiss was also their last, for after this – if he lived through this – whatever had been growing between them would wither. Or perhaps Lilla was alone in that . . . memory? Hope? Guilt-ridden desire?

Lilla took some deep breaths in through his nose and let his chin slump onto his chest. Perhaps he should be keeping his head raised as long as possible, in defiance of what was going to be done to him, but his pride wasn't sufficient for that. Better to save as much strength now as he could. Ignoble but sensible.

The wood beneath his feet was rough and Lilla dug his toes into it, focusing on the grain rubbing against his soles. The sun beat on his head, reminiscent of his mother's palm, big and warm and soothing when he'd fallen. The back of his neck and upper back were strangely exposed; his hair had been bound up high on his head so that it wouldn't tangle with the whip and be torn out by the roots.

His breath came too quick; he couldn't slow it. Behind him, the slither of leather on dirt, then an eternity of nothing, and then fire ripping across his shoulders in a line of incandescence, as if his back was the sky and the whip was lightning.

Lilla had been lashed before – he didn't know a slave in the Eighth who hadn't – and normally the eagles who carried out the punishment made them count the strikes aloud. He was pathetically grateful for the gag Ekon had given him; he didn't want to know what his voice sounded like past thirty strokes, which was the most he'd ever received before. Thirty had been tough. Thirty had put him on his belly on a cot in the healing hall. He couldn't even begin to imagine what a hund— The second blow fell, ripping him out of his thoughts and back into his body. He grunted.

He might not be expected to count aloud, but he would keep a tally anyway. Something to hold on to; something that would indicate when this would be over.

Three.

Lilla wondered if it was Ekon himself whipping him or one of the dog warriors. He wondered if a hundred blows would exhaust the whipper. Perhaps the strikes would get weaker?

Four.

The first bead of sweat rolled down the Tokob temple and he wiped it off on his inner arm.

Five.

The breeze cooled his skin, though it could do nothing for the fire in his back. Lilla worked his tongue against the cotton, trying to find a position that didn't suck the moisture out of his mouth. He'd be thirsty enough by the time this was over. If he was still alive.

Six.

Whoever was wielding the whip was extremely talented. It took twenty lashes before Lilla finally felt the blood begin to run. His punisher varied the placement of the strokes to keep the skin as intact as possible, but the sheer quantity they needed to inflict meant that it was impossible not to lay stripe on top of stripe.

Lilla's head was pounding in time with his heartbeat, and his heart itself seemed to be centred somewhere near the surface of his back, the flesh throbbing from his nape to the waistband of his loincloth. So far, his legs were still steady beneath him and he hadn't had to take his weight through his bound wrists, but he knew that would get harder as the punishment dragged on. Thirst and the heat of the sun were additional torments and the material gripped between his jaws was beginning to stick to the dryness of his tongue. Soon he would have to spit out the gag just so that he could breathe and then there would be nothing to muffle the noises he made.

An eternity later, he reached thirty lashes and heard the order for the whip to be passed to another wielder. Lilla had the hazy thought that he didn't want his tormentors to tire out their arms too much and something close to a hysterical giggle rasped its way out through the gag.

Thirty strokes and he was still standing. How would he feel at fifty, at seventy? Would he still be standing then? Would he be unconscious? Would they really deliver all one hundred lashes or stop if they thought it would kill him? Was this where Lilla's dreams of rebellion and freedom and Tayan would end? On this blood-spattered scaffold under a brassy, unforgiving sun and a song that crowed of Pechaqueh dominion?

The next warrior to wield the whip was fresh and seemed to have a point to prove. Their first stroke landed as precisely as all the others but with what must be twice the force. Lilla jerked against his restraints, throwing himself away from the source of pain so that the crossed beams he was attached to dug into his belly. His hands tightened convulsively on the ropes, burning the flesh from his wrists. The noise he made was higher pitched, closer to a scream.

This warrior struck faster too, fast enough that unconsciousness threatened by the time they reached forty lashes. The Tokob legs were beginning to shake and he had to brace his thighs against the cross and let it take some of his weight.

The more blows that landed, the dizzier he got and the harder it was to keep count. They might have reached fifty lashes when Lilla passed out for the first time. Only for a moment – the jerk of his wrists taking his weight brought him back, but not fast enough for him to prevent the gag falling out of his mouth. Shuddering, he forced his legs to bear him up again as he worked his jaw and tongue, searching for a little moisture.

When the next blow fell, his cry was a hoarse bellow of sound that echoed from the closest wall. Still the lashes came and by now he had no idea what number they were on. He tried to count again, just to keep his mind fixed on something that wasn't the agony in his back or the agony of waiting for the next strike, strikes that were somehow always a surprise.

Tears ran as fast as sweat as the blood that streaked his back soaked into his loincloth and trickled down his legs.

His knees buckled again, and again he forced himself to stand. Couldn't remember why that was important now; could barely remember what he'd done to be punished.

Saved Ekon.

A ragged bark of sound – part-laugh, part-sob – spilt from his lips and a second later the whip fell, turning the end of the noise into a shout. Lilla rolled his forehead against his bicep in wordless, pleading denial. Surely they were done. Surely this was a hundred lashes? More, even. He'd been here for hours, days. A lifetime.

It took another seven blows – how many did that bring it up to? Who knew – to make him begin to sob in earnest, hanging by his wrists even though that put more pressure on his torn and broken-open back, stretching the gaping wounds further. They paused then and there was a rising murmur of sound as a shadow fell over Lilla. A finger under his chin, lifting his head. Eyes meeting his, assessing. He knew his face but had lost his name; it had been whirled away in the fire.

'Nearly there, Lilla. Hold on,' the man said quietly and then, 'water,' he added with the crackle of authority in his voice. 'Douse him and give him a little to drink.' He stepped backwards and folded thick arms over a strong chest. 'There's no point in punishing an unconscious slave.'

Lilla tried to laugh, to spit at him, anything, but instead he let his head hang to his chest again until someone else – a shaman? – lifted it by the hair and put a gourd to his lips. The first swallow stung like bones in his throat, trickling into every scrape and abrasion carved by the force of his muffled screams. The second was easier, tasting less of blood and more of sweet life. He groaned at the third, chased for a fourth – but the gourd was gone.

More water, this time a great sheet of it, thrown against his back with such suddenness that he tried to twist away, bellowing. Was it water or venom or burning ash? No, salt-water, every drop a torment from the Underworld.

The pain was monstrous, sharper somehow than even the whip, but it didn't shut down his mind in the same way. Instead, a little sense and clarity returned to him, enough for Lilla to come back to himself. Again, he forced his legs to hold him.

'Fea-Feather,' he croaked, his voice barely there. The man returned, wary. 'How . . . many?'

Ekon – that was his name, Lilla remembered – pursed his lips and glanced away, then back. Lilla didn't know what his face was doing, but the Pecha must have seen something in it, for he nodded once, decisively. 'The next strike will be the sixty-fifth.'

Lilla's face crumpled and he dropped his head quickly, breathing hard through his nose until he had control. 'Thank you,' he muttered.

Ekon nodded again and then disappeared. The Toko let the beams take his weight, wedging his ribcage into the juncture to take the pressure from both his wrists and his legs. It wrenched his shoulders even further back, another misery that felt small now but which he knew would grow to be impossible to withstand. For now, though, he hung draped across the scaffold and gritted his teeth, determined not to puke up the precious water under the last strikes of the whip.

He failed.

Lilla swam up into consciousness just in time to see someone fiddling with the rope at his left wrist. The binding came free and he collapsed, swinging sideways from his right arm, his left knee smashing into wood. His ankles were already free.

It was over?

'Slave Tinit of Yalotlan has begged to take the last of pod-leader Lilla's punishment into her own skin. Twenty-one strikes,' the Feather shouted, his voice loud but still swallowed up by the vastness of the compound.

A dog warrior was worrying at Lilla's other wrist when Ekon's words filtered into his brain and arranged themselves into something he could understand. 'No,' he croaked, but there was no strength to his voice. He flailed his left hand and rolled his head weakly on his neck. 'No.' A little louder this time, enough that the dog paused and leant down.

'What?' he asked blankly.

Shuddering, Lilla gripped the wood in his left hand and stood, sweat breaking out all over his body and screams painting his tongue and teeth that he refused to let out of his mouth. He pivoted on his bound wrist and faced Ekon and the Eighth and his pod. Faced Tinit.

'No,' he managed, loud enough this time to cut off the murmuring and root Tinit to the dirt. 'My pod; my punishment.'

'Lilla, no,' Tinit cried, but he somehow managed to glare her into silence and stillness.

'Why?' Feather Ekon asked with a curious tilt to his head.

Lilla couldn't answer, wasn't even sure he had an answer. He just had to. He turned back to the scaffold and reached up to grasp the loosened binding in his free hand. He bowed his head and squeezed shut his eyes and waited. He didn't have to wait long.

The next blow landed and he arched and screamed, and the next and the next until his hand fell away from the rope and he looped his arm over the beam instead so he wouldn't fall.

'Malel bless you!'

The shout was faint with distance and thin with emotion, but he heard it. The whip seemed to land harder in retaliation.

'Ancestors guide you, Lilla,' another voice yelled, closer this time. The whip fell again and the voices rose, stronger and louder, more and more of them and the whip came faster, the blows harder, until he couldn't scream any more, until his legs gave out for the last time and he took the last eight, or twenty, or thousand blows while dangling from one wrist.

'One hundred lashes,' he heard someone say from an impossible distance. Dimly, he thought he could hear cheering. A hand in his hair, pulling his head up. He blinked, stared at the face, stern and forbidding. The man's mouth twitched, almost a moue of distress, but that couldn't be right. 'Take him away and treat him well,' he said. 'He has honoured his pod and his Talon. He has honoured himself.'

Someone cut the rope around his wrist; someone else caught him when he fell and draped him belly-down on a stretcher. The cheers rang into the sky. Lilla fled into the dark.

He woke to fire. Fire in his veins, fire in his bones, and fire raging in his back. He woke to thirst, the water in his body burnt away by the flames until he was shrivelled and desiccated; smoked meat.

'Tayan?' he croaked, the sharp, familiar bitterness of medicine reaching his nostrils.

There was a rustle of movement nearby and he forced open one eyelid to see a face, lined and framed by a long fall of grey-shot hair, hovering sideways next to his. 'You're alive then,' the man said in a distinctly unimpressed tone. 'Thought you Tokob were hardier than this. It's been two days.' He straightened up and fiddled with something that caused a flare of agony to burn bright in Lilla's back; the Toko groaned from deep inside his core and tried feebly to squirm away.

The man bent forward again and stared at him. 'The eagles know what they're about, so although you're going to have a very pretty set of scars, they didn't fully rupture any muscles. With time, rest and good training, you should make a full recovery. Once the wounds have sealed and the flesh has grown back, I'll give you some oil to rub into them so that the scars don't tighten as they heal. Otherwise you'll have limited mobility.'

Lilla didn't care how much mobility he had after this. Didn't care about anything but an end to the pain. 'Hurts,' he croaked and the shaman snorted.

'What would be the point of the lesson if it didn't? You can have more medicine in a few hours.'

Lilla sobbed. He'd die from the hurt before then.

Someone else appeared beside his cot and Lilla blinked slowly at him. 'Feather . . . Feather Ekon,' he croaked and tried to push himself upright. 'Malel, forgive me.'

'Hush.' Ekon crouched beside the cot and put his hand on the nape of his neck to still him. 'Don't move.'

The gentlest of pressure from the Feather's palm flattened him and he let it. 'How is my pod?' he mumbled, cheek squashed against the cotton-stuffed mattress.

'Worried about you,' Ekon said with a quirk of his lips. 'Slave warrior Tinit and the rest of your pod have begged me each day to come here and see whether you were awake yet. They have really been quite insistent, considering their status, and so I am glad that I will be able to report your continued existence to them.'

'This slave apologises for their behaviour,' Lilla managed, fear writhing within him, and then paused to cough, grateful it choked off his words before he could beg not to be hurt further. The Feather pressed a cup with a narrow spout against his mouth and tilted it gently so that he might drink.

'You do not need to apologise for your pod's devotion to you, pod-leader. I had suspected it during the flogging, but I am grateful to see that it was not simply born of your sacrifice. You have crafted them into a cohesive unit, which is exactly what we wanted from you and from them. You have done well, Lilla.' Ekon glanced away as if checking the shaman's presence and then leant in closer and lowered his voice to a whisper. 'I am proud of you.'

'This slave does not deserve such praise,' Lilla croaked even as his chest warmed with it. But it was a hollow warmth. He had bought their loyalty with his blood, and how genuine was pride that only manifested when he was beaten half to death for the crime of saving a life?

Perhaps Ekon realised his hypocrisy, for he bit the tip of his tongue and then heaved a sigh. 'Don't think I have forgotten what you did for me, Lilla,' he added quietly. 'I am deeply aware that I might well be dead or injured now if not for you. If not for you choosing loyalty to the Melody and the Empire over loyalty to your friends. To have acted against your own people and allies to save my life is something I will not forget. When you are recovered enough to leave the healing halls, I will acknowledge it publicly in front of your pod.'

Lilla smeared his cheek against the mattress in an approximation of a nod. He didn't much care, although he knew that he should.

'What would their punishment have been, Feather?' he mumbled, desperate to think of anything other than the pain.

Ekon blew out his cheeks and shook his head, and then

tucked a strand of sweat-lank hair behind Lilla's ear with a rueful smile. 'Twenty lashes each. If you had not begged to take their punishment into your skin, you would not be lying here now. Yet you did it so publicly, I had to agree. And the punishment needed to be severe. Twenty lashes for each of your pod, but a hundred for one individual.'

Lilla's breath wheezed in his throat and alarm creased Ekon's face before he realised he was laughing. 'Maybe think twice before you next ask for their punishment,' he added with a chuckle.

Lilla shook his head weakly; sleep was approaching fast now, but it was important to say this. He reached out and grasped Ekon's wrist in a clumsy, sweaty grip. 'Would do it again,' he whispered. 'Save them; save you.'

Ekon's eyes widened in surprise and then crinkled at the corners. His dimple flashed and he bent forward and pressed dry lips to Lilla's temple, another to the point of his cheek-bone, and a third that just grazed the corner of his mouth. There was a faint blush staining his face when he pulled back, one that matched the heat curling through Lilla's body. *Not the only one to remember the kiss, then.*

'Heal well and quickly,' Ekon said and put his hand over Lilla's, where it still held his wrist. 'I want to see you back on the training ground as soon as possible.'

Lilla was flat on his belly for another four days and then sitting up and walking slowly across the room for two more before the shaman announced he was well enough to return to his barracks. He would be out of training for a month, the longest he had ever gone without lifting a weapon. Lilla had no idea what he was going to do when the Eighth was drilling for most of every day, but a part of him looked forward to the rest, even though it would give him far too much time to think and brood and make wild plans that would never come to anything.

And sleep. The wounds exhausted him, as did forever bracing against the pain that not even the strongest medicine could dull.

When he finally exited the healing halls and made his way into the Eighth's training compound, nobody noticed. He was walking slowly with his back held exceptionally straight; even the slightest rounding of his shoulders caused pain in his abused muscles and torn flesh. Crisp cotton bandages swathed him from neck to waist and he couldn't bear even the weight of a tunic over the top of them.

A dog warrior whirled at the sound of his scuffing sandals, brandishing a whip, and Lilla flinched on instinct, raising a hand at the threat. The dog lowered his weapon when he identified Lilla and beckoned him forward, then pointed towards Feather Ekon, who was standing a few hundred paces distant. Beyond him, the Eighth Talon were drilling in vast lines and squares.

Lilla walked wide around the man with the whip, his back crawling with sense-memory, and made his way towards his Feather. He was fifty paces distant when Ekon saw him out of the corner of his eye and snapped his head around with the same wariness the dog warrior had exhibited. His face split into a grin and he pounded on the drum set up next to him to call a halt to the training. The Eighth fell into stillness and then snapped to attention.

Ekon hurried to Lilla and made himself a barrier between the Toko and his Talon. Hidden between their bodies, he took his hand and gave it a brief squeeze. 'How do you feel?'

Lilla swallowed the first answer to come to his mouth and managed a dip of his head. 'This slave is honoured by your concern, Feather,' he said formally. 'This slave feels much better and has been dismissed by the shaman except for daily visits to have his bandages changed and his wounds treated.'

'And how long until you are able to return to training?' the Feather asked even though surely the shaman would have told him. Perhaps he thought to catch Lilla out in a lie, but if so, then he understood the Toko less than he thought.

'Four weeks, Feather,' he replied evenly. 'Though of course if I am well enough and the shaman agrees, I would like to return earlier. Until then, if there is anything which you would find useful for me to do, I am pleased to work. In the kitchens, perhaps, or repairing weapons if you would allow this slave to touch such. Of course, I can read and write also.'

Ekon smiled again. 'You are injured and you should rest, Lilla,' he said gently. 'Though the offer is appreciated. I should expect no less from one with such honour.' He squeezed Lilla's hand once more and then let go and turned to face the Eighth Talon. Lilla's pod had been brought to the front once more and he could see them watching him with intent focus, their eyes lingering on the layers of bandages wrapping his torso. He managed a smile for them.

Ekon led him forward and then insisted that the Toko stand at his shoulder as if they were of equal status. A murmur rippled through the front ranks and Lilla squirmed. 'Pod-leader Lilla's punishment is concluded but his reward is yet unstated. He saved my life against one of his own. There are three ways for a slave warrior to reduce the term of their service. *What are they?*'

He roared the question and the Eighth Talon responded. 'By acts of bravery; by capturing slaves; by saving lives.'

Lilla found himself shouting along and those warriors too far back to hear the Feather's question soon understood what was required of them. The drill yard echoed with the chant.

Ekon was nodding. 'Pod-leader Lilla displayed two of those qualities – he committed an act of bravery by putting himself between me and a blade, and that act of bravery saved my life. As a reward for his actions, I will strike one sun-year from his service as a slave warrior.'

Lilla felt his mouth drop open in surprise. Of all he had expected, it had not been this. There was a moment of stunned silence and then his pod erupted into cheers, the sound spreading through the Talon as word passed of Ekon's generosity.

The Pecha turned to him with an expectant grin. 'What say you, Lilla?' he asked. He held up his arm and silence fell once again so that the front ranks might hear the Tokob response.

Lilla looked from Ekon to his pod and then beyond them to the rest of the Eighth. A sun-year; an entire sun-year. Gritting his teeth against the pain, Lilla faced the Feather and lowered himself slowly onto his knees and then pressed palms and brow to the dirt. Then he sat back on his heels and looked up and into Ekon's face. 'Rewarded together; punished together. I could not accept such a boon for myself alone.'

Ekon was already waving away the suggestion. 'I cannot give such to an entire pod,' he said and there seemed to be genuine regret in his tone.

Lilla took a breath as deep into his lungs as he could, the flesh and bones of his back howling at the pain. 'Of course not, Feather. This slave would never ask such. Would the high one offer them each a month off their service instead?' He kept his voice low enough that not even the closest of his pod could hear him. He did not want Ekon to feel he was being forced into a corner.

The Pecha stared down at him impassively for long enough that Lilla put his palms back on the dirt and began to bow.

'Sit up,' the Feather said sharply. He sucked his top lip into his mouth, studying the Toko kneeling at his feet. 'Yes,' he said eventually. 'I can do that.' He turned to Lilla's pod. 'Pod-leader Lilla declines my offer of a year off his service in favour of each member of his pod receiving one month off their terms instead.'

The silence was profound and then the cheers, when they came, were even louder than before. A month was nothing in the length of their service. A month won through Lilla's pain and sacrifice and gifted to them at his own expense was everything.

Ekon gestured him back to his feet. 'Well done,' he said quietly and that damn dimple flashed again in his cheek. 'Very well done.'

ENET

The source, Singing City, Pechacan, Empire of Songs
216th day of the Great Star at evening

'Great Octave Enet, Chosen of Xac, requests entrance into the holy lord's presence.'

There was no reply, so Enet approached with her eyes cast down, stopping a dozen paces away to kneel and press her forehead to the mats. When she sat back, she looked up just far enough to find the Singer's location. He was reclining in a mountain of pillows with the Toko slave sitting in his lap and hand-feeding him bites of fruit. So not out flaunting his tattoos today, then. Pity.

It was a highly unconventional method of announcing a Shadow, albeit with a single advantage: when he was in public, no one could approach him. So far, nobody knew his name or identity. Nobody outside the source was aware of the Singer's . . . choices.

Neither of them paid any attention to her arrival, but the slave did look up just then, his eyes narrowed. Enet breathed through a spike of anxiety and then stared fixedly at her lap

282

when he raised his chin to deliberately expose the feathers inked into his skin. *Just a coincidence. He has not learnt to Listen.* Still, she carefully ordered her thoughts and filled them with the love and adoration that was the Singer's due. And later today she would take the time to learn the Shadow's shape and feel within the song, so that if he did somehow come poking around, she'd know it.

The Chorus warrior who appeared to be assigned to the sla— to the Shadow stood near a wall, studying her, alert for the merest twitch that would indicate danger to the holy lord or his successor.

Enet was unused to being scrutinised so openly. It had been a long time since anyone had had the courage to be suspicious of her and she had forgotten how much she disliked it. She did not need to be watched and suspected and judged as if she was some no-blood free selling pots in the market. She was Great Octave and her loyalty to the Empire of Songs was without question.

Still, better to be scrutinised by a Chorus than by Pilos, whose survival of an assassination attempt, albeit injured, was a – she glanced again at the holy lord – was a fortuitous blessing of the holy Setatmeh.

'Great Singer, my heart rejoices to see you so healthy. And you, Shadow, I had thought you might be further enjoying the delights of our fair city?'

The Shadow arched an eyebrow. He was naked from the waist up again, blue-striped kilt sitting snug to his slender hips, and the paint of his people on his arms and chest and brow. 'Not today,' was all he said and then dismissed her presence, bending close to murmur in the Singer's ear. The holy lord laughed, low in his throat, and put his hands on the Tokob hips, possessive.

Enet licked her lips. 'Great Singer, the date of the Great

Star's little absence from the sky is approaching. My divinations, and those of a dozen Listeners and shamans throughout the Empire, all point to it as being a most auspicious time to wake the world spirit.'

The Toko looked up at that, but the Singer didn't, instead making smacking noises with his mouth until the Shadow turned back with a fond smile and fed him another slice of fig.

'My sweet love is healthier than he has been in years, but his illness was long, Great Octave. Are you sure now is the time?'

The muscles around Enet's eyes tensed and she forced them to relax, keeping her expression mild. 'I am sure only that the Singer knows his own self best. If he decrees the ritual be performed, then it shall be. It is not my place to question the decisions of our god. As I have yet to hear otherwise, I have begun transcribing the ritual for the participants myself, but we will soon need to—'

There was a splash from the offering pool and they all turned to look.

'Hello, my old friend,' the Toko said to the holy Setat looking back at them. It sang, a brief rising run of notes, and he laughed and nodded, and then bent to press a kiss to the Singer's throat before sliding off his lap.

Enet watched in consternation and growing fury as the slave crossed the room towards the pool and dropped to both knees in front of the god. 'What are you doing?' she hissed, completely unable to mask her simmering outrage and the nerves fluttering in her belly. 'Holy Setat, sacred spirit, ask and we shall answer,' she added pointedly.

The Shadow assumed a similar posture to the holy Setat, crouching on his haunches with his fingertips touching the stone floor. They watched each other as if communicating without words and Enet, through sheer force of will, forced her gaze away from the scene to observe the Singer and the Chorus warrior. The holy lord was sitting up in the pillows, looking intently at man and god crouched opposite each other. Ilandeh was face down in prostration as protocol demanded. As Enet should be.

The holy Setat raised a hand to the slave's face and pressed the pads of its fingers to the scars dotted around his eye. He came from a race of god-killers and yet the holy Setat touched him as if he was a friend. It had placed a mark upon him that seemed to honour him, to single him out as precious, as if the twin feather tattoos were not enough.

'What are you thinking, Great Octave?' the Singer rumbled in a low voice, as if unwilling to disturb the communion between slave and Setat.

Her stomach turned over. 'Your Chosen thinks only that she is not worthy to be amongst such divinity, holy lord. It is overwhelming to be surrounded with such power. I wonder . . .' she added carefully and sat up a little more. The Singer grunted for her to continue.

'I wonder whether the holy Setat is here in response to my words about the waking of the world spirit, great Singer. Your song is stronger than ever and all Ixachipan is now yours. The prophecies have been fulfilled and we have peace and stability across the Empire, from sea to sea. Perhaps now is the time to make the formal announcement?'

The Singer hummed and tapped his fingers against his thigh as he watched the Toko and the holy Setat in their silent, intense communion. Enet could see the sweat trickling down the Tokob ribs and suppressed a smile. He was not as unaffected as he pretended, then. She was perversely pleased.

'You are right,' the Singer said, startling her and filling her with a hot flood of anticipation. It was happening. The last thread weaving into the whole so that the pattern would finally, *finally* be revealed. The world was going to change. She was going to change it.

'On the first day of the little absence,' he added.

'As the holy lord commands. And during the eight days the Great Star is missing, you will remake the world.' She couldn't suppress a shiver.

The holy Setat let out a string of liquid notes and the Shadow swayed forward into its embrace. The Great Octave herself rocked on her knees with the urge to approach. She held still, muscles locked tight, watching in fascination and religious fervour, for the god to take the Tokob life. It didn't.

The slave pressed his face to the holy Setatmeh chest as if embracing a cherished friend and then sat back on his knees. The Singer's divine ancestor raised a claw-tipped hand to his face one last time and ran its fingers across the curve of his cheek and the plush fullness of his lower lip, before letting itself fall backwards over the edge of the pool and into the water. A great splash went up and soaked him and he laughed delightedly and then bowed to the wet stone. Enet and the Singer likewise abased themselves and when they sat up once more, the god was a shadow slipping out through the channel that tumbled down the side of the pyramid.

The Toko returned to the Singer's side, wiping water from his face as he came. He was smiling, his cheeks flushed with pleasure and smeared with paint as he sat after only the barest pause for an invitation. 'Did you see, my love?' he asked. 'The god is playful today.'

Enet stared between them and the pool and waited for an explanation that didn't come. 'What was that?' she asked when she couldn't bear it any longer. There was a touch of petulance to her tone that neither of them missed and she flushed. *Stay calm. Stay in control. The Singer is a glory to us all.*

The slave made an inquisitive noise and looked up at her. 'What was what? Oh, that?' He waved a hand in dismissal and grinned, at ease in his power. Enet hated it. Hated him. 'That particular god and I go all the way back to Tokoban. I was learning from it back there and when I was brought to the Singing City, it followed me through the rivers. We have been talking. Before my love and I became one, I couldn't quite understand, but now it is much clearer.'

'Blasphemy,' Enet gasped, shock prickling through her scalp. 'How dare you utter such lies here in the very source?'

The Shadow opened his dark eyes very wide and then they crinkled at the corners as he smiled. 'It is no lie, Great Octave,' he said and she could hear the laughter in his voice. 'Your gods speak to me; is that not wondrous? I feel truly blessed by their regard.'

'"Your" gods? Not "our" gods, then?' she demanded, snake-quick.

This time he did laugh. 'I spoke merely to try not to rouse your ire. Clearly, I was unsuccessful. Our gods, then.'

'Impossible,' she rasped, almost choking on her words in her haste to get them out. 'Even were it possible, the holy Setatmeh would not speak to the likes of you.'

The Singer's attention snapped to her with that, the song flexing and taking on a dangerous growl. The air in the source grew thick. 'The likes of what, exactly?' he demanded in a quiet voice. 'Tayan is my Shadow. He is my other half, my strength where you have brought only weakness. He is my loyalty where you have brought only betrayal. If the holy Setatmeh speak to me, the Singer of this Empire, why would they not speak to Tayan? Why, Enet?'

The Great Octave had no choice but to press her face to

the mats once more and mumble an apology that she strove to mean. When she dared to sit up again, Singer and Shadow were immersed in each other once more. Enet sat in impotent silence and growing rage. Deliberately, she took deep breaths and calmed herself. 'As well as transcribing the ritual so that there are enough copies for all the participants, Kapal and Chotek are practising the arrangement of glyphs to be painted on the floor. I have the book of dances ready for your viewing, holy lord. The magic for the waking, though, of course I have no power over.'

'Of course,' the holy lord agreed with that casual malevolence that had once laced his every utterance. Enet shivered again. 'Deliver the books to my sweet love, my Shadow. He will be the one to stand at my side when I wake the world spirit. I will need no other.'

'The ritual requires at least four,' she began and the Singer's body flashed gold – not the faint little flickers of the past months but a brilliant, blinding light, brighter than he might ever have shone before. The Toko clapped his approval and Enet closed her eyes against the Singer's radiance and his Shadow's black nothingness.

'As the holy lord commands,' she managed without a quaver, as if such displays were commonplace. She bowed a final time with as much lithe grace as she could muster from a body as unresponsive as wood. 'Under the song.'

The sun had long set by the time the Great Octave returned, brooding, to her estate. The council and Chorus were hers and she could depend on them to vote and act as she told them to, but Pilos and the slave were beyond her control. Having the council in the palm of her hand gave her greater power and influence than Pilos, but she no longer had the Singer's ear: that was firmly within the Tokob grasp.

If Pilos could win over the slave – or, worse, the other way around – they could still ruin everything she'd spent decades weaving.

Enet held herself poised in her litter until the gates clattered shut behind her and then slumped against the cushions, staring sightlessly at the sprawling building that her wealth and status had secured her.

Every day, it seemed, the ground shifted beneath her, wet and trembling on the verge of a mudslide that would drag her into its sucking, suffocating depths.

The songstone. The tonic. The Toko. Fucking Pilos.

The last attempt on the Feather's life had been badly managed and born of panic. He knew that she had ordered it, and she knew he knew, and so they continued the dance that would lead to one or the other's death. He was a threat and the Toko an even greater one, not that he realised it, too enamoured of his newfound power to notice. He was like a man who stumbled drunk over a hand-loom, tangling the threads beyond salvation and heedless of the devastation he had caused.

Her estate slave hurried out of the front door and along the path. Enet let him take her arm and ease her out of the litter. One of her mad gambles – *the last mad gamble, gods be good* – had paid off, at least. There was a capstone on its way and a master mason living in confined luxury in her palace. Along with her own, broken songstone, her treason was now complete.

Enet's ambition would be unmistakable if any of it was discovered. Never mind that all she did and all she had ever done since she was a girl was for the good of the people of the Empire. She did nothing for her own glorification. She never had; she never would.

She stalked down the corridor to the garden room. The evening birdsong held no beauty for her ear. The lush greens and bright flashes of wings limned in sunset were as tasteless as a badly patterned kilt to her eye. The song ran its fingers through her spirit and beneath her skin, winding through her, speaking of Pechaqueh superiority and coming glory.

All of it worthless. If she failed.

'Will it be enough?' she muttered. 'Will it get here in time?'

'It will, high one,' the slave said in a soothing tone as he stood at her side and then dared to put a comforting hand on her shoulder. 'Everything else is in place. All will be well.'

Enet clung to his words and watched the night fall across her city.

XESSA

Almost a month had passed since Xessa had killed Eja Oncan.

The wound in her chest had been long but shallow, and the tear in her palm was to her non-dominant hand. Both had healed enough that she had been selected for a death match the following day in honour of the new moon. There would be slaves thrown to river-monsters and others killing for the privilege of living just a little longer. An Empire built on suffering.

Most fighters got two moons off between death matches, but Kalix had said something about getting her back in there now that she had come to her senses. The trainers seemed confident she wouldn't use the fight as a way to die; perhaps seeing how she'd thrown herself back into practice as soon as Shaman Tleote allowed her to had convinced them that their lies had worked on her.

She snorted at their arrogance. Xessa had sworn to save Tiamoko from the fate laid out by Ilam, and she had defied

291

the ancestors she'd made and promised to live long enough to see it come to fruition. Her plan was spiderweb thin and as likely to break, but it was all she had.

She shouldn't be fighting this month, but it was the first step to saving the boy who symbolised Tokoban.

She would feel nothing, not before the fight or during it, and certainly not afterwards. She refused to ever feel anything again, not guilt or anger or regret. Certainly not loss or grief; she had no right to those.

Each day, she built stone walls around her heart that were better armour than the salt-cotton the Pechaqueh would dress her in. Walls as tall and impenetrable as the three sides of her cage, while her body was as strong and flexible as the bamboo bars at the front. Xessa would bend; she wouldn't break. She couldn't, not until Tiamoko was free.

Pilos owned her body and required that body to fight and kill for him. He did not own her mind or her spirit and those she would fence away carefully where nothing – not even Tiamoko – could reach them. Once he was saved, she could sink into herself and find an ending.

A pit-slave arrived with dawnmeal to find Xessa kneeling patiently three paces back from the bars of her cage. The slave refused to meet her eyes as she shoved the dish through the gap and put the cup of water next to it. When the woman had stepped back, Xessa dipped her head in thanks; the slave fled without responding. It was different to how it had been before she'd murdered Oncan. Back then, some of the slaves had had a sympathetic smile or a nod for her, but ever since she had promised she would live only for Tiamoko, they seemed to have seen something in her face or spirit that they didn't like. None of them made eye contact with her any more.

Before Oncan, Xessa had been bitterly amused that Pilos, who she knew refused to keep slaves on his estate or farms, saw no hypocrisy in having them live and work here, in a place dedicated to death. For all his noble talk, he saw the use in slaves; he just preferred to use them where he didn't have to see them every day. Fucking hypocrite.

Still, Xessa didn't care about those things now. She stood and crossed to the dish and cup and settled down to eat. The food was hearty and of decent quality, if lacking in seasoning, and the water was cool and sweet. The eja ate and drank without tasting and licked her bowl clean before sliding them both back through the bars and kneeling once more.

She had discovered the trainers and under-trainers found her silent, patient regard unnerving. Although she had promised herself and Malel she would take no joy in life any more, that her entire existence was dedicated to keeping Tiamoko alive as the sole representative of her home and tribe, she couldn't help the small, vicious stab of pleasure she got every time Ilam or Kalix came to her cage and found her waiting, as patient as Snake-sister, to be let out.

It was no different this morning: under-trainer Ilam covered his instinctive flinch with an elaborate shrug, and then flicked out the long coil of his whip before untying the gate and swinging it open. He pointed her towards the underground training pit and Xessa rose to her feet and stalked out and along the dim corridor without a care. What was there to care about? Her death? That was coming for her sooner or later; all she had to do was hold it off long enough to free Tiamoko.

Early morning light filtered through the plank roof above her head, more arching in through narrow openings lining each side of the wide area so that motes of dust winked gold in their beams, the very air sparkling as if Malel blessed it.

Xessa snorted. Only the lords of the Underworld would bless what went on in this place. *Pretty, though*. The eja shook her head and concentrated on the other fighters.

The Tlaloxqueh twins, Casiv and Vorx, were already in the training pit, deep in conversation. A few others that Xessa recognised; none she'd spend time with. Not that anyone could understand her.

Which doesn't matter any more. Train, fight, kill, live. Until Tiamoko is free.

And then . . .

She didn't allow herself to contemplate what would come after that, too afraid that if she looked it in the eye, she wouldn't be able to resist it. She had to live as long as it took for her friend to win his freedom from this place. His own skill would keep him alive through his matches and with her help – and Pilos's agreement – he'd buy his freedom that much sooner. *I can rest then, not before.*

The big Toko himself came in not long after. He took one glance around and then rushed to her side, boyish face made even younger by his delighted grin. He swept her into a hug and Xessa felt a little of the stone wall she was patiently constructing around her heart crumble and fall away. She hugged him back, burying her face in his meaty shoulder and inhaling the scent of him, the only home she had left. She drank it in but refused to allow herself to relax into his arms the way the small, weak, shameful part of her wanted. She didn't deserve this, but neither would she take this contact away from Tiamoko. He needed it.

Eventually he stepped back enough to sign. 'How are your wounds? I heard you fight tomorrow?' She nodded. Tiamoko's face twisted. 'Malel curse them. You should have at least another moon; two, seeing as you were so badly injured. But there's talk the Shadow will come to watch us. A patron like that, even just an approving nod if nothing more, and we could win enough on our next fight to get free.'

Xessa blinked. If Tiamoko could be freed tomorrow . . .

He scowled. 'But no one knows who he is, not even the trainers. The first time he was here everyone was kept away from him for his protection. But he's been seen several times in the city since. And I know Pilos spoke to him that first time.' He moved her gently so that her back was to most of the fighters, screening his hands from view.

'You know they're saying he's not even Pechaqueh?' he signed, awe in his face. 'Think of it, Xessa. Think how high they let us rise when they see our potential. What might this mean for the rest of us, for a no-blood to be the next Singer?'

Xessa grabbed his hands in hers, stilling them. 'No-blood?' she signed, making her face as disgusted as she could. 'How can you use such language about other people? Are we all defined by whether we are or are not Pechaqueh? Are they the pinnacle we should strive to reach? Would you swap your proud Tokob heritage for theirs?'

Tiamoko flushed. He shook his head. 'Sorry, Xessa. It's . . . it's how everyone speaks. I hear it a lot. I'm sorry.'

He didn't answer her question, though, about who he wished to be. Xessa quashed her suspicion. Her own inability to hear what was said to and about her was, in this, a blessing. 'Never mind,' she signed reassuringly. 'What else do you know about this Shadow person?'

He pouted. 'Nothing. That's it. How do people live, not knowing what's going on around them?' he complained and Xessa almost laughed. Tiamoko's love of gossip hadn't been dimmed despite his captivity, and she was grateful for it. It meant he wasn't as broken by this place as his earlier slip indicated. Still . . . *how high they let us rise. Let us.*

He touched her arm and then pointed: the trainers were beckoning fighters over to collect weapons. Xessa accepted the combination of stabbing spear and axe – ridiculous – and found an empty space on the packed earth at the front, where she could see Kalix and Ilam. She took several slow breaths and sank into her focus. She needed to learn so that she could keep Tiamoko safe. She needed to be strong so that she could kill tomorrow.

The session had been hard, the awkward weapon configuration fatiguing both mentally and physically, and Xessa just nodded when Kalix sent her off to the healing hall to have her wounds checked for the last time. Her right hand throbbed, the muscles aching from her palm all the way up her forearm, inside and out, but she'd managed the axe and the transitions well enough. As long as she was permitted to fight with her favoured weapons of spear and small shield – *or net, why won't they give me a fucking net; it's what I know* – then her hand would stand up well in the fight tomorrow.

Shaman Tleote beckoned her in and she peeled off her tunic and then slumped onto the stool, letting the sweat trickle down her temples and drip from her chin. It had stained her breast band and Xessa's nose wrinkled when she heaved a sigh and caught the smell of old sweat rising from the cloth.

Tleote checked the wound. The stitches had come out a while ago and she no longer wore a bandage, but it itched and the shaman had to slap her hand away as she automatically tried to scratch at the long red scar. Xessa stared over Tleote's head and kept her hands still in her lap.

Finally, the shaman tapped her arm and then nodded. She took Xessa's right hand and made her flex and curl the fingers, pointing each in turn and then spreading them wide before clenching them into a fist. She nodded again and then gestured at the bucket and cloth in a corner and mimed washing herself.

Xessa slid off the stool and went over to the corner and stripped off the rest of her clothes. Squatting, she wetted the cloth and then scrubbed it across her skin. When she was clean, she scrubbed her kilt and breast band and tunic in the bucket too, and then put them back on dripping wet. She lifted a few palmfuls of water to her lips and drank greedily. It tasted bad, gritty with dust and other people's blood, probably, but the water rations were never quite enough and the slave fighters were used to stealing water whenever and wherever they could.

A guard was waiting to take her back to her cage and she went placidly. The free fighters and those who were indentured but nearing the end of their contracts would be relaxing in the training halls or even outside. Xessa, Tiamoko and the other second-year slaves were fed in their cages and not permitted to socialise without heavy bribes. Xessa was glad of it. She had a person to kill tomorrow and didn't much feel like reminiscing with Tiamoko beforehand.

Back in her cage, the eja took off her wet clothes and hung them on the bamboo bars to dry, then wrapped the thin blanket from her cot around her hips. She lay back on the thin, rough mat on its wooden frame and stared at the tiny lizard that lived with her. It was high up on the back wall this time, above her feet, waiting in stillness for spiders or insects. For a reason to move or live. She knew how it felt.

Duskmeal was corn gruel sweetened with honey and two roasted palm hearts. She ate and then lay down with her back to the cage door. Some time later, she felt the faintest vibration as of someone banging on the bamboo bars sunk deep into the dirt floor. Xessa didn't bother to turn over – if it was one of the trainers, or even Pilos or Elaq, they would come in and alert her with a touch. If not, then it was one of the free fighters come to try and torment her some more. Probably the twins.

No one did come in, and so the eja went to sleep. Easily, as if the morrow held nothing but more of the same.

The lizard was hidden out of sight when Xessa woke before dawn. She stretched on her cot and then stood, rolling her neck and spine before crossing to the bucket for a piss. Bladder empty, she dressed and sat cross-legged in the middle of her cage and performed her morning prayers and promises, her hands beating a very gentle tattoo upon the floor.

The increase of light on the back wall told her the door leading to the cages had opened. Xessa took some final deep breaths and twisted until her shoulders clicked. Then she faced the front. Kalix was there, her mouth sour, eyes wary. Two guards slid into the cage and beckoned Xessa forward; they carried clubs and whips.

The ejab lip curled in disdain and she stalked between them as if they didn't exist. Kalix led them to the armoury and Xessa gulped down three cups of tepid water and a cornmeal bun stuffed with meat and peppers. It was still warm from the ovens: they always served the fighters decent food before their bouts. Some sort of pre-emptive reward for the blood to be shed by their hands and from their bodies.

Kalix's sudden stiffness alerted her. When she looked up, Elaq had entered the room. He'd been away from the pit for weeks and then returned as if he'd never left. Tiamoko burnt with curiosity about that too, but they'd never learnt the reason for it.

The trainer and the guards left and Xessa stepped backwards, putting distance between herself and the warrior.

Elaq smiled and raised his palms. 'Just came to wish you luck on behalf of pit-master Pilos,' he said. Xessa frowned and then nodded and bared her teeth in an approximation of a smile. It was more likely that he had been sent to assess her mental state and the likelihood of her using this fight as an elaborate suicide. There would be little they could do if she had chosen that trail and she'd known – and respected – the few who'd done it back in the early days of her captivity, but she had Tiamoko to think of.

She could have tried to tell Elaq this, to reassure him and his master that she had every intention of surviving the day, but there was no point. Either she fought and killed or she fought and died, but both of those things were up to Malel.

'There may be important guests watching,' he added carefully and she noted how tense he was. No doubt they wished for some way to swap her for another fighter, but what little she knew of the rules of this bloodshed made it a difficult and costly endeavour. It seemed they'd decided to take the risk with her.

Xessa let her lip curl and shrugged elaborately, then checked herself. *No emotion. That includes taunting him.*

Elaq pursed his lips and then checked her spear and small shield for quality. He passed them to her and Xessa tested the weight and balance of the spear herself, the bannerstone and obsidian tip, searching for cracks or loose bindings. They seemed sound.

Belatedly, she looked back up at Elaq. Was he angry that she didn't trust his ability to examine the weapon? To her surprise, the man just gave her a single nod of respect. 'Fight hard. Win for your pit and your pit-master. Pay no attention to the crowd, special guests or not. Focus on your enemy.'

They aren't my enemy, she wanted to tell him. And, *I'll win for Tiamoko,* but what was the point? He wouldn't understand her and even if he did, he probably wouldn't care.

Instead, she nodded back and then followed him out of the armoury and up the sloping corridor towards the holding cell a short walk from the bloody earth of the pit's arena.

It was just past noon, the hottest and most humid part of the day, and the air was so close it was like trying to breathe soup. They sprinkled the arena's floor with water between each fight to try and keep down the dust. Not for the benefit of the fighters of course, but so that the spectators had a clear view of the pairs attempting to carve each other open below them.

Xessa could smell the fresh tang of wet earth from inside the tunnel where she waited. Wet with water and wet with blood. That smell, too, heavy on the thick air. Cloying. It always used to make Ossa's hackles rise, the smell of blood, make him stay close to protect her, his big head pressed to her thigh. Malel, but she missed him.

The tiers of benches were full except for one area directly opposite, curtained off to either side for privacy but also, strangely, with another curtain between the occupants and the pit. As if the blood would offend a delicate stomach. As if the blood wasn't the point.

The pressure of the crowd's noise beat against the ejab skin; the constant movement and drumming of sandals was a dull rumble through the soles of her feet. Coldness spread out from her centre as she got the guard's nod and stepped through the gate and onto the cool, shadowed dirt. The line of sunlight a few paces distant held sparkling menace, as if crossing it would forever mark her as something other. A murderer, perhaps.

The thought was ridiculous: she had fought and killed ten people in this pit so far. She was already a murderer. Perhaps the difference lay in the fact that before she had fought only so that she might live. Today she would actively seek the death of another and a swift and merciful ending for them. She didn't know whether that made her a better or a worse person and didn't dare think too hard about it.

Her opponent was a woman, shorter than Xessa but much broader in the shoulder. One side of her head was shaved and the rest braided in Tlaloxqueh fashion. Her front teeth, though, hadn't been filed to points. A Tlalox in name only, perhaps, wearing the traditions of her people purely to attract attention and bets.

Xessa breathed a prayer to Malel that she would find this woman's gods and make it right with them. Whoever those gods might be.

Even Drowned?

The question made her flinch and then settle deep into her skin. She was eja; she was also a child of Malel and the world.

I'm going to kill her, so yes, even if they're Drowned. I owe her that.

She halted, staying in the shadowed area as much for the coolness on her skin as to make it hard for her opponent to see her. An under-trainer shoved her in the back and she twisted to face him even as she stumbled, but couldn't read what he said. Had the fight started? She whirled back around to face the Tlalox, but the woman remained still.

She guessed he wanted her further into the pit, so she crossed the line of shadow and squinted as the sun lanced into her eyes, the heat suddenly pressing on her scalp. Xessa concentrated on her left hand, forcing the fingers to loosen one by one around the haft of the spear. Then she focused on her breath until it was slower, normal. Deliberate.

Blurs of faces in the tiers above, mouths open in derision

or hate or to be filled with fruit by nimble slave fingers. Expressions of disgust and avarice and a terrible, dark blood-lust as they examined her, looking for her injuries. Looking for weakness, like a coyote circling a wounded jaguar. Xessa's skin prickled. She ignored it and ignored them, searching instead for Pilos and Elaq who would give her the signal. Before she could find either of them, the Tlalox erupted into motion, racing across the earth towards her.

Xessa snapped into stance, left hand firm on her spear, small shield held up in her right. A settled calm draped like wings across her. The sun had lost some of its glare and she could see the Tlalox clearly. Her salt-cotton was thick and came to her upper thighs, slashed to the hips for ease of movement. Padding on her forearms and a thick flexible band of leather around her throat. Part-collar, part-protection.

The woman rested her spear on the top of her shield and advanced into range. Xessa stepped out of it, maintaining distance to learn how she moved: was the Tlalox faster or smoother; did she favour one leg over the other? Her opponent didn't give her much time for analysis, leaping forward and stabbing the spear straight for Xessa's chest.

Xessa flipped it aside with her own spear – *should've used the shield* – and thrust back, but the other fighter was already scrambling away. Her right hand itched for a net, not a shield, and she had to resist the urge to look down for Ossa. *Dog's dead,* she told herself savagely as her opponent circled to her right and she twisted on the balls of her feet to keep her in view.

The fighter attacked again, her lips writhed back in a snarl of hate. Again, the eja deflected – using the shield this time – and struck back. Let her opponent exhaust herself with hard, fast strikes and lunges. Let her think Xessa was still wounded and only able to defend.

But this fighter was too canny to fall into that trap. When it was clear Xessa wouldn't commit to a swift exchange of blows she slowed. Then she stopped. They faced each other, unmoving, crouched behind the paltry protection of their little shields, eyes locked. And then the Tlalox smiled, broke her gaze and glanced behind Xessa. The eja flinched but refused to turn; she'd fallen for ruses like this before and wouldn't be distracted now.

The end of a whip lashed into the back of her thigh, the pain equal to the surprise. She twisted towards the new threat on instinct and the other fighter stabbed for her. The obsidian tip of her spear punched into the salt-cotton protecting Xessa's flank. Instead of pulling back, the Tlalox ripped it downwards and the armour tore, a ragged rent exposing her side, her kidney and guts.

Xessa hurled herself sideways in a tumble and came up near the under-trainer who'd whipped her. Whipped her for no reason. He was from the Tlaloxqueh pit, not Pilos's, and he'd tried to distract her. This fighter wanted to be the one who killed an eja.

Xessa lunged, whipping her spear up in a diagonal line, and took out the under-trainer's throat in a spray of crimson. She leapt sideways before he'd even begun to clap his hands to the gushing wound, spinning her spear in front of her to parry any thrust the Tlalox might make, but the woman had paused, genuine shock and a flicker of fear racing over her flushed face.

Xessa threw her spear with everything she had. The Tlaloxqueh shield came up but too high and the spear took her in the thigh. She staggered back, mouth open in an agonised howl.

The Toko snatched up the under-trainer's whip and flicked it at the fighter's head. It was longer than she'd thought and instead of ripping out an eye, she lashed an arm's length of leather into her face. The Tlaloxqueh pulled out the spear and tossed it away, clamping her hand to the bleeding hole in her leg. Not bleeding fast enough, as far as Xessa was concerned.

She was three strides away when the Tlalox recovered and stabbed out with her spear. Xessa slapped it down with the shield – two strides – and she spun it to drive the butt up towards Xessa's chin – one stride – and the eja slipped the strike. Right hand punching the shield forward to protect her face, she crashed into the Tlalox and they both went down.

Xessa scrambled onto her knees and got the whip around the Tlaloxqueh neck as she tried to roll away, presenting her back. The eja squirmed until she got a knee between her opponent's shoulder blades and then she pulled and pulled until the woman was limp beneath her. As soon as she was unconscious, Xessa released the whip, got her arm around her neck instead, and with a twisting pull and the grinding of bones, snapped her neck. Swift. Merciful.

She paused for a long moment, praying over the dead woman's body, and then pushed herself to her feet, retrieved her spear and strode to the pit-gate. The audience wanted a performance. The Shadow, whoever he was, probably demanded one. He could demand it of another.

This cold, emotionless killer was what they had made her. It was time they got used to it.

The gate swung open and Xessa walked into the gloom of the under-pit. She didn't look back.

ILANDEH

Pilo's fighting pit, Singing City, Pechacan, Empire of Songs
216th day of the Great Star at evening

The Shadow had become . . . imperious in the last few days, and against Ilandeh's respectful advice, had insisted on visiting the fighting pit on new moon for an afternoon of entertainment. He knew they were death matches and still he'd insisted that was the best way to spend his time before making an offering to the holy Setatmeh at dusk. The Singer had allowed it, vicarious death to sate his desires. And with the Singer's approval, Ilandeh could do nothing but obey.

The Feather had been given some warning by the cheering crowds when Tayan's litter was spotted, but by then it was too late to swap out his fighters – and so there was Xessa. She'd fought and won with beautiful precision, including her decisive execution of the under-trainer who'd tried to distract her. Unexpected, but not unwarranted. If not for Xessa's contemptuous slaughter of the man, Pilos would have interrogated him and they could have discovered if Enet had instigated this additional little entertainment, or if it had been the work of the rival pit-master to aid his fighter.

305

Ilandeh's jade was on Enet. Because it had worked. The Shadow had thrown himself out of his seat and torn at the curtain as the under-trainer advanced, shouting for Xessa to beware, and everyone in the crowd had seen his distress. They'd heard his voice, too, and the northern accent that marred it. Pilos had done his best to smooth things over, but the Shadow of the Singer shouting warnings for an eja of Tokoban was not easily explained.

And now, outside the pit, Tayan was brooding. Arguing. Demanding to see Xessa. Pit guards and the Melody warriors that Pilos had assigned him as escort were blocking both ends of the road to keep away curious onlookers, but Ilandeh's skin prickled with the sensation of being watched anyway.

A particularly strident comment reached her and she looked back to see the Shadow gesticulating back towards the high wall of the pit. The words "don't you know who I am" were written clearly across his face, and Pilos registered them as she did.

'Shadow of the Singer,' the Feather said in low, harsh tones, 'would you shame the holy lord by consorting with ejab god-killers? The Mute—'

'Her name is Xessa,' the Shadow growled.

'*The Mute* is a slave condemned to my fighting pit. She is a self-confessed murderer and dedicated her life to slaughtering the holy Setatmeh, with whom I understand you have a unique relationship.' He gestured to the claw scars around Tayan's eye. 'I cannot allow you to bring the Singer's honour and status into question by permitting you to consort with such as her.'

'*She is my friend.*'

'Once, certainly, before your people were brought under the song and into civilisation. Now, your elevation beyond

306

anything either of you could have dared dream precludes you from her company.'

Tayan let out a howl of pure frustration and bunched his fists; Pilos merely inclined his head, prepared to accept the man's violence without reciprocation. 'She nearly died,' the Shadow said in a softer voice, thick with emotion. His hands stayed at his sides, flexing.

'You are Shadow now,' the Feather said kindly. 'The holy Setatmeh are your ancestors. Can you condone the M— condone Xessa's actions now that you know them so intimately? Is she more important than all those gods she and her kind have killed? More important than those who still live because there are no more ejab hunting them?'

The question was risky, because what could they do if the Shadow said yes, actually, she is more important? If he demanded once again to see her, even to free her?

'I—' The Shadow stopped himself. Slowly, the angry tension in his posture weakened until he slumped. 'She's my friend,' he repeated miserably.

'I'd venture to say that you no longer have that luxury, Shadow. You can trust Chorus Ilandeh, and you can trust me, but as for friends, I wouldn't look further for companionship than the Singer himself. With respect, you have no real idea of the position he has awarded you or the enemies it has bred. All your friendship, your love and loyalty, belong to him now. He is your family; he is your god.'

It seemed Pilos had decided that the only way to deal with the Shadow's identity and former life was to ignore it and pretend he was a worthy successor to the holy lord.

Ilandeh winced. *Of course he is worthy, the Singer would not have chosen him otherwise. And . . . he is clever and kind and talented. The holy lord has seen his potential. How much does his blood really matter?*

But if that's true, how much does anyone's *blood matter?*

Ilandeh clutched her spear until her knuckles cracked and checked the pit guards and eagles again. The Shadow's safety was her responsibility and in this she had seniority over them and even Pilos. Seniority granted by the lie she was a Chorus warrior. She had to be worthy of her position and ideas of blood and status wouldn't serve her. Despite herself, though, the thought crouched at the edge of her waking mind like a black jaguar on a night-time game trail. Sensed rather than seen. Deadly. And somehow alluring.

She studied Tayan's throat again as he shrank in on himself in the face of Pilos's accurate but gentle recrimination. Two elegant, finely drawn feathers, one either side of his windpipe, beginning in the dip between his clavicles and ending curled just below his ears. As art, they were exquisite. On him, they were obscene.

They were also far more beautiful than the single one sported by the Great Octave. It, too, had been tattooed by the Singer's own hand, but it was clumsy and ragged. Another example confirming that whatever they all thought about the Tokob status, he had done something remarkable in giving the Singer back to himself.

And hasn't he been rewarded for it?

'Take me back to the source,' the Shadow said, making no effort to hide the pout in his voice. He gave Pilos one last withering glare and then clambered into the litter and jerked the curtains roughly closed. Ilandeh exhaled silently, with relief and irritation both, and then signalled the eagles closest to her that they were moving out. They pushed forward, clearing the crowd that was waiting at the end of the road in the hopes of catching a glimpse of the elusive Shadow of the Singer.

The tension among the warriors as they shoved through

the throng was so thick it sat heavy in her lungs, low and cloying like smoke from fires set to clear the jungle.

My life means nothing in service of the Empire and the Singer, she reminded herself just in case, but the words rang a little hollower with each repetition. She couldn't help it; the higher Tayan rose, the more she wondered what she could be capable of if only she could slip her leash. If only she could serve in every way in which she excelled, instead of just within the narrow limits imposed by Pechaqueh prejudice. Why did Tayan get this – get *all this* – and she got nothing but a rope and the whip? Why was the Empire so intent on denying her abilities? On denying her worth? Why was she so much less valuable than *him*?

Ilandeh choked on her bitterness but took her place beside the litter nonetheless, the shouts of the crowd mostly confused. There were a few jeers and more than a few calculating, narrow-eyed stares in Pechaqueh faces as they shuffled reluctantly out of the way. She singled out a vocal protestor and glared at him until he blanched and ducked away. Her blood thrummed in her veins, hot and sparkling, and the soles of her feet itched with the need to move. Danger was a featherlight caress against her skin.

The eagles signalled and the litter-bearers set out, Ilandeh striding to one side with Pilos on the other and Tayan sulking within the shadowed confines. Officially, the Feather didn't need to accompany them, but Ilandeh was glad of his presence and the Shadow didn't seem to care one way or the other.

The entertainment district was finally emptying of Pechaqueh and second-generation – or more – free as the sun drifted to earth: it was almost time for the new moon offering. Soon only the drunk, the destitute and the desperate would be left while the brothels, drinking huts, and vision-sellers and the game-runners all reduced their prices in an effort to make people linger. To keep them from the rivers and the proper worship of their gods.

It disgusted Ilandeh, as did those Pechaqueh and others who took advantage of those reductions. She was disgusted – *she was* – but . . . if you didn't have much wealth to begin with and all you wanted was to forget the pain of your circumstances and Pechaqueh broken promises, even if you were Pechaqueh, then . . . *enough. Enough, Ilandeh. Fucking focus. Guard your mind and remember your duty. Chorus to the Shadow.*

She told herself it was enough, and she glanced at the Shadow's shadowed form within the litter instead of watching the road – and that's when they attacked.

Afterwards, she'd never know how much of it was her fault.

One instant they were surrounded by eagles in an empty street and the next the air was full of darts, humming past her to rip into the curtains. Rip into the eagles. One grazed her thigh, leaving a burning trench through her flesh. Ilandeh gasped and threw herself into the litter and on top of Tayan. The Shadow's shriek of alarm turned into a grunted wheeze as she crushed the air from his lungs. He made no attempt to dislodge her, if anything curling tighter beneath her weight.

She heard Pilos choke out a curse and the image of his face, already slashed beneath the jaw, leapt behind her eyes. She twitched, desperate to go to his defence, but forced herself to remain still. 'Quiet,' she snarled as the Shadow squeaked at another dart tangling in the curtain behind him. 'Feather?'

'*Protect the Shadow,*' he bellowed and then there was the clash of wood and obsidian and the bitten-off curses of combat. Thuds and grunts and shrieks from ahead, behind and the side, echoing from the buildings and the empty, unobservant roads.

'Stay down,' she hissed into Tayan's ear and then braced herself on forearms and feet, her body stretched over him but no longer pressing him into the cushions. The litter-bearers had somehow adjusted for her increased weight and were still moving, jolting as they lost their rhythm but hurrying forward.

Ilandeh rose onto her knees, straddling the Shadow's waist, and then pivoted off him to kneel facing away from Pilos, spear held across her body. She tried to make sense of the vague moving shapes visible through the curtain. Her leg was burning where the dart had scored it, the skin around it going numb. 'Fuck. Shaman? Tayan, are you listening to me?' she demanded. The Shadow startled and looked up at her with huge, terrified eyes.

Ilandeh slapped her thigh. 'Poison,' she said. 'Do something about it or I'm dead. And if I'm dead, so are you.' She used the tip of the spear to part the curtains just enough to get a sense of what was happening, twitching when Tayan's mouth fastened on the wound and began to suck. He spat quietly onto the cushion and sucked again, drawing death and pain out of her body and into his mouth. If they lived through this, he could have her killed for how she'd spoken to him.

She decided to worry about that if they did live. Right now, she wouldn't lay jade on any of them getting out of this alive.

'Darters on the roofs,' she shouted as her eyes registered movement. Half of Pilos's eagles had bows and began shooting back as they closed in on the litter and its occupant, making themselves a screen between Tayan and his enemies. Screams rose from the roofs and a few figures fell to the hard-packed dirt road, their limbs flopping and shrieks cut off with impact.

'I probably got most of it, but you still need medicine. The others might have an hour before paralysis and death,' Tayan said and spat again to clear the poison residue from his mouth.

'Feather, darts are poisoned, we've got an hour,' Ilandeh yelled through the curtain. 'Back to the pit?'

'Back to the pit,' Pilos roared just as the litter lurched and one of the bearers went down. Ilandeh and Tayan tumbled backwards at an angle, sliding off the padded seat in a tangle of limbs and the warrior's spear. She hit the dirt first, the Shadow thumping down on top of her a heartbeat later and driving the breath from her lungs with an explosive grunt. She grabbed his shoulder to flip them over and got a handful of his shawl, which tightened around his throat. A dart flickered past her head and she cursed, tore away the material and rolled them so he was pinned beneath her again.

'Get the fucking litter up,' she shouted as someone kicked her in the face as they stumbled over her. 'Move it,' she shouted again, spitting blood, and then the bearer who'd dropped his carrying pole was hauled out of the way – out of the circle of protection. He wailed and then screamed as darts sprouted in his chest. An eagle heaved on the pole, righting the litter, and Ilandeh bundled the Shadow into it without ceremony.

'We're secure, back to the pit, *move, move!*'

The litter lurched again, arrhythmic and staggering, but they hurried back towards the pit entrance with its barred gate. Ilandeh lay over Tayan again, her spear lost somewhere behind them and a flint knife in her hand that would do fuck all unless their attackers came down off the roofs to engage.

Their attackers did just that, swarming down ropes or exterior stairs in a desperate bid to cut them off from the shadowed safety of the under-pit. 'Setatmeh preserve us,' she breathed as half a dozen ran howling at the litter, visible through the torn curtain. The eagles surrounding it held their positions rather than charging to meet them, their bodies all that stood between Tayan and darts or thrown spears or axes. 'Stay the fuck down,' she threatened although it didn't seem like the Shadow had any desire to move. She tore at the laces of her salt-cotton, hunched on her knees and one elbow over the Tokob prostrate form, and eventually used the knife to rip it open, then she wriggled out of it and wrapped it over his head and back.

'Curl up, small as you can,' she instructed over the fresh clash of weapons and bodies ahead. 'Pull it around you and if we need to run, hold the fuck onto it, you hear me? Do not drop my armour, Tayan.'

'I won't, thank you, I won't,' he babbled, scrunching up beneath the salt-cotton and Ilandeh. Someone burst in through the curtains and sprawled across her legs. She began to twist and kick at the same time as they dug a knife into the back of her thigh. Ilandeh yowled and kicked again, scrabbling over onto her side and off Tayan, who yelped and drew his legs higher up out of the attacker's reach. She managed one good, on-target kick before the woman was hauled backwards off the litter. She vanished with a curse that became a scream.

'Get ready to run,' Pilos shouted without warning and Ilandeh swore and dragged Tayan up onto his knees, settling the salt-cotton firmly around him and getting his arms through it.

'When I say, we run and we stop for fucking nothing, you hear me?' she demanded and he nodded, shaking with panic, his lower lip chewed raw.

'Three. Two! *One!*' Pilos howled and Ilandeh threw herself out of the side of the litter into the shadow of the pit and dragged Tayan after her. Her leg shook and threatened to buckle, but she wrapped her fingers in his armour and sprinted for the shadowed gate where Trainer Kalix was waiting, armed and beckoning. Pit guards flooded out past her and even a few of the free fighters, throwing themselves on the desperate ambushers with frenzied yells.

Ilandeh and Tayan piled past Kalix into the dim tunnel and kept going, the warrior pounding through the gloom into the heart of the fighting pit. 'Feather?' she bawled over her shoulder and could have sobbed with relief at his roar of affirmation. She skidded into a right-hand turn, Tayan crashing into the wall and screeching in pain as she yanked him around it, then ducked through an open bamboo gate and into a row of cells, most standing open. Fuck. Fuck, he was no safer here than out there if this was where the slave fighters lived.

She slowed to a halt, knife tight in one hand, the other locked around Tayan's armour and her own blood squelching in her sandal as it ran from the knife wound in her leg. And then Elaq burst into the other end of the corridor, armed and armoured. Despite the old eagle's animosity towards her, she was flooded with relief at his sudden presence. His return from the Melody fortress was impeccably timed. He skidded to a halt, gaping, and then beckoned them forward, peering over their heads.

'I heard him. He made it through the gate,' she panted and he gave a single, brief nod and then gestured Tayan between them so he was guarded front and back. He led them deeper into the under-pit, past locked cages peopled with fighters crowded against the bars and watching in wide-eyed silence.

'Where's Xessa?' Tayan suddenly demanded. Elaq didn't reply and the Shadow halted so abruptly Ilandeh walked into his back. 'Where is Xessa?' he asked again. 'I'm not moving any further until I've seen her.'

'Shadow, we are under attack,' Ilandeh tried desperately. 'Now is not—'

'Shut up. Take me to Xessa,' he snapped and, impossibly, horrifically, his skin began to glow gold with song-magic.

'High one,' she said and Elaq turned with an urgent frown, for in her guise as a Chorus warrior, they had equal status and the honorific was inappropriate. He caught sight of the golden sparkles in Tayan's skin and blanched.

'She's in Pilos's office. After her performance earlier . . . and it is defensible,' he added reluctantly.

'Shadow, this is not a good idea,' Ilandeh tried again, but he just gestured with his golden hand and Elaq led the way, rigid with tension. What else could they do when Tayan displayed his power so openly? The Singer's power in his veins, his body. Unmistakable. Irresistible.

Xessa was standing facing the door when Elaq opened it. She began to kneel immediately, then stopped when Tayan shoved past him. Ilandeh followed him in and put her hand on his arm, stilling him. 'For your protection, I cannot allow you closer to an unrestrained slave fighter,' she said, and if it was a little petty, well, he deserved it. They were *under attack*.

'High— Elaq, please fetch the translator,' she added and the eagle hesitated and then ducked back out of the office.

Tayan wrenched his arm free. 'I need no fucking translator,' he snarled.

'No, but I want to know what you two say to each other. I will have to report this to the Singer.' *Your breach of etiquette*, she didn't add, but the way he hesitated and then glanced sidelong at her told her he understood. He gave an elaborate shrug, as if unconcerned, but made no attempt to speak or sign.

Ilandeh looked at Xessa, who was staring at Tayan as if he was an ancestor come to impart wisdom. She waved until the woman looked at her. 'Do not approach, do not touch him, sign nothing until I say so,' she said clearly. The muscles around the Tokob eyes tightened and she raised her hands. Ilandeh took Tayan's arm again. 'We're leaving,' she said, making sure Xessa could read it; she shook her head quickly and put her hands behind her back. There was such naked hope – such *need* – in the ejab face that the Whisper had to swallow against a sudden lump in her throat.

'You fucking bitch,' Tayan breathed.

'Just trying to keep you safe, Shadow,' Ilandeh said. 'From yourself as well as others.' They waited in hostile silence until Elaq returned with Tiamoko, who choked when he saw Tayan and then snarled when his eyes met Ilandeh's.

'You fucking—'

Elaq kicked him in the back of his knee and put a knife to his throat before he'd steadied himself. 'Translate exactly what they say or you and the Mute both die,' he said. Ilandeh didn't wonder whether Pilos would have anything to say to that.

'Very well, Shadow, say hello to your friend.'

Tiamoko jerked and tried to stand, then hissed when Elaq's knife parted skin. 'Shadow? You're the Shadow of the Singer? Gods and ancestors, Tayan, what? How?'

'Speak only to translate,' Elaq repeated. 'Chorus, your blade at the Mute's neck.'

They did an awkward little dance when Ilandeh refused to leave the door – she needed to be between it and the Shadow in case the attackers forced their way in – and then they were settled, Tiamoko on his knees and Xessa facing

Tayan, the tip of Ilandeh's knife against the side of her neck. 'Make it fast, Shadow. We're not safe here.'

'Are you well?' Tiamoko said rapidly at Xessa's frantically moving hands. 'Why are you here? Are you a slave? Why is *she* here?' His voice twisted at that last one and Ilandeh's face heated.

'I'm the Singer's anointed successor,' he continued at Tayan's response, excitement growing in his voice. 'I have power now; I can get you out. Free you. You can go home—'

'No, they can't,' Elaq interrupted. 'They don't belong to you, Shadow, and you can't make promises like that. It's . . .' He trailed off.

'It's cruel to give them false hope,' Ilandeh added as Tiamoko translated their words for Xessa. At least she hoped that's what he was translating.

'I am the Shadow,' Tayan insisted, gold flickering in his skin again. The other Tokob gasped and flinched away from him. 'I can do whatever the fuck I want.' He didn't get any further, his face suddenly twisting with pain. He clutched at his chest and staggered.

The door slammed open and Ilandeh whirled to face it; Xessa darted for Tayan at the same instant and Ilandeh hauled her back by the arm. It was Pilos. 'Get these slaves out of here,' he snapped. 'Shadow, you disrespect the trust and love that the Singer places in you,' he continued in the cold, even voice he used when he was angry enough to kill. 'Ask the historians in the source for a treatise on the duties required of your status. Until then, you are best not to say or do anything.'

He dismissed Tayan's simmering outrage as if it belonged to a squalling child and turned to Ilandeh, who almost winced on Tayan's behalf before remembering the Shadow was Tokob and a slave. 'The pit is secure and there are two pods of eagles on their way. They'll escort you back to the great pyramid and I will have a written report for the Singer ready in an hour. I'll follow you over then. My recommendation will be that the Shadow doesn't leave the source again.'

'You can't do that,' Tayan said immediately, as Elaq herded the other Tokob out of the door; they both looked back repeatedly, but if they signed anything, the words were blocked by the Pechaqueh broad frame. 'The holy lord himself wants me out in the city living life, experiencing all the things forever denied him. The holy lord himself—'

'You think if you are injured or killed that he will not experience that too, through your link?' Pilos demanded. 'I will not allow him to be harmed by your death, therefore I will not allow you to die, and if the only way I can do that is to keep you in the source, then that is what I will suggest.'

'You have my voice in this, Feather,' Ilandeh added.

Tayan laughed, the sound grating and unamused. 'You think I am any safer in the source?' he demanded. 'With Enet and Acamah and all their cronies?'

'Safer than you are wandering the streets,' Ilandeh insisted, but the look she shared with Pilos was troubled.

'I want them freed,' the Shadow insisted, changing the subject as if he knew he'd lost that argument.

Pilos shrugged. 'Certainly. I will free the god-killing eja immediately. She can walk out of this pit right now. Those who just tried to kill you will delight in tearing her apart.' Tayan began to protest and the Feather spoke over him. 'Or she can fight and kill for me every second moon and be completely safe the rest of the time. As I told you earlier.'

'Fuck you,' Tayan said bitterly. 'Fuck you both. Fuck you all. This isn't over.'

'As the Shadow commands,' Pilos said and Ilandeh had to bite her lip to swallow her smile. The Feather could be petty too, it seemed.

TAYAN

It was dark by the time Tayan returned to the source and he had missed the first new moon offering since being named Shadow.

Xac had been watching the death matches through him, and the song and the bite of his appetite had steadily increased throughout the day. It had jumped, sharply, at the ambush even though Tayan hadn't seen most of the fighting himself. It had been that distracted hunger, he thought, that had allowed him to seize a little golden magic and use it for himself. Much good it had done him. *Or Xessa.*

The spirit-pain that had ripped through him in the fighting pit had been slow to fade and he'd realised with a lurch of terror that his actions could lead to the Singer demanding both Xessa's and Tiamoko's deaths. His own arrogance haunted him.

As he stepped into the source proper, the increased force of the song took away his breath, as it did each time he returned from his excursions. Power and want and majesty and need and glory and Pechaqueh superiority and hunger pulled him in a thousand different directions. His feet faltered and he put his hand against his chest again, though not in pain this time. It was so much, the magic and the song coursing through him, the vine growing from the Singer into him, ever-strengthening. Binding them tighter.

The holy lord was waiting for him, impatience, worry and anger mixing in his body language and the song itself. 'My Singer,' Tayan said, hurrying across the mats and dropping to his knees before Xac, all the disparate parts of himself slotting back together in his presence, within his orbit. Two halves of a whole and the song the seed at their centre, pregnant with life and possibility so long as it was watered with blood.

'My sweet love, forgive me. Your Shadow made many mistakes today and forgot himself. Forgot you.' Tayan paused to swallow against the thick, cloying taste of regret. He really had forgotten himself. Pilos had been right: everything he was, the Singer had given him. 'I was ambitious and I was wrong, holy lord. Your Shadow begs your forgiveness.' Tayan pressed his face to the mat, his heart thudding at the base of his throat.

The wait stretched long as the song rumbled into something lower, predatory. Sweat seeped across Tayan's ribs and gathered at his hairline. There was nothing stopping the Singer from rejecting his plea. There was nothing stopping him from doing anything. *I was too arrogant. I forgot myself in the rush of freedom. In the . . . delight.*

Saliva filled his mouth when he remembered the death matches he'd watched, and the song's own hunger – the Singer's need – spiked with it. He should never have gone and couldn't remember now whether the idea had been his or the Singer's. What if . . . what if he'd wanted it?

Amusement rippled through the link between them. *We are one, my sweet love. We want the same things.*

We want Xessa's freedom? Tayan dared to think and then grunted when the Singer's foot stamped down between his shoulder blades, crushing his chest against his own knees. He was far heavier than Ilandeh.

'You venture much, little shaman,' the Singer crooned as the song spiked and rippled with rage. Tayan could feel the magic moving, but not through him. He knew if he dared look, he'd see the holy lord incandescent with it. 'Be careful lest I show my claws.'

'Forgive me,' he begged again. 'I love you.'

The Singer laughed. 'Of course you do.'

There was one final downward pressure from his foot, and an internal twist from their link that forced the last bit of air out of Tayan's lungs, and then the holy lord let him go. He remained where he was long enough to show proper – and heartfelt – deference, and then slowly sat up, eyes cast down. 'Feather Pilos will be here soon with a report about the attack,' he murmured. 'I don't know whether he took any of the culprits alive, but I am hopeful he will have answers. He fought with honour, and Chorus Ilandeh too.' He indicated the silent warrior who stood to one side in borrowed salt-cotton, a strip of bandage tied roughly around her leg. The Melody detachment's shamans had come with the pods and treated those who'd been poisoned by the darts, working alongside the pit's own shaman, Tleote.

Ilandeh, to Tayan's lack of surprise, had refused more than the most basic treatment until he was back safe in the source. He tried to remind himself that didn't mean anything: she was just doing her duty. They certainly weren't friends. *We weren't even friends in Tokoban, remember. She was using me and all the rest of us.*

Tokoban.

Xessa.

The Singer twitched and Tayan tried to put her from his mind.

'Enet, Great Octave and Chosen of the Singer, requests entrance into the holy lord's presence.'

'Shall we draw the curtain, my love?' Tayan murmured to the Singer before he could give her permission. After everything that had happened so far today, he couldn't bear to see that beautiful, lying face. Xac blinked once and then the corner of his mouth lifted in a smirk; he nodded and the Toko took great pleasure in pulling across the rose-coloured cotton and screening them from view. Enet had used to sit here, whispering her plots and schemes and poisons into the Singer's ear. Now it was Tayan's place.

'Enter,' Xac said and despite himself the Tokob gaze snapped to Ilandeh. She limped forward, planting herself between Singer and Shadow and the woman entering the source. Her intent was clear; the meaning behind it, too. Tayan relaxed and watched Enet's outline through the translucent material. If she paused in consternation at the drawn curtain, he couldn't detect it.

'Great Singer, I heard of the ambush of your Shadow earlier at the fighting pit.' She managed to inject venom into the last two words, somehow insinuating that both Pilos and Tayan himself were at fault for what had happened. The Tokob irritation grew, but so did the Singer's amusement. Tayan sought to emulate the holy lord's state of mind. 'May I ask if he is well?'

'My Shadow can answer for himself.' Tayan hadn't felt the Singer's words in his own mouth this time, and he smiled at this tacit permission to answer Enet as he saw fit.

'Quite well, Great Octave,' he said with malicious glee. 'I owe my life to both Chorus Ilandeh and Feather Pilos.'

'Ah. Yes. How interesting that I hear those two names spoken together,' Enet said easily. Tayan frowned, confused at the sudden change in topic. Was his health of no concern to her? 'And not for the first time, either.' There was another rustle of skin on mat and Ilandeh stood a little stiffer. 'Tell me, Chorus, why did you fetch Feather Pilos here when the holy lord elevated my slave to Shadow? Chorus Leader Acamah did not give you permission to leave the source.'

There was a flutter of impatience from the Singer, but Tayan was intrigued. Had she? He'd believed Pilos had come here to beg forgiveness for his capstone nearly being stolen.

'For the same reason you were notified by Chorus Lisek, Great Octave,' Ilandeh said steadily. The Toko watched her. 'To properly honour the Shadow's elevation. The Feather of the Singing City is responsible for the Shadow's safety – as he was today. It was important for him to be made aware the great Singer had chosen his successor, and you were not here at the time to pass him word.'

Tayan choked on a laugh at the thought of Enet scurrying to inform the Feather that her former slave was now destined to surpass her in greatness. What he would have given to bear witness to that exchange.

'Are you accusing the Chorus of something, Great Octave?' the Singer rumbled, Tayan speaking along with him again as the holy lord's spirit tightened its grip on his once more. A beautiful strangling.

'Not an accusation, holy lord. Merely the observation that Chorus Ilandeh left her duty to you, her Singer, to flee the great pyramid to bring a message to Feather Pilos. I would ask where her loyalty lies.'

There was a silence. 'Go on, then.'

More silence. 'Holy lord?'

'Ask her,' the Singer and his Shadow said with malicious sweetness. Tayan smothered another laugh, less successfully this time. Xac's playfulness danced in his veins, a delicious warmth.

'Feather Pilos of the Singing City requests entrance to the presence of the holy lord.'

The Singer grinned, wagging his finger at Enet although she couldn't see it through the curtain. 'Come in, Pilos. The Great Octave was about to question Chorus Ilandeh.' Their voices were jovial but laced with danger and the room flexed with the Singer's power in time with the whispers of gold in their skin. The heartbeat of magic.

'Oh?' Pilos's tone was mild as his shadowed form bowed to the curtain and then settled back on its heels. 'If it is a report of the ambush you want, Great Octave, I have it here for the holy lord. Along with my recommendation that, for his own safety, the Shadow be confined to the source from now on. It is clear that he – or you, holy lord – have powerful enemies.'

'I will decide that later,' the Singer said, dismissing the Feather's concerns over Tayan's life. Perhaps with enough warriors to protect him, he'd be able to continue venturing into the city, for both their sakes. And if so, there had to be a way to contact Xessa again. There had to be a way to help them. Help all Tokob, even. Surely he could do that, had the power for that? Perhaps if he pledged himself to their good behaviour? Would they settle and lead quiet lives under the song and leave the holy Setatmeh to their own lives and pursuits in return for freedom?

'Continue, Great Octave,' Xac said, interrupting his thoughts and sending a pulse of warning along their link at the same time. No pain, though. No crushing. A reminder to pay attention, no more.

'Why did this warrior come running to you when the Shadow was first elevated?' Enet demanded and Tayan made a surprised sound. He'd expected her to back down, to mumble an apology or excuse, not to actually go through with the questioning as if Pilos was some no-blood in the marketplace. Was she expecting a different answer from him, or to discomfit the pair in some way? Ilandeh's success at deception would see her come through the encounter unscathed, he was sure; perhaps the Great Octave expected to see some lie in the Feather's face.

'It is standard procedure for the Feather of the Singing City to be—' he began and Enet cut him off with an outraged snort. 'I was already on my way here, if you remember, to discuss with the holy lord both the attempted theft of my songstone and the attacks in Tokoban from over the border. As such, I would have found out anyway. Chorus Ilandeh was merely thinking for herself and performing her duty as she thought best, I expect. Why?'

'She is close to you.'

Pilos hummed. 'The Chorus is an exceptional warrior and we fought together in Yalotlan and Tokoban, but we are not close. There are fifteen thousand eagles in the Melody; do you expect me to know all of them?' His shadowed figure twisted to Ilandeh. 'Why did you come to me, Chorus?'

'It was my duty, Feather.'

'Well, there you are,' he said, as if that explained everything instead of nothing. Tayan regretted suggesting they draw the curtain – he wanted to see Pilos's face. Ilandeh's gave away nothing, as expected, but there had been something, the merest flicker in her stance, when he denied there was any intimacy between them. Again, he was seized with the urge to attempt a Listening. To Ilandeh this time. Perhaps later, when he had time. For now, he needed to ensure his sweet lord would continue to permit him access to the Singing City.

'And as for that unrest I mentioned in Tokoban, holy lord, I have received further reports on it. The Zellih – we presume Zellih as their land is closest to the Ixachipan border – are increasing the number and scale of their incursions. Farmland has burnt and villages been destroyed. A pyramid, too.'

Tayan felt the Singer's outrage in his own chest, but it was followed closely by a glow of hope. The Zellih had rarely been the Tokob friends, but perhaps they had finally seen the threat inherent in the Empire's incessant expansion. They could not still believe themselves safe beyond the mountains and the salt pans. Who knew what would really happen when the world spirit was awoken? Maybe it would demand further conquest. First Zellipan, and then all Barazal could well fall to the Empire of Songs. *If only they had allied with us back when I went to weave a peace . . .*

A twisting yank to his heart brought his attention back to his body and the holy lord, whose amber gaze gleamed with dislike. Tayan bowed his head. *My love. My sweet lord. My thoughts wander; forgive me.*

'I tire of this dissent. *Your* dissent.' The Singer's voice doubled and then trebled with music, reverberating off the walls of the source and the words in his mouth alone. Tayan suspected none of them knew whether he was referring to them, but he did. Tayan knew this was directed at him: the agony tearing at his spirit made it clear. 'Great Octave, your meddling bores me, as do your poisonous words. And Shadow, my little, little Shadow. Align your thoughts with mine or you will have no more thoughts at all. I will not warn you again; there will be no forgiveness for another lapse.'

Tayan pressed his face to the mat, panting through the pain as the red vine growing from the Singer's golden vastness tightened even further. Something in him – mind or spirit – gave way with a crack he almost heard. Drool ran from his mouth as he welcomed the Singer's might and majesty into him. As he let him obliterate all but love and worship. There was no Zellipan, no Tokoban or Xessa. No husband or Sky City, no shamanic oath or spiral path. No Malel.

He was what his Singer made him, that and no more.

No more.

'Chorus Ilandeh, you saved my Shadow today, along with Feather Pilos,' the Singer continued pleasantly, no indication in his tone that Tayan was a writhing collection of broken thoughts and desperate adoration flailing for life and forgiveness. 'You have my gratitude and I am pleased to see that at least some of those who surround me are worth my regard. Pilos, approach. I will read your report directly.'

There was a rustle and then the padding of feet and Pilos rounded the curtain bowed at the waist, with the report held in front of him. The Singer's spirit jerked Tayan upright as if by the hair; the Toko raised a shaking hand to wipe the saliva from his cheek and stared fixedly at the ground, struggling to breathe, to stay upright. To stay whole within the Singer's mighty love.

Pilos knelt and extended the report, but Xac bypassed the bark-paper to grab the Feather by the jaw, pressing his thumb cruelly hard into the healing slash beneath it. Tears sprang to Pilos's eyes, but he made no sound.

The magic roared and thrummed in Tayan's limbs and mind as the Singer poured himself into the warrior in a great golden rush, the movement of magic restoring his strength in a heartbeat. A sacred gift and a test. Tayan caught glimpses that must have been the Feather's thoughts. He felt along the connection between him and the Singer and from there poked tentatively against Pilos's mind. It gave easily, like a thumbnail through the yolk of an egg. The images cleared, became more numerous.

Was this Listening? If Xac felt him there, he gave no indication, but Pilos made a distressed sound, his body twisting like a snake pinned beneath a forked stick.

Magic erupted in Tayan's skin, ripples and streamers of gold racing from his fingertips up his arms to his chest, probably into his face. He shuddered, breathing in power and exhaling music as Pilos's thoughts came to him – his memories of the ambush, what he'd seen and done. Glimpses of attackers, shouted commands, Tayan himself prostrate under Ilandeh before the litter's curtain cut off his view. And injured or cornered ambushers killing themselves so they could not be tortured and spill the secret of who had hired them. He plunged deeper, ignoring the Feather's pained gasping, picking up random faces and places and putting them down again, further and deeper, seized with curiosity.

He was Listening for the first time, all Pilos's thoughts laid bare without Tayan even having to try. He was Listening – and he was good at it.

When it was over and the Singer pulled away from the Feather's mind, Tayan knew he could stay and how he might get back in whenever he chose. And if he could do it to Pilos, he could do it to anyone. Ilandeh, certainly. Enet, perhaps, though he already knew her defences would be mighty. Pilos had willingly opened himself to the Singer; the Great Octave would fight the Shadow with every weapon she possessed. Still, the possibilities were endless and Tayan's own status would increase with each thought read, every secret learnt.

Would it be enough to secure his position? If he could present his lord, his Xac, with the secrets of those closest to him? His palms sweated with possibility and anticipation and he breathed a prayer of thanks to Malel for teaching him to journey, and to the holy Setatmeh for imparting their wisdom that led to the Singer choosing him. Tayan had found his place and his reason in the world. Paid for not with jade but with secrets.

'I hunger.'

He blinked, jerking out of his contemplation of what he'd learnt of Pilos. The Singer's features were slack with need, though his eyes were sharp and cruel as all around them and within Tayan the song began to change. *The images of the ambush. They have stirred him again.*

Pilos looked to Ilandeh, alarm in the jerkiness of his movements. The Chorus warrior's face was shuttered, remote.

'Holy lord, today is not the appointed day,' Enet tried from behind the rose-coloured hanging. There was no appointed day any more, there was only however long they could delay the Singer's urges and it had already been by far the longest period between indulgences.

'The Great Octave is right,' Tayan said as the bright possibilities of power and control withered in the sudden black fire of the Singer's hunger. That power wasn't worth the deaths of innocents. It wasn't worth his participation in those deaths. He couldn't, not again; he had to get away. Free himself. Panicked, Tayan seized the red vine linking them and began to tear at it. The Singer reached out with hand and spirit, the former grabbing a handful of Tayan's hair and wrenching his head back, the latter whipping coil after coil around him, a constrictor far larger and stronger than the small, fearful prey it crushed.

'We don't need it, my love,' he croaked, tears running back into his hair from the pain in his scalp and his spirit. 'We have all the power and strength we need. Please, my love, let us not. Such an indulgence is no longer necessary to—'

'We?' the Singer asked, his tone soft but stretched with insatiable greed. He shook Tayan by the hair. 'Mere heartbeats ago you were nothing but a drooling heap on the floor, an extension of my will and desires. Now, once again, you fight me. You fight the inevitability of my strength and you speak of "we". There is no "we", little shaman. I'm inside you and I know exactly the small, pathetic limits of your ambition. I have allowed it to proceed this long to judge for myself to whom you give your loyalty, love and life. And I think it is not to me.'

'It is, holy lord, it is,' Tayan gasped as the crushing pressure increased. 'You have it all, everything I am. You have me.'

Xac drew him close by the hair and nuzzled Tayan's jaw with his nose, then licked over his chin and into his mouth. The hunger swelled further, overwhelming his defences until he was panting with need and his fingers curled into claws.

The Singer ripped away the curtain and Enet hunched lower. 'We hunger,' they said together. '*We need.*'

'As the holy lord commands,' Enet said and snapped her fingers. Her slave, waiting at the source's entrance, vanished through it to fetch offerings for the Singer – and his Shadow.

Tayan writhed gently in place, his mouth watering and his stomach churning with hunger and revulsion until acid scoured his chest and throat. He whimpered and the Singer's hand gentled in his hair until he was cradling the back of his skull, pulled against his chest.

'Hush, my love,' the Singer crooned. 'We'll feel better soon. We'll be full and happy and our song will ring across the Empire and none shall doubt our power.'

The holy lord's lust rose in the Tokob belly and Tayan stretched up to kiss Xac again, to twine their tongues together and wrap his hands in his tunic. Desperate. Needy. Distantly, he heard someone muffle a sound of distress. Xac broke the kiss when two slaves stumbled into the source, their terror melting immediately into love and want. They approached easily, the song a caress that drew them forward.

The Singer's burning gaze swept the source. 'The rest of you: out.'

The Great Octave and Feather Pilos bowed and fled. The Chorus remained, as was their duty. Tayan remained, as was his desire. A slave slid into his lap and a knife, pale quartz blade and jaguar-bone handle, slipped into his hand.

'My sweet love,' he murmured as the slave wrapped long, slender legs around his hips, arms around his neck. 'Come, my sweet. Give me everything you are.'

THE SINGER

The source, Singing City, Pechacan, Empire of Songs

We are the Singer and our song is blood. See how it strengthens us and crafts the song into ever-higher glory. We are the song and it shines red with life and majesty and power.

Yet I feel . . . less present than before, holy lord. Drowsy and a little lost. How can this be strength? How is it glory when it dulls our edges?

Ah, little shaman, it does not matter how you feel. You are my Shadow, not my self. Not my body or my mind or my power. My Shadow. Do not make me blaze so bright that you are burnt away, my love.

I would not. I will not. But is there not another way to strength and glory? We already – *you* already – have so much more control than before. You are so . . . here, so alive again. The blood may not be the medicine you think it is. I am a shaman; let me—

Enough! Still you fight it, fight me? You have been given more opportunities than anyone ever before in the story of

Pechacan and the song-magic. You will have no more. If you love me, make me believe it. For I am the Singer. And my song – your song – is blood.

PILOS

The source, Singing City, Pechacan, Empire of Songs
216th day of the Great Star at evening

Pilos didn't flee the source when the Singer threw them out. He knew what was coming and a shiver rose from the soles of his bare feet all the way to the crown of his head. His fingers clutched at empty air, seeking a weapon.

Still, when he left the great oval chamber for the long, beautifully painted and utterly empty corridor, instead of hurrying along it, he found an alcove and slipped within. He was familiar with how the song was stronger within the pyramid, but even so, he wasn't prepared for the emotions that burnt in him because of its hunger. Anger fizzed through his veins, an anger put there by the holy lord. Need, too, a cruel, arrogant desire to take and take without regard for others.

'Feather,' Chorus Leader Acamah said as he ducked into the alcove, already tense with what was to come.

'Should you not be attending upon the great Singer?' Pilos asked, surprised.

334

'Chorus Ilandeh has it in hand,' Acamah said quickly, unable to quite suppress a shudder, and Pilos wondered how many of his other duties he shirked or put on her shoulders. 'Actually, now that you are here, I need to speak to you in private. What I have to say is not something for other ears.' He paused, anticipating a reaction.

Pilos gifted him a single raised eyebrow. Was this really the time for a confidential conversation? The song sparked and jumped and he gritted his teeth against the urge to punch Acamah in the throat just to shut him up.

'Feather, while who you take to your bed is your own concern, I fear Chorus Ilandeh's loyalty is given too much to you as a result. Her mind and spirit should be directed towards me and the great Singer, not you. I can no longer allow it.'

Acamah braced as if expecting to be attacked, though whether in response to his outrageous statement or the spiralling song, Pilos neither knew nor cared.

He allowed his other eyebrow to rise to join the first and thanked the holy Setatmeh he wasn't allowed to carry weapons within the source. Ilandeh? Of all people, Acamah thought they . . . *Ilandeh?*

'You will not allow it, you say?' he repeated, instead of any of that. 'What exactly is it that you will not allow?' He leant in and Acamah leant back, his throat bobbing as he swallowed. 'Whatever my private relationships are, Chorus Leader, and whoever is involved in them, they remain exactly that. Private.'

Acamah shifted awkwardly on his feet and they both flinched when the song suddenly twisted out of its now-frantic rhythm into something even wilder. Rage and lust surged in Pilos and he snarled in Acamah's face.

'She came to you without permission—' the Chorus Leader tried.

'Chorus Ilandeh has protected the Singer for longer than you have; today she saved the Shadow's life. Her loyalty is undoubted. And she came to me because it was her duty, even if you neglected to inform her of it.'

'Saved the Shadow? She saved the savage who has stolen the Great Octave's position, you mean,' Acamah said with a complete lack of self-preservation. Pilos let the song tempt him and punched the man in the gut, doubling him over and ripping the spear out of his hand at the same time.

'The Singer can have you executed – or kill you himself – for dishonouring his Shadow,' Pilos threatened. 'Where is *your* fucking honour? *You disrespect the Melody; you disrespect the Chorus; you disrespect yourself.*'

Acamah's words were lost along with his breath and he made no attempt to speak or wrest his weapon back out of the Feather's hand. He looked away instead, finding the mural on the opposite wall a source of sudden fascination as he straightened against the pain. There was anger but also fear sketched across his features.

'You have sold your honour in return for the Great Octave's favour,' Pilos said softly, almost lost beneath the song's howl. Again, Acamah didn't respond, but his cheeks flushed at the implication.

Pilos let the topic die, though knowing there were rumours about him and Ilandeh circling through the source – and therefore the city – made him itch. Still, better this gossip than questions about the purity of her blood which, for one heart-stopping moment, he'd thought was what Acamah was going to say. This was merely salacious gossip; that would see them both executed.

The song screeched again, pulling his thoughts back to the source, and then it began to claw at him, a sudden and inescapable onslaught: lust and hunger and cruelty and the need to hurt and rend and bite and tear. A sound between a whimper and a groan slid from his throat and he found himself clutching his temples in both hands, his fingers buried in his hair and the confiscated spear clattering to the ground. Acamah gasped and squeezed shut his eyes, turning his face to the wall and hunching his shoulders.

It was a storm of emotions wilder than any Pilos had ever felt even in the middle of combat. He didn't know how long it lasted: somewhere between an hour and an eternity passed before it finally settled, the song drifting into satiation and a sleepy sort of contentment. The Feather found himself slumped against the wall, panting as if he had run the entire perimeter of the Melody fortress. He spared a glance for Acamah. The need to hurt him had faded with the song's violence, but the knowledge that he was Enet's creature and utterly unfit to lead the Singer's guards remained true.

Pilos pushed away from the wall and prayed his legs would hold him. They did, just, and he walked back into the source with barely a wobble.

Singer and Shadow lay tangled together as if the orgy had been one of sex, not killing, although perhaps it had been that too. He'd watched the Shadow kiss the holy lord as if in love with him, with a tender greed that spoke of want. Ilandeh and Shaman Kapal were dragging the remains of a corpse out into the gardens, and even the Great Octave was tugging up the mats that were most saturated with blood. She glanced up, distracted, when Pilos entered and then straightened.

'Why are you still here?' Her voice was flat and curiously weary, its usual aggression missing.

Pilos, too, had been wondering what excuse he might give – and, in truth, why he had stayed. Was it concern for the Singer's safety or a voyeuristic curiosity as to what actually happened during an offering? If it was the latter, he regretted it now. 'I need to debrief Chorus Ilandeh on the ambush,' he said.

Enet stared at him and then, to his surprise, turned away and tugged up another mat. It was blood-slick and slipped from her stained fingers to slap wetly back into the puddle that had seeped through it to the stone beneath. She muttered something under her breath and dragged at it again.

Pilos studied the graceful curve of her back as she bent. He'd been expecting an interrogation or a clumsy attempt to divert his suspicions from the obvious and logical mind behind that ambush – Enet herself. Perhaps she was overly confident that none of the attackers had survived long enough to implicate her. In that, unfortunately, she was correct.

Pilos switched his attention to the two men spattered with blood and entwined in each other's arms. The holy lord and his Shadow looked lazy and sated, as sleepy as infants. Swaddled in death. The song had settled into a steady, contented thrum that surged with power and clarity. It was the clearest and closest to its previous majesty since its breaking.

He no longer had to wonder why, on that fatal day, everyone within the walls of the pyramid had been helpless to resist the Singer summoning them into death. If there had been so much as a whisper of command in the song today, he'd have run into their arms himself.

Ilandeh returned from the garden where she'd dragged the corpse and Pilos hurried to her side. 'Are you all right?' he murmured, too low for others to hear him.

Ilandeh gave him a tired smile that cracked at the edges. 'Thank you, Feather, I am well. It was . . . restrained compared with previous offerings.'

It took Pilos a few seconds to parse her meaning and then his eyebrows rose. 'The Tokob doing?' he breathed.

'I am neither a shaman nor a Listener, but it seems likely. He is the only new factor in the offerings.'

The scent of blood sharpened as Enet dropped a sodden mat at Ilandeh's feet with a pointed look. The Chorus stared at her impassively for an instant and Pilos bent down and picked it up before they could begin circling like dogs.

'Allow me,' he said smoothly, rather than explain that he would prefer Ilandeh to keep her eyes firmly fixed on the Great Octave and her proximity to the Singer. 'Easy,' he murmured under his breath and Ilandeh shot him a look. Pilos headed into the gardens with something like relief. He dropped the mat on the small pile next to the bodies and allowed himself one single analysing look at the ruin of two lives. It was worse than a death in battle, no matter how brutal that often was. This looked more like an attack by a jaguar or a pack of coyotes, though he noticed the marks of stab wounds. He wondered whether they'd come before or after the bite marks. But Ilandeh had said restrained, so maybe, Setatmeh willing, they'd been slaughtered first and . . . chewed second.

The Feather coughed and drew in a deep draught of fresh air to clear the stink from his nostrils. The carefully clipped gardens were, aside from the corpses and bloody mats, pristine and breath-taking, a slice of wilderness without the fangs or chaos of true jungle. An illusion, like so much else in the source. *Excepting the holy lord's majesty.*

Pilos squared his shoulders and returned to Ilandeh. Enet, too, appeared toothless in the aftermath of the offering and that gave him a chance to move.

'Acamah believes us lovers,' he murmured and clearly heard the Whisper's shocked inhalation. 'At least he isn't questioning the strength of your blood, and it explains your actions in telling me of the Shadow without orders.'

'I understand, Feather.'

One more deception for her to weave into the cloth of her disguise, only this one directly implicated Pilos. At least the idea of a Feather and a Chorus warrior put them almost equal in status. His mouth twisted at what people would think if they knew her as a macaw. Ilandeh's father and thousands of others may see little wrong in bedding a no-blood, but such an act held no interest for Pilos.

Now that the fury was over, slaves and more Chorus warriors were appearing back in the source, Acamah with them, sidling in as if hoping no one would have noticed his absence in the first place. Two pretty young slaves brought blankets and cushions for the Singer and his Shadow, who appeared to have no intention of moving for quite some time. The slaves were nervous, but they wrapped the men with gentle hands and rested their heads on the cushions. No one attempted to bathe the blood from them.

Ilandeh saw the direction of Pilos's gaze. 'The Singer will rest now,' she said in a neutral voice and he exhaled silently, unsure what he would have done if she'd decided to begin a subtle flirtation intended to be noticed.

'He rests so that he may weave the offering's strength into the song and make us all stronger. Make our Empire of Songs more glorious and more powerful. Make himself a little more ready to wake the world spirit.' Enet's voice rang through the source and Pilos was impressed at the level of self-deception she displayed. That she continued to say such things would, under other circumstances, be laughable. There couldn't be a single person left in the great pyramid who believed that anything the Singer was doing was in any way for the world spirit or to the Empire's glorification. Or sacred.

'The Singer will not rest. He does not need to, for he has taken much strength. Much medicine.' The holy lord and his

Shadow rose to sitting as one, with that eerie synchronicity Ilandeh had told Pilos of, but which he'd never seen. Everyone in the source excepting the Chorus warriors fell to their knees.

'The magic builds,' the Singer added and he and the Shadow gestured together for Great Octave, Feather and Shaman Kapal to approach and sit. Ilandeh stood to one side, spear at the ready. After a long, awkward pause, Chorus Leader Acamah hurried over to take his proper place opposite her.

Pilos was consumed with second-hand embarrassment for the man and mortification that an eagle could be so oblivious to their duty. He tutted, very softly, but in the lingering silence of the source, the sound carried. Acamah flushed; Enet glared. The Shadow grinned and the Feather felt another brush against his mind, softer this time but no less invasive than the one that had ripped into him during his communion with the Singer. He carefully constructed the image of himself as a boy, kneeling on the stinging-hot stone of the grand plaza with his brow pressed to it, being presented to the great pyramid for the first time. Scents and sounds and the roughness of the grit under his knees; the awe and majesty of the song and the pyramid itself, gleaming blood-red in the bright sun; the Singer, a tiny figure poised beneath the white glimmer of the capstone at its summit. His most cherished memory and a powerful barrier.

The scratching fell away and the Shadow stared at him, surprised and then thoughtful. Pilos didn't miss the tiny flicker as he cut his eyes towards the Singer and then away and wondered if he'd made a mistake. But while he had nothing to hide, he also had no desire to be so thoroughly invaded just so the Shadow could sate his curiosity.

'I will perform the ritual to wake the world spirit on the first night of the Great Star's little absence.'

341

The Singer's words were entirely unexpected and, on instinct, Pilos looked to Enet. Her mask had cracked, just a little: her hands were clenched tight in her lap. No doubt he wasn't supposed to know.

It's happening, the one thing she can't allow if she hopes to be Singer. She needs to take power before the ritual or she'll never ascend. The threat to the holy lord's life just became acute.

'After much deliberation, I have decided that Enet, Kapal, my sweet love, and Chotek will assist. Do we have everything we need?' The Singer looked at Enet as if they were picking up the threads of a conversation broken off only a moment ago. Pilos did some quick calculations: it was just over one month away. *Setatmeh preserve us, she'll be like a cat in a trap now, wild and more dangerous than she's ever been.*

'We do, holy lord,' the Great Octave said with serene calm. 'You will weave a mighty magic and change the world.'

Pilos bit the tip of his tongue and then spoke anyway. 'Do you have the songstone?'

The Singer frowned, the Shadow looked between them in puzzlement, and Enet twitched. A minute movement he would have missed if he wasn't watching for it.

'The ritual doesn't require songstone,' the holy lord said.

Pilos inclined his head. 'Ah, forgive me, great Singer. It seems my education has abandoned me. My old tutor would be ashamed at this one's poor recollection of her valuable teachings.'

'You saved my Shadow's life, today. There is no need for forgiveness.'

Pilos bowed deeper. 'The holy lord is too generous. If anyone should be praised, let it be Chorus Ilandeh. Her dedication has been exemplary. If she was one of my eagles, I'd—ah, I beg the holy lord's forgiveness. This one spoke out of turn.'

This time Enet's glare was poisonous.

'You'd what, Feather?' the Singer asked, placing a proprietary hand on the Shadow's leg. They were both still covered in blood, which was flaking off in small red clouds as it dried. The smell hung heavy in the air despite the breeze through the colonnade.

'I would have recommended her for elevation to Feather and a command of her own.'

'And yet you are not, and she is not, and so the words themselves are empty,' the Great Octave said with a hint of fake regret. 'Perhaps it is affection that makes you speak so. Chorus Leader Acamah is—'

'With respect, Great Octave, you are not a warrior. Acamah's performance has been less than I would expect of a Chorus Leader.' Pilos's voice didn't shake and Ilandeh didn't look at him, though she had to be wondering what the fuck he was doing.

'Acamah was a fine eagle, but he has no head for command. I doubt his performance and, being honest, his loyalty. Why was it Ilandeh who had to take it upon herself to alert me to the Shadow's elevation? That was the Chorus Leader's job, yet the only person he informed was you. Why was it Chorus Ilandeh who stayed in the source to protect the Singer and Shadow during the offering? That, too, should be Acamah's responsibility. Out of the two of them, only one performs their duty and measures up to the standards required of eagles of the Melody, let alone leader of the warriors dedicated to the Singer's own safety.'

Pilos waited for Acamah's outburst, but all the man did was look to Enet for confirmation of how he should act. The Feather waved his hand. 'There. He doesn't even attempt to defend himself.'

'Chorus Ilandeh's loyalty is only to you,' Enet said. 'The doubts you have about Acamah, I have about her.'

'She has never shown the slightest hint of disloyalty during my time here,' the Shadow said, startling them all. 'She has undertaken every single duty required of her without complaint. She was wounded today in my defence and despite that, she removed her own salt-cotton to give to me. When the time came, she kept me safe and still treated me with respect.'

Pilos had a vivid memory of Ilandeh shouting threats at the Shadow, and from the amused glitter in his eyes, her words hadn't gone unnoticed by the man himself, but it seemed that he, too, would rather have Ilandeh in charge of their safety. The warrior herself was blushing, the thin scar below her eye and across her nose standing out pale against the flush.

Pilos looked to the Singer, who was watching him. He prostrated himself immediately.

'I agree,' the Singer said and the Feather was glad his face was hidden by the mats. 'Acamah stays, but Ilandeh is Chorus Leader.'

Shit. That hadn't been quite his plan. And yet it was done.

Ilandeh shifted her spear just long enough to touch belly and throat before resetting it in her hands. 'The Feather does me too much honour,' she said in a strong voice. 'And the great Singer does me even more. I shall endeavour to live up to your trust in me and I will protect you and your Shadow until my dying breath. Against all enemies. Chorus Acamah, I would be pleased to learn from you to ensure a smooth transition of command. As the holy lord commands.'

'A wise decision, my love,' the Shadow said, pressing a kiss to the Singer's bloody cheek.

'I thank the great Singer for his wisdom,' Pilos said while Enet bristled enough to rival a porcupine but was unable to add her voice to the discussion. 'Chorus Leader Ilandeh, in response to these shocking events, I suggest that you deliver a weekly report to High Feather Atu on the temperament of your fellow warriors. Any signs of disloyalty must be dealt with immediately. The Chorus has always been incorruptible; I trust you to ensure it remains so.'

'My life to serve, Feather. I will submit my warriors and also myself to weekly inspections so that you might assure yourself of the holy lord's safety,' she added, and in that moment Pilos could have kissed her and proven the rumours right. An open line of communication between himself and the source – the one thing he'd never had, that he and then Atu had always wanted – she had handed to them.

Pilos nodded. 'A wise suggestion and one that, with the holy lord's permission, I will accept.'

You can start by watching Enet for us. Her ambition isn't choked; her lust to become Singer isn't dimmed. She's going to try for power soon. She has to, if she is to be the Singer who wakes the world spirit.

Thirty-five days until the ritual. She must strike before then. And she will.

They watched each other, polite masks in place and weapons hidden behind their backs. Except for Ilandeh. She was extremely visible and she knew it. Pilos trusted her to watch her own back; he just didn't know how long she could do that while also watching the Singer's.

Until the Great Star's little absence and the world spirit is awoken by Singer Xac, he reminded himself. *If she dies after that, it'll be a sad loss, but a bearable one. Her life is mine to use as I see fit and we both know it.*

So live a little longer, Ilandeh. Just a little longer.

XESSA

Tayan was alive.

Tayan, the friend of her heart, was not just alive but was also, apparently, someone very important in the Empire of Songs. Xessa had never cared for the politics or hierarchy of her captors and in the immediate aftermath of the meeting, when Elaq dragged them both away, there hadn't been time to question Tiamoko. She'd spent hours restlessly pacing in her cage, worrying at how Tayan had been freed and elevated so fast, when the glimpse she'd had came back to her – the shaman's spiral path tattoo inked into his shoulder and branded with a narrow triangle. A slave brand that hadn't been scarred through.

That made even less sense and by the time she saw Tiamoko at the next morning's training, she was almost frantic. He told her how rumours had flown through the pit in the aftermath of the attack on Tayan, with fighters shouting guesses and theories to each other along the

corridor of cages. Those who were second-or-more-genera-
tion citizens of the Empire of Songs were outraged that a
foreign slave would be named Shadow, with most concluding
that he was an imposter or it was some sort of test by the
Singer of his people.

Told her, too, how he'd admitted his and Xessa's friendship
with Tayan and the Shadow's full identity. The animation in
his face had faded a little and he'd been aggrieved at how
few pit-fighters believed him, most believing him to be lying
outright, or claiming a status by association where there was
none.

Tiamoko had fed her as much information as he had in
the snatched moments before and after training, though
neither of them knew what was true and what invented. It
hadn't been long before Tayan was being painted as a foreign
shaman who'd cast some evil northern magic on the Singer
to kill him. Only the Singer's great strength and mastery of
the song-magic was enough to stop him.

They'd laughed at that one, the idea of Tayan using magic
for evil intent, but as the days passed and the rumours
grew ever wilder and the great pyramid did nothing to curb
them – and Tayan himself sent no word – Xessa began to
worry. She'd watched with increasing anxiety over the last
year as Tiamoko's language changed, his talk that of status
and honour granted by pit-master Pilos, of the song's
majesty and the glory it promised in return for obedience.
One thing everyone agreed on was that being close to the
source of magic itself made it impossible to resist. If Tayan
really did regularly visit the great pyramid as his position
as Shadow suggested, maybe his ability to remain clear-
headed was compromised.

Maybe Tayan was no longer her Tayan, Lilla's Tayan.
Maybe he was a cheap Pechaqueh version of Tayan. The

thought made her mouth twist, but the way Ilandeh and Elaq had held knives to her and Tiamoko, not to him – the way he'd been wearing armour clutched around him and the fine dyed cotton of his clothes . . .

Doesn't matter. He promised to free us, to help us, even if Elaq said he couldn't. He'll find a way and he'll still be him and we can go and find Lilla and, and, and Toxte—

Xessa couldn't finish the thought. *I'll never be free*, she reminded herself, picking at the raw wound in her heart. *I am eja and that is my death sentence, no matter what Tayan could say or do.*

Despite herself, despite the peace she'd made with that, she couldn't help the tendril of hope, as small and tender as the first unfurling of a pea shoot, that whispered that maybe, maybe, things might be different now. Because Tayan was going to save her.

Deliberately, Xessa examined the stone and bamboo walls of her cage and ran her fingers over the raised brands on each upper arm. She felt the thick supple collar around her throat and then she stamped, very deliberately, on that soft little tendril of hope. She would fight and train and kill and eat and free Tiamoko with the strength of her arm and the cunning of Snake-sister. There was nothing else in her future, and no hope to be found from the people of her past. Xessa was in her cage, and Tayan was in his and only chance had brought them together that one time. It wouldn't happen again.

Reassured that her purpose and her will remained intact, Xessa settled down cross-legged to await dawnmeal and that day's practice.

According to Tiamoko, there were other rumours from that day, and they were all about her. How differently she had fought and how cold she'd been afterwards. How she'd slaughtered the under-trainer who had sought to distract her. Word was that Pilos had had to pay the man's worth in jade to pit-master Mazte and that debt had been added to Xessa's. She shrugged at that, as she did at everything being said about her. The pride she'd felt as an eja had no place here. She wasn't like Tiamoko and the other fighters, who craved recognition from the crowd and the trainers. What did it matter to her, the reluctant approval of the people of this pit?

She took up her usual place at the front of the underground training hall and Tiamoko found her there a few moments later. 'Tayan's name is all over the Singing City. Zimio over-heard Casiv, who'd had a visit from his and Vorx's cousin. Everyone knows he's the Shadow.' Tiamoko's excitement was obvious and he was practically bouncing on his toes as he signed. 'How many others do you think have earned their freedom? It's so much faster than I expected. I thought we'd be here years, but he did it in two, probably even less to get elevated so high so fast. We might be only months away from our own freedom, Xessa. Think about it, think about all we'll be able to do when we're free in the Empire.'

His grin was big and enthusiastic, inviting her to join in his delight. 'Tayan can't have been condemned as we were,' Xessa signed deliberately, refusing to admit how much it hurt to destroy his hopes. But they needed to be practical. 'He hasn't seen the inside of a fighting pit or the Melody fortress. Likely he made medicine to save his owner's life and was freed for that. As for this Shadow business—' She cut herself off when Vorx stalked past her. She stared back, dead-eyed and fearless, until he blinked and made an elaborate show of greeting his twin instead.

'You're beginning to frighten them,' Tiamoko signed when she faced him again. 'I like it; they don't know what to do about it. At this rate you'll be taking my own status from me. But I pray you're wrong about Tayan. We just need to work hard, as he did.'

Xessa tensed. 'Your status?' she signed. 'Since when did Tiamoko of Tokoban remember his honour? I recall you showing up for your first hunt in Lilla's Paw with your salt-cotton on backwards.' He swatted at her, laughing and not at all embarrassed. 'But I am sorry,' she added, confused and a little wary that her friend now viewed her as a rival.

He waved it away and grinned. 'Don't be sorry, little eja. You have finally learnt to protect yourself from at least one of the evils of this world. I'm proud of you.'

Xessa pursed her lips against a smile and raised one eyebrow. 'I'm ten sun-years older than you, boy,' she signed primly. 'But thank you for being proud of me.'

Tiamoko laughed again and nudged her and she felt the warmth of him – skin and humour and affection – scrabble at the stone walls around her heart that even the sight of Tayan hadn't been able to knock down. It would be so easy to let them both in and so very, very dangerous. Xessa's heart wasn't made to be hidden away, but if she left it bare to the world, she'd never find the strength she needed to save Tiamoko.

Kalix walked to the front of the training area, cutting off their conversation, and under-trainer Ilam positioned himself in front of the Tokob. They didn't make Tiamoko move away, so he translated for Xessa as the trainers ran through the sequence of blocks and locks and the eventual throw they would be practising so that she had a rare full under-standing of the drills to come. They began by moving slowly against imaginary opponents, allowing the trainers time to come and correct each movement and stance before they partnered up and began to practise properly.

They were dismissed just before highsun to rest and drink water. Kalix tapped the Tokob on their shoulders as they began to leave with the rest. She murmured something Xessa didn't catch and then beckoned.

'The Feather wants to see us both,' Tiamoko signed quickly and gestured for her to precede him down the corridor towards the room where Pilos spoke to fighters and entertained guests. She'd hoped for this, or something like it, since coming up with the plan to save Tiamoko, but she'd never expected it to happen so soon. She'd expected to fight at least a few bouts, whether to first blood or death, before Pilos ran out of patience and summoned her. But maybe the summons was because of Tayan and nothing else.

Pilos was already seated on a low stool when they entered and knelt to press their faces to the floor. Tiamoko put his fingers on her wrist to indicate she could sit back up and then moved to sit at the third point of the triangle so she could see him and Pilos at the same time. He fixed his gaze on Pilos's feet, but Xessa watched the pit-master's face.

'You fought well in your last encounter, but it has not gone unnoticed that you fought very differently from your usual style,' Pilos said without preamble and Tiamoko translated. 'Not just then, but in your training sessions since, too. I am curious as to why.'

Xessa breathed out. Not Tayan, then. Her. She looked from Tiamoko to Pilos and then to Kalix standing against the wall. 'Did my victory disappoint you?' she signed deliberately. Tiamoko sucked in a breath but translated for her.

Pilos gnawed on his lip as if giving her question serious consideration. 'It did not,' he said eventually and clearly enough that she didn't need to look at Tiamoko's hands.

'Then what does it matter?' she asked, distantly aware that her words could have repercussions for Tiamoko as

351

much as for herself. But she needed to move this conversation in a particular direction and this was the only way she could think to do it.

'As I said, I am curious,' Pilos replied with more patience than she had expected.

'Before, and despite my skill, my victory was never assured. I fought in the style I used when I killed' – she broke off abruptly and had to shake out her hands to still their tremble – 'I was too emotional. It no longer suits me.'

'It could be argued that your new style suits you even less,' Pilos said. Tiamoko translated his words and added that his tone was mild and seemed genuine. Xessa appreciated the additional information: most people within the pit delighted in keeping their faces neutral when they spoke to her and she had long since given up trying to discover if they meant more than they seemed to.

'I fought and won for you, pit-master. Did I not bring you jade?'

The question was presumptuous and she knew it. From the sudden tension, so did Tiamoko, but he translated anyway. Xessa remembered an almost identical situation back in the great pyramid when she had first been brought to this stinking city. Then, she had been tied in a line with other ejab and presented to the Singer for his inspection. She had signed many angry words and threats of violence and Elder Rix had translated for her. Translated every threat and jeer and then died because of them. Because of her.

'You won me much jade, yes,' Pilos said, surprising her. 'But I think you will win me less each time if you continue fighting this way.'

Because I fight like Tiamoko now, the warrior you have translating for you? she thought and could see from his fixed expression that her friend had realised the same. That he was imagining them both being worn down and eventually killed by this life that didn't respect their abilities. His brow wrinkled as he looked at her, but Xessa refused to acknowledge his concern.

'I am sorry you feel that way. You own my body and you order me to kill: I do that. I am your weapon and have not yet failed in my task. How I perform that task is up to me.'

'Is it?' Pilos snapped and then visibly calmed himself. Still, anger flashed in his eyes and his fingers tapped a staccato rhythm against his knee before stilling. 'What is it you want, Xessa?'

Xessa and Tiamoko both twitched at his use of her name, though for the eja it was shock mingled with triumph. It was unheard of for a pit-master to address a slave fighter by their given name and not the number of their cage or some nickname given to them by the crowd. *The Mute.*

Still, this was what she'd wanted, prayed for. This was her chance.

'I want Tiamoko to be freed,' she signed quickly. The Toko hesitated, stricken, and Xessa gestured for him to translate. He did so, blushing as he spoke her words. Pilos arched an eyebrow and then shook his head. 'Then the jade that is my portion for every fight won,' she signed and waited for Pilos's reluctant nod. 'Most of it already goes to secure the freedom of my husband Toxte' – her hands trembled at his name – 'and my friends Tayan and Lilla.' Another pause as she realised that if Tayan had been freed in fact, despite the unmarred brands on his shoulders, then surely that portion of her winnings would have been returned to her. She looked to Pilos for an answer, but his face was blank. Fucking Pechaqueh.

'The rest of my portion, all of that set aside for my own freedom, I wish to go to Tiamoko that he might be freed sooner. That is what I want.'

Again, the big Toko paused and would not translate, but he had got halfway through the explanation and now Pilos himself demanded the rest of it. Tiamoko answered and, in case he had twisted her words, Xessa pointed at him and nodded, miming handing over jade and then pointing again.

Pilos shifted back on his stool and folded his arms. His face might have been carved from wood, it was so expressionless and still. He stared into Xessa's eyes as if attempting to read the words on her spirit. She held herself still and open, projecting sincerity and not above pleading if she had to.

Get him free and get him safe, the sooner the better. Get him out of this antechamber to the Underworld.

When it seemed Pilos would not break his silence, Xessa began to sign again. 'I mentioned the jade I am owed, but we all know that I will never earn my freedom. I am eja, what you call god-killer. Even if I was to earn my freedom, I would be torn apart by your people the moment I set foot outside this pit. You know that, and I know that. I am at peace with it. But that does not mean I am not owed that jade. And if I am owed it, then I can choose what to do with it.'

Pilos ran his tongue across his lower lip as he watched her, calculating. He dropped his hands back onto his knees and leant forward. 'And if I agree to this, to a talented fighter earning his freedom twice as fast – and the jade I will lose as a result unless he signs back on as a free fighter – will you revert to your previous fighting style?'

Xessa felt the jaws of the trap close around her. How neatly he had laid it and baited it, and how blindly she had walked into it. 'Why?' she asked.

'Passion,' Pilos replied immediately. 'Give me fire and creativity and intuition. Give me the passion and flair that forces people to bet against and even for you and I will give away your jade as you have asked.'

Make myself a spectacle. Something that Pechaqueh loathe but cannot help admiring. I hope they feel grubby and sick when they bet on me to win. I hope it fucking shames them.

'I will not risk myself unnecessarily,' she signed and Pilos held up his hands in agreement. 'Very well. Not masked, though. Never masked. And no masks for Tiamoko either.'

'You ask much.'

Xessa licked her lips. 'I am giving you the rest of my life for as long as it lasts,' she signed. 'I am giving my life to and for this pit. I am giving my jade away so that I will never be free. I ask only that we no longer fight our own people. And, and for news of my husband.' The final words came out of her hands before she could stop them and she held her breath. This, surely, was too much. Almost, she wanted to take it back, to beg Tiamoko not to translate, but it was too late.

The pit-master tilted his head to one side, exposing the long, fresh scar beneath his jaw. 'You have not asked for news of him before, even though you named him with the others. You have not asked for news of anyone. Why now?'

'Because she needs something to live for besides this foolish trade,' Tiamoko said and signed at the same time, anger clear in his face. 'Pit-master, please—'

'Do we have a trade?' Xessa interrupted and glared at him until he translated.

Pilos stroked his forefinger across his lower lip. 'We have a trade,' he said, nodding as he spoke. 'You fight at the next new moon. Both of you.'

Three fights in a row, no month off in between. Pilos wanted to see her back at what he considered her best. Xessa blinked away the sting in her eyes and nodded back.

'Are you moon-mad?' Tiamoko demanded as soon as they left the room, Kalix leading them back towards the hall for the afternoon's training. 'You don't make trades with Pechaqueh. And you don't ever trade away your freedom for mine.'

He was so angry he was shaking, and Xessa clasped his hands in hers to still his tirade. They'd paused in the corridor and Kalix would notice any moment. 'It's true. I'll never get out. As soon as I got close to earning my freedom, Pechaqueh would be sleeping in the streets waiting for me to leave this pit. You think I didn't work it out within the first month? I dedicated my life to killing their gods,' she signed but gently, because while he must know the truth too she didn't want him to feel obliged to offer her false hope. 'But I can get you out. I can keep you safe.'

'But Toxte is eja—' Tiamoko began.

'I told them he's a warrior,' Xessa signed, cutting him off and then gestured at her ear. 'It's different for me: no one would have believed that. So if Toxte's not stupid – and he's not – he'll have told them the same when he was captured. All ejab will, Malel guide them. He'll be serving in the Melody and my jade will help him buy his freedom that much earlier, the same as you.'

He'll be serving there as long as he was captured. As long as he didn't die in the Sky City on that awful, awful night. Malel, would Pilos even tell me if he was dead? Will I be able to trust the news when it comes? If it comes?

'You shouldn't have done what you did for me,' Tiamoko signed; his bottom lip was wobbling and he sucked it between his teeth, bit hard. 'But once I am free, I'm going to find him. I swear to you by Malel and my ancestors, I will find Toxte and the rest and I will watch over them for you until you can do it for yourself. Because you will get out of this pit. Somehow. We'll come back and break you out. We'll—'

Xessa patted his cheek and stopped his hands with hers again. She caught a glimpse of Kalix in the corner of her eye. The trainer was striding back down the corridor, looking angry. 'I know you will,' she lied and walked away before he could reiterate his wild promise. He'd never manage any of it, but she allowed herself the indulgence of pretending he told the truth.

Xessa had always been willing to die for her people, her city, her homeland. Now she had to live for them, and she was discovering that it was much, much harder.

LILLA

Eagle compound, Melody fortress, the dead plains,
Tlalotlan, Empire of Songs
225th day of the Great Star at evening

They'd chased the last of the breeze, sitting on the roof of Ekon's quarters and sharing a pitcher of water and tales of conquests past as they watched the sky darken. Lilla had listened, sick at heart and at stomach, to Ekon's stories even as his skin breathed in his closeness and something he'd thought long-dead flowered into new life, opening its poisonous leaves to the Feather's sun.

Despite the pain that stitched through the muscles of his back, despite their relative statuses, there was something building between them and he knew the Pecha was as aware of it as he was. Lilla wondered if Ekon's nerves prickled with imagined touch as his own did every time their glances caught, held, before flicking away. Guilt and anticipation – and guilty anticipation – swirled in his stomach.

I want him. Malel forgive me, but I want him.

It was a sick joke that the man whose life he'd saved, and

358

who had ordered him whipped unconscious for it, was the same man who could stir such long-buried desire, but the brush of his hand when he'd gestured Lilla down the stairs and back into his quarters had been like lightning – illuminating, terrifying, and impossible to ignore. For one wild, incandescent moment, he hadn't ignored it. He'd welcomed that lightning, welcomed Ekon's arms and warmth and mouth – and then torn himself away.

'Forgive me, high one. I . . . you are kind and I would, I want to but, but I cannot. This slave apologises.'

Lilla braced himself for the explosion of anger and violence, breathing a silent prayer to Malel that the punishment wouldn't fall on his back again. He wasn't sure he could stand another whipping and he cringed into the soft mats.

The taste of Ekon's mouth lingered like poison and his skin tingled with the remembered touch of those fingers and the heat of chest against chest. The hands gentle on his hips and the hitch of Ekon's breath when Lilla's lips parted for his tongue.

The want had thrummed through him – still did, if he was honest – low and pleading, but the Feather's hand on the knot tying his kilt had been too much, too soon. Not unwelcome, just not . . . yet.

Now, Ekon was silent but for his ragged breathing, and then there was a rustle and thump as he sat and the long, slow exhalation of control. 'No need to apologise,' he said, his voice low and rough. 'Please sit up.'

Lilla raised his head. The Feather sat cross-legged facing him, the flush of desire still in his cheeks but no longer fogging those midnight eyes. He gestured. 'Sit and talk some more.'

'Forgive this slave,' Lilla began again as he straightened on his knees, his eyes fixed on the expanse of warm brown skin at the neck of Ekon's tunic. He swallowed, wanting, his blood screaming at him to give in, to take and be taken. Surrender.

Ekon waved it away. 'You are a slave, yes, but you are more than that: you are a *slave warrior*, sworn to the Melody. The Melody owns your body, not any individual. Not me. Do you understand?' Relief flooded through Lilla's gut and he nodded, jerky and graceless.

'You are a part of the greatest fighting force in the world,' Ekon continued, surprising him. 'No one may disrespect the bond between you and the glory of our Empire's might without punishment.' He grinned suddenly like a cat, playful and predatory both, and Lilla's stomach flipped over again. Two dimples, the second only appearing when he grinned openly, careless of who might see, dimples that made him boyishly handsome. Lilla had to try very hard not to stare at Ekon's kiss-bitten lips.

'I won't say I'm not disappointed, but I hope that in time you will come to me freely. I suppose up to now I have been nothing but your commander, after all. And the one who ordered . . . that.'

The stitches had come out of the worst wounds a few days before, and the surface pain, at least, had begun to fade. The hurt still lingered deep inside his muscles – and, treacherously, his heart – but every day it faded a little more. Lilla was healing. Bored out of his mind and with little to do, but healing.

'That is not the reason,' he stammered and meant it. The Feather's eyebrows raised. 'The fault for my punishment belongs only to Fang Kux, Malel guide her to rebirth.'

'That does surprise me,' Ekon said softly. 'And pleases me. It can be difficult to navigate a relationship when statuses are very different.'

Lilla startled. 'Relationship?' he blurted, before hastily looking down. 'Ah, forgive—'

'If you say that one more time today I think I'm going to go mad,' Ekon said, laughing. 'Here, now, we are just two warriors. Two people who, I'm fairly sure, share a mutual attraction. But it was the thought of a relationship that surprised you?' He blushed suddenly. 'I apologise, Pod-leader, if I have misinterpreted things. If, when you are ready – if you are ever, if you want – if you would prefer there to be no attachment or obligation, then of course. Whatever you want,' he finished softly, adorably earnest despite his tongue-tied delivery. Lilla shivered. What did he want?

Freedom and vengeance. And him. Malel forgive me, but I want him.

And Tayan? Pain stabbed through his chest, sharper and deeper than Kux's little blade. *Tayan is dead. Fucking Ekon will further my plans and make him trust me.*

Lilla didn't want to further his plans by fucking the Feather. Lilla wanted to fall apart in his arms, so consumed by pleasure that the rest of the world and all its shames and indignities faded into nothing. He wanted his body to be the world and Ekon the sunlight stroking it back to life. He wanted to feel the man's weight on him, hard fingers locked around his wrists, pinning him down until he had no choice but to die of the ecstasy of it. He realised he was staring at Ekon's mouth again and wrenched his eyes away.

'You would be . . . since my husband,' he said with a clear hitch in his voice. 'I'm sorry,' he repeated helplessly.

'Ah,' Ekon said, understanding muting some of the returning heat from Lilla's focus on his mouth. 'Yes, I know that pain well. I was married once. She was killed six years ago in a Quitob uprising against the song. She was an eagle too. Since then, well, there have been encounters, but no more than that.'

Lilla put his hand on Ekon's knee. 'Your loss hurts my heart,' he said and it wasn't a lie. He managed a small, tentative smile. 'I must ask your forgiveness again that you sought pleasure from someone who isn't quite ready to provide it.'

The Feather closed his warm, broad palm over the back of Lilla's hand and held it against his leg. 'Does that mean that, perhaps, one day you might be? Ready?' His thumb was tracing over the back of the Tokob wrist, a slow delicious drag impossible to ignore.

The low heat simmering in Lilla's gut flared to life again, even just at this. Though many people in the barracks didn't care about the lack of privacy, whether they pleasured themselves or took pleasure with others, Lilla had never been comfortable following their example and now just this, the simple caress of a thumb on his wrist, set his blood alight in a way that was impossible to ignore.

'One day,' he tried to say, but what actually came out was: 'kiss me'. Ekon seemed as surprised to hear the words as Lilla was to say them, but he didn't hesitate. He pushed up onto his knees and took Lilla's face between his palms, pressing a soft, hungry kiss to his mouth. Lilla sucked in a breath through his nose and gripped Ekon's wrists to keep his hands on his face, letting him tilt his head to better kiss him again. Ekon's lips parted slightly in encouragement.

Instead, Lilla drew away. 'I don't know how far,' he began, but Ekon was already nodding.

'Of course,' he said. He stared into his eyes, making sure he knew that everything he said was genuine. 'I am a patient man, Lilla. I can and will wait for you. But right now, I would very much like to kiss you again. With your permission.'

Lilla couldn't help the groan that slipped from his throat and this time it was he who pushed forward, bringing their faces back together. He slid his hands along Ekon's arms up to the shoulder and then back into the soft, heavy fall of his hair. His chest was tight and his lungs hurt with suppressed emotion, but the rest of him hummed with heat and want. He groaned again at Ekon's tongue in his mouth, his fingers tightening in the man's hair and drawing a grunt from him. Quickly, he loosened his fingers, but Ekon made an encouraging sound and so he gripped it again.

The Pecha was kneeling up over Lilla so that he had to stretch up and tilt his head back and he was aware again that Ekon was taller than him. It was different enough, both in height and in the way he kissed, for Lilla to lose himself in it without comparing it to other kisses and other people. One person.

They kissed until they were dizzy, and then Ekon pressed his mouth, hot and wet, down the side of Lilla's neck. Lilla was aware of his own harsh panting and the molten heat pooling in his belly. With Tayan being in Pechacan as a peace-weaver and then Lilla's own capture, it had been more than two years since anyone had wanted him and he was burning up from the inside with the need of it. The hesitation from before was burning too – burning away.

Ekon's next kiss to the side of his neck had a hint of teeth in it and Lilla hissed in a breath, his hand pressing at the back of the Feather's neck in a silent request for more. More kisses. More bites. He felt rather than heard Ekon's pleased hum at finding a pleasure point on which to lavish attention. His hands had fallen to the Tokob shoulders and now one slid over and down across his shoulder blade. Lilla winced and instantly Ekon broke off from his neck and drew back.

'Gods, I'm so sorry, Lilla. Are you hurt? Do you need a shaman?'

Lilla was dazed, unable to draw his eyes away from Ekon's mouth, flushed and swollen from kissing. 'It's fine, I'm fine, just kiss me again.'

Ekon surged up against his mouth and pulled him in, fists tight in his tunic this time and Lilla pushed forward until they were both kneeling up and he could slide one hand tentatively around Ekon's waist. The man gave another appreciative hum and so he slid his fingertips beneath his tunic to encounter skin shockingly hot and shockingly soft.

The Pechaqueh hands flexed in the front of his tunic and then the left one trailed down Lilla's flank to his hip, bypassing the torn flesh and muscles of his back. His hand rested there, squeezing with every kiss and brush of tongues until Lilla was half-crazy with it, his hands tightening on Ekon's back and dragging him closer. Chest to chest and belly to belly, not even enough room for air between them.

The Feather broke away again to press more kisses to the other side of his throat, teeth catching and dragging against salt-wet skin and Lilla couldn't help the needy little twitch of his hips, a twitch that caused the Pechaqueh fingers to tighten convulsively on his flank.

'Fuck,' he panted against his neck and Lilla couldn't help a snort of amusement.

'I want . . .' He swallowed his words and a moan as Ekon pressed their hips together, his erection pressing hard against Lilla's thigh.

'Sorry,' the Pecha gasped and shuffled backwards. Lilla's hands tightened on his waist and pulled him back in so that they both let out startled little moans.

'What do you want? Tell me,' Ekon asked, his fingers tight on Lilla's hip and then moving slowly, tentatively, around to grip at the muscle of his arse. Lilla sucked in a breath and let his head fall back and the Pecha attacked his throat with more kisses until he had no choice but to slide both hands up under Ekon's tunic to grasp at the muscles of his back and haul him even closer, crushing them together.

'Please, tell me,' he begged. Instead of replying, Lilla pressed his thigh between Ekon's and the man groaned at the pressure against his cock and shoved his hips forward. His fingers tightened in the meat of Lilla's arse as he dragged him into another kiss, this one hard and filthy, desperate. Lilla kissed him back with reckless abandon, trying to say with his body what he couldn't with his mouth. He didn't know the rules of this, what he was allowed; it was easier to show than to speak and risk offence.

It had been so long and he just wanted to forget, forget all of it except for the building pleasure and the strength in the body against his. Shoulders and arms and back thick with muscle and the thigh slotted between his own broad and steady. Nothing at all like Tayan.

Lilla blinked, the name a lightning bolt through his head that threatened to blast him to ruin. He closed his eyes and sank into another kiss and pressed his hands to Ekon's hips, urging him closer and faster until they were moving rhythmically against each other. Lilla was gasping into Ekon's mouth as the pleasure pooled in his belly and at the base of his spine and he focused on that, only that.

Ekon still had one hand in Lilla's hair and the other squeezing his buttock, avoiding the expanse of his back. There was something about that – about not being held or surrounded – that made it easier. He didn't feel cherished like this, or even particularly liked. It was just a need that they could fulfil together. He didn't have to think about emotions, which made it easier not to think about Tayan.

'Lilla,' Ekon moaned, his name laced with hunger. He dragged up the front of his kilt and pressed it securely between their bellies. 'Can I?' he asked, tugging at the hem of Lilla's own. He nodded and Ekon pulled the material out of the way and they both made choked-off noises at the drag of skin against skin.

Ekon was wet and scalding hot where he pressed against Lilla's thigh, feather-soft skin over his hardness and the Tokob hands clenched convulsively on his hips. 'Ah.'

'Yes,' the Pecha breathed. 'Fuck, that's so good.' He hauled Lilla even closer, pressing his thigh more firmly between his and dragging a noise very like a whimper out of the Tokob chest. 'Are you close?'

Lilla nodded and Ekon surged forward as if he wanted to knock him over onto his back and press down on top of him. They rocked and steadied and then the Feather was kissing him, kissing the noises right out of his mouth and replacing them with his own, harsh and needy.

Lilla's hips stuttered out of rhythm and both Ekon's hands went to his arse and pushed him hard against him. 'Yes, that's it,' he murmured. 'Don't stop now, Lilla. Come. Come for me.'

A raw cry tore from his throat and he did as ordered, everything within him drawing tight, muscles locking up, the pleasure bursting outwards through his limbs and squeezing his lungs in his chest.

'*Fuck,*' Ekon said yet again and then followed him. They held on tight through the shocks and twitches of their orgasms, shaking in each other's arms. Lilla wanted to laugh and scream and sob all at once, the release not just of pleasure but of tension and self-control and everything he had to be in this place coursing through him like honeypot and then evaporating.

He dropped his head onto the Pechaqueh shoulder and panted through the last flutters. Ekon's skin was hot through the thin material of his cotton tunic, and Lilla nosed it aside and pressed his lips there. His tongue. Tasted salt and sweat and breathed in warm masculine musk. Made a small, pleased noise on his next exhalation.

Ekon dragged his head back up by his hair and Lilla's eyelids sagged at the rightness of the pressure on his scalp. They kissed again, deep and languid this time, all the urgency of before gone. The Toko had been half expecting to be dismissed immediately, so the kiss was a pleasant surprise and he sank into it, winding his arms around Ekon's neck and chasing his mouth with his own. He managed a rueful laugh when they finally broke apart, still pressed tight together but able to meet each other's eyes.

'I'm shaking,' he whispered.

'I'm glad,' Ekon replied and used the grip on his hair to tilt his head sideways so he could bite his ear.

Lilla drew in a long, slow breath. 'That's been building for a while,' he murmured and, to his surprise, Ekon ducked his head and blushed before managing a shy smile.

'Yeah.' He fumbled for Lilla's hand and then brought it around to his kilt. 'Hold that out of the way while I get a cloth to clean up,' he murmured and bunched up his own skirt before finally pushing onto his feet.

Lilla sank back onto his heels and couldn't help giggling at the mildly ridiculous nature of what they had just done, as if they'd been boys navigating the first flush of lust and hadn't been able to wait long enough to undress. It was only once Ekon came back and tried to wipe him down that the Toko realised he should be the one to do that.

'Feather,' he said, shocked, grabbing for the cloth. Ekon snatched it away, consternation and disappointment darkening his face. 'Your status,' he tried. 'You shouldn't. I'm a slave.'

'What? Lilla, no,' Ekon said, genuine shock in his tone. 'Here, for . . . for this, we have no statuses. Setatmeh, you think I would use that, that I would even *want to* use that, between us in private? Is that what you think of me?'

Lilla shoved his kilt back down over his legs, heedless of the mess, and got halfway into a bow before Ekon grabbed him by the shoulders and pulled him upright again. 'Forgive this slave,' he began and snapped his mouth shut on any more; there was hurt now in the Pechaqueh eyes.

The Toko gestured helplessly, his heart thudding sick and slow in his chest. There was anger, too, that it should be up to him to explain; that Ekon couldn't see or understand. 'I don't know how to be,' he said. 'I don't know what I'm allowed, or what you want now. Whether I should go; if I'm allowed to stay. I don't even know what to call you.' Shame filled him then, drowning the anger and chasing away the last embers of pleasure and contentment. He could feel the supple leather collar resting low on his neck, something he rarely noticed any more.

'You said I belong to the Melody, not to you, but that knowledge that I am owned, a slave, doesn't go away just because of . . . great sex. You mentioned a relationship before, but I know what the other eagles will think of you if you do that. A quick fuck, a dalliance perhaps, is one thing, but can your status bear the dishonour of a Toko lover? A slave lover?'

The words ran out, pus draining from a wound, and Ekon didn't answer. Instead, he lifted Lilla's kilt back up and wiped his skin with the cloth, gentle. Lilla blushed and fidgeted but didn't stop him. Was he allowed to stop him? A muscle jumped in his jaw.

Finally, the Feather looked up again and there was a glimmer of something in his expression. 'Great sex?' he murmured, and then carried on before Lilla could even think of how to reply. 'Out there I am Feather and you are Pod-leader, and nothing we do in here will change that. If you don't want to do this again, that still won't change. You don't need to worry about displeasing me, or about being punished if you end whatever this is. Whatever it might become. As for what the others think, it doesn't matter.

'And in here,' he added, tossing the cloth into a corner and taking Lilla's hands, 'you are Lilla and I am Ekon. Two people; two warriors. There is no status between us when you are here.'

The Tokob breath was trapped in his chest; it hurt to inhale. 'That may not be as easy as you assume it to be.'

To his surprise, Ekon nodded. 'I know, Lilla. And I know you will probably find it difficult to believe that there will be no punishment if you change your mind about any of this. I only hope that over time you will let me prove my sincerity.'

'You could have anyone,' Lilla burst out, though he didn't let go of Ekon's hands. 'You're Pechaqueh, you're a Feather. Someone your own status would—'

'I want you, Lilla. If you'll have me,' he interrupted gently.

The Toko stared at him helplessly. Now that his initial desire had been sated, guilt twisted as sharp as flint in his belly. 'I don't— I haven't—' His eyes stung and he clenched his jaw and stared across the room instead.

Ekon squeezed his hands and then kissed them both. 'You don't need to make a decision right now. Why don't you go back to the barracks? I'll give you some time to think. It's not because I don't want you here,' he added hastily. 'I've told you I want you, but what happens next is up to you. I want to give you the space to decide.'

In silence, they rearranged their clothes and finger-combed their hair, then stepped out into the early evening sun and into their sandals. The Feather walked him back to the narrow passageway leading to the Eighth Talon's compound.

'Under the song, high one,' Lilla said automatically, not quite meeting his eyes.

There was the tiniest hint of a pause, barely there at all, as if Ekon was waiting for him to look up. 'Under the song,' he murmured, and then he was gone.

'I'm with you.'

'What?' Lilla asked as they shuffled along in the queue for dawnmeal.

Tinit leant up to whisper in his ear. 'I'm with you. When you rise up. I've lost everyone already; why the fuck wouldn't I fight against these, these kin-killers? I'm yours. Whatever you need.'

Lilla licked his lips and murmured his thanks. Nearly seventy warriors of the Eighth had pledged their lives to the rebellion in the aftermath of his punishment, as if watching him be whipped had shaken the Pechaqueh lies out of their heads. It was the biggest influx of rebels since the earliest days of their imprisonment here in the fortress and brought their numbers to almost one in three of the Eighth Talon.

And it had been, at least partly, because of Lilla's deception. In the immediate aftermath of Kux's death, the Toko had known that it could mean the end of his rebellion. He might have been reported as a traitor by one of Kux's closest friends; he could lose the warriors already committed to the cause who'd watched him prioritise Ekon's life over that of the Yaloh.

In the bright rush of panic and pain and battle-madness, he'd begged Ekon for the pod's punishment to fall only on him in the hopes of retaining their loyalty at least, a foundation from which to build again. When it became clear instead that many in the Talon saw his request as an act of nobility, defiance against Pechaqueh cruelty, he'd been forced to play along. And it had worked – sixty-six new converts to the cause – but it left him feeling grubby on the inside. Tricking them into rebellion was surely as reprehensible as the lies of the song.

No, they just finally realised that nothing they or their kin can do will ever be enough; we'll never be truly free unless we take that freedom and destroy the concept of Pechaqueh superiority.

He wasn't sure how much he believed it, but then Tinit muttered an oath and Lilla followed her gaze to Feather Ekon. The man wasn't watching them, or if he had been, he'd looked away even as the Toko turned towards him. Lilla worried at his lip. The idea of Ekon watching him lit up both his desire and his shame, especially when Tinit spat deliberately on the ground. His pod and the new rebels wouldn't forgive the Feather for his punishment even as some – most, all – of them understood why it had been ordered.

Lilla himself didn't blame Ekon; he blamed Kux, as he'd said the day before. But he couldn't voice that to Tinit or his pod. He didn't like how that made him feel, either, complaining to a Pecha about a member of his pod, even one who was now dead. As if Ekon's opinion was more important than theirs. He gusted a sigh and turned his face up to the sun. It was all such a fucking mess.

Lilla took his dawnmeal and went to lean against the wall in the shade. The heat made his tunic stick to his back and he lost more than a few scabs pulling it off each night. Easier to just hide out of the sun. And it kept people away from him.

The wounds were enough to explain his abrupt mood swings, and while he made an effort with his pod and the rest of the Talon in the evenings, he didn't have the energy in the mornings, when sleep was still pain-filled and elusive and he woke grumpy and short-tempered.

Today was worse, and he found it impossible to concentrate on anything other than the memories of Ekon's hands gripped tight on his face and in his hair. He had finger bruises on his hips and couldn't resist pressing against them, the dull ache a delicious, forbidden reminder that he liked more than he should.

His dreams had been full of Ekon and Tayan, a hot and wanting mixture of images that he couldn't separate and which left him hard and aching and guilt-stricken.

The Eighth Talon were called to order shortly after dawn-meal and marched out of the barracks compound and into the vast drill yard connected to it. His pod went last to stay near him as long as possible. As he had each morning since leaving the shaman's care, Lilla stood at the rear and waited to see whether he would be summoned. He'd been told four weeks until he could return to training, but he wanted them to know he was prepared to do all they asked of him. He was a loyal slave warrior, dedicated to the Melody's glory and the Empire's peace.

The Talon, aside from those injured like himself and confined to the healing hall, marched through the gate and narrow passage until he was left alone once more – apart from Ekon.

Lilla's stomach turned over when he realised the Feather had waited for him. He walked over slowly, and any tentative decision he might have made during the sleepless hours of the night faded. Ekon was striving for nonchalance, but there was hope in his eyes he seemed unable to quell and a blush high on his cheeks. The combination lightened his face, and though the man was clearly older than Lilla, it gave him a boyish vulnerability that he found hard to ignore. Hard not to be affected by.

'Pod-leader Lilla, how are you today? How goes your recovery?'

Lilla dropped to his knees and pressed his brow quickly to the dirt before rising again. 'The Feather's concern honours me. This slave's recovery proceeds according to the shaman's satisfaction. I thank the high one for his concern.'

The words were painfully formal and they both knew it, more formal than Lilla usually employed.

'I am glad to hear you are feeling better.' Ekon hesitated and then glanced casually towards the gate; it had been shut after the last stragglers and the vast compound with its ten barracks buildings lined up inside was still and silent. Ekon took two paces forward and Lilla's mouth went dry. 'How are you truly? Not just your injuries?' he murmured.

'Feather?' Lilla asked, his voice a rasp.

Ekon took his meaning. 'We are alone, Lilla. My name is Ekon.'

Even with that tacit permission, he didn't know how to answer; Tayan had been the talker out of the two of them, but Lilla had never felt tongue-tied like this before. Perhaps it was because if he heard words of desire fall from his own mouth, something inside him would rupture and never again be fixed. So, coward-like, he didn't speak; he took two paces of his own until they were standing close enough to feel each other's body heat.

He looked up into the Pechaqueh eyes and Ekon saw what he needed to do. He grabbed Lilla by the tunic and pulled him in, stepping backwards until his back was pressed to the wall and they were lost in shadow.

It had to be a risk for him, not just that someone would see him with a slave but that Lilla himself might take vengeance upon him. In this position, pressed tight together with the Feather's back to a wall, it would be no great difficulty to snap his neck. Lilla didn't snap his neck. He let himself be dragged into a kiss, one that set him aflame again in an instant, a kiss hard and hot from the start.

Eventually, Ekon heaved a sigh and pushed him gently away, evading Lilla's mouth with a rueful smile.

'I have a Talon to train,' he said with clear regret. 'Ask one of the dogs to escort you to the scribing hall; we've had some orders through from the Singing City that need copying.'

'As the Feather commands,' Lilla replied, throaty with want. He forced himself to focus on Ekon's words. Orders from the Singing City. This was exactly why he'd asked to be kept busy during his recovery; what might he learn from the secret correspondence from the heart-city of the Empire?

Ekon flashed a dimple and then stroked his fingertips across Lilla's cheekbone. 'You're a good man, Pod-leader,' he murmured and strode away. Lilla stayed where he was, in the shadows, until long after he was gone. His palm ghosted over his cheek where he could still feel the echo of that caress. A good man? He was a liar, a cheat, a killer. A man who'd betrayed his husband and was going to betray his lover.

'He deserves it. They all deserve it.'

There was no one in the empty compound to believe the lie. Not even him.

ILANDEH

The source, Singing City, Pechacan, Empire of Songs
231st day of the Great Star at evening

The Singer had bowed to pressure from his council and there was going to be an official event at which the Shadow would be presented to them all. And not only councillors, but also selected nobility from around the Singing City.

Ilandeh didn't know whether it would be enough to hold back the landslide of gossip threatening to bury the city and wider Empire, which had turned ugly within hours of the attack outside Pilos's pit and showed no signs of dying down.

Someone had seen the Shadow's slave brands – she remembered grabbing his shawl during the fighting – and the news of his status had spread like maize blight. Not just a no-blood, but a *slave* no-blood. Pechaqueh were openly questioning the Singer's choice and the Choosers were being kept busy breaking up large, angry gatherings. More than once they'd been forced to summon Feather Pilos and his eagles to their aid. The city simmered with potential and with violence.

Ilandeh stood stoic and watchful – and exhausted – three paces behind the holy lord, as befitted her status as Chorus Leader. The whole city seemed convinced Tayan was using evil northern magic to ensnare the Singer. Everyone in the source had thought the same in the immediate aftermath of the spirit-joining, which itself was still under Shaman Kapal's daily scrutiny. She spent hours every day inside the song with Chotek, the two of them trying to work out where and how the link had been made. And how it might be unpicked.

They were twenty days away from the Great Star's eight-day absence from the skies. Twenty days from the ritual to awaken the world spirit and transform Ixachipan, which by now should be a peaceful and contented Empire. Instead, rumours that a no-blood occupied the second most powerful position in society had inflamed the rebellious tendencies of slaves and even free across Ixachipan. High Feather Atu was moving Talons to cities and restless towns, preparing for the worst. The Great Octave herself had suggested a postponement of the ritual, citing the outrage in the city, and the holy lord had flown into a spectacular rage, his song a clangour of fury and power and superiority that had driven them all to their knees.

Tayan had preened at his side as Ilandeh tried to hold the disparate parts of her spirit together through the onslaught of Pechaqueh might, as if the song no longer cut at him the way it used to. The link between them was strong indeed.

She had overheard Kapal speaking with Chotek about the spirit-bond: it was like flesh growing together after an injury, sealing over to leave a scar. It would need to be slashed anew to separate them, but who could predict the results of such medicine? Yet none of them knew whether the Singer could work his great magic and wake the world spirit with the Toko attached to him like a leech.

It's the other way around.

Ilandeh quelled the thought with savage speed, glancing automatically towards the holy lord. Tayan was watching her as the slaves hurried around the source putting the final touches to the preparations for the gathering. His smile was enigmatic and a little pained. He hadn't been hurt during the ambush, but the Singer had drawn on their link that day, and many times in the days since, every time the Shadow's thoughts grew too loud or the holy lord merely wanted to flex his power or indulge his divine malice. The Tokob eyes were bloodshot and his skin waxy. The blue line he'd drawn from the middle of his lower lip to the point of his chin wasn't quite straight.

However the link benefited the Singer – Ilandeh let her gaze skim over the holy lord's healthy brown skin and broadening arms and chest and made an educated guess – it was doing the opposite to Tayan.

Perhaps they won't need to be separated. Perhaps the holy lord in his power will . . .

Would what? Drain Tayan's spirit of its strength until he was a husk, a body without the spark of sacred life to animate it? Would his flesh survive that? Would he wander around behind the Singer like a shambling corpse, like . . . Ilandeh shivered. Like Otek, Xessa's father, and all the other spirit-haunted Tokob ejab she'd had the misfortune to meet in the Sky City?

Ilandeh blinked and checked the source again. Why should it matter what happened to a slave, even if he was the Shadow? That was the fatigue talking, nothing more.

Only two weeks as Chorus Leader and already she wanted to claw out her eyes. Nobody knew her real identity, but Acamah carried his resentment as openly as his spear and he had the Great Octave's endorsement. That had done much to keep the Chorus allied to him and they followed Ilandeh's orders only with reluctance.

In recent months, her disguise had become almost too perfect. Where she remained the exemplar of a Chorus warrior – and now Leader – the rest had become lax and inattentive as Enet tightened her grip on their loyalty and the source. The Great Octave had made overtures of friendship to Ilandeh that she had acknowledged but not returned. In response, rumours of her relationship with Pilos had sprung up: it couldn't be a coincidence.

Now, Ilandeh drilled them as if they were warriors of the First Talon under Atu's direct command and they disliked it. Disliked her. Could do nothing about either one.

They could kill me.

The Whisper's carefully cultivated paranoia was another reason for her exhaustion. She wouldn't trust anyone else with the Singer's safety, and she had direct orders from Pilos to protect the Shadow, but it was the calculation in the faces of the Chorus, the low-voiced conversations abruptly cut off at her arrival, that stole the majority of her sleep.

The Chorus Leader shifted in place, easing the ache in her feet, and checked the position of the sunbeams slanting through the colonnade. The presentation of the Shadow was to begin at highsun: the bustling slaves had an hour at most to adorn the source. There were new, lavish cushions in vibrant dyes scattered around the room in an elegant arch around the rose-cotton hanging that would conceal the Singer. Low tables beside each one already held a platter of fruit and a pitcher of cool water. Meat and bread, beer and honeypot would arrive as guests took their seats. Before the hanging sat another cushion, wide and deep blue: the Shadow's seat.

He didn't sit there now, keeping his place at the Singer's side instead. They bent their heads together, whispering softly like new lovers. Touching, too. The Singer laughed, boyish and joyful, and the Toko grinned. He glanced up at Ilandeh again and she felt her lips curve – she remembered that smile and its infectious ease, always inviting her to join in the joke. It dropped from the Shadow's face as if it had never been and an unfamiliar feeling washed up the back of her skull and tightened like a band around her head: shame.

Ilandeh had always done all that the Empire of Songs had required. Given her life to the Melody and dedicated herself to bringing the uneducated under the song for their own benefit. The year she and Dakto had lived in the Sky City had been hard but not unusual: make friends, earn trust, learn secrets, move on. The last two years in Tayan's company, a reminder every day not of what she'd done – she didn't feel bad about that. *Don't I?* – but of the people she had done it to. The face and form of Tokoban itself, here before her day and night.

She cleared her throat. 'Chorus Acamah, I want every single person, no matter their age or status, checked for weapons before they enter,' she snapped as the warrior appeared at her side with an obsequious little smile.

'As the Chorus Leader commands,' he drawled and vanished again before she could say any more, and she fought the urge to call him back and make him show her the deference she was due. She refrained. There were bigger battles to come. No point wasting breath and strength on such as him.

It was just before highsun when the guests began to arrive, the members of the council and their families first, and then other nobles and prominent citizens of the Singing City, Choosers and the administrators who kept the records of slaves and their movements across the Empire. Feather Pilos, of course, and his subordinate, a tall, rangy woman named

Xochi that Ilandeh vaguely remembered from the fall of the Sky City. She prayed Xochi wouldn't remember her.

Great Octave Enet greeted everyone with kind words and smiles, even the eagles. Ilandeh could hear her musical laugh from where she stood beside the hanging concealing the Singer and his Shadow. Enet mingled and chatted and flirted as necessary, leading guests to refreshments, seating them according to some complicated pattern that likely only she knew. Her advice was asked a dozen times in the first hour and she listened to each grievance or complaint before offering solutions.

Ilandeh had to admire the way her mind worked, even as she stared down each person to turn hostile or mistrustful gazes on the hanging and the figures seated behind it. Unlike the Great Octave, she wasn't here to make friends and had no qualms about being the visible promise of violence should anyone make an unsanctioned move towards the Singer.

No one gossiped within the source itself, but it was clear from how people sought each other out just to exchange significant looks that none of the guests approved of the holy lord's choice. Especially not with the beautiful, clever and generous Great Octave flitting among them like a jewelled butterfly.

'I'm hungry.'

Ilandeh's hand tightened on her spear. 'I will have a slave bring you a platter, great Singer,' she said, half-turning towards the curtain. 'Is there anything in particular you wish to eat?'

The Singer's eyes were hooded and calculating. 'The song hungers.' Next to him, the Shadow gasped and then began to murmur, too low-voiced for Ilandeh to hear. Even so, she could see the flush rising in the Tokob cheeks as the song dropped into something lower, darker. Something needy and cruel. Conversations died and the bright swirl of kilts and tunics and beaded, feathered hair stilled. Scores of nervous faces turned to the hanging.

Ilandeh did a quick count – two weeks since the last. How could Enet have been so stupid as to organise something like this before the Singer had, had . . . *received his offering*. Was this her plan? Did she want everyone to see what the Singer and his Shadow had become? Was that how she'd secure the magic for herself when the time came for the holy lord's ascension?

Or is this how she gets rid of every possible rival at once, by gifting them to the Singer in another orgy of death like the one that broke him?

Pilos was watching her, unblinking and intent. He'd made Ilandeh Chorus Leader; he had to believe she was capable. Not that all the ability in the world would be enough to stop a blood-hungry, rampaging god if he decided to feed.

'Music,' Enet called brightly. 'This is a celebration. Our glorious Singer has chosen his Shadow and the stability of our great Empire of Songs is assured. Music,' she called again and the musicians who had been playing in the gardens hurried in and struck up a lively hymn of praise.

The distraction worked on the guests, but the Singer and his Shadow were still engaged in whispered, and sometimes silent, communion. Gold began to pulse through the holy lord's fingers, and Tayan redoubled his pleas. He reached out and held Xac's hands, raising them to kiss the knuckles.

Movement in the corner of her eye had Ilandeh's attention snapping back to the room at large. The Great Octave stepped closer with a platter of delicacies and a cup of beer. She knelt beyond the curtain. 'Holy lord, please eat so that we might all bask in your strength and glory. Perhaps afterwards would be the right moment to present your Shadow to the assembled guests?'

Ilandeh beckoned a slave to taste the food and beer and, after a suitable wait, she passed them to the Shadow who coaxed the holy lord into taking small bites, cajoling and teasing and pressing butterfly-light kisses to his cheek and temple as he fed him. The Great Octave bowed to the hanging and glided away among the guests again, a holy Setat among the water grass. The tenor of the song softened and the guests slowly relaxed into chatter once more.

Ilandeh quartered the source again, checking her warriors were alert and staying aloof from the guests as instructed. Acamah was slinking through the crowd; when he noticed her watching him, he changed direction. Ilandeh tracked where he'd been heading – towards Spear of the Singer Haapo. She frowned and looked for Pilos; he'd moved closer during the swelling of the song. Close enough that they could speak.

'Good to see you, Feather,' she said amiably as Xochi engaged a gaggle of noble children with tales of warfare and good-natured banter nearby, riling them up enough that they became rowdy and provided a decent screen under which Pilos and Ilandeh could speak.

'Is all in order, Chorus Leader?' he enquired politely. 'The great pyramid seems well protected.'

'Thank you, Feather, I am honoured you think so. We're training hard these days to protect the holy lord from all dangers. Speaking of which, do I need to be concerned about the increasing unrest in the city?'

Pilos pursed his lips, considering. 'It's mostly brawls and arguments over prices, though we are seeing increased friction between Pechaqueh and free. The Choosers and my detachment are handling it. If anything comes close to the great pyramid, we will beat the war drum relay across the city and send every warrior here.'

Ilandeh breathed out in relief and then recalled herself. 'Your, ah, your diligence is noted and appreciated, Feather,' she said awkwardly and hoped no one noticed how flushed she was.

'I'm more concerned with the news from Tokoban,' Pilos said casually and sipped from his beer, glancing at the posturing youths and throwing a comment their way to encourage them to greater performances. 'The Zellih attacks are increasing, though they are struggling to secure territory. Still, Feather Calan tells me there have been attacks on pyramids, with two more burnt and one completely destroyed.'

'Setatmeh preserve us,' Ilandeh murmured. 'The song?'

There was nothing casual about Pilos now. 'You have not heard of this while guarding the Singer?' Ilandeh shook her head, her eyes wide. 'The song remains in Tokoban, though its strength is lessened in the areas of destruction. Calan has warriors protecting the pyramids surrounding the damaged ones to prevent further weakening in the song there, and labourers clearing ground to erect replacements. She's recalled the part of her Talon stationed in Yalotlan to bolster her forces, yet I fear that without the Sixth's presence, that land may descend into further disobedience.'

'And if the song weakens further in Tokoban, we could be looking at more unrest.' Pilos nodded, grim. 'The Zellih have never heard the song's majesty, though, excepting those few merchants who have traded with Tokoban over the generations. They are walking into our Empire; they are walking into our strength. That will do much to steal their spines from them. I have faith Feather Calan will end their threat swiftly and act to subdue Yalotlan if necessary.'

Ilandeh spoke as if what the Zellih felt was foreign to her, as if the song didn't tear at her too, promising half of her that subjugation and obedience were her only options while the other half revelled in the coming annihilation of all non-Pechaqueh. For that was what the song seemed to promise, stronger each day.

She took a pace backwards and glanced behind the rose-cotton, marvelling again that Tayan, a no-blood, could withstand the song's ravages with such ease. But he was the Shadow of the Singer, almost as far above her as the holy lord himself. Tayan had more power than she could begin to imagine and, whatever his blood whispered to him in the night, he could drown it out with the thrum of that golden magic that sparkled beneath his skin. Envy smoked in her gut as she stepped close to Pilos again and belatedly noted the approval glimmering in his dark eyes. She blinked.

'You speak as one of our truest, Chorus Leader,' he said warmly and Ilandeh lit up from the inside before blinking again, this time at the strange twist to his mouth. Her words – her truth – should be coming from a Pechaqueh. That they did not, even if he publicly said otherwise, evidently made him uncomfortable. Enet's ambition and Acamah's disloyalty, all those Pechaqueh spreading rumours in the markets and the mob and assassins outside the pit, and it was Ilandeh's unwavering belief in the Empire of Songs that disgusted him.

The ember he'd lit in her guttered. 'Do you expect a swift conclusion to hostilities in the north, Feather?' she asked with a stony politeness he didn't notice.

'Of course. The Zellih are of Barazal – that whole continent is peopled with savages, even worse than the Tokob. They won't be able to stand against us for long.' He paused, his gaze faraway and wistful; as Feather of the Singing City, he'd see none of the action. Some of her irritation faded. Pilos snapped back to himself. 'High Feather Atu will send the First and Third Talons to lead the defence should it become necessary.'

Before Ilandeh replied, she glanced behind the curtain to find the Shadow kneeling up, excitement lightening his blue-painted features. She stared at him, the distinctive Tokob patterning of his paint and his unblemished slave brands, and felt battle-readiness flood her limbs. It was one thing for people to know the Shadow was Tokob and quite another for them to see evidence of it in the very source itself. She didn't know why the Singer allowed him to dress so. She wondered if she'd feel differently if he was Xentib.

'Feather, it's time,' she said, swallowing her animosity at Pilos's prejudice. She was the one standing here, honoured and trusted, not him.

But because of him.

'And Acamah seems friendly with Spear Haapo,' she added, as duty demanded.

Pilos grunted and inhaled through flared nostrils. 'Xochi,' he said as Ilandeh signalled the nearest Chorus warriors. 'Enough playing.' The eagle smiled at the group of enamoured youths and just as quickly turned her back on them. They milled in confusion and then faded back, picking up on the warriors' tension.

'Honoured councillors, nobles and guests,' the Great Octave called, having somehow appeared at the perfect moment to attract all the attention to herself, 'our holy lord, the great Singer Xac, asks you to greet with all humility his Shadow, Tayan, called the stargazer, shaman of Tokoban.'

There was nothing in her voice or body language other than joy and adoration, but she had to be seething. Naming him as Tokob was proof enough of that; she was priming the audience to dislike him. Ilandeh concentrated on her surroundings. Everyone here was an enemy until proven otherwise.

There was a pause as Chorus warriors slid forward to put a protective cordon between the hanging and the audience. The silence was thunderous and the councillors crowded forward first, followed by their families, then nobles, Choosers, and everyone else. Ilandeh's mouth dried at the multitude of eager faces gazing at her – and the Shadow behind her.

When Tayan stepped around the hanging with a bright, eager smile, the clamour was instantaneous. Whispers quickly became low-voiced comments, and then louder and louder still, until: 'So it's true? A Tokob slave? A *Toko*? I had thought it a jest of the holy lord's. I had thought there was a real Shadow, not this mockery of sacred tradition. How can *this thing* be our next Singer?'

'Who speaks?' the Singer asked from behind the hanging, his melodious voice cutting through the babble and leaving nervous silence in its place. Tayan's face had darkened with each word until anger rose from him like heat-shimmer.

Enet played her role to perfection. She arched one perfectly sculpted eyebrow towards the speaker. 'The councillor for Quitoban,' she said crisply, and then knelt and bowed to the Shadow and the Singer behind him without the slightest hesitation.

'Remove him and his family. Their lands, businesses and wealth are gifted to the source. Anyone who shelters them will suffer the same fate.'

'H-holy lord!' the councillor squawked. He fell to the mats and banged his forehead against them repeatedly. 'Forgive me, holy lord. Forgive this one's foolishness. Spear of the—'

'No,' the Singer said and his Shadow with him. Tayan's skin flickered with gold and there was a susurration of awe around the source. 'There is no forgiveness.'

Ilandeh let her face go hard as she swept the assembled

throng with a glare until they knelt in a panicked rush, like bats spilling from the mouth of a cave at dusk.

Tayan wore his displeasure as openly as the magic in his skin. The guests' obeisance did nothing to soothe him, nor did the councillor for Quitoban's ignoble removal from the source, his partner and children weeping and pleading as administrators and Chorus warriors dragged them away.

'Does anyone else protest my choice of Shadow?' the Singer demanded. 'He began to say something about a Spear? Haapo, perhaps? Or you, Enet? You still retain the title of Spear of the City, do you not?'

Enet sat back on her heels. 'Your wisdom is as great as your magic, holy lord, and as bright as the sun. I protest nothing and willingly open myself to you should you wish to Listen to my truth.' She closed her eyes and tilted her face up in supplication.

Ilandeh let out a held breath and sucked in another, re-adjusting her hands on her spear. A bold move from the Great Octave, who all knew desired to be Singer. How far did her hold over the rest of the Chorus go? Would they converge on Singer and Shadow and tear them from this world if the holy lord moved against Enet? Was now the moment she acted?

Unlikely. She'd want as few Pechaqueh in the source as possible to give her the best chance of being chosen by the song-magic.

But unlikely didn't mean impossible. Ilandeh readied herself for violence. Pilos and Xochi would stand with her; perhaps that would be enough to get the holy lord away. If they left the Shadow to Enet's claws, his death would buy them some time.

'If not for Tayan, I would still linger within my illness. Instead, because of him, my strength grows by the day and my magic with it. Because of him, I will awake the world spirit on the day that my brother, the Great Star, leaves us for his little absence. *You owe us both your worship.*'

The Singer's voice was like a jaguar's paw – soft and hiding a lethal strength. It slid inside them all, took hold of their reverence, and twisted it tight and hard until it bled love for the holy lord and his Shadow. Reluctant adoration swept the crowd.

But not Enet. Shock, fury, and then blankness ripped across her face one after the other and Ilandeh's gut churned with unwilling sympathy; she knew exactly how it felt to have her efforts overlooked and ignored or deemed as less important than another's actions. On the other hand, it had been Enet who broke the Singer and Tayan who put him back together again, however unconventionally, or even unwillingly, he might have done so.

'How may we ever thank you, great Singer?' Councillor Haapo shrilled into the disbelieving silence. 'You will transform Ixachipan, perhaps the entire world, for us. You will bring us into the splendour which we were promised. Great Singer, your glory and dedication knows no bounds.' Haapo moved into a full prostration, loudly proclaiming his thanks and begging the holy Setatmeh to watch over Singer Xac and Shadow Tayan. It was dramatic in the extreme, but necessarily so to deflect attention from what the Councillor for Quitoban had so nearly said. Not that Ilandeh would forget it. She mentally moved Haapo up her list of threats.

Guests eager to curry favour followed, crying out their support and love for the Singer in loud voices, the tension bleeding from the room as they began excited speculation as to how the world would change once its spirit awoke. And so soon!

The Shadow stood before the rose-coloured cotton, resplendent in his fine kilt and bright paint. Forgotten.
And furious.

ENET

Great Octave's estate, Singing City,
Pechacan, Empire of Songs
235th day of the Great Star at evening

It should be today. Her people had sent word that the capstone was only a few sticks outside the Singing City after its long, secretive journey from the border of Tokoban. When it was here, she would have sixteen days before the ritual to wake the world spirit. Sixteen days to make herself ready to serve the Empire of Songs.

'How much stronger will the holy lord grow in that time?' she mused aloud. 'I pray strong enough to wake the world spirit and change all our lives,' she added, and then hesitated at a flicker, a tickle, against the edges of her mind.

Enet opened herself wide. 'Holy lord? How may I serve? Do you require me back at the source?' She projected love and adoration and waited for the Singer to make known his will. While she did, she looked out over the garden of her estate, her eyes unfocused. The holy lord needed her full attention.

The flicker grew stronger and the tickle became a sharp stabbing pain and the Great Octave whimpered. The Singer was angry, or tired perhaps. A touch less deft than usual. She opened her mind wider, welcoming him, and then he was there, inside her head and scattering the pages of her thoughts like a frightened turkey.

The Shadow.

Enet jerked on her cushion and began to close her mind, but he had fingers and toes gripping the edges and was using them to haul himself closer, deeper inside her.

'*Get out,*' she shrieked with mouth and mind both. '*Get out of my head.*' She was dimly aware of shouted alarm in the room that her body occupied, and then someone began to sing in a deep, strong voice. A drum accompanied it and then other voices joined in, the chorus growing. Enet tried to cling to it, to sink her consciousness into it.

She had no right to exile the Shadow from her thoughts and yet she could do nothing other than that. How dare this filthy no-blood slave steal into her mind? *How dare he?*

The Shadow took to Listening as if he'd been born Pechaqueh, and though the music formed a gleaming barrier between him and Enet, it was not enough. Not strong enough. She slapped herself in the face.

Still not enough.

So many secrets, Great Octave, came his voice, slick with greed and glee. *Let me see how many I can pry open.* Enet slapped herself again, same cheek, the sting deep in her face and her palm. She focused on the hot hurt of it to the exclusion of all else but still he wriggled in, overwhelming her defences slowly until he found what he wanted. *Singer Enet? You think that lies within your future?* the Shadow demanded with infinite amusement and an edge sharper than obsidian. *You think I will let you take my destiny from me?*

391

No matter how many other thoughts and images she threw at him, the Toko clung to that one, to her imagined future: regal in the source, beautiful and golden beyond compare and more powerful than anyone else in Ixachipan.

You will never take it. You will never have the magic. It is mine. Mine.

Every thought-word from the Shadow was a blade, wielded with the precision of a shaman cutting out sickness. Enet screamed as he studied her hopes and plans to succeed Singer Xac when he ascended.

Mine, he snarled again, and then he was gone.

The Great Octave slumped into the arms of her slaves, weeping. The singing faltered and then picked up again at the rough gesture of her estate slave. She clung to him. 'Shadow Tayan is strong indeed,' she gasped. 'There must be singing, chanting or reading around me at all times when I am here or out in the city. Understand? *At all times.*'

'As the Great Octave commands,' he murmured soothingly and brought one of her hands up to his mouth to kiss her knuckles. 'To Listen now, here,' he said tentatively. 'Do you think he knows?'

'He knows I desire to be Singer,' Enet said, letting him take her weight for a moment. The enormity of it threatened to overwhelm her. 'He is but the Shadow. The holy lord in his infinite wisdom has known I am ambitious for many years and still made me his Chosen. It is the Singer who I obey and love. The Shadow has influence, yes, but no real power. And he has his own ambitions, of which the great Singer is well aware. We are blades at each other's throats and every day we spend in combat is another day closer to the waking of the world spirit. The more the slave focuses on me, the more secure becomes Singer Xac's fate as its eternal consort, which is my fondest wish.'

'Dangerous, high one.'

'Everything is,' Enet snapped and sat up, straightening her spine so that she relied on no one once again. 'He will be back there now, crowing over his supposed victory. He will not come again.'

'Are you certain?'

Enet flashed a warning glare at his presumption and then softened, just a little. 'No. But nothing in this life is certain. We have sixteen days until the world changes. Sixteen days until Tayan of Tokoban learns just how much he means to the holy lord.'

'It's here.'

Enet twisted to face her estate slave, stumbling in her haste. She'd been stalking around the garden room for the last hour while one of her slaves read the history of Singer Tenaca to her in a loud voice. An hour that had passed more slowly than any of her entire life – including the eternities she'd spent labouring to bring her son into the world. The boy who was now gone because of her decisions. *My diamond child. My Pikte. When I see you again, will you forgive me? Will you look at all that I have wrought since your death and deem it worthwhile?*

There was sweat on the Chitenecah upper lip and his eyes were big in his face as he stood just inside the door. 'Shall I put extra guards on the estate's perimeter?'

'No,' Enet snapped, and then again, quieter. 'No. We mustn't draw attention.'

'As the high one commands.' He drummed his fingers against his breastbone and stared sightlessly out of the window.

'Xini. It's going to work.' He startled at her use of his name – strange and uncommon in her mouth – and met her eyes with a worried smile.

'As the high one commands,' he said again, softly this time. She nodded once and the moment of familiarity was over: Xini opened the door for her and bowed as she strode through, falling in behind her. Two score warriors thronged the garden, escorting a dozen slaves carrying a wide, shrouded litter.

'It's actually here,' she murmured to herself, a shiver of religious awe moving down her spine. 'And I've got two weeks. That's enough, surely. Surely that's enough.' Enet took a deep breath and squared her shoulders, settled her face into its familiar, imperious lines. 'Hurry. Get it inside. No, you idiots, the litter won't fit. You'll have to carry it by hand. Do not touch it directly – hold only the ropes. I said *hurry*.'

The sweating slaves lifted the waist-high object wrapped in layers of cotton and grass ropes. The litter itself was abandoned on the path beside the offering pool as they strained beneath the burden.

Enet forced herself to precede them when what she wanted to do was flutter around and even lend her own strength to theirs. They weren't moving fast enough. What if someone knocked on the gate now? What if fucking Pilos demanded entrance? Or a Chooser? Even her position as Great Octave wouldn't be sufficient to deny them entry.

Xini led the way to the secret room, hauling the painted screen out of the way and slamming back the door. The broken songstone cap was within, covered and pushed back against the wall to make room.

'Carefully,' she snapped as one corner of the wrapped bundle clattered into the edge of the door as they manoeuvred it inside. Sweating, panting low-voiced, strained commands, the bearers performed a complicated dance to squeeze in through the doorway and lay the object on the prepared platform. Finally, it was done.

'Out,' Enet said, ragged. 'You, see to them. They're to rest and eat, the guards included.' Xini nodded and ushered the slaves back out through the door, casting her a single enquiring glance as he went. She nodded once and he left her alone with her prize.

Enet walked around the shrouded mound, her heart somewhere in her throat. Carefully, precisely, she filled her mind with adoration of the Singer, almost oblivious to the actions of her hands as she carefully picked at the knots of the ropes. Eventually, she took a knife from one of the shelves and, screwing up every strand of discipline and patience and will she had left, knelt and very, very carefully cut through the ropes one by one, setting aside each piece as it came free.

Enet breathed slow and controlled, centring herself in her power, her convictions, and what little magic she had left from her tonic. It thrummed weak as a cup of badly brewed beer through her veins, almost vibrating in time with the magic she could just about sense from the object before her. Eventually, the last rope parted beneath her knife and Enet set it aside. After another three deep breaths, she began unwrapping the many layers of fine cotton and the padding that obscured its true shape.

The last layer fell away to reveal milky-white stone gleaming with chips that looked like quartz or mica. *Songstone.* Not just that, but carved songstone. A capstone already imbued by the rituals of Listeners to connect it to the spiderweb of pyramids that stretched across all Ixachipan and united it under the song. A living, working capstone of the Empire of Songs, fresh from a supposedly Zellih-destroyed pyramid in Tokoban.

Enet exhaled, sick with adrenaline and nerves. Her hands shook as she extended them towards the pristine lines of the capstone resting in its nest of blankets. Tears welled in her eyes: it was so beautiful. The sum and pinnacle of Pechaqueh achievement. Reverently, she placed her palms against it and then, softly, leant her brow between them.

Xini found her like that an unknown time later. 'High one? High one, do you wish the mason to be brought in now?'

No, she wanted to say. To scream. This songstone's power was so much greater than the one she'd carved herself, even though it felt different. Impersonal, where the broken stone was hers, body and mind. Broken as she was broken; powerful as she was powerful. *Powerless now, which I refuse to be.*

Yet this stone's magic was undeniable and, with the mason's help, could be bent to her will. Still, she was reluctant. She wanted to attune to it herself, wanted to reach out and connect and feel it reach back.

But we don't have time for that.

Enet and the broken songstone had a long, intimate history. It had taken her eight sun-years – an entire Star cycle – to carve it to the point it had reached before she had, at the very final moment before its ultimate incarnation, shattered it beyond recall. Her spirit was like that capstone, she thought, every decision she'd made and every person she'd lost a crack, a chasm, marring her perfection.

It's worth it. Everything I've done will be worth it. It has to be.

'Bring me the mason,' she rasped. 'And sufficient guards but I want them outside the door. We're not leaving this room until I know what I need to.'

'As the Great Octave commands. You should know that we have the location of her family. If you suspect her of lying, use it.' Xini paused, fists clenched in distaste. 'We can bring them here if necessary so that you might make the point but . . . she was carefully selected, high one. Supremely talented, but better with stone than with people. Suggestible.'

'I understand. Put arrangements in place to bring the family here but wait for my word.' The Chitenecatl gave her a tight smile and a little bow.

Enet waited in serene silence, refusing to pace or swear or pray. Her attire was perfect, her cosmetics skilfully applied and the mask beneath them firmly in place. Just before the door opened, she wiped the palms of her hands on the back of her kilt.

'Master mason,' she greeted smoothly as the woman was brought in. 'Under the song.'

The mason had the broadest shoulders she'd ever seen, meaty arms and thick wrists and a barrel chest, but she wore them lightly and without threat. Instead, she hunched her shoulders and stared at Enet with clear anxiety – until her gaze fell on the capstone. Professional concern took over in an instant. 'High one? Is there an issue with the capstone?' she asked, stepping forward, all her attention already on it rather than the Great Octave. She knelt and bowed to the stone, muttering prayers, before laying her hands against it.

As Enet had done, she appeared to reach for the magic within it, though Enet knew the mason would understand it far more innately than she could. Idly, she wondered how much of it was down to years of inhaling songstone dust as well as the rituals taught her by the Listeners, historians and diviners who trained the masons.

'The capstone is serving its sacred purpose, high one,' the woman said, a furrow between her brows. She looked at Enet for the first time. 'It should be . . . why is it here? Why am I here?'

'Mason, do you know who I am?' Enet asked. The woman shook her head, mute. She was still worried, but the presence of songstone seemed to have convinced her that she was here for work. 'My name is Enet. I have the honour of being Great Octave to our holy lord, the Singer Xac.'

The mason gaped and then hurriedly pressed her forehead to the mats. 'Forgive me, high one, I didn't know.'

'There is no reason why you should,' Enet said easily. 'May I have the honour of knowing your name?'

'Nux, high one. I have the honour of working in the mine in the west of Xentiban. I . . . am I in trouble, high one? Is there an issue with my work? This capstone is not mine, but it is flawless.'

Enet raised an eyebrow. 'Not yours? You can tell?'

'Yes, high one. The, ah, signature of the mason is clear in the magic.'

'Good,' she said briskly. 'That is what I was hoping to hear. I am sorry that you were brought here in secret and I know you have been worried while you have been a guest on my estate. I promise you there is nothing to fear. Nux, you have been chosen out of all the master masons within Ixachipan. The great Singer is working a mighty magic and I have the honour of assisting him.'

She leant close, inviting confidence. 'We are going to wake the world spirit soon,' she murmured and Nux was gratifyingly awestruck.

'To do this, I must strengthen my connection with the song-magic and this capstone must be modified, just a little. Do you understand?'

'Modified, high one? It is perfect already; it works.'

'I know that. It channels the magic perfectly. But of course, the ritual requires the magic to move differently. Do you understand?'

'Ah,' Nux said, though she didn't seem completely convinced by Enet's explanation. 'Then modified how?'

'I need you to identify a safe place for me to carve a series of glyphs in the capstone that won't damage its structure or interrupt the flow of magic, but rather intensify it and channel it, not outwards from all sides as normal, but only out through those marks. I know it can be done,' she added as Nux began to protest, huge hands flailing.

'It is forbidden,' Nux wailed. 'Glyphs? Containing the magic and channelling it? No, no, it must never be done.'

'Master mason,' Enet said with outward patience. 'Why do you believe it is forbidden? For this very reason. It is a mystery contained purely to the ritual to wake the world spirit. A ritual the details of which are kept secret from ordinary Pechaqueh, let alone any of the peoples we have brought under the song. A ritual known to the Singer, to me and the historian of the source. No one else. Tell me, mason, do you know the requirements of the ritual?'

Nux faltered. 'I do not, high one. But we are told – the first lesson we are told—'

'Is not to carve glyphs or direct the magic in the capstone. Of course. Think of the damage you could do if you inadvertently harnessed the song in the wrong way. Do you trust me, Nux?' Enet added, suddenly enough that the other woman flinched.

'What? Of, of course, high one. Of course, you are our Great Octave. The Singer himself chose you. It is just . . . the ritual? Really?'

'When the world changes, Nux, when the world spirit awakes and we see an end to suffering, and all Ixachipan becomes a garden for us to play in, you will be able to tell your family you helped make it. I can't do this without you, Nux. *The Singer* cannot do this without you. Will you help us?'

Nux was slack-jawed and starry-eyed. 'My wife will be so proud,' she breathed.

'She will,' Enet agreed softly. 'You're going to help us change the world, Nux. If you agree.'

The woman blinked at that. 'Yes, of course I will,' she said quickly. 'What are the glyphs? What do you need me to write?'

'No, Nux. I must do the carving myself. I need you to tell me where and how deep so that the glyphs direct the magic only in one direction, not from each face. And we don't have much time, either. The ritual must take place in just over two weeks.'

The mason blinked again and her dreamy expression faded and was replaced with determination. She ran a critical eye over the capstone, then stood and walked around it, examining each of its four faces. Enet let her work, watching closely as she touched seemingly random parts of the stone, muttering under her breath.

'How many glyphs?' she asked absently.

'No more than six,' Enet said, uncaring of the mason's lack of respect. She appreciated the woman's focus.

'Deep enough to access the magic but not so deep as to take months to carve,' she muttered. 'You'll need to trace them in charcoal first and not deviate. No deeper than the first knuckle of your little finger.'

Enet felt an uncharacteristic blush heat her cheeks and put her left hand – the one with the missing finger – behind her back. Nux held out her hand. 'The charcoal?'

'I said you couldn't,' the Great Octave began.

'I need to mark out where you can carve,' the mason said. 'There are veins within songstone, channels for the magic. If you go into one, or go too deep, you'll crack the whole piece. Shatter it. I'll mark the places where you can carve. Do not stray outside the lines.'

Enet found her a small stick of charcoal and watched the

mason's huge hands cradle it delicately and then draw gentle lines that swam and flowed across the milky stone. 'In here, Great Octave. Nowhere else. And only pick one side – you can't carve all of them or it won't work.'

'I will not forget,' Enet promised.

'Let me see your tools, your carving tools,' Nux said when she had marked each side of the capstone. Wordlessly, the Great Octave handed them over and the mason turned them over in her hands. 'Absolutely not,' she said, disgusted. 'You can't get any delicate work done with these.' She dropped them on a shelf and strode to the door and pulled it open. Xini and six burly guards jumped in surprise.

'High one?' Xini asked, his hand up to still the guards, awaiting Enet's order.

'My tools that came with me,' Nux said. 'We need them if we are to be successful. One of you, hurry and get them.' The woman turned back into the room and crouched by the capstone again, paying no attention to the murmuring outside. 'This side,' she said decisively, and set about tenderly wiping the charcoal scuffs from the other faces.

Enet and the estate slave exchanged a look and then she flicked her fingers, sending him to fetch the mason's tools. She watched Nux mumble happily to herself as she crawled around the capstone, occasionally tapping it or skimming her fingertips down the pristine edges. Xini had made a good choice.

Enet held the glyphs she needed to carve in her mind, not looking at them directly, not acknowledging anything that was happening here in her palace. It was the thinnest of disguises, more translucent than the rose-coloured hanging that kept the Singer hidden from view, but it was all she had against the prying of the Toko or even the Singer himself, should he choose to come looking for her. She had not been to the source all day; despite the holy lord's preoccupation with his Shadow, her absence would soon be noticed.

Xini came back with Nux's tools and the mason took them eagerly and spun to face Enet. 'Here,' she said excitedly. 'Let me show you.'

'It is always useful to learn a new skill that will bring glory to the Empire of Songs,' the Great Octave agreed as, behind them, her guards began a song praising Singer Xac, one of the new compositions that she was unfamiliar with. She listened closely to the words as her eyes tracked Nux's hands, letting the motions settle into her consciousness without her input.

Looking sideways at the future. Looking sideways at her path to changing the world.

PILOS

Xessa was fighting today. Her first fight since they'd made their agreement.

Pilos had a knot in his belly as he sat in the seats and waited for her to come out; despite the coming ritual to wake the world spirit and his ongoing suspicion of Enet, this fight – the wealth it would bring him – was important. The gate opened and Yerit's fighter trotted onto the dirt, to a roar from the crowd. He squinted down at them and stiffened.

'Pit-master,' he said tightly even as Elaq beckoned urgently to one of the pit guards. 'Pit-master, who is your fighter?'

'Ah, did I not say?' Yerit asked nonchalantly and swirled beer in his cup. 'My scheduled fighter took a bout of fever yesterday. It was difficult, but I managed to get another ready in time. Couldn't have you losing prestige among the pits if your prize frog-licker didn't get a chance to stick her spear in someone, could we?' He waved his fingers down at the hard-packed dirt. 'No, no, this will be a fine match.'

403

'It isn't done to switch fighters without proper warning,' Pilos said through gritted teeth.

Yerit clapped him on the shoulder, his flapping hand grazing the scar across his jaw. Pilos flinched despite himself. 'Don't fret, pit-master. They're evenly matched. I know all your fighter's statistics and have brought a worthy opponent. It will be fine entertainment. Slave, pass the pit-master the report.'

Yerit's body slave handed Pilos a sheet of bark-paper, which of course he could have done first thing, before even the warm-up bouts had been fought. Yerit thought to force Pilos's hand, but as he scanned the glyphs, the man seemed to have spoken true: they were evenly matched. They were . . . Pilos went cold. He leapt to his feet, but it was too late; the second gate was already opening and Xessa had stalked out into the arena.

'Turn her away!' he shouted. Kalix squinted up at him, confused. 'Put her back to her opponent, right now.' The trainer didn't hesitate, lunging for Xessa's arm and dragging her towards the gate. The slave balked but then Ilam was there too, grabbing her other arm and hissing questions at Kalix.

'Feather?' Elaq demanded, also on his feet and his hand on his knife.

'Get her out of there,' Pilos snarled. 'This parrot-fart's put her in against a Toko.'

Yerit stared up at him with a frown. 'Is there a problem with your fighter, pit-master?' he asked mildly, ignoring the insult. 'She's stepped onto the dirt; you can't swap her now. Not unless you forfeit all bets already placed.'

'You fucking no-blood son of a slave,' Pilos grunted, making sure this insult was very clear. 'They will fight to first cut only,' he decided, his attention flickering between

Xessa and her tense shoulders and the other Toko stalking her half of the arena.

Loud protests rose from the seating around them, urged on by Yerit himself. 'They've stepped onto the dirt! The fight cannot be changed. Start it now! Start it now!' It quickly became a chant, echoing around the pit.

Pilos couldn't go against the audience and the bets already placed for one slave fighter. But how much status would he lose if she rammed her spear into her own throat in front of them all? It's what she'd sworn to do if faced with one of her own, and that was something he'd sworn wouldn't happen.

'Get me the big lad, the translator,' he snarled to Elaq. 'Go.' Yerit's fighter could translate herself, he assumed, but he couldn't trust anything she signed.

Elaq had done the same calculations and knew the risk they faced, because he didn't hesitate, hurrying along the row and down the stairs. The Feather moved to the edge of the pit. 'You, Yerit's slave. Name and home.'

The woman turned to look up at him. She had a scar across her face and a chill in her eyes. 'Lutek of the Sky City, Tokoban. Warrior.'

'And have you fought Tokob before for pit-master Yerit?'

Lutek's eyes cut towards Xessa's back and then she jerked her chin upwards. 'Yes. I know what this place is. What you turn us into. You have broken our people and I will not let you break me. I will live whatever it takes.'

'I admire your determination, but my fighter thinks differently. She has vowed to suicide if she is put in against her own.' Pilos wasn't sure what he was asking this woman – this slave of a rival pit – to do.

'Sounds like my fight will be easily won, then,' Lutek replied, shifting sideways so that she could keep Xessa and the trainers in view in case this was a ruse. Pilos admired that about her too.

'Right now, she doesn't know who you are or what's happening. If you press her the instant the fight begins, she'll react on instinct, too busy fighting to stay alive to remember to die.'

Lutek paused. 'Doesn't know? Ah, it's Xessa, isn't it? I did wonder if we'd ever face each other.' She paused to run her thumb across the hatching in the spear's grain, examining Pilos's face. 'She was a friend, you know, back home. Suicide would be a mercy for her.'

Pilos dropped his voice and leant over the wall. 'Give me a show and I'll buy you from Yerit. I swear it on Xessa's death. On my honour. On . . . Malel.'

Lutek blinked. 'You *want me* to kill her?' she asked, drifting closer.

Pilos snorted. 'No, I want her to kill you, but I already know that's not going to happen. You've fought here before, and we've fought at your pit. You know how I treat my fighters. I can give you that, but only if you give her a death in battle, not a suicide. You won't be a slave fighter, either. Indentured. Two years and you're free,' he added, a final gamble.

The woman shook out her shoulders and licked her teeth. Then she tipped her head onto one side. 'I accept. I'll kill Xessa for you – and you'll do what you've promised.'

From the corner of his eye, Pilos saw Elaq dragging out the male Toko and waved him back. 'Fight!' he roared and Kalix and Ilam shoved Xessa hard and ducked into the passageway beyond the gate as she righted herself. She spun, wild and snarling and confused.

Lutek was already on her, flint spearhead gleaming. Tiamoko screamed something; Xessa leapt away, defensive and then flowing into the first attack, instinctive and lethal. The crowd roared.

And Pilos prayed.

'She asks what you said to Lutek, pit-master,' Tiamoko said in a monotone. He was ashen, but Xessa looked even sicker, as if she was suffering from an unseen wound. The shaman had said she wasn't: her injuries were surface and minor, despite the ugliness of the match. Tiamoko stood beside him, with Ilam and his knife a few paces away. Xessa was back in her cage, for while Pilos hoped she might be reasonable, he wasn't willing to test that assumption without a sturdy barrier between them.

The Feather's ruse had played out better than he had hoped. By the time Xessa had identified Yerit's fighter, they'd already been exchanging a flurry of vicious blows, Lutek pressing her so hard she couldn't think or plan or do anything other than obey her years of training and her body's desire to live. It was what Pilos had made her, and he thanked the holy Setatmeh he had been successful.

The fight had been fast, bitter and brutal, and when Xessa used that unpredictability he'd never managed to train out of her to flow beneath an attack and come up slicing her spear tip into Lutek's groin, they'd both been surprised. She'd severed the artery and Lutek had collapsed to one knee, Xessa too busy pressing her hands to the wound to open her own throat before the under-trainers wrestled her away. They shouldn't have been in the pit that fast – it was a death match and both fighters still lived – but not even Yerit had protested. He had made it clear that Xessa had to watch Lutek bleed to death, though, a little extra added cruelty to make up for his loss.

A little extra added cruelty so that she kills herself and we both lose, more like.

407

Pilos focused back on the Mute. Her eyes glittered with unshed tears, as dead and unblinking as a snake's. She flung up a hand, demanding he answer her.

He should have been angry at the questioning but instead he was relieved to have a chance to explain. *As if I owe her anything. As if she is worth my words, my breath.*

And yet . . . warrior to warrior, I do owe her this. If she was one of my slave warriors, if she was in a Talon, I would find her in the aftermath of a battle against her own people and I would let her know she'd done the right thing. As I did with my Quitob dog warriors during the uprising six years ago.

This is no different.

He put on the cloak of Feather, even High Feather, and met her gaze without flinching and without shame. 'I asked Yerit's fighter to give you a worthy death, not a worthless suicide. Something your ancestors would be proud to witness. You gave her that instead.'

He watched Xessa's face as Tiamoko translated, though he thought she got at least some of it from his lips. Either way, his meaning seemed lost on her. The familiar frustration bubbled up, the same he felt every time he tried to communicate with her. Vaguely, he found himself resenting her; all of this would be easier if he could only talk to her properly.

'I did not know, I swear that on my gods, on the holy Setatmeh and the world spirit. We have an agreement.'

She began signing even before Tiamoko finished his own translation.

'You broke the agreement,' Tiamoko said for her, as Pilos expected.

'I tried to stop it. And as I promised, I gave your portion of the winnings to those you claimed, and the rest to your friend's debt.' He indicated the big warrior, whose face softened and then went hard again. 'And . . . I have news of your husband. I promised that too.'

Tiamoko sucked in a breath and despite how obvious a deflection it was, Xessa still approached and grabbed the bars of her cell. Her face was ugly with hope and fear and a poisonous shame that was eating away at her. He knew her thoughts as if they were his own: why do I get this when a Toko is dead at my own hand? Still, she hauled on the bamboo in an ecstasy of impatience.

'Toxte of the Sky City, warrior,' Pilos said, reading from the list he'd obtained from the central slave records here in the Singing City. It had been easy, in the end, just six days of cross-referencing for the scribes – but Xessa had claimed him, and he'd claimed her, and that always helped. He'd kept the knowledge to himself until after this fight, which he could admit was unfair – there'd been a possibility she could have died without knowing. Still, it had all worked out in the end.

'He was crippled during the fall of the Sky City and failed selection for the Melody. He works on the chinampas in Quitoban, among the tidal marshes. He lives; he is healthy despite his injury. He works to pay off his debt and yours.'

Xessa fell as if someone had cut her legs from under her. Raw, ugly sounds of grief tore from her throat, and then Tiamoko was kneeling opposite her, hands reaching through the bars and gathering her close.

'He's alive, sweetheart,' he murmured, his voice breaking. 'He's alive.'

Pilos felt like an interloper; he turned to leave when Tiamoko began speaking, confusion and then horror in his voice as he translated.

'Toxte should not waste his jade on my debt. It should go back to him so that he might be free sooner. Tell him I'm dead, high one' – he choked and then spoke on – 'tell him to forget me.'

The Feather came back to the cell and watched Xessa drag herself to her feet as if she was a greyhair who'd lived a dozen Star cycles. 'Promise me you'll do it. He needs to understand there's nothing left for him to believe in,' Tiamoko whispered as she signed.

Pilos raised his eyes to the roof and inhaled through his nose, fighting for calm. *That fucking Yerit. I'll kill him myself for wasting my time on this. If she wasn't so valuable . . .*

'I will do no such thing,' he said deliberately. 'How dare you seek to destroy your husband's hope for the future. Who are you to be so cruel? Is Toxte of Tokoban's happiness worth so little to you?' He might as well have been speaking one of the languages of Barazal for all the comprehension in Xessa's face. He grabbed Tiamoko by the arm and hauled him upright. 'I thought you were living for your friend?' he demanded and then shook him. 'Translate.'

'She's not – she won't,' the Toko stuttered and then gave up, signing instead.

To Pilos's surprise, Xessa lunged at the bars, clawed fingers catching in his tunic and pulling so fast and hard that he slammed into the bamboo, the mostly healed wound beneath his jaw taking the brunt of the impact. His eyes watered and his hand dropped to his knife even as hers reached for his throat.

'She thinks you're threatening my life!' Tiamoko shouted as Ilam yelled and sprang to the gate, hurrying to untie it. Tiamoko jammed an arm in between Pilos and the bars, too busy trying to drag him free to sign anything that might have calmed the raging woman.

In spite of every instinct screaming at him, Pilos let go of his knife and her arm and held up both hands, palms open and turned towards her. He could feel the blood in his face, the pounding of his pulse in his temples, and just managed to shake his head against the grip of her hand. Setatmeh, but she was strong.

Tiamoko was straining to push her away with one hand, snapping the fingers of the other in her face to attract her attention so she could read his lips. Pilos's vision was beginning to blur at the edges before Xessa's grip slackened enough for him to take a breath. The effort it had taken to stand still and wait – hope, pray – she'd let go had shaken him. He'd been heartbeats away from giving up on patience and slamming his knife into her chest. Pilos stepped back and dragged Ilam away too, striving for the appearance of calm as he coughed.

'Forgive her, high one, please I beg you, I'll do anything. She's mad with grief. Please, high one, please,' Tiamoko was babbling as Xessa slumped to her knees again, hands wrapped around the bamboo and brow pressed against it as her shoulders shook with sobs.

Pilos flicked his fingers in dismissal and the Toko hesitated long enough to be insolent before squeezing Xessa's wrist and walking to his own cell. The other slave fighters were in the under-pit, discussing the day's bouts and waiting for news from the shamans on injured friends. The Feather was glad they hadn't witnessed this.

He crouched opposite Xessa, Ilam mumbling a warning he ignored. He checked in both directions again, eyeing Tiamoko's cell, and then put his hand over Xessa's where she gripped the bars. Her hitching breaths stilled; everything stilled. As if she was carved on the side of a pyramid or painted on a wall.

She looked up through wet lashes. 'Live for your husband and Tiamoko,' he said clearly. The slave shook her head, miserable. 'Live for Lutek's memory,' he tried and she snarled, though it lacked any bite.

Pilos patted her hand once and stood up, his knees clicking. He stared down at her, making his face implacable. 'Then live for me – and for your dog. He misses you.' He walked away while she was still gaping.

'Pilos, Feather of the Singing City, requests entrance to the holy lord's presence to meet with Chorus Leader Ilandeh.'

'Welcome, Feather Pilos,' the Shadow said. 'Rise and approach. I'm sure you have much to discuss with the Chorus Leader, what with the ongoing unrest in the city. We do hope you will put an end to it swiftly, don't we, my love?' Pilos bowed a little lower. 'We have sufficient guards today; you may stand at a distance for your discussion.'

'You honour me with such consideration, Shadow,' he said and stood, walking around the seated pair with his eyes averted. The Chorus Leader watched him approach with a neutral gaze, eyes tracking from him to the Singer every few breaths to assure herself of his safety. They were, indeed, heavily guarded, but Ilandeh was taking no chances. He was pleased.

'Great Octave Enet, Chosen of Xac, requests entrance into the holy lord's presence.' Enet's voice was quiet but clear and Pilos tensed, as did his Whisper, but the Shadow greeted her easily and there was nothing they could do but obey his command and move deeper into the gardens, out of earshot. Still, there was heavily guarded and then there was Enet, sitting almost within touching distance of the Singer. A muscle flickered in Pilos's jaw.

'Chorus Leader, it is a pleasure to see you again. You honour me with your company. Under the song.' Ilandeh was getting better at accepting his words and the status of equality they conveyed; even here when none could overhear them, it was best to keep up the pretence.

'And you, Feather Pilos. Under the song.' She stood facing towards the holy lord, while Pilos turned side-on so that the Great Octave could not see his face. He had become more conscious of lip-reading since Xessa had come into his pit. He doubted Enet had the skill of it, even less so at this distance, but he would take no chances.

'Are you well, Ilandeh? Things proceed smoothly with your new position?'

'Chorus Acamah has accepted his change in status. As for the others, I have no concerns about their loyalty to the Singer.'

Ah, then there was an issue with their loyalty to her as Chorus Leader. Pilos had suggested Ilandeh because to do otherwise would be suspicious: why wouldn't he recommend her in the aftermath of her actions to save the Shadow's life? Yet he and the Whisper had years of acquaintance behind them. She'd proved herself again and again to him and earned his trust through fire and blood. He couldn't expect his eagles to feel that same trust when they'd never fought alongside her.

But if she couldn't control the Chorus, especially as they both knew Acamah, Lisek and the rest were dangling from Enet's jade-strings, then perhaps a new face altogether would be wiser. Xochi, perhaps. The problem would be finding a good enough excuse to install her in the great pyramid before the Great Star's absence.

Perhaps it's time for Ilandeh to have an accident.

'You've had a difficult few years,' he said in a low voice. Ilandeh startled, eyeing him and then lifting one shoulder in a small shrug. 'And despite your blood, I want you to know that I'm proud of you. You've never acted with anything less than perfect honour and complete dedication and—'

'Despite my blood?' Ilandeh's voice was flat when she interrupted, low but throbbing. Pilos blinked. '*Despite* my blood? Do you think it's my fault my blood isn't pure, Feather? Do you think I wouldn't change it if I could, that I don't regret every single day that my father fell in love with a Xenti?'

'That's not what—' he began.

She was still watching the Singer, but her voice dripped with scorn and Pilos felt anger kindle in his belly. 'You say you trust me as if it is some great reward, as if it will make up for the fact that I'm going to be torn to pieces by this Chorus sooner rather than later. You think they're not moving against me? I came to you, *I begged you* to take action against Enet or to get me out and put a real eagle in my place, and you didn't. You made me fucking Chorus Leader instead. And now, although I am the impure one, it is your eagles who are Enet's creatures, not me. *I* am the loyal one; *I* am the Singer's best and only hope of survival. I have always put the Singer, the Empire, the Melody and you before myself. And you stand there and tell me I'm a good little warrior *despite my blood.*'

Pilos clenched his jaw. 'Ilandeh,' he growled, 'I only meant—'

'You only meant I've surprised you, that I've outperformed the promise of my parents. One parent, anyway. That I've done well no matter how limited my natural abilities might be.' She paused to suck in air through flared nostrils and Pilos was seized with the urge to clap his hand over her mouth. How dare she. *How dare she* speak to him like this. First a no-blood fucking slave and now a half-blood Setatmeh-damned Whisper!

'Your trust is precious to me, Feather,' she continued in a lower tone, 'and I have never wanted to do anything but serve the Empire and win your approval, but your condescension is humiliating and unwarranted. I am better than you believe. Is it the idea of a half-blood being within the source when the world spirit is awoken that disgusts you? Or it is just me?'

Her words cut deep and cut true. It did distress him. 'Watch your tongue,' he snapped, but there was little fire in it. 'Who do you—'

'The song hurts, Feather, did you know that?' Ilandeh spoke on, relentless. 'Every day and night I am within this pyramid, it is a physical pain, telling me I am lesser, that I should throw myself to my knees before every Pecha I see and beg their forgiveness for my father's crime of loving a savage. For my crime of being born of that love.' She finally turned from her steady regard of the Singer to face him, taking one soft, dangerous step closer. Pilos flinched. 'And yet I do my duty regardless. With love of the Singer in my heart.'

A muscle jumped in Pilos's jaw and fury boiled from his skin like steam. 'We are done for this week,' he grated.

Ilandeh's lips peeled back in a smile that showed too many teeth. 'As the Feather commands,' she said softly. 'Under the song.'

'Ah, Feather, are you leaving?' the Shadow asked as Pilos stalked away from Ilandeh and knelt to his Singer. His jaw was clenched so tight his teeth hurt. *How dare she.* 'My sweet love and I have been talking, haven't we, holy lord?' he added and the Feather forced himself to pay attention.

'You are Spear of the Singer,' the Singer rumbled and Pilos rocked on his knees, his mouth falling open in genuine shock and all of Ilandeh's vicious, improper heresy wiped from his thoughts.

'Holy lord?' Enet asked carefully into the silence. 'Do you remember his—'

'He is Spear of the Singer. Haapo is a fool who looks to others to tell him how to think. Pilos is neither. Are you, Pilos?' the Singer added as the rich red-brown of his skin began to glow from within. 'I can trust you again, can I not?'

'Always, holy lord,' Pilos choked, his mind a hot blank. 'You do me too much honour. I swear to repay you with my loyalty, my life and the best advice I can offer.' *Like a change in fucking Chorus Leader for a start.*

The Shadow grinned at the Singer and then Pilos. 'You will remain Feather of the Singing City as well,' he said easily. 'We know there is still unrest about my identity, but the ritual to wake the world spirit approaches. We expect the Singing City to be peaceful when it does.'

Ah, so not an empty role, then, but a promise that he would spend the next weeks being run ragged finding rumour-mongers and rounding up vocal opponents of the Singer's choice of successor.

'I will ensure it is so,' Pilos promised and bowed. 'Under the song.' He forced his face to reveal only his gratitude before he stood again, packing away the pride and acknowl-edgement that it was *about fucking time his efforts were recognised* into a tight, hot ball in his chest for later examination. He looked at Ilandeh, who had resumed her place behind the Singer as was proper. Her expression was closed, but something brightened her eyes. Tears? Or the gleam of disloyalty?

'Great Singer, Shadow, Great Octave Enet, I will see you at the next council meeting. Please do not hesitate to call on me should you require anything before then.' He took a swift breath. 'Chorus Leader, I leave the holy lord in your capable hands. Under the song.'

The Shadow grinned again, perfectly aware of how much the announcement had riled his former owner and entirely unrepentant of that fact. Despite himself, the corner of Pilos's mouth twitched.

He made one final, deep obeisance and then returned through the garden and into the source, and then down the long, empty corridor, his mind reeling.

Spear of the Singer again. Well, fuck me. This'll put a scorpion up Enet's kilt and no mistake.

He grinned, slapping his fist gently into the palm of his other hand, before his mood soured with the force of a mid-Wet rainstorm. *Ilandeh.*

LILLA

Lilla stepped out of his sandals and into Ekon's quarters, anticipation mingling with trepidation in his belly. They'd spent a handful of evenings together, passionate, intense evenings, but then there'd been nothing, not even a message or a stolen moment after training, for ten days. Something had happened to keep Ekon at his duty every evening until night fell. Or he had changed his mind and was simply ignoring Lilla until he understood that it was over.

The Toko had tried to focus only on what that meant for the cause and the rebellion, but his thoughts had turned, again and again, to the hollowness inside him carved by the withdrawal of Ekon's affection. The empty hurting.

But then, now. Tonight. Here.

The early evening was still hot and that's why Lilla's palms were sweating; no other reason. A guard had escorted him and then left him outside Ekon's quarters, the late sun shining like a lump of gold just above the compound wall.

418

The Feather was standing with his hands clasped behind his back, his tunic and kilt fresh and vibrant when he called for Lilla to enter. His hair was loose, not just cascading down his back, softer than midnight, but framing his face. No eagle feather ornament or coloured strings holding it back from his temples. Bands of light angled in through the high openings beneath the roof, throwing gold into his hair and down the line of his jaw. It didn't touch his eyes, though, which were as black and fathomless as an underground pool.

Lilla dropped to his knees, but before he could put his head down in obeisance, Ekon was drawing him up by the shoulders and back onto his feet. He didn't let go and Lilla's heart sped up. 'Feather?'

'Lilla, please.' Ekon's voice was smoke and honey, and instead of its habitual edge of command it was soft; hungry. 'My name is Ekon. Have you really forgotten? Again?'

He hadn't, but he enjoyed hearing Ekon give him permission; enjoyed stripping away that last barrier of status between them. That wasn't the reason tonight, though. Lilla fixed his eyes on the Pechaqueh mouth. Watched him lick his lips. 'It has been . . . some time, Feather.'

'It has, but this has not changed. When you are here, I like it when you use my name.' There was an awkward pause. 'Even if you have changed your mind.'

Arousal was a dart striking Lilla in the gut. 'I thought perhaps it was you who had changed his mind. These last days—' He realised what he was saying and instinctively went to bow again. Again, Ekon prevented him. 'Forgive this . . . you owe me no explanations, Feather Ekon, you—'

'Kiss me,' Ekon said suddenly, fiercely.

Hateful, Lilla tried to remind himself, *impersonal at best*, but it had been neither of those things even that first time and certainly not now, with his treacherous heart kicking under his ribs with the intensity of his relief. *He still wants me.*

Ekon's hands were warm on his shoulders, their strength leashed and yet obvious. Not hidden but restrained, and Lilla knew that those hands were not often restrained when they were laid on a slave. His thumbs were making slow circles across the muscle – across the brands – on the Tokob shoulders. Lilla pushed that away. The last ten days without him, without word or glance or touch, had made him doubt himself and everything he was and wanted. The last ten days *. . . are over and I am here again, with him. With Ekon.*

And he still wants me.

'You summoned me, Ekon?' he managed through the tightness in his throat instead of kissing him the way he had asked. Because Lilla had spent the last ten days doing more than just fretting over Ekon's distance. Another score of rebels had trickled into his hands, convinced by others and by his punishment on the scaffold. They numbered a third of the Eighth Talon now; the time was ripening like corn in the sun for when they would rise up and commit slaughter.

Of everyone.

The Pechaqueh mouth twisted. 'No,' he whispered urgently. 'No, not summoned. Invited. You can leave if you want to.' His right hand drifted to Lilla's chin and lifted it. 'Please look at me. If I have done something wrong . . .'

The "please" nearly undid him and he did look, his gaze travelling slowly from the Feather's chest to his throat, his mouth – lingered, involuntary – and on until he stared into those lovely eyes in their nest of fine lines and saw not only desire but respect. Patience. Hope. Lilla didn't realise he'd bitten his lip until Ekon's gaze flickered down and then back, hotter than before. The finger under his chin shifted, softly beckoning, and butterflies took off in Lilla's gut. He rocked forward on a stuttering breath, shifting his weight until their lips touched. They inhaled together, broke a kiss softer than dew, and kissed again, long and chaste. A question begging an answer, despite what they'd already done together here in this room.

Lilla answered the kiss's question, placing a trembling hand on Ekon's chest, not pushing away but daring to touch. He ached with the tenderness that filled his chest and stole his senses. It was a tenderness that would break him, an affection that shamed him, because this man, this fierce, beautiful man, was Pechaqueh, and owner, and enemy.

And wanted.

For two years that had felt like a lifetime, he had controlled Lilla's every move and word, had punished him and starved him, beaten him and humiliated him. Praised him and raised him up, taught him and fed him. Watched him until the weight of his gaze was like a stone on Lilla's chest. Smiled, so rarely it was the break of sunlight in the middle of the Wet, and as dazzling. And now kissed him.

Ekon's hand slid from beneath Lilla's chin to cup his cheek, the other still on his shoulder. Aware of the renewed imbalance of power they'd worked to eradicate before and doing what he could to redress it. Lilla tilted his head and pressed forward, opening his mouth. Ekon inhaled, a little sharper, and his tongue flickered out and Lilla caught it with his own. There was still air between them and he only had one hand on Ekon, and yet the Feather didn't press for more. Lilla's decision; Lilla's pace. Again.

Lilla's decision. *I'm going to kill this man soon.*

He stepped forward, stinging eyes drifting shut and his hand sliding up Ekon's chest and around the back of his neck beneath the fall of hair, gripping at the nape and pulling him close. His other hand landed on his waist and Ekon

421

cupped Lilla's face as if it was precious jade, as if it was his life's fortune within his grasp. Gentle but firm and willing to let go if the Toko so desired. Of everything Lilla desired with all the intensity of a drum celebration, Ekon letting him go wasn't it.

It was so much more than the last time he'd been here, even just this kiss. So much emotion held between their bodies that Lilla thought he might crack open because of it, shatter apart and blow away on the breeze. The soft flutter of tongue made him dizzy and they were pressed together in the slick evening heat, his chin tilted back in order to reach that expert mouth.

And then Ekon broke the kiss and Lilla stumbled, clinging to him. His eyes opened slowly. 'What?' he managed and found the Pecha smiling fondly at him, and he cracked a little more at the clear affection, something sweet and guilty flooding his chest with warmth.

I'm going to kill this man. I'm going to kill you, Ekon. I have to.

I have to.

'Sit, Lilla. I have . . . the shaman gave me some oil and' – he flushed scarlet and stepped out of the Tokob arms, his eyes comically wide – 'fuck, that's not, not that sort of oil . . .' He rubbed his brow. 'The shaman gave me some oil *for your back*, to help ease the scarring now that the bandages are off. You'll need some help applying it.'

Lilla's amusement at Ekon's mortification faded into a pleased sort of embarrassment and a sudden vulnerability that made him fidget. 'You want to rub my back?' he asked.

'I want to make you feel good,' the Feather said with a shy smile and it was Lilla's turn to blush. 'May I?' he asked, tugging at the hem of Lilla's tunic. The Toko chewed at his lip again and then nodded, caught between need and shyness of his own. He looked away as the tunic was lifted over his head, ridiculously tongue-tied. The last time Ekon had seen his naked back, warriors had been striping it with a hundred lashes. Whatever it had looked like before, it was a ruin now. There was a long moment of silence and then Ekon exhaled, shaky, and bent to lick a broad stripe across Lilla's chest.

He gasped.

'Sorry,' he said, not sorry at all if his grin was anything to go by, and the Toko huffed out a laugh. The Feather pressed a series of kisses to his chest and up his neck, nosing against his jaw.

'Ah, I see what this is,' Lilla murmured breathlessly as he clutched the back of Ekon's neck. 'There's no salve at all, is there? Just an excuse to finally get me naked.'

It was a gamble to say it, to acknowledge the desire, but Ekon's mouth curved into a smile against his cheek. 'There is, actually. You just distracted me.'

'This slave apologises,' Lilla said automatically and they both stilled, tension suddenly crackling between them. 'Ah . . .'

'Please sit, Lilla,' Ekon said, pressing another kiss to his jaw before releasing him. 'Let me take care of you.' It didn't quite paint over his mistake, but the Toko liked that he tried anyway.

He dropped down to sit cross-legged on the mats, moving as the Feather directed him to get light on his back. He let Ekon brush his hair forward over his shoulders and then . . . nothing. No words or movement. Shame unfurled its poisonous leaves within him and Lilla let out a strangled laugh and reached for his tunic again.

'Never mind, it's fine, I know they're ugly,' he began. Something touched his back and he stilled, barely breathing. The Pechaqueh mouth was as soft as butterfly wings as he kissed the scars laid across Lilla's shoulder blades.

'They're not ugly,' he whispered, so low Lilla could barely hear him. 'They are my shame.'

Lilla twisted, ignoring the dull ache in his back, to face Ekon. 'What? No! Don't say that,' he tried, but the Pecha clearly hadn't intended for him to hear; his face was pinched and he was concentrating on the small clay jar of salve, rolling it between his palms to warm the contents.

'Ekon, please don't say that. Or think it,' Lilla insisted, despite the bitter, roiling core of him that agreed with the Feather. He gestured helplessly. 'It is my life, the consequences of my pod's actions. You had no choice.'

I'm going to kill this man. He has to trust me and so I have to convince him I don't blame him for this. So that I can kill him.

Despite what he told himself, Lilla ached to kiss away the unhappy twist to Ekon's mouth. The Feather gently turned him back around, unspeaking, and his hands, warm and slick with oil, stroked across his back. The medicine stung a little, but it faded as Ekon massaged it into skin and scar and the muscles beneath, drawing out tension and conjuring a deep, not unpleasant, ache in its place. Lilla sank into it, willing to let Ekon's words and his own slide away under that expert touch.

'There is unrest in Tokoban, along the border with Barazal,' Ekon said into the meditative quiet. 'The Zellih have been probing at our borders for some time and are increasing their activity every day. High Feather Atu is leading the First and Third Talons north to support the Sixth under Feather Calan, who you might know has been there since the end of the war. There's going to be even more chaos in the fortress in the next few days as other Talons rotate out to key locations. It's keeping me busy.'

Lilla wondered if it was an oblique apology for his absence over the last days. He also committed the information to

424

memory. An emptier fortress, Talons on the move. This could be the perfect opportunity – their only opportunity. 'I pray the Zellih are beaten back easily,' he said. 'It has been years since they threatened us – apologies, since they threatened the Tokob – but our elders and histories confirm they are talented warriors.' He tipped his head forward without thinking and Ekon chuckled, kissed the nape of his neck and then dug his thumbs into the twin bands of muscle. Lilla hissed in pleasure-pain.

'You must think the threat significant to have sent the First and Third,' he managed as his eyes sagged closed in pleased surrender to the strength in Ekon's hands. Six thousand warriors marching across the hills and jungles of his homeland, strangers fighting to defend a land they didn't belong to, one that meant nothing to them except as another line on a map, another boast over beer.

'The finest eagles and finest dogs should be more than enough to subdue the Zellih,' Ekon agreed. 'Though the High Feather regrets . . . Ah, never mind.'

'Regrets?' Lilla pressed into the quiet.

Ekon sighed, warm air ghosting across his skin. 'Regrets there are no Tokob who speak the Zellih language who could be . . .'

'Trusted in Tokoban,' Lilla finished for him. 'My husband knew—' He cut himself off and Ekon's hands stilled on his skin.

'Well, this is painfully awkward,' the Feather managed. 'I apologise.' His hands didn't leave his skin, though, so Lilla shoved back against them in a little unspoken plea. He felt another sigh against his back, this one perhaps relieved, and Ekon resumed the massage, long slow strokes Lilla could lose himself in.

He did so, trying to get back to that place he'd been in before, hungry for sensation and uncaring of his responsibilities.

For a few moments – or hours – where he didn't have to think or watch his words and actions. Where he could just be.

And be with him. Lilla's mouth went dry. *The man I'm going to kill.*

'With the Second Talon already in Xentiban and the First and Third heading north, the High Feather had to ask Listener Citla to contact the Listeners in all the major cities to put up announcements that the intake of fresh Pechaqueh blood into the Melody would need to be delayed. We'll probably still get a few turn up here who missed the message, but the rest will stay away. It's hard when this happens. Those youths will have been training all their lives and counting the days until their trials. Now they're looking at a wait of months. Maybe even longer.'

Lilla dragged his mind away from wondering what Ekon tasted like and pricked up his ears. 'How many were you expecting? Does everyone automatically get in?' His voice trailed off into a hiss as Ekon pressed in under his right shoulder blade, where the muscle was always tight from weapons work. 'More,' he grunted and then whined when the Pecha complied.

'Usually a couple of thousand, but probably only half make it through selection.' Ekon's voice was tight with the strain of working at the knot. 'The quality of eagle warriors cannot be allowed to drop, and nobles and even councillors attempt to bribe the High Feather into letting a favoured but untalented child join our number. It tends to echo, more or less, the number of eagles who leave each sun-year, whether through age, injury or death, song bless them.'

'What happens to the rest?' Lilla asked, trying to pay attention: eagles were leaving but no more were joining, at least this year. Their numbers would be reduced and then lessened further by the Zellih in his homeland. Malel was watching over him, sending him opportunities – more rebels, fewer eagles, a Feather who allowed him to get close enough to kill.

'Most will return to their family trades or attempt an advantageous marriage to increase their status. Some will sign on as bodyguards or even free fighters in the pits. Many see it as a source of shame, but to even attend the selection is in fact an honour. Their blood and talent have carried them far, just not far enough. Is it so with you?'

'No. Anyone who wishes to walk the jaguar path may do so. We are warriors and hunters; those who are less talented in combat focus on bringing back game to our villages and cities. They still join in our training, though: every warrior is needed – was needed – during time of war.'

This time Ekon didn't flinch or pause, and Lilla let the conversation die there. There was little more to be said, anyway. They knew who they were and what their people meant to each other. At least the Pecha seemed similarly determined to save the atmosphere and it was a long time before his hands slowed on Lilla's skin. 'There. How does that feel?'

Lilla made himself stretch and twist, shivering lightly when the Feather's hands remained on his waist, hot and gentle. 'Good,' he said. 'Feels good.' He swayed backwards a little and Ekon moved forward, pressing very gently against him, his fingertips drifting up and down his flanks. Lilla slid his hand back behind him until he encountered a knee and grazed up over it to a thigh, squeezing, and then turned his head to meet Ekon's mouth with his.

The Zellih, Tokoban, the movement of the Talons and his need to kill the Pecha kissing him all vanished in a dizzying rush of heat as his body came to life again, struggling out of the deep lethargy from the massage and flinging itself towards Ekon. He made a noise, half-wanting, half-frustrated, and then got his feet under him, stood and twisted and dragged Ekon up.

The Feather wrapped a long, hard arm around his waist and pulled him even closer and Lilla's breath caught. He stretched back to look up at him and found his lips were damp and soft, begging to be bitten, and so he caught Ekon's lower lip and sucked it into his mouth and pressed his teeth into it. Someone whimpered.

He slid his hands beneath his tunic and Ekon gasped and arched into his touch as he stroked the dip of his spine. Hands slid up to Lilla's hair and carefully, patiently, untied the cord that held it back from his face and pulled it forward. It was a strangely solemn moment, heavy with intent, and the Toko took his hands out from under the tunic to hold on to Ekon's wrists and watch the tiny frown of concentration between his brows as he arranged Lilla's hair to his satisfaction. When it was done and the Feather put his head on one side to study the effect, Lilla blushed and had to fight to hold his gaze.

He grabbed Ekon's tunic. 'Take this off,' he said in a rough voice, needing to step out of that moment and into one driven by simple, uncomplicated want. Ekon complied, and the bars of evening light glimmered in the sheen of sweat across the hard planes of his chest and flanks and, as Lilla had hoped, the sight stopped every thought in his head. The Pecha smiled at his appreciation and pulled them together, skin to skin.

Lilla gasped and Ekon let go as if he was burning. 'I'm sorry.'

The Tokob eyes widened and then a grin spread over his face. 'It wasn't a protest,' he murmured and splayed his hands over the expanse of hot skin before pressing their chests together again. The fires in the Pechaqueh expression were no longer banked and Lilla cast himself headlong into their heat, begging to be devoured. They kissed hard, hands roaming flesh and tugging at kilts, and then Ekon's came undone and Lilla smiled against his mouth – that had been tied *very* loosely – and the Pecha laughed at himself in shameless admission.

Lilla let the kilt fall from his hands and then followed it, dropping to his knees in a voluntary act of worship that caused the Pecha to make a strangled noise of protest. They hadn't done this yet.

'You don't need to,' he tried, and then choked on air as Lilla took him into his mouth, gentle but all in one go, hands pinning his hips in place. *I'm going to kill you*, he thought, a defence against the pleasure surging in him at Ekon's taste and musky scent. Malel, but he'd wanted this.

The Feather clutched at his hair and let out a soft cry, hips stuttering, but seconds later he moved back. 'Not yet,' he gasped and dragged Lilla onto his feet, into a kiss, and across to the bed, fumbling at the knot of his kilt as they went.

Lilla wondered whether the medicine Ekon had rubbed into his back had some magic in it, because he felt drunk and slightly outside of his body as they fell in a tangle of limbs and tongues and roving hands, curtained in each other's hair until they were stifling and sweat-slick. Lilla wanted nothing more than to taste him, possess him, be possessed. Surrender to him, their statuses be damned. This wasn't that, and they both knew it. Or maybe it was. He didn't care.

He got Ekon on his back and slid down his body and took him into his mouth again, unrelenting this time until the Pecha was whining and arching off the bed, until he had to forcibly drag Lilla off him by the hair. 'Are you trying to kill me?' he demanded breathlessly, startling a burst of laughter out of the Toko. 'Come up here. Now.'

Lilla shivered at the command in his voice and complied, not examining the reasons why he wanted to obey too closely. He draped himself on top of the Feather, both of them groaning at all the places where they touched. Despite everything, Ekon's hands gentled every time they stroked his back, constantly aware of the injuries – even more so than Lilla himself.

When he couldn't stand it any longer, the Toko rolled them, needing to feel Ekon's weight pressing him down. It took all of a few heartbeats before he was wrapping his legs around the man's hips and clinging on, scraping the hair back from Ekon's face so he could kiss it. 'Tell me there's some of that oil left,' he said and the Feather let out a heart-felt groan and hid his face in Lilla's neck.

'You are going to kill me,' he muttered again, the words resonating uncomfortably in the Tokob chest. He shoved them away, suddenly desperate to forget, and growled appreciatively when Ekon stretched up to a shelf above the bed and took down a different pot of oil, a gleam of mischief in his eyes.

'What does the honoured warrior want me to do with this?' he teased. Lilla bit his shoulder.

Ekon laughed and then knelt up long enough to tip oil onto his hand. His eyes asked the question and Lilla's answer was to lift his hips; the Pechaqueh breath shuddered out of him and he propped himself on one elbow so they could kiss while his slick finger teased and coaxed and then pressed in.

Lilla grunted at the sting and made himself relax, concentrating on the languid sweep of tongue and fingers, the lean muscled form hovering over him and the arousal simmering in his belly. Ekon worked with focused, deliberate patience until he was pliant and twitching at the pleasure of each teasing stroke, needing more, more, and then withdrew his fingers. Lilla whined his disappointment.

'Can I . . . Do you want . . . What do you want?' the Feather asked, panting with the strength of his own desire. Lilla drank in his expression, the open need in his face that nevertheless didn't contain a demand. He hesitated a bare instant, because they definitely hadn't done this yet, nothing even close, but he knew instinctively that he could change his mind and Ekon would let him. He didn't. He wanted it, wanted Ekon and the promise of his body.

'Yes,' he breathed, tightening his legs around the Pechaqueh waist and beckoning him in. Ekon shuddered out another breath and leant forward for another kiss while he used the oil again before pulling the Tokob hips onto his lap and easing in.

Lilla cried out and he paused. 'Is this—' Ekon began.

'*Don't stop,*' Lilla begged and the Feather's worry slid into delight and the hunger returned to his face and he began to move, slowly at first, carefully, until Lilla urged him on with kisses and whimpers and hands pulling him closer, faster. Harder.

They moved together with the endless shifting motion of the sea, Ekon's brows drawn tight in agonised concentration, determined to wring pleasure from Lilla's body before giving in to his own.

'I did not expect such devotion to a slave's desires,' Lilla teased when the Feather lavished kisses and bites on his sensitive throat, nosing against the leather collar.

Ekon bit hard enough to hurt – and not the pleasurable sort of hurt. 'Do not. You are . . . I don't see such things.'

The burgeoning pleasure vanished, replaced by a stone-heavy coldness in his chest. Lilla's teasing had perhaps been ill-judged, but so was Ekon's reply. 'What things?' he demanded even as he forced his body to stay relaxed for Ekon's intrusion. Was it pretence or self-preservation?

The Feather blinked away the fog of lust. 'No, no, kitten, I didn't mean it like that,' he insisted, dragging himself from the pleasure with visible effort and stilling his movements. 'Lilla, I want you – I thought I'd made that clear. I want you no matter what, I don't care what others say. My status . . . it can bear this.'

He winced as he said it, knowing how it sounded, and nausea swirled in Lilla's chest. *Of course he knows how it sounds; he's the one who said it.*

Malel, please, why must he make it so easy for me to kill him? And yet. And still. I want him. I want this, even if I only get it this one time.

So. 'Don't stop,' he whispered again, clinging to Ekon's shoulders. 'I've only ever wanted to forget. If you truly don't care what anyone thinks, please, please don't stop now.'

'Oh, kitten,' Ekon murmured, and began a slow, hypnotic rhythm once more, one that kindled a fire deep in Lilla's belly and which he stoked, mercilessly and with expert precision, until the Toko was lost within its flames.

He gasped at the fullness and clung to Ekon as tears gathered, pooled and overspilt and the Pecha kissed them away. Lilla reached up to touch his face. 'I'm not your slave,' he said, even as he surrendered, completely and without regret. Even though he would do anything Ekon asked of him. Still, 'I'm not your slave,' he repeated, and Ekon turned his head and kissed his palm and then drew his thumb into his mouth and bit it.

Pressure – pleasure – *want* – built wave upon wave upon wave until Lilla was sobbing with it and Ekon slid a hand between them to stroke him. The Tokob back arched and he panted into Ekon's neck as the pleasure swamped him and then crested, crested some more until he came hard, every muscle clenched and Ekon cursing and frantic within him until seconds later he followed, shuddering, whimpers rolling from his throat until he collapsed, boneless, on top of him.

Finally, they stilled and Ekon managed to force himself up onto one elbow, panting and golden with sweat, one dazed dark eye visible through the curtain of hair that shivered with his quick breaths.

They watched each other, sweetly exhausted, Ekon's body a precious weight on him and in him, more important than the ache building in Lilla's back or the words that still echoed in his head. Still, he didn't protest when the Feather slowly withdrew and then stretched out by his side and held him close. He kissed Lilla again, their eyes open, then pulled back so there was nothing but a wisp of air between their mouths. He brushed the pad of his thumb across Lilla's cheek, wiping away fresh tears.

'You are not my slave,' he murmured. 'Kitten, *you are not my slave.*'

How badly Lilla wanted to believe him. How badly he wanted this to be real, that this illusion of safety might never end. He closed his eyes and buried his face in Ekon's chest. If he was lucky, maybe the Feather would let him pretend that this sliver of happiness was true, just for a while.

Just a little while.

Before the day came when he had to put a blade in him.

ILANDEH

The source, Singing City, Pechacan, Empire of Songs
246th day of the Great Star at evening

Pilos had attended their weekly meeting and conducted himself with distant formality, allowing no hint of their former friendship to soften his edges. Had they ever been friends? Ilandeh wasn't sure any more. He'd spoken of opportunity and status, of gratitude, as if she were a raw recruit shirking a tedious duty. As if this were her fault.

He'd also brought Feather Xochi with him, the warrior newly elevated to assist him in his twin duties as Feather of the Singing City and Spear of the Singer. Ilandeh had known she was looking at her replacement and felt nothing but a sick, exhausted relief. The more she thought back to the hissed conversation – the hissed argument – the harder she found it to regret what she'd said. She had given Pilos and the Melody everything she was, every last good thing including her pride, and still he couldn't see past her blood to who she really was. Who had failed who, really? Every time he judged her by her blood and

434

not her service, he betrayed her. Worse, he betrayed the Empire of Songs.

Flight Ilandeh, Whisper Ilandeh, half-blood Ilandeh, had served in the Chorus for over two sun-years. Served, survived, and fed Pilos and Atu the information they needed to strengthen themselves and defend against Enet and her allies. She had saved the Shadow's life and Pilos had saved her life, and now they were . . . what? Enemies? The thought was a stone in her stomach, but like a stone cast into a pond, it caused ripples. Anger. Bitter satisfaction.

Relief.

She was surprised Xochi hadn't already replaced her, but Pilos had made no mention of it to the holy lord, whose approval he would need. With each day they moved closer to the ritual and the waking of the world spirit, she wondered whether he was just too busy. The unrest in the city – the isolated uprisings, the little desperate riots and the Pechaqueh ruining one another across the whole Empire – must be occupying much of his time, especially with High Feather Atu marching for Tokoban to drive out the Zellih war parties.

And now here they were, with only five days left until the Great Star's eight-day absence from the sky. Ilandeh was facing the possibility she might still be in place when the ritual was conducted, a ritual she knew well by now, with the amount of time she'd spent listening to the Shadow and the Singer discuss it and recite portions of it. Her skin pebbled with superstitious awe every time.

Five days and still Enet had not acted. Her ambition had always been clear and yet now she did nothing other than attend upon the holy lord and his Shadow, idling away the mornings in their company and overseeing council meetings at highsun. And then, each afternoon, she retired to her estate with a graceful obeisance and polite farewell.

Her absences niggled like toothache; Ilandeh didn't trust her at the best of times, but even less so when she couldn't see her. Enet held her secrets closer than her skin and despite the approach of the day that would herald the Singer's ascension to eternal consort – a Singer that wasn't Enet – she did nothing. Or seemed to do nothing.

And so, it didn't matter what had happened with Pilos, Ilandeh would still help him and the Empire that didn't value her. His suspicion and contempt were a knife blade in her heart, but she knew her duty. As Whisperer, as eagle, and as a Chorus Leader.

Once the world spirit had woken, there would be no gods left but it, the holy Setatmeh and the Singer. No more Malel for the Tokob and Yaloh, no more Mictec for the Chitenecah, Tlaloxqueh and Axib. And no more Nallac for the Quitob – and the Xentib.

Ilandeh remembered little about the stories and rituals of her mother's people, a conscious choice on her part to fully immerse herself in her father's life and world and blood. Even so, she felt a flicker of disquiet at a future in which Nallac, the multi-gendered god of storms and sun, who she remembered from night-time tales as a very small child, would cease to be.

It was likely around the time the tales stopped that Ilandeh also ceased dressing and styling her hair in the Xentib fashion. Or her mother was forced to stop dressing her like that. Now, she wished she knew more about that half of her heritage, despite how it had held her back and shamed her. She ran her thumb across the small tattoo of the chulul on the inside of her wrist, the mark of a Whisper innocuous among her others but which conveyed a status she'd always valued, and tried to focus on the tasks ahead of her. She had rejected her mother and her mother's ways; she had no right to regret now. Nallac had abandoned her as surely as she'd abandoned them. Ilandeh had made her choice.

What about Tayan, though? She couldn't help but wonder, her eyes drawn to the Shadow where he was laughing help-lessly beneath the weight of the Singer's burly arm. *Can he really have fallen so far that he has forgotten his Malel?*

Fallen was the wrong word, but once Ilandeh thought it, she couldn't come up with another. The Shadow wasn't the Tayan she'd known and befriended, albeit under false pretences. He wasn't even someone she recognised any more.

She pursed her lips and cleared her mind; she was eagle Ilandeh, Chorus Leader Ilandeh for as long as the Spear of the Singer or the holy lord himself desired. Her loyalty was absolute; her integrity unmatched. Her thoughts pure.

There was a burst of laughter from the Singer this time and Ilandeh stared at them as if they were strangers. He and Tayan were playing dice among a confusion of empty cups and discarded items of clothing. Ilandeh didn't understand the rules and suspected neither did they; at this point in the evening they were both far too drunk and seemed to be arbitrarily swigging liquor and slowly disrobing.

Tayan groaned and knocked back another tiny cup of honeypot. He put it down with unsteady fingers and then swayed in to lean against the holy lord's side. Their mouths met in a sloppy, giggling kiss and Ilandeh looked away to assess the rest of the vast oval chamber. The holy Setat that had somehow befriended Tayan was in the offering pool, chin propped on its crossed forearms at the edge, the rest of its body floating invisible. Its great liquid black eyes were fixed on Tayan and the Singer as if their actions were a source of vast amusement.

A shadow moved in the corner of her eye and Ilandeh's attention snapped sideways. Something moved in the gardens and she took several rapid steps in that direction until she could identify Chorus Acamah. He beckoned and she drifted closer, moving sideways so she could keep the holy lord in her line of sight. Ilandeh paused between two columns, a welcome breeze stirring her hair.

'Is all well, Chorus?' she asked, caution tensing her spine. 'No danger in the gardens?' He shook his head and she relaxed slightly, twitching at another burst of laughter from the holy lord. 'You are not on duty this evening, Acamah. What brings you here?'

The words were brusque but she didn't have it in her to modify her tone. If Acamah could have been trusted to perform his duty, Ilandeh would never have had to step into his sandals, and the argument with Pilos might never have happened. *He would still have thought all those things about me, though. Has always thought them.* Her lungs tightened with nameless emotion once more. Why blame Acamah? At least his hatred of her was honest.

'Chorus Leader, I came to apologise. There has been tension between us recently, and it is my fault. I have acted inappropriately and not accorded you the respect you are due. I should always put the Singer's needs first and I forgot that. It will not happen again.'

For the space of a single heartbeat, Ilandeh believed him, but she was a Whisper and she lied for a living. She was lying here, each and every waking moment; she lied even in her sleep. And she could smell another's lie a stick away. Whatever Acamah was here for, it wasn't to make peace.

What his words did do were distract her just enough. The long tail of a whip snaked from the darkness on her other side and around her throat so fast she didn't even hear the hiss of leather. It jerked cruelly tight, cutting off breath and voice, and pulled her between the columns and into the dusk-laden gardens. Two more Chorus warriors stepped inside to cover her absence, though whether they were entering to protect the Singer or to assassinate him, she didn't know.

Ilandeh clattered her spear against the column in an instinctive attempt to raise the alarm before Acamah tore it from her hands and threw it deep into the gardens. She doubted it would be enough to alert the holy lord. If the Singer died because of this, because of her . . . Ilandeh dug her heels into the rich earth and attempted to brace but there was no denying the insistent pull of the whip. Every time she planted her feet, the supple leather tightened further.

Acamah lunged from her right and she kicked at him, but the whip jerked her off her feet and she landed hard on her left hip. The warrior hauling on it didn't even slow, dragging her bodily through the dirt and shrubs by the neck. Acamah paced her, his features ugly with hate and triumph. Wherever they were going, it was somewhere far enough from the source that the holy lord wouldn't hear their violence.

The Whisper threw herself towards a decorative stone bench and managed to brace the sole of her sandal against its base. She came to an abrupt halt, her left knee wrenching sideways. Pain seared up her leg, but the arrested motion was just enough to allow her to get her other foot beneath her. Ilandeh threw herself upright, vaulted the bench and ran towards the wielder of the whip, ignoring the leather still cutting off her air until she'd closed the distance enough to get some slack in the length.

Ilandeh wrapped the whip around her right arm and pivoted, snapping it sideways with the force of her turn. The warrior holding it lost their grip and she kept running, closing the distance and gathering up the long coil of leather as she went. Her left knee was blazing with pain and her lungs were tight with lack of air, but she reached him before he could do more than grope at his belt for an axe. It was Lisek, one of Acamah's closest friends. No surprise. The whip's heavy handle cracked into his face, sending him over backwards with a cry.

Ilandeh followed him down and he rolled; her throbbing knee slammed into his shoulder instead of his windpipe and she skidded off him into the dirt. She knelt there just long enough to unwind the whip and suck in a great draught of sweet air through her crushed throat before she was up again and rounding on the approaching Acamah. Ilandeh drew her knife and flicked out the whip as she slid behind a massive fern.

Acamah's spear jabbed through the foliage at her belly and then stabbed down at the last moment, trying to open her thigh. She danced backwards, stumbling on her left leg and turning it into a dive behind a stand of bamboo. He lunged after her and she flicked the whip at his head; he dodged backwards and she spun on her aching knees to confront Lisek.

The Chorus lunged in with his axe and Ilandeh's whip hand came up on instinct. The blade bit deep into the web of flesh between her thumb and first finger. She bellowed and let go of the whip to grab his wrist and drag him forward onto the point of her knife. The obsidian blade broke under the impact, but there was enough of it left attached to the handle to pierce his salt-cotton and reach his belly.

Lisek let out a shriek that would surely alert everyone within earshot. Acamah roared and leapt onto her back. His spear came around beneath her chin and he jerked it tight against her throat and began to pull, cutting off her air once again. Ilandeh grabbed his hair and the salt-cotton under his armpit and twisted around and down, tucking her chin to her chest. Acamah overbalanced and tumbled half over her hip and Lisek's next axe-blow went into her upper arm instead of her face.

All three of them were a writhing tangle of grunts and blood when there were shouts from nearby and someone began to beat the huge drum that alerted the Singing City eagles to an attack on the great pyramid.

Ilandeh had lost the remnants of her knife somewhere in the struggle but when she flipped Acamah, he'd loosened the chokehold with the spear and she wriggled out of his embrace. Lisek was a heavy weight on her lower body, but he wasn't doing much other than holding her down and shouting; the wound she'd dealt him had stolen his taste for the fight. She gasped in air and slammed her elbow backwards again and again until Acamah rolled away. She snaked a leg free and kicked Lisek off her.

Ilandeh rolled in the opposite direction, found Acamah's own spear and clubbed him in the temple with it. Panting, dizzy and bleeding from a head wound she didn't remember getting and her left upper arm, Ilandeh forced herself onto her feet, reversed the spear and placed the tip against the former Chorus Leader's throat.

'What the fuck—' she began.

Lisek slammed into her back and she rocked forward. Before she could regain her balance, he shoved down on her shoulders and the tip of the spear sank into Acamah's throat. Ilandeh gasped and jerked backwards, but it was too late. The former Chorus Leader clutched at his throat and stared up at her, bewildered, as blood pumped between his fingers.

Ilandeh met his gaze and then turned to face Lisek. The man was hunched over the wound in his belly but he gave her a cruel little smile before straightening and punching her in the jaw. She stumbled backwards over Acamah's prostrate form, slipping in the spreading pool of his blood, her left knee still throbbing with pain. She shook away the stars in her head and brought up the spear to defend herself and then they were surrounded by the rest of the on-duty Chorus.

Lisek pointed at her. 'She murdered Chorus warrior Acamah and nearly killed me when I tried to save him. She's a traitor. Restrain her.'

'That's not true,' Ilandeh began but it was too late. Half a dozen spears pointed at her throat and chest and rough hands grabbed her arms and forced them behind her and up her back until she grunted in pain. 'Spear of the Singer Pilos will already be on his way in response to the sounding of the war drum,' she shouted, the words echoing off the distant stone of the pyramid. 'Only he has sufficient status to judge me; none of you may do so. I do not submit to your authority.'

Lisek spat between her feet. 'Status and authority? We can kill you here and now, save him the effort.'

'What is going on out here?' Great Octave Enet stalked towards them with her slaves and a dozen off-duty Chorus warriors trailing her.

Ilandeh's stomach dropped into her sandals. 'Great Octave, I demand—'

Lisek punched her again and this time darkness fell over her eyes.

The blood from the cut above Ilandeh's right eye had mostly congealed by the time Pilos and several hundred eagles arrived in response to the alarm. The wound to her right hand and left arm had been stitched and bandaged by Shaman Kapal and her knee was wrenched rather than dislocated. It was wrapped in wet maguey and bound to prevent swelling. She didn't care about any of that.

The Chorus Leader stood in a ring of guards in the lowest level of the great pyramid, as far from the holy lord as Enet could get her without actually leaving the source. Chorus warrior Lisek had been taken away for treatment; Ilandeh didn't know what had happened to Acamah's corpse. She hoped the bruises around her throat were clear to all, proof that she had been attacked, but she expected everyone here in this room was either part of the plot to kill her or wouldn't protest when she was condemned.

She wondered whether Acamah would have been so keen to lure her away from the Singer's side had he known he was to be the sacrifice to ensure her downfall. But at whose hands – Enet's or Pilos's? Who had decided her loyalty to the Singer was her death sentence?

The barred gate slammed back against the wall and Pilos strode in. He didn't wait for anyone to speak. 'I have assured myself of the holy lord's safety, as well as that of his Shadow, and stationed eagles around the source to protect him seeing as it appears every Chorus warrior has gathered here. Tell me why I am the only one in this fucking pyramid who takes their duty seriously?'

'This prisoner was seen murdering a member of the Chorus, Spear,' one of the guards behind Ilandeh said. 'Chorus warrior Lisek almost lost his life stopping her rampage. The great Singer owes his life to Lisek and the fallen Acamah. She was planning on slaughtering our holy lord next.'

'Was I?' Ilandeh demanded in a hoarse rasp. 'And where is your proof of that?'

'Here.' This voice came from the doorway and they all turned to look. Ilandeh was bitterly unsurprised to see Great Octave Enet standing there with Lisek by her side. The man was pale with pain and sweating but there was a desperate triumph marring his features. Enet's face, in contrast, was as serene as ever, as if all this was beneath her and she wasn't weaving Ilandeh's fate with skilful fingers. Did that mean this was her plot? But why? What had Ilandeh ever done but protect . . . Ah.

Enet proffered a rolled sheet of bark-paper. 'This person has been communicating with a known rebel group here in the Singing City. She is planning on murdering the Singer and his Shadow and attempting to seize the song-magic for herself.'

Ilandeh couldn't help it; she barked a strangled laugh at the absurdity. 'Let me see?' Enet passed the paper to Lisek, who limped forward and held it up. The Chorus Leader snorted. 'That is Acamah's hand. He has a very distinctive brush-flick when writing the Singer's name. I can show you a dozen examples from correspondence in my room. Either he forged that letter to implicate me or he was the one conspiring with rebels.'

'You are lying,' Lisek snarled. 'You're a traitor and a murderer. You plotted to kill the great Singer.' He had her knife – the Chorus Leader's knife – tucked into his belt. As if he could wield the power and status embodied in that blade, even broken as it was.

'*I plotted?*' Ilandeh demanded, gaze flicking away from the knife and resting on Enet with deliberate intent. The Great Octave looked back with a polite puzzlement so genuine that Ilandeh was reluctantly impressed. The woman could be a Whisper, she could lie so well.

She looked to Pilos. He would never believe such a transparent fabrication; whatever he thought of her now, he had placed her here to save the Singer, not kill him. She had never once let him down. 'Spear, I was ambushed and—'

'Spear Pilos,' Enet spoke smoothly over her. 'It was you who reduced Acamah's status and elevated this woman to

Chorus Leader. Order her execution and present yourself to the holy lord to confess your crimes.'

Ilandeh felt the first cold touch of true fear. After everything she'd done for him, everything she had sacrificed and all of the blood she had spilt in his name, let alone the Melody's name, Pilos owed her a way out. He owed her more than the ignominious death of a traitor. No matter the words that had passed between them, he owed her the same loyalty she'd always given him. So why did he look at her as if she was a traitor in truth?

Enet switched her gaze between the silent Pilos and the Chorus Leader. She shook her head sadly. 'Spear of the Singer, what were you thinking to insert such a flawed creature into our most sacred space? How could you not have seen the poison of ambition flowing through her? You are reluctant to admit your error of judgement to the holy lord and that can only go poorly for you. Will you not reconsider? The warrior's fate is already decided. I suspect yours will be as well if you do not throw yourself on the Singer's mercy.'

'My life belongs to the Empire of Songs and its Singer, Great Octave,' Pilos said without a hint of trepidation. 'There will be no need for you to run to the holy lord with tales of my misconduct; I will speak to him myself. As for this traitor,' he waved a hand in Ilandeh's general direction, 'kill her and be done.'

As for this traitor, kill her and be done.

As for this traitor.

Traitor.

Ilandeh's pulse throbbed in her wounds. Heat tingled through her limbs and cold anger chased it.

'I sorrow that your judgement could be so flawed, Spear. I worried at your unexpected elevation and it seems I was right to do so. I do not believe you are capable of fulfilling the duties required as Spear of the Singer.'

Pilos turned a cool gaze on Enet. 'That is not for you to decide, Great Octave. You are merely Chosen; my elevation was suggested by the Shadow and implemented by the holy lord. Be content in his wisdom.'

Enet gave him a small, patient smile and stepped forward, Lisek at her shoulder. She conducted a slow, assessing circuit of Ilandeh and then reached out and ran her fingers through the warrior's hair; Ilandeh shuddered.

'You were remarkable in your deception,' she murmured. 'I had known there was something wrong with you for some time, but even I did not suspect your ambition would rise so high.' She leant very close and dropped her voice even further. 'I could have made you a marvel. Instead, you will simply be a corpse. And not even a pretty one when these fine warriors are done with you. How dare you betray our Singer.'

'If you seek to anger me to violence, Great Octave,' Ilandeh said calmly and loud enough for all in the room to hear, 'you will have to work significantly harder than that. I have dedicated my life to the Singer's safety and have neither failed in my duty nor deviated from it. Acamah lied to you; Lisek is lying to you now.' She met Pilos's eyes in a challenge: when was he going to side with her? *Was* he going to side with her? He'd pronounced her death, but surely . . . surely?

'You speak of lies? You speak of failure? *What is this?*' Enet ripped the eagle feather from Ilandeh's hair. 'This is your pride, warrior. This is your status and your greatness, proof of your dedication to the Empire of Songs.' Deliberately, Enet snapped the feather in half. The feather Ilandeh had worn for so long, gifted to her by Pilos himself when he commanded her to protect the Singer with her life – and death. Enet might as well have snapped Ilandeh's bones.

Ilandeh gasped in unfeigned outrage and a strange, complicated sense of loss. She had earned that feather and the status that went with it. Earned it a thousand times over, and yet the urge to tell them who she was boiled in her chest. To do so would condemn Pilos alongside her; she was beginning to think he deserved that.

Enet's voice came from very far away. 'Kill her, Feather Pilos. Prove your loyalty.'

Pilos held out his hand. There was no emotion in his glittering gaze, no hint of remorse or a tiny wink to say this was part of his plan to save her. 'Spear,' he demanded and a warrior passed their weapon to him.

'Chorus Leader Ilandeh, you have brought violence to the source and have reached beyond your status for something that is not yours to take.'

Your status. He may as well have just shouted her parentage from the pyramid's top.

'You have broken the law of Pechacan. I condemn you to die.'

Ilandeh moved without thought. A ring of armed guards was only useful before a sentence of death was passed, because now she had nothing to lose. She was dying either way: may as well make them work for it.

She ran at Enet. Lisek, fawning sycophant that he was, moved to intercept her. She kicked him in the gut, into the wound she'd given him out in the gardens, and Lisek's mouth dropped open on a soundless scream. He crumpled; other Chorus rushed to protect Enet; and Ilandeh ripped her knife out of the man's belt.

She spun and Pilos was already lunging for her – his strike

would have taken her in the back. Killed from behind: he meant it, then. He meant for her to die.

Ilandeh deflected the thrust with the outside of her left forearm, batting it down and away, and then spun behind him and wrapped her right arm around his neck, pressing the broken sliver of blade into the thick muscle running up the side of his neck.

'Drop the spear,' she snarled into his ear.

'Kill her, kill her right the fuck now,' Pilos said, but he did as she commanded.

'Back up! No closer or I'll slice him. You, shut up,' she added, squeezing her arm tighter around his neck. He was bigger, taller, stronger than her, so she used the leverage to bend him backwards and make him vulnerable. 'You call me a traitor?' she snarled in his ear, too low for the crowding Chorus warriors to hear.

'I'm going to peel your fucking skin off your bones.'

'Shut up. Stay back or he dies. Stay back!' They didn't, so Ilandeh gritted her teeth and dug the knife into Pilos's neck, hard. He grunted and stiffened, the instinctive flinch from pain, and the warriors around them cursed and faltered. She smelt blood.

'You're not helping yourself, eagle,' Enet said. The woman was amused, standing carefully on the far side of the room. Her arms were folded beneath her breasts and she appeared to be enjoying the show immensely. Lisek was a mewling huddle against the same wall.

Pilos snorted and the Whisper dug in the knife again. 'You want to tell them my identity, Spear Pilos? What will they do when they know it was you who placed me here? You who trusted me with this?'

The words were more breath than speech, but he heard

them. She felt the bob of his throat as he swallowed against her blade. Swallowed words. Swallowed defiance.

Carefully, precariously, Ilandeh and Pilos shuffled backwards down the corridor and then the short staircase leading out of the great pyramid's slave quarters. Night had fallen.

'Let him go. Let him go now!' someone bellowed. The Chorus warriors following them were brandishing blowpipes, darts already loaded; Ilandeh kept Pilos firmly between herself and them. It was the only way she was getting out of here alive. 'Let him go or die. The Singer will string you up by your own guts, you fucking traitor. Let him go now and make it easy on yourself.'

'Shut up,' Ilandeh panted. 'Shut up or he dies. I swear it, I'll fucking kill him here and now if you don't stop talking.' She tightened the knife under Pilos's chin again and this time the blood ran over her fist. The Chorus halted, quietening instantly. 'That's better. Your precious fucking Spear will live as long as you do what I say. Stay there. I'll release him halfway down that road. Only if you stay there.'

'You let me go and I'll kill you where you stand,' Pilos promised and she jerked hard on his neck, bending him further backwards as she moved down a step, his arms flailing as he struggled for balance and his weight pressed against her chest.

'You chose Enet over me. Fucking *Enet*. Everything I've done, all the sacrifices and lies, the lives taken, the promises I made knowing I'd break them, they were all for you and the Melody. All of it. And this is your response? *Fucking coward.*' She spat the last words, saliva hitting his cheek and dusting his hair.

Ilandeh chanced a look back over her shoulder. Four more steps and then the narrow road between two temples. She tightened her arm around his neck again until he was in danger of falling and they staggered the final steps down to level ground. The Chorus warriors leapt after them but she was already dragging him into the shadowed street.

'*Get back,*' she screamed again and then gritted her teeth and dug the point of her knife in under Pilos's ear, right into the healing wound from the earlier assassination attempt. The irony wasn't lost on her. The Spear howled and their pursuers halted again, shouting threats. Ilandeh pulled Pilos backwards into the dark street and edged along it, checking in both directions and up at the roofs. Clear, she thought. She prayed.

'I gave you my life,' she hissed and slammed him face first into the wall. 'I'll never forgive you for this,' she added as he crumpled.

'Fuck you,' Pilos wheezed. 'I should've known blood would tell eventually. Why couldn't you just have died?'

'So it was you?' she demanded, kicking him in the ribs.

He grunted. 'Was it?'

The scuffling from the end of the road told her she was out of time. Ilandeh slammed his head into the wall again and he slumped, unconscious. Unable to speak or drip poison in her ear. Unable to make his disgust plain.

'I hope you're fucking dead,' she lied.

Heart in her throat, Ilandeh ran and didn't look back.

TAYAN

The source, Singing City, Pechacan, Empire of Songs
1st day of the little absence of the Great Star

The middle of the night was long past but still Tayan lay awake, the Singer tucked into his arms and legs, his breath beading into moisture and sweat against the Tokob chest. He hadn't slept properly in weeks, and barely at all since Ilandeh had been accused of treachery and escaped both the pyramid and her execution. She'd had ample opportunities to kill him or let him die when out in the city; she could have killed him and the Singer during the night here in the source and no one would have known until the song vanished. She hadn't. Tayan had never thought, not for one instant, that she would.

He missed the steadiness of her presence. He missed how safe he'd felt knowing she was watching over him despite her actions and words when he'd first come here. The new Chorus Leader was a woman he'd never met before, Feather Xochi. She'd been recommended by Pilos, and Listener Chotek had taken her thoughts apart one by one to search

451

for any hint of the same disloyalty that had allegedly infected Ilandeh. There was nothing to find.

Tayan didn't like her and she didn't like him. He was the second most powerful person in the Empire of Songs and he was a slave. And a Toko. Xochi had helped bring his homeland under the song; she'd fought and killed countless Tokob and it frustrated her that she had to protect and obey this one.

It wasn't just Xochi's performative obedience and the intact brands on his arms that reinforced his status with every breath; Tayan was a slave to the Singer in body, spirit and mind, irrefutable and unbreakable. It was only here in the darkest part of the night when the holy lord was deeply asleep that he could think his own thoughts without fear of Xac hearing.

Others might, he supposed. Listener Chotek, Enet, any of the Listeners in the Empire who had returned to the currents of the song now that it had stabilised and become something magnificent once more – bloody and hungry, sharp with teeth, but breath-taking in its majesty nonetheless. Beautiful as a blade was beautiful, as a jaguar was beautiful. As the lightning strike that lit you up with incandescence so you died bright and burning and terrible in your glory.

And Tayan had helped make it so.

In the depths of the night, in the depths of his exhausted wakefulness, he knew all the things he'd done and become. Perhaps that was one of the reasons he tormented himself by denying sleep; maybe there was one tiny corner of his spirit that hadn't completely been stained through by blood and that screamed at him of redemption, even forgiveness.

The other reason he couldn't sleep was far more selfish. The power he'd been convinced was his he knew now was only borrowed and could easily be removed. Tayan had nothing but his title, and that would be obsolete once Xac woke the world spirit. Would he live to see another dusk or would the Singer or Enet finally put an end to him? Xac wouldn't need him once he was the world spirit's consort, not as a weapon pointed at Enet or as a source of strength and clarity. Perhaps they'd toss him to the holy Setat that found him so intriguing? Or throw him down the pyramid steps for the Pechaqueh who so hated him to tear apart?

The Singer might even give him back to Enet; out of all the possibilities that haunted his wakefulness, that was the most horrifying. He was the Shadow of the Singer and he was helpless.

Not entirely.

Tayan shifted carefully, rolling onto his back. Xac nestled into his armpit and didn't stir and the shaman lay staring up into the shadows above. His heart beat slowly, sick and heavy, and the red vine between him and the Singer pulsed in time with it. Growing.

Here and now, with the Singer's hold on his mind if not his spirit loosened, Tayan tried again to convince himself that nothing he'd done had been his fault, but the truth was that he *could* resist Xac and his wants. It hurt and fatigued him beyond anything he'd known, but it was possible. Not in everything, but some things, and so he had. At first. But Xac's desires and Xac's twisted logic and Xac's overwhelming presence were inescapable and it became easier to turn his face away and give in and pretend he had no choice.

And then. *And then . . .* it became easier to actively choose. It hurt less to embrace those choices. To seek out secrets and lies in the minds of councillors and Chorus warriors and gift them to Xac like tiny jewels. To want what the Singer wanted.

What the Singer wants? Or what I want?

How much of what Tayan had done was the fault of the Singer, or the greedy song? How much was him?

He'd killed people. Killed slaves. He'd . . . eaten people. He'd spoken to slaves and Chorus warriors, administrators and courtesans as if they were insects. He'd made demands that increased their hardship. He'd promised Xessa and Tiamoko that he'd free them and then done nothing. He'd discovered how to contact Lilla and hadn't. He'd been selfish and greedy and arrogant.

No, I have been practical. The alternative was agony and fatigue and a lingering death. The longer he lived, the more Xac trusted him. That gave him options. Or it had, until now. Because Tayan was out of time.

Today, Xac, my love will wake the world spirit and Malel, Snake-sister and Jaguar-brother will die. Mictec and Nallac and all the lesser gods. The wild spirits, perhaps. Tokob ancestors. Even the lords of the Underworld.

Will I stand by and do nothing then as well?

Tears trickled down his temples and he made no effort to wipe them away. He had given in when he should have fought. He had held his tongue and suppressed his thoughts when he should have convinced Xac that there was another way. Surely there was another way. If the world spirit had created all things, then it had created the gods, too. So why did people say all gods but those of the Pechaqueh would die?

The Singer made a sleepy noise and rolled over, freeing Tayan's arm. Quickly, he sat up and slid out of the bed while he had the chance, acting on instinct and desperation. As Shadow and shaman, and possessed utterly by the Singer and therefore safe, he had his own box of medicine and most of the ingredients he'd need. As for the rest, he'd just have to hope practice and need made up for them.

Whoever Tayan still was, whatever tattered remnant of the man and shaman and husband he'd once been, he still had this one choice: he could fight the connection and the magic and disavow the power and privilege and love he'd been accorded; or he could bite his tongue and bear witness to the dimming of the world.

He wished it was an easy decision. He wished he was stronger. The holy lord slept and Tayan had just this little space of time to change the course of the world. If he was brave enough. This or nothing. Now or never. Stop it or embrace it.

Tayan knelt at a low table and mixed the magic with water and a drop of honey and swallowed it down, then sat cross-legged and began beating the journey rhythm on his knee. He didn't have the diluted frog poison or the figures of his spirit guides, but he'd increased the amount of fungus in the hope that would allow him an easier journey to the spiral path. It might kill him, but he was going to die later anyway. At least he was trying.

For once.

A golden glow began to rise around him as the spirit world shimmered into view atop the flesh world. The spirit world, not the song-world. The second world he'd spent two decades visiting, that was almost as comfortable as this one. Golden and familiar, with familiar, golden adversaries. Tayan could have sobbed; he leapt onto the first path he saw, no matter that the thread leading his spirit back to his body was brittle and weak. So be it; he was committed now. He'd be brave, for the last time. Or perhaps, if he was honest, for the first time. Not because of what awaited him in the spirit world, but because of what he was leaving behind in this one. Everything he was giving up.

I have to. I should. For Lilla, though he didn't claim me. For Xessa and Tokoban. For Malel.

He barely remembered how it felt to mingle his spirit with Malel any more. He hadn't even thought about it in . . . so long. Now, as his spirit walked the twisting path towards the mother goddess and he called upon his guides for aid something, some scar tissue, loosened and fell away in his chest. He called, and then entreated, and then begged, until with a roar and a swirl of black fur, Young Jaguar leapt onto the path ahead of him. The least predictable – the most dangerous – of his guides.

'Young Jaguar, I honour your presence here and offer you my thanks. I seek a merging with Malel to beg her aid in undoing the harm the Singer will perpetrate. Will you show me the way as you have before?' The words were garbled in his haste and, worse, threaded through with a self-doubt that Young Jaguar would scent and respond to.

As expected, the great black cat's tail lashed and he bared his fangs, swiping at Tayan's spirit with his paw, claws extended. The Toko dodged but Young Jaguar followed in a low-bellied stalk, his ears flat and intent clear.

'Young Jaguar, honoured spirit guide, I am Tayan, called the stargazer, shaman of Tokoban. I have journeyed with you and Old Woman Frog and Swift Hawk many times before. Please, Young Jaguar, I must merge with Malel so that I might know how to protect her.'

The cat roared at him, swiping again and this time when Tayan dodged, he saw the thick red vine that connected him to the Singer, tendrils of which now crept along the thread leading from his body. 'No,' he tried. 'You don't understand. I won't let this reach Malel, I won't bring her harm. I'm trying to save her!'

'You, who have contributed to her downfall, now wish to save her?' The voice was familiar and Tayan recognised the form of Lutek, warrior and friend. Around her were others, scores and perhaps hundreds, who he knew and who he'd last seen alive in Tokoban. He wept to see them here on the spiral path, for it meant they were lost. They had died far from the soil that birthed them, and without the sense of place and belonging and home to guide them, the spiral path was a confusion and a danger. They would wander endlessly downwards until they reached the Underworld – and then these ancestors would never be free from torment.

He made sense of Lutek's words a moment later. 'Contributed? How?' he demanded and the ancestors swirled, the motes of light in their ragged forms moving faster as they clumped around him. Young Jaguar snarled and paced, his ears back. Overhead, Swift Hawk appeared and let out a single, piercing shriek. Two spirit guides – were they here to watch his demise?

'You forget Malel and her teachings,' another ancestor snarled: Eja Oncan, one of Xessa's friends. 'You perpetuate the song and its magic that destroys Malel's connection to the world. You make that magic stronger. You heal him that wields it. You have forgotten Malel.'

'I have not,' Tayan's spirit shrieked and Young Jaguar pounced, bearing him down onto the path and fixing his fangs in him. Tayan screamed again. Above, Swift Hawk echoed him. 'Home,' he gasped. 'Home, I can take you home. I can – with Young Jaguar and Swift Hawk – we can get you to the Realm of the Ancestors. Help you. Can't we, honoured guides?'

Young Jaguar shook him so hard the thread connecting him to his flesh frayed. He felt, for an instant nauseating in its intensity, what it meant to be severed. Lost.

'Please, please,' he stuttered. 'Forgive me. Let me help them. I can do that. Let me do that.'

'Keep your blight from us,' Lutek snarled. 'We need nothing from a song-lover such as you.'

Young Jaguar finally let him go and Tayan's spirit sprawled on one of the many spiral paths and he knew he would never be allowed to come even this far again – supposing there even was a spiral path after today.

Carefully, he picked himself up and checked the thread back to his flesh – with Malel's grace it would hold. He changed the rhythm he was tapping on his knee to the one that called him home.

'Young Jaguar,' he began and the spirit guide roared again. 'Young Jaguar, Swift Hawk, take them home, I beg you. Take them to their ancestors that they might know peace. I will . . .' His voice broke. 'I will leave. And I will pray for them and for Malel. I will not come again. But take them home. For them, not me.'

The cat watched him with eyes glowing like flames, and then he blinked and leapt up onto another path directly above the one on which they stood. Swift Hawk dived down, wings trailing iridescent magic, and then swooped up to hover above Young Jaguar. The shaman pointed and one by one the ancestors clambered up, a long, heart-breaking stream of dead Tokob. Lost Tokob. 'My body and breath, Young Jaguar and Swift Hawk,' Tayan murmured in the spirit and flesh worlds, 'my thanks and adoration.' His voice cracked on a sob.

'Honoured ancestors, rest in your realm in peace and seek not to return to life,' he murmured and stumbled back along the disintegrating thread towards his body. The scarlet infecting it had almost reached his spirit-shape as he turned his back on the spiral path and Malel, lost to him forever. *And to us all.*

Sick in spirit and shaking in body, Tayan let the spirit world sink and the flesh world rise as he climbed back inside the shell of his skin and bones. His fingers stuttered and finally fell still and he let himself settle into his weeping, pain-wracked body, remembering its shape and limits and how muscles and organs worked. Remembered breathing only when his lungs spasmed and he sucked broken air. Remembered sight when pink light pressed against his eyelids and he opened them to find dawn was an open wound bleeding into the world. He had journeyed the second half of the night away and accomplished nothing.

Not nothing, he insisted fiercely as he stretched cramped legs and felt, as if for the first time, the pain of blood returning to his feet. *Those ancestors are safe. The guides will do right by them. That they are lost is not their fault – they died too far from Malel.*

And now Malel will die.

Tayan's mind was empty and exhausted, his eyes swollen with weeping and despair a stone in the pit of his stomach. He drank water, grimacing at the dryness the magic had left in his throat and the axe-bright pain in his skull that was too much fungus magic. He distracted himself with the lazy contentment and growing awareness that seeped through him. Power trickled into his limbs, filling the channels where his shamanic magic lived – but this magic tasted different. His neck muscles creaked as he turned to look at the bed. Xac was watching him through slitted eyes, and arousal was an arrow through his guts.

No. Leave me alone.

He'd tried and failed. No one could blame him.

Come here, little one.

Tayan shifted. He'd done what he could, everything he could. It wasn't his fault that the world would change and besides, no one had actually said what would happen to Malel or the Realm of the Ancestors. It could be he was worrying over nothing.

'My sweet little Shadow,' the Singer murmured and Tayan shuddered, sinking into the waters of want and love and adoration. He crawled to the bed and onto it, seeking beneath the blanket for his sweet Xac.

'Malel does not want you,' the Singer whispered. His warm palms spanned Tayan's slender hips and drew him down. 'But I am the Singer. I am power and desire, possibility and immortality. Do you deny me?'

Tayan slipped beneath the surface and let Xac's love fill his lungs and skin, brighter and sharper than the magic of Malel. Vibrant and here and insistent.

An exquisite drowning.

If he was no longer welcomed by the gods of his people, then he would have this instead. All of it. He'd offered help and been rejected. The past was gone; dead. The future – this future – was bright and dazzling and Xac was both over-whelming and impossible to deny. Easier to give in. Easier to love, not fight.

He seized Xac's face and kissed it, a golden glow rising from their shared skin. 'I could, would, will, never deny you, my love,' Tayan whispered, his tears falling like tiny jewels upon the Singer's face.

'*You are my only god.*'

Chorus Leader Xochi was waiting outside their chamber when the Singer and his Shadow emerged, the sun already well up in the sky and the song lazy and sated.

'I'm so hungry,' Tayan said, despite the dawnmeal they'd finally got around to eating in bed.

'Then we shall eat,' Xac said, but with the same remote-ness that had settled on him as they bathed and dressed. His brother, the Great Star, would not rise this evening, and after the solemn celebration to mark that event, the Singer would perform the greatest and most complex piece of magic in the history of Ixachipan. And Tayan would help him; it was his sacred duty.

And it is my desire.

'What will happen to me after the world spirit is awoken?' Tayan asked as they strolled along the lavish corridor. 'You will have no need of a Shadow then; you will have eternity.'

'You would ask for freedom?' Xac asked with only a little fire.

The Shadow shook his head, bewildered. 'Never. I ask only to remain at your side and aid you, to help you grow ever stronger and the song with you. To heal all the worries of this world.'

'We shall see, little shaman. There is much to do before that moment comes.'

'Then I will do whatever you require, my love.' Tayan smiled at the rightness of his place in the world and that he had been given the gift of loving the Singer. It was the duty of his life and its pride. He followed Xac into the source, inclining his head towards the empty offering pool and then sitting on a cushion a little distant – a little behind – the Singer's. That was new.

Enet was waiting for them and the corner of her mouth turned up at his wary confusion. 'You will not distract the holy lord. Today is momentous. You will be his silent support and no more.' She stepped closer and he flinched despite himself. Xochi slid between them and Enet stopped moving.

He nodded, affecting an air of impatience. 'I already know my duty, Great Octave. I do not need you to remind me.'

She gave him a tight little smile that couldn't warm the coldness in her eyes, but neither could she hide the little twitches of her fingers that betrayed her excitement. Tayan snorted and turned away from her, Xac's arrogant confidence thrumming through his blood. Enet was toothless here in the source without her foolish followers to commit violence on her behalf. And she would never disrupt this day. The Great Octave was, if anything, even more fanatical about the waking of the world spirit than Xac.

And yet, he had seen inside her head and uncovered her secret desire to be the Singer who performed that great magic. But of all the things she had attempted – killing Pilos, killing Tayan, probably getting rid of Ilandeh, he still wasn't sure – she hadn't raised a hand against the holy lord.

Yet.

Which means I need to watch her. I will step between her blade and my sweet love if needed. I will do all that is required.

Food arrived and Tayan fell on it, starved. The source crackled with excitement. The choir sang hymn after hymn of triumph and glory; the Chorus warriors were bright-eyed and alert, not just because Xochi demanded it but because they would bear witness to the changing of the world. Even the slaves were flushed with importance and energy, carrying out their duties with joy.

The ritual to wake the world spirit was engraved on all their minds by now. Tayan knew the precise sequence of steps that the Singer would undertake, the chants and dances he must perform, the burning of incense and offering of smoke and light and precious stones and woods at the right times. He knew his own part in it, too. He was to be the Singer's strength and support. It was a complex and draining piece of magic, harnessing the song and using it to call forth the world spirit from its sleep. Tayan would struggle to perform it when he was at his best; he was grateful to be only a crutch for his love, whose strength had grown each day but who still . . . no. It would be well. All would be well and the world would change.

Malel.

Tayan blinked at the intrusive thought and cast it away. Another rose in its place, one of equal if not greater danger. What if the day did not end as predicted? Despite himself, the Tokob hand rose to stroke the twin feathers decorating his throat.

Malel!

What if the magic actually passes to me? What if a Toko shaman becomes the next Singer?

Then Enet will kill me and take it from me.

If the holy lord died. Which he would not. He would accomplish everything the day promised, waking the world spirit – *Malel, we cry to you, O Malel* – and become its undying consort for eternity. And Tayan was going to help him do it, no matter what.

The Singer's influence and the song's strength had grown throughout the day, as if reassuring the Empire of Songs that there was no need to worry during his brother the Great Star's absence.

The source had been filled with an afternoon of solemn procession and music, under which thrummed an almost manic excitement among the privileged, noble-born Pechaqueh guests. Though all would be sent home before the ritual began, still they would be able to claim they were there the day the world changed for the better and peace became eternal.

Tayan had felt increasingly wrapped in the Singer's growing strength and increasingly sleepy as the holy lord drew on their connection to prepare for what was to come. He was content to be the holy lord's trusted help and not to have to think far beyond ensuring he accomplished all of the greatness that was to come.

Vaguely, he wondered what the Great Star would see when it returned in eight days to find the world spirit awake and Xac its eternal consort. What would Ixachipan look like from its vantage in the sky? The garden of the world and the harmony of an eternal peace, an eternal music.

Tayan had never seen the Great Star, his vision far too poor to allow it. He'd never seen any stars, or even the sunset with any sort of clarity. Perhaps, one day, his love the holy lord would let him look through his eyes and see the world in all its magic and splendour, sharp-edged and clear.

The last song of entreaty for the Great Star's quick return swelled through the source, carried in the throats and on the breaths of the richest and most influential Pechaqueh in the Singing City. The High Feather should have been here; so should Spear Pilos. Neither were, for no one could say what might happen in the hours to come and it was best for Pilos to be with his Melody warriors. Atu, of course, was marching the First and Third Talons to Tokoban to drive back the Zellih. Despite that clear evidence of unrest, the Empire was deemed peaceful enough for the waking of the world spirit to be attempted.

But what if—the Singer's hold on his Shadow tightened strangling-tight, clamping down on his thoughts. His voice began to falter as he sang, lost among harsh rasps for breath, but the sweet lethargy weighing down his limbs made it impossible to protest and he couldn't quite remember what he'd been thinking about, anyway. Why would he want to when everything was so warm and contented? Tayan let the song-within-the-song roll on without him and concentrated on standing still at the Singer's side, blinking slowly at the gathered guests.

When the full complement of songs and prayers was completed, the Chorus warriors stepped away from the walls and ushered the guests away without ceremony. Almost before the last notes of their hymn had faded, the source was empty of all but those with a role to play in the coming ritual and the warriors and slaves who would protect and serve them.

The song – his song – *our song* – was swelling and urgency gripped them all, even Tayan. It was time. It was here. The magic, the world spirit, the ritual that would change the world. The city was a roar of mania at the promise of the coming hours. The promise of the coming paradise. Across Ixachipan, Pechaqueh and all right-minded half- and no-bloods would be celebrating. Waiting. Anticipating. And Tayan would be a part of what was to come.

He blinked and clutched at Xac's arm. 'My love, my sweet love, a little less, I beg you. Please, holy lord, just a little less.'

Enet slapped his hands away and he stumbled. 'Do not presume to command the great Singer. You have no understanding of what he is about to accomplish.'

Tayan mustered up a glare. 'Do not presume to tell me what I do and do not understand, Great Octave. I am Shadow; I am *inside* this ritual.'

A muscle jumped in Enet's cheek but instead of replying she stalked to the other end of the oval source, where Shaman Kapal and Listener Chotek were drawing the sacred symbols and glyphs upon the stone floor in various pigments. Words of power and awakening, symbols of strength and majesty, calls to the world spirit to begin the great magic bringing it from the sleep that had claimed it since it had made the world and the sky and all things on and in between.

Tayan watched them fixedly, swaying slightly.

Enet was back in front of him again. 'You're exhausted, Shadow. Perhaps you should sit somewhere quietly. The holy lord can weave the mightiest magic Ixachipan has ever seen with the assistance of just myself, Shaman Kapal and Listener Chotek. Holy lord?' There was the faintest sheen of sweat on her upper lip and Tayan focused on it.

Maybe I've been poisoned. Maybe a . . . sleep medicine? My love? Xac?

'Find him some cushions. I want him close but not close enough to interfere.' The Singer didn't so much as look at him. 'He will give me everything he has. Won't you, my sweet?'

Something twisted in the Tokob chest and he grunted. Blood welled around his teeth as he smiled. 'Anything you desire, holy lord. My life to serve.'

It wasn't sleep medicine. It probably wasn't poison. If Tayan could have visited the spiral path again – if he had the strength or the permission – he suspected he would have seen almost all of his spirit encased in the red vine, the strangler fig of the Singer's love. He might even have seen it inside the song, if only he had the energy to enter it.

He sat slumped in the cushions, imagining his life as a cracked clay pitcher slowly oozing water. *I am Shadow of the Singer. I pledged him my life.*

I just never thought he'd take it.

He hiccupped a laugh and slumped a little further, his hands palm down on the floor between the cushions. In front of him, Xac moved through the ritual that built the first layer of magic, the brush of it warm against the Tokob skin. The Singer was beautiful, chanting and dancing and making offerings, spinning between the glyphs without a misstep.

I gave him that, the grace and strength to do that. I made him strong enough to wake the world spirit, not Enet. Me.

Ponderously, Tayan's head swung from the holy lord towards the Great Octave, standing with Kapal and Chotek in a semicircle around the ritual space. She chanted the responses to the Singer's ceremonial questions whenever they were required, touching feathers and incense to a brazier so that stink and then sweet wafted through the source.

She was sweating more now, her movements having lost some of their natural grace. Still, she didn't have the look of a person who had spent her political life striving to steal the song-magic only for it to slip through her fingers here at the last possible moment. *Maybe she actually isn't going to . . . Wait.*

The song-magic. Tayan could feel it, not within him as he'd been able to ever since the holy lord had joined them together, but outside his body. Feel it *with* his body: a shivering in the air; a vibration in the ground. He swallowed a mouthful of blood and flattened his palms against the bare stone. Magic moved within it, drifting towards the ritual space like a feather on the wind.

'I can feel it,' he whispered. Xochi jerked and looked at him. 'I can feel the magic building. In here.' He patted the stone and then frowned. 'Not in here. What . . .' The Chorus Leader hushed him and he bit his lip and closed his eyes, seeking through the muffling layers of cotton in his head for that elusive smoke-wisp of magic. Xac's presence was stronger than ever and it took a huge effort to block him out enough to concentrate.

'What is that?' he breathed. 'Chorus Leader, help me up,' he added, trying to focus. 'I need to know what's happening.'

'You can't go near the ritual,' Xochi began, squatting next to him and keeping her awestruck gaze on the Singer who was glowing bright with magic and stolen life.

'Don't need to,' Tayan mumbled. 'Need to go down. Need to find what it is.' He took a deep breath and wiped bloody spit off his chin. 'Need to find what's stealing my magic.'

467

He flapped his hand and Xochi looked again at the Singer, then helped him quietly to his feet and jerked her head so the other new Chorus warriors – the eagles loyal to Pilos and so to the Empire, apparently – moved closer and took her place.

'Protect him with your lives. We'll be back soon,' she murmured.

'Hurry,' Tayan insisted. 'Following threads of magic, following twisting paths unlike any in the song . . . it's what I do. I'm a Toko shaman.' He giggled and leant on Xochi's arm, his gaze flickering to Enet again. Whatever this was, she was at the heart of it. She was making her move after all.

'Didn't plan for me, though, did you, Great Octave Enet? You never did know what to do about me.'

THE SINGER

The source, Singing City, Pechacan, Empire of Songs

I am the Singer. The song. The blood and the glory. I am the beginning and end of all things, the strength of this world and its waking.

This waking I perform, I alone, for which I take all the strength needed. All the song's strength. All your strength, little one. And you give it so sweetly, do you not? Your love is almost as bright as the shape of your life. Almost.

. . .

You are silent, little shaman. You think you can hide from this? From me? I own you, sweet one, my gentle Shadow. I am you, inside you and around you. Show yourself.

Show yourself!

. . .

Your silence is telling. You seek to avoid your fate, little shaman? You think to outwit your Singer, your god? Very well. If you will not bend, then you must break. And if you will not break, then I will watch you shatter.

I am the Singer and the song, the blood and the Empire.

I am the world and my destiny is greatness so far above you that I am as the sun. I will shine so bright you will burn. I will burn everything you are and everything you love if you do not answer. If you do not submit.

. . .

So be it. You are mine to do with as I wish. And I hunger, my sweet.
I hunger.

ENET

So many things had fallen into place, but so many had not, and their lack was a stone in her throat, heavy and painful and hard to chant around. Yet all would be as the gods decreed and just as she could not stop the Great Star's procession across the sky, nor could she stop what happened this night. She prayed only that she was worthy enough to fulfil her part in it, that the modified capstone hidden in the lowest level of the pyramid and the dust she'd harvested from carving it and consumed over the past sixteen days in ever-increasing amounts would together give her enough magic to do what she needed to do.

There could be no further errors. She, Kapal and Chotek formed the shape of the three stars that made up Tenaca's Dance, the constellation named after the first Singer to wield the magic and learn of the world spirit's promise to return. The holy lord was Tenaca's hands, leaping between the four directions and towards the centre of the world painted upon

471

the stone. He was at the heart of power and magic and life itself and his movements stirred and woke each direction until the world spirit itself would awake and surge upwards with the Singer as its focal point.

The holy lord began the second layer of magic that needed to be woven; the second of nine. His voice was stronger than she had heard it in months and it contained that edge of power and arrogance that she remembered from the days before the breaking of the song. Yet he was sweating freely, despite the strength he was drawing from the Toko. A few months of increasing health weren't quite enough to overcome the effects of languishing so long within the song's own bloodlust. He would slow and he would falter.

Enet allowed the chant to blanket her thoughts and gave herself up to the ritual and the building magic – magic that teased along her veins and tickled her muscles. She had drunk so much tonic in the last two weeks. Surely it was enough?

'Who speaks for the world?' the Singer demanded.

'The Singer speaks for the world,' Enet said along with Kapal and Chotek. They were all sweating with the effort, even though they had nothing to do but remain still. The holy lord leapt at them, feet skipping as nimble as a dancer's between the chalked and painted glyphs.

He reached the second call and response and there was a clear upsurge in the magic contained within his body, their bodies, and the source itself. Enet sucked in air that glimmered at the edges, sweet as pollen.

The trickle of magic was growing, brushing up through the soles of her feet from the capstone resting so far below. Her attunement to it wasn't as strong as it had been with the broken songstone – she hadn't had long enough carving it and consuming its dust – but it was there, etched with the glyphs that bound it to her and her to it. As the Singer completed the second layer of magic and began the third, the trickle became a tiny stream bathing her feet and moving up into her calves. It would fill her from the feet up until she was crowned in its glory and ready, finally, to act.

Enet's gaze travelled around the source, marvelling at the brightness of colours and the clarity of sounds, from the Singer's feet slapping the stone to the individual beads of sweat dripping from his brow onto his naked chest. Her eyes swept past the cushions and Chorus warriors, hesitated, and went back. The slave was gone. When, where had he gone? Why? Had the holy lord sapped the last of his strength and he'd collapsed? She hoped it was that simple, but the unease lurching in her gut told her it could be more.

The tiniest shimmer caught her attention and Enet blinked, puzzled, and then blinked again in dawning recognition. Barely there, and yet there indeed, a whorl of gold crept beneath the delicate skin inside her wrist. Song-magic.

A settled calm fell over her. All would be well. It didn't matter that Tayan had left the source; he couldn't know about her capstone. No one knew about it other than Chorus Acamah, who had escorted the guards carrying it inside the pyramid and down into the lowest storeroom before losing his life to the traitor Ilandeh. A tragedy.

Even if the Shadow somehow found it, her guards were still there.

She smiled as she chanted the third response, turning her wrist to press against her stomach where the gold was hidden. Close now. Close to the changing of the world.

They'd reached the sixth layer of magic and all of them were struggling under its weight. The magic from Enet's tonics supported her, but even so the breath rattled in her chest. Shaman Kapal was suffering far more than Enet, unable to keep her feet and kneeling in position with her hands braced on her thighs, while Listener Chotek fared only a little better. Even his lifetime of training and immersion in the song weren't sufficient to hold so much magic with ease.

The holy lord himself had slowed both his dance and the chant, sweat smearing his paint into unrecognisable swirls. He was bent over with his hands on his knees, stomach undulating as he sucked in air, face hidden by the lank fall of his hair. Not even the gold surging beneath his skin could steal away his exhaustion. He would never be able to finish all nine layers.

Enet beckoned and Chorus Lisek approached with four cups. He stopped a respectful distance away, his features screwed up against the storm of magic surrounding them.

'Holy lord, water,' she croaked and gestured. Lisek drank from each cup in turn and then handed them to the shaman, the Listener, and the Singer. The fourth he offered to Enet with a tiny nod and she drank deeply, the gritty taste of songstone dust burning in her chest and belly. The magic jolted in her, up to her waist now as if the lower half of her body lay in the sun while the rest was in shadow. She drank again and again until the cup was empty and her stomach was hot and sore, but she could feel the magic brighter than ever, no longer a streamlet rushing over her but a waterfall pounding against her senses.

Her magic, the tonic's magic, and the magic the Singer was crafting all merged into one and suddenly, between one heartbeat and the next, she could grasp it. Take hold of the ritual's power. But could she wield it?

Magic lived in everything, song-magic glowing and twisting and linking them all together in a complex pattern Enet couldn't hope to unravel. At its centre the songstone – the one beneath her feet and the one above their heads and all the others, fireflies in the dark or the pattern of stars fallen to earth. Her exhalations glimmered with life; her inhalations were molten with it. Strength flowed into her, connection and power and the ability to manipulate, to *change*, everything she touched and saw and smelt. The backs of her fingers were sparkling too, now, and she wiped them on her kilt and then held them down at her sides where they were less visible. She hadn't expected this and there was no way to counter it; she could only hope that no one would notice before she took the rest of it for herself.

Three more layers of magic to open the door to the world spirit. Only three.

The Great Octave looked at the Singer and amid the burning light of magic she saw the thick red vine stretching out of him that led to the Toko. It pulsed with energy, all of it heading one way – into the holy lord. Cut that off and he'd fall in an instant. Undone. Unmade.

She wouldn't need his stone knife. She wouldn't need any weapon. She could reach out and snap that connection, here and now. Enet gathered will and magic and took a step towards him.

'Stop! Holy lord, stop. She's done something, she's gathering power for her own purposes.' The Singer looked up, his face lined with fatigue and running with sweat. His eyes gleamed amber and malevolent as they fixed on the Shadow. 'Singer, there's a second capstone carved with the Great Octave's name in the lowest level of the pyramid. Holy lord, she means to kill you.'

Everything, all movement in the source, stopped. Enet closed her eyes for the briefest of moments.

This fucking Toko. This fucking, fucking Toko.

She faced the slave, the Shadow, the shaman, and her magic allowed her to see his power coiled within him for the first time. It was golden-blue and vast as an ocean, and even though his spirit was falling to the predations of the Singer, his magic was a separate and awe-inspiring thing. Deeper and stranger than she'd ever imagined, even without the aid of the frog-juice on which she'd thought all his power depended. How completely he had hidden it from her, only to show it here, now, at the worst possible moment.

This fucking *Toko*.

'You are interrupting a ritual and a magic you cannot possibly understand,' Enet said, her voice low but throbbing with outrage. 'Chorus Leader, take him away this instant. We are at a critical point. The world and its spirit hang in the balance.'

'Your guards are dead, Great Octave,' Xochi said instead and her salt-cotton was spattered with blood. 'And I have seen the capstone with my own eyes.'

Enet felt the full weight of the Singer's regard upon her and something small and afraid quivered in her chest. 'What do they say?' he demanded and the magic fluctuated, all the power they'd built veering wildly as his attention slipped from the ritual. She gasped at the pain of it, Kapal and Chotek and even the Toko swaying beneath its force.

'Holy lord, please! The magic; you mustn't. The ritual must be finished,' she shouted and gathered up the ropes and coils of her own power, strengthened through prayer and exposure to the songstone dust, channelled through the capstone beneath her feet, and readied herself.

The deception, the distraction, didn't work. The Singer lunged for Enet with a screech of outraged recognition. He could see his power gathered in her hands, not realising that it had never really been his. Should never have been his. She lashed out with it, spirit and mind and body inexperienced but instinctive. The Shadow leapt between them and shoved the Singer sideways. Shoved him out of the ritual space, scuffing the carefully drawn glyphs and knocking over the brazier of wood chips and incense.

The six layers of magic they had woven together exploded, casting everyone in the source to the mats with screams of pain. The magic, wild and unconstrained, whipped about them in a rending frenzy and then, as the books and prophecies and masons themselves had told, was sucked into Enet's capstone and directed back out in a beam like sunlight.

Straight into her.

Six layers of magic. Nowhere near enough to wake the world spirit but more than enough to kill Xac. The holy lord was writhing and screaming as Enet took all the magic, took his magic, *took the song itself*, from him. She was standing in a lightning bolt, in a forest fire, in the heart of a mountain that spewed molten rock – but she had control. Carefully, she wrapped herself in power and began to pluck at it, learning the pathways of the song and how to manipulate it.

The magic responded, pooling within her and threatening to overflow. A sense of vastness – the world spirit itself – rose up in place of the living world that it had created. A sleeping god? A sleeping disease, more like, one that would destroy not save and Enet had the power now, had all she needed. Not to wake the world spirit, but to subdue it.

The Great Octave grasped the song-magic and, as the song itself veered into one single, high-pitched, unchanging wail of confusion, she shoved the world spirit backwards, downwards, into a sleep so deep it would never awaken. Never return. Never threaten. A sleep only one step from death. No garden for Ixachipan. No subjugation to some great, ancient, unknowable being with the power to create – or destroy – a world.

The effort drained the magic from her in one sickening lurch, but as soon as she was empty, more rushed to fill it from the capstone below. Enet retched at the mighty ebb and flow of magic, a tide within her threatening to sweep her away. Her eyes watered and nausea coiled within her, but as soon as it was replenished, she reached for her power.

The world spirit was gone, buried in its own magic never to return. Not even if it was called. Now for the rest of it. Enet clenched her fists. Xochi was a wobbling barrier between her and the thrashing Singer, Lisek a crumpled form at her feet. They did not have the same affinity for magic as the ritual-weavers and so it affected them differently, not tearing their spirits but stripping strength from their bodies.

The Shadow, though, despite bleeding from the ears, eyes and nose, was still standing and advancing on her. Kapal and Chotek were dead or dying, insects crushed beneath a weight they'd never even comprehended, let alone thought to wield.

The Great Octave drew more power into herself, so much that she was incandescent with it, glowing gold as the Singer dimmed. Drawing it out of the world, out of Xac, out of the Shadow. She could reach out and stop the Singer's heart. Anyone's heart, no matter how distant they might be. There was no distance within the magic, within the song that began to mould to her shape and will. She could—

The Toko appeared before her, his lips stretched in a hungry maw and his eyes as flat and dead as a lizard's. 'No,' he said calmly despite the tremors running through his slender frame. 'No. You will not take my magic from me. You will not take my power.'

'You have no idea what this is,' Enet panted, preparing to crush the heart in his chest. 'I gave everything for this, I gave my fucking son for this, and I won't let you—'

'No,' he said again, and in his hand was the stone knife of ritual. They struck together, she with magic, he with quartz.

They both missed.

The holy Setat, however, who leapt in a graceful arc from Enet's left, didn't miss.

Its claws tore through her belly and back out even as its other hand swept Tayan out of danger. Magic – her magic – lashed the holy Setat inside and out and only a creature that had been immersed in and then changed by that magic could withstand such an attack. Even so, the noise that tore from its throat was pure agony, a denial of her very existence.

The holy Setatmeh shriek did more to steal Enet's strength than the claws that had ripped her open. She stumbled under the scream that, together with its strike, stole her from the world and shattered a scheme so huge she'd long ago lost sight of its edges. Hadn't even known most of them.

A fucking Toko slave had seduced a holy Setat to his cause and between them they'd destroyed everything. Destroyed so much more than they could possibly know, and in Tayan's case, simply for greed.

A hysterical laugh sobbed in Enet's throat as she cupped gleaming red in her palms, brighter than the pyramid's own paint. It trickled between her fingers and pattered hot on her shins and feet. She'd thought the Toko a problem to be solved, a support to be levered carefully away from the Singer, but never a threat. What could he ever have done against her power and prestige?

'You can't stop it,' she mumbled in Tayan's face as the magic fell from her control to lash against them all. The song was a wild, untameable beast screaming through the night and shaking the walls of the source. The Singer whimpered, a collection of writhing limbs somewhere impossibly distant,

479

yet impossibly near. The holy Setat fled into the offering pool and away through the stream. Screaming; gone.

'Not even you can stop what is put in motion this night.' Enet toppled onto her side. 'You learnt to play the game, little shaman,' she breathed and jerked her chin after the god. 'It's a pity that in the end you played for the wrong side.'

The Shadow crouched, fingertips touching the floor for balance and his knees cocked up to either side; the pose of a holy Setat. 'I learnt to play from you, Great Octave,' he murmured, wiping blood from his eyes, 'a lesson well-taught and well-learnt.'

He poked through the mess of her tunic and she shrieked and writhed away from him. 'Get your fucking hands off me,' she choked. The magic was pulsing out of her even faster than her life, no matter how hard she tried to contain it, to fashion it into a bandage that would save her and everything she'd worked to achieve.

'You've ruined more than you can know. But you'll see; you'll see and then wish you'd waited just an hour longer. Just a single fucking hour and you'd have been free.' The words were strangled, coming in gasping lurches, but they gave him pause.

He looked away from her belly, frowning. 'Live long enough to tell me what in the Underworld you're talking about and I'll treat that wound,' he said. 'Once I've seen to the Singer, my sweet love.'

Another laugh bubbled in Enet and she swallowed it down along with the taste of blood. Stared at the murals painted on the ceiling and did her best not to look at the ruin of her body and her plans. Did her best not to regret her rash bravado and empty threats.

Did her best not to scream.

*　　*　　*

The song was . . . a voice. A weeping, gibbering, moon-mad shriek. A howling of vengeance, a pitiful murmur. A lingering death in the dark, alone and afraid.

The song was a voice.

And it was lost.

It was supposed to have been Enet's. The song-magic; the power. All hers.

But at least it's not his.

The Toko was shuffling across the source with Xochi taking most of his weight and his medicine box in her other hand. The Chorus Leader was practically dragging him, desperate to get him to the Singer to heal him.

The magic was still wild and flailing at them all – Enet jerked under its lash and Tayan sagged a little more in Xochi's grip with each blow, but finally he reached the Singer. Xac was lying on his back, much like Enet, only without the accompanying pool of blood. His limbs flopped and twitched as hers did, seemingly at random. Because the magic had left him, or because she had destroyed his ability to wield it?

Was that why the song cried?

Chorus Leader and Shadow collapsed next to the holy lord, Xochi ripping off the lid of the medicine box and thrusting it at Tayan, almost knocking him over. He rocked on his knees and the warrior steadied him, her hand flashing out to grip his arm. She seemed oblivious to the enormous breach of protocol and Enet managed a tiny snort at herself: *still thinking of propriety as your life dribbles out of your belly? What a Singer you would have made.*

The thought caused a pain in her chest, separate from the body-hurt of her opened guts. This was a spirit-hurt, a hurt that encapsulated everything she should have achieved and had let slip away. Again, she grasped for the magic, but where before it had flooded into her directed by her

481

capstone, now – she didn't know why; it didn't make *sense* – it was like trying to grasp a scorpion's tail. Every touch brought pain as it skittered from her grip. She could hold on to nothing.

'Doesn't matter,' she whispered to herself. 'The world spirit's gone and can never be brought back. I didn't do all I promised, but I did that.'

'You did enough, Enet.'

The Great Octave blinked until the face above hers came into focus. She smiled and reached for it, smearing blood across a cheek. 'Xini.'

'I have bandages. Itzil has gone for your medicine box and we can—'

'Stop. It's over.' Perhaps she hadn't spoken aloud, because the Chitenecatl ignored her words and began tenderly peeling back her tunic. He sucked in a breath and then fixed a smile in place that was uglier than her opened gut.

'This is going to hurt,' he murmured and slid hands and linen beneath her and then began binding it tightly. Enet yowled and would have arched away if she'd had the strength. 'You didn't fail, though,' he continued. 'Did you? The world spirit?'

'Is gone,' she confirmed and his smile softened into something more genuine, wondering. It was a barrier against the cold seeping into her limbs.

'And everything else is in place. That's why you have to live,' he insisted. 'This is just the beginning and we need you. All of us. We need you, Enet.'

'I've missed my name in your mouth,' she whispered.

There was no pain any more. Sleep pulled at her, wrapping her in softness as Xini wrapped her torso in linen. It would slow the bleeding, perhaps. Give her a little longer. The song still limped and roared and wailed, untethered from a consciousness that could control it. It should have been hers. Perhaps, if Itzil was quick with that medicine box, the gods would smile on Enet one last time. Perhaps she could still take it and make it hers. Change everything, as she'd always said she would.

Perhaps . . .

TAYAN

The magic was wild and unconstrained, but the song –
warped though it was – still clattered across the Empire, so
the Singer wasn't dead.

Tayan knew he wasn't dead because of their link, but that
same link was possibly the only thing keeping his sweet love
alive and he knew, too, that it couldn't support two spirits
for long.

*He lives, despite what Enet did. Despite everything she's
destroyed, he lives and she won't. She failed.*

But Setatmeh, she was close.

Setatmeh . . . one had saved his life and suffered agonies
because of it. Had leapt between them when Tayan's fumbled
strike with the stone knife missed and taken the brunt of
Enet's wielding of the magic. And wasn't that a thing? He'd
only felt the edge of it and still it had burnt and twisted his
insides. He hadn't known the magic could do that; not even
the Singer had ever hinted at it, and surely, if that knowledge

484

had been within his grasp, he'd have used it to enforce his Shadows obedience.

Tayan blinked and refocused. The Singer. Xochi was alternating babbling urgently in his ear with shouting commands at the few Chorus who had so far ventured into the source. All of them were shaking under the song's alien sickness, but she sent some to the offering pool to chant prayers to the god who'd saved him and others to stand guard over Enet. Her slaves were working feverishly to save her, but as everyone else had been ordered to stay away, shamans included, it was likely the Great Octave would bleed to death before he could get back to her. *But I want to know what she did. How did she use the magic? How did she bend songstone to her will? How—*

'Shadow!'

Tayan's hands had fallen still. The Singer. Yes. 'Get me honeypot and water, hot cacao spiced with chillies – not too many – and corn gruel. We need to stimulate his system and then nourish it. Go!' he snapped. Xochi relayed his words to another so she could stay with them and the Toko forgot about her as he slid his consciousness along the link into the Singer.

He could have entered the song first and from there joined with Xac's mind, but he knew instinctively that to enter the song at this moment would be the last thing he ever did. Still, it had only ever been the Singer in his head, not the other way around.

It was shockingly easy. Every barrier the holy lord had constructed around his mind was gone, rubble and flame and ash. The red vine encasing their spirits was flaking, pulsing and cracking as it sought life wherever it could. Tayan's own strength was failing rapidly now; if the holy lord relied solely on their spirit-link, they'd both be dead within the hour. He needed another source of life-essence. An offering? No, they didn't have the strength for that, either.

'Xochi, the blue jar in my medicine box. Mix it with half a cup of water,' he rasped. Tayan held the Singer's mind in the cupped palms of his spirit and waited, both of them weakening, for the score of stuttering heartbeats it took the Chorus Leader to comply. She sloshed the cup into his hand. 'Fuck,' he muttered, 'this is going to hurt.' He drank the journey-magic down in three long swallows, the insides of his cheeks pinching at the bitterness.

The Toko handed back the cup and then got the lid of the medicine box. He began tapping a rhythm. 'Like this,' he said. 'Do not deviate from this rhythm until I say. When I do, drum this instead' – he tapped a different beat – 'and keep going no matter what. We both die if you fail.'

The spirit world was rising already, Tayan's weakness lowering his flesh's resistance to the magic. Xochi's face was intent as she watched his hand and then nodded. 'As the Shadow commands.'

'The Singer will die,' he emphasised.

The Chorus Leader began drumming in time with him as he switched back to the journey beat. 'I understand.'

'When the cacao arrives, put it in my hand and help me get him to drink. But *keep drumming*.' There wasn't time for more; Tayan gasped and sank beneath the surface of the spirit world, filled with dread at the enormity of what he was attempting. Young Jaguar and Swift Hawk had promised him violence if he dared return, but already he could see the many trails of the spiral path stretching before him. He turned his back on them.

He turned from the song, too, the currents that had been teeth before and now were death itself to brush against. The millions of spirits he'd found hanging apathetic and unaware within the song were gone, and the realisation of their purpose was appallingly clear. They were food, nourishment for the world spirit as it was drawn from slumber. Xac had brought the world spirit close enough to the surface of waking that it had consumed every spirit trapped within the song for the hundreds of years since its inception. *Not just them. How many Listeners were lost? How many spirits, alive and knowing, did it eat? Was it a blessing to them or did they die shrieking?*

Clinging to Xochi's drum beat and the frail thread of his spirit, he followed the red vine back into the Singer's body. His mind. His spirit.

Followed it into madness.

The Singer was in shock, his body shutting down and his mind lost, unable to control the magic tearing through the source and across every stick of Ixachipan. The writhing, screaming song bore none of the feral majesty that accompanied an offering to the Singer, but nor did it sound like anything Tayan had ever known before.

He didn't know what the song sounded like when its Singer was beginning to ascend, but he suspected it wasn't dissimilar to this. Pechaqueh would know. Councillors could be running through the night to the pyramid even now, hoping to be chosen in Xac's last moments of mortal life to go to the waters with him. And go to the waters he might if his Shadow couldn't save him. Or perhaps die without transforming at all. Die in truth; die human. Despite his lifelong knowledge that the holy Setatmeh could be slaughtered, Tayan knew they lived for hundreds of years if spared attack or injury. Xac should have that. He deserved it, for bringing all Ixachipan to peace beneath his song.

Then it's up to me to see that he ascends as he is destined to do.

When it is his time, of course. Only then.

There hadn't even been the faintest tug on the link between them, but Tayan amended his thoughts with instinctive speed. He was the Shadow, Xac's most loyal and devoted slave, and he would restore him to health and glory or die trying. And he knew how to do it, too. He hoped. He prayed.

Xochi's drumbeat was steady and unerring, anchoring Tayan to his flesh by the thinnest gossamer-gold, and he prayed for that, too, that it would not snap under the immense pressure of what he needed to do. How far he needed to go – and through whom.

The holy lord had drunk cacao and water and eaten a little gruel, the Tokob hands trembling as they held cups and spoon to the Singer's mouth. The effort of keeping so much in motion – the work to heal the Singer, to feed him, to listen to the journey rhythm, to be aware of the predations of the song circling ever closer, to not lose himself – had brought Tayan to the very limits of what he could manage.

The song-magic lashed out at unpredictable moments, threatening disaster and death, but there was a thread still binding it to the Singer. And the Singer, of course, was bound to his Shadow.

'Don't falter,' he panted in the flesh world. 'No matter what. It gets harder from here.'

'As the Shadow commands,' he heard, the words sliding off him like water. He was already turning inwards, unspooling the thread of his spirit behind him as he entered the holy lord's mind once more and followed it to the last connection he held with the song.

Death there. Death lies through there.

Magic lies there, and I am shaman and peace-weaver and Shadow. I bend magic to my will.

There could be no fear, as there could be none in the face of Young Jaguar or the wild spirits of the spiral path or those hungry ancestors in their realm, seeking his flesh to live again. There could be none of that. There was only the sacred task of making medicine for the holy lord, the great Singer, his sweet Xac.

Tayan pushed through the Singer's consciousness and out into the song-world, the fifth world. It looked like the Underworld.

It was an alien landscape, utterly unlike the song in which he'd spent so much time before. The flesh world faded and the great golden ocean, the disc of the Singer, that he'd been expecting to find was, instead, a dried-up pond. The majority of its surface was marred with veins of rot, the cracks from before more like fissures in limestone, canyons opening between cliffs. The golden Singer himself was dull, glazed in hopelessness, his sheen long vanished.

Oh, my love. What has she done to you?

Tayan was rocked by a pathetic scrabbling, a frightened drawing away. He looked down at himself, at the faded, tired blue where once he'd been so vibrant. *Do not fear, great Singer. I mean you no harm.*

The cracks that had once been golden threads stretching from the holy lord to his pyramids, his songstone, were bleeding magic and emotion, draining him into the song. Tayan needed to stop the flow. Reverse it, even. Borrow the song's own strength until the Singer's was replenished.

'Shadow? Are you well?'

Xochi's voice came from far away; he flapped a hand to dismiss her concern. He was not well, but only because his love was suffering. He couldn't merge their spirits as he'd done on

489

that fateful day that had led to their linking; they were already merged in every way that counted. Which meant . . .

Gently, Tayan reached out with spirit-fingers and brushed them against one of the towering, lethal walls of song-magic that rushed and slammed and sliced through the fifth world, wild and uncontrolled. A wisp of his spirit was severed immediately, but he got a grip on the magic and drew it, with love and gentleness, away from its mad dance and into himself. If he and the Singer were already one, and the Singer was unable to control the magic, then his Shadow would do it for him.

The first smoke-fine puffs of magic slipped inside Tayan and found a space within spirit and body, a home ready-made by his joining with Xac. Like birds flocking, more magic followed, and then more and more and more, suffusing him, restoring his energy and salving his exhaustion, filling him to the brim and overflowing until he was a gushing waterfall of golden magic. Until he was god.

Until he was god.

With a monumental effort of will, Tayan focused on the Singer. His spirit had been shattered by Enet's theft of his magic, and although the vine pulsing between them was feeding him, he remained small and dull. It would take time. Tayan could give him that. Tayan had all the time in the world, and all the strength, all the knowledge of the magic and the songstone.

The song itself began to stabilise, still ugly and discordant but no longer a raging animal loosed from confinement. Even so much was an improvement and a necessary one to calm the Pechaqueh and reassure the Empire of Songs that the great pyramid had control.

Xochi's drumbeat faltered for an instant before recovering. In the flesh world, Tayan slapped at her. 'Focus. This is not him; I do it for him, so that he can recover. Without the beat, I cannot.'

It was no longer true; he could swim these waters without effort or needing a way home. He was home. *The song* was his home now. And with its strength, he could finally get his answers. Leaving the greater part of himself to watch over the holy lord, Tayan sent a splinter of consciousness through the steadying song to Great Octave Enet. Spear of the City Enet. Dying Enet. He would ease her passage from this world – once she had told him everything.

The Shadow slid into Enet's mind like a blade, past the defences falling into ruin as she weakened. She was speaking with her slaves, her words slurring, and he could see why: the holy Setatmeh claws had injected their venom, but only when they were deep inside her. Injected into organs that didn't feel, she had no idea she was poisoned as well as bleeding to death.

She didn't have long, but he would ensure it was long enough. He would hold her spirit suspended in the song past death if he had to, until he had his answers.

'Get the books and take Itzil and go. You know where. Tell them I failed, that after all of it, I failed. Tell them to keep going and . . . that I'm sorry.'

Always speaking in riddles, Great Octave. Is plain speech as alien to you as the tongues of Barazal?

He felt her hitch and then smile. 'Ah. Toko slave, I wondered how long it would take you to find a way in.'

She wasn't speaking aloud and her inner voice retained all the strength and arrogance of a lifetime of privilege and scheming and deceit.

Did you really think you'd succeed? he demanded. *Here, in the heart of my love's power? You thought you would steal his song and the magic?*

'Your love? He was mine well before he was yours, slave, but I gift him to you now, to do with as you will. As you already are, I think.' She spoke on before he could reply. 'And in return, I ask one thing.'

Despite himself, two years of obedience had left their mark. In spirit and flesh worlds, Tayan bowed his head.

'Control the Singer for as long as possible. Keep him pliant; keep him weak. Whatever you do, modify the song so it doesn't screech of Pechaqueh superiority.'

What are you talking about? Tayan demanded, alarm pulsing in waves through his spirit and tinging black at the edges with fear. He refused to acknowledge the sudden sharp spike of interest her words caused. *Keep him weak? My purpose – my only purpose in this world – is to restore the song, to heal it and the Singer with it. I cannot do that by making him weak. Healing the song is the purpose given me by the holy Setatmeh themselves. I am—*

'Then you have fallen in truth, Tayan of Tokoban, once friend to ejab and now selling yourself to their enemies. Fallen too far to ever climb back. I pray your gods can forgive you, for your people never will.'

Enet coughed, deep and agonising, little sips of air in between all she could manage. Tayan could feel her life fading, drifting through his fingers like coils of incense smoke.

'You really are the worst slave I ever owned. Suppose I can't, can't be surprised you betrayed me and everyone in Ixachipan. Xac gave you power, after all. And you have ever been greedy.'

Tayan bobbed in her mind like a leaf on a stream, riding the fading currents of her thoughts. *You didn't answer my question,* he said. *Why seize the power? Why do . . . what did you do?* he amended, feeling the magic tingling through the expanse of his spirit, now the bright, shining blue of shamanic paint and vaster than an ocean. Vaster than Xac's. *The spirits in here are all gone. What did you do? What about the world spirit? Answer me!*

Enet ignored him, speaking to her slaves again and making no effort to protect herself as Tayan ripped through her mind for the final secret in a frenzy. She'd wanted to be Singer, schemed, and killed for it, but why had she taken the magic in such a way the world spirit was banished?

'You need to go, Xini. Itzil, too. Take the books and go. No more arguments; no more excuses.'

'Come with us,' someone said as Tayan tore her open, searching, searching.

'I'll stay. It's time to atone.'

'You have nothing to atone for,' Xini insisted.

'Two hundred and fort— forty-three.' Tayan found the truth and burst inside it, desperate.

What is this, what were you doing?

'Two hundred and forty-three. Do not add to my tally. Go, both of you, please go. For all who would be free.'

'For all who would be free,' Xini said, his voice strangled, as Tayan took the secret from Enet's dying mind and found he could not understand it. Turned it over and over as she faded, examining it and unable to believe it. No. *Impossible.*

How could they all have been so wrong, for so long?

'Great Octave, Enet. I can hear it. It's beginning. You did that. Your name will be remembered forever.'

'Of course it will,' Enet said, but it was shame, not arrogance or triumph, that soaked her thoughts when she spoke.

Tayan showed her the secret she'd kept hidden beneath all the others, decoy secrets that had somehow been truths. She'd worn her ambition so openly, held her desire to be Singer so firmly in her heart that none of them, not Tayan, not even Xac, had thought to look deeper.

What is this? Two hundred and forty-three what? he shouted in her head, to no response. *Tell me what you've done.*

'You know what I've done, Tayan of Tokoban, shaman and husband. Shadow and traitor. I've done what you couldn't, what you're too greedy to ever understand. For my diamond boy, my Pikte, For all who would be free. Keep him weak, Tayan. Keep him weak and we can win this.'

Win what? he tried, but she was fading, venom and blood loss killing her organs one at a time until her heart stuttered, stumbled, and stopped.

'For all . . .'

Tayan felt her spirit loosen and tore himself out of her mind lest he be stolen from life as well. He flung himself back into the song. A song that buoyed him up; a song that gave him power. The Singer was small and querulous in the back of his mind, demanding power and answers and worship. The Toko hushed him, casting himself outwards into the city. *I can hear it. It's beginning.* Xini's words.

And, *keep him weak and we can win this*, from Enet.

'Recall beat,' he said and Xochi changed her drumming. He no longer needed it, but it was better no one knew that. He raced back along the thread of his spirit and into his flesh and opened his eyes to find himself glittering gold, a cascade of sparkles chasing through his skin. He inhaled magic; exhaled glory.

And became aware of hurrying Chorus warriors and a few breathless, excited councillors kneeling around him and competing to pray the loudest in the hopes of ascending at the Singer's side. He ignored them, focusing on Xochi's panicked face. He put his hand over hers, stilling the rhythm.

'Shadow? Shadow Tayan?' she gasped. 'Did the world

spirit awaken? Where is the transformation we were promised? Is the holy lord ascending?'

Tayan of Tokoban, called the stargazer, looked at Xac
unconscious next to him. With barely a thought and less
effort, he snapped the red vine the Singer had stitched into
his spirit, separating them once more. The Singer twitched
and his presence faded from the Tokob consciousness.

Tayan gathered up all the coils and loops of magic and
snugged them around himself like a cocoon. The song
veered and stumbled and the councillors leant forward as
one, alight with greed and ugly hope. Frowning, the
Shadow allowed a small trickle of magic to pass into the
holy lord and the song trembled and settled. So. The Singer
and the song needed each other as much as they needed
him. For now.

He looked Xochi in the eye and could see his own reflec-
tion: he was gleaming. 'The Singer failed. The world spirit
will not wake today. He gave all his strength to the attempt
and his recovery will be long and painful. I will support him
until he regains his health.' He glared at the avaricious
councillors. 'The holy lord is not ascending. Return to your
homes immediately.'

'There's fighting in the streets, Shadow,' Xochi said.

Ah, yes. Enet and her audacious, outrageous plan. He
would ensure that failed too. 'Pilos can deal with it. You will
look to me for instruction until such time as the Singer is
recovered; is that clear?'

'As the Shadow commands.' Xochi gestured at the crest-
fallen councillors and urged them away. Tayan stared at
Enet's corpse, his song surging and dropping like waves on
a beach, a little higher, a little steadier, each time. A little
more in control.

For the good of the Empire of Songs, Tayan would take up the sacred burden of the song-magic and wield it for Ixachipan's glory. Just until the Singer was well and the Great Octave's followers were put back in their place.

Keep him weak.

Just until then.

THE SINGER

The source, Singing City, Pechacan, Empire of Songs

Shadow?

Shadow, where are you? The silence, Shadow, it burns me. The absence inside me cuts. Where is it? Where is my magic, my song, my destiny? Where is the world spirit I was to awaken?

Shadow?

Answer me!

. . .

Enet? Enet, are you there? I'm afraid, Enet. Such things I've done, such terrible, bloody things. Our boy, Enet. Our Pikte.

. . .

Answer me. Someone, anyone. I'm afraid.

Please?

497

LILLA

'Shut up and follow me,' Ekon said and his voice was hard, brooking no dissent.

'Have I done something wrong, high one?' Lilla tried, though he was pretty sure he knew what this was about. The ritual to wake the world spirit had happened and then the song had . . . Lilla had no words. It wasn't even as it had been during the monthly magic-weaving they'd endured before. There was no lust for cruelty and violence in it. It sounded like the earth itself was screaming, begging for an end to a pain so great it would blot out the sun.

The frenzied celebrations they'd heard coming from the Fifth Talon's drill yard – where the eagle, hawk and dog Talons had gathered – had degenerated into confusion as the song that had built and built in majesty and power shattered into madness.

In contrast, the tense, grieving silence of the Eighth Talon's barracks buildings had, after a disbelieving pause, broken into

498

jubilation. Warriors spilt out of the buildings into the compound in a whooping mass, giddy with relief even as the raging, unleashed song whipped at them, uncontrolled bursts of emotion that had them flinching, laughter stuttering into pained gasps. Cowering under the song's fury, still they laughed in its teeth, laughed at its failure and whimpered at its cutting.

Lilla's vicious pleasure at the failure of a ritual that would have stolen Malel from them had lasted until Ekon's long-legged, predatory stalk through the Eighth Talon's compound to fetch him. He'd come himself; he hadn't sent a slave. Whatever order was coming, Lilla wasn't going to like it. There could be no other reason Ekon would come for him himself.

The Feather walked faster and Lilla matched him; if the Pechaqueh were humiliated by the failure of their ritual, they'd mete out punishment to remind the slaves who was in charge. A lesson in power and possession, in "I can and so I will".

Not even their relationship would see him spared and might even be what had driven Ekon to select him. The Tokob ears weren't stopped by ejab spirit-magic; he knew what others were saying about them. About the Feather and his questionable appetites. The eagles Ekon lived among saw only the slave brands. He wasn't even a dog warrior. He was property and they supposed Ekon used him as such.

And, despite all his protestations of not caring, Ekon had shrunk beneath their taunts and become harsher in his treatment of the Talon. Perhaps he didn't know he was doing it; or perhaps Lilla was being overly generous.

Besides, he had endured enough whispers from his own warriors that he knew how Ekon felt. Even those dedicated to rebellion had sent him sidelong looks as if they couldn't quite believe he'd gone so far to gain his enemy's trust.

Lilla grimaced. If only it was that simple. Why had he had to complicate things with feelings? What was this bubble of happiness that popped in his chest every time Ekon's face or voice or touch rose in his memory?

There was no bubble of happiness now, though. The song laid into him with the same fiery bite as the whip that had ruined his back. Even Ekon hunched beneath it. The tall, lean eagle looked neither left nor right as he marched Lilla out of the slave compound, along the passages to the eagles' quarters and in. He didn't speak or slow down until he was in his house, sandals kicked off and abandoned outside.

Lilla took off his own more slowly, trying to calm his heartbeat. It didn't work. He hadn't been brought into the presence of other eagles as sport or spectacle, but that didn't lessen the sense of danger prickling the hairs on the back of his neck. He stepped through the curtain and immediately knelt and pressed his face to the mat. He stayed there; he didn't know why Ekon was angry, but he wasn't prepared to exacerbate it.

'Stand.'

The Feather's voice was heavy with something that Lilla couldn't name. Something weighing on his spirit. He stood carefully, looking up far enough to see the Pechaqueh thighs and the fists clenched at his sides. Ekon stepped forward, pushed him against the wall and kissed him.

Lilla made a surprised noise as a rush of heat flashed from his belly out into every limb. Want vied with anxiety and he opened his mouth to Ekon's insistence and slid his arms around his back.

'Ekon,' he gasped when he had to break away just to breathe, almost dizzy. Sweat and dust, spice and sunlight, drifted from the Feather's skin and wrapped him close.

The Pecha grabbed his chin in one strong hand and pulled him close again. 'Just a little longer,' he murmured and kissed him again, tenderly this time, the passion under tight control. Lilla melted into it, a breathy almost-sound easing from his throat. It was easy to forget the Pechaqueh tension and the hardness of his voice under the slow, mesmerising brush of his lips and tongue.

Lilla pressed his hips forward and Ekon pulled away, flushed. 'Have I,' he began, uncertain, and the Feather put his fingertips across his mouth, hushing him. Lilla resisted the urge to lick between his fingers and instead held Ekon's gaze until he stepped away, towards the door-curtain. He cocked his head and listened, then nodded once to himself. 'Good,' he muttered. 'Lilla, sit. We have to talk and there isn't much time before it begins. Despite the failure in the source, for failure it must be. She'd never—' He cut himself off and gestured abruptly, sinking onto his heels on the mats.

Lilla blinked rapidly, the wall at his back the only thing keeping him upright. His mouth was buzzing. 'What? Ekon, I don't understand.'

The Feather just pointed; Lilla knelt opposite him, close enough to reach out and touch, though his awareness was returning and with it he could see that Ekon was tense again, his gaze skating over Lilla and then flashing away. A muscle was flickering in his jaw.

'What's wrong?' Lilla blurted, the flesh beneath his ribs fragile and tender. *That was our last kiss. He's ending it. He can't stand the taunts any more. I'm not worth it.*

'You're planning a rebellion,' Ekon said and it was like being thrown into a river full of Drowned. Every muscle in the Tokob body tensed with the urge to flee or fight. Every thought of relationships and the tender shoots of affection, of . . . more than that, were scorched to ash. His gaze flicked to the corner of the room near the door and the spear propped there. He'd have to step past Ekon to reach it and the Feather would never let that happen.

'You don't have enough people, but more than I expected,' Ekon continued as if every word wasn't a shard of obsidian flaying Lilla's flesh.

There was a knife sticking out of Ekon's belt. He'd have to go for that. He pressed himself to the mats. 'High one, whatever you have heard, let me—'

'Sit up,' Ekon snarled and Lilla paused, nausea flashing through him, but then complied. He shifted on his knees, readying himself. What else could he do? With the song spiralling further towards violence, it wouldn't be unexpected for brawls and murder to occur. With luck, he'd be executed without too many questions and the rebellion could continue without him.

Without luck . . . well, he wouldn't name anyone, no matter what they did to him. He'd die before he betrayed his people. He refused to acknowledge the idea that he'd betrayed them in this building a dozen times and more already. Betrayed them with every heated kiss and press of fingers in flesh, with every breath and gasp and begging plea of 'more, gods yes, more'. Despite the coming violence, a blush rose in his cheeks.

'I said there isn't much time. You are not the only ones planning such an uprising.' Lilla blinked at that and Ekon scoffed at his expression. 'You think others have simply been waiting for you brave, noble Tokob and Yaloh to come and lead us to freedom? You think we haven't been planning this *for generations?* Your arrogance rivals that of the Pechaqueh.'

Lilla bristled, because that was exactly what he'd thought, that all those who'd been decades or longer under the song had lost their desire for freedom. Still, Ekon's words were impossible, a clumsy trap he wouldn't fall into. They couldn't be true. He forced himself not to look at the knife handle.

'However many you have, it isn't enough unless you are allied to a bigger force, one more organised. One that stretches across every stick of Empire.'

'I don't know what—' he tried again.

'Quiet. Slaves have lived and died entire lifetimes waiting for the right moment, never knowing an instant's freedom. They've died knowing their children may never know that freedom either, but they've done it. And do you know why?'

Lilla swallowed hard. 'No,' he croaked, frantically trying to sense the trap. What game was the Feather playing? Cold sweat had broken out across his body, swamping the heat from moments before.

'Because a third-generation slave or servant is precious,' Ekon said, disdain dripping from every syllable. 'Good, loyal bloodlines are handed down in families like precious artefacts or pieces of jewellery – and those families' fortunes rise and fall. Some end up on councils or governing cities and large towns. Some end up Chosen. This game has been played for so long to ensure enough loyal servants are owned by enough powerful or strategic people. Now, finally, we are here and we are ready.' Ekon paused to press his fingers into his knees, grounding himself.

Bewilderment coiled through Lilla's dread. Dread at the conspiracy being discovered; dread at sliding Ekon's knife through Ekon's ribs.

'Sunset on the day of the waking of the world spirit was the signal to prepare, with the uprising to begin three hours later. It doesn't matter that we failed to seize the song, we rise anyway. Everything else is in place; it cannot be stopped now. It's actually happening.' Ekon's voice was bright with excitement, his whole body alight with it. 'Your rebels will storm the Fifth's drill yard. Don't worry, you'll have support. They're confused, struggling under this version of the song. Kill everyone. We'll deal with the remaining high command and the Listeners.'

'I will not . . .' Lilla began again and then stopped. Looked at Ekon. 'What?'

The Feather leant forward, urgent now. 'Listen to me, Lilla of the Tokob, warrior of the jaguar path, because we are running out of time. An Empire-wide rebellion begins tonight and it will do so with or without you and your rebels. I know you had your own plans, though I don't know how advanced they were, but I'm asking you to commit to us, fight with us. Together we can break the Melody's back, destroy it from within. Those who—'

The lies sat ugly on Ekon's tongue, unworthy of one with so much honour. 'I don't believe you. You're Pechaqueh; you're a Feather of the Melody. I watched you kill Kux! You've killed dozens, perhaps hundreds, of people and enslaved them, enslaved me.' Lilla didn't know if he meant literally or emotionally. 'You're full of shit.'

Ekon took a very deep breath through flared nostrils. 'I have,' he admitted. 'I've killed more than you could possibly know. Maybe I'll tell you that number one day, my tally; probably I won't. But let me tell you why and how I made that choice, over and over again: nineteen sun-years ago, a Pechaqueh family were executed on the way here to present their son for induction into the Melody. Ekon was the sole survivor of his family's slaughter by rebel slaves. Those slaves had been killed in the assault, one by himself despite his injuries.'

He pulled his tunic up and pointed to the jagged, ugly scar seaming up his side from his hip towards his bottom ribs.

The scar that just the night before Lilla had pressed his tongue against, licking salt from its knotted contours.

'Ekon was found two days later as he lay among the corpses of his family. He was near death, unable to do much more than give his family lineage and intention to join the Melody. By the time the shamans had declared he would live, Pilos had heard of his – *of my* – bravery and automatically welcomed me into the Second Talon as an eagle. It took me a Star cycle to become the Feather in charge of a slave Talon so that I might encourage rebellion. A Star cycle in which I and a few others brought slave warriors and dog warriors into the conspiracy and seeded them among nearly every Talon in the Melody. For this very day.'

Lilla stared at him, his mind an uncomprehending blank. 'What are you saying?' he whispered. 'Who are you?'

'My name is lost to everyone, including me. I no longer speak or think it. I am Ekon now, but before I was Pechaqueh, I was – I am – Chitenecah. We are rebels and we are in every noble household in the Empire and some of the highest positions within the Melody. And tonight, we tear down Pechaqueh dominance and take back our lives and freedom.'

To their mutual surprise, Lilla began to laugh, ragged and wheezing, as the consequences of all his actions bore their fatal fruit. 'I'm married,' he croaked and hot, angry tears choked his voice. The enormity of his betrayal was a mountain falling on him, and it been for nothing. For less than nothing. 'I'm married to Tayan and you made me fuck you, made me betray my promises so I could get close enough to kill you. Made me feel . . . And you're, all this time you've been . . . Tayan's never going to forgive me.'

'But Tayan is dead?' Ekon tried, doing his best to follow Lilla's tangent.

'I lied,' Lilla almost shouted. 'I lied so that he wouldn't be killed if I was caught.' He put his head in his hands and dragged at his hair, a formless screech muffled against his bicep. 'They never found his body at the ambush site. For all I know, my husband is alive and waiting for me, and I've betrayed him and every promise I ever made. For the chance to kill you. For nothing! This is what you fucking people have made me. How could you? *How could you?*'

'That's not,' Ekon began, reaching out and grabbing Lilla's leg; he shook him off. 'That's not what I meant to happen. I didn't know you'd done that, kitten, or I never—'

'Don't call me that,' Lilla choked. 'Fuck, I'm going to be sick.'

The Pecha – *or whoever he is* – recoiled as if Lilla had, indeed, vomited in his lap. 'Is that how I make you feel?' he asked, his voice small and hurt. 'Lilla, I'd never have kissed you that first time if I'd known you were married, let alone anything more. But you didn't claim him. When I began to, to care for you, I made sure you were unwed.'

'Well, I'm not fucking unwed,' Lilla hissed as bile scorched his throat, 'and if you think I'm going to . . .' He closed his eyes and pressed the heels of his hands against them, fighting the hurt tangling in his chest. 'How do I know anything you're saying is the truth?' he asked in the end. His own life was forfeit one way or the other, but he refused to condemn the rebels along with himself.

'I swear it on my ancestors, on the Chitenecah goddess Mictec. I swear it on my own life.' He drew the knife from his belt and laid it in front of Lilla. 'You're not as subtle as you think, Lilla. I saw you spot this immediately, so here it is. If you think I'm lying, kill me. The rebellion will go ahead regardless, here in the fortress and all across Ixachipan. Nothing can stop it. I will not regret dying for freedom; I well know my privilege in living this life compared with yours or any of the slaves throughout this swamp of an Empire. I have been one of the luckiest. Luckier even than many that Pechaqueh call free. Luckier than some Pechaqueh themselves, perhaps. The things I've had to do are the price I pay for this freedom and if it ends here, at your hand, then Mictec will judge me and no one else.'

He sat still, his face calm, as Lilla picked up the knife. As he held it out and pressed the tip beneath his chin, denting the soft, tender flesh where the Toko had pressed lips and fingers and teeth. 'I could,' he whispered. 'It would be so easy. For everything; for the lies. For fucking me just to secure my rebels.'

'That's not why I fucked you,' the Feather said. 'I wanted, want, you because you're decent and good and honourable—'

'Not any more,' he snarled.

Regret flashed across Ekon's face, but his voice was steady. 'Mictec will welcome me and so will my ancestors. Nothing you do will stop this uprising. It is bigger than any one person, bigger than you or me, and I only hope you will rise with the rest when the killing starts. If you want all those things you're so passionate about, all the things you must have promised your people, then you'll fight alongside us. And I'm sorry that things between us could not have been . . . purer of motive. I hope you find your Tayan, Lilla. I hope you find your happiness when the blood has stopped flowing.'

Jaw clenched, Lilla tightened his grip on the knife. 'The blood will never stop. Not as long as people like you live.'

'People like us, you mean.' Ekon raised his chin. 'I'm sorry, kitten, but it's the truth.'

'You killed Kux.'

'And then had you whipped, yes. And told my warriors not to hold back with the lashes. But how many rebels did that spectacle bring you? How many came to your side when you forfeited your reward of a year off your service?' There was, of all things, sympathy in the Feather's eyes, even as his words showed Lilla the truth about himself.

Lilla stared at the point of the knife, pressing against flesh, and then dropped the blade. 'No. I'm not like you,' he insisted, knowing he lied. 'And I won't play the noble, self-sacrificing warrior who's the hero of a story no one will ever read because that's easier than facing up to what he's done. When this is over, I'll find Tay, and I'll be able to look him in the eyes and tell him I'm a better man than you are.'

Ekon's breath shuddered out of his lungs but he didn't contradict him.

Lilla had thought of the years ahead and the things he'd have to do. He'd thought he might spend them with this man, lie though it would be – *would it have been?* – until he killed him. Now he was staring at the knowledge that, instead, he was going to have to live and fight alongside him. Live with how he felt, with the lightning Ekon had seeded under his skin with no more than the weight of his gaze.

'As you wish, Lilla,' the Feather said, and there wasn't even a rebuke there, or a defence. 'I'm going to take you back to the Eighth now and we're going to kill the guards on the gate. Once inside, get your rebels moving while I distract the archers on the wall. Get into your drill yard – the gate will be open – and take out the dogs guarding your armoury. They're not ours. Arm everyone and then just follow the screams to the Fifth's training compound. Kill every eagle and hawk you can find and every dog or slave warrior that stands against you – and there will be hundreds, perhaps thousands. I know you know that, but I want you to really understand what it means. They're either with us or against us. Kill them all and I'll meet you in the middle.'

508

'And that's it? You take my rebels from me the way you've taken everything else?'

Ekon paused halfway to his feet. 'What?'

'Who put you in command, Feather Ekon? You don't know the number or temperament of the people with me, but you're throwing them into the Fifth's compound against thousands of Pechaqueh? Are our lives so expendable?'

'Had you planned your own rebellion to be bloodless, then?' the man asked, frustration creeping into his voice.

'. . . No.'

'I'm not taking your warriors from you, Fang. We have a plan for how this needs to go; I'm asking you to be a part of it. And we are really running out of time, so make your choice.'

Still Lilla hesitated, but Ekon was shrugging into his salt-cotton. 'Fine,' he growled and then lowered his voice to the coldest, flattest snarl he could muster. 'But betray me and I will spit you on a blunted spear.'

'I would expect no less,' Ekon said. He pointed to a second set of armour. 'Dress.' He knotted the laces along the sides, picked up a bow and quiver, a second knife and his spear. 'For the Chitenecah and Mictec,' he prayed over the weapons, his eyes tightly closed. 'For all who would be free.' He reached a long arm outside and dragged their sandals in. 'Dress,' he snapped again, 'it's nearly time. Stay behind me and don't speak.'

Numb fingers fumbled with ties as Lilla dressed in an eagle's armour, picked up live weapons and then strapped on his sandals and followed Ekon into the dusk. There were five of them at the high, heavy gate, dog warriors whose grumbling faded the instant the Feather appeared. 'Open it,' he said and four stepped back to press against the wall while the fifth turned to untie the gate. Ekon stepped in close and slung his left arm around a dog's neck; his right hand punched a blade into the base of his throat and he threw him at the next without a pause.

Lilla watched, shocked into immobility at the casual violence, the lack of any sort of warning, and then vengeance and fury and guilt and shame burst free from his chest and he charged past and rammed his spear up into a gut, through the salt-cotton and back out. The man at the door turned at the commotion, puzzlement slipping into fear before the Toko ripped his spear tip across his face. His scream was loud and Lilla flinched; the sound echoed and carried through the narrow passageway. Ekon made a frustrated noise and killed the next with a stab through the lung that stole his voice along with his breath. The fifth was pressed against the wall and Lilla drew the feint so Ekon could stab him under the arm.

'I'm sorry,' he panted but the Feather ignored him, ripping open the gate.

'Go, and pray to your gods that I can distract the archers.' He didn't wait for a reply, vanishing back between the high walls.

Lilla ran inside and found scores of faces turned in his direction; they'd heard the scream despite the hammering, howling song. His gazed skittered over them, looking for one of his pod or any of the warriors he knew was sworn to the cause even as he moved away from the gate – the open gate – and further from the wall bristling with enemies.

'Tinit,' he called with relief and silence fell around him, some warriors edging closer and others away, unnerved by his appearance in bloody eagle armour and carrying weapons. He shoved through the crowd and the woman blinked and began to kneel before recognising him.

'P-pod-Leader? Lilla?' she stammered.

'It's happening. Don't ask questions, don't ask me how, but we have more allies in this fortress than we ever believed. It's happening now.'

Even in the dusk and the distant glow of torches, he saw her pale. 'Now?'

'Now,' he confirmed. 'Get everyone on our side to mass at the gate through to the training compound; we're taking the armoury and then we're taking this fortress.'

'Monkey shit,' snapped someone to his left. Lilla stared him down.

'The archers,' said someone else.

'Archers are being dealt with but yes, they'll be a threat, so be fast. Hold up blankets if you can quickly reach them to spoil their aim and if you're sworn to us, pass the word. If not, get out of my face and get ready to hide when they come for you. It's likely they'll kill you and for that I'm sorry. Or you can join us and fight them. Fight for your lives.'

'That's it?' the speaker from before muttered.

Lilla rounded on him. 'There's no time for more. You pledged your lives to the Melody so that your kin would live. You pledged to kill innocents and die guilty to save them, and that is on your own consciences when you stand before Malel.' He slashed his hand through the air, only belatedly noticing the blood spattered across it. He clenched it into a fist, adrenaline making him jittery. 'None of that matters now; none of it. There is a rebellion about to start that will set this empire ablaze. There are no bystanders. Whatever we think of those who've set this in motion, we are warriors. We can fight and kill and rescue our kin at the point of a bloody spear, or we can die on our knees at the hands of our "owners".'

Lilla wrenched at the collar around his throat. 'Die wearing these.' He slapped his brand. 'And these.'

'But if we surrender—'

'You think they will wait to check the central records? You think they will carefully match up our names and loyalties with those of our families? If this uprising is as big as I have been told, they'll be killing slaves the Empire over in an effort to break us. So we kill them first.'

'You're sure?' Tinit demanded and Lilla held up his bloody hands in mute explanation. 'Malel be praised.' And with that she was gone, darting through the crowd and pausing to whisper in ear after ear.

'If we surrender,' the man tried again and Lilla shoved him hard, cutting off his words and then pushed past, interrupting conversations and dragging people to him, pausing only long enough to ensure they understood.

The word spread fast and warriors began to head for the gate in a slow but purposeful drift, and those far back around the barracks buildings sensed the commotion and began to converge as well, shouting questions, hurrying. The darkness grew a little more and no arrows found them, so Ekon must have kept his word.

The song veered again and then steadied. The wild clamour and painful screeching smoothed suddenly, like a frightened dog feeling its owner's firm hand. It calmed and even found a strange, familiar cadence all its own.

There was a resounding cheer from deep within the fortress and shouted praise to the Singer. Lilla swore and broke into a run. Screams marred the sounds of celebration before he'd gone more than a dozen steps, one or two and then more, and more and more, a rising pitch of anger and disbelief threading through the clamour.

'*Malel!*' he bellowed and sprinted for the gate, praying it would open as Ekon had promised. The rebels followed his lead and suddenly he was dragging a cloak of righteous fury behind him, scores and then hundreds and then more Tokob and Yaloh running with him, their hands empty of weapons but their hearts bright with vengeance.

The gate slammed back and he sprinted through, clearing it fast to allow the next and the next to follow. The armoury was built into a corner of the training compound, its door usually tied shut from the inside by the guards stationed within, who accessed it from a second door through the outer wall of the compound.

Arrows began falling when perhaps a third of their number had made it through the gate – Lilla heard the screams begin behind him – but he didn't dare stop. Open the armoury, get weapons, get up to the wall and kill those archers who'd killed or evaded Ekon. Had he fallen already? He put on a burst of speed just as the building opened from the inside and a woman stepped out.

She raised both hands. 'Feather Ekon – Ekon the Chitenecatl – sent me. On my ancestors and Mictec, I swear it. For all who would be free,' she added, the same phrase Ekon had used. Lilla's headlong charge slowed and he lowered his spear as he reached her, wary but willing to wait a few more seconds.

'There are archers on the wall. Ekon was supposed—'

'We'll deal with it. Armoury's yours, Fang Lilla. Get to the Fifth Talon's training compound – that's where the killing is. And your gods go with you.'

He blinked that she knew his name but didn't question it; Ekon must have placed a lot of faith in his ability to convince him to join the rebellion. Something sharp twisted in him at that, but he shoved it aside and darted into the armoury, through it and straight to the other door to stand guard. He didn't need weapons. He had Ekon's weapons.

He paused just long enough for a dozen rebels to arm

themselves and line up behind him, tension rolling from them in waves. He let every swallowed hurt, every insult and degradation, every questioning of his people and his faith, boil up in his chest until it was burning brighter than the ache of his still-healing back. The back flayed at Ekon's order. Ekon the Chitenecatl, who had done unspeakable things to further his deception of his Pechaqueh companions. Ekon, who had loved him.

'Malel,' he said and heard the warriors behind repeat it, heard it ripple backwards through the armoury.

'Follow the screams,' he said, barely recognising his own voice. 'And fucking kill them all.'

PILOS

The eagle barracks was full to bursting because, despite the magic and the transformation of the world that the Singer would bring about, Pilos had ordered every one of the thousand warriors under his command to be in attendance in case of . . . unforeseen events. *Enet.* He'd allowed their families to join them, though, because after all it would be the largest celebration the Singing City had ever seen and he wouldn't take that from his eagles.

As the sky flared pink and peach and red and purple, Feather Pilos led everyone gathered, warrior and civilian, in the solemn songs mourning the Great Star's vanishing from the sky. At the feast afterwards, during which all solemnity fled and wild speculation built as the night darkened, he allowed each of his eagles a cup of beer with their meal. No doubt hundreds had got friends to pass them extras, but there was little he could do about that. He had to trust them not to end up drunk, and they'd repaid that trust – for the most part.

515

They'd all felt the building magic within the song and the celebrations within and without the compound grew more raucous until, in a moment of horror that had shivered in Pilos's bones and which he knew he'd never forget, all that potential, all that sacred building wonder, had shattered and in so doing shattered something within each right-minded Pecha. Snuffed out some holy spark that lived within them all and resonated with the song, the songstone, and the world spirit.

Snuffed out a part of what *made them Pechaqueh*.

Listener Zecatl had screamed and convulsed as if possessed by a wild spirit, her eyes rolling back in her head, foam spilling between her teeth.

Pilos himself was driven to his knees among dropped plates and scattered food with his head clamped between his hands while the song sobbed and wailed and roared, its claws unsheathed and striking them all, full-blood and no-blood alike. Indiscriminate in its rage and pain.

For some endless period of time, the Melody compound was nothing but whimpers and shrieks and twitching limbs as the eagles and their kin cowered and shivered under the song's lash, a spiritual flaying that made it impossible to think or plan or move.

And then a steadying. A smoothing of the song and a lessening of the spirit-hurt. As one, the eagles staggered to their feet and formed up in the compound, grim and pale and sweating. Hard-eyed and tight-jawed and determined. Pilos's pride; Pilos's command. He sent ten bands of twenty into the city to keep people calm and enforce a curfew.

With Listener Zecatl still unconscious, he had no way to reach anyone in the source short of going there in person. The watchers in the drum tower had line of sight on the distant pyramid: the signal fires weren't burning. Listener

Chotek didn't contact Pilos directly and Xochi didn't send a message either. And so they waited, as protocol demanded, while the song thrashed and gibbered and the world spirit very definitely did not wake.

Perhaps three hours had passed when Pilos heard a distant swelling roar, shot through with screams like a cloud wreathed in lightning, sudden and blinding. The compound was on the northern edge of the city, a straight run through to the great pyramid at its heart, and the noise was rising from the west and then the east. It was more than confusion, more than apprehension at the awful violence of the song. This was fear and rage and a terrible, twisted righteousness.

This was Pilos's worst fears brought to hideous, firelit life.

'Drum tower, report!' he bellowed. Not for the first time, the Spear found himself despairing at the city planners of old. The great pyramid was defensible, but its location in the centre of the city was a huge disadvantage.

'Fire, Spear. Something's burning east of our location.'

'I don't like this,' Pilos muttered to Elaq as another warrior reported another fire, this time to the west. And then a third. 'Signal fires?' he demanded.

'No, Spear. They're all over the place, not following our towers. They look . . . I think it's a riot.'

'City-wide?' he asked, aghast, and then swore, long and viciously, at the urgent beating of a distant drum. The alarm call to the west. Another took up the beat, and then another: either the eagles he'd sent into the city or its Choosers were calling for help. The sound spread like a necklace of disease, swelling with pustulence until it threatened to choke him.

'Protect the Singer! Protect the source!' Pilos shouted. 'Tower, beat the general alarm; I want it echoing across the whole city and pulling in every retired eagle, on-leave dog and newly made free who isn't piss-drunk.

'Elaq?' he added, clapping him on the shoulder. 'You're in charge of defending the compound. Three hundred here at all times protecting the civilians – don't send them home until we know the streets are safe. I'm taking five hundred to the pyramid. The eagles already in the city will be heading to the alarm locations – send another hundred as well. When the free and retired start reporting in, send them out in pods to put down these rioters. We need to cover ground and we don't have the numbers to do it, so pick your fights. You've got the Listener, if she wakes, and pray Setatmeh she does. Either way, I'll be in touch when I reach the Singer. Keep safe; don't take risks.'

'We'll be here when you've settled the city, Spear, song willing,' Elaq said. He glanced at the sky behind Pilos's head. 'You should get going. Find out what's happened at the source. The world spirit, Spear, and the song . . .' He trailed off and Pilos nodded in grim agreement. He offered a swift prayer to the holy Setatmeh that it wasn't as bad as he feared, but then Elaq gripped his shoulder hard.

'There's no room for mercy, Spear, not with the numbers we have – or don't have, rather. No matter their tribe or status, if you can't trust them, you kill them.'

Pilos's throat clicked with dryness. 'Under the song, Eagle Elaq,' he said formally and inclined his head.

Elaq grinned like a jaguar and touched belly and throat. Then he winked. 'Under the song, Spear Pilos. Don't get yourself dead without me to watch your back.'

Pilos huffed a laugh and then stepped out from under his friend's hand. He raised his voice. 'First five pods, with me,' he ordered. 'We stop for nothing!'

He spun on his heel in the flamelit, beer-sticky compound and signalled for the gate to be pulled wide, then set out at a run towards the pyramid, the distressed cacophony of the city and the howling, imbecilic wail of the song beating against his ears and shredding his spirit. He fought against it with the same grim determination he'd fought everything all his life. There was no other choice.

They streamed into the streets in tightly packed pods with archers flowing along ahead and behind. Pilos carried his war club as well as a spear. There were knives in his belt and he prayed this was all just some big drunken revel got out of hand when the song did . . . whatever it had done. He suspected the holy Setatmeh weren't going to answer that prayer. Pilos wasn't that fucking lucky, not even on the night peace was supposed to descend on the Empire forever.

They turned on to the Street of Fighters to find it eerily deserted, though there were fires lighting up the sky to either side of the wide road leading to the Way of Prayer and then the great pyramid itself. Not just fire but noise, and not just noise but screams. Shouts. The clash of weapons and the slick wet *snicks* of cleaving flesh.

The pyramid was still far in the distance, blotting out the stars at the end of the long straight road. It was also bright with flame: the watch fires had been lit in the time it had taken to run this far. The red-painted stone bounced the torchlight back on itself until the pyramid glowed crimson and gold. Beautiful. Frightening.

They encountered no one all the way to the pyramid, but that absence of enemies didn't reassure Pilos. The sounds of violence were increasing across the city even as the song began to smooth again, into something softer. They reached the pyramid's grand staircase without encountering a single person, the enormous plaza in front of the building empty but for the smoke drifting across its surface.

Chorus warriors occupied each of the seven levels of the pyramid and were vocally relieved when Pilos identified himself.

He ordered fifty eagles to both the warriors' and servants' entrances to hold them against potential attack and another hundred to line the steps themselves. The remaining three hundred he placed in a double ring around the pyramid's base.

The song was strong now but directionless, battering at him with random emotions – anger, hurt, loss, anger again – but without imperative. It didn't tell Pilos who to be or present the glory and status that would be his in return for his love. It didn't speak of Pechaqueh strength and wisdom or the world spirit's awakening. It was lost.

That fucking Enet. I'll peel her face from her skull if she's behind this.

The pyramid as protected as he could make it with a mere five hundred warriors, Pilos raced up the steps to the grand entrance, identifying himself at each archery platform so that he could proceed to the next.

'What the fuck is happening, Spear?' one of the Chorus stationed at the main entrance asked, and Pilos forgave his lack of propriety in the circumstances.

'Best guess is drunken riots but they're spreading fast,' he replied. 'We passed at least a dozen separate fires on the way here and that's just in the north of the city. What happened in the ritual? Is the holy lord unwell?'

The warrior sagged and Pilos's alarm flared higher. 'It's a fucking mess, Spear. Minimal distractions in the source itself, so most of us were stationed elsewhere and no one knows for sure what happened except Chorus Leader Xochi.' Pilos clenched his jaw against the urge to tell the man to speak fucking faster.

'Best we can tell the ritual broke halfway through when the Great Octave was killed. We don't know for sure what she did. But . . . then it went bad. Or worse, anyway. Kapal and Chotek are dead. The Singer's alive, barely, and the Shadow is doing what he can to hold it all together, but then, well.' He gestured and Pilos, numb with shock after shock, turned to look.

Twenty, fifty, maybe a hundred fires were burning across the Singing City. The stars in the west – minus the missing Great Star, of course – were entirely hidden behind veils of smoke, choking and viscous even this high up. His city was burning. *Burning.*

'This is not— this has nothing to do with the failure of the ritual,' he mumbled, whether to himself or the Chorus he didn't know, before the rest of the warrior's words caught up with him and he spun back to face the man, grabbing him by the salt-cotton and hauling him close despite his spear and garbled protest. 'Wait. The Great Octave is *what?*'

'Pilos, Spear of the Singer and Feather of the Singing City requests entrance, armed in time of unrest, to the holy lord's presence.'

Not even when they'd been at war in the north had Pilos stepped into the source in his sandals and salt-cotton, and armed. A shiver of religious terror gripped him and he fought it down. He needed to be able to move fast and there was protocol for this if the heart-city was ever threatened. Still, he felt bulky and too big even within the huge, opulent space of the source itself.

'Let him in,' came a voice and the warriors guarding the entrance stepped aside. Another score were clustered tightly around the Singer at one end of the source, far from the colonnade out into the gardens. The holy lord was lying on a low bed dragged in from somewhere, layer upon layer of blanket swaddling him despite the night's warmth.

Xochi was standing behind the bed and naked relief flashed across her face when she saw Pilos. 'Spear, praise the song you're here,' she croaked. Her kilt was bloodstained and there were bandages swaddling her shoulder and knee. 'Please, what is the situation out there?'

Pilos took a second to touch his belly and throat and bow his head for the Singer, though the man was an unmoving lump beneath the blankets. The Shadow sat on a cushion at the foot of the bed and it was hard to look at him. He burnt with golden light, so bright that he lit up the bed, the floor, the mats.

The Feather looked at Xochi again; she lifted one shoulder in an infinitesimal shrug. Whatever had happened, or was still happening, the song was slowly calming. That was the most important thing.

Enet's dead, he reminded himself when his gaze was drawn to a section of bloody matting not far from the cleared area where the ritual must have been performed. *She's fucking dead and . . . I don't actually know how I feel about that. Because the city's rioting and the holy lord looks broken and what we need now is strength. And despite everything else she was, Enet was strong.*

He would need a debrief from Xochi, but for now, the Great Octave was dead, the Singer was comatose, the Shadow was holding so much magic he looked otherworldly, and the city was on fire.

Priorities.

'I have sent out as many patrols as we have warriors for to enforce a curfew, and Elaq is in command of the compound and the defence of the civilians. We've sounded the general alarm to summon all off-duty and retired warriors of all castes. The Street of Fighters and Way of Prayer were both deserted on the way here, but there were fires to either side and, from the summit of the grand staircase, they're on at least three sides of the great pyramid. It looks . . . city-wide.'

The words burnt as they left his mouth, burnt as his city was burning. He swallowed a mad urge to giggle.

'I brought five hundred eagles to protect the source and I cede them to your control, Chorus Leader. As for the rest, they will put down what riots they can and protect the Melody compound.'

Xochi looked momentarily horrified at being put in charge of five pods. Pilos didn't blame her; he'd made her his second in command and then almost immediately elevated her to Chorus Leader. But she was experienced and she was calm under pressure. And she was all he had.

Ilandeh would have—

No.

'If you require anything at all from me, I am at your disposal,' Pilos added and nodded at her obvious relief. He could imagine how unnerving it had been to wait here, unable to call for aid other than through the bonfires in the gardens, unable to leave and ascertain the situation for herself.

Pilos looked around the source, assessing. 'Have you been in contact with High Feather Atu?' he asked. 'Depending on their progress through Chitenec, they might be closest if we require reinforcements.'

Xochi shook her head. 'Not yet. Listener Chotek and Shaman Kapal are dead and the holy lord has . . . No, we haven't managed to contact anyone.'

'Then that is our first task,' Pilos said, his heart sinking. 'Though my Listener is unconscious back at the compound; I wasn't able to bring her.'

'Then we have no means of communication,' Xochi said. She looked sick.

'I'll have to get Zecatl. Somehow, I'll get her here. Or at the least, I'll get her to contact the High Feather first, in case . . .'

They stared at each other in silence. It was three sticks back across a burning, dangerous city and he couldn't take his pods with him. They were needed here.

He slid his hand beneath his hair to scrub the back of his neck and used the motion to glance sideways at the Singer again. He had so many questions, not just about Enet but the ritual itself. The Shadow. He dragged his focus back to the rioting; all else could wait. The Singer lived, so did his song. Pilos had to make sure the city did too.

'Bring everyone, not just the Listener. Bring all your warriors and all those who respond to your summons. The Singer must be protected.' The Shadow's voice was rich with the harmonics the song lacked.

Pilos hesitated, his mind whirling. 'Shadow, we need warriors in the city to dissuade people from causing a disturbance,' he said carefully.

'Kill them all,' said the Shadow, his tone indifferent. 'Kill every fucking no-blood who has risen against our might.'

Pilos inclined his head, in equal parts shocked and relieved. How could he accomplish such a thing while also protecting the pyramid? And "no-blood"? *The Shadow* was a no-blood. 'As the Shadow commands,' he said instead of any of that.

He made a hasty obeisance and strode from the source. Despite the grunting wail of the song that scratched at him like a mad person, something akin to excitement fluttered in his gut. He flexed his fingers on club and spear.

'Right,' he said to himself. 'Let's get out there and find out what the actual shit is happening.'

* * *

What was happening was, indeed, a city-wide uprising. Not just of slaves, though, which was what he'd expected, but servants too. Even, incomprehensibly, free. Free former warriors, free merchants and artisans, free weavers and potters, free flesh-traders. How? Why? What did free even have to rebel against anyway? They were *free*.

Pilos had no idea how it had started, or where, or why, but there were fucking thousands of no-bloods rioting in the streets. And they were very clearly targeting Pechaqueh homes and businesses, and so far as he could tell from the myriad glows of burning and the gut instinct he'd learnt to listen to over four decades, they were in every quarter at once so that his eagles wouldn't be able to force an open engagement.

And it wasn't only property they were destroying. There were Pechaqueh corpses in the streets and if they were in the streets then there were more – scores, maybe hundreds more – in the houses and on the estates and in the temples.

The wall of the Melody compound came into view and he and his half-pod, all that could be spared from the defence of the great pyramid, halted. In silence, they stared at the broken gates and the twisted bodies and the smoke rising from within the scarred walls. He'd been gone less than two hours.

There were heads above the top of the wall and Pilos coughed away smoke, preparing to shout up, when the shifting wind caused the fires to flare and show him the scene in better detail. There were heads on the top of the wall. They just weren't attached to bodies.

The eagle on his left howled a warning and lunged in front of Pilos before three arrows punched him off his feet. He crashed into the Feather, who staggered back under his weight just as a second flight came in from the right.

'Form a square,' Pilos yelled. He shoved away the dying warrior, set his spear and engaged the first to come at him as his eagles slotted into position to either side. Nobody came out of the broken compound to help them. Then again, no one came out to kill them, either. But still, three hundred eagles, Elaq, all those civilians. How could they have fallen so fast?

The general alarm.

Pilos swore. How many retired dog warriors had Elaq let into the compound before enough traitors masquerading as loyalists had gathered inside to begin a slaughter? They'd invited their own deaths in through the gate, at Pilos's order.

There was no more time for self-recrimination or reluctant approval of the enemy's strategy. Warriors descended on them from two sides and Pilos was thrown into a fight for survival. He hated the thrill that rippled through him as screams and the clash of weapons erupted, knowing it was inappropriate, but he couldn't help it. He'd never thought he'd get this again, this chance to prove himself among warriors. This chance to lead in combat. To be what the song had made him to be.

What about them? More arrows that they couldn't properly guard against, and he knew what it would do for their attackers' morale to see eagles running from them. But he knew, too, what it would do for them if they wiped out fifty warriors in a single ambush. 'Scatter,' he shouted and they charged the enemy, cutting through them in all directions and vanishing into the side streets. Standard practice was they'd relocate five streets back towards the pyramid; their attackers would know this too. They'd be fighting a running battle all the way back to the source. Or they'd die here, strides from what should have been safety.

And so it proved. Pilos was around a third corner and out of sight – he thought – when a club came down on his shoulder and drove him to one knee, pain flashing up into his head and all the way down to his fingertips. He dived forward, rolled over his shoulder and bounced back to his feet, spear in his hands. His own club had been abandoned at the ambush site and the spear wobbled in his weakened grip as he flailed it at his attacker, who danced away and then knocked it down and lunged back in. Her club arced up and although he jerked backwards, it skimmed his chest and took him beneath his chin, snapping his head back.

Lightning exploded in Pilos's skull, the sharp, hot pain of a bitten tongue and a flood of metal in his mouth. His knees wobbled beneath him and then a second figure darted in, between him and the woman.

'Finish him!' his attacker screamed. There was a flash of firelight on obsidian, or possibly highly polished flint, and a spray of red so dark it was black, and it was the woman who collapsed, hands going to her neck but unable to stem the flood that ended her life. The warrior who'd saved him tensed and then spun to face him; only the fact that Pilos was cradling his jaw prevented it from dropping open.

'Ilandeh?'

The Whisper made an aborted movement, a half-lunge towards him with her spear, and he flinched away. Her teeth gleamed, her eyes too; the snarl of a half-wild animal fearing a trap. They stared at each other for an endless moment tainted with smoke and too many harsh words, and then someone called his name. Ilandeh dropped his war club at his feet, backed into the darkness and was gone.

Pilos worked his mouth, checking for loose teeth. One at the bottom, maybe two at the top. Two eagles converged on him, bloody and panting, and they hustled to the next meeting point. There were no more than thirty eagles gathered there, guarding the roads and covering the roofs with bows and blowpipes.

'Spear?' one panted.

A severed head was hurled into their midst, landing with a squelch and rolling to a stop near Pilos. He ignored it, waiting for the brawl that would follow, but instead there was a shower of arrows and a scream, suddenly cut off, as an eagle was dragged into the darkness of an alleyway.

'Move!' Pilos roared, but despite the command, he hesitated – just long enough to recognise Elaq's face on the head lying on the stone. 'Fuckers,' he snarled, almost choking on grief and rage and his own swollen, bloody tongue. '*Fuckers.*'

They moved out again, running in formation this time. 'Back to our last position,' he roared, spitting blood. The eagles would know he meant the pyramid; perhaps their attackers would not. Pilos moved in their midst, fury simmering in his gut.

Fury. And the first stirrings of fear.

XESSA

Pilo's fighting pit, Singing City, Pechacan, Empire of Songs
2nd day of the little absence of the Great Star

Xessa stood with her face pressed to the bars of her cage, straining to see down the corridor to the gated exit. Ossa lay at her feet, chin on her instep, and she felt him whine. *I know, Ossa. I'm thirsty too.*

Pilos had, to her surprise, been as good as his word. If she ignored the fact that he'd kept her dog at his estate for *two fucking years* and only told her about him when he was out of ways to convince her to live, then she couldn't help the gratitude that sat, warm and soft in her chest, at this most unexpected of reunions.

In the days since Lutek's death and the revelation of Ossa's survival, Xessa had found herself desperate to earn Pilos's approval. The need for her dog was constant, gnawing, almost poisonous in its strength. It had destroyed the walls around her heart in the space of a single breath and she'd been unable – and unwilling – to build them up again. Not if there was a chance.

529

And there had been. Yesterday, the first of the eight days of the Great Star's little absence, Pilos had arrived at the pit early, not long past dawn. There would be no training that day and the fighters, even the slaves, were allowed to mingle and feast and celebrate. She'd been looking forward to spending it with Tiamoko, until the shadows on the wall opposite told her someone was coming. Of all she'd expected, Ossa dragging Pilos along the corridor on the end of a rope, her dog slavering and barking and frantic, hadn't been it.

Such joy in his every line and movement as he leapt at the bars and Xessa flung herself at him from the other side, trying to gather him to her, to drag him through the bamboo in the endless seconds it took for a smiling Pilos to untie the gate.

Even now, a day later, the wonder of it had still to leave her. Ossa had still to leave her. Pilos had said something she hadn't really seen, something about coming to collect him later, but it hadn't happened. As soon as the cages were opened after dawnmeal, Tiamoko raced in and threw himself on the dog, sobbing uncontrollably. They'd spent the day there, despite their relative freedom, the big Toko hurrying out to fetch them food and beer and water, reluctant to stray far.

But then duskmeal had been served and the slave fighters – and only the slave fighters – were sent back to their individual cages, unless they'd amassed enough jade to bribe the guards. Neither Xessa nor Tiamoko had such wealth and she'd braced for the exquisite agony of having Ossa taken from her too, but nobody came. Not even knowing that she'd bought Ossa's presence in her cage with Lutek's life could stifle her joy at being able to keep him close through the night.

He was medicine to her every wound, whether of the flesh, the mind or the spirit. A desiccated, long-barren part of her had flooded when he'd raced into her cell and thrown himself on her, his broad, blunt head slamming into her jaw hard enough that she saw stars. By the time she'd blinked them away, he was a wriggling, slobbering streak of black lightning and no matter how much she'd tried to grab him, to instinctively wrap her arms around this lost limb, this part of her heart, he'd been too full of joy and love to stay still and be held.

Two years, and he hadn't forgotten her. Xessa hadn't been forgotten.

Yet her elation had faded in the hours since she'd woken, squeezed onto the very edge of her cot while Ossa sprawled across the whole of the thin, cotton-stuffed mattress in canine slumber. No one had brought her dawnmeal, or taken away her shit bucket, or even brought a gourd of water.

Ossa's ears had been ever on the move after night had fallen, flickering against her neck as they lay squashed together. Growls had shivered through her ribs and he'd paced the front of the cage several times, wary. She'd thought it was being in a strange place full of the worrying scents of old blood and strangers, but now she knew something must have happened.

Xessa crouched and tapped the dog's nose where it lay on her foot; he looked up, alert despite his dull eyes, and she asked him to listen to the left. He stood and loped into the corner of the cage, then dropped his head; no sound. She did the same on the right, with the same result.

Which meant – unless he'd lost so much training that he'd mixed up his responses – that there were no fighters in the cages along this corridor. Including Tiamoko four cages down. Which was impossible.

Not impossible. Zimio didn't come past last night on the way to lock-in.

Xessa occupied the second-to-last cage and had become used to the Chitenecah cheery greetings each morning. She was only one fight away from freedom and the eja had assumed she'd marked the Great Star's little absence in the bed of one of the other contracted fighters. But even if Zimio was still asleep in a different cage after having been well-fucked, that didn't explain the lack of trainers or slaves moving through the pit. Not even the stirring in the air that was doors and gates further along being opened and closed reached her. The air was still and thick and heavy. Empty of life.

She tried clapping and thought about commanding Ossa to bark, but he was as thirsty as she was, so instead she stretched her arm through the bars and fumbled for the ropes that tied the gate shut. Xessa hadn't tried this in months, because she knew no matter how much she stretched and twisted, she couldn't reach the knot where it sat in a recess of hollow bamboo fixed to the bars. It was simple, and clever, and frustratingly effective and none of that had changed since the last time.

Xessa flailed a bit longer, fingers seeking, but she grasped only air. She withdrew her hand and slapped the bars in frustration. She grabbed her blanket and lashed it against the bamboo in frustration, then kicked it, sparking a full-body leap sideways from the dog.

The eja ground her teeth at being so helpless, knowing she was entirely reliant on someone coming and letting her out. She paced the edges of her cage yet again, stalking back and forth, back and forth, back and forth. Ossa retreated to her bed and watched. Her thirst grew.

* * *

When the dog's head jerked up, Xessa thought he'd spotted the tiny lizard that lived on her wall, before remembering he'd caught it around highsun and swallowed it almost whole, only spitting out the bony end of its tail. She put her hand on the back of his head but he wriggled off the cot and stalked to the bars of her cage, ears pricked.

Hope and then fear woke in Xessa's breast, and she snapped her fingers and asked for information, wondering if he'd— but he was already signalling "friend" and her heart leapt again, hope renewed. This time she did give the order to speak and he barked, his big front paws up on the bars and his tail wagging furiously.

Xessa joined him, face pressed to the bamboo and one hand on the scruff of the dog's neck, ready to pull him away just in case. And then Tiamoko appeared at a run, returned at last. The eja reached through the bars but he evaded her hands, pointing at Ossa and demanding she silence the dog. She cupped her hand over the top of his muzzle in the command for quiet.

'What's happened? Where is everyone?' she signed as he worked at the ropes. He got the gate open and strode in and grabbed her shoulders, giving her an excited shake until she had to bat him away and repeat her questions.

'Slave rebellion!' he signed, his eyes dancing. 'City-wide, slaves and servants and, apparently, even free are rising up and killing every Pechaqueh they can find. It's carnage out there but we're freeing ourselves, Xessa. We're going to kill them all and be free!'

The ejab jaw hung slack. 'What?' she managed.

'It's because of Tayan, it must be. He did something, or he inspired enough of us that we can take back our freedom. Maybe it's Tokob leading the whole thing.' Tiamoko was bouncing on the balls of his feet. 'When the fighting started

533

last night, Kalix and Ilam tried to make everyone go back to their cages, but the free fighters refused,' he continued before Xessa could even begin to process that. 'They let us out and the trainers and pit-guards were outnumbered so they ran, tails between their legs, and locked the gates from the outside. It's some sort of standard procedure in times of unrest, whether within or without. We're too dangerous for them to take the risk we might get free, so they shut everything up and leave us here until the emergency's over.'

'No one let me out,' Xessa began to sign but Tiamoko stepped suddenly back out of the cage at the same time as Ossa's big triangular ears pricked. She stilled.

'Factions formed and scores were settled through the night,' Tiamoko signed after a long, tense moment. 'The fighting happened in the pit itself, in the armoury and the kitchen. It's taken me this long to reach you since the killing began. Casiv and Vorx were in favour of leaving you here.' Xessa felt her stomach twist, reminded again that many of the free fighters who'd contracted with the pit had adopted Pechaqueh beliefs and their way of life. Of course they wouldn't want an eja to walk free. Who did?

'Zimio and I spoke for you, but no one else did. It got bloody.' He signed this without emotion, once again the dead-eyed boy from the Sky City who'd killed with a lack of remorse ugly in one so young and good-hearted. The only thing Xessa felt about it now was relief. 'But we need to leave. It's only because the others started forcing the gates that I managed to get away; with luck we'll have a clear run out of here, but even if we do, there's no saying what it's like on the streets. We'll go via the armoury and see if they've left us any pickings.'

Xessa struggled to comprehend the flood of information and impossible suggestions – *on the streets; via the armoury.*

'I need water and food as much as weapons,' she signed as the slew of emotions suddenly retreated enough for her to feel her body again. She was almost shrivelled with dehydration, her eyes gritty and her tongue dry. 'Ossa too. And then we need to decide what to do next. Where do we go?'

Pilos's words came back to her. Toxte, crippled but alive, a farm slave in the chinampas of Quitoban. Her husband. If she could get out of the city – if she survived long enough – she could go and find him. The enormity of the idea gave her vertigo so that she staggered as she stepped out of her cage for the last time. So many emotions crowded her throat that she choked on them and had to bend double, bracing on her knees just to breathe. Ossa licked her face while Tiamoko's warm, broad palm rubbed soothingly at her back.

She straightened and stared at her friend as a horrible, hysterical thought seized her. 'Is this real?' she signed. 'Ossa. You. This supposed uprising. Is it really happening?'

Tiamoko tipped back his head and laughed. 'All true, all happening,' he signed. 'So we should move fast, yes? As for where we go, that's obvious. We go to Tayan. He'll be leading this rebellion; he has to be. Didn't he tell us he'd free us? And now look!'

Xessa nodded, a little shaky. Tayan was in the city and in a position of power that had led to him organising a rebellion. Toxte was in distant Quitoban. Both were options, and as much as her spirit yearned for Toxte, it made sense to find Tayan first and then all travel together. Whatever he'd done, being named the Singer's successor would surely hold enough power that they'd be unmolested on their journey east.

Despite the incessant circling of her thoughts, Xessa's body knew what it needed. Her stomach cramped with hunger and thirst clawed at her and she gestured shakily for Tiamoko

535

to go first, keeping Ossa at her side to alert her to danger from behind.

The pit's kitchen was big and it was deserted, shelves broken and baskets emptied and overturned. Everything of use had been stolen. She found a half-broken jug that still had a little water in the bottom and drank greedily, savouring the coolness, and then gave the rest to Ossa – who ignored it and jerked his head up, lips pulling back.

Xessa ducked and her unseen attacker's strike missed, going over her head to smash into the empty shelves lining the wall instead of into her back as must have been intended. Ossa leapt up at them, teeth flashing and the eja spun with a cry, because to lose her dog now, after everything, was more than she could bear, but he was already dancing out of range. It was Casiv.

Tiamoko said scores were settled; I guess this is mine.

She'd never known what it was about her that the twins hated so much, but she didn't waste time worrying about it. Casiv wanted her dead and she wanted – for the first time properly and deeply and with every part of her being since she was captured in the Sky City – to live. Casiv wielded an axe and Xessa backed steadily across the width of the kitchen, Ossa stiff-legged at her side. Where was Tiamoko? Had Casiv killed him on his way in, or was he fighting the Tlaloxqueh brother? He and Vorx did everything together, after all. Maybe that included killing Tokob.

Casiv swung at Ossa, assuming, correctly, that hurting him would hurt Xessa. But the dog had spent his life fighting Drowned and they were faster and less predictable than a Tlaloxqueh pit-fighter. And he was fighting alongside Xessa again. The eja felt everything in her and about her slide into place, her lost limb not only returned but functioning as Malel made it to function. Ossa twisted sideways and she ducked the other way, splitting Casiv's attention so his axe-blow missed them both.

The dog circled and Casiv turned with him, weapon out as both protection and threat. Xessa jumped in and hooked around his neck, yanking him up and back so fast his spine arched and before he could twist into or out of it and use his greater strength to throw her, Ossa tore up into his groin and lower belly, a rip and jerk before he flitted out of range.

And that was all it took. Casiv's scream vibrated against Xessa's forearm; she spun, changing her grip to a headlock, and slammed his face into the edge of the stone-lined fire-pit. Teeth and nose shattered and he slumped, axe falling from his hand, blood spurting from his torn groin.

The eja picked up his axe and sent Ossa out on a run, the command coming easily even though the terrain was like nothing he'd ever quartered before. Still, the dog went will-ingly, sprinting to the kitchen's entrance and then spinning in place to signal "friend". Xessa kept the axe up just in case, but it was Tiamoko. He was wielding a heavy wooden platter, but he tucked it under his arm when he saw the man bleeding to death by the fire.

'You going to end him? He's screaming pretty loud.'

Xessa thought about just leaving him, but that was the sort of thought Pechaqueh had, not Tokob, so she chopped the axe into the back of his neck, severing his spine, and then passed it to Tiamoko. 'Find me a spear so I can work with Ossa the way Malel intended,' she signed as soon as her hands were free and she'd assured herself of her dog's health. The ruby droplets coating his fur weren't his. The broken pitcher had mostly survived, and Ossa licked greedily at the last drops of water. 'And then let's get out of here.'

* * *

In the end, the gates from the under-pit had proved too sturdy and the fleeing trainers had piled debris against them to further hold them shut. The fighters, free and slaves alike – those who hadn't been killed during the madness of the night – had broken into the arena, climbed the pit wall into the seating and made their way down the public stairs and out of that, less fortified, exit.

The Tokob followed the same route, Xessa grunting under the weight of lifting Ossa high enough for Tiamoko to snake a long arm under his ribs and hoist him, wriggling, over the pit wall. They'd even managed to find her a spear: it wasn't perfect – slightly too long and heavier than the ones she'd used as an eja – but she was stronger now, too. It would serve.

They paused at the lowest tier of seats to look down into the pit where they'd both fought, bled and killed. Nearly died. It looked small from up here, and shabby. A place that had once been made from death and power and torment and was now just an oval of beaten dirt with stepped seats ringing it and two gates leading into it. Unremarkable. Boring. And a place that would haunt her dreams for as long as she had left to walk Malel's skin. Would she remember it when she was an ancestor? Would she remember it forever? Xessa shivered.

The urge to take the fastest route to freedom was strong, but instead they climbed to the highest row of seating and looked out over the edge of the retaining wall at the Singing City. Smoke rose from dozens of places across the entertainment district alone and the great pyramid itself glowed red with paint and bright with the fire crowning it at the heart of this vast, corrupt place of stone and arrogance and death. Three small pet monkeys had escaped from one of the more expensive brothels and were fleeing across the roofs from the smoke, their tails held in elegant curves over their backs as they stretched and leapt, small furry hands grabbing, pulling, climbing. Racing towards the distant promise of the public gardens.

Towards freedom.

Xessa's eyes and heart followed them until they vanished. She'd never been this high up before, and even on those occasions she had travelled to other pits to fight, she'd always been under heavy guard and hurried through the streets with barely any time to examine her surroundings. Now it felt as if the entire city was laid out for her curiosity. It was both like and unlike home. The open plazas and administrative buildings were familiar enough that she felt something bruise beneath her breastbone, but the temples were alien, not just in colour and shape but in meaning. Despite what Pechaqueh said, no gods lived there; only the lords of the Underworld occupied those death-houses. If this really was a rebellion of all the peoples who yearned for freedom, why weren't the temples the first places to be set on fire?

Doubt closed a bony fist around her heart.

'That's the songstone cap, see there?' Tiamoko interrupted her thoughts and drew her attention back to the great pyramid, by far the largest building in the city. The largest building she'd ever seen.

She looked back at him. 'See it rising above the bonfires? That sparkle? That's the source of the song and the magic, they say. That one block of stone. And Tayan's the heir to it. He'll take that magic and use it to remake the world, maybe, the way the Singer was supposed to last night and failed.'

It was hard to believe the fate of a million people was determined by that pale triangle of rock, or that something so simple could carry so much evil within it. Xessa found she couldn't look away. Perhaps it contained a particularly powerful spirit, one trapped in the stone by Pechaqueh magic and forced to sing. She didn't know; she didn't really understand the relationship between the Singer and the songstone. She'd never cared enough to try and learn. Her early fantasies of slaughtering the Singer had been foiled upon learning that the magic would simply choose a replacement. Xessa couldn't break the song in any way she knew how, but as she also couldn't hear it, it was easy to forget it existed.

Now, though, she was very much aware of it again. Could Tayan really do what Tiamoko was suggesting? 'What is the song telling you right now?' she asked.

The big Tokob face soured. 'It's been . . . weird ever since the ritual failed and the uprising began. Wild, painful. It's getting steadier and stronger again now and it says we should stop fighting. Give up our weapons and beg for forgiveness. Submit. Lie down. Surrender.'

Xessa blinked against the sting of smoke on the wind and stared at the red pyramid. 'But, Tayan,' she signed, confused. Tiamoko wouldn't meet her eyes. 'You said this was his rebellion. You said he has access to this magic. Are you telling me he's letting the song make us believe we can't win? Or are you lying to me?'

'I'm not,' Tiamoko signed in protest, his young face wrinkling with hurt. 'Ever since the song was broken, it hasn't had the same flexibility, they say. It can't do what it used to, like a snapped limb improperly healed. Good for basic tasks, not for anything more than that. Tayan will do what he can,' he added confidently, but Xessa didn't feel it in her gut the way she had before. The friend of her heart would have sounded a clarion call to war through the song if he'd had the power Tiamoko believed he had. He'd have done it no matter what happened to him as a result. Tayan wouldn't leave them like this, listening to something that told them they should shrink and apologise and cower.

He *wouldn't*.

'So . . . will the song stop you fighting?' she pressed. The savage glint in the boy's eye was all the answer she needed and it soothed a little of her worry. She looked out over the city again, drawing acrid air deep into her lungs. No green smells, just people and stone and filth and smoke and death. They were so very, very far from Malel's skin.

'What do you think?' Tiamoko signed after another few moments. His face was alight with gleeful savagery at the sight of the smoke and burning buildings. 'I can hear fighting from all directions, but there will be ways through. Where do you think Tayan will be? In the great pyramid itself? I think he'll be there, but it's going to be heavily guarded.'

Pilos's pit was near the middle of the entertainment district, the rival pits all within a few sticks. In between were other arenas dedicated to animal fights and tracks for racing dogs, as well as lavish stone buildings where people could drink and dance and hire lovers by the hour or the night.

The wind changed direction and brought a whiff of burning meat to their noses; Xessa wrinkled hers and sneezed violently. Ossa planted his paws on the edge of the wall and stood on his hind legs, peering out at the city with just as much interest. Her hand fell automatically to his broad head and she scratched between his ears. If they stayed and fought their way to Tayan, she'd be putting the dog in danger again, the way she had in the Sky City. But if they ran, she'd never find any of her kin again. There had to be more than just Tayan and Tiamoko in this city.

'We should find other Tokob. There must be hundreds here. Ally with them and then fight our way into the pyramid and to Tayan. Give him the protection and time he needs to, to destroy the song, or whatever his plan is. He'll have one, I know that much. And . . . I want to kill the Pechaqueh who stand against us. Kill all of them. Kill Pilos.'

Tiamoko laughed and punched her in the arm. 'Ah, Xessa,' he signed with exuberance, 'I do love the killer they've made you.' He swept her into a hug and she was grateful for it, burying her face in his broad chest and hiding the expression twisting it. Even she didn't know if it was disgust or delight she felt at his words. And at him who spoke them. Her friend's gentle, innocent heart had long since been burnt in the fires of Pechaqueh cruelty and what was left was shrivelled, but it was strong and burnt with a fire of its own.

And mine? she wondered. *Who am I now? Xessa the eja, or Xessa the pit-fighter, killer of kin and hungry for Pechaqueh blood?*

She held Tiamoko a little tighter as Ossa tried to shove his snout between them. She was both, and the sooner she embraced that, the better. The Pechaqueh had sown this crop in arrogance and over-confidence. Now it was time they harvested their bloody fruit.

TAYAN

The source, Singing City, Pechacan, Empire of Songs
2nd day of the little absence of the Great Star

Enet was dead and the Singer was still unconscious, clinging to the last thread of magic stretching between him and the songstone. The thread Tayan allowed him.

It was for his own good: too much magic would overwhelm his already burdened body and weakened spirit. He could have a little more as his strength returned, but until then, for the duration of the holy lord's illness, Tayan was in charge. Of everything. Of the magic and the Melody and the Singing City. Of the Empire of Songs – which was burning.

It had become increasingly clear throughout the night and the interminable hours since dawn that the rebellion was far larger and better organised than the Pechaqueh had dared to contemplate. Listeners, unable to contact Enet or Chotek, had been clamouring at the holy lord's consciousness – and by extension, Tayan's – to report uprisings among slaves, servants and free across the entire width of the Empire, ocean to ocean. Even, astonishingly, within the Talons of the Melody itself.

543

According to those who'd managed to report in safely, every land under the Empire's rule was ablaze with rebellion. Some small, some raging, but all burning. Pechaqueh and any who stood with them were enemies, no matter their innocence or their blood.

It had been planned on a scale Tayan couldn't begin to imagine, involving countless people at every level of society. Months of unrest and infighting, driven by the fracturing of the song, had exploded into violence.

And at its heart, Enet. So many things over the last two years suddenly made an unexpected, audacious sort of sense when viewed in this new light. How carefully she had led the Singer on the path to self-destruction to the point where his song was weak enough to inspire unrest. The songstone tonic she'd been openly consuming in front of her slaves to strengthen and prepare her for some great task or magic, which she feared. The assassination attempts on himself and Pilos and her subtle manipulation of the Singer to attempt a magic he wasn't strong enough for.

And, finally, as she lay dying: *For all who would be free*, and, *You've ruined more than you could know*, and, *Keep him weak.*

She had wanted to be Singer, Tayan was sure of that, but she hadn't wanted it out of greed or ambition. Everyone else had assumed that was what drove her and Enet had let them. Her enemies convinced themselves she was a threat, Enet didn't disabuse them of the notion, and no one bothered to look any deeper.

'Masterful.'

And yet . . . she'd also bought slaves and given them over to the Singer's ravening madness. She'd gifted Xac the death of *her own child* and sent countless more to the holy Setatmeh over years of new moon offerings. *Perhaps two hundred and forty-three more. She spoke of a tally she needed to atone for.*

'Such strength of will,' he muttered. Tayan stretched out his hands and plucked at the magic, relishing the golden flickers in his fingers. The song twisted as his hands did, dancing through the air. So much magic bending to his will. Malel would—

Malel and the spirit guides no longer wanted Tayan of Tokoban. He would never see them again, never feel Malel's presence or hear Old Woman Frog's amused laugh. He was cut off from his ancestors and the spirits. He flexed his fingers again, sending the song soaring, lighter and higher, calling on all who heard it to worship it. Worship him.

'Spear Pilos again requests entrance, armed in time of unrest, to the Singer's presence.'

Tayan blinked and focused on his surroundings again. The Singer was unconscious still, on a lavish bed surrounded with painted screens for privacy. His Shadow sat in front of the screen and Xochi stood to one side where she could see them both. There were eagle warriors in the gardens as well as Chorus.

Tayan gestured his assent and Pilos strode in, bruised and bloody, haggard with exhaustion. He'd been missing for hours. 'We are pleased to see you still live, Spear.'

'Great Singer, Chorus Leader . . . Shadow. Forgive my long absence. The Melody compound has fallen. There are five hundred warriors here and, pray Setatmeh, there should be a few hundred putting down riots in the city and aiding the Choosers, but the rest, Listener Zecatl, Eagle Elaq, the civilians' – he swallowed and bowed a little lower – 'forgive my incompetence, holy lord. They are all dead.'

The holy lord didn't so much as twitch in acknowledgement.

'You estimate no more than eight hundred warriors spread across the entire Singing City?' Tayan asked. His song juddered and he wrapped the magic tighter around himself, reduced the amount passing to the Singer to a dribble. It was easier to control the more of it he had and, in such circumstances, the source needed to project strength. Tayan was honoured to do that for the holy lord.

'Yes, Shadow. There are entire districts on fire and the traitors are fortifying their positions where they can.' Pilos's voice cracked with some restrained emotion, or perhaps it was just thirst. He was bloody, sweaty and smoke-stained, his bare legs and the hem of his kilt streaked with grime.

Behind the Singer, Xochi swore quietly and began muttering low-voiced orders to another Chorus warrior.

'The Singing City must not fall,' Tayan said and the song's harmonics and strength echoed through his voice. It flooded into him, golden and seductive. Pilos, Xochi, even the Singer seemed to swell as the song did. *My gift to you. My promise of loyalty.*

'It must remain a beacon of Pechaqueh might and majesty, a beacon of hope. Your fate and that of everyone you know depends upon ensuring its survival, Spear. Go out there and slaughter as many fucking no-bloods as necessary to bring them to their knees. *As I told you to last night.* I don't care how you do it, I don't care how many bodies lie rotting in the streets to achieve it, but you will bring my city to heel.'

Shock was written plain across Pilos's features and Tayan's own words echoed back to him – *my city.* He stared at the Spear, daring him to question his Shadow. Pilos did not. He looked at the golden swirls dancing through Tayan's arms and across his chest and he pressed his face to the mats. 'As the Shadow commands. Please, with Listener Zecatl dead, I have been unable to contact the High Feather. With so few warriors under my command, may I ask how long until he reaches the Singing City?'

Heat suffused Tayan's cheeks. 'You can hold for a week?' he demanded instead of answering.

Pilos sat back on his heels and flicked his gaze to Xochi and the Singer, then back. 'I may be able to hold the source for a week, Shadow. The census earlier this year confirmed thirty thousand people living in the Singing City. Only around twelve thousand of them are Pechaqueh and three-fourths of that number will be civilians. Retired eagles are making their way here and will increase our numbers, but the city is going to burn. We need the High Feather and the First Talon.'

'They will be here in a week,' Tayan said. 'Go and organise your warriors, Spear. Hold the source – hold as much of the city as you can – until Atu arrives. You will not enjoy the cost of failure.'

The words of dismissal came easily, power thrumming through the Tokob veins. Pilos's lips tightened but he bowed again, almost to the mats. 'As the Shadow commands. Chorus Leader Xochi, with your permission, my warriors will take over the temple to the world spirit in its aspect of bringer of harvest. It is the closest and largest building and we can sortie from it against large groups of traitors.'

'I agree, Spear. The pyramid's stores are healthy – more than enough to feed us all for a month. Several hundred Pechaqueh, many retired eagles, and a few hundred no-bloods, have pledged to fight with us too. I'll send them to you at the temple.'

'I'll be watching the no-bloods,' Pilos said heavily. 'They're how the compound fell. If I can't trust them, I'll kill them. We can't risk anything else.'

'Be safe, Spear. Under the song.'

'And you. Under the song.' He bowed to the Singer once more and then rose fluidly to his feet.

Tayan waited until he'd left and then reached for his magic, wrapped it tightly around himself, and tore his spirit free of his flesh.

The song was powerful, but it had lost some of the smoothness and harmony that he and Xac had crafted when they had been as one. Aside from a single, wailing thread, this song was Tayan's alone, and it had teeth and jagged edges that could flay an incautious spirit. He traversed it with ease, blazing blue-gold.

He found the High Feather and slid into his mind without warning. Tayan could see out of his eyes: the thousand different shades of green that was a lush jungle canopy, the ground he was kneeling on sharply sloped. Distant birdcalls and people murmuring.

Almost home. Almost Tokoban. He tried to smell what Atu smelt, to taste the air, and couldn't.

'Atu.'

'Sh-Shadow? Setatmeh be praised. Listener Citla has been searching the song for Listener Chotek or the Great Octave. The song, Shadow, the holy lord.' He paused and Tayan sensed him calming himself. 'I have heard from Feathers at the fortress and in Axiban and Quitoban of rebellion. Thousands rising up in the fortress, Shadow, led by *eagles and Feathers*. Warriors we have trusted with commands, with our lives, have risen against the song and their honour. We—'

'I want the First Talon marching to the Singing City immediately. You are to be here within the week. The rest of your Talons are to stamp out the flames of rebellion across the Empire. They have two weeks.'

Atu glowed a sickly, anxious yellow. 'We are already on our way, Shadow. But two weeks may not . . . The skirmishes in Tokoban are increasing, Shadow. Latest reports have warriors massing at the border. Too many to be just Zellih. We fear there is an alliance of tribes in Barazal.'

Tayan rocked, images of his homeland on fire dancing across his mind. But if the rebellion was there, too, then it was already burning. Did it matter who set the torches? 'The savages from Barazal can wait. The Empire is already in flames. Pilos has no more than eight hundred warriors, probably fewer. Would you have the great pyramid taken by no-bloods? The Singer killed?'

Atu was silent, struggling with the news and the strain of the communication. 'As the Shadow commands. The Third and Sixth will have to hold Tokoban.' There was another pause, a hesitation. 'I will be there in a week.'

'Don't be late,' Tayan warned and tore himself back out of Atu's mind, already wondering whether two Talons in Tokoban were one too many. He pulled himself back inside his body. His heart was thumping but other than that, he had navigated the song – his song – with ease. As Xac might do. As a Singer would.

He stared at the mural on the far wall: Ixachipan and all the lands and people the song governed. Eight lands and nine Talons, though two consisted of slaves and couldn't be trusted. The First was coming here and would subdue not just the Singing City but all Pechacan, perhaps. The Third was going to Tokoban, where the Sixth already fought. That was the extent of his knowledge.

He glared at Xochi. 'Chorus Leader, you are an eagle and a Feather. I expect you to offer me advice when Pilos isn't here. Do you understand?'

Xochi knelt and put her head in the mats. 'Forgive me, Shadow. I will advise you to the best of my ability in the future.'

'Don't let me down again.'

'This one dares not.'

'The Empire of Songs needs you, Xochi. I need you.'

Her shoulders rose and fell and she sat back and then rose smoothly to her feet. 'This one understands, Shadow.'

Tayan barely heard her. Eight lands and nine Talons, but really only seven that could be trusted. Possibly fewer. They needed more warriors.

The Empire of Songs was burning and the holy Setatmeh were waiting for him to heal the song that granted them immortality.

They would not wait forever.

THE SINGER

You are ill, my sweet love. And tired, so tired. Aren't you? But you need not fear, my love. The Empire and the song are in good hands. I will watch over everything until you are well. I will make you strong again in time. As soon as I can. As soon as the current unrest is dealt with. You have nothing to fear, my love.

Shadow? Shadow, what is going on? I feel . . .

Hush now, my sweet. Rest and get well. Shaman's orders.

But—

No. Rest, my love. You don't need to worry about anything. Recover your strength and your Empire will be here to worship you if you do.

"If?"

Hush, my sweet. Sleep now in the arms of . . . our song. Sleep.

LILLA

'Remember who you are. Remember that this song is a lie. It can no more see into your hearts and know your worth than you can see into the Singer's. How does he know the measure of your life? How does he know the strength of your will or courage? How can he, when he and all Pechaqueh see us as nothing more than ants beneath their sandals?' Ekon winked at Lilla and spread his arms to the warriors gathered at the side of the road ready to move out; Lilla recoiled, stone-faced, at the Feather's – *the Chitenecah* – gesture. 'Yet well do we know the particular hot agony of a black ant's sting.'

There were murmurs of derision and others of discontent. *We are more than ants, even those fucking ants, and that you liken us to them confirms you still think like Pechaqueh. Manipulate like them.*

Use others like them.

But Lilla had pledged to bring down the Empire, and Ekon had brought far more to the cause than he had. Ekon had

552

given all – name, tribe, life – to it. Lilla might hate him for making him a liar and a betrayer, but he had to respect him, too. He just didn't have to like it.

'I cannot tell you not to listen to the song, for that is impossible. But I can tell you that it lies. That every time you begin to believe we cannot win, or we are not worthy of walking the same ground as Pechaqueh, those thoughts are not yours. That is the song lying to you. We live now as free people under the sun and never will we feel the collar on our necks again. Never again will we bow to Pechaqueh. We have a war to fight, warriors, free warriors of Ixachipan. A war to fight and a war to win. Never doubt that. Never doubt yourselves. Look how far we've already come!'

His gesture encompassed the wide limestone road heading northeast and the vast tracts of burning farmland. There was jungle in the distance, just a thin strip probably not even a stick wide, but Lilla couldn't stop looking at it. Not only was it easier than looking at Ekon, but it was the first uncultivated jungle he'd seen since they'd committed bloody slaughter in the Melody fortress and fought their way free. They'd been running ever since, it felt like, Ekon grim and distant apart from when he needed to inspire the warriors, as now. And they needed inspiring because they were about to reach a sizeable town. They would demand its surrender and the freedom of its slaves; if they didn't get it, they'd start killing.

It was the fourth town they'd come across in three exhausting, exhilarating days and Lilla still wasn't sick of the slaughter. A grim joy bubbled in him now at the prospect of killing Pechaqueh, a distraction from the one he wanted to kill. *Only he isn't Pechaqueh. Is he?*

The unrest that had been building through the Empire for the last half sun-year had, with some gentle nudging from

Ekon, convinced High Feather Atu to reassign the strongest Talons to Tokoban and Quitoban. That redeployment meant thousands of Melody warriors were between cities when the uprising began, giving rebels a chance to consolidate ground before the enemy arrived.

The ruthless slaughter they'd perpetrated in the Melody fortress was something Lilla knew would haunt him once this was all over. They'd killed their way into the Fifth Talon's compound and murdered thousands of drunk, unarmed eagles, hawks and dogs. Thousands more had fought back, and then Ekon had been there with his rebels and they'd killed enough to force a way out, setting fire to what they could as they fled. They'd left thousands of Tokob and Yaloh of the Eighth and Ninth Talons cowering in their barracks, refusing to fight.

Lilla wanted to hate them. He couldn't. Freedom meant the freedom to choose; he could not take that away from them, however little he liked their choice.

But if not for Ekon's quiet manipulation of the High Feather, the freedom fighters would have been facing four Talons and they'd have died. As it was, perhaps two thousand of them had made it out alive. Two thousand warriors in their ancestral paint, with collars sawn from their necks and justice warring with vengeance in their hearts.

The rebels broke up into smaller groups once Ekon stopped speaking, passing his words to those who'd been too far away to hear and forming into their pods.

'Our necks,' Lilla said when Ekon was, momentarily, alone amid the sea of warriors. His voice was hard with mockery. 'You said we'd never feel the collar on *our necks* again. Only you've never worn one, have you, Feather?'

Ekon met his eyes steadily in the little space that had grown around them. 'No. I haven't. I helped put them on hundreds of others instead. What's your point?' Lilla inhaled sharply. 'We are fighting a war, Fang Lilla, all of us together, all for the same cause. Wars require unity, in deeds as well as words. I didn't want to complicate things with qualifications and excuses.'

The Tokob fingers brushed at his own throat, bare after so very long, and then down the barely sealed cuts through his slave brands. 'You don't know what it's like,' he said and hated that his voice was so fragile. Hated Ekon seeing him like this.

He's seen you more vulnerable than this. He's seen you fall apart beneath him and kissed you back together.

Shut up.

Ekon chewed on his bottom lip and then lifted his chin. 'Collar me, then,' he said and Lilla flinched. 'Put a collar on me; own me for as long as you want. *Make me* understand.'

Lilla's cheeks flamed and he folded his arms over his chest, rocking back on his heels. His back ached today – it ached more with every confrontation with Ekon, every interaction with him. 'You seek to make me Pechaqueh?' he demanded, to push away the other, shameful thoughts that had come to mind when Ekon said "own me". The images. The memories.

Ekon scrubbed his hands over his face. 'No, Lilla. Not every conversation needs to be a fight, you know. We can just work together, secure our freedom together. Can't we?'

The Tokob lip curled. 'As the Feather commands,' he spat and began to turn away. Ekon grabbed his elbow and spun him back around and Lilla found himself staring up into eyes narrowed with fury.

'Fuck you, Toko. You think your pride is hurt, your feelings, because we fucked a few times after you lied about your husband being dead? *I killed my own wife* because she found out I'm Chitenecah. I loved that woman with all my heart; I'd have died for her and instead I slipped a knife under her ribs during a fucking slave uprising where I had to kill good people, innocent people, to maintain the lie that led me here, that led us all to *this one chance* to make it all worth it.

'You chose, Lilla of the Tokob. I gave you time and space and every opportunity to turn me down. *You chose*; now live with it. I carry enough guilt for my actions; I won't carry yours too.' He paused for breath, chest heaving, and then all the fight went out of him. 'How could I feel guilty at what we shared, anyway? It was . . . everything I wanted. Everything I still want.'

Lilla snarled, at the sudden twist of heat in his belly as much as at Ekon. 'It doesn't excuse what you did,' he said, low-voiced. Angry.

'What I did?' Ekon's own anger flared up again. 'What was that, exactly? Respect you and your wishes, gain your consent over and over, stop when you asked me to stop?'

'Lied. You lied to me.'

They were starting to attract attention now, concerned faces looking in their direction. The rebels of the Eighth knew Lilla as the warrior who'd brought them together, the leader they looked to. The others followed Ekon for the same reason. For the two of them to be publicly quarrelling barely three days into the rebellion and hours before a fight to free a town didn't look good. Still, Lilla clung to the idea of Ekon's lies to keep his anger hot, because anger was all that kept the guilt at bay. The shame.

'You lied too,' Ekon said reasonably. 'You fucked me for the single reason that you wanted to get close enough to kill me. How much of what you wanted was you, Lilla of the

Tokob, wanting me, Ekon of the Pe— of the Chitenecah?'
The slip brought a fresh scowl to Lilla's face, but the question was dangerous, calling forth memories and feelings he couldn't afford. 'I lied about who I am, yes, but I never lied about my reasons for wanting you. I never pretended to feel something I didn't, kitten. That was you, your lie.'

'*I didn't pretend either,*' Lilla burst out and Ekon stepped back, shock marring his features. And then cautious hope. He shifted to come close again and Lilla flinched, and then flinched again when a warrior cleared their throat loudly and announced the pods were ready to set out. The Toko breathed out in relief; he couldn't, *couldn't*, have a conversation about feelings now.

'Don't call me that,' he said, his voice dull, and stepped away.

Tinit was waiting for him. 'Don't know why you put up with that,' she said as his pod took the lead and began to run. 'Don't know why you're allowing a Pecha to give us orders – oh, I know he says he isn't, but really? The way he speaks; the way he moves. Why are we still in pods? This isn't the Yaloh or the Tokob way of fighting. Three days into our freedom and we're taking orders from a Feather again? Not that we ever really stopped,' she added.

'He brought more warriors to the cause than I did. And he's a great leader,' Lilla tried.

'You're a great leader, Fang. You nearly died for us; all he did was nearly kill you. And his warriors are too like him, too set in Melody ways. We should—'

Lilla cut her off with a gesture and they ran in silence for fifty paces. She wasn't wrong, though. Ekon had given up everything to become an eagle, even his name, and now he was struggling to fit back into his previous skin. He'd taken charge when they'd fought their way free of the Melody fortress several bloody hours after the uprising began and Lilla, reeling under everything he'd learnt and heady with unexpected freedom, had been content to follow his command – sensible, cautious, with the promise of vengeance at the end. Now every instruction grated, just a little, as Ekon snapped out orders with casual ease and in full expectation of their being obeyed.

'At least let us fight the right way, our way,' the Yalotl tried.

'We lost against Melody tactics, Tinit,' Lilla said. 'Every people in Ixachipan lost. We're going to be facing Melody warriors again soon, maybe even today. Melody against Melody gives us a greater chance of success than Paw against pod. Just for now,' he added when he saw her scowl. 'Once we've got momentum, once we've linked up with others, we'll have the numbers. But for now, I think it's best that we fight as we've been trained.'

'We were trained before,' she muttered but then dropped back a pace to leave him alone, isolated at the front of his pod. Lilla could feel the weight of her gaze, assessing. Perhaps wondering how much he'd been infected by Pechaqueh thinking. By Ekon himself.

The town had fallen too easily. It wasn't until they'd rested for a few hours, amassed some supplies, and were preparing to move out that they realised why.

Ekon and Lilla crouched in the lee of a building and peered into the treeline. They'd swept the thin strip of jungle when they'd taken the town and it had been empty. It wasn't now. 'There,' Ekon breathed, pointing. He was so close the Toko could feel his body heat, but he shifted closer and pressed his cheek to the Pechaqueh – *the Chitenecah* – to look where he was pointing. There were people, warriors, emerging from beneath the shrubs and low ferns.

'Clever little fuckers,' Lilla muttered. 'Tunnels?'

'Or storage pits. Suspicious in and of themselves. I'd say this town was involved in smuggling before this.'

'So instead of protecting their civilians, their warriors hide the better to lure us in and then surround us,' Lilla finished. He realised they were still pressed together and jerked away. 'How many do you think?'

Ekon shrugged; it was impossible to tell. 'They wouldn't risk an attack without numbering five hundred warriors if they're eagles, more if they're dogs. But, by Mictec's grace' – he paused and a small, private smile crossed his face, as it did each time he spoke aloud the name of his goddess – 'none of the Feathers will entirely trust the dog Talons any more. They'll be questioning the loyalty of everyone who isn't an eagle, and if they know about me and the few others like me, they might even be wary of their own.'

'None of which helps us here and now,' Lilla pointed out. 'But unless those tunnels are the start of an extensive cave system, they can't have more than five hundred. That said, aside from the town and those trees, there's no cover. It'll be toe to toe out in the open and we're supposed to be saving our strength for the Singing City.'

Again, Ekon had that distant, shifty look. He beckoned and they slipped away into the town, past hurrying warriors pulling fences and palm-leaf roofs down to refashion into flimsy barricades that would stop darts but little else. Poisoned darts.

'There is . . . another solution,' Ekon said when they and the other leaders had gathered in a small plaza. Someone had chopped their axe through the dedication to the Singer painted on the obelisk standing at its centre.

Lilla's stomach dropped into his feet. He didn't like that tone. 'What solution?'

'Sacrifice,' Ekon said simply. 'Half of us hold them here so the rest can run for the Singing City. That's where the fate of this rebellion will ultimately be decided: as long as they retain control of the song-magic, they've got a chance. But if the Singer falls—'

'*What?* Absolutely not.' But the other commanders, all dog warriors or Coyote leaders, were already nodding. As if Ekon's words made sense. As if this had been the plan all along.

It has, he realised with a sick twist. *It has been his plan.*

Ekon smiled sadly. 'I have much to make up for, Fang Lilla. I've known for a very long time that I would not live to see the Singing City. I hadn't expected to leave the fortress.'

The Toko stared at him, outraged and strangely breathless. 'Or how about this: you fucking don't, we repel this attack and then get back on the road? There's a time and place for suicide, Ekon, and this is neither.' Lilla's disbelief was tainted with panic and he didn't dare examine why.

Ekon glared at him as if offended that the Toko disagreed with his plan to commit suicide by way of dog warrior. 'All right, gather the civilians,' he said eventually. 'If they wouldn't protect them, I don't see why we should. I want Pechaqueh under heavy guard at our defensive positions; if the enemy tries to pick us off with arrows or darts, shove a few out into the open and use the rest as shields. That should buy us some time. Lilla, take three pods and circle around the trees, see if you can come in behind them. Once we've won, we'll discuss whether the decision reached Star cycles ago, about rebels in the Melody sacrificing themselves to stop that Melody reaching the Singing City, holds true here and now.'

There was tension in his voice and Lilla wondered how long he'd spent working towards a moment just like this, knowing it would be his death. Perhaps it was easier to make some of the decisions he'd made, knowing his life had been offered up as sacrifice by others, possibly even before he was born.

Unwilling admiration tried to climb Lilla's throat and he swallowed it down. His impassioned outburst from before had been a response to Ekon's ability and nothing more. *He's a good leader. We need him.*

He was planning to fuck me and then die. Seduce me and then leave me. Would he ever have told me what he planned or would I simply have discovered he wasn't with me at some point on our march?

Or was that why he was so desperate to get me in his bed? One last fling before his life was forfeited.

The Toko clenched his teeth, took up a spear and made his way towards his pod, beckoning and then holding up two fingers for others to follow. They came eagerly, keen to fight under him instead of Ekon, and he could feel the beginnings of a rift forming. Worse, he wasn't sure he wanted to stop it.

He relayed their orders as they flitted to the southern edge of the town where, so far at least, no movement had been spotted. The green of the jungle, almost painful to look upon among the parched and hacked-back fields, was a stick to the west.

Lilla hesitated. 'Break into Paws,' he said in a low voice. 'Spread out and stay low and circle wide. Half a stick out, I want you down on hands and knees, on your bellies a quarter-stick after that. Do not be stupid,' he added as their faces lit up. 'If you're facing a pod, reform into the same to meet it. The Melody fight this way for a reason; let's not lose to them now because of pride or nostalgia. The victory is what is important.'

'Our ancestors—' Tinit began.

'Winning will honour our ancestors,' Lilla broke in. 'Dying because of stubbornness will not.' He stared her down until she grunted reluctant agreement. 'I want to go back to my proper way of life too, Tinit. But we don't get that until we've won.' He didn't add that none of them would ever get it, not truly. That there was no way back to how they'd lived before. Not for them; probably not even for their children or children's children. Wounds of the spirit didn't heal that fast and the land had a long memory.

His neck prickled; he was choosing his words with the same care Ekon had used earlier and which had disgusted him so much. He checked the field between the town and the trees was still clear instead of saying anything more and then signalled. The Paws drifted over the road and spread out, running in a crouch with their spears held low so that they appeared to be fleeing the town completely.

Lilla's Paw went last, with Lilla himself at the very rear. Watching the warriors; watching the trees. Brooding.

It was impossible to estimate numbers, but Lilla thought they probably outnumbered the warriors besieging the town, though barely. They'd attacked at two separate points and Lilla's three hundred had fallen on them from behind and destroyed four pods before hurrying back to the town's defence.

They'd dug in there, strung across the roads and covering alleys from above, until Ekon had sent a runner requesting reinforcements and they'd had to abandon their position. Now they held two plazas linked by a wide avenue and a handful of smaller streets near the western edge of the town and no more.

The shape of the territory they occupied worked against

them and Lilla was constantly on the move, checking his warriors and lending his spear where it was needed, making sure no one was cut off. He ducked out of the front line, his chest heaving as he fought to draw the hot, dusty air into his lungs. Twenty paces away was another front line and in this one Ekon spun, hacking and leaping, lightning and storm and wind made flesh.

News of his identity had spread and the dog warriors – and the eagles who commanded them – were desperate to land the killing blow on the man who had fooled them all and risen to be one of the elite, trusted by High Feather Atu himself. A man who'd fought alongside them, drank with them, slept with some of them, and who turned out to be a no-blood child of slaves. A man who had enmeshed himself so deeply in the disguise of a Pecha that he had mercilessly slaughtered free tribespeople, including his own, to secure his place.

The fighting swirled closer and Lilla could see Ekon was tiring. He intercepted a spear punching for the Pechaqueh – *the Chitenecah* – back with his own, the hard impact shivering through the wood and the bones of his hands. His opponent's lips drew back and she flung herself at Lilla, howling curses as Ekon raked his spear through the face of another, dragging it down and out and punching it back into the man's thigh.

Lilla didn't see any more. The woman's spear work was fast and precise, her thrusts powerful, and it was all he could do to parry the lethal glass blade away from his flesh. His foot came down on something and his ankle rolled, the same one he'd cracked fighting Kux what seemed a lifetime before, and which the long days running had aggravated. Agony flared up through his leg and his knee buckled.

The dog warrior's spear was as inevitable as sunrise and

all Lilla could do was wrench his shoulder back, turn his torso, and pray. The blade ripped through layers of salt-cotton and sliced through the front of his shoulder. He braced for pain and felt no more than a hot sting.

Thank you, Malel.

The warrior yanked back on the spear but the binding where the obsidian was secured to the shaft caught in the torn armour. Lilla lashed out and she tried desperately to palm it away, but his thrust was strong enough to push past her defence. His spear tore into her flank, punched out through her kidney, and retreated before her fingers could close around it.

Lilla surged to his feet, twisted ankle forgotten, and the spear tip took her beneath the chin, up through mouth and tongue and into her brain. She collapsed and he kicked her off his spear, dragged hers out of his ruined armour, and leapt again to Ekon's defence.

They ended up back to back, spears whirling, ducking and stabbing as if they'd trained together all their lives. More rebels crowded around the pair, slowly but surely pushing them out of the front line to where they were safe. Died saving them, as if he and Ekon were worth something greater than themselves.

They leant against each other, panting and cataloguing their injuries, the numbers they still had up and fighting, the wounded within the circle of protection, and the dead littering the plazas and roads. To their left, the sounds of fighting stuttered and then stopped. A Toko popped up in Lilla's line of sight and signed they'd pushed back the enemy yet again. He raised a hand in acknowledgement.

'One more push?' Ekon asked and Lilla nodded, scrubbed sweat and dust from his face, and side by side they waded back in.

* * *

It was dark and Lilla hadn't known it was possible to be this tired. He hadn't been in the Sky City during those last, frenzied days, but he imagined it had felt something like this – an agony of waiting, trapped by the walls meant to keep you safe, the next attack and the next and the next, each coming from a different quarter without rhyme or rhythm or any way to predict them. Allowing no rest, no relaxation. Just waiting, and then killing and trying not to die, then waiting again. Over and over.

They'd fought back the same, sending warriors out to ambush and assassinate, the dark blade in the black night, stealing among the dog warriors keeping watch and sowing mayhem.

Lilla had slept for an hour, perhaps two, despite their falling numbers and the sharp brightness of wounds sustained through the afternoon and evening and into the night. He groaned and tried to roll over, but pain pulsed through his arm and he gasped, remembered dislocating his elbow and a frowning Yalotl wrenching it back into place and then shoving his spear back into his hand.

Ekon, slumped by his side, wordlessly handed him a half-empty gourd of water. 'We're nearly out,' he warned and Lilla did his best to sip slowly. Thirst instantly became the worst of his pains and the precious mouthfuls he allowed himself were nowhere near enough. He held the last one in his mouth as long as he could, trying to soothe the dryness of his tongue and throat.

'Those dog warriors,' Ekon said suddenly and then stopped. He gusted a sigh and stretched his shoulders, wincing. 'We knew we wouldn't get them all, but I did think, hope, that out here where they can see the rebellion, see civilians rising and fighting for freedom, they might join us. It was different in the fortress, hemmed in by walls and surrounded by eagles. But it hasn't happened. I know we can't do more than guess at the numbers we've got, but I don't think it's enough, Lilla. I don't think we have enough.'

Lilla stared up into the sky. The song had been a thing of horror to them all, Pechaqueh in particular, on the night of the Great Star's return and it had been that that had brought hundreds of fresh rebels to their side in the fortress, but it was stable now. It was fucking relentless and growing more harmonious with every hour that passed. *Put down your weapons. Beg for Pechaqueh mercy. End this petty, hopeless little uprising. Embrace the song and your place under it. Under our sandals.*

Ekon put his face in his hands and Lilla realised how exhausted he was. He reached out and patted his knee awkwardly; the Chitenecatl sniffed and looked up, managed a smile and then caught Lilla's hand and pressed it to his cheek.

The Toko swallowed and then, more gently than he'd intended, pulled away. 'So what's the plan?' he asked. 'We can't hold here forever, not just because we don't have the numbers, but because that's exactly what they want. And don't talk of suicide again.'

'Why not? The eagles will sacrifice every dog warrior they've got to kill us,' Ekon said. 'And the dogs know it; they know their duty is to hold us here and exterminate us, no matter how many of their own number die. Even if we surrender, they won't accept it. We've rebelled; our only fate is death, no matter how much the song lies otherwise. Why not—'

'If you ask for volunteers, you won't get any,' Lilla interrupted, angry but doing his best to keep his voice – hoarse from shouting orders – quiet.

'We'll get some. Enough, perhaps.'

'Ekon . . . you can't mean this,' he tried, shifting to sit up with a groan. Malel, but he ached, from scalp to soles.

Ekon's smile was weary. 'Would you die for your people?'

'Of course.' The man tilted his head as if to say, then what is the difference? 'Fuck. Look, you're a Feather – no, listen, you are. Were. Whatever. The point is we need you, even if none of us like your Feather act or how you're always ordering us around. You understand Melody tactics better than us and you know exactly which Talons are being moved and to where. I imagine you've marched to every land in Ixachipan during your years as an eagle. You know the roads and towns and cities. We need you if we're going to win this.'

'I can't ask people to do what I'm not willing to do myself,' Ekon said with a quiet dignity that made Lilla want to push him in a river.

'You don't have to,' a voice said and the Toko twisted to look up. 'There are a few hundred of us, maybe as many as five hundred, who'll keep these monkey-fuckers occupied long enough for you to get out.'

Lilla scrambled to his feet. 'Tinit? Tinit, no, you're—'

The Yalotl put her palms up in a barrier between them. 'I didn't follow you and I still lost everyone, *everyone* I've ever cared for. Partner and children; parents. What does it matter to me if I live on now? I should have listened back when we were in the pit, when you tried to convince us not to claim our kin. That way, they'd be dead but I wouldn't know. I'd still have the illusion of a future and so maybe I wouldn't be volunteering for this now. But I didn't, I don't, and I am.' Her palms became claws and she hooked them in his salt-cotton and dragged him close, stared up at him. 'Go now, in the dark, and we can probably fool them until dawn, but that's as much of a head start as

567

you'll have. Get to the Singing City and fucking cut them down, Lilla. For me and mine.'

'For all who would be free,' Ekon said behind him. 'I swear on Mictec, Tinit, your sacrifice, and the sacrifices of those who stand with you, will not be in vain. We'll end the song for you. We'll end it all.'

'For all who would be free,' Lilla echoed with an effort, but his voice was as hollow as his heart.

XESSA

The grand plaza, Singing City, Pechacan, Empire of Songs
5th day of the little absence of the Great Star

Of all the things Xessa had expected from rebellion and freedom, it hadn't been this. It hadn't been wild, untargeted, senseless slaughter. Tiamoko had made it sound as if the uprising was organised and methodical, but in the last four days they'd joined five different groups while trying to connect with other Tokob or get news of Tayan. And each time they'd got caught up in fighting, looting and murder.

The groups seemed to have little interest in anything other than vengeance and destruction, and Xessa understood that – the need to break and kill and visit suffering upon her tormentors was a constant pressure in her chest – but it wasn't focused. Tiamoko was the one well-versed in tactics, not her, but even the eja could see that the random lootings and burnings and killings weren't causing the right damage in the right places. They weren't going to gain a victory of any size like this, no matter how much they outnumbered the Pechaqueh.

They weren't making a difference, because those they killed might have been slave-owners, might have offered people to the Drowned, might have committed a thousand atrocities, but they weren't warriors. And it was the warriors who needed to die first if Ixachipan was to be free. The warriors, the nobles and the Singer. The song.

Tiamoko suggested strategic targets such as the Melody compound, the Choosers' offices, and the nobles' estates, but each time he was laughed off. The groups were all made up of house- or market slaves, not warriors. They were armed with skinning knives and homemade clubs and digging sticks, not spears or axes. They didn't fight in Paws; they broke and fled the moment one of their victims picked up a weapon and fought back. They were civilians killing civilians and only succeeding because they outnumbered their victims. They burnt food stores instead of defending them; they were lost in an orgy of violence but none of them would survive a dozen heartbeats in a fight against a Melody warrior, a pit-fighter or even an estate guard.

Xessa was filled with guilt and relief each time she and Tiamoko slipped away from another group. They wouldn't manage anything meaningful among these people, but she also wouldn't come between them and their vengeance. She just hoped that they wouldn't run into any of the roving bands of warriors fighting for the Empire of Songs. Everywhere they went, non-Pechaqueh were seizing people off the streets and delivering them to the flesh markets to be held in cages for execution. In return for a few shattered pieces of jade, the peoples of Ixachipan were turning on each other.

It reminded Xessa uncomfortably of the last days before the Sky City fell, when Tokob, Yaloh and Xentib had stopped working together against their common enemy in favour of arguing with each other. Not all of it could be blamed on fear and desperation. The cracks in alliances were never so clear as when those alliances were under strain.

But today was going to be different. A few hours after dawn they'd found hundreds of people all moving in concert towards the great pyramid, people who'd defiantly sliced blades through the brands on their shoulders to mark themselves as free. People who'd looted for dyed and woven cotton instead of plain maguey and wore strips of it around their biceps and wrists and knees. People wearing their tribal paint on limbs and faces.

Not all of them were warriors, but she could tell enough were from the way they carried themselves. This, *this* was what Xessa had wanted. And in the press of bodies all moving in the same direction, they'd found Yaloh. They'd found Tokob. No one she knew personally, but a dozen familiar faces from the markets back home. Didn't matter. The sheer, dizzying pleasure of being able to sign with others was close to overwhelming. They'd been house slaves, but they clutched weapons with murderous intent, malice and justice carved into the lines around their mouths. The more Xessa signed with them, the more she realised just how few warriors of the northern tribes had been sold to the fighting pits. Putting them in the Melody far away from civilisation seemed to have been the preferred method of killing them or converting them to the song, but Pechaqueh were nothing if not curious for spectacle and new entertainments, and so a small proportion had come to the fighting pits and the homes of the wealthy instead.

Xessa already knew from bitter experience how her deafness classed her as other and exotic; now she realised that if not for Pilos's pit, she would likely have been executed or thrown to the Drowned. Too dangerous to be a house slave, she was too limited – supposedly – to be a Melody warrior.

Yet here she was, alive and free among her people and heading into a fight with Ossa at her side and Tiamoko at her back. A warrior regardless.

Ossa pranced among the Tokob and more than a few tears were shed at the sight of him. An eja and her dog: Toko after Toko licked their thumbs and pressed them to her temple, gifting Xessa with a splinter of their spirit for strength and luck.

She and Tiamoko had avoided the centre of the city so far, not only because the groups they'd been with had refused to head in that direction, but also because there was nothing they could do there. Tiamoko could have scouted the pyramid, but without anyone to report his findings to, it was wasted time and dangerous. They were glad to discover from the people around them that they were being led by free: retired dog warriors, pit guards – Xessa's lip curled despite herself – and house guards. Real fighters taking real orders from the unknown figures who'd planned this rebellion. They learnt, too, to their initial disbelief, that the uprising wasn't just confined to the Singing City. It was Empire-wide, from one side of Ixachipan to the other.

Xessa didn't know if she could believe it, but as she read the same story over and over from Tokob faces and hands as they proceeded, something small and delicate unfurled its wings inside her. Hope. She read other stories too, of horror and loss and humiliation, and in those faces and gestures she found her rage given shape and form. Her eyes caught again and again on familiar, beloved gestures, on tattoos with the distinctive Tokob curls and embellishments, and each sight fed her spirit and her fury in equal measure until she was shaking with the need to kill these agents of the Underworld and seize the land back from them.

A Xenti thrust a jar of paint into Tiamoko's hands, urging

them to call their gods to their flesh. He, Xessa and Ossa huddled in the lee of a building and drew the symbols of strength and courage on each other with reverent movements. Xessa dabbed the slinking shape of Snake-sister between Ossa's shoulder blades to gift him cunning and speed in the strike, and then had to lean against the wall and breathe. And pray. Feeling the familiar tightness of paint on her brow and cheeks, the backs of her hands, caused a flurry of emotions, tangled and impossible to distinguish, to tighten around her ribs.

'You look . . . real again,' Tiamoko signed when she glanced at him. 'You look right.'

Xessa sniffed and nodded. 'You too, warrior. Your feet on the jaguar path once again. Bringing honour to your ancestors.'

She was about to sign more when his smile faltered and he looked over her head, back the way they'd come. He flushed, eyes narrowing with murderous intent, and lunged past her, Ossa spinning into a low crouch, his hackles up, to protect her.

Xessa clutched her spear and ran after Tiamoko. Whatever was out there, he wasn't facing it alone. Ossa sprang forward, rounding the corner just ahead of her, and she would have run into him if the sight before her hadn't stopped her in her tracks. Her spear came up and she checked along the alley and then up at the roofs. And then she stepped forward and pressed the stone tip of her weapon in alongside Tiamoko's forearm, where it was crushing a woman's throat as he pinned her against the wall.

Ilandeh.

Tiamoko shifted sideways, releasing some of the pressure and twisting his body so he could see Xessa. The eja adjusted her spear and nodded to indicate that she had her, and he let go. 'She says she wants to fight with us,' he signed and

573

Xessa twitched, an aborted impulse to drive the spear into the Pechaqueh throat.

Instead, she clicked and put Ossa in guard and the big dog snapped at Ilandeh's legs until she was cowering against the stone, hands out in paltry protection. Ossa would tear them off at the wrists if given the order. How badly Xessa wanted to give that order.

She rested her spear in the crook of her elbow. 'She fucking what?'

Ilandeh began to speak, Tiamoko translating. 'I'm sorry for everything. For what I did in the Sky City. It wasn't all a lie' – the eja sucked in a breath and Ilandeh flailed her hands desperately – 'sorry, sorry! Please, I'm Xenti. That wasn't a lie. I'm half-Xenti, look.' She pulled at her hair until a brightly dyed snake's rattle was revealed. As if that proved anything at all. She hadn't worn it in Tokoban, some story about how her village elder was the only one who could replace the one she'd lost. So what did it mean now? Nothing. Less than nothing.

'You killed high elder Vaqix and Eja elder Tika,' Tiamoko said and signed, and it wasn't a question.

Ilandeh licked her lips, her gaze flickering between them. She nodded once. 'My orders. I was sent to destabilise your city, to cause unrest. But since, so much has happened and Pilos has done . . . I don't want to fight for them any more. I want to fight with you. For you. For freedom.'

Tiamoko's signs were as hesitant as Ilandeh's words must be, but Xessa snorted at this flimsiest of excuses. They'd spotted her spying for the Melody, as she had done before, and now she was lying her way out of it – as she had done before.

'Why would we trust anything you say?' Xessa signed. 'After everything you did, all those betrayals for your

Pechaqueh masters? I'd say you're a better trained dog than Ossa, but he at least understands right from wrong.'

Ilandeh's face darkened with anger but she swallowed it down. 'They betrayed me, the Pechaqueh, I mean. Used me and discarded me. I want—'

'Now you know how it fucking feels,' Tiamoko said and signed. 'Maybe now you've got a taste of what you did to us. How you caused us all to be here. How your actions led to us killing each other, not trusting each other. You cost us our homes, our ancestors!'

'I'm sorry,' Ilandeh repeated and rubbed a fist in the centre of her chest. Xessa jerked as if the woman had slapped her; *how dare she* use Tokob sign? She clicked, preparing to give Ossa the kill command, when Ilandeh hurried on. 'I kept Tayan safe, protected him, would have died for him. Doesn't that mean anything?'

The eja looked at Tiamoko and raised her eyebrows.

'Kill her,' he signed immediately. 'It's a trick.'

'Do you believe her? About protecting Tayan?'

'Does it matter even if she did?' he asked and her response was vehement and instant. Tiamoko nodded. 'I'll do it, don't worry,' he added, as if putting a blade in Ilandeh would be at all difficult for Xessa. 'We need to hurry if we want to be in on the fighting,' he added and the eja looked back over her shoulder. There were only stragglers passing the end of the alley.

When she turned back, Ilandeh had a knife pressed to Tiamoko's throat and the man's body in between her and the leaping dog. 'Call him off,' she said clearly over the Tokob shoulder.

Fury seared through Xessa's limbs, but she whistled and Ossa slunk back to her side, stiff-legged, ears back.

'You think I didn't understand enough of that little

exchange?' Ilandeh demanded, Tiamoko once more translating in response to the jerk of the knife closer to his neck.
The Xenti looked like she was going to cry, her eyes glittering.
'Why won't any of you just listen? Why doesn't anyone want
me on their side? I made mistakes, I listened to their lies,
and now I just want to make up for it. If you won't let me
prove I can be trusted, then what more do you want?'

Tiamoko snarled something Xessa didn't catch and Ilandeh
brought the knife away from his neck just long enough to
club the handle and the bottom of her fist into his windpipe.
The big Toko went down choking and she kicked him in
the back, sending him sprawling into Ossa as the dog leapt
forward, his protective instincts overriding Xessa's command.

The eja followed a heartbeat later to catch Tiamoko; Ossa
wriggled from under his collapsing form and tripped her. She
went down over the dog's back, over Tiamoko, and in the
time it took them to untangle themselves, Ilandeh vanished.

Xessa could smell smoke when they finally reached the rebels
crowding through the temple district and its burnt-out,
half-collapsed buildings. Once she knew Tiamoko wasn't
badly hurt, she'd been set on hunting down Ilandeh, but he
said they'd do more good in the battle to come. She wasn't
sure she agreed – she had unfinished business with that, that
spy – but he'd been insistent. They'd been searching for a
way to make a difference and this was it, not chasing one
supposed half-Xenti across the city. As if her heritage made
a difference, made her one of them. Xessa's fury boiled anew.

She and Tiamoko began threading their way to the front
as the crowd milled, uncertain. They were warriors and their
duty was to confront their enemies and put their bodies
between them and civilians, no matter how determined they
were to fight for themselves.

Ossa padded at Xessa's side, occasionally slipping ahead through small gaps but always waiting for her to catch up. In the last five days, they'd begun to move together like water again, flowing and intuitive, a single lethal entity. Today would be no different, even though today they'd be facing trained warriors once more. Xessa refused to think about the scars the dog already bore and how many more he might have before this was over. If he lived.

She knew from Tiamoko that the song was a relentless urge to peace through surrender, that the only way forward was to lay down weapons and bend their necks to their collars and their owners. To beg for forgiveness and the right to serve Pechaqueh as they were destined to do. She was both profoundly pleased she couldn't hear and consumed with guilt: Xessa had been impatient, even condescending, with Tiamoko and many of the freed slaves they'd come across, angry at them for letting it get in their heads. Now she watched the way the civilians began to hunch their shoulders and slow their steps, wincing, and she was ashamed.

And it was Tayan doing it – or at least, he had a hand in it. They were no closer to understanding his role as Shadow and whether he truly had any control over the magic and the song's message, but these were *Tokob* flinching under its weight.

The press of warriors ahead of them slowed and Xessa looked first for Ossa and then at Tiamoko. 'We're close to the grand plaza,' he signed. 'Dog warriors and eagles. A few thousand. We outnumber them, but . . .' His hands fell still and he jerked his head at the mass to their rear. If they were facing unarmed, injured eagles, they'd probably be able to kill them. Anything more than that and the civilians that made up the bulk of their number were likely to break and run. And somewhere back there was Ilandeh, probably waiting to pick them off one by one, all her words just lies. As they always had been.

Xessa gnawed the inside of her cheek. 'Best make sure this lot don't break our line, then,' she signed with more confidence than she felt. Tiamoko's answering smile was strained, but then he squared his shoulders and coldness seeped into his expression – when he turned back to face the growing daylight at the end of the road heralding the grand plaza, Xessa let herself shiver.

The warriors in front sped up once more and then they were running, pouring out of the road and those on either side, three streams of them racing into the huge open space dotted with obelisks.

Opposite loomed the great pyramid, blood-red and ominous, capped in flame and sparkling white. At its base stood row upon row of warriors, Pechaqueh eagles and Chitenecah dog warriors, Axib free and Tlaloxqueh flesh merchants. Not just Pechaqueh, but all the tribes of Ixachipan were arrayed against them. Except, Xessa hoped and prayed, Tokob and Yaloh.

Someone stumbled into her on her right and she shoved at them, trying to make space for herself and Ossa, but they kept on pressing and she looked over their head to see more of the enemy racing out of the side streets between the burnt-out temples. They might no longer have roofs from which to shoot arrows and darts, but the buildings themselves and the roads between could still be used as cover.

Xessa tried to angle left away from the second threat, only for Tiamoko on that side to shove at her arm. So, they were coming at them from three sides. Not good, but not the end before it had even begun, either. The eja slowed as the warriors in front did and they entered a formation she'd fought against outside the Sky City. A Melody formation, different from the thirty-strong Paws that Tokob and Yaloh favoured that gave them manoeuvrability in thick jungle.

She glanced at Tiamoko for confirmation and then slid in behind them, ready to support or take the place of a fallen warrior as necessary. Behind stretched the mass of armed civilians. Many at the rear had slowed when they'd seen the enemy and there was a gap opening between those huddled against the walls of the buildings and the warriors pressing forward. Some hurried to catch up, darting forward in a scurrying hunch, and others faded back into the roads. They'd take no part in the battle after all.

The memory of the Sky City came back to her again and she found she couldn't blame them. How many civilians back home had, when it came to it, been too afraid to raise weapons? There was no shame in it.

The Pechaqueh sent their allies at them first, perhaps in an effort to dismay them with the prospect of fighting their own people, or more likely to preserve their own numbers. If the rebels were already exhausted by the time the eagles swept down on them, the battle would be a massacre.

Then we can't let that happen, Xessa thought confidently, not that she knew how to combat the tactics being thrown at them. She didn't have long to ponder it before the first warriors reached their lines and they swayed and shifted under the impact. The eja looked down instinctively and saw Ossa flinching and backing away, his left forepaw held up; someone had trodden on it in the crush. That was another way in which they weren't suited to this type of warfare.

Xessa made herself big and spread her feet, the right braced forward for balance, then dragged him between them where she could protect him with her body and the butt of her spear. They might be fighting for freedom, but Ossa was as much a symbol of what Xessa had lost and could have again as anything else. She wouldn't risk him breaking a foot or a leg before he'd even had the chance to sink his teeth into the enemy.

Warriors were shoving at her from all sides and it didn't take long for gaps to begin to open in the line ahead. She glanced again at Tiamoko, got his nod, and together they charged into the hole before the enemy could force their way through. Ossa moved with the same lethal grace he'd always had, and even after five days of fighting alongside him again, Xessa still marvelled at his lithe speed.

She only had a second to watch him before someone was leaping at her. Xessa ducked the swing of the axe and ripped her spear tip down the front of his lead leg, opening up the inside of his knee. He went down with his mouth gaping and she rammed the spear into it, blood exploding along the haft, and let his body block the warriors behind him straining to reach her.

Xessa gave herself up to the cut and chop and slash and duck of combat, her eyes darting everywhere as she tried to anticipate the next attack. A spear drove through the press and she jinked sideways, but it still came so close it almost took off her ear. She batted it away with her own, only for it to come back in for jab after jab, swift and unpredictable and each one aiming somewhere different, so she was constantly parrying instead of fighting back.

She was wearing stolen salt-cotton that was far too big for her and when the spear broke through her defence and slammed into her side, the armour twisted around her body with it, stealing the blow's force and unbalancing her attacker. Xessa's return thrust struck the warrior in the chest just as Ossa tore out their hamstring. She ripped the spear out of her opponent's hands and passed it backwards to the rebels behind her, and an instant later a bloody hand punched her in the side of the head.

Xessa rolled with it, spinning in a complete circle and coming back with her spear half-raised. The face of this new enemy was familiar, known, and impossible. Vorx, dead Casiv's twin. Out of the pit and fighting for the Pechaqueh. The Tlalox had no honour and even less sense of duty.

He grabbed her spear and wrenched it; Xessa held on and managed a short, awkward kick into his thigh, before his own spear spun with a sinuous twist and flip that took her feet from under her. Xessa crashed onto her back on the plaza, the battle raging all around and above her. She'd be trampled by her own if Vorx didn't stab her first.

Ossa raced between the Tlaloxqueh legs, teeth opening his calf as he passed, and Vorx spun, limping, to find what had hurt him. Xessa scrambled onto all fours, jabbed with her spear at a different warrior and then found the hot, wet holes of the bite in Vorx's leg and hooked her fingers into them, ripping.

The Tlalox reared back, his leg jerking from her slippery hand and the spear butt crunching down onto her forearm. She went for another grab and missed when Vorx brought the spear sharply back up into her face. Xessa's jaw snapped shut under the impact. Lightning forked in her head and blood burst against her palate and out of her lips. She slipped back onto her knees and then threw herself forward, the crown of her head slamming into his groin. Vorx collapsed on her back, driving her into the stone, but she wriggled free and kicked whatever part of him she could reach.

Ossa came in again, grabbed her by the right forearm and began dragging her back to rebel lines, but she screamed and twisted free: Pechaqueh-issued salt-cotton didn't come with the arm padding used by ejab, though the dog didn't know that. Vorx grabbed Ossa by his scruff and flung him away, twisting in the air. Xessa screamed again and then the Tlalox fell on her, knees in her chest and his spear punching for her face.

The eja gave a single twisting convulsion and jerked her head sideways. The spear shattered next to her face, fragments of flint peppering her cheek and ear. She punched him in the mouth, twisted the spear haft from his hands and clubbed him awkwardly around the head. Someone fell over them, knocking Vorx off his knees, and for a crushing moment Xessa had the weight of two people driving her into the stone before the other person flailed away.

Her spear was jammed between their thrashing bodies. The wicked edge was close to her face and Vorx saw it at the same time she did. Muscles bulging, he grabbed her by her hair and wrenched upwards, at the same time trying to shove the spear tip down into her face. Her eye.

Xessa's right hand was under his chin trying to push him away, her left digging into the wrist of the hand gripping her hair, but neither were enough to stop the slow, inexorable movement of her head towards the spear tip. Vorx leant in further, closer, so close she could taste the saliva splattering from between his gritted teeth. The pain in her neck and scalp was growing as fast as her neck muscles were fatiguing, her vision juddering as she shook with the effort.

Ossa leapt onto Vorx's back then and sank his teeth into the side of the Tlaloxqueh neck. The fighter reared backwards, flailing and releasing his grip on Xessa. She grabbed his shoulder and yanked, twisting her hips at the same time. He and Ossa fell sideways and she rolled from under him and bounced to her feet, hands settling on her spear.

Vorx kicked her legs from under her again and Xessa went back down, face first this time, splitting her chin on the stone. The air blasted from her lungs; the spear jolted from her grip. She rolled onto her back in time to see Vorx silhouetted against a sky so blue it was white.

And then he was staggering as something big, black and muscular landed on his back. Ossa clung with his big paws just long enough to tear out the side of the Tlaloxqueh throat and then he was jumping away, landing over Xessa's legs and standing there, bloody and hackles up, snarling his challenge.

Someone dragged her up onto her feet and out of the front line, the swirl of battle putting it beyond her. She whirled, fist pulled back to her jaw, but it was Tiamoko. He shouted something that she didn't catch. She shook her head. He pointed back the way they'd come and then signed it: *another wave. Enemy*.

Xessa felt her heart kick once, hard, and stretched up onto her toes to stare over the heads of the panicking armed civilians. Hundreds of warriors pouring out of the streets behind them, dressed in Melody salt-cotton with eagle feathers in their hair.

Led by fucking Pilos himself. Xessa felt a thrill of savage glee jolt through her and dragged at Tiamoko's arm, pointing wildly at the man who'd made them fight and kill for entertainment – fight everyone but the true enemy. Fight her own. Tiamoko's face contorted and together they began shoving their way through the melee of warriors, Ossa slipping among legs like a shadow.

No matter how Xessa struggled, she couldn't fight through the press of allies in time. There were some warriors interspersed in the ranks at the rear, but not enough to force discipline into the civilians in the face of the eagles' charge. They crammed forward, towards the pyramid, pushing their own front line into the enemy there, and then broke and fled to either side, like water from a cracked pipe, spilling into the narrow roads off the plaza and away. More and more followed as they were infected by the same fear. Some eagles gave chase; others continued to advance.

The pyramid was *right there*, Pilos was *right there*, and they couldn't reach either one. Xessa grabbed for Tiamoko in a wordless plea. Surely they could still do this? His lips were pressed thin and bloodless and his nostrils flared as he looked down at her. He shook his head once. 'It's over for today. Retreat.'

'No,' Xessa signed, 'no, it can't be. Tayan's in there. He'll help us. You'll see, he'll do something!'

'If he was going to help, don't you think he would have already?' Tiamoko replied, his gestures angry and his expression lost, betrayed. He looked up at the great pyramid and then grabbed her by the arm before she could reply. Relentlessly, he dragged her away, making sure they stayed deep among the fleeing civilians, out of spear range. It was brutal, but it was necessary: let those who couldn't or wouldn't fight die first and preserve the warriors who would do both for the next engagement.

Please, Malel, please don't turn your face from your first children. Please stand with us. With Tayan, wherever he is.

Angry tears burnt the ejab eyes, but Tiamoko was implacable and Ossa a tail-tucked, ears-back fleeing form. They ran.

They were in the shadows of a side street, the scent of smoke and burnt stone heavy on the still air – they were almost away – when Xessa dug in her heels. She felt something. A . . . presence. A taste on her skin, as if her spirit was calling out to another's.

Tiamoko pulled on her arm and she pulled back, resisting, and this time he let her, checking ahead and catching his breath as she scanned behind. She quartered the corpse-strewn plaza and the small knots of civilians and warriors fleeing the ravening Pechaqueh and their song-leashed allies, but it wasn't that. It wasn't there. Ossa circled her, his hackles raised. He was limping slightly on his right foreleg, but not enough to make her too worried. Most likely he'd cut his paw on some broken stone or obsidian, but he didn't cease his vigil.

Her gaze rose from the plaza to the pyramid, up the levels occupied with warriors, all the way to the top and the song-stone cap on its four pillars. There was a slender, long-haired figure standing beneath it dressed in bright cloth. A finely woven tunic shimmered gold across their chest and arms and their kilt was shamanic blue, matching the blue on their forehead and the line she could just make out running down their chin. The wind stirred their hair into a flag and they reacted with an impatient flick of head and hand in concert to brush it behind their shoulders. A familiar gesture. A known, beloved gesture. Whatever it was that had called to her confirmed what her heart already knew.

Tayan.

There was a second figure further back on the platform, armed and armoured and wearing the yellow kilt of what she'd learnt was a Chorus warrior. A bodyguard to the Singer. They leant in to speak to Tayan, gesturing down into the plaza below. Tayan nodded and the gold of his tunic flared brighter. People in the plaza – Tiamoko, next to her – flinched.

Xessa snapped her fingers and grabbed him when he came to her side. 'What is the song doing right now?' she demanded.

'It just . . . strengthened. Gave me a jolt of, of the knowledge that I'm less than Pechaqueh. That if I want peace, I need only surrender.'

Numb, she pointed to where Tayan stood under the capstone of the great pyramid. Unable to tear her eyes from his distant figure, she didn't know what Tiamoko's expression was when he saw the shaman, their friend – this Shadow of the Singer who'd promised to free them – and realised that the song was no different for his presence. That it had, in fact, just made him feel worse.

Xessa knew Tayan better than she knew herself. She'd grown up with him and could recognise his shape and movements even from here, all the visual clues that allowed her to pick him out of a crowd, to identify him when he faced away from her or was crossing out of her path.

That was Tayan. The friend of her heart.

A Tlalox limped past, hand clamped to a wound in his shoulder and one ankle already swelling from some injury. He stared curiously at them and then back the way they'd come. Numb, Xessa pointed at Tayan and the Tlalox nodded, said something.

Tiamoko translated. 'He said that's the Singer. He's glowing gold with his magic.' The eja stared at Tiamoko's hands as if they might attack her, her heart a sickening thud in her chest and cold sweat prickling between her shoulder blades. Because that wasn't the Singer; that was Tayan, his Shadow. Glowing with song-magic that was telling everyone who heard it that only Pechaqueh deserved to be free.

'That's not the Singer,' she signed, to be sure he understood. The Tlalox limped past, uncaring.

'No,' Tiamoko signed, stricken. 'It's Tayan. But how is he doing that? *Why* is he doing it?' He rubbed at his chest, grimacing. Carefully, slowly, so that she didn't shatter into pieces and blow away on the wind, Xessa knelt and put her arms around Ossa's neck, breathing in the warmth of him.

He'd lied to them in the fighting pit. Tayan wasn't going to save them; Tayan was with the Singer, sharing his magic and his life and his purpose. He'd chosen a side and it was the wrong one. He'd betrayed her and Lilla.

He'd betrayed them all.

LILLA

Sound carried far on the still night air, over streets pregnant with the silence of frightened people very deliberately holding still and quiet. Lilla had only passed through the Singing City once, when he'd been sold in the flesh market to the Melody despite his broken head, the promise of his physique and the circumstances of his capture enough for the eagles to take a chance on his recovery. Even now he got occasional headaches, some blinding in their intensity, and the high whine in his ears had never really gone away, but other than that, the Melody had got exactly what they'd bought – a warrior. Lilla's lips lifted away from his teeth in a smirk. Perhaps they were regretting their investment now.

They don't even know who you are, fool. And there's no place for arrogance in what's to come.

It made him feel better anyway.

And he needed that confidence, because they were finally

588

here after battling their way out of the Melody fortress, across Tlalotlan and through the hills and farmland to the heart-city. Everything they'd faced so far was as nothing compared with what was to come. As satisfying as it had been to kill eagles and the dogs who refused to abandon their masters on the road, it was here that they would seize their freedom and end Pechaqueh domination forever.

'Where do we go?' Lilla breathed into Ekon's ear. The relentless horrors of the march had done a little to grow delicated scabs over the sharp wounds of betrayal, both Ekon's and his own, which Lilla had been forced to acknowledge. While both had lied their way through the relationship, only the Toko had had murder in mind for his lover.

Lilla had managed, through sheer bloody-mindedness, to prioritise what they were doing and think of ways to ensure, not just their survival, but their ultimate victory. It didn't stop him lying awake for too long during each too-short rest period to relive every choice and every mistake he'd made since his capture, but it was getting easier, at least, to plan and speak with Ekon as they once had.

'There's a huge mahogany tree growing next to the wall of Great Octave Enet's estate. It will be watched. We go there and our allies will let us know where they need us for whatever they have planned.'

Lilla looked at him in surprise, squinting through the darkness. 'Enet? Is that wise?'

'That's not something we need to worry about. Once we meet up with the leadership or one of their commanders, we'll find out how things stand.'

'You speak as if you'll defer to them,' he murmured. 'Surely it should be the other way around? You are a warrior and leader of warriors; you should take command, especially as we'll be facing eagles.'

Ekon was already shaking his head. 'As I command here?' he asked but without rancour. Lilla blushed; two days out from the town where Tinit and the others had sacrificed themselves, Lilla's rebels had refused to take any further orders from Ekon, insisting the Toko be the one to lead them. Lilla's response had been to offer a shared command, a compromise that pleased no one but, he reasoned, if he were to fall in the next skirmish, ambush or battle, at least his warriors would be more inclined to stay with Ekon and help overthrow the song.

'They'll already have commanders in place. We're not important, Lilla, not really. We're just warriors to throw at the enemy until they break. If you thought we'd all be heroes by the time this is over, well, let's just say it won't be our names that get remembered.'

'I don't care about that,' Lilla muttered and gestured for Ekon to lead the way. They left their force in concealment and, together with twenty warriors, slipped as soft as shadows through the streets towards the noble district of the Singing City.

It was riskier going through the city than around it, but they needed to get a feel for the general terrain and any help or hindrance they might encounter from non-combatants.

The Toko hadn't seen this part of the city before. Plazas and temples and buildings whose functions he couldn't guess at were laid out in a grid with smaller roads leading off to the nobles' palaces, hidden behind high walls screened by lush public gardens. Lilla smiled. He could see where trees with overhanging branches had been used to gain entry to some estates since the uprising began. No doubt the Pechaqueh within had been most surprised when they were cut down. How many buildings beyond those walls would be smoking ruins by now?

Shapes flitted across the road ahead and vanished – civilians or enemies? Fleeing or luring? There was no way to tell unless they hunted them down and a swift shake of Ekon's head confirmed Lilla's own reluctance to seek out trouble so early on.

They made careful progress but there was no ambush or sudden flight of arrows winging their way, and they reached Enet's estate – and its attendant mahogany – without incident. The area was empty of life.

Lilla looked to Ekon in silent question, anxiety crawling in his gut, but the Feather gave him a reassuring smile and crouched in the inky shadow of the tree. He drew his knife and made a small cut in the back of his forearm and squeezed it until the blood ran. He dipped his finger in the blood and made a series of marks on the trunk low down at the base.

Ekon sucked at the cut and then licked away the last traces of blood. He stood and shifted closer to Lilla. 'Now we find ourselves somewhere comfortable to watch from and wait for our answer,' he murmured. 'Might take an hour; might take the rest of the night. You should try and sleep while you can this time,' he added with a pointed look. Despite himself, Lilla flushed: he hadn't realised his inability to sleep had been noticed, let alone by the man who was causing it. He shrugged and ducked his head.

Ekon led them to the gate into Enet's estate, surprising him again. Surely this place would be occupied? The gate opened under his hand and they slunk in, scanning the darkness. It seemed deserted; Lilla didn't trust it. Inside were more gardens, black and grey in the darkness but smelling rich and alive. The building, the *palace*, was a dark sprawling lump just visible through the foliage.

Lilla found a Tokob arm and used touch-sign to indicate *caution, watch, danger*. Ekon pointed upwards; there were platforms built into the trees closest to the wall and he climbed into one and then snapped his fingers to indicate it was clear and he had line of sight across part of the gardens. Lilla and two others joined him and the war party separated into small groups to occupy the rest. They set up with two facing in and two out, giving them a view over the whole front wall of the estate and the front aspect of the palace.

Ekon leant close enough to breathe in Lilla's ear. 'I've got this watch. Sleep.'

'I'm fine—' the Toko began.

'We share this command. I need you at your best. Sleep.'

Lilla thought about simply ignoring the order, but his limbs were heavy and his eyes gritty with fatigue. Reluctantly, he curled himself onto the platform and closed his eyes. He was convinced he wouldn't sleep and bitterly unsurprised to prove himself correct. Still, it was pleasant to lie still and not be running or fighting or hiding. Pleasanter still to listen to the rustle of leaves and the soft rubbing of branch on branch. Night birds and insects trilled, night-blooming flowers scented the air. If he tried hard, it almost reminded him of home. Almost.

Despite himself, Lilla shifted very slightly into Ekon's warmth under the pretext of finding a more comfortable position. A hand came down and brushed, featherlight against his temple, sweeping back a strand of hair. Lilla shivered and then held very still, wanting and hating that he wanted. But he was here in the Singing City, where the central records of all slaves were held. Like every other warrior who'd travelled with them, they were desperate to access those records and find where their loved ones had been enslaved. How easy would it be to find Tayan among the thousands of other names? They didn't even know what form the records took. Ekon did, and he owed Lilla that much at least.

The Feather didn't remove his hand from the curve of Lilla's skull, and as if it was medicine, the Toko relaxed under its warm weight. He even slept for a while. He woke to that same hand sliding down his cheek to gently grip his shoulder and a voice murmuring in his ear: 'Someone's here.'

Lilla opened his eyes and looked into Ekon's face, far too close to his own. The warrior smiled an apology and let go, shifting lithely onto his feet and out of the Tokob space. Lilla rolled onto his feet to peer over the wall: a single figure crouching at the base of the tree, face pressed almost against the bark to identify the marks the Feather had left. They stood and looked up, starlight not quite enough to limn their face, and then held their hands out from their sides and approached the gate into Enet's estate.

'Something's wrong,' Ekon murmured. 'They should leave a mark telling us where to go.'

Lilla swung down out of the tree and darted into the lee of the gate even as it opened. The person came through and he lunged at their back and wrapped his arm around their throat, pressing his knife to their inner thigh where the salt-cotton didn't reach.

'Hello, Lilla. I thought it was you.'

Lilla didn't even register the clatter as he slammed Ilandeh into the gate, not until Ekon was by his side and dragging the knife away from her flesh. 'Lilla, stop.' And then he recognised her and stilled.

Ilandeh stared back, her eyes comically wide. 'Feather Ekon? *Feather Ekon?* You're, you're with the rebels? How?' She sucked in a breath as Lilla pressed his knife beneath her eye, her gaze landing on him with so much weight and history and . . . frantic hope that it stopped him plunging it in.

'You traitorous fucking shit,' he growled. 'How dare you show your face to me.'

'Please, Lilla, please, let me explain.'

'I've had a bellyful of Pechaqueh lies,' he snarled, digging the point of the blade into delicate skin. She flinched.

Ekon put his hand on Lilla's shoulder. 'Let her talk,' he murmured.

'You don't know what she's done,' he insisted.

'Is it worse than what I've done?' the man asked. 'I fought in Tokoban too.'

Lilla shoved him with his free hand hard enough that he stumbled back a pace. 'You didn't sneak into our city and befriend us and then destroy us from within! You didn't share food and beer, ritual and our lives with us. You weren't there when we sacrificed to Malel for aid in the war.' His hand found Ilandeh's throat and the knife was unwavering on her face. 'I hope you said your prayers to the Drowned, for you'll be meeting them soon enough.' He pulled back to strike, Ilandeh making no move to defend herself, and Ekon grabbed his arm.

'Enough! Ilandeh is a Whisper, a macaw. Half-blood.'

'Half-Xenti,' she whispered.

'Half-fucking-Pecha,' Lilla corrected, twisting to free himself. Ekon held fast, his other arm snaking around the Tokob chest to haul him bodily backward. 'All traitor. Liar. How many promises did you break in the Sky City? How many did you kill? *How many died by your hand in my home before the war even started?*'

'In total? Seventeen over the year. Vaqix and Tika included.' Her voice was small but she didn't hide from what she'd done.

'I killed five times as many to secure my place as a Feather,' Ekon said in his ear. Lilla thrashed in his arms and felt

Ilandeh twist the knife from his grip. He kicked, hit the gate instead of her, and had to bite back a scream.

'You're telling me she's one of you?' he choked. 'A rebel?'

'I'm . . . I'm not,' Ilandeh said. 'Or I wasn't, then. I believed wholeheartedly in what I was doing, in the Empire and the peace it could bring you under the song. But I don't believe that any more. I gave them everything and that's exactly what they took. Now I want my vengeance.'

The Toko lashed out again and this time his sandal caught her in the thigh. She grunted, staggering, and Ekon tightened his grip and wrestled him back a step. 'Calm down, Lilla. Kitten, please, take a breath.'

'Don't fucking *call me that*,' he swore, struggling, but Ekon was taller and stronger and there was no way out of his hold. His eyes stung with frustration and betrayal, the tears burnt away in the raging heat of his anger. 'Get your hands off me, Pecha. Get your hands off me *right now*.'

A dozen of the warriors who'd come with them had gathered nearby to stop them killing one another. Ilandeh was still pressed against the gate, her palms turned out to them to show they were empty. Her mouth was a thin slash in her face. 'Spear Pilos has perhaps six hundred eagles left, plus another thousand who are retired and have flocked to the source to support him. There are at least two to three thousand free or retired dogs who've sided with them, too. So far they're mixing the dogs in with the eagles to keep an eye on them in case they prove false' – she glanced at Ekon as she said it and shook her head again – 'but they'll have called for help. My guess is High Feather Atu's closest, though I haven't been privy to Talon movements recently.'

A private, bitter smile crossed her face. 'The High Feather and the First were in Chitenec last I heard. If they were recalled immediately they could be here any day. You need to—'

595

'Lies,' Lilla said, but it was weaker now. He stopped fighting Ekon's grip, memories of Ilandeh and Dakto in his and Tayan's home eating and laughing through the long evenings combining with memories of Ekon, pressed against his back like this but more, so much more and closer and precious. One a friend, the other a lover. Both betrayers. 'Get off me,' he whispered, his heart breaking. 'Get off me before I fucking kill you both.'

Ekon complied and Lilla stumbled away into the dark, away from the gate and the warriors and the past. His feet splashed into a stream and he leapt back on instinct, then stared at the ribbon of moving blackness curling through the gardens. Enet had a stream on her estate. A stream for the Drowned to visit her. He bent double, hands on his knees, and gasped for breath, sparkling dots crowding his eyes and the constant distant whine in his ears increasing in volume. He was going to pass out and then a Drowned would come and take him. Perhaps it would be better that way. Perhaps it already had and this was some awful nightmare perpetrated by his dying mind.

'. . . Rebels are housing many of their warriors at the northern flesh market . . . no, not that one, people are holding captive no-bloods there . . .' Her voice faded in and out; Lilla couldn't even hear Ekon's low-voiced questions.

His breathing steadied, his vision clearing, and the Toko risked straightening up. His head swam unpleasantly and the familiar pain began to build in his temples. He hadn't had an attack in months; it didn't surprise him he'd have one now. He just had to act before it got too bad. He strode back to Ilandeh and Ekon, shouldering the Feather out of the way. 'Get out. Leave.'

Ilandeh flushed and reached out to grab his arm; he stepped away. 'Lilla, please. Please, I just want to fight. I want to make up for—'

'Well, you can't,' he said. 'I can't even stand to look at you.'

'Then what should I do?' she snapped. 'Pechaqueh don't trust me; rebels don't trust me. What the fuck should I do?'

'You want to make it up to me? To all Tokob?' he demanded as Ekon murmured futile pleas to calm down. Surprisingly, Ilandeh nodded. 'Then go to Tokoban and put a stop to the mining. They're digging into Malel's skin, carving her open. Songstone mines. You want to do something to make up for your past and help the rebellion? Stop your precious Pechaqueh getting hold of any more songstone.'

'But I want—' she began. Lilla had had enough. His hand closed around her throat again, cutting off words and air.

He leant very close. 'No one cares what you want. No one in all Ixachipan gives one good shit about you. Do you understand? You're nothing. Less than nothing. I pray Malel herself kills you, but if she doesn't, then end the mining operation in Tokoban.'

'That's impossible,' she croaked, fingers scrabbling at his wrist.

Lilla bared his teeth. 'I know. Now fuck off before I snap your neck.' He dragged her off the gate, pulled it open and hurled her into the street.

Ilandeh fell and rolled twice, limbs flopping, and then dragged herself to her feet. She looked back for one endless moment, her face shadowed but her eyes glittering. She fled.

It was the still hour before dawn when Ekon and Lilla led their small army through the city to the northern flesh market. Lilla had protested violently against trusting Ilandeh's directions, but whatever a Whisper was – none of the Eighth Talon had heard of such a warrior – Ekon trusted her information. Trusted her, perhaps, despite everything Lilla had told him of her crimes.

He wondered whether the rebels had chosen the flesh market because of its size, or whether there was a more symbolic element to the idea of basing their freedom in the place of their greatest degradation. It was the same market Lilla had been sold in although when they reached it, the vast bamboo cages had been torn down and now it was just an open space with scarred, stained stone underfoot. It still stank of misery and desperation, as if fear and humiliation had sunk into the very stones of the plaza itself.

The hairs stood up on the back of the Tokob neck. The spirits of the dead were still here and they were angry; wronged; vengeful. It was a place made of suffering as much as stone and bamboo and it perfumed the air until Lilla thought he would be sick from it.

But aside from the unknown ancestors haunting the place, there was no one else.

Ekon signalled for them to hunker down in the shadows and then stepped into the plaza alone. He dropped his spear and knife and then unlaced his salt-cotton, pulling it over his head and flicking his hair free, walking three paces in between each action. He dropped the armour and kept walking. 'For all who would be free. Feather Ekon of the Chitenecah, traitor in the Melody's heart and true son of Mictec, brings warriors to kill the song.' He turned in a circle with his arms outstretched. 'For all who would be free.'

'Eyes open, stay alert,' Lilla murmured and heard the command passed backwards. There was a bright flaring line in the sky and a burning arrow arced from a building opposite and shattered on the ground at Ekon's feet. The Toko had to bite back a cry of alarm, his fingers twitching on the string of his own bow.

Ekon flinched but didn't run. He turned to the building from which the arrow had come and stripped off his tunic, holding out his arms again, the garment dangling from his right fist. Inviting another arrow. Lilla guessed all these gestures were a code much like the one he'd drawn on the tree at the Great Octave's palace. Passwords could be tortured out of suspected traitors, but any Pecha warrior who echoed Ekon's words but didn't accompany them with this elaborate dance of gesture and movement would be killed.

A door at the base of the building opened and Ekon dropped to his knees, right then left. He put his tunic on the ground and then stretched out on his stomach. Lilla was so tense he thought his spine would snap as the figure approached Ekon and spoke to him too quietly for the Toko to hear. He didn't know how much time passed before the Pecha – *Chitenecatl* – pushed back onto his knees and then stood. He embraced the figure and then suddenly people were pouring out of the building.

Ekon turned to where Lilla and their warriors were hiding. He put one hand palm up in front of his chest and the other edge-down on top of it and drew them both towards him: the Tokob sign for safe. His shoulders hunched against the promise of arrows, Lilla stepped out and their warriors followed him. The freedom fighters gathered around Ekon were wide-eyed at their number.

'You have brought a larger force than we had dared to hope, although we had not expected to see you at all, son of Chitenec.' The figure who'd approached Ekon was a tall, thin woman of middle years, all sharp lines and piercing eyes. Her voice was softer and more melodious than her appearance suggested.

Ekon winced and ducked his head, looking ashamed to be alive. Lilla wanted to shake him; wanted to kiss him; wanted to kill him. 'This is Fang Lilla of the Tokob. If I had fallen at the fortress or on the way here, he would have led our warriors to the Singing City and done his best to find you.'

Lilla blinked and realised that Ekon, despite his protestations at being destined to die, was higher up in the rebellion's hierarchy than he'd let on. That elaborate ritual wasn't something every rebel knew; it was reserved for certain members of the uprising. He certainly hadn't taught it to Lilla on the way here.

'It will take time to get you all under cover,' the woman said, ignorant of the Tokob internal re-evaluation of everything Ekon had done since the night of the Great Star's vanishing. The secrets he'd carried closer than his skin. Like Ilandeh. She offered him a small smile out of a lined face that didn't seem familiar with the expression. 'You are Tokob?'

Lilla hesitated, glancing at Ekon, who nodded encouragement. 'I am, ah, high one,' he mumbled.

A look of affront crossed the woman's face. 'Please never call me that again, and also don't apologise,' she added when he began stumbling over his words. 'We are all of us relearning our own rhythms of speech and the names of our gods. I ask only because we have had some hundreds of Tokob and Yaloh swell our ranks. I pray you may find kin and friends among their number. Most of our forces are spread throughout the city so as not to attract attention, and so that we might launch attacks at seemingly random points. We do have a main body of warriors here and we'll house you with them for a few hours so that you might rest in safety. You can call me Weaver.'

Lilla looked once more to Ekon for reassurance and couldn't help returning the man's smile when he nodded. They were among friends and, more importantly, there were friends among these friends.

* * *

The safe place Weaver had spoken of turned out to be a series of squat, thick-walled buildings a stick north of the flesh market. She told them they'd stood empty ever since Tokoban fell, a dusty, echoing monument to the horror of empire – there were no more people to conquer and drag here in ropes to sell like turkeys or bolts of cotton. Lilla knew he'd cost the Melody far less than a bolt of cotton.

Like the market itself, it was as poignant as it was practical: the buildings had housed thousands of slaves at once and were now home to thousands of freedom fighters. They were dark and claustrophobic and filled with silent, watchful faces and here, too, torment was baked into the very walls.

Some of those they passed wore expressions of fear, others determination, and many cool assessment – warriors. Lilla walked with a deliberately relaxed gait and shoulders, as unthreatening as it was possible to be in filthy, bloodstained armour and carrying four visible weapons: two spears in his right hand, a bow in his left, and a blowpipe strung over his back.

Ekon marched at his side, grim but awestruck. Lilla caught his eye. 'Weaver?'

'A lot of those with responsibility within the hierarchy are known only by their slave trades,' he whispered. 'So that if any of us were captured, all we could tell the Pechaqueh was that name. Until tonight I didn't know Weaver was a woman. The true commanders will be somewhere in the city, but none of us will ever know who they are. Weaver is the face of the rebellion here, as I was in the Melody.'

The woman herself gestured them to a small open space at the rear of the building and they hurried into it, their warriors piling in behind until they were pressed up against the far wall by the multitude of bodies. Voices never rose above the quietest murmur, but the entire building echoed with a breathing, lilting sort of susurration.

Weaver crossed to another small group and Ekon inhaled, grabbing at Lilla's forearm. He jerked his head in their direction. 'That's Xini and Itzil, Enet's estate and body slaves. The three of them together were responsible for weakening the song in the months leading to the uprising. Itzil is Enet's birth mother – Chitenecah, like me. Enet was infamous in Pechaqueh society for having removed Itzil's tongue as a punishment when just a girl. Knowing who Itzil really was and still doing that . . . I can't even guess what they went through together, the strength of will they must have had to hide in plain sight and do all that they did for the cause.'

There was unconscious pride in Ekon's voice and it squeezed Lilla's heart; was this the first time the man had been able to be proud of his blood and lineage? And then his words caught up with him.

'*Enet?*' he hissed and Ekon nodded, holding up a finger to cut him off.

'I know. Their stories are some of the bloodiest and the bravest,' he murmured. 'But forgiveness for her is . . . Enet's name will forever be tarnished. Think of the courage it took to be that cruel,' he added, more to himself than Lilla.

Lilla just managed to prevent himself from commenting on Ekon's own innate skill in that area. He stared at the tiny space they had left for themselves now all their warriors had crowded in behind them and then took off his salt-cotton and laid it down as some protection against the stone floor.

Ekon copied him and then squeezed down onto the stone on his back, his feet drawn up to make himself small. Lilla curled on his side, putting his back to the Chitenecatl and trying without success to get comfortable. The close press of bodies, the dark and the smell cast him back in time to the pit under the Melody fortress where he'd been confined on his arrival. Countless weeks in that stinking, cramped Underworld, scuffling for food and breathing the stench of unwashed bodies, of urine and shit and hopelessness until it coated his tongue and the inside of his lungs and he choked on every breath. Until he'd never be clean or safe or alone again.

Lilla's chest began to constrict, his throat too, and he curled tighter, trying not to touch anyone, not to let the memories overwhelm him. Kux, who'd helped him maintain peace in that pit for five months, even though she never agreed with what he was planning. Kux, who'd tried to kill him and then tried to kill Ekon. Kux, whose last act before the Feather cut her down was to gift him a hundred lashes for her crime, lashes that were still thick and purple against his skin and that never stopped aching, no matter what he did.

'I'm going to touch your shoulder, Lilla,' Ekon murmured from behind him and despite how low his voice was, the Toko still flinched and had to bite back a cry. 'Focus on that, on my hand and the stone beneath you, all right?'

He flinched again when the hand came to rest on his upper arm. Ekon shifted, but he wasn't touched anywhere else, couldn't even feel the Chitenecah body heat pressing against his back.

'Good. Just breathe, nice and slow. Count to six to inhale and eight to exhale. My hand, the stone, the count. That's all. Good.'

'I don't . . . need,' Lilla tried, his voice a strangled rasp, and Ekon's fingers tightened in the meat of his shoulder. His breath stuttered out of his chest, and then again, softer, when the man gripped firmer, a rhythmic, slow squeeze and release that was easier to concentrate on than counting. In for three squeezes, out for four, until the dots in his vision cleared away and the shadow of the collar loosened its grip on his throat.

'Enclosed spaces?' Ekon asked when Lilla finally relaxed under his touch. He rolled onto his back and the Chitenecah hand briefly slid onto his chest before he took it away.

Lilla refused to miss it when it was gone. 'No, this place is too big for that. It's . . . memories. The pit under the fortress,' he whispered, unsure why he was answering. 'I'm just – we're so tightly-packed, it's the same sort of feeling. The dark, the forced proximity. The smell of fear.' He made himself smile, forced and ghastly. 'Though that might just be me.'

Ekon very slowly rolled to face him, careful not to touch him. 'It'll be me you're smelling, too, I promise,' he murmured and then knuckled at an eye. Lilla was absurdly grateful that he didn't mock him for his weakness, but it didn't even seem to occur to Ekon to do so. He supposed the Feather was right, too: they were all afraid, to some extent. This was more than war; this was the Pechaqueh very way of life burning down around them. They'd do anything – everything – to restore what they saw as the proper order. If they didn't have slaves to tend their crops and make their clothes and build their houses and feed their gods, they'd have to do it all themselves.

'Spear Pilos is out there somewhere,' Ekon said abruptly, his voice low but still clear enough that Lilla heard the tension winding through it like liana. 'And in just a few hours, maybe, or at most a few days, I'm going to face him over a battlefield and he'll know . . . everything. About me. About the scale and depth of my betrayal of him. They'll come for me – every eagle that recognises my face and real-ises what I've done will come for me, just like the fortress, like the town. And Pilos . . . he was my High Feather. My friend. Him and Atu and Detta and Calan and more.' He cut himself off with a twist of his lips. 'And they are Pechaqueh and slavers and conquerors and—'

This time it was Lilla who reached out. 'And they were your friends,' he whispered, fingertips just grazing Ekon's clavicle. He was so warm, skin softer than down. 'You had to do many things in the Melody. Becoming friends with Pechaqueh is . . .' he trailed off, suddenly realising where his thoughts were leading him.

Ekon's jaw tightened and he shifted away. Still close enough to touch – there wasn't room for any less – but he folded his arms over his broad chest and stared past Lilla's ear. '. . . Is the least of the hundreds of atrocities I committed,' he finished for him. There wasn't bitterness or reproach or even anger in his tone, any of which Lilla would have been glad of in that moment. Just resignation. Agreement. A self-loathing that ran far deeper than he'd ever seen in anyone before, including himself. Deep enough to drown in. A sparkling green cenote, beautiful and lethal and full of teeth.

Lilla leant up on his elbow and grabbed Ekon by his tunic, dragging him closer, almost under him. Ekon stared up with wide, shocked eyes. 'We're here now, free and fighting, because of you,' he growled. 'You did this, brought two thousand of us safely out of the fortress and past the corpses of our enemies and into the very heart of the Empire we're going to destroy. So yes, you did things that I can't even imagine and honestly don't want to, and no you'll never wash off that blood, but, but isn't that the lot of every warrior? War makes monsters of us all. None of our hands are clean and all of us have regrets.'

He was panting with the effort of keeping his voice low and had to force his hand to unclench from Ekon's tunic, the muscles of his forearm relaxing under the Chitenecah own grip – when had he grabbed Lilla's wrist?

'So you're going to face them – we'll face them together – and you'll look them in the eye and proclaim yourself a proud child of the Chitenecah, a devout son of Mictec, and then you're going to—'

'Lilla?'

The voice was low but it carried, rolling his name in a rich Tokob accent, and it was a voice he hadn't heard in . . . so long. He jerked up and around so fast his head spun and it was hard to focus, but then he saw him, looming over the nearest standing warriors. And beside him, tall but slight—

'Tiamoko? *Xessa?*'

'I'm going to what?' Ekon murmured quietly from behind him, almost plaintive, but Lilla paid him no mind, scrambling to his feet and then dodging sitting and lying bodies, weaving through knots of those still standing, moving on instinct it felt like: he couldn't tear his gaze away in case they vanished.

Others saw him coming and shuffled out of the way and then there was a clear path and Xessa and Tiamoko were both running along it and he threw himself into a sprint and hurled himself into their outstretched arms, catching them both by the backs of their heads and pulling their faces into his neck. Arms came around him, crushing tight, but it didn't matter because his lungs weren't working anyway.

'Malel, oh, Malel, thank you, thank you,' he was babbling in between peppering them both with kisses. 'Spirits and ancestors, I can't believe it. You're here. You're alive.' A giddy laugh broke from him and even though people around him were smiling at their reunion, a few winced at the volume and he muffled his laughter into Tiamoko's broad shoulder and let his tears fall there, too.

Xessa, for once, seemed content not to immediately begin asking questions, clinging around his waist like a constrictor, and Tiamoko was sobbing audibly. Lilla did what he could to soothe him and then a hot and wriggling form was burrowing in between their legs and he yelped as something wet shoved under his kilt. He looked down.

'Ossa?' he breathed, quietly so as not to frighten away the spirit, for surely he wasn't real. And then he saw Xessa's wet-eyed, grinning face. His mouth was hanging open. All three of them knelt then, in a little circle of home and family at the centre of which spun a grinning, blissful dog, his fur watered by all their tears.

They each had a story to tell, ones that would have lasted days, but no time in which to properly tell them. Lilla couldn't stop touching their arms and faces, clicking his tongue over their new scars and holding their hands when the shadow of memories grew too dark.

Eventually, the news travelled through the building that they would be marching to the great pyramid around highsun and that, with the additional numbers of warriors, they expected to finally break Pechaqueh dominance, take the pyramid, kill the Singer. A frisson of excitement and anxiety rippled through the building and it was into that atmosphere that Ekon slunk across to their little group.

Lilla could see the anxiety simmering beneath his skin and stood up to introduce him. 'Both of you, I'd like you to meet Ekon of the Chitenecah. He is in charge of the free Talon that marched from the Melody fortress. Ekon, meet Xessa and Tiamoko. Xessa is an eja and Tiamoko fought in my Paw. They are both fine warriors and both were condemned to Pilos's fighting pit here in the Singing City. Xessa can read your words from your mouth as long as you face her and speak clearly, not too fast.' He tapped his finger to his earlobe.

Ekon actually flinched at Pilos's name, but the smile he mustered seemed to fool the new arrivals. 'It is an honour to meet friends of Lilla's. Though he is too modest: this Talon is as much his as mine and the work he did to secure the numbers we have is a debt that all the free people of Ixachipan will never be able to repay.'

Lilla blushed and then again, harder, when Xessa's gaze switched between the two of them, her expression calculating. He prayed her hands would not twitch in a question he didn't know how to answer, but then Tiamoko was asking Ekon about their numbers and Xessa gestured Lilla a few paces away. She set them deliberately so that Lilla had his back to Ekon and he felt a stone solidify in his stomach, weighing it down.

'Are you safe? Do you know where Tayan is?' she signed abruptly.

'I'm as safe as any of us can be, and no, I don't know,' Lilla signed with sweaty hands. Worry over what Xessa might ask faded beneath the blinding sun of hope. 'Do you know? What do you know? I, I didn't want anyone to get hurt when I rebelled – I didn't know about any of this, it was just Tokob and Yaloh back then – so I didn't claim anyone as family. Including Tayan. I'm sorry, Xessa, it was for your protection, not mine. This way they had no one to threaten me with and my actions wouldn't lead to anyone's deaths.'

His hands ran out of words and he waited in miserable silence for her censure. Instead, she drew him into another fierce embrace and followed it up by licking her thumb and pressing it to his temple. Renewing their bond as family. He smiled helplessly as he returned the gesture – of course – but then she took a pace backwards and a deep breath.

'That was sensible, Lilla. I didn't do that because there was never going to be a chance for me to escape once I knew where I was going, so I did claim you.' He winced and she quirked the corner of her mouth in sympathy. 'Don't worry. I'm not blaming you; you did the right thing at the time. We've all done things and made choices. I doubt any of them have been good, really, but we had to make them and so we did. But that goes for Tayan too, and I need you to pay attention now. Because I'm not sure how much . . .' She paused for another deep breath and a tear tracked from the corner of her eye down her cheek.

Instinctively, Lilla wiped it away and then braced.

'I've seen Tayan, but only from a distance. Here in the city. He's made a choice, too, and you need to know about it. About where he is and what he's doing. And for who.'

'I don't believe you,' Lilla signed with shaking hands. 'You didn't see what you thought you did. Or if you did, it doesn't mean what . . .'

Doesn't mean what? That he has put himself in a situation to effect a coup and has done things he's probably not proud of while surrounded by enemies who can kill him if he so much as breathes wrong? I did all that. I have no right to pass judgment.

I won't pass judgment.

'We've spoken to some people since then to work out exactly what he's doing, including a Chitenecatl who worked for Enet, and who was there during the ritual. Tayan is *with* the Singer,' Xessa signed. 'How can you just forgive that? How can you pretend it doesn't matter when he's—'

'When he's what?' Lilla signed, his movements cold and angry. 'When he's been surviving? We've all had to do things we're not proud of, Xessa. Make choices that change

609

who we are, that violate promises we made to others and to ourselves.'

'Yes, that's clear,' Xessa signed with cold malice and he couldn't help but ache for the impetuous, funny and loving woman she'd once been even as he flushed at the implications of her words. She always saw too much. 'What you don't seem to understand is that it's not just that he's fucking the Singer, and doing who knows what else, it's that he is the *Singer's successor*. He's the heir to the magic that controls you all, and he's not using that to help us. He's not helping us at all, Lilla. This is his song you're hearing. His and the Singer's combined.' She flailed a hand in the air to emphasise her point.

Lilla recognised the malice for what it was now, a brittle shell over the soft rawness of her hurt. 'Xessa,' he said, reaching for her. She slapped his hands away.

'Fucking someone to stay alive, or even because you need the comfort in a hard world, that I can understand. Forgive. But Tayan has real, true power and he's not bending it to our aid. He's supporting the Singer – he's the reason why the song is so powerful. *Tayan* is the one telling you all you're worthless.'

Lilla found himself, as he always had done, siding with his husband against the fiery eja. She couldn't know any of the things Tay had had to do; none of them could even guess at it. 'I suppose it was different for you, being a pit-fighter,' he signed coldly. 'Not having to make allies, having Tiamoko close all the time. Not trying to plan a rebellion the way the rest of us were. The way I know Tayan was. Is.'

Xessa stepped back, her face cycling through a variety of expressions. 'You think your life has been harder than mine since we were captured? How many people have you killed during your time in the Melody, *Pod-leader Lilla?*'

Her hands were shaking. 'How many *Tokob* have died so you might live?'

Lilla felt the blood drain from his face and then Tiamoko was at Xessa's side, a hulking shadow. He put his hand on the nape of her neck and glared at Lilla. 'We've all suffered, Fang,' he said, 'Xessa and I have fought and killed and nearly died a dozen times each in that fucking pit. We've been forced to fight our own for Pechaqueh entertainment, and we've both seen Tayan standing at the top of that fucking pyramid glowing gold with song-magic. She's angry and frightened and if you have no—'

Xessa twisted to look up. 'What are you saying?' she signed.

'I'm telling him to fuck off because he doesn't understand what happened to us any more than we understand what he or Tayan have been through,' Tiamoko said clearly, and she tensed and then slumped, at the acknowledgement and the gentle reprimand both. She hid her face against his chest, done with the conversation.

'I don't know what your husband is up to, Lilla, but I would have thought the time for him to act would be when the whole fucking Empire rose against the Pechaqueh. That he hasn't is telling. Worrying. He said he'd free us, told us to our faces at the fighting pit he'd see us free, and now he sits up there in luxury, in the heart of Pechaqueh power, and does nothing.'

'Enough,' Lilla managed, his voice cracking even on that single word. 'We don't know what he's already attempted or put in place. You're naming him a traitor to the Tokob based on one glimpse of him? I had thought you both to be cleverer than that. You've made it very clear I don't understand your experience in the fighting pit. Well, you don't understand mine. And none of us understand Tayan's.'

Lilla took a deep breath and shook the buzzing out of his fingertips. 'If you can't speak well of the man you've been friends with for years, then don't speak of him at all in my presence.' He jerked his chin at Xessa. 'And make sure she knows the same,' he added.

Tiamoko glared at him but didn't speak. They'd been reunited less than an hour and all it had showed Lilla was what the Pechaqueh had done to them all. Broken and ruined them, filled them with doubt and suspicion. He looked at the easy intimacy between Xessa and Tiamoko and very deliberately didn't allow himself to be that petty. Instead, he nodded once and threaded back through the crowd to Ekon, who was sitting cross-legged and watching him approach, tension in his neck and shoulders.

'Are you all right?' he murmured and Lilla flinched at the quiet concern in his voice and the almost overpowering urge he had to climb into his lap and demand Ekon make him forget the world for a while.

He dropped down into a graceless sprawl on the stone instead. 'My husband is alive,' he said bluntly and it was Ekon's turn to flinch before he mustered a smile. He opened his mouth to begin some empty platitude but Lilla cut him off. 'He's alive and he's the Shadow of the Singer.'

Ekon let out a long, slow breath and hunched his shoulders, twisting the hem of his kilt between his fingers. 'I'm sorry.'

'Sorry?' Lilla began and then rocked where he sat. 'You knew, didn't you?' he breathed. 'Fucking gods, you knew it was him. There's no way the news that the Singer had taken a foreigner as his Shadow wouldn't have spread through the Melody. You fucking knew and you didn't tell me.'

Ekon had the grace to look ashamed. 'I knew a Toko called Tayan was Shadow, yes. But I didn't know it was him. You told me he was dead; you told me that yourself. I had no reason to disbelieve you. And Tayan isn't an uncommon name in the north. There are two in the Ninth Talon alone.'

Lilla held up his hand in a mute plea for silence. 'Don't,' he managed. 'Just . . . just don't. How much more can you try and break me?' he added, mostly to himself. Ekon inhaled, sharp, pained, and then crossed his arms over his chest and looked down. A muscle flickered in his jaw.

He didn't know what to believe, what would hurt less – that Ekon knew and didn't tell him because he wanted his rebels; or because he wanted Lilla himself. The shock on Ekon's face on the night of the uprising when he'd told him Tayan still lived took on a new significance. He'd been horrified, yes, but he'd been ashamed too. A shame that haunted Lilla because it was so familiar. In their own way, they'd each betrayed his husband.

'What else did they say about the Shadow?' Ekon asked after a decent interval. His tone was delicate, but the Toko understood what he meant. He just shook his head, concentrating on holding himself together; he felt cracked open, as if his heart might slide from his chest into his lap at any moment. The things he'd done. The things he'd *felt*.

Weaver appeared then, seeming unbothered by the tension crackling between them. 'Spear Pilos has called a parlay,' she said without preamble and held out a bundle of turkey feathers. 'You're coming with me, Ekon. Lilla, I want you to draw up the rebels of the Eighth Talon to let our enemies know you've arrived. That'll help lend weight to our arguments.'

'Lilla's husband,' Ekon began.

'Later,' Weaver said. 'We have a chance to end this without further bloodshed.' She grinned at them both, the expression youthful on her lined, weary face. 'We've forced their hands; we've bled them so much they want to talk. Now let's finish it.'

EPILOGUE

PILOS

The grand plaza, Singing City, Pechacan, Empire of Songs
1st day of the Great Star at morning

Pilos had never been more grateful for the sanctity of the turkey feathers in his life. With them tied in his hair, he was forbidden from raising weapons against the warriors opposite him. Against Feather Ekon of the Second Talon, the man he'd personally trained and taught and elevated and, finally, put in charge of the slaves of the Eighth. *Who he'd turned into traitors.*

There'd been rumours in the city, and confirmation from a few Listeners across the Empire who managed to reach the Shadow, of dog warriors and macaws joining the rebellion. By now he'd heard enough of the Shadow's muttering to think that even Enet herself might have been a part of this. But an eagle? A Feather? It was too much.

But it would also be short-lived, both the rebellion and the rest of Ekon's existence. Already, a few reports had been received confirming that some cities and towns in Pechacan and Chitenec were back in proper hands. The lands most soaked in song-magic, with the longest history of Pechaqueh rule, were already falling back into the natural order. Once they took back control here in the Singing City, the rebellion would die out.

And here they all are, conveniently gathered together to be killed.

'Spear Pilos,' Ekon said formally and although his voice was steady, there was a glisten of sweat across his brow and upper lip. 'You called for this parlay. You are willing to hear our terms?'

'No. I called for this parlay,' came a voice from behind Pilos. A voice tinged with harmony and rolling with northern roundness. 'Tayan of Tokoban, called the stargazer. Shaman, peace-weaver, and Shadow of the Singer.'

Less a shadow, more the sun itself these days.

Tayan made to step past Pilos, offering him a warm smile as if he'd read the thought, and the Spear put out his hand to stop him. The Shadow came to an obedient halt, but he was in full view of the traitors' delegation and their warriors drawn up in formation behind. They could see his turkey feathers; they could also see the gold of magic rushing beneath his skin. Naked from the waist up and painted in the colours and tattoos of his people and his calling, he was healthy and bright-eyed, big with magic and thrumming with power. As far from a normal Toko as it was possible to get. Even Pilos felt a touch of awe at his proximity. He looked more like a Singer than—

There was a choked-off cry from the traitors' ranks and the Toko looked that way. 'Hello, husband,' he called, voice pitched loud. Pilos tensed, ready to leap in front of the Shadow. 'It pleases me to see you still live. You should be a part of this peace-weaving; you have always been sensible. Come here.' Tayan imbued the command with all the force of the song until it carried the sort of imperative more often heard from the holy Setatmeh. There was a shuffling in the warriors and civilians gathered opposite them; this parlay was partly a way for the Shadow to test the limits of his power.

The man the Shadow had addressed flushed and twitched, rocking forward onto his toes and then staggering back a step. Not as decisive as he no doubt wished it to appear. Still, to have caused such a ripple among their enemies while the Shadow was outside the source, away from the full strength of the magic was . . . thought-provoking. *Worrying.*

'Why are you weaving a peace for them, for the people who destroyed Tokoban?' the Shadow's husband demanded, a crack running through his voice.

'Why didn't you claim me as your husband when you were captured?' the Shadow struck back.

Ekon winced and Pilos braced for violence. The man made a choked-off noise and didn't answer and Tayan waved away his own words. 'It doesn't matter. I weave a peace for all peoples, to bring us together, united on one land, under one sky.'

There was a stirring of derision from some of the traitors. 'Spear Pilos,' Ekon said hurriedly, 'this is Weaver, one of our commanders. She will—'

'She is no commander,' Pilos interrupted. 'She is not even a warrior. If there is to be a parlay, it will be between us, warrior to warrior.' He sneered. 'Even though you are a traitor.'

'No traitor, Spear, merely a man who loves his people, his gods, and his freedom. And if it is peace we are to discuss, and this negotiation is at your request, not ours, then why not Weaver? Peace should not be spoken of by the likes of us.'

'You're right,' Pilos snapped despite himself, 'one such as you is not worthy to speak to me.'

'But we are worthy to speak to Tayan of Tokoban,' Weaver said. 'He is not Pechaqueh, after all. I would hear what he has to say about this peace he proposes.'

This was it. Pilos's heart kicked against his ribs regardless of the turkey feathers they all wore. The delegations were in the clear space between two forces, his own warriors arrayed before the great pyramid, the slaves in straggling lines across the great plaza – except for the traitors of the Eighth Talon and the retired dog warriors, who all stood in unconscious imitation of his eagles.

See, he wanted to point out, *we gave you this. We gave you discipline and honour and pride. We gave you tactics and intuition and you think to turn them on us? We will grind you into the dirt.*

'You all know your place in this world,' the Shadow said and the harmonics in his voice strengthened so that it bounced and echoed over the heads of the assembled rebels and all could hear him. His skin sparkled and glowed until he was a small sun standing next to Pilos's shadow, and the Spear heard the murmurs of awe from the people gathered opposite. He located the husband in the front line and smirked at the mix of despair and desire on his face.

'You all knew peace up until nine days ago,' the Shadow called. 'You all knew comfort and security. You chose to throw all of that away and now you come here and ask what peace is? Listen to your hearts and the song in your heart. Listen to each other; listen to me. Peace is in laying down your weapons. Peace is the very act of *choosing peace* over violence. Peace is contentment with your proper place in the world. You have known that, and you can know it again. Peace and stability, and the satisfaction and honour

618

that comes from a duty well performed. Love and devotion and children were all yours before and can be again. You shattered your own peace, and now—'

The arrow was already losing power and speed, shot from too far back to be of much danger, but Pilos stepped forward and raised the small shield tied to his left arm. The arrow thunked into it and then fell to the stone with a clatter. To his surprise, Ekon whirled to face his rebels with his arms up.

'Respect the sanctity of the peace feathers,' he bellowed.

'That is no peace,' someone shouted back. 'That is a return to slavery.'

'Of course he would advocate it when he has freedom and power and magic,' another yelled. 'It's easy for him.'

'I am the Singer's most loyal, loving and devoted slave,' the Shadow shouted back, his voice doubling and trebling with song. He shrugged off his shawl to show his intact slave brands as proof. 'In service I have found contentment; in thinking of another first I have found peace. I beg you to do the same. Throw down your weapons and bare your necks. Return to the homes of those who loved and cared for you. Don't—'

The man he'd identified as his husband shoved through the crowd and sprinted forward. Pilos and his honour guard tensed. He was charged with keeping the Shadow alive and unhurt, but if all the rebels followed this one's lead, they'd be in trouble. He glanced back and raised his fist towards Xochi's distant form. She waved her readiness: if there was an attack, she'd signal the newly arrived First Talon, under High Feather Atu, who were assembled behind the pyramid out of sight. If it came to it, they outnumbered these ungrateful fucking slaves three to one.

'Tayan! Tayan, what are you saying? The song is evil!' his husband shouted. Feather Ekon caught him around the waist as he crashed into the group and wrestled him into stillness. 'Xessa told me you'd lost yourself, that you'd become Pechaqueh in your heart and I refused to believe her, I said you'd never do something like that, that you were planning your own rebellion.' He wasn't struggling in Ekon's grip, but he did wriggle an arm free and hold it out imploringly. 'Tay, please. Now is the fucking time if you have a plan. And if you don't, then, then just come back. Come back to me.'

Ekon was whispering desperately in the Tokob ear. The Shadow smiled. 'Listen to your lover, husband,' he said and Pilos's eyebrows rose. He looked at Ekon again, at the tight clutch of his arms that was more than an attempt to save the peace-weaving.

'You took off your marriage cord,' the Shadow continued. 'You have always been wiser than me, Lilla, and in this you are no different. Let us end it, then. Unless you would have peace under the song and peace for all Ixachipan?'

The Shadow put his hands to his neck and the tattered cord that rested against his clavicles. The Toko, Lilla, had fallen still and was watching with wide, pleading eyes. 'I . . .' he began and then licked his lips.

'Help me convince them, Lilla, and I'll come back to you,' Tayan said, low enough this time that only the peace delegations heard him.

Lilla sounded as if his heart was being torn from his chest. 'This is not you,' he begged. 'Don't let this be you. Please.'

The Shadow waited, patient and still, gold in his veins and the song building to an echoing crescendo that promised peace within service.

Lilla slumped and tears ran to drip from his jaw. 'I will not trade my freedom and the freedom of my people,' he croaked. 'Not even for you. The song lies, and it has corrupted your tongue.'

'So be it,' the Shadow said without emotion, and he lifted the cord from around his neck and dangled it between two fingers. Then he dropped it deliberately to the stone and looked at Pilos. The song swelled, sweet and thundering and victorious, and the gold in his skin swelled with it.

'Kill them all.'

AFTERWORD

Grand plaza, Singing City, Pechacan, Empire of Songs

I can feel the song growing in power a little more each day. Growing deeper into me. A song that will unite all people in glorious purpose, in beauty and harmony. Medicine for all the world.

Once Ixachipan is stable again, we will extend our reach into Barazal. The Zellih will have already heard it, those who have dared to set foot in Tokoban. They will know of my might and growing strength. They will know they cannot win.

I will not allow them to win.

There will be peace for all peoples under my song. For I understand its magic now; I understand the contentment it brings and I know how to fix it so that my immortal kin can live free.

I am Tayan of Tokoban, called the stargazer – for now. Called the Shadow – for now.

I am Tayan of Tokoban and this is my song.

And my song is good.

The End

623

ACKNOWLEDGEMENTS

There was a bigger than expected gap between *The Stone Knife* and *The Jaguar Path*, so thank you to all the readers who've been so patient. I hope it was worth the wait and you're wallowing gloriously in the emotional devastation.

Thanks as always go to my fabulous agent, Harry Illingworth, for his tireless work, and to the team at HarperVoyager past and present – Jack Renninson, Vicky Leech, Natasha Bardon, Elizabeth Vaziri, Jamie Witcomb, Emily Goulding – with thanks to Anna Bowles for their epic proofreading skills, and to Stephen Mulcahey for this bold and beautiful cover.

2021 and 2022 were as tough as 2020 in their own ways, so thanks on a personal note to the Bunker for sterling work in keeping me sane and plying me with AO3 fic recommendations and unhinged TV shows. In particular, thank you to Leife Shallcross and EJ Beaton for giving *The Jaguar Path* an early read and to all who cheered me over the finish line.

Big thanks to Stewart Hotston for advice, conversations about racism and colonialism, book recommendations and a thorough beta read. And to David Bowles for his ongoing cultural expertise with respect to the civilisations which are the inspiration for the peoples of Ixachipan.

And last in the list but first in my heart, to Mark, my family, loved ones and friends. Thank you all for continuing to support me on this craziest of journeys and offering wisdom, sympathy and gin when needed.